James W. (James Washington) Sheahan

The Life of Stephen A. Douglas

James W. (James Washington) Sheahan

The Life of Stephen A. Douglas

ISBN/EAN: 9783743310650

Manufactured in Europe, USA, Canada, Australia, Japa

Cover: Foto ©Raphael Reischuk / pixelio.de

Manufactured and distributed by brebook publishing software
(www.brebook.com)

James W. (James Washington) Sheahan

The Life of Stephen A. Douglas

THE LIFE

OF

STEPHEN A. DOUGLAS.

BY

JAMES W. SHEAHAN.

NEW YORK:

HARPER & BROTHERS, PUBLISHERS,

FRANKLIN SQUARE.

1860.

PREFACE.

In the following pages it is proposed to present as full and as complete an account of the life and public services of Stephen A. Douglas, of Illinois, as the limits of this volume will allow. The events of the last six years have given to his name a world-wide fame, but his entire public career, as well as the incidents of his boyhood, furnish an example of success following a determined purpose to adhere to fixed political principles that has rarely had its equal. So intimately has Mr. Douglas been connected with the most important legislation, and with the history of the political parties of the last twenty-five years, that it has been found difficult at times to confine this work to a record of his acts. But as far as it has been possible to do so, the writer has abstained carefully from comments upon the acts of others, except when to do so was necessary to present clearly and truthfully the history of Mr. Douglas.

It is due to candor to state that these pages have been prepared without having been submitted to Mr. Douglas, who, if he read them at all, will do so for the first time after the issue of the book. They have been written by one who agrees fully with Mr. Douglas in political views, and who, since the passage of the Kansas-Nebraska Act, has been engaged in maintaining before the people of Illinois the wisdom, justice, and expediency of the policy of the Democratic party upon the question of Slavery in the Territories.

With these words of explanation the book is submitted to those who may choose to read it.

CONTENTS.

CHAPTER I.

CHAPTER II.

CHAPTER III.

CHAPTER IV.

CHAPTER V.

CHAPTER VI.

CHAPTER VII.

CHAPTER VIII.

CHAPTER IX.

CHAPTER X.

CHAPTER XI.

CHAPTER XII.

CHAPTER XIII.

CHAPTER XIV.

CHAPTER XV.

LIFE OF STEPHEN A. DOUGLAS.

CHAPTER I.

EARLY LIFE.

"The issues of all human action are uncertain. No man can undertake to predict positively that even virtue will meet with its full reward in this world; but this much may be said with entire certainty, that he who succeeds in marrying his name to a great principle, achieves a fame as imperishable as truth itself." Such was the language in which a senator from Virginia concluded an able and most eloquent speech upon the Kansas-Nebraska Bill. The prediction has been verified by history. By that act of legislation, the name of STEPHEN A. DOUGLAS was "married" to the principle of Popular Sovereignty; and, even had he no other claim upon the grateful memory of the American people, that indissoluble blending of his name with the most vital principle of constitutional liberty would alone render his name as imperishable as truth itself. The name of STEPHEN A. DOUGLAS, therefore, has, by that single and most memorable act, been stamped ineffaceably upon the pages of his country's history, and, though contemporaneous writers may have recorded the most widely differing judgments upon his conduct, and future historians may differ as widely as those who were present at, and who were participants in the consequences of the passage of that great act as to the measure of censure or praise that should be awarded to him, still the assertion of the senator from Virginia will stand verified, and, in defiance of all the bitterness of his enemies, throughout all coming time the name of DOUGLAS and the great principle of Popular Sovereignty will be so linked in the records of the past, and so closely identified with the memories of the present, that the fame of the former can only perish in the overthrow of the latter—an occurrence only possible in the total destruction of truth itself.

A

That branch of the Douglas family from which the subject of this work is a descendant emigrated from Scotland, and settled at New London, in the province of Connecticut, during the earlier period of our colonial settlements. One of the two brothers who first came to America subsequently removed from New London, and settled in Maryland, on the banks of the Potomac, not very distant from the site of the present city of Washington. His descendants, now very numerous, are to be found in Virginia, the Carolinas, Tennessee, and other Southern States. The other brother remained at New London, and his descendants are scattered over New England, New York, Pennsylvania, and the Northwestern States. Doctor Stephen A. Douglas, the father of the statesman of the present day, was born at Stephentown, in Rensselaer County, New York, and when quite a youth removed with his parents to Brandon, Rutland County, Vermont, where, after his regular course at Middlebury College, he studied medicine, and became distinguished in his profession. He married Miss Sarah Fisk, the daughter of an extensive farmer in Brandon, by whom he had two children—the first a daughter, and the second a son. On the first of July, 1813, without any previous illness or physical warning, he died suddenly of a disease of the heart. At the very moment of his attack and of his death, he was playing with the daughter at his knees, and holding his son Stephen in his arms.

In 1813 the country was at war with Great Britain—had undertaken a war with the most powerful nation in the world; at that time the United States, with an unprotected coast, with an overbearing, and insulting, and powerful enemy menacing both seaboard and frontier; with hostile navies swarming upon the lakes, and commanding every sea where the enterprise of American commerce had unfurled a sail, and veteran armies, fresh from Continental fields of renown, landing on our shores—at that time, when the infant republic, trusting in the justice of her cause, had risked every thing to preserve the sacred principle that an American citizen, no matter where he might be, who stood upon an American deck, was to be secured, at all hazards, in all the great rights guaranteed to him by the Constitution of his country — while this war was waging, and while the contest between absolute power and popular right was maintained with fire and sword from De-

troit to Key West, in the midst of this struggle, on the 23d
day of April, 1813, was born STEPHEN A. DOUGLAS, who, forty-
one years thereafter, became the great champion of that same
sacred principle,—not, indeed, in behalf of the gallant men
who tread the decks of the American fleets, but in behalf of
those other and no less gallant heroes—the pioneers of American progress, the founders of American states, the builders
of American sovereignties—the People of the American Territories.

The grandmothers, maternal and paternal, of Mr. Douglas
were of the name of Arnold, and were both descended from
William Arnold, who was one of the associates of Roger Williams in founding the colony of Rhode Island, and whose son
was appointed governor of that colony by Charles the Second,
when he granted the famous charter under which the state
continued to be governed until even after the establishment
of the American Union, and until the adoption a few years ago
of the present Constitution of Rhode Island. The descendants
of Governor Arnold are at this day very numerous in Rhode
Island, and, indeed, throughout the whole country.

Immediately after the death of Dr. Douglas, his widow, with
her two children, removed from their native village to a farm
about three miles in the country, where she resided with her
bachelor brother, Mr. Fisk, on their patrimonial estate. From
his earliest childhood, Stephen was raised to a regular course
of life—attending the district school during the winter seasons,
and working steadily on the farm the residue of each year.
When fifteen years of age, finding that a number of his school-
mates of his own years were about to enter the academy to
prepare for college, he applied to his uncle, whom he had always been taught to respect as a father, for permission and
means to enable him to take the same course. This request
was made in pursuance of an understanding which he supposed had existed in the family from his earliest recollection,
that he was to be educated and sent to college; so strongly
was this plan for the future impressed upon his mind, that it
had never occurred to him that his uncle's marriage a year
previous, and the very recent birth of an heir to his estate, had
in the least changed their respective relations; nor had he
seen in these events that cloud which was to darken the hitherto bright visions which had stimulated his youthful am-

bition. An affectionate remonstrance against the folly of abandoning the farm for the uncertainties of a professional life, accompanied by a gentle intimation that he had a family of his own to support, and therefore did not feel able to bear the expense of educating other persons' children, was the response made to the boy's request. Instantly the eyes of young Douglas were opened to his real condition in life. He saw at once that he could not command the means requisite for acquiring a collegiate education without exhausting the only resources upon which his mother and sister must rely; he also saw that if he remained on the farm with his uncle until he became of age, he would then be thrown upon the world without a profession or a trade by which he could sustain them and himself. Realizing the full force of these considerations, and perceiving for the first time that he must rely upon himself for the future, he determined to leave the farm and at once learn a mechanical trade, that being the most promising and certain reliance for the future. Bidding farewell to his mother and sister, he set off on foot to engage personally in the great combat of life; on that same day he walked fourteen miles, and before night was regularly indentured as an apprentice to a cabinet-maker in Middlebury. He worked at his trade with energy and enthusiasm for about two years, the latter part of the time at a shop in Brandon, and gained great proficiency in the art, displaying remarkable mechanical skill; but, in consequence of feeble health, and a frame unable to bear the continued labor of the shop, he was reluctantly compelled to abandon a business in which all his hopes and pride had been centred, and to which he had become sincerely attached. He has often been heard to say, since he has been distinguished in the councils of the nation, that the happiest days of his life had been spent in the workshop, and, had his health and strength been equal to the task, no consideration on earth could have induced him to have abandoned it, either for professional or political pursuits.

He entered the academy of his native town, and commenced a course of classical studies, to which he devoted himself for about twelve months with all that energy and enthusiasm which are a part of his nature.

In the mean time his sister had married **Julius N. Granger**, Esq., of Ontario County, New York, and shortly afterward his mother was married to Gehazi Granger, Esq., father of Julius, and at the close of his first year at Brandon Academy, young Douglas, at the earnest solicitation of his mother and step-father, removed with them to their home near Canandaigua, New York. He at once became a student in the academy at that place—an institution which for more than half a century has been celebrated for its thorough academical course of studies, and for the large number of eminent professional men and statesmen whose names once appeared on her catalogue. He remained at Canandaigua nearly three years, applying himself with untiring energy and zeal to the pursuit of his classical course at the academy, and, during a portion of the same time, followed a course of law studies in the office and under the instruction of the Messrs. Hubbell. Some idea may be formed of his proficiency in the classical course, and of the energy with which he pursued his studies, from the fact that, while the laws of New York at that time required a course of seven years to entitle a student to be admitted to practice law, four years of which might be occupied in classical studies, Mr. Douglas, on a thorough examination upon his whole course of study, was allowed a credit of three years for his classical attainments at the time he commenced the study of the law, leaving four years only as the period which he would be required to continue as a law student to entitle him to be admitted to the bar of that state. He kept up his collegiate course, however, during the whole time he was studying law, so that when he removed to the West in June, 1833, he had mastered nearly the entire collegiate course in most of the various branches required of a graduate in our best universities.

While at Canandaigua, that taste for political controversy, which had shown itself in him when a boy, had a wider field. The re-election of General Jackson took place in 1832; and the animated, vigorous, and, at times, most heated discussions of the day, developed and matured that taste, until he made the study of the political history of the country a subject of as deep importance as he did the scholastic exercises of the academy. We have not been able to ascertain whether, during the exciting canvass of 1832, he made any address to any political meeting in Canandaigua or elsewhere; but we are informed that in the debating clubs, and in all gatherings, large

or small, the cause of the old hero found in him a most enthusiastic champion. It was in the discussions which took place
before the societies composed of his fellow-students at Canandaigua that he made his first public speech; and it was there,
after having conquered the natural diffidence of all youthful
orators, that he first obtained that confidence and self-reliance,
as well as that ready and constant flow of strong and forcible
language, which mark the speeches of his more mature age.

A gentleman, now residing in Illinois, who was a fellow-stu-
dent of Douglas at Canandaigua, states that he was universally
beloved by all his companions—loved for his impulsive gen-
erosity, his frankness, and the genial kindness of his disposition. He was recognized and admitted to be *the* politician of
the circle; and, though the students were of all political parties, to Douglas was conceded the distinction of being the best
posted student in the place. Indeed, a taste for politics was
evidenced at an early day. It is stated that one of his earliest
essays in behalf of the Democratic party was the organization
of a band of "Jackson boys" in Vermont, who proclaimed a
war upon the "Coffin handbills," and who managed to destroy
those placards as soon as they appeared on the walls and fences
of the town. He has lived to read the declaration to the people of Illinois, in 1858, of a "life-long democrat," who was actively engaged in the circulation of those infamous libels upon
General Jackson, that Stephen A. Douglas was not a safe or
reliable member of the Democratic party!

In June, 1833, Mr. Douglas, then a few months over twenty
years of age, left Canandaigua to earn for himself a livelihood
and independence. His destination was that uncertain region
then designated by the general and somewhat comprehensive
term "the West." He left home and friends without any purpose of locating at any particular point. His intention was to
go to a new country, and by identifying himself with its interests, and devoting his talents to the development of those interests, he hoped to be successful. Such a home, he concluded,
could not be found in the old-settled states, where the walks
of the profession were crowded with men already eminent, but
a man of energy and industry might hope for one in the new
settlements on the Ohio and Mississippi. Provided with a
small sum of money, he left Canandaigua, and his first resting-
place was at Cleveland, Ohio. It was not his intention origi-

nally to remain at Cleveland, but, as he had letters of introduction to persons residing there, and also personal friends, he thought he would profit by such advice and counsel as he could obtain as to other and more distant points. He made the acquaintance of the Hon. SHERLOCK J. ANDREWS, at that time a practicing lawyer, and since then a member of Congress from that district. Mr. Andrews was pleased with the youth; gave him all the information he could furnish, but advised him to remain in Cleveland, and, as an inducement to do so, tendered him the use of his library and office until he should have pursued his law studies for one year within the state, as required by the laws of Ohio, when he would be entitled to admission at the bar, at which time, such was Mr. Andrews' liberal offer, Douglas was to be associated with Mr. Andrews as a member of the firm. To be met at the very threshold of his undertaking by such a brilliant promise of success was truly gratifying, and the offer was at once accepted. But the engagement was not to be completed. Young Douglas at once entered upon his duties as law clerk in Mr. Andrews' office, but in less than a week was prostrated by an attack of bilious fever—the scourge of the Western country during the period of its early settlement—and was confined to his room for many weary months. It was not until October that he exhibited any signs of permanent recovery. The physicians who had attended him advised him to return to Canandaigua, as, in all probability, he would be attacked by the fever again in the spring, which his feeble health and delicate frame, both now so disastrously impaired, would not be able to sustain. Under these circumstances, he concluded to leave Cleveland—then but a small village, now the beautiful forest city of the Lakes. In leaving there, he never thought of taking the back track and becoming a dependent upon his friends at home, but he determined to leave Cleveland by a forward movement, by a further step into the great West, resolved never, never to return until he should attain and firmly establish a respectable position in his profession. With this purpose firmly fixed in his mind, he left Cleveland during October, 1833, and never returned to visit his friends there until, ten years later, he carried with him his certificate of election as a member of Congress, having, in the mean time, been state's attorney, member of the Legislature, register of the Land-office, secretary of state, and judge of the Supreme Court in the State of Illinois.

He left Cleveland on a canal-boat, on which he traveled until he reached Portsmouth, on the Ohio River, where he took steam-boat and proceeded down the river to Cincinnati. For an entire week he sought some respectable employment in that city, from which he could derive means to support himself until such time as he could recruit his health and regain his strength to enable him to commence the practice of the law. His short stock of funds was nearly exhausted. Finding no encouragement in Cincinnati, he pushed on to Louisville, Kentucky, where he spent another week with no better success than had rewarded his search in Cincinnati. Nothing but his firm resolve not to return until he had accomplished a success at the bar nerved the heart of the friendless, moneyless, health-less boy. He never despaired of success, though from what quarter and when it was to come bid defiance to his conjectures. Turning his back upon Louisville, he proceeded by steamer to St. Louis. During this trip he for the first time witnessed and realized to their full extent the casualties incident to the navigation of the Western rivers—casualties with which, on several occasions subsequently, it was his misfortune to become too familiar. Near the mouth of the Ohio the boat was detained a whole week in consequence of running upon a "snag" and breaking her machinery; and just below St. Louis she barely escaped destruction by fire. During this trip, thus prolonged to nearly twice the time usually occupied in going from Louisville to St. Louis, he made several acquaintances, and formed friendships which he has ever cherished with affection, and of which he always speaks with gratitude, particularly when referring to Dr. Linn, the distinguished senator from Missouri, and Colonel Miller, at that time governor of the same state, both of whom were his fellow-passengers.

Arrived at St. Louis, he made the acquaintance of the Hon. EDWARD BATES, then, as now, an eminent lawyer and an ornament to his profession. Mr. Bates was kind to the young stranger, encouraging him by his advice, and tendering him the free use of his office and library until he could get into practice on his own account. The immediate and urgent necessities of the youth did not permit an acceptance of this generous offer. He had but a few, very few dollars left, and some immediate employment yielding a pecuniary compensation was necessary. With thanks, he reluctantly but necessarily declined Mr. Bates's offer, and, seeing no opportunity of obtaining employment in St. Louis, he concluded to seek without delay some country town, where, if his earnings were small, his expenses at least would be far less than in the large city. His present search was an engagement as a teacher until spring, by which time he hoped with renewed health he might enter upon the great field of his ambition—the practice of the law.

Having recently read a book of travels in the Western States by a Scotchman, in which was given a charming description of that part of Illinois about Jacksonville, and having counted his money, and finding that he had barely enough left to enable him to reach that place, he resolved to make the last effort in that quarter, and trust to Providence and his own energies for the future.

At the time to which we refer, Illinois was settled principally in what is now the lower half of the state—in that part lying south of a line drawn east and west across the state, at what is the present northern boundary of Sangamon County; the counties of Sangamon and Morgan embracing the territory then included in the limits of half a dozen of the present counties of the state. The seat of government was at Vandalia, in Fayette County, but Sangamon and Morgan were the leading counties in point of population. In 1830, three years previously, the population of the state was as follows:

White inhabitants	155,061
Free negroes	1,637
Total free	156,698
Negroes held in bondage	747
Total population	157,445

By a census taken under the authority of the Legislature of 1836–7 the population was ascertained to be:

White males	141,667
White females	125,558
Total white	267,225
Free negroes	2,261
Negroes registered as apprentices and held in bondage	488
Total population	269,974

The Hon. John Reynolds was governor, and Hon. Zadock

A 2

Casey lieutenant governor, they having been elected in August, 1830, to serve four years each.

The state was represented in Congress by the Hon. Samuel McRoberts and John M. Robinson in the Senate, and by three members in the House of Representatives.

The judiciary of the state consisted of a Supreme Court of four judges, holding office during good behavior, and a number of circuit courts. The circuit courts, having been erected by the Legislature, were within the control and subject to the action of the power that created them. They might be abolished or increased from time to time, as the Legislature might determine. The Supreme Court, however, being a tribunal erected by the Constitution, the judges held office by a tenure which could not be disturbed by any legislative action. The only possible modes by which the Legislature could reach that tribunal was by voting an address, to be voted for by two thirds of the members, asking for the removal of the judges; by impeachment, trial, and conviction of the judges; or by increasing from time to time the number of judges constituting the court. The judges of the Supreme Court, with the governor, constituted a Council of Revision, a majority of which council could approve, or could exercise a veto upon all acts of legislation. The Supreme Court at that time consisted, as has been stated, of four judges, viz., William Wilson, Thomas C. Brown, Theophilus W. Smith, and Samuel D. Lockwood. The state in 1832 had voted for General Jackson, and the Democratic party was in a decided majority.

The state had for a number of years been agitated upon the subject of internal improvements. That was the subject of local politics, entering more or less into the election of all state officers, particularly of members of the Legislature. Railroads and canals at that time were a subject as prolific in excitement, in speeches, in resolutions, and in politics as they have been at any subsequent period in the history of the state. At every session of the Legislature charters without number were granted for all manner of works of improvement, but these produced no results. A charter to build a road or cut a canal was almost valueless without the means or the credit to commence and go on with the work. As an indication of the extent to which this business was carried, the following table of railroads and canals authorized by acts of the Legislature previous to the final adoption of a system in which the state was to become the paymaster will suffice.

In December, 1835, a special session of the Legislature was held. Previous to that time the following railroads had been authorized by law, companies having been incorporated with liberal charters for their construction:

Names of Roads.	Miles.
Vincennes and Chicago Railroad	240
Alton and Springfield	80
Jacksonville and Meredosia	24— 344

At that special session the following were added to the list:

Belleville and Mississippi	16
Pekin, Bloomington, and Wabash	150
Mississippi, Springfield, and Carrollton	125
Alton, Wabash, and Erie	240
Central Branch—Wabash	80
Galena and Chicago	175
Wabash and Mississippi	260
Shawneetown and Alton	180
Alton and Shawneetown	190
Mount Carmel and Alton	150
Wabash and Mississippi Union	180
Warsaw, Peoria, and Wabash	275
Waverly and Grand Prairie	30
Rushville	15
Pekin and Tremont	8
Illinois Central	300
Beardstown and Sangamon Canal	150—2524

And at the next session the following:

Illinois and Mississippi	90
Naples and Jacksonville	24
Chicago and Vincennes	240
Springfield and Beardstown	50
Winchester, Lynnville, and Jacksonville	40
Bloomington, Ottawa, and Keshwakee	125— 569
A grand total of 24 railroads, with an aggregate length of 3287 miles, and one canal of 150 miles, making together of miles	3437

Charters were liberal in their terms, and contractors were ready and willing to go on with the works upon the first appearance of money. But money there was none, and the issue had gradually been growing up before the people whether the state should or should not become a party to the construction of these works. The prospect of railroads or canals construct-

ed by individual enterprise or capital was daily becoming more
and more remote; and as that prospect receded, the policy of
having the state embark in the grand enterprise assumed more
significance, until at last it took shape and form, and became
the eventful topic of the day. It had its friends and it had its
opponents; for years the latter were the stronger, and Legislatures, reflecting the popular will, refused to commit the state
to the internal improvement policy. A particular series of
works formed the body of each proposed scheme, but these
works were not of overruling local importance to those portions of the state having the main portion of the people, and
consequently controlling the State Legislature. To overcome
this great difficulty, the scheme of public works was each year
increased by the addition of a new railroad, or branch connecting two or three counties, or giving the means of transportation from interior counties to creeks and streams, which were,
with very little regard for truth, declared by act of Legislature
"navigable rivers." We believe a steam-boat captain, deceived
possibly by one of these acts of Legislature, attempted to as-
cend the "navigable" river Sangamon, and did succeed in
reaching a small place called Portland, near Springfield, but
the trip was never repeated, the boat having been compelled,
for want of room to turn, to back down stream until it reached the Illinois River. Those who now pass the railroad bridge
over the Sangamon River, on the Chicago, Alton, and St. Louis
Railroad, a few miles north of Springfield, will have some difficulty in discovering the advantages of that point, the site of
Portland, for a city with an extensive river trade. Yet, in
olden times, that prospect was not deemed more visionary than
that Chicago would be a city of a hundred thousand inhabitants. The advocates of the internal improvements to be constructed by the state grew stronger each year. Many counties, once strong in their hostility to the great scheme, were
revolutionized in sentiment by including in the general plan a
railroad or a branch which was to enhance the value of the
farms a hundred-fold, and give to each producer a cheap and
rapid ride to market with his products. Who could withstand
the temptation? Who could refuse to vote for a railroad to
pass by his own door? The history of the last five years has
shown that the men of 1835–6 were at least no more unwise
than the men of 1859. Cities borne down with debt, counties

reduced to repudiation, and individuals utterly ruined by liberal subscriptions to railroads, indicate that the seductions of grand works of internal improvement have been as potent of late years as they were in the days when Illinois so unfortunately embarked in the business. In vain, however, was the plan of a general system presented. The flying bids for local support became so numerous and so heavy that they threatened destruction to the whole. The removal of the seat of government was agitated, and eventually that project became a powerful auxiliary to the improvement system. It is believed that the delegation of a county having six members in the Lower House were enlisted in support of the improvement bill by the promise of the removal of the capital to the county seat of that county. Nor did this even turn the scale. Another and a more extensive bid for local support was included in the scheme. This was, that out of the first moneys borrowed on the faith of the state for works of internal improvement, a large sum (eventually fixed at $200,000) should be paid, in proportion to a census to be taken, to *all the counties in the state through which no railroad or canal was provided to be constructed by the state!*

The state was also, to some considerable extent, agitated upon the subject of General Jackson's bank policy. The bank had many interested, as well as political friends in the state. The policy of General Jackson was represented as fatal to the best interests of the people, because it destroyed the only reliable banking capital of the country. How was Illinois to prosper without roads and canals, and how were roads and canals to be constructed if the banks—the only capitalists of the country—were destroyed? These questions were propounded at every town-meeting and court-day, and many of the most devoted friends of Jackson shrank from a defense of what they knew not how to defend.

Pending these great questions, pending the consideration of measures fraught with so much evil to the state, and whose consequences are yet so severely felt, on a morning late in November, 1833, STEPHEN A. DOUGLAS stepped from a steam-boat at the town of Alton, and for the first time trod the generous soil and breathed the pure, free air of the Prairie State, Illinois.

He lost no time in Alton, but at once proceeded by stage-coach to Jacksonville, where he arrived next day. He still lacked six months of being twenty-one years of age.

CHAPTER II.

FIRST STRUGGLES IN ILLINOIS.

ONCE arrived at Jacksonville, he had reached that point in his journey where, whether fortune was to smile or to frown upon him, he was to meet his destiny. He saw no prospect of succeeding at the law, no prospect of immediate success, and pecuniary aid was indispensable. He had but thirty-seven cents in money, and was a total stranger. Gentlemen now in Illinois, who at that time held high position—socially, politically, and officially—state that, even a year later, there was but little in the personal appearance of the delicate, wasted form, and the pale, anxious face of the youth, to attract any special attention. His first essay was to find employment in a law office, where for a time, in consideration of his services as a clerk, he could obtain enough to defray his personal expenses. He remained in Jacksonville some days, and was forced by necessity to sell such of his school-books as he had brought with him. Failing to obtain any employment, even as a teacher, at Jacksonville, he started one morning in December on foot, and walked to the town of Winchester, now the flourishing county seat of Scott County. The morning after his arrival he left his lodgings to inquire for employment. As he approached the square, he saw a crowd of persons assembled, and curiosity led him to the spot.

Some time previously a merchant in Winchester had died, and his stock in trade, consisting of a great variety of articles, had been advertised for sale by the administrator; the sale had attracted a large attendance. The morning on which Mr. Douglas made his advent into the public square of Winchester was the morning fixed by previous notice for the sale. The administrator and the crier were present, but a clerk competent to keep a record of the sales, and to make out the bills of the several purchasers, was indispensable. The hour had arrived and passed; no person in the assemblage competent was willing to undertake the duty; the administrator was embarrassed, and the multitude impatient. At this critical moment

Mr. Douglas approached the scene; he was a stranger; one of the persons present suggested that perhaps he could "read, write, and cipher." The administrator at once addressed Mr. Douglas, representing the embarrassments of the case, and the urgent necessity for the sale, which could not proceed without the aid of a competent clerk. He begged his services as a personal obligation, and tendered the liberal salary of two dollars per day. After a brief struggle, in which the promised fee had, doubtless, its full force in determining his mind, he consented, and the sale at once commenced. The auction continued three days, and the impression made by the young clerk was a most favorable one. His youth, his superior attainments, and particularly the promptness with which he discharged his duties, won for him the kind regards of all parties; and, in addition to this, the readiness and ability which he displayed in the political conversations which took place at every interval during the sale and in the evenings, gained for him a respect and an admiration not generally extended to persons of his age. The warmth and force, yet the perfect good-humor displayed by him in defense of "Old Hickory" in these discussions at once marked him as a valuable acquisition to the one party, and a formidable opponent of the other. The old farmers, who were Jackson men because they felt Jackson was right, though unable to argue the case with the Bankites, found in Douglas an object of special admiration. They expressed their willingness to serve him in any way that was in their power. His three days' services as clerk of the auction yielded him six dollars in money—no small sum in those days, particularly when they constituted a man's entire fortune. His want of means, and his desire to get a school, were soon known, and as soon canvassed among his new-found friends and admirers; and in a few days he was provided with a school of forty pupils, at the rate of three dollars each per quarter! He engaged to conduct this school for three months, and, on the first Monday in December, 1833, he commenced his labors as a teacher.

In the few days he had remained at Jacksonville he made the acquaintance of General Murray M'Connell (his first friend in the state which has since conferred so many honors upon him), and who was appointed fifth auditor of the Treasury by President Pierce in 1855, at the request of Judge Douglas, without General M'Connell's solicitation or knowledge. The particular favor which General M'Connell rendered Mr. Douglas, which he has never ceased to acknowledge, was the loan of some old law-books and copies of the statutes of the state. These books were indispensable to him, and he had not the means to purchase them.

While teaching school, he devoted his evenings and leisure time to the study of these borrowed books, and frequently, on Saturday afternoons, acted as counsel before the justice's court in Winchester. Before leaving Jacksonville, he had filed his application before the Supreme Court for admission to the bar. The proceeds of his school, together with the fees obtained for legal services before the justice of the peace, justified him, at the end of the three months, in giving up his school and in removing to Jacksonville, where he opened an office for the practice of the law.

On the fourth day of March, 1834, then lacking some seven weeks of his majority, he was licensed as an attorney by the judges of the Supreme Court. Little did those judges think, when they issued a license to the stripling who stood before them on that bleak March day, that in a few, a very few years, he would become the leader of a great, growing, and eventually triumphant party, having for its aim the reorganization of that court and the destruction of its political power; much less did they suppose that, in seven years from that day upon which they granted him their license to practice law, he would be elevated by the almost unanimous voice of the representatives of the people to a seat upon the same bench they occupied, possessing the confidence and the approval of the people to a degree never previously enjoyed by any judge in the State of Illinois.

At that time there was published at Jacksonville a Democratic paper, called the "Jacksonville News," edited by S. S. Brooks, Esq. Mr. Brooks, in a letter before us, after stating that he commenced the publication of this paper in February, 1834, says: "My prospectuses were circulated throughout Morgan and the adjoining counties, and, immediately after the publication of the first number of the paper, most of them were returned with lists of names of subscribers on them. Among the returned copies of the prospectus was one from Winchester, with a large number of names, accompanied by a very complimentary and encouraging letter, signed 'Steph. A. Douglas.' Naturally desiring to know something more of my unknown friend than the name, I found, upon inquiry, that he was a young man from the State of New York, engaged in the humble but honorable occupation of school-teacher. A few days afterward, say about the first of March, Mr. Douglas visited Jacksonville, and a personal introduction followed. In anticipation of his visit, I expected to see a young man, for of such was composed the corps of 'Yankee schoolmasters' in this state at that time; but in this, my first interview with Douglas, I was surprised to see a youth apparently not exceeding seventeen or eighteen years of age. He was not quite 'twenty-one,' but was beardless, and remarkably youthful in appearance for that age. I was more surprised, however, in the strength of his mind, the development of his intellect, and his comprehensive knowledge of the political history of the country."

As has been stated in a former part of this book, although the state was Democratic, and had voted for General Jackson in 1832, public opinion was in a very unsettled and excited state respecting some acts of his administration. The "Bank Question" was the all-pervading topic of national politics. The removal of several cabinet officers, the withdrawal of the government deposits from the custody of the United States Bank in September, 1833, were the leading acts of aggression charged against the administration. The bank was contracting its discounts and circulation, producing panic and consternation throughout the state, whose people were expecting internal improvements through the aid of external capital. No locality in Illinois was exempt from the excitement. Parties were designated "Jackson party" and "Opposition." The hostile feelings of the two parties in Illinois were intense, and were exhibited in all the relations of life. Social and business intercourse was confined, as far as was practicable, to political friends. To be a political opponent was, to a great extent, to be a personal enemy, and an enemy to the country. At that time, in Jacksonville, the supporters of the bank policy of the administration were very few. The editor of the "News," and perhaps two others, were the only men who dared openly justify and maintain the cause of General Jackson. A few men, farmers of intelligence in different parts of the county, who were independent, and under no obligations of a pecun-

iary character to the bank or its friends, were fearless in the
assertion of their political sentiments. It was the custom in
those days for nearly the entire population of the county to
visit the county seat on Saturdays—the men to sell produce,
trade horses, and talk politics, and the feminine portion to see
the fashions and do shopping. Consequently, almost every
Saturday was a kind of seventh day political jubilee for the
Jackson party, who, if not numerous, gloried in their individual and collective pluck, in the justice of their cause, and, of
course, were not afraid to make a noise. Mr. Douglas opened
his law office in a room in the court-house building. He soon
became the political cynosure toward whom the eyes of the
Democracy of the county were directed. His open, frank, and
respectful manners, the extraordinary ability and vehemence
with which he defended the acts of the administration, and the
remarkable self-possession and confidence which marked all
his political controversies—and they occurred almost daily—
soon made him the object of attraction and admiration on one
side, and of fear and abuse on the other. The Opposition—
just about that time called "Whigs"—were so arrogant in the
superiority of their numbers, and so overwhelming in the control of public sentiment, that it became necessary for the friends
of General Jackson to "define their position" in some public
manner, and effect an organization. After consultation, it was
deemed by Mr. Douglas and the editor of the News expedient
to call a mass meeting of the Democrats of the county, to test
the question whether General Jackson was to be entirely abandoned or heartily supported. The proposition, however, met
violent opposition from the residue of the party, under the impression that the people would not turn out to sustain the
President under the existing panic. The proposition met with
more favor from the Democrats outside of Jacksonville, but
still a majority thought the experiment a hazardous one. Notwithstanding the fierceness of the Opposition, and the openly
proclaimed objections of Democrats, hand-bills were issued
and posted in every town in the county, calling a mass meeting two weeks hence at the court-house. In the mean time
resolutions were prepared, endorsing the policy of the President in refusing to recharter the bank and in removing the
deposits—two points upon which thousands of Democrats differed from the administration. The majority of the Democrats

thought a bank of some kind indispensable, and the other side thought and declared the charter of such an institution to be clearly unconstitutional. The resolutions met with fierce opposition in the little caucus. When the day of meeting arrived, the court-house was thronged; people poured into town in wagons, on horseback, and on foot. At twelve o'clock a larger concourse of people had assembled in Jacksonville than had ever met there before. Douglas had previously declined the duty of offering the resolutions, pleading his youth, his short residence in the town, and various personal considerations; but when the hour of meeting arrived, when the court-house was filled to its utmost capacity, when the windows were taken out to enable those outside in the square to hear the proceedings within, the gentleman to whom had been assigned the duty of presenting the resolutions handed them to Douglas, telling him that the opportunity now presented to make an impression was an extraordinary one, and should not be neglected, and was of such personal importance to him (Douglas) that he ought not to allow it to pass. At all events, it was soon ascertained that unless he presented them they would not be offered at all. The meeting having been organized, Douglas boldly advanced, stating that he held in his hands certain resolutions which he supposed would meet the approval of all Democrats: these resolutions he then read, and, in a brief speech, explained and supported them.

As soon as he had taken his seat, Josiah Lamborn, Esq., a lawyer of considerable reputation, subsequently attorney general of the state, a Whig, and a man of great personal influence, followed in opposition to the resolutions. He was severe and caustic in reference to Mr. Douglas, and flatly contradicted a statement of fact made by him. He addressed the meeting for some time. Douglas immediately arose, and at once applied himself to a reply to Lamborn. The question of fact he soon disposed of by calling up several Whigs, who declared Lamborn to be wrong. He then for an hour or more addressed the meeting in his own peculiar style. The effect was irresistible. Lamborn precipitately left the room; and when Douglas concluded his speech, the excitement of the meeting had reached the highest point of endurance; cheer upon cheer was given with hearty vigor; the crowd swayed to and fro to get near the orator, and at length he was seized by them, and, borne on the shoulders and upheld by the arms of a dozen of his stalwart admirers, was carried out of the court-house and through and around the public square with the most unbounded manifestations of gratitude and admiration. He was greeted with varied but most expressive complimentary titles, such as "Highcombed Cock," "You will be President yet," "Little Giant" —which last title, originating at this first public occasion of his defense of Democratic principles, is yet, with renewed confidence in its appropriateness, applied to him by his friends.

Such was the first appearance of Stephen A. Douglas on the theatre of Illinois politics—a theatre that for twenty-five years has been the constant scene of unbroken triumphs. As on his first appearance he was borne in triumph upon the shoulders of his admiring hearers, so, for a quarter of a century since then, he has been borne upon the hearts of a most generous people. He has made their cause his cause, and, in return, they have made his cause theirs.

That day, the personal and political triumph of the newly-discovered yet powerful champion of General Jackson's policy settled the political destiny of Morgan County for several years. The speech itself is remembered to this day; and the old veterans who heard Douglas that day, and who have heard him a hundred times since, declare that he has never yet equaled the first speech he delivered in Jacksonville in March, 1834. Morgan County, from that day forth, became Democratic; the Jacksonville News was sustained in its policy. It remained Democratic until Douglas had moved to another county, and the party, feeling secure in its strength, suffered the newspaper to fail for want of support, when it became Whig, and remained a Whig county until, in 1858, it gave a majority for Douglas and democracy.

The history of this meeting was published far and wide in the state, and there was a great desire to see and hear the man —the youthful David—who had compelled an orator like Lamborn to flee from a meeting in his own town. During that year an election was held for governor and lieutenant governor. Joseph Duncan, who for several years had been a representative in Congress, was elected governor, and Alexander M. Jenkins lieutenant governor. Neither had a majority: there being three tickets in the field, Duncan and Jenkins were elected by a plurality of votes. The election took place in August, and the new officers were installed in January, 1835. The Legislature at that session passed an act changing the mode of appointing certain officers. State's attorneys had previously been appointed by the governor; this act made them elective by the General Assembly in joint convention. The name of Douglas was suggested for the office of attorney for the first judicial district. His friends—and they were all friends who knew him —if few, were ardent in his support. As soon as the act was passed, Mr. Douglas went up to Vandalia, where the Legislature was in session. His competitor was JOHN J. HARDIN, one of the most accomplished lawyers in the state, a gentleman universally esteemed and respected, a speaker of the highest order, an experienced prosecutor, and one who had been favorably known to the people of the district for years. On the 10th of February, 1835, the Legislature met in joint convention to elect officers. The vote for state's attorney for the first judicial circuit being taken—we quote the Journal—"Mr. Stephen A. Douglas, Esq., received 38 votes, and John J. Hardin, Esq., 34 votes for that office; scattering, 2."

In the recorded list of the names of those voting for Mr. Douglas on that occasion is that of the now venerable John S. Hacker, at that time a member of the State Senate; Mr. Hacker, in 1858, was dismissed from a small federal office because he refused to support the Republican candidate and oppose Douglas. He had a son in the Legislature of 1858–9 who voted for Douglas's re-election to the Senate. Another name recorded in the list of those who voted for Douglas in 1835 is that of James Hampton, who, in 1859, as a member of the Legislature, had the pleasure of again voting for him—on this latter occasion for his re-election to the Senate, over the combined fury and bitter hostility of the Republican party and federal authorities.

The election of Douglas to the important office of public prosecutor in the most important circuit of the state, over the celebrated Hardin, caused great discussion throughout all Illinois. Those of his political friends who knew him were extravagant in their joy and confident of his success; those who did not know him were doubtful if a mistake had not been made, and his enemies openly declared the election an outrage. One of the Whig judges of the Supreme Court, who has long since expressed the highest opinion of Mr. Douglas's ability, declared that the election was wrong. "What business," he asked, "has such a stripling with such an office? he is no lawyer, and has no law-books." A few months sufficed to change the judge's opinion, and a few years more found him recognized as one of the ablest practitioners at the bar of the Supreme Court. We have seen it stated on high authority that during the time Mr. Douglas filled the office of state's attorney, not a single indictment drawn by him was ever quashed; and there was probably not a term of the court in any one of the many counties comprising the large circuit in which there were not more or less criminal cases, embracing, in the aggregate, crime of almost every grade. His success as a public prosecutor, and his personal deportment at the bar, and socially with the people of the several counties to which the duties of his office carried him, rapidly confirmed the high opinions expressed by his friends, and gradually removed all the prejudice which had been created against him by opponents at the time of his election.

An incident that took place during the early days of his attorneyship will illustrate the difficulties he had to encounter, and the promptness and energy with which he met and converted what was intended as a painful humiliation into a proud personal and professional triumph. It was his first term in M'Lean County. There had been some local law violated, and the number of offenders were numerous. The attorney proceeded in the discharge of his duty with great zeal. He sat up all night writing his indictments, and actually closed the business in a short time. The Grand Jury found the bills as prepared, and were *forthwith discharged.* The bar, having obtained a hint that the new attorney was to be caught and publicly disgraced, waited the denouement with anxiety. The morning after the Grand Jury had been discharged the crisis came. A member of the bar, then, as now, one of the most distinguished lawyers of the state, at the opening of the court, moved to quash all the indictments found at that term, fifty in number, on the ground that they alleged the offenses charged in them as having been committed in "MClean County," a county unknown to the laws of the State of Illinois, the county in which the court was then sitting, and in which the parties were residing, being "M'Lean County." In other words, that the prosecuting attorney had misspelled the name of the county. The objection, if valid, was a fatal one; and the Grand Jury having been discharged, there was no opportunity to correct the error in spelling. The triumphal glances of the bar, the sharp inquiry of the court if the state's attorney had any thing to say, would have disheartened even a more practiced attorney. The objection was stated in clear and forcible terms; not a lawyer at the bar could see how it was to be overcome; and when the counsel who made the motion took his seat, the laughter and merriment at the counsel-table was only equaled by the loud satisfaction expressed in the lobby by the friends and neighbors of the accused. The motion was an entire surprise to the attorney—at least he so expressed himself. He insisted that before the court should decide the question, the original act of the Legislature establishing the county should be produced; when that was done, he informed the court he would possibly have something to say on the motion, if, indeed, that motion was persisted in. This was said with so much confidence and earnestness, and, withal, the position taken was so correct, that the court decided that the attorney was entitled to what he had asked, and that, as the proof required was so easily obtained, counsel should produce the act establishing the county. A number of acts of the Legislature were at once produced, all referring to the county as "M'Lean" County, and the evidence that that was the proper legal name of the county, and had been so recognized through several years of legislation, was positively overwhelming. During the reading of these acts, the remarks of counsel, the emphasis with which the orthography of the name of the county was delivered, was terrible. Several persons approached Douglas and whispered that he would save himself much useless mortification by giving up the contest, and allowing the indictments to be quashed. He refused. There happened at that time to be no copy of the statute establishing the county in Bloomington; Mr. Douglas insisted that the name of the county could only be determined legally by the recital of that act, and, until it was produced, he must insist that the court could not decide that the indictments were fatally defective. He bid the counsel who made the motion, as well as the crowd who seemed to think the escape of criminals but a small matter compared with the professional discomfiture of an attorney, to beware of the consequences of thus pandering to a contempt of the appointed officers of the law. He rejected promptly the proposition to accept the series of statutes read as defining the proper name of the county. The matter dropped for the present.

That night, and the next day and evening, the legal fraternity, including jurors, witnesses, and litigants, were made merry over jocular criticisms upon schoolmasters turned lawyers, upon schoolmasters being unable to spell the name of one of the largest counties in the state. Witticisms flew fast and thick, and counsel repeatedly urged that they dare not proceed with business until the question was settled how to spell the name of the county. Mr. Douglas kept his own counsel: that he felt the importance to him personally and professionally of this point was evident to all. His friends could not understand the courage with which he met the motion, nor the boldness with which he repelled every open assault. They imputed his defiant tone to bravado, and his demand for the statute as a mere excuse for delay, to gain time in which to make up his mind whether to resign his office and leave the state, or to go back to keeping school. In the mean time, messengers had been sent to Peoria and elsewhere for a copy of the acts of 1830–1.

The one party was confident that its production would be the last nail in the professional coffin of an aspiring individual who, a few months ago, had defeated one of the best lawyers in the state, and had attained the best attorneyship in the gift of the Legislature. The court was in session when the messengers returned; one glance at the book, and counsel rose and asked the court to dispose of the motion to quash the indictments. All was excitement. The state's attorney had also glanced at the book. He rose as defiant as ever, and demanded the reading of the statute. Lawyers crowded around the counsel who held the statute in his hand, and were perfectly astounded at the effrontery of the prosecutor. Profert of the statute was made; the court asked counsel to read it, and counsel read, amid profound silence, the words, "An Act to establish M'Lean County," and turned triumphantly toward the attorney for the state. That gentleman, instead of being annihilated by the tone or manner, or by the words read, quietly stated that the title of the act was not the act itself, and demanded that the whole act should be read. The court said that counsel must, as it was demanded, read the statute. He at once read the first section:

"Sec. 1. Be it enacted by the people of the State of Illinois, represented in the General Assembly, that all that part of country lying within the following boundaries, to wit, Beginning," etc., etc., "shall constitute a new county, to be called *McLean*."

There was a pause—a suspension of public opinion—and the silence was broken by the demand of the prosecutor that the other sections be read. Section 2 did not contain the name of the county; section 3 repeated it twice, and each time by the name of "McLean;" sections 4 and 5 made no mention of the name, and section 6 and last named Bloomington as the "seat of justice of said county of McLean." The attorney, in drawing his indictment, had omitted the apostrophe, and capitalized the C, using a small l. He had employed the exact letters of the body of the statute; the other side, seeing a capital C, a small l, and no apostrophe, had been caught in the very trap in which they thought the attorney had placed himself. Of course, the motion was overruled. The joke was turned, the laugh was on the other side; and the crowd, now regarding the whole thing as a most dexterous plan deliberately laid by the prosecutor to catch the able lawyers with whom he had to contend, gave him an applause and a credit vastly increased in enthusiasm by the previous impression that he had been thoroughly victimized by his opponents.

In the winter of 1835–6—the one following his election as state's attorney—the expediency of uniting the party, and effecting an organization so as to concentrate its powers, and enable them to elect the candidates to be chosen at the succeeding election, was duly presented by Mr. Douglas. The Jacksonville News, editorially and by communication, urged the propriety of holding a county convention to nominate candidates to be supported by the whole party. The result of these proceedings was that the Democracy did unite, did effect an organization, and did call a county convention, the first ever held in Morgan County. It was a new and hazardous movement. The county was entitled to six members of the Legislature, and the county offices to be filled were valuable. It had been customary for all candidates to run relying upon their personal popularity and their personal exertions to obtain support. The proposition to limit the number of Democratic candidates to one individual for each office was a startling proposition. Often as many as ten or fifteen candidates would be before the people for the same office, and Mr. Brooks assures us that he has seen no less than eighteen names announced as candidates for the office of sheriff. The county was decidedly Whig, and the only hope of success was to unite as far as possible the Democracy upon one candidate for each office.

The county convention was held in April. The day having arrived for its assemblage, Jacksonville was filled with people, drawn thither by the novelty of the occasion. The Whigs were there in large numbers; they confidently expected that Douglas would be defeated in his effort to reduce the aspirations of individuals to the measure of party success. The failure of the convention was predicted from the beginning. The candidates to be selected were numerous: two senators, six representatives, one sheriff, three county commissioners, one coroner, and perhaps others of minor importance. The number of aspirants for these nominations was large. The convention was conducted with great dignity and decorum. The nominations were received with great approbation, every precinct being represented by delegates, and by a large attendance of lookers-on. Much to the disappointment of the Opposition, there was but one dissatisfied man—one of the candidates for sheriff " bolted" the nomination, run as an independent candidate, and, though personally popular, and encouraged in his course by the Whigs, suffered a most inglorious defeat. The Whigs, alarmed at the union of the Democrats, united upon a ticket also. At the head of the ticket for representatives they placed the gallant John J. Hardin. There was no man on the Democratic ticket who was able to oppose Hardin in debate. Douglas at once took the stump, and met Hardin every where. He was asked why he, who was not a candidate, should canvass the county when the whole Democratic ticket was afraid to meet their opponents. The taunt at that time had its force. The Democracy wavered. At length, so disastrously did the contest appear, that one of the candidates on the Democratic ticket consented to give way, and, by unanimous desire, Mr. Douglas was placed on the ticket. He then met Hardin, and together they canvassed Morgan County as it had never been canvassed before, and perhaps not since. The convention system inaugurated by Douglas was the object of special attack. He bore the brunt of the battle as he has ever done, and repelled the assaults of his opponents. He appealed to the people to elect, not himself, but the ticket. He fought the first fight in behalf of regular nominations, and the people of Illinois have fought that fight for him on repeated occasions since then. The contest continued up to the day of election. The result was that the entire Democratic ticket was elected, save and except one of the candidates for representative. General Hardin, leading his ticket, was elected over one of the Democratic nominees. This determined the success of the convention system, and the success of Douglas in thus redeeming an old Whig county was properly appreciated by the Democracy throughout the state.

CHAPTER III.

LEGISLATOR, LAWYER, POLITICIAN, AND JUDGE.

On the first Monday in December, 1836, Mr. Douglas took his seat in the most important Legislature that ever assembled in the State of Illinois. It was at that session that the great project of internal improvements was brought to a successful legislative approval. The country was wild with speculation. Schemes of improvements were pressed from every quarter. We have already given a list of the acts incorporating railroad and canal companies passed at the two previous sessions. The United States Bank was no more; state banks were expanding with a fearful momentum; the State of Illinois was pressed to become a partner in the institutions which were to furnish capital to the state and her citizens to enable them to prosecute an advancement that was to equal almost in celerity and magnificence the magic achievements of the genii that obeyed Aladdin's lamp and ring. The people had gone beyond their representatives. Many counties instructed unwilling or reluctant representatives to vote for the schemes of promised wealth and grandeur. The Legislature met, a majority of its members pledged personally or by instructions to vote for the Internal Improvement Bill. The Legislature met on the 5th of December.   In the House were W. A. Richardson, John J. Hardin, James Semple, Robert Smith, Abraham Lincoln, S. A. Douglas, John Calhoun (of Lecompton memory), John A. M'Clernand, Augustus C. French, James Shields, and other men whose names have since been written brightly on our national history.   At that session the Hon. R. M. Young was elected United States Senator for six years from March, 1837.   The governor, in his message, reviewed in terms of strong condemnation the financial policy of General Jackson, impeaching his conduct, and censuring his motives and purposes.   After a warm debate, that part of the message referring to federal affairs was referred to a select committee.   On the 23d of December, the committee, through the Hon. John A. M'Clernand, its chairman, made a report, concluding with resolutions approving the general course of General Jackson's administration, and disavowing the correctness of the charges made in the governor's message.   The debate on these resolutions was protracted and warm.   It was participated in by nearly all the prominent men on both sides.   The main contest, however, was between Douglas and Hardin, the rival representatives from Morgan County.   The debate covered the entire policy of General Jackson.   The resolutions were adopted.

Mr. Douglas was appointed chairman of the Committee on Petitions.   Early in the session a petition was presented, praying, on behalf of one Henry King, that he be divorced from his wife Eunice.   That petition was committed to Mr. Douglas's hands.   The Legislature had for several years been accustomed to granting divorces, and applications for that kind of relief were annually increasing in number and importance.   Mr. Douglas made a report upon the subject of divorces, and the powers and duties of the Legislature in relation to the matter, concluding with the following resolution : "*Resolved*, that it is unconstitutional, and foreign to the duties of legislation, for the Legislature to grant bills of divorce."   This was debated, Mr. Hardin approving of the resolution, but objecting to the word "unconstitutional," which he moved to strike out.   Douglas replied, and the House, by a vote of 53 yeas to 32 nays, adopted the resolution as reported.   That was an end to divorces by the Legislature in Illinois.

It having been soon demonstrated that some system of internal improvements, to which the state was to be a party, was to be passed, the question became important which of the two leading plans suggested should be adopted. These plans were substantially as follows:

1st. That the state should select certain leading and most important works, which should be owned, constructed, and worked exclusively by the state. 2d. That the state should subscribe to a certain share—one fourth, one third, or one half—of the stock of the several railroad and land companies then incorporated, or which should thereafter be incorporated by the state.

These plans had their advocates and friends. The latter plan was the favorite of the speculators; under it the several companies could organize by the payment of a few dollars on each share, and then obtain the subscription by the state in full. Had this plan been adopted, the state would have been the contributor of all the actual cash capital, and would have had no proprietorship or control of the works. We have shown that, at the time the Legislature met, there were companies incorporated authorized to construct over 3400 miles of railroad and canal; the capital to do this work, estimated at the moderate sum of $30,000 a mile, would have made an aggregate (supposing no other works to be proposed) of over $100,000,000, into which enterprise the state would soon be led to at least one third of the entire amount.

Mr. Douglas was personally opposed to any system to which the state was to be a party; but, in obedience to instructions, and yielding to the necessity of favoring the least objectionable to prevent the adoption of the greater enormity, he favored the first-mentioned plan. Accordingly, early in the session he submitted the following resolutions indicating the plan which he viewed most favorably:

Resolved, that the Committee on Internal Improvements be instructed to report a bill for the commencement of a general system of internal improvements, as follows:

The bill shall provide,

1st. For the completion of the Illinois and Michigan Canal.

2d. For the construction of a railroad from the termination of said canal to the mouth of the Ohio River.

3d. For the construction of a railroad from Quincy, on the Mississippi River, eastward to the state line, in the direction of the Wabash and Erie Canal.

4th. For the improvement of the navigation of the Illinois and Wabash Rivers.

5th. For making surveys and estimates of such other works as may be considered of general utility.

Resolved, that as the basis of the system, the improvements shall be constructed and owned by the state exclusively.

Resolved, that for the purposes aforesaid, a loan of   millions of dollars should be effected on the faith of the state, payable in such installments and at such times as shall be required in the progress of the works.

Resolved, that portions of the lands granted to the state to aid in the construction of the Illinois and Michigan Canal should be sold from time to time, and the proceeds applied to the payment of interest on the said loan, until the tolls on the proposed improvements, together with such other means as the state may provide, shall be sufficient to pay the interest on such loan.

These resolutions were referred to the Committee of the Whole, and upon them, as well as upon the bill which was subsequently reported, long, eventful, and important discussions took place. This plan was unfortunately rejected. It proposed the commencement of two roads, one traversing the state from north to south, the other from east to west, leaving to future Legislatures the task of providing for such other works as time, experience, and practical surveys and explorations might recommend. The idea of constructing two railroads only was too insignificant for the magnificent views of that day. A hundred roads would not have answered the pressing demands of an excited people, flushed with the deceitful prosperity of an inflated system of paper currency. To confine the works to these two roads would also have prevented the necessity for the state to embark as a partner in the state banks. The state was asked to authorize an increase in the banking capital of the state, to become a large stockholder in the state bank, and to make the state bank and its branches the depositories and fiscal agents of the state. All these propositions, presented in their most seductive forms, met with a firm, uncompromising hostility from Mr. Douglas. But the state was mad; no man could resist the storm which swept over it; and the entire system—internal improvements, increase of bank capital, subscription to the stock by the state, all passed by the most decided majorities, in February, 1837, and the Legislature adjourned on the 8th of March following.

A brief synopsis of the "Act to establish and maintain a general System of Improvements," approved February 27, 1837, may not be out of place here.

The act directs a survey of the route from Charleston, via the county seat of Clark County, to the most eligible point on the Great Wabash River between York and the line dividing the states of Illinois and Indiana. It makes appropriations as follows on account of the works enumerated:

1st. Improvement of the navigation of the Great Wabash River. $100,000

2d. For removal of obstacles to steam-boat navigation in Rock River.. 100,000

3d. For the Illinois River west of the 3d principal meridian.... 100,000

4th. Kaskaskia River.. 50,000

5th. Little Wabash River.. 50,000

6th. For a great Western mail route from Vincennes to Saint Louis.. 250,000

7th. For a railroad from Cairo to some point on the southern termination of the Illinois and Michigan Canal, via Vandalia, Shelbyville, Decatur, Bloomington, thence via Savannah to Galena 3,500,000

8th. For a southern cross-railroad from Alton to Mount Carmel; railroad from Edwardsville to Shawneetown, via Lebanon, Nashville, Pinckneyville, Frankfort, and Equality...................... 1,600,000

9th. For a northern cross-railroad from Quincy, via Columbus, Clayton, Mount Sterling, Meredosia, Jacksonville, Springfield, Decatur, Sidney, Danville, and thence to the Indiana state line... 1,800,000

10th. For a branch of the Central Railroad from a point between Hillsboro and Shelbyville, thence through Coles and Edgar counties to the Indiana state line.. 650,000

11th. For a railroad from Peoria, through Fulton, Macomb, Carthage, to Warsaw... 700,000

12th. For a railroad from Lower Alton, via Hillsboro, to the Illinois Central Road.. 600,000

13th. For a railroad from Belleville, via Lebanon, to intersect the Alton and Mount Carmel Railroad... 150,000

14th. For a railroad from Bloomington to Mackinaw, in Tazewell County, there to fork—one branch to connect with Peoria and Warsaw Railroad at Peoria, the other branch to pass Tremont to Pekin 350,000

A person who will take up the map of Illinois will see in the above scheme of improvements how carefully Chicago is avoided. South of and including Peoria, every representative and senatorial district is provided with one or more railroads passing through them. But, to make the bill even more palatable, the following provision was inserted, being the 15th appropriation:

15th. There shall be appropriated the sum of $200,000 of the first money that shall be obtained under the provisions of this act, to be drawn by the several counties in a ratable proportion to the census last made, through which no railroad or canal is provided to be made at the expense or cost of the State of Illinois, which said money shall be expended in the improvement of roads, constructing bridges, and other public works.

Section 21 authorized the board of fund commissioners to contract for loans, etc., of eight millions of dollars at 6 per cent., redeemable at any time after January 1, 1870. Another section provided that all moneys obtained by the board from loans and otherwise should be deposited in some *safe* bank or banks. Section 33 authorized the commissioners, in locating the several roads where the lines did not touch county seats or important trading towns, to construct lateral branches of said railroads to said towns.

Another important measure of that session was the continuation of the Illinois and Michigan Canal, which had previously been commenced by the state, a grant of land to aid in its construction having been made by Congress. Douglas was an active and earnest supporter of this great work. Upon the best plan for constructing it there was a wide diversity of opinion. The "deep cut" was one plan, and eventually was adopted. It proposed a canal to be fed from the lake at Chicago, and to run along the Illinois River to its present termination, having all the necessary lockage and dams. The other plan was to put locks and dams upon the Illinois River, making it navigable for steam-boats up to the very highest point, and then connecting it by a canal to be constructed thence to Chicago. Douglas favored the latter plan. After a long and animated contest, the two houses found themselves unable to agree. The House of Representatives adopted and adhered to for many weeks that plan which had been so strenuously urged and approved by Douglas, while the Senate as strenuously adhered to the other plan. For several weeks the contest between the two houses waxed warm; at last, there being great danger that the whole measure would fail, the Senate bill was somewhat modified (though its main features were retained) by a committee of which Douglas was a member, and was passed, he giving it his support, as better than no bill at all. Subsequent experience has not confirmed the wisdom of the Legislature. The plan adopted of a deep cut from the lake was in after years abandoned. Had the plan proposed by Douglas been adopted, the canal could have been completed for a sum less by several millions than would have been required to carry out the plan adopted by the Legislature. His speeches on this and other subjects at this session of the Legislature won for him the highest credit; his fame as an orator, but especially as a ready debater, was universal, and public men in all parts of the state sought his acquaintance and friendship.

The Legislature adjourned in March, having laid the foundation of a public debt which, for nearly a quarter of a century, has loomed up, in all its hideous proportions, an object of terror and of oppression to the people of the great and fertile State of Illinois. All was excitement; the Legislature, before adjourning, elected the commissioners for the several works of improvements, and the number of officers necessary to carry on the grand system was by no means a small one. For a few weeks all seemed prosperous and brilliant. In May the banks of the entire country suspended specie payments, and then came a revulsion. The state bank and its branches went down with the others; the alliance between the state and the banks proved an unfortunate one. It is unnecessary to state more than the general result. The Illinois banks never resumed payment; the stock sunk very low; their paper depreciated as low at times as fifty or forty cents on the dollar; the state lost all, or nearly all that it had subscribed; and, after five or six years, the charters were repealed, and Illinois continued without banks until, under the new Constitution some years later, a general banking law was adopted. The Legislature, at that same session, passed an act providing for the removal of the seat of government from Vandalia to Springfield, the removal to take place on the 4th of July, 1839.

In April, 1837, Mr. Douglas was appointed by the President register of the land office at Springfield, to which place he removed at once, and consequently vacated his seat in the Legislature.

In consequence of the panic and its prospective effects upon the system of internal improvements, Governor Duncan called a special session of the Legislature to meet in July of that year. The signs of the times were portentous of a storm such as the country had never experienced; the commercial world had already experienced some of its most destructive force. The political sky was dark unto blackness. On the 4th of March a Democratic president had been inaugurated. He had been elected by a majority most decisive. A Congress had been chosen, in which those elected as his party friends were in a large majority. Financial ruin and general bankruptcy stood vividly conspicuous in the imagined future. Mr. Van Buren called an extra session of Congress. His first message proposed, as a remedy for the present and a preventive for the future, that long-abused and now cherished scheme, the Sub-Treasury. It was popularly styled the "Divorce Bill." It was to separate forever all connection between the banks and the national government. Mr. Van Buren soon found himself deserted by his party friends not only in Congress, but throughout the country. Nowhere was the defection greater than in Illinois. The delegation in Congress (all Democrats) refused to vote for the Divorce Bill—two of them giving as their reason a desire to consult with their constituents. These two subsequently continued Democrats, and one of them is now an honored and venerable member of the party in Illinois; the other never returned, and finally went over to the Opposition. The governor of the state, elected as a Democrat, renewed the assaults upon Mr. Van Buren which at the previous session he had made upon General Jackson. Members of the Legislature quailed before the storm. Many faltered, and a few openly joined the Whigs. Mr. Buchanan, with his peculiar faculty of finding and rewarding old traitors to the Democratic party, in 1858 rescued from an oblivion of over twenty years, to which he had been consigned by the Democracy of Illinois, one of these men who had so basely abandoned his party in the dark hour of its peril, and conferred upon him an office from which an honest, honorable gentleman was removed because he was a friend of Douglas! In 1837 the traitor was applauded by the Opposition for opposing his party, and in 1858 Mr. Buchanan heaped honors upon the same man for a like treachery! The Democracy was dismayed. For years they had had possession of the state government and all its patronage. The Legislature and the governor, both elected as Democratic, were now opposed to them. Necessity demanded earnest and prompt measures for defense. The Opposition were strong, united, and led by able, gallant men. As soon as the Legislature assembled Mr. Douglas proceeded to Vandalia. The benefit of the convention system, in uniting and concentrating the party in a close contest, had been demonstrated by him in Morgan County. No state convention of either party had ever been held in Illinois. A meeting of the Democratic members of the Legislature and other persons was held on July 27, 1837, to adopt some means to produce concert of action by the party in the elections of the ensuing year, and to prevent, if possible, any farther disintegration of the party. The result of this meeting was a call for a Democratic state delegate convention, to meet at Vandalia in the December following, to nominate candidates for governor and lieutenant governor. A committee of thirty of the most distinguished Democrats of the state was appointed to prepare and publish an address to the people of the state upon the existing condition of affairs, political and financial. Douglas, Shields, Richardson, M'Clernand, and Smith were members of this committee. A state central committee of five from each congressional district was also appointed. Thus was formed the organization of the Democratic party in the State of Illinois—an organization which has remained unbroken and unconquered for nearly a quarter of a century. In another place will be found its progressive history from 1837 to 1860.

The address shortly after appeared, and was published and circulated extensively throughout the state. It had much effect in staying the disaffection in the party produced by the general prostration of business and the urgent counsels of those public men who had abandoned the party. In the mean time, political discussions, generally of the warmest character, were frequent; and at most of these, now in Springfield, and now in some other city or county, Douglas braved the storm and upheld the banners of the Democratic party. The financial remedy proposed by Mr. Van Buren was particularly defended. It fully agreed with the policy which, during the winter before, he had so laboriously but so unavailingly urged upon the Legislature with respect to state affairs. He had opposed and denounced the connection of the state and its finances with the banks, and had predicted that the results of such a union would be disastrous. Time unfortunately proved that the predictions were well founded.

The state at that time had three members of Congress, elected from separate districts. That part of the state lying south of Morgan and Sangamon counties included two districts, while the vast region extending northward to the lake and to the Wisconsin line was all embraced in one district. The convention system was again put into operation, and the several counties sent delegates to Peoria in November, 1837, to nominate a candidate for Congress from this large district —the election not to take place until August, 1838, and the member elected not to take his seat until December, 1839. The convention was held, and the contest for nomination was an active one. Mr. Douglas was nominated; he was under twenty-five years of age at that time. The vast territory embraced within the district had been rapidly increasing in population during the previous five years; the work on the canal had drawn thousands of laborers to that part of the state. Politicians had heretofore confined their operations to the central and southern part of the state, and the north had been suffered to go uncared for. The great contest of 1840 was approaching, and it was necessary that this extensive region should be visited and secured for the party. Mr. Douglas was thought to be the man for the task. At the election in 1836, that district had given Harrison a majority of above three thousand over Van Buren. Unless it were attended to, the whole state would be in peril. With but faint hopes of an election, but with strong determination to strengthen the party by urging a union and combination hitherto unpracticed, if not unknown, he accepted the nomination. His opponent was the Hon. John T. Stuart, an eminent lawyer, a fine speaker, and a gentleman long and favorably known to the people. During the winter the contest was rather of a "scattering" character, but as soon as the spring opened sufficiently to admit of traveling, the two candidates set out upon their campaign, which, commencing in March, did not close until the very night before election.

This canvass is regarded as the most wonderful, under all the circumstances, that was ever held in the West. The candidates rode from town to town, speaking together every day except Sundays. The man who takes up the map of Illinois and looks at the territory embraced in that district, will not be surprised to know that, although the candidates spoke six

days a week for five months, they were still unable to visit
every place. The excitement produced by the contest was
very great. The Democrats at first had but little hope of
electing their candidate, but as account followed account of
the wonderful effect produced by Douglas's speeches, their expectations took a different turn. As the day of election approached the anxiety became intense. It required great powers of endurance to go through the contest, and thousands
who had firmly believed that the slight frame of Douglas
would fail under the protracted effort were astounded to hear
that he continued as fresh to all appearances as his large and
finely-formed opponent. In August the election took place;
the excitement was only increased by the imperfect returns
received. There was no telegraph nor railroads at that time,
and returns were slow in reaching county seats, and still slow-
er in reaching the seat of government. For weeks the state
was in suspense. It was soon ascertained that the aggregate
vote exceeded 36,000, and that the majority either way would
not exceed twenty. Returns came imperfectly made up, and
were sent back for correction. Errors and mistakes were discovered, and friends on both sides were industriously engaged
for weeks in having these corrected. Hundreds of votes were
cast for "Stephen Douglas," and for Douglas with various other and misplaced initials. Votes were in a like manner given
for Mr. Stuart with his initials and given names transposed
or misstated. The majority, however, of these errors were on
the Douglas tickets. At one precinct on the canal Douglas
lost a large vote by a trick of one of the bosses, who had tickets prepared with the name of S. A. Douglas printed in large
type, but placed as a candidate for the Legislature. At last
the state officers announced the official canvass, and by it Stuart was declared to have a majority of five votes.

On the 4th of March following (1839) Mr. Douglas addressed a letter to Mr. Stuart, setting forth the difficulties existing
in ascertaining the true wishes of the majority of the people
of the district, and proposing that they should sign an agreement to the following effect:

1. That the state officers should again canvass the vote according to the returns, and give to Stephen A. Douglas and
John T. Stuart respectively all the votes polled for them, without reference to the spelling of their names; or, that the

state canvassers should throw out all the misspelled names, and count only those where the votes were recorded for John T. Stuart or Stephen A. Douglas.

2. That, in case the state officers declined, the recount be made by friends chosen by the parties.

3. That three persons be chosen to visit each county and examine the original poll-books, and report the number given for Stuart and Douglas respectively, by whatever initial; or report the number given for John T. Stuart and Stephen A. Douglas.

4. That both resign all claim to the election, and run the race over again.

These propositions, he said, he made to " avoid the trouble, excitement, delay, and expense of a contested election."

Mr. Stuart, on the 13th of March, answered by respectfully yet firmly declining each and every of the propositions, as he had no doubt as to the fact of his election. That ended the matter so far as Mr. Douglas was concerned. He had resigned his office to enter the canvass in 1838, and had, during the whole year, neglected his professional pursuits. He had neither the time nor the means to expend in prosecuting a contest for the seat.

The Democratic State Convention, which met in December, 1837, nominated James W. Stephenson for governor, and John S. Hacker for lieutenant governor. In April, 1838, Mr. Hacker withdrew from the contest, and Mr. Stephenson, who was charged with being a defaulter, also withdrew. Being a public defaulter had not, at that time, become such a political virtue as to entitle an individual guilty of it with the exclusive management and control of the party. It remained for a president in 1858 to make official crime the badge of executive approbation in Illinois. The state convention was recalled to assemble June 5th, 1838, and Thomas Carlin was nominated for governor, and S. H. Anderson for lieutenant governor. These gentlemen were subsequently elected, and entered upon the duties of their office in January, 1839.

The renown achieved by Douglas in his campaign with Mr. Stuart was most extensive. He was not considered as defeated; his election was claimed by the Democratic party; and the state officers, all of them belonging to the Opposition, were charged with having patched up the returns in order to give the certificate to his opponent. This charge, however, was untrue as far as the state canvassers were concerned, though, doubtless, it was justly made against some of the county officials. On the 9th of October, 1838, there was a great banquet given at the city of Quincy to Governor Carlin and Mr. Douglas, at which the latter was the great object of interest. One of the active men at that demonstration was the Hon. I. N. Morris, who now represents that district in Congress. The Opposition were not indifferent to the result. On the 29th of September a grand barbacue was given at Springfield, in celebration of the great victory gained in the defeat of Douglas. It was attended by all the leading Whigs of the state, and so important was the result considered that one of the judges of the Supreme Court left the bench and presided on the occasion.

Mr. Douglas, after the election was over, entered into partnership with a Mr. Urquhart, and announced his intention to devote himself exclusively to the law. But it was idle for him to attempt to withdraw from politics. Already he had become the acknowledged champion of democracy, and the ablest debater on the stump. Nor was the acknowledgment of his ability confined to his efforts on the stump; he already was distinguished at the bar, and in all important cases he was found on one side or the other; yet, whenever the party demanded a defense, whenever Democratic principles required an advocate, he was called from his office, and put forward to meet the array of the opposition. At that time some controversy arose about the famous "resolutions of '98," which had been assailed or ridiculed by the Whig orators of that vicinity, and on the 9th of March, 1839, an immense meeting was held at Springfield, and Mr. Douglas addressed it in a learned and able explanation and defense of those resolutions. The speech is represented by the newspapers of the time as having silenced the Opposition in their derisive assaults upon those venerable landmarks of Democratic truth.

The Legislature met in the winter of 1838–'39, and, on the 9th of January, Governor Carlin appointed the Hon. John A. M'Clernand secretary of state, and communicated the nomination to the Senate. The Senate, instead of confirming or rejecting the nomination, adopted a resolution declaring that, as there was no vacancy in the office of secretary of state, the governor could not appoint any person to the office. The effect of this action of the Senate was to keep Mr. Alexander P. Field, the then secretary of state, in his office, and to deny to the governor the power of removal. The feeling growing out of this action was very great. After repeated efforts to obtain the office, after the adjournment of the Legislature, a bill was filed before the Circuit Court, and the case of the People, *ex relatione* John A. M'Clernand *vs.* A. P. Field, came up in the Circuit Court before Judge Breese, and was argued elaborately. Judge Breese delivered a very able opinion, confirming the power of the governor to remove the secretary of state. An appeal was taken to the Supreme Court. In July, 1839, the Supreme Court met at Springfield, and the appeal was taken up. The array of counsel was brilliant: Levi Davis, Cyrus Walker, Colonel Field, and Justin Butterfield represented Mr. Field, and Wickliffe Kitchell (attorney general), Jesse B. Thomas, S. A. Douglas, J. A. M'Clernand, and James Shields appeared for the relator. The argument occupied four entire days, and is represented by contemporaneous writers as having been of the very highest character. Mr. Douglas's argument was regarded as so conclusive by the parties agreeing with him that it was published in extenso in the papers of that day.

The court consisted of four judges. Judge Brown set up the plea of being a relative of one of the parties, and refused to sit in the cause; Judges Lockwood and Wilson overruled the decision of Judge Breese, thus confirming the right of Mr. Field to retain the office in defiance of the governor. Judge Smith dissented from this opinion.

For some considerable time previous to this decision, a party had been gradually forming, and daily growing more numerous, having for their purpose a constitutional reorganization of the Supreme Court. This decision confirmed many in the impression that the court had become a mere political instrument, which, through the exercise of judicial functions, was to be used to promote party ends. The court, invested as it was, together with the governor, with the veto power, was a formidable auxiliary of the Whig party. Its members, as the Council of Revision, could hold governor and Legislature in check, and accomplish indirectly all the ends sought by the minority. A new issue was from the date of this decision formally presented to the people, and that issue was a reorganization of the Supreme Court, and in favor of that proposition the entire Democratic party in the state soon found itself arrayed.

On the 19th of November, 1839, the Whig candidates for presidential electors having already been nominated, the great presidential campaign of 1840 was opened at Springfield. Cyrus Walker, the Whig candidate, opened the debate, and Douglas was summoned to reply. The effect of that reply, though perfectly satisfactory to the Democracy, was not so to the Whigs. Mr. Lincoln was sent for, and, in the evening, made a long speech, to which Douglas again replied. The debate became an animated one, and was continued till midnight, Douglas replying to Lincoln and Walker as they successively relieved each other in the discussion. On the next day he addressed a Democratic mass convention, and made a very elaborate speech on the subject of the United States Bank. On the 9th of December the second Democratic state convention assembled at Springfield, and among the delegates were Judge Breese, who had by that time avowedly united with the Democracy, Willis Allen, J. A. M'Clernand, W. A. Richardson, Lyman Trumbull, James Shields, J. D. Caton, now of the Supreme Court, S. A. Douglas, Murray M'Connell, and others well known in the history of the state. In March, General Harrison having been nominated for the presidency by the Harrisburg Convention, the political fires were blazing extensively. A political discussion, continuing a whole week, took place at Jacksonville, in which Colonel Hardin and Colonel Baker, now of California, took the Whig side, and Mr. Lamborne and Mr. Douglas the Democratic side. On the last day of the discussion Mr. Douglas was announced to make the closing speech, and a newspaper now before us containing the account of the meeting states that the people came even from adjoining counties on horseback and in every description of vehicle to hear him. In April he was nominated for the Legislature in Sangamon County, but declined.

On the 6th of January the House of Representatives investigated certain charges preferred against the Hon. John Pearson, one of the circuit judges. Mr. Douglas, together with Messrs. Lamborn, Shields, Turney, and M'Connell, undertook the defense, and the result was a complete vindication of the persecuted gentleman. During the summer of 1840 Mr. Douglas's services were in almost daily requisition. The hard cider and log-cabin campaign was prosecuted with the most violent energy. Harrison was a Western man ; Democrats in all parts of the Union were abandoning the party, and it was confidently proclaimed, and nowhere than in Illinois more strongly believed, that "Van was a used up man." Yet the gallant Democracy of Illinois remained true to their flag, true to their principles. The contest was a severe one. Illinois had many able and accomplished Whigs—men powerful in debate, and powerful with the people because of their personal character and professional abilities. The Democratic candidates for electors had as much as men could do to follow up and meet their opposing candidates, and well and ably did they perform their duty. But to Douglas was in a great measure confided the task of encountering several able and distinguished Whigs, who, though not on the electoral ticket, were indefatigable in their exertions on the stump. For seven months Mr. Douglas devoted his time to the attempt to prevent Illinois falling into the hands of the Opposition. He traversed all the doubtful counties, strengthening the desponding, and giving new hope to the fearful. The result is known. At the August election Democratic majorities in both branches of the Legislature were elected, and the popular vote, though close, was Democratic. From August to November the battle was waged with renewed vigor. The August elections pointed out the localities in which the respective parties were weak, and to these points Douglas was dispatched, and not until the day of election in November did he rest from his labors. The state was saved to the Democratic party. In the general defeat throughout the Union, Illinois was one of the seven states that chose Democratic electors, and, save New Hampshire, stood alone in the Northern States in maintaining a Democratic supremacy. It is no disparagement to the hundreds of noble spirits who, in behalf of the Democratic party, fought the glorious fight of 1840 on the soil of Illinois, to say that to Mr. Douglas was due much of the honor and credit of the result. His strong constitution and powers of physical endurance rendered him able to perform labors which other men, no matter what might be their mental gifts, would have been unable to withstand. From one end of the state to the other, the "Little Giant" was recognized and applauded as the most conspicuous of the many heroes of that contest. His reputation as an orator, and as the forcible exponent of political principles was, by his deeds in this memorable campaign, raised to the highest point in the opinion of his party. He had already outstripped men who were veterans when he entered the state, and seven years from the day he—a sickly, feeble stranger-boy —first trod the prairies of Illinois, his name was as familiarly known, and his great abilities as fully admitted, as were the name and abilities of any other man in the state.

In the State of Illinois there had been for many years a custom of holding, during the sessions of the Legislature, a "third house," in which the lobby, composed of all persons attending at the seat of government, were admitted as members. Those who have witnessed the scenes at the sessions of the "lobby" of late years will not discover in the broad jokes and general hilarity that importance and great benefit which in olden times resulted from "Lord Coke's" assembly. The best minds and the best hearts were not always to be found in the legislative halls. The best lawyers in the state were generally in attendance on the Supreme Court during the meeting of the Legislature, and these men were often found in the meetings of the lobby. Here were discussed all the great measures pending before the Legislature, and it was often at these meetings that members of the Legislature heard arguments which, for ability and research, were never equaled within the Senate or the House. Douglas was an active member of this house. In the discussions of the many questions there presented, he was one of the ablest and one of the most conspicuous. Here was discussed the bank question, the internal improvements, the reorganization of the judiciary, the subject of alien suffrage, and, by no means the least important, the great question of repudiation.

The Legislature met on the 7th of December, 1840, both branches being Democratic. A majority of the Senate now being in favor of sustaining the governor in the removal of the secretary of state, Mr. Field abandoned the struggle and resigned the office. The governor, on the 27th of January, 1841, appointed Mr. Douglas secretary of state.

This session was destined to be one of great importance to the state, to the Democratic party, and to Mr. Douglas personally.

were on the ground of expediency. The governor dissented from his associates in council, but was overruled by the majority. The bill was, however, considered, and passed both houses by the requisite majority.

Under this act the state was divided into nine circuits, that being the number of judges of the Supreme Court ; and on the 15th of February, 1841, the Legislature met in joint convention to elect the five additional judges provided for by the act. In that convention, Sidney Breese, Stephen A. Douglas, Thomas Ford, S. H. Treat, and Walter B. Scates were chosen. In the allotment of circuits, the fifth, being the Quincy District, was assigned to Judge Douglas. On the 4th of March, 1834, a poor stranger, without friends, books, or money, he obtained, what was supposed to be a favor, from the four judges of the Supreme Court, a license to practice law ; and in less than seven years from the date of that license, by the force of his own unaided abilities, he had so won the confidence and respect of the people that he was chosen a member of that same court.

It was at this session of the Legislature that the Hon. LYMAN TRUMBULL, now of the United States Senate, introduced his resolution advising the practical repudiation of a portion of the state debt by refusing to pay interest on certain bonds of the state for which the state had received no equivalent. This measure was advocated by Trumbull in the House, and was discussed in the lobby, and in a powerful speech in the latter Mr. Douglas administered a crushing rebuke to the arrant demagoguism evinced by the mover of the resolution. The proposition was made so odious that it was soon abandoned as an unsafe hobby even for a demagogue. The state, through inability, for a number of years afterward omitted the payment of interest, but never at any time repudiated the debt ; and subsequently, when the state was in a condition to pay, the accrued interest was funded, and stock for its amount was issued bearing interest. All honor to the gallant men who met the insidious and perfidious proposition to repudiate at the threshold, and strangled it even in the hands of its author.

The circuit to which Judge Douglas was assigned was the most perplexing and annoying. It included the Mormon settlements, and there was a constant conflict between the "Saints" and the "Gentiles." Some of the most exciting scenes of his life were spent in the judicial and other proceedings growing out of the turbulence of the people connected with the Mormon leaders. Joe Smith and his people were accused of all the crimes in the calendar, particularly with all the horse-stealing committed in that section. Whether true or false, it was almost impossible to prove by sufficient legal testimony the guilt of the parties accused. The consequence was that an embittered state of feeling gradually grew up between the Mormons and the rest of the people, and these exasperated feelings often led to deeds of violence. Joe Smith was the head of the Mormon Church and people. The people held the court responsible if the prisoners escaped conviction, and the Mormons denounced the court for inclining always to the oppressors of that chosen race.

One trying scene in his judicial career will suffice to illustrate the difficulties attending the administration of justice in cases where the Mormons were parties, and at the same time serve as an illustration of the boldness and Jackson-like determination of Stephen A. Douglas. Joe Smith had been indicted for some offense, and was put upon his trial before Judge Douglas. While the case was proceeding, the people, who had collected from all parts of the country to see the prisoner, and, as they hoped, to rejoice at his conviction, became excited by the thousand stories told of Mormon outrages. Smith was represented to be, as he was in fact, the moving spirit of the sect, and it was supposed that if he were put out of the way, the entire settlements, being deprived of their leader, would break up and leave the country. Moreover, Smith was by the populace held individually responsible for all the crimes charged against his people. On this occasion the multitude had become greatly excited, and it being whispered that the evidence would hardly justify a conviction, it was proposed by some one to enter the court-house, seize the prisoner, and hang him. A gallows was at once constructed and erected in the court-house yard, and a body of four hundred men entered the court-house for the purpose of taking Smith and hanging him. As the mob boisterously and tumultuously entered and crowded toward the bench, near which Smith sat, the judge directed the sheriff to clear the court-room, as these men interrupted the proceedings. The sheriff, a small, weak man, requested "the gentlemen" to keep order and to retire, and attempted to enforce the request, but very soon informed the court that he could not do it. Gaining confidence by the confession of powerlessness on the part of the sheriff, and maddened still more by the sight of the prisoner, several of them climbed over the bar, and rushed toward Smith. The judge at once rose in his place, and, addressing by name a large-built man, who stood six and a half feet high, a Kentuckian by birth, and of great muscular strength, said, "I appoint you sheriff of this court. Select your own deputies, and as many of them as you require. Clear this court-house; the law demands it, the country demands it, and I, as judge of this court, command you to do your duty as a citizen bound to preserve the peace and enforce the laws." The newly and rather suddenly appointed sheriff "obeyed orders." He ordered the crowd to leave, the judge encouraging him all the while. The first, second, and the third who refused to quit the court-room were instantly knocked down by the powerful arm of the Kentuckian. Others were thrown out of the windows by him and his deputies, and the great crowd, baffled and discouraged by the repulse of their leaders, crowded out of the doors. In less than twenty minutes from the first entrance of the mob the court-room was cleared. A murder had been prevented. The administration of law had been protected from a violent invasion. The prisoner's right to a fair trial by the courts of his country had been vindicated, and all this by the prompt action of the judge. A feature in the case that renders it more striking is, that the judge had no power to appoint a sheriff, the duly appointed sheriff of the county being present; and in his extempore appointment he had exceeded his authority, or, more properly speaking, had assumed an authority that did not belong to him. This he well knew. But the emergency was a great one. A moment's delay would have been fatal; the least sign of hesitation would have sealed the prisoner's fate; in five minutes he would have been hanged, if, indeed, he was not killed before taken out of the building. It was no time for debate as to the limits of his power. Like Jackson at New Orleans, he assumed the responsibility of doing what necessity required. He did the only thing that was possible to prevent a murder in the precincts of the court, and a gross violation of the laws.

The gratitude of Smith was unbounded. On many previous occasions he and his followers had denounced Judge Douglas for his frequent decisions adverse to their interests in cases where they were parties, but from that time out he always treated Douglas with respect. He had learned that the best judge was not the man who decided in his favor, but the man who decided as justice demanded, and who, to protect the prisoner and preserve the laws from violence, had driven back a murderous mob! The respect of the Mormons, won by this event, was of infinite service to himself and others on a very memorable occasion. We give the story as we find it, having no doubt of its general accuracy:

"In the year 1846, the excitement against the Mormons at Nauvoo reached its height. The people of the surrounding country determined to drive them away. The Saints determined to defend themselves. A civil war seemed imminent. Governor Ford dispatched a regiment to put down both belligerents. This regiment, consisting of 450 men, was under the command of Colonel John J. Hardin, the old political opponent, but warm personal friend of Mr. Douglas, who held the post of major.

"As the little body of troops approached Nauvoo, they saw the Mormons, 4000 strong, drawn up to oppose their advance. Every man of them was known to be armed with a 'seven-shooter' and a brace of Colt's ' revolvers'—twenty-one shots to a man besides a bowie-knife.

"Hardin halted his troops just out of rifle range, and addressed them :

"'There are the Mormons, ten to one against us. I intend to attack them. If there is a coward here who wishes to go home, he may do so now. Let any man who wishes to go step to the front.'

"Not a man came forward.

"'There were, I dare say,' says Mr. Douglas, 'just 451 of us, including our colonel, who would have been glad to have retired; but not one of us had the courage to own that he was a coward.'

"'Major Douglas,' said the colonel, 'will take 100 men, will proceed to Nauvoo, arrest the twelve apostles, and bring them here !'

"'Colonel Hardin,' asked the major, quietly, so that no one else heard, 'is this a peremptory order?'

"'It is.'

"'Then I shall make an attempt to execute it. But I give you warning that not a man of us will ever return.'

"'The apostles must be taken, Major Douglas,' replied the colonel.

"'Very well, colonel. If you will send me alone you will be much more likely to get them.'

"'But you will lose your life.'

"'I will take the responsibility. If you send me alone, I will pledge myself to reach the city. As to bringing in the twelve, or getting back myself, that is quite another question. I will try.'

"'Major Douglas,' said the colonel, after reflecting a few moments, 'will proceed to Nauvoo, taking such escort as he sees fit.'

"The order was hardly given when the little major—for he was not then a 'Little Giant'—dashed off at full speed and alone. As he approached the Mormon legions, General Wells came forward to meet him, and, after a brief conversation, escorted him through the hollow square of troops into the city. He was not long in finding Brigham and the twelve. All of them were old acquaintances of his. Most of them had, in fact, been before him for trial, as judge, upon some charge or other.

"The judge is famous for his taking manners, and in a very brief time he succeeded in inducing Brigham and his associates to accompany him. They all packed themselves into the 'apostolic coach,' drawn by eight horses, and presented themselves in the camp.

"The fighting was postponed, and negotiations for the removal of the Mormons were entered upon, Judge Douglas being chief negotiator on one side. Brigham himself said but little; and, at length, said he would go out for a while, directing his associates to settle the terms. These were soon informally agreed to by the twelve, and they were committed to paper.

"Brigham returned, and asked how matters had succeeded. He was told that every thing had been settled.

"'Let me look at the terms,' said Brigham, quietly.

"He read them over hastily.

"'I'll never agree to them—never!' he exclaimed.

"The vote was formally put, and the whole twelve, without

a dissenting voice, declared against them, though they had as unanimously accepted them not five minutes before.

"The negotiations were then renewed between Brigham and Douglas. New terms were settled; and, when the vote was taken, the twelve agreed to them at once. The treaty was duly signed, and the Mormons prepared to leave the state."

The election to a seat on the bench of the Supreme Court was as unexpected as it was undesired by Mr. Douglas. He had already attained a heavy practice, particularly in the larger cases. He was located at the seat of government, and was holding an office of honor, whose duties were comparatively light, and which afforded him the use of the public library. As secretary of state he could practice law; as judge he would be compelled to perform a great amount of labor at a very disproportioned salary. But friends asked the sacrifice, pressed it, urged it, and he consented. He did not take his seat until the last day of that term; and, as soon as the court adjourned, removed his residence to the beautiful city of Quincy, on the Mississippi, and commenced his circuit duties. He had, independent of his Mormon constituents, a large district; his duties on the circuit, and at the semi-annual meeting of the court at Springfield, occupied nearly all his time. He was holding court at least ten months in each year, and the journeyings from county to county were by no means trips of pleasure. Some of the most important cases were brought before him. We have heard it stated that there was but one case of the many decided by him that was ever reversed, and that was one involving some question of practice. He was, as judge and as a member of the Council of Revision, determinedly hostile to all the attempts by legislation to prevent the collection of honest debts. In those days, when money was scarce and credit destroyed, there were demagogues who, not bold enough to imitate Trumbull in his proposition for direct repudiation, still sought, like him, popularity with the rabble by propositions for stay laws and assessment laws. One of these laws provided that, before a man's property should be sold for debt, it should be appraised by a certain number of his neighbors, and then it could not be sold on execution for less than that appraised value.

Against these and all similar acts of legislation Judge Douglas remonstrated in the Council of Revision; and whenever they came before him judicially, whenever he could do so conscientiously, he decided them to be unconstitutional, as violative of that great principle that the Legislature should not pass laws impairing the validity of contracts by *ex post facto* regulations. These and like decisions, often pronounced with striking emphasis and warmth, lost him the friendship and support of the few, but endeared him to the many, and eventually gained for him that warm confidence of the public which is sure to follow an upright adherence to the right.

The extent of his popularity at this time may be judged by an event that took place at the session of the Legislature in December, 1842. He had then been a judge nearly two years, and had been absent from the seat of government, and from the political caucusing and managing that was ever going on at that place. When the Legislature met a United States senator was to be chosen. He was then twenty-nine years of age —would not be thirty until April, 1843. The senator to be chosen was to be elected for six years from March 3, 1843. There was a demand from various parts that he should be selected. He was a friend and a supporter of the Hon. R. M. Young, then holding the place. There were several competitors for the place, and their friends urged Douglas's non-eligibility. The Constitution required senators to be thirty years of age; he would not be thirty at the time of his election. His admirers, in his absence, urged in reply that he need not, even if there was a called session, take his seat until after he had reached the required age. But such questions were not, in those days, as familiarly understood as at the present, and his nonage was used with great effect against him.

The Democratic members of the Legislature met in caucus on the evening of Friday, December 16, 1842, to nominate a candidate for United States senator. The excitement was high, and was shared in by the hundreds of leading men of the state not members of the Legislature, but present at Springfield. There were nineteen ballots before a nomination was made; and as the result of each was announced to the multitude outside, the cheering for the candidates by their respective friends added greatly to the excitement. The following was the result of the first and last ballots:

	1st.	19th.
R. M. Young	38	1
Sidney Breese	28	56
S. A. Douglas	29	51
J. A. McClernand	18	3

The Hon. Sidney Breese, having on the nineteenth ballot obtained a majority of *one*, was declared nominated, and next day was elected by the Legislature.

In December, 1841, a Democratic state convention had assembled to nominate candidates for state officers, and had nominated the Hon. A. W. Snyder for governor, and John Moore for lieutenant governor. During the canvass Mr. SNYDER died, and the Hon. THOMAS FORD, one of the judges of the Supreme Court, was placed on the ticket in his place. Messrs. Ford and Moore were elected, and entered upon the duties of their offices in January, 1843.

In the spring of 1843 Judge Douglas's health became very much impaired, and he contemplated resigning his office and spending the summer in the Indian country—that country with which, under the title of Kansas and Nebraska, his name has subsequently become so familiar! But the exigencies of the Democratic party required his services again. The state had been redistricted under the new census, the number of representatives in Congress to which Illinois was entitled had been increased to seven, and the district in which he resided was one in which the Democrats had but little hope of success. Several counties had nominated him for the office, but, in consequence of his ill health, and the seeming impossibility on his part to canvass the district, he had declined the use of his name. But on the meeting of the counties he was nominated; the persons voted for, besides Mr. Douglas, on the first ballot, were William A. Richardson, A. W. Cavarly, Ex-governor Carlin, and Ex-senator Young. The convention met at Suggsville, in Pike County. Judge Douglas was nominated on the second ballot by a most decided vote. A committee was appointed to wait upon him, and urge his acceptance, as the only hope of carrying the district.

He was, when informed of his nomination, holding court at Knoxville; he was advised, considering the doubtful chances of the election, to retain his judicial office, and resign it only in the event of his election. He rejected this advice, and, having accepted the nomination, as soon as the term was closed he resigned his office as judge.

The Hon. O. H. BROWNING, of Quincy, one of the ablest lawyers in that district, was the opposing candidate. Mr. Browning was attending court at the time, and, as soon as the judge resigned, they made out a list of appointments for joint discussion, commencing at Charleston (now Brimfield), in Peoria County, on June 23d. The district was a large one. It included the following named counties, with those which have since been formed out of them, viz., Jersey, Green, Macoupin, Calhoun, Pike, Brown, Schuyler, Adams, Marquette, Fulton, and Peoria. The two candidates from that day until the day before election traversed the district together. The election took place in August, and the contest was an excited and animated one, and the result was that Mr. Douglas was elected by a majority of 445! So great had been the exertions and labors of the candidates, that on election-day both were prostrated with illness from which neither recovered for nearly two months.

As soon as his health permitted, some time in November of the same year, he left Quincy on his way to Washington. Ten years had just elapsed since he had entered the state a poor, friendless, and unknown youth. During those ten years what an eventful life had been his. In November, 1833, he had gone from one town to another on foot, seeking employment that would yield him enough to pay for his board and washing. In November, 1843, he bore upon his person his commission as a member of Congress! In the winter of '33–4 he had accepted, as a gracious deed of kindness, the place of teacher to a school of forty pupils, at three dollars per quarter each; now he was the duly commissioned and honored representative in the councils of his country of a hundred thousand of his fellow-citizens. In 1834 he had obtained from the Supreme Court, with their sneer upon his pretensions, a license to practice law; within a few months he had resigned his seat as a colleague of those same judges to accept of a higher and more important trust confided to him by the people of Illinois. During those ten years, how strong must have been the will, and persevering the energy, that enabled him successfully to encounter all the opposition and overcome all the obstacles which met him at every path. From the day of his memorable speech in the court-house at Jacksonville he had been a marked man by friend and foe; that speech drew upon him the attention of all envious rivals in his own party, and aspiring men in the Opposition. It was the stepping-stone to an unbounded and unequaled popularity in his own party, and drew upon him the first shaft of the Opposition. When Mr. Lamborn rose to address that meeting that day, he had not the slightest doubt of " killing Douglas" before he concluded. But Douglas was not " killed;" the very means employed to destroy him he used with unequaled power in strengthening and elevating himself. The work attempted by Lamborn on that occasion was taken up by many during those first ten years of Douglas in Illinois, but the men who engaged in it failed, as have all other men who attempted the task. Where are the men who sought his political destruction in those years? They have been forgotten, or, being remembered, are remembered only because they encountered Douglas and were vanquished by him. It is unnecessary to mention names; it is unnecessary to ask what became of the men who, during those years, sought to destroy him in the estimation of the people; the only answer that need be given to such a question is to point to the tombstones that stand conspicuously upon every political battle-field of those ten eventful years.

Mr. Douglas, after his ten years' absence, visited, on his way to Congress, his friends at Cleveland and his relatives at Canandaigua. He had redeemed his promise—that he would carve out his own successful career. Unaided and alone he had gone forth; he now returned as the chosen representative of the generous people with whom he had taken up his residence. Since he had last seen his relatives, he had, from the condition of a penniless, homeless youth, been admitted to the bar, chosen state's attorney, register of the land office, secretary of state, judge of the Supreme Court, and now a member of Congress. Had he been idle? had he wasted his talents? had he misapplied his time? Was there one of the hundreds who, surrounded with all the aids of wealth and family influence, had started in life with him, could show a more brilliant or successful career, or more honorable proofs of ten years' earnest labor?

Since December, 1843, Mr. Douglas has been a representative of Illinois in one or other house of Congress. He took his seat in December, 1843, and again in December, 1845, as a member of the House. In August, 1846, he was again elected to the House; but at the session of the Legislature commencing December, 1846, he was elected to the United States Senate. In January, 1853, he was again elected to the Senate,

and in January, 1859—after the memorable contest of 1858—
he was a third time elected for a term of six years. After the
first convention which nominated him for Congress, there was
no opposition to his nomination, the party taking him up as
their candidate by universal consent. So with his election to
the United States Senate. After the caucus had nominated
him in 1847, he was elected as a matter of course; and in
1853 and in 1859 no opposition in his own party was ever
urged against his re-election.

Perhaps no man, not excepting even the great Clay, Webster, and Benton, has taken a more active part in the debates
of Congress during the time that he has been a member, than
Mr. Douglas. No branch of the public business has occupied
his whole time. He has been an untiring business man upon
all the great subjects that have been before Congress since
1843. Upon all these questions he has entered largely into
the debates, and the attentive reader of the discussions in Congress will find that Mr. Douglas's speeches are *all* devoted to
the accomplishment of *practical* ends, to be attained by following fixed principles; and that in no instance has he departed
from this policy, even when by so doing he could avoid personal hostility or obtain personal favor. His intrepidity as a
statesman has marked every step of his public career, and the
stronger and more violent the storm directed against him, the
stronger and more unyielding has been his determination to
work out the great end he had in view.

Another distinguishing mark of Mr. Douglas's career has
been that he has NEVER FAILED in any proposition which he
has undertaken seriously to have accomplished. He has introduced many measures that he has never pushed to a successful issue; but when the right time arrives for any measure
that he deems appropriate and necessary, he never has failed
to give to it all his energies, and in such case has never failed
in seeing it successful over all opposition.

In reviewing the public history of a man who, like Mr.
Douglas, has taken such an important part in the legislation
of nearly twenty years, covering a period of agitation and excitement never exceeded in the previous history of the country, it is necessary, in a work like this, to condense narratives,
when the whole story should be told, and to give the substance
only of speeches, when the entire speeches ought to be read.

Much that is valuable in the history of the country, and much that would be useful in forming a true and just estimate of Mr. Douglas's great abilities as a jurist, a statesman, and an orator, is reluctantly yet necessarily omitted in this volume. In preparing the sketch of his services in Congress, it has been found more convenient, and possibly more advantageous to the reader, to arrange them under subjects, without any strict reference to chronological order; and the reader must remember that the subjects treated of in the following pages are not all, but only a few of the leading measures in which he has taken an active part.

CHAPTER IV.

MR. DOUGLAS AND GENERAL JACKSON.

It has already been stated that Mr. Douglas's first speech of a political character in Illinois, and his first public political triumph, was at a public meeting at Jacksonville, in the spring of 1834, where he encountered the ablest of General Jackson's opponents, and in a county where the influence of the bank had paralyzed the Democracy, had silenced the old hero's champions, and was carrying unopposed all political power to the side of the monopoly. Young, inexperienced, unknown to the people, he vindicated the policy of the old veteran, and turned the tide of popular opinion in his favor. That was not the only speech, nor the only time that he encountered the gallant and eloquent orators of the Whig party in the defense of General Jackson. On the circuit while prosecuting attorney, on the stump as candidate for the Legislature, in the Legislature as a member, before the people as a candidate for Congress, on the stump as a Democratic orator, every where, on all occasions, from 1834 until the expiration of General Jackson's term of office in 1837, Mr. Douglas was selected by his political friends, and recognized by his opponents, as the especial champion of the administration, and of the personal and political character of General Andrew Jackson. It has also been stated that in boyhood, when serving as an apprentice in Vermont, he was found in the workshop, and in all congregations of youths of his own age, and even of a larger growth, the defender of Jackson. His exploits in tearing down the infamous coffin hand-bills are still remembered. Afterward, while at Canandaigua, he was noted for the fervor with which he espoused the cause of Jackson, and during the canvass of 1832 for the zeal displayed in behalf of Jackson and Marcy.

Nor was his advocacy of the principles of General Jackson terminated by the retirement of the old hero from the presidency. In Mr. Van Buren's administration, and in the trials and vicissitudes that attended its earlier days in financial matters, the old hero's cause was tried over and over again. During 1837, 8, and 9, Mr. Douglas was indefatigable on the stump and in convention in the defense of the financial policy adopted by the party. In these matters he occupied the very first position as an orator before the people of his state.

In December, 1843, he took his seat in Congress. For several years preceding there had been a struggle over a bill proposing to refund to General Jackson the fine of $1000 imposed upon him by Judge Hall, at New Orleans, during the defense of that city. Some of the best minds in Congress had considered the question, and it had been, as was thought, thoroughly discussed. The bill had never become a law. Early in the session of 1843–4 a bill was introduced, and the subject was again debated. General Jackson was extolled on all sides; most of the friends of the bill supported it as a measure of gratitude—a boon due by a grateful country to her patriotic and successful defender. On this ground it was mainly supported by its friends. On the 7th of January, 1844, Mr. Douglas obtained the floor. He was then unknown to Congress. His was a new face, and his was a strange voice in those halls. He did not follow the beaten path in his advocacy of the bill. He at once took high and strong ground in defense of General Jackson's conduct. He denied the legality of Judge Hall's judgment. This position was a bold one; the speaker attracted attention; and, as he warmed with his subject, he soon obtained the ear of the House. His speech was a success. It established his character as a lawyer and as a debater. From that time to the present day he has never been compelled to address empty benches, or an impatient, inattentive audience. As a monument to indicate his starting-point in the parliamentary history of the country, the speech is here inserted in full.

Mr. Douglas said :

When this bill was introduced by the learned gentleman from Pennsylvania (Mr. C. J. Ingersoll), I entertained the hope that it would be permitted to pass without discussion and without opposition. But the character of the amendment submitted by the gentleman from Georgia (Mr. Stephens), and the debate which has taken place upon it and the original bill, have been of such a nature as to justify and require the friends of the bill to go into a discussion of the whole subject. For one, I am not disposed to shrink from the investigation of any question connected with this subject, nor am I prepared to acquiesce silently in the correctness of the imputations cast upon the friends of this measure by gentlemen in the Opposition. They have been pleased to stigmatize this act of justice to the distinguished patriot and hero as a humbug—a party trick—a political movement, intended to operate upon the next Presidential election. These imputations are as unfounded as they are uncourteous, and I hurl them back, in the spirit which they deserve, upon any man who is capable of harboring, much less expressing, such a sentiment. It ill becomes gentlemen to profess to be the real friends of General Jackson, and the exclusive guardians of his fame, and to characterize our effort as sinister and insincere, while in the same breath they charge him with violating the Constitution and laws, and trampling with ruthless violence upon the judiciary of the country. They seem to act upon the principle that the most successful mode of blackening the character of a great and good man is to profess to be his friends while making unfounded admissions against him, which, if true, would blast his reputation forever. If these are to be taken as the kind offering of friendship, well may the old hero pray God to deliver him from the hands of his friends, and leave him to take care of his enemies. I insist that this bill has been brought forward and supported in good faith as an act of justice—strict, rigid, impartial justice to the American people, as well as their bravest defender. The country has an interest in the character of her public men—their unsullied fame gives brilliancy to her glory. The history of General Jackson is so inseparably connected with the history of this country, that the slightest blot upon the one would fix an indelible stain upon the other. Hence the duty, the high and patriotic duty, of the representatives of the people to efface every unjust stigma from the spotless character of that truly great man, and transmit his name to posterity adorned with all the charms which the light of truth will impart to it. The charge of exerting arbitrary power and lawless violence over courts, and Legislatures, and civil institutions, in derogation of the Constitution and laws, and without the sanction of rightful authority, have been so often made and reiterated for political effect, that doubtless many candid men have been disposed to repose faith in their correctness, without taking the pains to examine carefully the grounds upon which they rest.

A question involving the right of the country to use the means necessary to its defense from foreign invasion in times of imminent and impending danger is too vitally important to be yielded without an inquiry into the nature and source of the fatal restriction which is to deprive a nation of the power of self-preservation. The proposition contended for by the Opposition is, that the general in command, to whose protection are committed the country, and the lives, property, and liberties of the citizens within his district, may not declare martial law when it is ascertained that its exercise, and it alone, can save all from total destruction. It is gravely contended that in such an awful conjuncture of circumstances, the general must abandon all to the mercy of the enemy, because he is not authorized to elevate the military above the civil authorities, and that, too, when it is certain that nothing but the power of the military law can save the civil laws and the Constitution of the country from complete annihilation. If these are not the positions assumed by gentlemen in so many words, they are unquestionably the conclusion to which their positions necessarily and inevitably conduct us; for no man pretends to venture the assertion that the city of New Orleans could, by any human agency or effort, have been saved in any other manner than the declaration and enforcement of martial law. For one, I maintain that, in the exercise of this power, General Jackson did not violate the Constitution, nor assume to himself any authority which was not fully authorized and legalized by his position, his duty, and the unavoidable necessity of the case. Sir, I admit that the declaration of martial law is the exercise of a summary, arbitrary, and despotic power, like that of a judge punishing for contempt, without evidence, or trial, or jury, and without any other law than his own will, or any limit to the punishment but his own discretion. The power in the two cases is analogous; it rests upon the same principle, and is derivable from the same source—extreme necessity. The gentleman from New York (Mr. Barnard), in his legal argument to establish the right of Judge Hall to fine General Jackson one thousand dollars for contempt of court, without the forms of trial, has informed us that this power is not conferred by the common law, nor by statute, nor by any express provision, but is inherent in every judicial tribunal and every legislative body. He has cited the decision of the Supreme Court of the United States in support of this doctrine, and I do not deem it necessary, for the purposes of this argument, to question its soundness. The ground upon which it is held that this extraordinary power is original, and inherent in all courts and deliberative bodies, is, that it is necessary to enable them to perform the duties imposed upon them by the Constitution and laws. It is said that the divine and inalienable right of self-defense applies to courts and Legislatures, to communities, and states, and nations, as well as individuals. The power, it is said, is coextensive with the duty, and, by virtue of this principle, each of these bodies is authorized not only to use the means essential to the performance of the duty, but also to exercise the powers necessary to remove all obstructions to the discharge of that duty. Let us apply these principles to the proceedings at New Orleans, and see to what results they will bring us.

General Jackson was the legally and constitutionally authorized agent of the government and the country to defend that city and its adjacent territory. His duty, as prescribed by the Constitution and laws, as well as the instructions of the War Department, was to defend the city and country at every hazard. It was then conceded, and is now conceded on all sides, that nothing but martial law would enable him to perform that duty. If, then, his power was commensurate with his duty, and (to follow the language of the courts) he was authorized to use the means essential to its performance, and to exercise the powers necessary to remove all obstructions necessary to its accomplishment—he had a right to declare martial law, when it was ascertained and acknowledged that nothing but martial law would enable him to defend the city and the country. This principle has been recognized and acted upon by all civilized nations, and is familiar to those who are conversant with military history. It does not imply the right to suspend the laws and civil tribunals at pleasure. The right grows out of the necessity; and when the necessity fails, the right ceases. It may be absolute or qualified, general or partial, according to the exigencies of the case. The principle is, that the general may go so far, and no farther, than is absolutely necessary to the defense of the city or district committed to his protection. To this extent General Jackson was justifiable; if he went beyond it the law was against him. But, in point of fact, he did not supersede the laws, nor molest the proceedings of the civil tribunals, any farther than they were calculated to obstruct the execution of his plans for the defense of the city. In all other respects the laws prevailed, and were administered as in times of peace, until the Legislature of the State of Louisiana passed an act suspending them till the month of May, in consequence of the impending danger that threatened the city. There are exigencies in the history of nations as well as individuals when necessity becomes the paramount law to which all other considerations must yield. It is that great first law of nature, which authorizes a man to defend his life, his person, his wife and children, at all hazards, and by every means in his power. It is that law which authorizes this body to repel aggression and insult, and to protect itself in the exercise of its legislative functions; it is that law which enables courts to defend themselves and punish for contempt. It was this same law which authorized General Jackson to defend New Orleans by resorting to the only means in his power which could accomplish the end. In such a crisis, necessity confers the authority and defines its limits. If it becomes necessary to blow up a fort, it is right to do it; if it is necessary to sink a vessel, it is right to sink it; and if it is necessary to burn a city, it is right to burn it. I will not fatigue the committee with a detailed account of the occurrences of that period, and the circumstances surrounding the general, which rendered the danger immediate and impending, the necessity unavoidable, the duty imperative, and temporizing ruinous. That task has been performed with such felicity and fidelity by the gentleman from Louisiana (Mr. Slidell) as to make a recital of the facts entirely unnecessary. The enemy—composed of disciplined troops, exceeding our force four-fold in numbers—were in the immediate vicinity of the city, ready for the attack at any moment. Our own little flotilla already destroyed; the city filled with traitors, anxious to surrender; spies transmitting information daily and nightly between these traitors and the enemy's camp; the population mostly emigrants from the different European countries, speaking various languages, unknown to the general in command, which prevented any accurate information of the extent of the disaffection; the dread of a servile insurrection, stimulated by the proclamation and the promises of the enemy, of which the firing of the first gun was to be the signal—these were some of the reasons which produced the conviction in the minds of all who were faithful to the country and desirous to see it defended, that their only salvation depended upon the existence of martial law. The governor, the judges, the public authorities generally, and all the citizens who espoused the American cause, came forward, and earnestly entreated General Jackson, for their sakes, to declare martial law, as the only means of maintaining the supremacy of the American laws and institutions over British authority within the limits of our own territory. General Jackson, concurring with them in opinion, promptly issued the order, and enforced it by the weight of his authority. The city was saved. The country was defended by a succession of the most brilliant military achievements that ever adorned the annals of this or any other country, in this or any other age. Martial law was continued no longer than the danger (and, consequently, the necessity) existed. At the time when Louallier was imprisoned and Judge Hall was sent out of the city, official news of the signing of the treaty at Ghent had not been received; hostilities had not ceased; nor had the enemy retired. On the very day the writ of habeas corpus for Louallier was returnable, General Jackson received official instructions from the War Department to raise additional troops, and prepare for a vigorous prosecution of the war. Hearing a rumor, on the same day, that a treaty of peace had been signed, he sent a proposition to the British general for a cessation of hostilities until official intelligence should be received, which proposition was rejected by the English commander. It can not be said, therefore, that the war had closed, or the necessity for martial law had ceased. All the considerations which induced its declaration required its continuance. If it was right to declare it, it was right to enforce and continue it. At all events, Judge Hall and his eulogists are estopped from denying the power or the propriety of the declaration or the enforcement of martial law. He advised, urged, and solicited General Jackson to declare it, and subsequently expressed his approbation of the act. Yes, even that learned, that profound, that immaculate judge, D. A. Hall, himself advised and approved of the proceeding. Did he not understand the Constitution and laws which it was his duty to administer? or, understanding them, did he advise General Jackson to do an act in direct violation of that Constitution which he was sworn to support and protect? Conscientious judge! Advise a military officer, when in the discharge of a high and responsible duty, to violate the Constitution, and then arrest and punish him, without evidence or trial, for that very violation!

Rare specimen of judicial integrity! Perfidiously advise the general for the purpose of entrapping him into the commission of an unlawful act, that he might wreak his vengeance upon him according to the most approved forms of the Star Chamber! I would like to hear from his most ardent admirers on this floor upon that point. It is material to the formation of a correct judgment upon the merits of this question. One of two things is necessarily true in this matter: either he was guilty of the most infamous, damnable perfidy, or he believed that General Jackson was acting within the scope of his rightful authority for the defense of the country, its Constitution, and laws. In either event, his conduct was palpably and totally indefensible. Having advised the course which General Jackson pursued—even if he had changed his opinion as to the correctness of that advice, and the legality of the acts which had been committed in pursuance of it, and even if, under these circumstances, he had felt it his duty to vindicate the supremacy of the laws and the authority of his court by inflicting the penalty of the law —yet a mere nominal fine (one cent) would have accomplished that object as effectually as one thousand dollars. In this view, it was not a case requiring exemplary punishment. He did not doubt—he would not doubt—that the general had acted conscientiously, under a high sense of duty; and if he had exceeded his authority, if he had committed an error, it was an error into which he had been led by the advice of that very judge, whose duty it was to know the law and advise correctly, and who afterward, with the shameless perversity of his nature, enforced a vindictive penalty. I boldly assert that the judgment was vindictive, because the amount of the fine, under the circumstances of the case, is conclusive upon that point. But if I should grant, for the sake of argument (that which I do not admit), that General Jackson exceeded his authority, and thereby violated the Constitution and laws, and that Judge Hall was clothed with the competent power to punish the offense, still I am prepared to show that, even in that event, the judgment was unjust, irregular, and illegal. The champions of Judge Hall on this floor have debated the question as if the mere declaration of martial law of itself was a contempt of court, without reference to the fact whether it actually interrupted and obstructed the proceedings of the court. Was there ever a more fatal and egregious error? Every unlawful act is not necessarily a contempt of court. A man may be guilty of every offense upon the whole catalogue of crime, and thus obtain for himself an unenviable immortality, without committing a contempt of court. The doctrine of contempts only applies to those acts which obstruct the proceedings of the court, and against which the general laws of the land do not afford adequate protection. It is this same doctrine of necessity, conferring power, and at the same time restricting its exercise within the narrow limits of self-defense. The rights of the citizen, the liberties of the people of this country, are secured by that provision of the Constitution of the United States which declares that " the trial of all crimes, except in cases of impeachment, shall be by jury;" and also the amendment to the Constitution which requires "a presentment or indictment of a grand jury." General Jackson, as well as the humblest citizen and the vilest criminal, was entitled to the benefit of these constitutional provisions. If he had violated the Constitution, and suspended the laws, and committed crimes, Judge Hall had no right to punish him by the summary process of the doctrine of contempts, without indictment, or jury, or evidence, or the forms of trial. It is incumbent upon those who defend and applaud the conduct of the judge to point out the specific act done by General Jackson which constituted a contempt of court. The mere declaration of martial law is not of that character. If it was improperly and unnecessarily declared, the general was liable to be tried by a court-martial, according to the rules and articles of war established by Congress for that purpose. It was a matter over which the civil tribunals had no jurisdiction, and with which they had no concern, unless some specific crime had been committed or injury done; and not even then until it was brought before them according to the forms of law. Some specifications have been made in the speeches of gentlemen against General Jackson, which I will notice in their proper order.

The first is the arrest and imprisonment of Louallier on the charge of instigating treason and mutiny in the general's camp. It is immaterial for the purposes of this discussion whether he was actually guilty or not. He stood charged with the commission of high crimes, the punishment of which was death. He was believed to be guilty, and consequently there was probable cause for his arrest and commitment for trial, according to the doctrine of the courts. If permitted to go at large, he might have matured and executed his plans of mutiny and treason by the aid of the British army, which was then hovering around the city. But, supposing this arrest to have been contrary to law, as gentlemen contend, yet it was no contempt of court. If it was an offense at all, it was a case of false imprisonment, which was indictable before a grand jury and triable by a petit jury. Why did they not proceed against General Jackson according to law, and give him a trial by a jury of his country, and obtain a verdict according to evidence? The answer is obvious: they could not procure a verdict of "Guilty" from an honest and patriotic jury who had fought in defense of the city under the operation of that "terrible martial law," and who had witnessed the necessity for its declaration, and its glorious effects in the salvation of the country.

The next specification which gentlemen make against General Jackson is, that he did not appear before Judge Hall in obedience to a writ of habeas corpus issued by the judge for the liberation of Louallier, who was in confinement on a charge of mutiny and treason. A simple statement of the facts of this case will carry with it the general's justification. The evidence shows that the writ was issued on the fifth of the month, and made returnable on the sixth, before Judge Hall, at eleven o'clock in the morning, and that it was never served on General Jackson, or shown to him, until the evening afterward. Hence it was impossible for him to have complied with the injunctions of that writ, if he had desired to do so. The writ had spent its force, had expired, was *functus officio* before it reached General Jackson. There was no command of the court remaining that could be obeyed, the time had elapsed. These facts were distinctly set forth by General Jackson, under oath, in his answer to the rule of court requiring him to show cause why he should not be punished for contempt; and they have never been denied. In fact, there is an abundance of corroborative evidence to the same effect. From these facts, it is clear, first, that General Jackson had committed no contempt of court; and, secondly, if he had, he fully purged himself of the alleged offense.

The next specification in the catalogue of crimes which gentlemen charge upon the hero of New Orleans is, that he forcibly seized and retained possession of the writ, and the affidavit on which it was issued. The facts are, that when the writ and affidavit were brought to him for service, after the time for its return had elapsed and it had become a nullity, he discovered that a material alteration had been made, in the handwriting of the judge, not only in the writ, but also in the affidavit, without the consent of the man who had sworn to it. These alterations of themselves rendered the papers void, even if they had been originally valid, and had not expired of their own limitation; but, as they contained the evidence upon their face of the crime of forgery, it was important that General Jackson should retain possession of them, lest they should be destroyed and the evidence lost. With this view, the general did retain the originals and furnish certified copies to the judge. These transactions did not occur in the presence of the judge or his court, nor when his court was in session, and, of course, could not legally be punished by the summary process of contempt. If they were illegal, why not give the benefit of a fair trial by a jury of his country, as guaranteed by the Constitution and laws? No; this was arbitrarily and unjustly withheld from him, thereby denying him the privilege of proving his innocence.

The next, and the last, of these high crimes and misdemeanors imputed to Jackson at New Orleans is that of arresting Judge Hall and sending him beyond the limits of the city, with instructions not to return until peace was restored. The justification of this act is found in the necessity which required the declaration of martial law, and its continuance and enforcement until the enemy should have left our shores, or the treaty of peace should have been ratified and published. The judge had confederated with Louallier and the rest of that band of conspirators, who were attempting to defeat the efforts of the American general for the defense of the city. Their movements were dangerous, because they were protected by the power of civil law, in the person of Judge Hall, by a perversion of the privileges of the writ of habeas corpus. The general was driven to an extremity, in which he was compelled either to abandon the city to whatever fate the conspirators might choose to consign it, or to resolutely maintain his authority by the exertion of his own power. He TOOK THE RESPONSIBILITY, and sent the judge beyond the lines of his camp. The question arises, was this act a contempt of court? The court was not in session, he did not interrupt its proceeding, he did not obstruct its progress, but he did imprison the man who had been exercising the powers of judge. If that imprisonment had been unlawful, the general was liable to be indicted for false imprisonment, and, like any other offender, to be tried and condemned according to the forms of law. But the judge had no right to say "vengeance is mine," and I will visit it upon the head of my enemy until the measure of my revenge is full.

Now, sir, I have disposed of all the specifications of crime, and oppression, and tyranny which have been charged upon General Jackson by his enemies upon this floor, in connection with his defense of New Orleans. I have endeavored to state the facts truly, and fairly apply the principles of law to them. I will thank the most learned and astute lawyer upon this floor to point out which one of those acts was a contempt of court, in the legal sense of that term, so as to authorize a summary infliction of punishment without evidence, trial, or jury? No gentleman has yet specified the act, and explained wherein the contempt consisted; and I presume no one will venture on so difficult a task. It is more prudent to deal in vague generalities and high-sounding declamation, first about the horrors of arbitrary power and lawless violence, then the supremacy of the laws and the glorious privileges of the writ of habeas corpus. These things sound very well, and are right in their proper place. I do not wish to extenuate the one or depreciate the other; but when I hear gentlemen attempting to justify this unrighteous fine upon General Jackson upon the ground of non-compliance with rules of court and mere formalities, I must confess that I can not appreciate the force of the argument. In cases of war and desolation, in times of peril and disaster, we should look at the substance and not the shadow of things. I envy not the feelings of the man who can reason coolly and calmly about the force of precedents and the tendency of examples in the fury of the war-cry, when "booty and beauty" is the watchword. Talk not to me about rules and forms in court when the enemy's cannon are pointed at the door, and the flames encircle the cupola! The man whose stoicism would enable him to philosophize coolly under these circumstances would fiddle while the Capitol was burning, and laugh at the horror and anguish that surrounded him in the midst of the conflagration! I claim not the possession of these remarkable feelings. I concede them all to those who think that the savior of New Orleans ought to be treated like a criminal for not possessing them in a higher degree. Their course in this debate has proved them worthy disciples of the doctrine they profess. Let them receive all the encomiums which such sentiments are calculated to inspire.

But, sir, for the purposes of General Jackson's justification, I care not whether his proceedings were legal or illegal, constitutional or unconstitutional, with or without precedent, if they were necessary for the salvation of that city. And I care as little whether he observed all the rules and forms of court, and technicalities of the law, which some gentlemen seem to consider the perfection of reason and the essence of wisdom. There was but one form necessary on that occasion, and that was to point cannon and destroy the enemy. The gentleman from New York (Mr. Barnard), to whose speech I have had occasion to refer so frequently, has informed us that this bill is unprecedented. I have no doubt this remark is technically true according to the most approved forms. I presume no case can be found on record, or traced by tradition, where a fine, imposed upon a general for saving his country, at the peril of his life and reputation, has ever been refunded. Such a case would furnish a choice page in the history of any country. I grant that it is unprecedented, and for that reason we desire on this day to make a precedent which shall command the admiration of the world, and be transmitted to future generations as an evidence that the people of this age and in this country were not unjust to their benefactor. This bill is unprecedented, because no court ever before imposed a fine under the same circumstances. In this respect Judge Hall himself stands unprecedented.

The gentleman from Louisiana (Mr. Dawson), who addressed the committee the other day, told us that General Wilkinson declared martial law at New Orleans and enforced it at the time of Burr's conspiracy. Where was Judge Hall then that he did not vindicate the supremacy of the laws and the authority of his court? Why did he not then inflict the penalty of the law upon the perpetrator of such a gross infraction of the Constitution which he was sworn to defend and support? Perhaps his admirers here will tell us that he did not advise, and urge, and entreat General Wilkinson to declare martial law. I believe that feature does distinguish the two cases, and gentlemen are entitled to all the merit they can derive from it. I am informed that in one of those trying cases during the last war, which required great energy and nerve, and self-sacrificing patriotism, General Gaines had the firmness to declare martial law at Sackett's Harbor; and when, after the danger had passed, he submitted himself to the civil authorities, he received the penalty of the law in the shape of a public dinner instead of a vindictive punishment. I doubt not many other cases of a similar nature may be found, if any one will take the trouble of examining the history of our two wars with Great Britain. But if the gentleman from New York intended to assert that it was unprecedented for Congress to remunerate military and naval commanders for fines, judgments, and damages assessed against them by courts for violating the laws in the honest discharge of their public duties, I must be permitted to inform him that he has not examined the legislation of his country in that respect. If the gentleman will read the speech of the pure, noble, and lamented Linn in the Senate, in May, 1842, he will find there a long list of cases in which laws of this kind have been passed.

He said, "There were precedents innumerable where officers have been found guilty of breaches of law in the discharge of their public duty, and therefore calling for the interference of a just government. Of these it is only necessary to introduce a few where the government did interpose and give relief to the injured officer. These cases commenced as early as August, 1790, and have continued down to the present time. Thus, in April, 1818, Major General Jacob Brown was indemnified for damages sustained under sentence of civil law for having confined an individual found near his camp suspected of traitorous designs.

"At the same session Captain Austin and Lieutenant Wells were indemnified against nine judgments, amounting to upward of $6000, for having confined nine individuals suspected of treachery to the country. In this case it was justly remarked by the secretary of war (John C. Calhoun), that 'if it should be determined that no law authorized' the act, 'yet I would respectfully suggest that there may be cases in the exigencies of the war in which, if the commander should transcend his legal power, Congress ought to protect him, and those who acted under him, from consequential damages.'

"In the case of General Robert Swartwout in 1823, the committee by whom it was reported stated that 'it is considered one of those extreme cases of necessity in which an overstepping of the established legal rules of society stands fully justified.'"

I will not occupy the time of the committee with further quotations, but will refer those who may wish to examine the subject to the speech itself, and the cases there cited.

These cases fully sustain the position I have taken, and prove that the government has repeatedly recognized and sanctioned the doctrine that in cases of "extreme necessity the commander is fully justified" in superseding the civil laws, and that Congress will always "make remuneration when they are satisfied he acted with the sole view of promoting the public interests confided to his command." The principle deducible from all the cases is, that when the necessity is extreme and unavoidable, the commander is fully justified, provided he acted in good faith; and, in either event, Congress will always make remuneration. Then, sir, I trust I have shown to the satisfaction of all candid men that, instead of this bill being unprecedented, the opposition—the fierce, bitter, vindictive opposition to its passage is unprecedented in the annals of American legislation. Are gentlemen desirous of making General Jackson an exception to those principles of justice which have prevailed in all other cases? They mistake the character of the American people if they suppose they sever the cords which bind them to their great benefactor by continued acts of wanton injustice and base ingratitude.

Why this persevering resistance to the will of the people, which has been expressed in a manner too imperative and authoritative to be successfully resisted? The people demand this measure, and they will never be quieted until their wishes shall have been respected and their will obeyed. They will ask, they will demand the reason why General Jackson has been selected as the victim, and his case made an ignominious exception to the principles which have been adopted in all other cases, from the foundation of the government until the present moment. Was there any thing in his conduct at New Orleans to justify this wide departure from the uniform practice of the government, and single him out as an outlaw who had forfeited all claim to the justice and protection of his country? Does the man live who will have the hardihood to question his patriotism, his honesty, the purity of his motives in every act he performed, and every power he exercised on that trying occasion? While none dare impeach his motives, they tell us he assumed almost unlimited power.

I commend him for it; the exigency required it. I admire that elevation of soul which rises above all personal considerations, and, regardless of consequences, stakes life, and honor, and glory upon the issue, when the salvation of the country depends upon the result. I also admire that calmness, moderation, and submission to rightful authority, which should always prevail in times of peace and security. The conduct of General Jackson furnished the most brilliant specimens of each the world ever witnessed. I know not which to applaud most, his acts of high responsibility and deeds of noble daring in the midst of peril and danger, or his mildness, and moderation, and lamb-like submission to the laws and civil authorities when peace was restored to his country.

Can gentlemen see nothing to admire, nothing to commend, in the closing scenes, when, fresh from the battle-field, the victorious general—the idol of his army and the acknowledged savior of his countrymen—stood before Judge Hall, and quelled the tumult and indignant murmurs of the multitude by telling him that "the same arm which had defended the city from the ravages of a foreign enemy should protect him in the discharge of his duty?" Is this the conduct of a lawless desperado, who delights in trampling upon Constitution, and law, and right? Is there no reverence for the supremacy of the laws and the civil institutions of the country displayed on this occasion? If such acts of heroism and moderation, of chivalry and submission, have no charms to excite the admiration or soften the animosities of gentlemen in the Opposition, I have no desire to see them vote for this bill. The character of the hero of New Orleans requires no endorsement from such a source. They wish to fix a mark, a stigma of reproach, upon his character, and send him to his grave branded as a criminal. His stern, inflexible adherence to Democratic principles, his unwavering devotion to his country, and his intrepid opposition to her enemies, have so long thwarted their unhallowed schemes of ambition and power, that they fear the potency of his name on earth, even after his spirit shall have ascended to heaven.

The bill passed the House, and subsequently passed the Senate.

After the adjournment of Congress, Messrs. Polk and Clay having been nominated for the Presidency by their respective parties, a monster convention was held at Nashville, Tennessee, to which delegations and distinguished men from all the Western States were invited. A large delegation from Illinois, including Mr. Douglas, went to Nashville. The attendance was immense. A letter now before us from one who was present states: "It was a monster gathering; forty acres were scarcely able to afford standing-room for the vast assemblage of men and women there collected from nearly every state in the Union. Some of the most brilliant orators in the country were there; the masses hung upon their lips day after day with increased interest, but at last the hour came for the adjournment.

Many had come from a great distance, not only to attend the convention, but also to see that GREAT MAN who had for so long a period and so prominently occupied the hearts of his countrymen. They could not leave without the long-wished-for pleasure of seeing ANDREW JACKSON. The moment the speaking had closed, the immense throng turned their steps toward the 'Hermitage.' I remember well the appearance of the vast procession—the countless multitude, as it came surging down the main road leading to the home of Jackson. As the people entered the avenue leading from the high road to the plain but capacious dwelling, the old patriot, though feeble from age, roused himself once more to receive the sincere and unbought homage of his grateful and confiding countrymen. He took a seat on a sofa in the large hall opposite to the porch and entrance. The multitude filled every standing-point in front of the mansion. Affectionate friends surrounded him; the throng asked but the privilege of seeing and taking him by the hand once more. They approached in files, shook hands with him, and then passed on through the hall. Thousands passed thus before the old hero. * * * * At last our friend, Judge Douglas, of Illinois, approached. I remember well how pale he looked, and how small and plain he seemed beside the hundreds of robust and gallant specimens of Tennessee manhood. Governor Clement C. Clay, of Alabama, a senator of the United States, had been for some time acting as the medium of introduction to strangers. The scene that ensued was one never to be forgotten."

One of the Illinois delegation who accompanied Judge Douglas was WILLIAM WALTERS, Esq., the editor of the "ILLINOIS STATE REGISTER," the most influential as well as the ablest conducted paper in the state. Mr. Walters was with Judge Douglas at the moment of his introduction to General Jackson, and on his return to Springfield a few days thereafter he published the following description of what took place:

"Every thing that relates to Andrew Jackson, the hero of New Orleans and the friend of his country, is of deep interest to the American people; and although the incident we are about to relate is in itself of no great interest, it becomes so to us in consequence of those connected with it.

"At the Nashville Convention of August last, we visited the Hermitage, only twelve miles distant, in company with Judge Douglas, of this state, and some others of our fellow-citizens. The Hermitage was crowded with people from almost every state, who had been invited thither by the venerable patriot on the day succeeding the convention.

"Governor Clay, of Alabama, was near General Jackson, who was himself sitting on a sofa in the hall, and as each person entered, the governor introduced him to the hero and he passed along. When Judge Douglas was thus introduced, General Jackson raised his still brilliant eyes and gazed for a moment in the countenance of the judge, still retaining his hand. 'Are you the Mr. Douglas, of Illinois, who delivered a speech last session on the subject of the fine imposed on me for declaring martial law at New Orleans?' asked General Jackson.

"'I have delivered a speech in the House of Representatives upon that subject,' was the modest reply of our friend.

"'Then stop,' said General Jackson; 'sit down here beside me. I desire to return you my thanks for that speech. You are the first man that has ever relieved my mind on a subject which has rested upon it for thirty years. My enemies have always charged me with violating the Constitution of my country by declaring martial law at New Orleans, and my friends have always admitted the violation, but have contended that circumstances justified me in that violation. I never could understand how it was that the performance of a solemn duty to my country—a duty which, if I had neglected, would have made me a traitor in the sight of God and man, could properly be pronounced a violation of the Constitution. I felt convinced in my own mind that I was not guilty of such a heinous offense; but I could never make out a legal justification of my course, nor has it ever been done, sir, until you, on the floor of Congress, at the late session, established it beyond the possibility of cavil or doubt. I thank you, sir, for that speech. It has relieved my mind from the only circumstance that rested painfully upon it. Throughout my whole life I never performed an official act which I viewed as a violation of the Constitution of my country; and I can now go down to the grave in peace, with the perfect consciousness that I have not broken, at any period of my life, the Constitution or laws of my country.'

"Thus spoke the old hero, his countenance brightened by emotions which it is impossible for us to describe. We turned to look at Douglas—he was speechless. He could not reply, but convulsively shaking the aged veteran's hand, he rose and left the hall. Certainly General Jackson had paid him the highest compliment he could have bestowed on any individual."

It has been stated publicly, and we know of no reason for questioning the truth of the statement, that General Jackson, at his death, bequeathed all his papers to FRANCIS P. BLAIR, the editor of the Washington Globe, and that among them was found the pamphlet copy of Judge Douglas's speech, with an endorsement, in Jackson's own handwriting, signed by him, in these words: "This speech constitutes my defense; I lay it aside as an inheritance for my grandchildren."

It is doubtful whether, in the long and eventful public life of Mr. Douglas, there has ever been a moment when words of applause and approbation have ever sounded so pleasant in his ears as those thrilling sentences of the venerable hero, General Jackson.

On the 8th of January, 1853, the magnificent equestrian statue of Jackson, by Clark Mills, was erected in Lafayette Square, Washington City, and the committee of arrangements had previously invited Mr. Douglas to deliver the oration on the occasion. As the orator was selected because of his well-known efforts in the cause of the patriot, and because of the high esteem in which General Jackson held him, the invitation was most appropriately directed to Mr. Douglas. On that occasion Mr. Douglas delivered a most polished and graceful address, in which he reviewed the policy of preserving the memory of the deeds of the great and good by the aid of the highest works of art. He gave, also, a graphic and eloquent sketch of General Jackson's history, personal, military, and political, and pointed with a touching power to his brilliant example as one which could never fail to deserve the approval of the American people. The following extract gives, in a few words, his rapid recapitulation of General Jackson's peculiarities as a statesman.

"The high qualities which, in a different theatre, had sustained him in every emergency, enabled him to rise superior to all resistance, never failed him in his civil administration. Calm, patient, and even deferential in counsel, when his opinion was matured and his resolution formed he threw all the fiery energy of his nature into its execution. The history of his civil career, like that of his military campaigns, consists of a rapid succession of terrific conflicts and brilliant achievements, in which he never lost a battle or failed in a skirmish. His state papers will stand forth, so long as the history of this republic shall be read, as imperishable monuments to his statesmanship."

The candid observer of Mr. Douglas's own course as a statesman will not be at a loss to know whose example he has followed so successfully as a public man and as a statesman.

CHAPTER V.

THE ANNEXATION OF TEXAS AND MEXICAN WAR.

Mr. Douglas was one of the most ardent supporters of the annexation of Texas. In 1844 the Democratic convention coupled the annexation of Texas with the Oregon question, and thenceforth Mr. Douglas, as well from his own judgment as because they formed part of the Democratic platform, strenuously supported both measures. A portion of the party surrendered 54° 40', much to his regret and against his earnest protest; but he still adhered to the other measure, and was one of the most able advocates it had in Congress. His speech on the annexation of Texas stands upon the record not exceeded, and rarely equaled, in point of ability, by any of the very many elaborate speeches made upon that subject.

While the joint resolution was pending, he proposed that the Missouri line of 36° 30' should be preserved as a settlement of the slavery question, and that it should be renewed and perpetuated in the resolution of annexation. Though the resolution subsequently adopted was not the one proposed by Mr. Douglas, yet his proposition applying the line of 36° 30' to the territory acquired by the annexation was incorporated into the measure, and subsequently became part of the law. His course upon this point is sufficiently elucidated in subsequent chapters, and it is unnecessary farther to refer to it here.

THE MEXICAN WAR.

Texas was annexed in 1845, and at the next session was admitted into the Union. The events following that action of the United States resulted in the invasion of American soil by Mexican troops.

On the 11th of May, 1846, President Polk informed Congress that war existed by the act of Mexico, and urged that Congress should authorize the President to call into the service of the United States a force of volunteer troops. In the House of Representatives (of which Mr. Douglas was then a member) the message was read. The reading of the most voluminous correspondence was called for. The message and correspondence were laid on the table, and, pending a motion to print, they were taken from the table and referred to the Committee of the Whole. They were also ordered to be printed. The House then went into Committee of the Whole. On the 27th of January the Committee on Military Affairs had reported a bill authorizing the President to accept the services of volunteers in case of the invasion of the soil of the United States, etc. The bill had not been prepared with any reference to a war with Mexico, but was a general bill, and had stood on the calendar from the day it was reported without any action.

This bill was taken up. The committee rose immediately, and a resolution was offered to close debate in committee on

D

that bill in two hours. The House adopted the resolution, refusing the yeas and nays on the question. The House again went into committee, and a large portion of the documents were read, occupying an hour and a half in the reading. The peril of General Taylor's little army was imminent, and immediate action was necessary. The bill was amended so as to authorize the raising of 50,000 volunteers, and appropriating ten millions of dollars. The difficulty was in arranging the preamble. Various propositions were made, and the preamble was eventually agreed upon in the following words:

" *Whereas*, by the act of the Republic of Mexico, a state of war exists between that government and the United States."

Mr. Delano, of Ohio, offered a proviso condemning the President in taking armed occupation of the territory lying between the River Nueces and the Rio del Norte. This was rejected. The bill was reported to the House. The vote on adopting the preamble was, yeas 123, nays 67. The bill then passed, yeas 174, nays 14.

The subject of the war was considered and debated on an appropriation bill, and two days thereafter, on May 13th, Mr. Delano having addressed the House, Mr. Douglas, in an impromptu reply, made a most thorough vindication of the war and of President Polk's policy. That speech was never surpassed, and, as it is part of his history, and of the history of the administration he supported so ably, it is here annexed entire. It is the most concise and yet thorough presentation of the title of the United States to the Rio del Norte as the boundary of Texas ever presented in Congress. The speech was regarded then, as it will be now, as a most powerful argument in justification of the war, and of the American title to the whole of Texas. Its effect upon the House was very great. It gave to Mr. Douglas an increased popularity, and added greatly to his rising fame as an orator and debater. His colloquies with the venerable JOHN QUINCY ADAMS drew from that gentleman subsequently the highest commendations for their readiness and ability.

Mr. Douglas rose to reply to the speech of the gentleman from Ohio (Mr Delano), who had just taken his seat. Several members proposed that the committee rise, with a view to adjournment, that he might speak in the morning, if he preferred that course. He declined to avail himself of their courtesy, as his remarks would necessarily be desultory and without preparation, and directed principally to the points which had already been touched in the discussion. My object (said he) is to vindicate our government and country from the aspersions and calumnies which have been cast upon them by several gentlemen in the course of this debate, in connection with the causes which have led to the existing war with Mexico. I prefer to meet and repel those charges at once, while they are fresh in our minds, and to demonstrate, so far as my feeble abilities will enable me to do so, that our government has not been in the wrong, and Mexico in the right, in the origin and progress of the pending controversy. The gentleman from Ohio has been so kind as to herald my expectant advent before my arrival, and to announce that I was about to follow him in the debate. I suppose he drew such an inference from the fact that I entered the hall while he was speaking, took a seat near him, and listened to his speech with the most respectful attention. He certainly had no other authority for the announcement. Acting on this supposition, he has addressed a large portion of his remarks to me, and invited a special answer from me to the main points of his argument. I propose to gratify him in this request; and while I shall speak with freedom and boldness of his positions and arguments, I shall endeavor to observe that courtesy toward him individually which is consistent with an appropriate reply to such an extraordinary speech. I commend the patriotism, if not the morality of the sentiment which he quoted at the beginning, and repeated several times during the course of his remarks : "I go for my country, right or wrong." I fear, however, that this sentiment, once so much applauded by our countrymen, is about to be brought into ridicule and contempt by the use which that gentleman and his coadjutors are now disposed to make of it. They tell us that they go for their country, right or wrong; but they insist that their country is and has been all the time in the wrong. They profess to support the war, but they vote against the law which recognizes its existence and provides the means—the money and the men—to expel a hostile army that has invaded our country and butchered our citizens. They profess great anxiety for the triumph of our arms, but they denounce the war—the cause in which our country is engaged—as " unholy, unrighteous, and damnable."

Mr. J. W. Houston. Who made use of that expression? Was it any gentleman on this side of the house?

Mr. Douglas. Yes, sir. The gentleman from Ohio (Mr. Delano), who has just taken his seat, made use of the identical words, and repeated them several times, with great emphasis, in the course of his speech, while the great body of his political friends listened with the most profound respect, and gave every indication of approbation and encouragement by expressions, looks, and nods of assent. Even now I see the venerable gentleman from Massachusetts nodding his approval of the sentiment.

Mr. J. Q. Adams. Yes, sir, I endorse and approve every word and syllable of it.

Mr. Douglas. So I supposed, from the marked indications of approbation which that gentleman and his friends gave to all the attacks which have been made, during this discussion, upon the rights, interests, and honor of our country. He is more bold and less politic in the expression of his opinions. They, after a little reflection, discover the expediency of concealment; but the lamentable fact is too palpable, that their feelings and sympathies are in perfect unison ; since he has had the hardihood to avow the sentiment, I suppose they will consider its profanity and moral treason perfectly consistent with their professions of Christianity and patriotism. What reliance shall we place on the sincerity of gentlemen's professions, that they are for their country, right or wrong, when they exert all their power and influence to put their country in the wrong in the eyes of Christendom, and invoke the wrath of Heaven upon us for our manifold national crimes and aggressions? With professions of patriotism on their lips, do they not show that their hearts are with the enemy? They appeal to the consciences and religious scruples of our countrymen to unite in execration of our government for supporting what they denounce as an unholy, unrighteous, and damnable cause. They predict that the vengeance of God will fall upon us; that sickness, and carnage, and death will be our portion; that defeat and disgrace will attend our arms. Is there not treason in the heart that can feel, and poison in the breath that can utter such sentiments against their own country, when forced to take up arms in self-defense, to repel the invasion of a brutal and perfidious foe? They for their country, right or wrong! who tell our people, if they rally under their country's standard, their bones will bleach on the plains of Mexico, and the enemy will look down from the mountain-top to behold the destruction of our armies by disease, and all those mysterious elements of death which divine Providence employs to punish a wicked people for prosecuting an unholy and unjust war! Sir, I tell these gentlemen it requires more charity than falls to the lot of frail man to believe that the expression of such sentiments is consistent with the sincerity of their professions—with patriotism, honor, and duty to their country. Patriotism emanates from the heart; it fills the soul; inspires the whole man with a devotion to his country's cause, and speaks and acts the same language. America wants no friends, acknowledges the fidelity of no citizen who, after war is declared, condemns the justice of her cause and sympathizes with the enemy. All such are traitors in their hearts, and it only remains for them to commit some overt act for which they may be dealt with according to their deserts. The gentleman from Ohio has condemned the action of his own government, not only on account of the war and the causes which produced it, but has assailed with equal virulence all efforts to restore the amicable relations of the two countries by peaceable means. He has arraigned the administration for the appointment of Mr. Slidell as minister to Mexico on an errand of peace, and dwells with apparent delight and triumph on the fruitless results of the mission. He is dissatisfied with both peace and war, is willing to embrace neither alternative, and condemns all efforts to adjust the matters in dispute by either means. He thinks that nothing good can come out of Nazareth, and seems determined to find fault with his own government, whatever its policy. Not content with assailing the administration and all its movements, peaceful and belligerent, he has passed from the Del Norte to 50° 40' for the purpose of paying his respects to myself, in his own peculiar way. He has been pleased to represent me as standing on an iceberg, breathing defiance to the British lion, while abandoned by a portion of my own friends, upon whose support I had a right to rely with confidence. If this be true, it was a grievance personal to myself, which I had a right to avenge in my own way, without the interference of the gentleman from Ohio.

I will assure you that I have never been disappointed in an expectation that he would stand by me in any struggle for maintaining the rights and honor of the country, whether in reference to Texas or Oregon. In regard to that portion of my political friends to whom he alludes, I am free to confess that I did sincerely regret that they did not take the same view of our rights and duties in respect to the Oregon question which I entertained and fearlessly expressed. I made no disguise of my sentiments and feelings. Our disagreement on that question was open and unequivocal. I did condemn their refusal to take up their position on 54° 40', and stand there, regardless of consequences. My opinions have undergone no change in that respect. But it is due to them that I should now say that I never questioned their patriotism, nor doubted for a moment that, the instant war existed, they would rally as one man to their country's standard, merging and effacing the slightest trace of a previous difference of opinion. Patriots may differ as to the expediency of a declaration of war, or the wisdom of a course of policy which may probably lead to such a result, but honor and duty forbid divided counsels after our country has been invaded, and American blood has been shed on American soil by a treacherous foe. Party strife and political conflicts should then cease. One sentiment should animate every heart; one object control every movement—the triumph of our country. Mr. Chairman, if I could have anticipated the extraordinary turn which has been given to this discussion, I could have presented to the committee and the country a mass of evidence, from official documents, sufficient to show that, for years past, we have had ample cause of war against Mexico, independent of the recent bloody transactions upon the Rio del Norte. I could have presented a catalogue of aggressions and insults; of outrages on our national flag—on the persons and property of our citizens; of the violation of treaty stipulations, and the murder, robbery, and imprisonment of our countrymen—the very recital of which would suffice to fill the national heart with indignation. Well do I recollect that General Jackson, during the last year of his administration, deemed the subject of sufficient importance at that time to send a special message to Congress, in which he declared, "The wanton character of some of the outrages upon the persons and property of our citizens, upon the officers and flag of the United States, independent of recent insults to this government and people by the late extraordinary Mexican minister, would justify, in the eyes of nations, *immediate war*." I have neither the time nor the documents before me to enable me to go into a recital of the details of these Mexican enormities. They were sufficient, however, in the opinion of General Jackson, to justify an immediate resort to arms. But her weakness and distracted condition softened our resentment, and induced us to endure her aggressions. It is characteristic of our country to be magnanimous where forbearance does not become pusillanimity or a gross dereliction of duty. I fear we carried our magnanimity too far in this instance. Certain it is that it produced no beneficial results; for at the very next session Mr. Van Buren was under the necessity of calling the attention of Congress to the subject, and adding to the old catalogue a long list of new grievances, asking for authority to issue letters of reprisal in case prompt satisfaction should not be made. I have in a book before me an extract from the report of the secretary of state (Mr. Forsyth) to the President, to which I will invite the attention of those who have not examined the subject:

"Since the last session of Congress an embargo has been laid on American vessels in the ports of Mexico. Although raised, no satisfaction has been made or offered for the resulting injuries. Our merchant vessels have been captured for disregarding a pretended blockade of Texas; vessels and cargoes, secretly proceeded against in Mexican tribunals, condemned and sold. The captains, crews, and passengers of the captured vessels have been imprisoned and plundered of their property; and, after enduring insults and injuries, have been released without remuneration or apology. For these acts no reparation has been promised or explanations given, although satisfaction was, in general terms, demanded in July last."

Aside from the insults to our flag, the indignity to the nation, and the injury to our commerce, it is estimated that not less than ten millions of dollars are due to our citizens for these and many other outrages which Mexico has committed within the last fifteen years. When pressed by our government for adjustment and remuneration, she has resorted to all manner of expedients to procrastinate and delay. She has made treaties acknowledging the justice of our claims, and then refused to ratify them, on the most frivolous pretexts, and, even when ratified, has failed to comply with their stipulations. The Committee on Foreign Relations of the Senate of the United States in 1837 made a report upon the subject, in which they said, "If the government of the United States were to exact strict and prompt redress from Mexico, your committee might with justice recommend an immediate resort to war or reprisal." The Committee on Foreign Affairs on the part of the House of Representatives, at the same session, say: "The merchant vessels of the United States have been fired into, her citizens attacked and even put to death, and her ships of war treated with disrespect when paying a friendly visit to a port where they had a right to expect hospitality;" and, in conclusion, the committee observe that "they fully concur with the President that ample cause exists for taking redress into their own hands, and believe we should be justified, in the opinion of other nations, for taking such a step." Such was the posture of our affairs with Mexico in 1837 and 1838, and the opinion of the several departments of our government in regard to the character and enormity of the outrages complained of. These transactions all occurred years before the question of the annexation of Texas was favorably entertained by our government. We had been the first to recognize the independence of Texas, as well as that of Mexico, before the national existence of either had been acknowledged by the parent country. In doing this we only exercised an undoubted right, according to the laws of nations, and our example was immediately followed by France, England, and all the principal powers of Europe. The question of the annexation of Texas to this country was not then seriously mooted. The proposition had been made by Texas, and promptly rejected by our government. Of course, there could be nothing growing out of that question which could have given the slightest cause of offense to Mexico, or can be urged in palliation of the monstrous outrages which for a long series of years previous she had been committing upon the rights, interests, and honor of our country. But our causes of complaint do not stop here. In 1842, Mr. Thompson, our minister to that country, felt himself called upon to issue an address to the diplomatic corps at Mexico, in which, after reciting our grievances, he said:

"Not only have we never done an act of an unfriendly character toward Mexico, but I confidently assert that, from the very moment of the existence of the republic, we have allowed to pass unimproved no opportunity of doing Mexico an act of kindness. I will not now enumerate the acts of that character, both to the government of Mexico and to the citizens, public and private. If this government choose to forget them, I will not recall them. While such has been our course to Mexico, it is with pain I am forced to say that the open violation of the rights of American citizens by the authorities of Mexico have been greater for the last fifteen years than those of all the governments of Christendom united; and yet we have left the redress of all these multiplied and accumulated wrongs to friendly negotiation, without having ever intimated a disposition to resort to force."

It should be borne in mind that all these insults and injuries were committed before the annexation of Texas to the United States—before the proposition was ever seriously entertained by this government. Of course, the subsequent consummation of that measure can afford no pretext for these atrocities previously committed. The same system of plunder and outrage was pursued, only on a smaller scale, toward France and England. For offenses of the same character, only less aggravated, and not one tenth as numerous, France made her demand for reparation, and proclaimed her ultimatum from the deck of a man-of-war off Vera Cruz. Redress being denied, the French fleet opened their batteries on the castle of San Juan de Ulloa, and compelled the fortress to surrender and the Mexican government to accede to their demands, and pay two hundred thousand dollars in addition, to defray the expenses of enforcing the payment of the claim. The

English government also presented claims for remuneration to her subjects for similar outrages. Wearied of the dilatory action of the Mexican Congress, the British minister presented his ultimatum, and, at the same time, informed the Mexican government that, in the event of non-compliance with the demand, he was instructed to inform the admiral of the Jamaica station of the fact, who had been instructed to act in that case, and employ force in compelling an acquiescence. The affair was speedily arranged to the satisfaction of the British government. Thus we find that remuneration and satisfaction were made to England and France for the same injuries of which we complain, where their subjects and our citizens were common sufferers. Still the wrongs of our citizens are unredressed, and the indignity to the honor and flag of the country unavenged. Our wrongs were ten-fold greater than theirs in number, enormity, and amount. Their complaints have been heard in tones of thunder from the mouths of their cannon, and have been adjusted according to the terms dictated by the injured parties. The forbearance of our government to enforce our rights by the same efficient measures which they employed has been considered as evidence of our imbecility, which gave impunity to the past and license to future aggressions. Hence we find that while Great Britain and France, by the energy and efficiency with which they enforced their rights, have commanded the respect of Mexico and re-established their amicable relations, the United States, by an ill-advised magnanimity and forbearance toward a weak and imbecile neighbor, has forfeited her respect, and lost all the advantages of that friendly intercourse to which our natural position entitles us. Under the operation of these causes, our commerce with Mexico has dwindled down by degrees from nine millions of dollars per annum to a mere nominal sum, while that of France and England has steadily increased, until they have secured a monopoly of the trade and almost a controlling influence over the councils of that wretched country. Such was the relative position of Mexico toward the United States and other countries when the controversy in regard to the annexation of Texas arose. The first proposition for annexation had been promptly rejected—in my opinion very unwisely—from a false delicacy toward the feelings of Mexico. When the question was again agitated, she gave notice to this government that she would regard the consummation of the measure as a declaration of war. She made the passage of the resolution of annexation by the Congress of the United States the pretext for dissolving the diplomatic relations between the two countries. She peremptorily recalled her minister from Washington, and virtually dismissed ours from Mexico, permitting him, as in the case of all his predecessors, to be robbed by her banditti according to the usages of the country. This was followed by the withdrawal of the Mexican consuls from our sea-ports, and the suspension of all commercial intercourse. Our government submitted to these accumulated insults and injuries with patience and forbearance, still hoping for an adjustment of all our difficulties without being compelled to resort to actual hostilities. Impelled by this spirit of moderation, our government determined to waive all matters of etiquette, and make another effort to restore the amicable relations of the two countries by negotiation. An informal application was therefore made to the government of Mexico to know whether, in the event we should send a minister to that country, clothed with ample powers, she would not receive him with a view to a satisfactory adjustment. Having received an affirmative answer, Mr. Slidell was immediately appointed and sent to Mexico. Upon his arrival he presented his credentials and requested to be formally received. The government of Mexico at first hesitated, then procrastinated, and finally refused to receive him in his capacity of minister. Here, again, the forbearance of our government is most signally displayed. Instead of resenting this renewed insult by the chastisement due to her perfidy, our government again resolved to make another effort for peace. Accordingly, Mr. Slidell was instructed to remain at some suitable place in the vicinity of the city of Mexico until the result of the revolution then pending should be known; and, in the event of success, to make application to the new government to be received as minister. Paredes being firmly established in power, with his administration formed, Mr. Slidell again applied, and was again rejected. In the mean time, while these events were occurring at the capital of Mexico, her armies were marching from all parts of the republic toward the boundary of the United States, and were concentrating in large numbers at and near Matamoras. Of course, our government watched all these military movements with interest and vigilance. While we were anxious for peace, and were using all the means in our power, consistent with honor, to restore friendly relations, the administration was not idle in its preparations to meet any crisis that might arise, and, if necessary in self-defense, to repel force by force. With this view an efficient squadron had been sent to the Gulf of Mexico, and a portion of the army concentrated between the Nueces and the Rio del Norte, with positive instructions to commit no act of aggression, and to act strictly on the defensive, unless Mexico unfortunately should commence hostilities and attempt to invade our territory. When General Taylor pitched his camp on the banks of the Rio del Norte, he sent General Worth across the river to explain to the Mexican general and the civil authorities of Matamoras the objects of his mission; that his was not a hostile expedition; that it was not his intention to invade Mexico or commit any act of aggression upon her rights; that he was instructed by his government to act strictly on the defensive, and simply to protect American soil and American citizens from invasion and aggression; that the United States desired peace with Mexico; and, if hostilities ensued, Mexico would have to strike the first blow. When the two armies were thus posted on opposite sides of the river, Colonel Cross, while riding alone a few miles from the American camp, was captured, robbed, murdered, and quartered. About the same time the Mexican general sent a notice to General Taylor that, unless he removed his camp and retired to the east side of the Nueces, he should compel him to do so. Subsequently General Arista sent a message to General Taylor that hostilities already existed. On the next day a small portion of our army, while reconnoitring the country on the American side of the river, was surrounded, fired upon, and the greater portion of them captured or killed. It was then discovered that the Mexican army had crossed the river, surrounded the American camp, and interposed a large force between General Taylor's encampment and Point Isabel, the depôt of his provisions and military stores.

Here we have the causes and origin of the existing war with Mexico. The facts which I have briefly recited are accessible to, if not within the knowledge of, every gentleman who feels an interest in examining them. Their authenticity does not depend upon the weight of my authority. They are to be found in full and in detail in the public documents on our tables and in our libraries. With a knowledge of the facts, or, at least, professing to know them, gentlemen have the hardihood to tell us that the President has unwisely and unnecessarily precipitated the country into an unjust and unholy war. They express great sympathy for Mexico; profess to regard her an injured and persecuted nation—the victim of American injustice and aggression. They have no sympathy for the widows and orphans whose husbands and fathers have been robbed and murdered by the Mexican authorities; no sympathy with our own countrymen who have dragged out miserable lives within the walls of her dungeons, without crime and without trial; no indignation at the outrages upon our commerce and shipping, and the insults to our national flag; no resentment at the violation of treaties and the invasion of our territory.

I will now proceed to examine the arguments by which the gentleman from Ohio [Mr. Delano], and those with whom he acts, pretend to justify their foreign sympathies. They assume that the Rio del Norte was not the boundary-line between Texas and Mexico; that the republic of Texas never extended beyond the Nueces, and, consequently, that our government was under no obligation, and had no right, to protect the lives and property of American citizens beyond that river. In support of that assumption, the gentleman has referred to a dispute which he says once arose between the provinces of Coahuila and Texas, and the decisions of Almonte, and some other Mexican general, thereon, prior to the Texan revolution, and while those provinces constituted one state in the Mexican confederation. He has also referred to Mrs. Holley's History of Texas, and, perhaps, some other works, in which we are informed that the same boundary was assigned to the Mexican province of Texas. I am not entirely unacquainted with the facts and authorities to which the gentleman has alluded, but I am at a loss to discover their bearing on the question at issue. True it is that in 1827 the provinces of Coahuila and Texas were erected into one state, having formed for themselves a republican constitution, similar, in most of its provisions, to those of the several states of our Union. Their constitution provided that the State of Coahuila and Texas " is free and independent of the other united Mexican states, and of every other foreign power and dominion ;" that " in all matters relating to the Mexican confederation the state delegates its faculties and powers to the general Congress of the same ; but in all that properly relates to the administration and entire government of the state, it retains its liberty, independence, and sovereignty ;" that, " therefore, belongs exclusively to the same state the right to establish, by means of its representatives, its fundamental laws, conformable to the basis sanctioned in the constitutional act and the general constitution." This new state, composed of a union of the two provinces, was admitted into the Mexican confederacy under the general constitution established in 1824, upon the conditions which I have recited. The province of Coahuila lay on the west side of the Rio del Norte, and Texas upon the east. An uncertain, undefined boundary divided them ; and, so long as they remained one state, there was no necessity for establishing the true line. It is immaterial, therefore, whether the Nueces or the Rio del Norte, or an imaginary line between the two, was the boundary between Coahuila and Texas, while these provinces constituted one state in the Mexican confederacy. I do not deem it necessary to go back to a period anterior to the Texan revolution to ascertain the limits and boundaries of the *republic* of Texas. But, if the gentleman has so great a reverence for antiquity as to reject all authorities which have not become obsolete and inapplicable in consequence of the changed relations of that country, I will gratify his taste in that respect. It must be borne in mind that Texas (before her revolution) was always understood to have been a portion of the old French province of Louisiana, whilst Coahuila was one of the Spanish provinces of Mexico. By ascertaining the western boundary of Louisiana, therefore, prior to its transfer by France to Spain, we discover the dividing line between Texas and Coahuila. I will not weary the patience of the House by an examination of the authorities, in detail, by which this point is elucidated and established. I will content myself by referring the gentleman to a document in which he will find them all collected and analyzed in a masterly manner, by one whose learning and accuracy he will not question. I allude to a dispatch (perhaps I might with propriety call it a book, from its great length) written by our secretary of state in 1819 to Don Onis, the Spanish minister. The document is to be found in the State Papers in each of our libraries. He will there find a multitudinous collection of old maps and musty records, histories and geographies—Spanish, English, and French—by which it is clearly established that the Rio del Norte was the western boundary of Louisiana, and so considered by Spain and France both, when they owned the opposite banks of that river. The venerable gentleman from Massachusetts [Mr Adams] in that famous dispatch reviews all the authorities on either side with a clearness and ability which defy refutation, and demonstrate the validity of our title in virtue of the purchase of Louisiana. He went farther, and expressed his own convictions, upon a full examination of the whole question, that our title as far as the Rio del Norte was as clear as to the island of New Orleans. This was the opinion of Mr. Adams in 1819. It was the opinion of Messrs. Monroe and Pinckney in 1805. It was the opinion of Jefferson and Madison—of all our presidents and of all administrations, from its acquisition in 1803 to its fatal relinquishment in 1819. I make no question with the gentleman as to the applicability and bearing of these facts upon the point in controversy. I give them in opposition to the supposed facts upon which he seems to rely. I give him the opinions of these eminent statesmen in response to those of Almonte and his brother Mexican general. Will the gentleman tell us and his constituents that those renowned statesmen, including his distinguished friend [Mr. Adams], as well as President Polk and the American Congress, were engaged in an unholy, unrighteous, and damnable cause when claiming title to the Rio del Norte? I leave the gentleman from Ohio and his venerable friend from Massachusetts to settle the disputed point of the old boundary of Texas between themselves, trusting that they may agree upon some basis of amicable adjustment and compromise. But, sir, I have already said that I do not deem it necessary to rely upon those ancient authorities for a full and complete justification of our government in maintaining possession of the country on the left bank of the Rio del Norte. Our justification rests upon better and higher evidence, upon a firmer basis—an immutable principle. The republic of Texas held the country by a more glorious title than can be traced through the old maps and musty records of French and Spanish courts. She held it by the same title that our fathers of the Revolution acquired the territory and achieved the independence of this republic. She held it by virtue of a successful revolution, a declaration of independence setting forth the inalienable rights of man, triumphantly maintained by the irresistible power of her arms, and consecrated by the precious blood of her glorious heroes. These were her muniments of title. By these she acquired the empire which she has voluntarily annexed to our Union, and which we have plighted our faith to protect and defend against invasion and dismemberment. We received the republic of Texas into the Union with her entire territory as an independent and sovereign state, and have no right to alienate or surrender any portion of it. This proposition our opponents admit, so far as respects the country on this side of the Nueces, but they deny both the obligation and the right to go beyond that river. Upon what authority they assume the Nueces to have been the boundary of the republic of Texas they have not condescended to inform us. I am unable to conceive upon what grounds a distinction can be drawn as to our right to the opposite sides of that stream. I know nothing in the history of that republic, from its birth to its translation, that would authorize the assumption. The same principles and evidence which, by common consent, give us title on this side of the Nueces, establish our right to the other. The revolution extended to either side of the river, and was alike successful on both. Upon this point I speak with confidence, for I have taken the precaution, within the last few minutes, to have the facts to which I shall refer authenticated by the testimony of the two most distinguished actors (one of whom I now recognize in my eye) of those thrilling and glorious scenes. Upon this high authority, I assume that the first revolutionary army in Texas, in 1835, embraced soldiers and officers who were residents of the country between the Nueces and the

Rio del Norte. These same heroic men, or so many of them as had not been butchered by the Mexican soldiery, were active participators in the battle of San Jacinto on the 21st of April, 1836, when Santa Ana was captured and the Mexican army annihilated.

Although few in number, and sparsely scattered over a wide surface of country, and consequently exposed to the cruelties and barbarities of the enemy, none were more faithful to the cause of freedom, and constant in their devotion to the interests of the republic throughout its existence. Immediately after the battle of San Jacinto Santa Ana made a proposition to the commander of the Texan army (General Houston) to make a treaty of peace, by which Mexico would recognize the independence of Texas, with the Rio del Norte as the boundary. In May, 1836, such a treaty was made between the government of Texas and Santa Ana on the part of the Mexican nation, in which the independence of Texas was acknowledged, and the Rio del Norte recognized as the boundary. In pursuance of the provision of this treaty, the remnant of the Mexican army was permitted, under the orders of Santa Ana, to retire beyond the confines of the republic of Texas, and take a position on the other side of the Rio del Norte, which they did accordingly.

Mr. J. W. Houston. Was that treaty ever ratified by the government of Mexico?

Mr. Douglas. I am not aware that it was ratified by any body on the part of the government of Mexico except Santa Ana and his subordinate officers, for the very good reason that he was himself the government at the time. Only one year previous he had usurped the government of Mexico, had abolished the Constitution of 1824, and concentrated all the powers of government in his own hands. To give stability to the power which he had acquired by the sword, he called a Congress around him, composed of his followers and adherents, and had *himself* formally proclaimed dictator of the republic, and, as such, clothed with all the powers of government, civil and military. From that moment the government of Mexico was a republic in name, but a military despotism in fact. She had no Constitution, no government, except the will of the dictator, and the instruments he chose to select to execute his will. In this capacity, he marched his armies into Texas for the purpose of reducing those people to subjection to the despotism which he had established, and exterminating the last vestige of freedom which remained in his dominions. The Texans flew to arms in defense of their liberties, in defense of the form of government which they had established for themselves by their state Constitution of 1827, and the national Constitution of 1824, in pursuance of the provisions of which they had been admitted as a sovereign state into the Mexican confederacy. The Texans had taken up arms in support, and Santa Ana for the destruction, of the Constitutional government in Texas. While engaged in this work of desolation with fire and sword, committing butcheries and barbarities unknown to civilized warfare, Santa Ana fell into the hands of the heroic Houston and his gallant little army, a captive to those whom he was striving to reduce to captivity. Then it was that the tyrant became a suppliant—a suppliant for his life and liberty —at the hands of those he had doomed his victims. Then the dictator bent his knee in prayer for mercy, and sued for peace, offering to recognize the independence of Texas if he could be permitted to rescue the remnant of his followers from destruction, and remove them beyond the Rio del Norte. A treaty to this effect, as I have already stated, was subsequently entered into in due form; and, in pursuance of its provisions, the Mexicans evacuated Texas, and retired beyond the Rio del Norte. This treaty was executed by Santa Ana as the government *de facto* for the time being, and, as such, was binding on the Mexican nation.

Mr. J. Q. Adams. I desire to inquire of the gentleman from Illinois if

Santa Ana was not a prisoner of war at the time, and in duress when he executed that treaty.

Mr. Douglas. Santa Ana was a prisoner and in duress, and so was the entire government of Mexico, for he was at that time the government *de facto*, clothed with all its functions, civil and military. The government itself was a prisoner and in duress. But will it be contended that that circumstance rendered the obligation less obligatory?

Mr. Adams. It is a strange doctrine that the acts of a prisoner while in duress are to be deemed valid after he has recovered his liberty.

Mr. Douglas. We are at war with Mexico. Our armies will soon march into the heart of that country. I trust they will penetrate as far as the capital, and capture not only the army, but the government itself in the halls of the Montezumas, that we may make them all prisoners of war, and keep them in duress until they shall make a treaty of peace and boundary with us, by which they shall recognize not only the Rio del Norte, but such other line as we shall choose to dictate or accept. Will the gentleman from Massachusetts contend that a treaty made with us under those circumstances would not be binding, because, forsooth, the government was a prisoner at that time? How is a conquered nation ever to make peace if the gentleman's doctrine is to prevail? Take the case of an absolute monarchy: the king is captured in battle at the head of his army. Both parties may then be willing to settle the dispute, but no treaty can be made because the king is in duress, and, of course, the victor would not release his royal prisoner until a treaty of peace had been executed, lest he might continue hostilities, and, by the fortunes of war, triumph in the contest. This doctrine would place all unfortunate belligerents in a most deplorable condition. They refuse to make peace before defeat, because they hope for victory. They are incompetent to do it afterward, because they are in duress. Surely a defeated nation would find itself in a lamentable predicament. Too feeble to resist, disarmed, conquered, and still incompetent to make a treaty of peace and adjust the matter in dispute on such fair and equitable terms as a magnanimous foe might propose, because the war of aggression which they had commenced had resulted disastrously, and made them captives. I fear, if the gentlemen on the other side succeed in establishing their doctrine, they will soon find their Mexican friends in a dilemma truly pitiable. Perhaps, if General Paredes and his military government should be reduced to captivity, these gentlemen would require that our armies should retire within our own territory, and set the prisoners at liberty, before negotiations for peace should be opened. This may be their view of the subject, but I doubt whether it is the view which the American government or the American people will feel it their duty to act upon. Our crude notions of things might teach us that the city of Mexico was a very suitable place for conducting the negotiations. I must, therefore, be permitted to adhere to my original position that the treaty of peace and boundaries between Santa Ana and the Texan government in May, 1836, was binding on the Mexican nation, it having been executed by the government *de facto* for the time being.

Mr. Adams. Has not that treaty with Santa Ana been since discarded by the Mexican government?

Mr. Douglas. I presume it has, for I am not aware of any treaty or compact which that government ever entered into that she did not afterward either violate or repudiate. The history of our treaty stipulations with her furnishes ample ground for this presumption. I have not deemed it necessary to inquire what particular acts of disavowal, if any, have been since adopted by the Mexican government. It is sufficient for my purpose that the treaty was entered into by competent authority at the time of its execution. The acts of a government *de facto* are binding on the nation as against foreign nations, without reference to the mode by which that government was established, whether by revolution, usurpation, or rightful and constitutional means.

Mr. Adams. I deny it.   I deny the proposition.

Mr. Douglas. I will not enter into an elaborate discussion of the laws of nations on the point with the learned gentleman from Massachusetts.   I will say, however, that I understand writers on international law to lay down the principle as I have stated.   Certainly the practice and usages of all civilized nations sanction it, of which history furnishes innumerable examples.   Does the gentleman deny the validity of the acts of the British government in the times of Cromwell because it was a mere government *de facto*, established in blood, in violation of the English Constitution?   Many of the most important treaties affecting the destiny of Europe were made with the British government during that period; and who ever heard of a European sovereign denying their obligation or failing to claim the benefits of them?   More recent and memorable instances may be found in our claims of indemnities against France, Naples, and Spain, for injuries which we sustained during the French Revolution.   We did not permit these countries to exonerate themselves from the obligation to make us compensation upon the pretext that Napoleon, Murat, and Joseph Bonaparte were military despots, who had ascended the thrones through blood and violence.   We recognized them as the heads of those governments *de facto*, while seated on the thrones of the legitimate kings of those countries, and subsequently held the nations responsible for all their invasions of our rights.   Spain, Naples, and France have each acknowledged the obligation and granted indemnities.   Will the gentleman deny the validity of the purchase of Louisiana upon the ground that it was made with a usurper, who was afterward taken prisoner and dethroned? With as little propriety may he reject Santa Ana's treaty with Texas, and our treaties with the presidents and dictators of Mexico, who have successively and alternately seized the reins of that government at short intervals, and banished or beheaded their predecessors, and changed the forms of government to suit their purposes.   In these and all similar cases the usages of the civilized world sanction the doctrine for which I contend, that the government *de facto*, for the time being, is recognized, and the nation held responsible for its acts, without inquiring into the means by which it was established, or allowing the obligation to be dissolved by subsequent revolutions or disavowals.   I am not now discussing the question whether the distinctions attempted to be established in England on the termination of the Wars of the Roses, between the rival houses of Lancaster and York, were well founded or not.   I do not pretend to say whether it is a settled principle of the laws of nations that there is such a distinction between governments *de facto* and governments *de jure* as some gentlemen insist upon.   I wish to avoid all immaterial issues, for I have had no opportunity for investigation or preparation on these points.   All I insist upon in this discussion is that the acts of the government *de facto*, for the time being, are binding on the nation in respect to foreign states.   It is immaterial, therefore, whether Mexico has or has not disavowed Santa Ana's treaty with Texas.   It was executed at the time by competent authority.   She availed herself of all its benefits.   By virtue of it she saved the remnant of her army from total annihilation, and had her captive dictator restored to liberty.   Under it she was permitted to remove, in peace and security, all her soldiers, citizens, and property, beyond the Rio del Norte.   The question is, had she a moral and legal right to repudiate it after she had enjoyed all its advantages?

The gentleman from Massachusetts attempts to apply the legal maxims relative to civil contracts to this transaction.   Because an individual who enters into a contract while in duress has a right to disavow it when restored to his liberty, he can see no reason why Santa Ana could not do the same thing. I shall not go into an argument to prove that the rights of a nation, in time of war, are not identical with those of a citizen, under the municipal laws of his own country, in a state of peace. But if I should admit the justness of the supposed parallel, I apprehend the gentleman would not insist upon the right to rescind the contract without placing the parties in *statu quo ;* for it must be borne in mind that Santa Ana was a prisoner according to the rules of war, and consequently in lawful custody. Is the gentleman prepared to show that the Mexican government ever proposed to rescind the treaty, and place the parties in the same relative position they occupied on the day of its execution? Did they ever offer to send Santa Ana and his defeated army back to San Jacinto, to remain as General Houston's prisoners until the Texan government should dispose of them according to its discretion, under the laws of nations? But I must return from this digression to the main point of my argument. I was proceeding with my proof, when these interruptions commenced, to show that the Rio del Norte was the boundary between Texas and Mexico, and has been so claimed on the one side and recognized on the other ever since the battle of San Jacinto. I have already referred to the fact that the country west of the Nueces had her soldiers in the Texan army during the campaigns of 1835 and 1836, and that the treaty of peace and independence between Santa Ana and the Texan government recognized the Rio del Norte as the boundary. I have also referred to the fact that the Mexican army was removed from Texas, in pursuance of that treaty, to the west bank of that stream. I am informed by high authority that General Filisola received instructions from the authorities in Mexico, who were exercising the functions of government in Santa Ana's absence, to enter into any arrangement with the Texan government which should be necessary to save the Mexican army from destruction, and secure its safe retreat from that country; and that, in pursuance of those instructions, he did ratify Santa Ana's treaty previous to marching the army beyond the Rio del Norte. My friend from Mississippi, before me (Mr. Davis), who has investigated the subject, assures me that such is the fact. My own recollection accords with his statement in this respect. These facts clearly show that Mexico, at that time, regarded the revolution as successful as far as the Rio del Norte, and consequently that the river must necessarily become the boundary whenever the independence of the new republic should be firmly established. Subsequent transactions prove that the two countries have ever since acted on the same supposition. Texas immediately proceeded to form a Constitution and establish a permanent government. The country between the Nueces and the Rio del Norte was represented in the convention which formed her Constitution in 1836. James Powers, an actual resident of the territory now in dispute, was elected a delegate by the people residing there, and participated in the proceedings of the convention as one of its members. The first Congress which assembled under the Constitution proceeded to define the boundaries of the republic, to establish courts of jurisdiction, and the exercise of all the powers of sovereignty over the whole territory. One of the first acts of that Congress declares the Rio del Norte, from its mouth to its source, to be the boundary between Texas and Mexico, and the others provide for the exercise of jurisdiction. Counties were established, reaching across the Nueces, and even to the Rio del Norte, as fast as the tide of emigration advanced in that direction. Corpus Christi, Point Isabel, and General Taylor's camp, opposite Matamoras, are all within the county of San Patricio, in the State of Texas, according to our recent maps. That same county, from the day of its formation, constituted a portion of one of the congressional districts, and also of a senatorial district in the Republic of Texas; it now forms a portion, if not the whole, of a representative district, and also a senatorial district, for the election of representatives and senators to the Texan Legislature, as well as a congressional district for the election of a representative to the Congress of the United States. Colonel Kinney, who emigrated from my own state, has resided in that country, between the Nueces and the Rio del Norte, for many years ; has represented it in the Congress of the Republic of Texas, also in the convention which formed the Constitution of the State of Texas, and now represents it in the Texan Senate. I know not what stronger evidence could be desired that the country in question was, *in fact*, a portion of the Republic of Texas, and, as a consequence, is now a portion of the United States. If an express acknowledgment by Mexico of the Rio del Norte as the boundary, is deemed essential, and the recognition of that fact in Santa Ana's treaty, and subsequently by Filisola, is not considered sufficient, I will endeavor to furnish further and more recent evidence, which, I trust, will be satisfactory on that point. I have not the papers to which I shall refer before me at this moment, but they are of such general notoriety that they can not fail to be within the recollection of the members of the House generally. It will be remembered that when we were discussing the propriety and expediency of the annexation of Texas some two years ago, much was said about an armistice entered into between Mexico and Texas for the suspension of hostilities for a limited period. Well, that armistice was agreed to by the two governments, and in the proclamation announcing the fact by the Mexican government, the Mexican forces were required to retire from the territory of Texas to the *west side of the Rio del Norte*. This proclamation was issued, as near as I recollect, in 1843 or 1844, just before the treaty of annexation was signed by President Tyler, and at a period when Mexico had had sufficient time to recover from the dizziness of the shock at San Jacinto, and to ascertain to what extent the revolution had been successful, and where the true boundary was. She was not a prisoner of war, nor in duress, at the time she issued this proclamation. It was her own deliberate act (so far as deliberation ever attends her action), done of her own volition. In that proclamation she clearly recognizes the Rio del Norte as the boundary, and that, too, in view of a treaty of peace, by which the independence of Texas was to be again acknowledged.

Mr. Adams. I wish to ask the gentleman from Illinois if the last Congress did not pass an act regulating trade and commerce to the *foreign* province of Santa Fé ?

Mr. Douglas. I believe the last Congress did pass an act upon that subject, and I will remind the gentleman that the *present* Congress has passed an act extending the revenue laws of the United States over the country between the Rio del Norte and the Nueces, and providing for the appointment of custom-house officers to reside there. As near as I recollect, the gentleman from Massachusetts and myself voted for both of those acts. The only difference between us, in this respect, was, that he, being a little more zealous than myself, made a speech for the last one—for the act extending our laws over and taking legal possession of the very country where General Taylor's army is now encamped, and which he now asserts to belong to Mexico. That act passed this Congress unanimously at the present session, taking legal possession of the whole country in dispute, and of course making it the sworn duty of the President to see its provisions faithfully executed. In the name of truth and justice, I ask the gentleman from Massachusetts, and his followers in this crusade, how they can justify it to their consciences to denounce the President for sending the army to protect the lives of our citizens there, and defend the country from invasion, after they had voted to take legal possession by the extension of our laws ? They had asserted our right to the country by a solemn act of Congress ; had erected it into a collection district, and the Constitution required the President to appoint the officers, and see the laws faithfully executed. He had done so; and for this simple discharge of a duty enjoined upon him by a law for which they voted, he is assailed, in the coarsest terms known to our language, as having committed an act which is unholy, unrighteous, and damnable! But I feel it due to the venerable gentleman from Massachusetts to respond more particularly to his inquiry in regard to the act of the last Congress regulating commerce and trade to Santa Fé. I do not now recollect its exact provisions, nor is it important, inasmuch as that act was passed before Texas was annexed to this Union. Of course Santa Fé was foreign to us at that time, whether it belonged to Texas or Mexico. The object of that act was to regulate the trade across our western frontier between us and foreign countries. Texas was then foreign to us, but is no longer so since her annexation and admission into the Union. Mr. Chairman, I believe I have now said all that I intended for the purpose of showing that the Rio del Norte was the western boundary of the Republic of Texas. How far I have succeeded in establishing the position, I leave to the House and the country to determine. If that was the boundary of the Republic of Texas, it has, of course, become the boundary of the United States by virtue of the acts of annexation and admission into the Union. I will not say that I have demonstrated the question as satisfactorily as the distinguished gentleman from Massachusetts did in 1819, but I will say that I think I am safe in adopting the sentiment which he then expressed—that our title to the Rio del Norte is as clear as to the island of New Orleans.

Mr. Adams. I never said that our title was good to the Rio del Norte from its mouth to its source.

Mr. Douglas. I know nothing of the gentleman's mental reservations. If he means, by his denial, to place the whole emphasis on the qualification that he did not claim that river as the boundary "*from its mouth to its source,*" I shall not dispute with him on that point. But if he wishes to be understood as denying that he ever claimed the Rio del Norte, in general terms, as our boundary under the Louisiana treaty, I can furnish him with an official document, over his own signature, which he will find very embarrassing and exceedingly difficult to explain. I allude to his famous dispatch as secretary of state, in 1819, to Don Onis, the Spanish minister. I am not certain that I can prove his handwriting, for the copy I have in my possession I find printed in the American State Papers, published by order of Congress. In that paper he not only claimed the Rio del Norte as our boundary, but he demonstrated the validity of the claim by a train of facts and arguments which rivet conviction on every impartial mind, and defy refutation.

Mr. Adams. I wrote that dispatch as secretary of state, and endeavored to make out the best case I could for my own country, as it was my duty; but I utterly deny that I claimed the Rio del Norte as our boundary in its full extent. I only claimed it a short distance up the river, and then diverged northward some distance from the stream.

Mr. Douglas. Will the gentleman specify the point at which his line left the river?

Mr. Adams. I never designated the point.

Mr. Douglas. Was it above Matamoras?

Mr. Adams. I never specified any particular place.

Mr. Douglas. I am well aware that the gentleman never specified any point of departure for his northward line, which, he now informs us, was to run a part of the way on the east side of that river; for he claimed the river as the boundary in general terms, without any qualification. But his present admission is sufficient for my purposes, if he will only specify the point from which he then understood or now understands that his line was to have diverged from the river. I have heard of this line before, and know with reasonable certainty its point of departure. It followed the river to a place near the highlands—certainly more than one hundred miles above Matamoras; consequently, if we adopt that line as our present boundary, it will give us Point Isabel and General Taylor's camp opposite Matamoras, and every inch of ground upon which an American soldier has ever placed his foot since the annexation of Texas to the Union. Hence my solicitude to extract an answer from the venerable gentleman to my interrogatory whether his line followed the river any distance above Matamoras, and hence, I apprehend, the cause of my failure to procure a response to that question. If he had responded to my inquiry, his answer would have furnished a triumphant refutation of all the charges which he and his friends have made against the President for ordering the army of occupation to its present position. I am not now to be diverted from the real point in controversy by a discussion of the question whether the Rio del Norte was the boundary to its source. My present object is to repel the calumnies which have been urged against our government, to place our country in the right and the enemy in the wrong, before the civilized world, according to the truth and justice of the case. I have exposed these calumnies by reference to the acts and admissions of our accusers, by which they have asserted our title to the full extent that we have taken possession. I have shown that Texas always claimed the Rio del Norte as her boundary during the existence of the republic, and that Mexico on several occasions recognized it as such in the most direct and solemn manner. The President ordered the army no farther than Congress had extended our laws. In view of these facts, I leave it to the candor of every honest man whether the executive did not do his duty, and nothing but his duty, when he ordered the army to the Rio del Norte. Should he have folded his arms, and allowed our citizens to be murdered and our territory invaded with impunity? have we not forborne to act, either offensively or defensively, until our forbearance is construed into cowardice, and is exciting contempt from those toward whom we have exercised our magnanimity? We have a long list of grievances, a long catalogue of wrongs to be avenged. The war has commenced; blood has been shed; our territory invaded; all by the act of the enemy.

I had hoped and trusted that there would be no anti-war party after war was declared. In this I have been sadly disappointed. I have been particularly mortified to see one with whom I have acted on the Oregon question, who was ready to plunge the country into immediate war, if necessary, to maintain the rights and honor of the country in that direction, now arraying himself on the side of the enemy when our country is invaded by another portion of the Union. To me, our country and all its parts are one and indivisible. I would rally under her standard in the defense of one portion as soon as another—the South as soon as the North; for Texas as soon as Oregon. And I will here do my Southern friends the justice to say that I firmly believe, and never doubted that, if war had arisen out of the Oregon question, when once declared, they would have been found shoulder to shoulder with me as firmly as I shall be with them in this Mexican war.

Mr. Adams. I thought I understood the gentleman some time ago, while standing on 54° 40', to tell his Southern friends that he wanted no *dodging* on the Oregon question.

Mr. Douglas. I did stand on 54° 40'; I stand there now, and never intend, by any act of mine, to surrender the position. I am as ready and willing to fight for 54° 40' as for the Rio del Norte. My patriotism is not of that kind which would induce me to go to war to enlarge one section of the Union out of mere hatred and vengeance toward the other. I have no personal or political griefs resulting from the past to embitter my feelings and inflame my resentment toward any section of our country. I know no sections, no divisions. I did complain of a few of my Southern friends on the Oregon question; did tell them that I wished to see no dodging; endeavored to rally them on 54° 40' as our fighting line, regardless of consequences, war or no war. But, while they declined to assume this position in a time of peace, they unanimously avowed their determination to stand by the country the moment war was declared. But, since the gentleman from Massachusetts has dragged the Oregon question into this debate, I wish to call his attention to one of his wise sayings on that subject, and see if he is not willing to apply it to Texas as well as Oregon, to Mexico as well as Great Britain. He recalled to the mind of the House that passage of history in which the great Frederick took military possession of Silesia, and immediately proposed to settle the question of title and boundaries by negotiation. During the Oregon debate he avowed himself in favor of Frederick's plan for the settlement of that question, "Take possession first, and negotiate afterward." I desire to know why the gentleman is not willing to apply this principle to the country on the Rio del Norte as well as Oregon? According to his own showing, that is precisely what President Polk has done. He has taken possession, and proposed to negotiate. In this respect the President has adopted the advice of the gentleman from Massachusetts, and followed the example of the great Frederick. The only difference in the two cases is that the President was maintaining a legal possession, which Congress had previously taken by the extension of our laws. For this he is also abused. He is condemned alike for using the sword and the olive branch. His enemies object to his efforts for amicable adjustment as well as to the movements of the army. All is wrong in their eyes. Their country is always wrong, and its enemies right. It has ever been so. It was so in the last war with Great Britain. Then it was unbecoming a moral and religious people to rejoice at the success of American arms. We were wrong, in their estimation, in the French Indemnity case, in the Florida war, in all the Indian wars, and now in the Mexican war. I despair of ever seeing my country again in the right, if they are to be the oracles.

On the 23d of February, 1848, President Pierce communicated to the Senate the treaty of peace with Mexico, negotiated at Guadalupe Hidalgo by N. P. Trist, calling attention to certain provisions in it which were highly objectionable. The debate on this treaty continued until March 10, when, it having been amended, the vote was taken, "Will the Senate advise and consent to the ratification of the treaty in the form of this resolution?" and the vote stood:

Yeas—Ashley, Atherton, Bagby, Bell, Bradbury, Bright, Butler, Calhoun, Cameron, Cass, Clarke, Crittenden, Davis of Massachusetts, Davis of Mississippi, Dayton, Dickinson, Dix, Downs, Felch, Foote, Greene, Hale, Hannegan, Hunter, Johnson of Maryland, Johnson of Louisiana, Johnson of Georgia, Mangum, Mason, Miller, Moor, Niles, Rusk, Sevier, Sturgeon, Turney, Underwood, Yulee—38.

Nays—Allen of Ohio, Atchison of Missouri, Badger of North Carolina, Baldwin of Connecticut, Benton of Missouri, Berrien of Georgia, Breese of Illinois, Corwin of Ohio, Douglas of Illinois, Lewis of Alabama, Spruance of Delaware, Upham of Vermont, Webster of Massachusetts, Westcott of Florida—14. Two thirds having voted in the affirmative, the treaty was ratified.

The objections to the treaty on the part of Mr. Douglas are stated in the extracts from his speeches in the various part of this volume.

CHAPTER VI.

POLICY WITH FOREIGN NATIONS.

SINCE the advent of Mr. Douglas upon the floors of Congress, he has always taken an active and decided part in the discussions upon the proper policy to be adopted and maintained by the United States with respect to foreign governments, and also respecting foreign possessions and foreign domination upon the American continent. While he has always been a strenuous defender of the Monroe doctrine, and a zealous advocate of its rigid maintenance on all occasions by the United States, he has never given his approval to any of the resolutions or propositions which, from time to time, have been introduced into Congress, with a view of having a declaration of what this government would or would not do under certain circumstances. His theory is that the declaration by Mr. Monroe was a formal notice to the world that thenceforth there was to be no *new* establishment of power or acquisition of territory on this continent by any European nation. By that declaration he is willing to stand. It is broad, explicit, and covers the whole subject. As to all other questions, he is for leaving the United States unfettered by declarations, pledges, or treaty stipulations. He is opposed to any agreement between the United States and any European power by which the United States will be bound to do or not to do certain things respecting the future of any part of this continent. He is for leaving the government perfectly free to act when the occasion arises, just as the circumstances and interests of the country shall at the time require.

When Mr. Douglas entered Congress the Oregon boundary question was causing considerable agitation. He had discussed the subject often at home in Illinois. It was no new subject for him. He at once entered largely into it. As the whole controversy has long since been finally disposed of by treaty, it is unnecessary to quote in a work of this kind his speeches on the question. They were many and able, and displayed a research for which those who were strangers to him were reluctant to give him credit. He was for 54° 40', and was the last man to yield in the memorable congressional struggle that ensued some years later. He had declared in his first speech his matured and deliberate opinion that the American title was clear and indisputable, and that he never would, now or hereafter, yield up an inch of Oregon to Great Britain or any other government. He was a warm supporter of the proposition of giving the notice required by existing treaty for the termination of the joint occupation of the disputed territory. He advocated the immediate organization of a territorial government for Oregon, and its protection by an ample military force. If these events, if this just enforcement of American rights were to lead to a war with Great Britain, he urged the strong necessity for putting the country in a state of defense. He reviewed, with strong and emphatic denunciations, the incessant progress made by Great Britain in extending and maintaining dominion on this continent. He described her power at the north and on the lakes; her possessions and dépôts in the Atlantic, and also on the Pacific; pointed out her intrigues to obtain Texas on the southwest—all these things he presented with great force and power.

On the 3d of June, 1844, he made a speech in the House contrasting the principles, and the opinions upon all pending national questions, of Messrs. Clay and Polk. This speech was made in reply to one delivered by Colonel Hardin, of Illinois; it was such an able exposition of Democratic principles that it was the campaign speech of the session, was printed in immense numbers, and was sent all over the Union.

THE OREGON BOUNDARY.

The following extracts from speeches delivered by him on the Oregon question of that day will serve to illustrate his *general* views:

"It therefore becomes us to put this nation in a state of defense; and, when we are told that this will lead to war, all I have to say is this, violate no treaty stipulations, nor any principle of the law of nations; preserve the honor and integrity of the country, but, at the same time, assert our right to the last inch, and then, if war comes, let it come. We may regret the necessity which produced it, but when it does come, I would administer to our citizens Hannibal's oath of eternal enmity, and not terminate the war until the question was settled forever. I would blot out the lines on the map which now mark our national boundaries on this continent, and make the area of liberty as broad as the continent itself. I would not suffer petty rival republics to grow up here, engendering jealousy of each other, and interfering with each other's domestic affairs, and continually endangering their peace. I do not wish to go beyond the great ocean—beyond those boundaries which the God of nature has marked out, I would limit myself only by that boundary which is so clearly defined by nature."

Again:

"Our federal system is admirably adapted to the whole continent; and, while I would not violate the laws of nations, nor treaty stipulations, nor in any manner tarnish the national honor, I would exert all legal and honorable means to drive Great Britain and the last vestiges of royal authority from the continent of North America, and extend the limits of the republic from ocean to ocean. I would make this an ocean-bound republic, and have no more disputes about boundaries, or 'red lines' upon the maps."

The Baltimore Convention, which in June, 1844, nominated Mr. Polk for the presidency, had passed the following resolution:

"*Resolved*, That our title to the whole of the territory of Oregon is clear and unquestionable; that no portion of the same should be ceded to England or any other power; and that the reoccupation of Oregon, and the reannexation of Texas at the earliest practicable period, are great American measures, which this convention recommends to the ardent support of the Democracy of the Union."

It subsequently became a subject of grave discussion and of warm controversy whether that part of this resolution relating to Oregon was or was not a part of the Democratic platform to which the party was committed. In the discussion upon that point, Mr. Douglas, while conceding to President Polk all possible patriotism, and admitting that the President could not have been aware, on his accession to the presidency, that the United States had at one time offered to compromise on 49°, contended, nevertheless, that all Democrats were bound by the resolution of the Baltimore Convention.

The history of the Oregon boundary question is one of the most interesting in the annals of our government. The limits of this work will not permit it to be given in full here, but its progress and final settlement may be understood from the following brief sketch:

The proposition to give the notice of the termination of the joint occupancy of the disputed territory was renewed during the first Congress of which Mr. Douglas was a member, and failed. In the twenty-ninth Congress it was again urged. This was the first Congress following Mr. Polk's inauguration. In his inaugural address the President had used these memorable words:

" Nor will it become in a less degree my duty to assert and maintain, by all constitutional means, the right of the United States to that portion of our territory which lies beyond the Rocky Mountains. Our title to the country of the Oregon is ' clear and unquestionable,' and already are our people preparing to perfect that title by occupying it with their wives and children."

By the 3d article of the treaty of October, 1818, it had been agreed that the country in dispute should be open and free for ten years to the citizens of both countries, without prejudice to the claims of either country. Several subsequent efforts were made to settle the matter by negotiation, but without success. In 1827 a convention was made, by which it was agreed to continue in force the existing stipulation for a joint occupancy, with a proviso that after October, 1828, either of the contracting parties, on giving due notice of twelve months to the other contracting party, might annul and abrogate this last treaty, which should, from and after the expiration of the twelve months' notice, be abrogated and annulled. The United States had, in all the negotiations, offered to fix the boundary upon the parallel of 49° north latitude, but the offer had been rejected. Great Britain offered the boundary of 49° to its intersection with the northeastern branch of the Columbia River, and then with the channel of said river to the ocean. This had been rejected, for obvious reasons, by the United States. In 1843 the negotiations had been renewed; and in August, 1844, pending the presidential contest in which Mr. Polk was a candidate, Great Britain, through her minister at Washington, made an offer having for its main feature the line of 49°. This was rejected by Mr. Tyler. Upon Mr. Polk's entering the office of President, he found that the United States, from 1818 up to a very recent period, had offered to accept the parallel of 49°, the difference between the two governments being upon questions involving the joint right of navigation of the Columbia River, free ports upon Vancouver's Island, and other points of detail. Mr. Polk again offered as a compromise the line of 49°, omitting what had been tendered by his predecessors— the free navigation of the Columbia River south of that line. He was, he said, unwilling to concede to Great Britain the free navigation of any river in the United States. The British minister rejected the offer, and Mr. Polk then asserted the American claim to the whole territory. He recommended that the notice be given for the termination of the existing convention.

In December, 1845, Mr. Douglas, being then chairman of the Committee on Territories, reported " a bill to protect the rights of American settlers in the Territory of Oregon until the termination of the joint occupancy of the same."

In January, 1846, the Committee on Foreign Relations in the House reported a joint resolution directing the President forthwith to give the twelve months' notice for the abrogation of the treaty of 1827.

Upon this resolution a protracted debate took place. Mr. Douglas advocated its passage. He took the high ground that the American title to the whole territory was indisputable, and he was for resuming its exclusive occupancy. He denied that such a course would afford cause for war; but if it was used as a pretext for war by Great Britain, he would not shrink from the contest. He denied that Great Britain had the slightest legal claim to any part of the northwestern coast, and, having no just or legal claim, he was for excluding her entirely from that coast. The records of Congress bear ample evidence of the interest felt by the country upon the question; and in the broad pages which contain the speeches, there are none that will better repay the time given to their perusal than those which contain the speeches of Mr. Douglas.

The excitement following these measures, and up to the day of the final settlement of the question in Congress, was intense, and the country was no less agitated. Peace or war, the integrity of the national domain or its severance, were the themes of daily and angry discussions in all parts of the country. State conventions and state Legislatures took action upon the subject, and throughout the land the declaration of "fifty-four forty or fight" was growing into popular favor, and was fast becoming an expression of national sentiment. In the second week of February, the House, by resolution, closed the debate in Committee of the Whole. In the mean time, while these propositions were pending before the House, the British minister, on the 27th of December, 1845, and again on January 16, 1846, proposed to the American government, 1st, to submit the whole question of an equitable division of Oregon territory to the arbitration of some friendly sovereign or state; and, 2d, to refer the question of title in either of the two powers to the whole territory; the arbitrator, in case he found the title to the whole to be in neither, to assign to each such portions as he might think it entitled. These propositions were promptly rejected by Mr. Polk, who declined the first proposition (among other reasons) because he could not admit Great Britain to have any claim to any portion, and, secondly, because he did not think the territorial rights of the nation a proper subject for arbitration. He could not consent to any measure which would withdraw our title from the control of the government and people of the United States, and place it within the discretion of any arbitrator, no matter how intelligent and respectable.

The debate closed at three P.M., Mr. Darragh having made the last speech, and then ensued a scene which is graphically described in the Congressional Globe. The question pending was on the joint resolution reported by the Committee on Foreign Relations, directing that the President forthwith give the notice. The first amendment proposed was to strike out the word "forthwith," which was agreed to without a division. The next amendment proposed was to authorize the President to give the notice whenever, in his judgment, the public interest required it. This was rejected; ayes 56, noes 136.

Mr. Dromgoole submitted a substitute for the resolution reported by the committee. It authorized the President to give the notice, but declared that nothing in such action was to be taken as interfering with negotiations for an amicable settlement of the controversy. Under the rules of the House, both the original proposition and the proposed substitute were open for amendment.

Mr. Dargan moved an amendment, providing, 1st, that the existing differences between the two governments were still the subject of honorable negotiation and compromise, and should be so adjusted; and, 2d, that the boundary-line between the Canadas and the United States should be extended due west to the coast south of Frazer's River, and thence through the centre of the Straits of Fuca to the Pacific, giving to the United States all the territory south, and Great Britain all lying north of that line. The first clause was rejected—ayes 96, noes 102; and the second clause by an overwhelming vote.

Mr. J. A. Rockwell moved an amendment declaring that, as the President had refused to accept an offer to refer the matter to arbitration, it was the sense of the House that the President should be permitted, upon his own responsibility, to take such further measures as he might deem expedient. This was rejected.

Mr. J. A. Black offered as an amendment for the substitute a preamble and resolution, that, with a view of fixing a limit beyond which the settlement of the question could not be delayed, and at the same time affording every possible opportunity for a just and final settlement, the President give the twelve months' notice, etc. Rejected.

Mr. Ramsey moved to amend by striking out all after the word "resolved," and insert,

"That the Oregon question is no longer a subject of negotiation or compromise."

This was the ultimate ground on the subject, and the House voted — ayes 10, noes 146. The proceedings having taken place in Committee of the Whole, and the vote by tellers, no record is preserved of the names of members voting on this or any other of the propositions; but Mr. Wheeler, in his History of Congress, writing from personal knowledge, gives as the names of the ten who voted in the affirmative the following:

Alexander Ramsey, of Pennsylvania.	Joseph B. Hoge, of Illinois.
Archibald Yell, of Arkansas.	Robert Smith, "
William Sawyer, of Ohio.	Stephen A. Douglas, "
Cornelius Darragh, of Pennsylvania.	J. A. M'Clernand, "
F. G. M'Connell, of Alabama.	John Wentworth, "

Finally, after the rejection of a large number of amendments, the committee, by a vote of ayes 110, noes 93, adopted the following: "*Resolved, by the Senate and House of Representatives*, etc., that the President of the United States cause notice to be given to the government of Great Britain that the convention between the United States of America and Great Britain concerning the territory on the northwest coast of America, west of the Stony or Rocky Mountains, of the sixth day of August, one thousand eight hundred and twenty-seven, signed at London, shall be annulled and abrogated twelve months after giving said notice.

"*Resolved*, That nothing herein contained is intended to interfere with the right and discretion of the proper authorities of the two contracting parties to renew or pursue negotiations for an amicable settlement of the controversy respecting the Oregon Territory."

E.

The committee rose and reported the resolution to the House. The House, by a vote of yeas 163, nays 54, ordered it to be engrossed, and then, without a division, the resolution passed. The Senate debated this resolution from February till the 16th of April, when it amended it by substituting another resolution for it. The House refused to concur; a committee of conference was appointed, and they reported a resolution which was finally agreed to by both houses. It authorized the President, in his discretion, to give the notice, which authority he promptly exercised. It is known that while the Senate and House were thus engaged, an active correspondence was going on between the representatives of the two governments, which finally ended in a formal offer, in the month of June, by the British government for a settlement of the boundary-line upon the parallel of 49°. As the rejection of that proposition involved possibly the issue of peace or war, the President, imitating the example set by Washington in several cases, submitted the offer to the Senate for their advice upon it. The Senate, by a vote of 38 to 12, advised the President to accept the proposal of the British government. On the 16th of June the President communicated the treaty to the Senate; and on the 18th, the Senate, by a vote of yeas 41, nays 14, advised and consented to the ratification of the same. Thus ended the exciting Oregon boundary question, in the discussions upon which Mr. Douglas earned an enviable reputation both as an orator and as a statesman.

The annexation of Texas and the Mexican war, though both questions bearing directly upon the foreign policy of the government of the United States, are subjects so intimately connected, and forming a distinct chapter of the history of the country at the time, will be found under a separate head.

MONROE DOCTRINE.—CLAYTON-BULWER TREATY.

The next great question affecting the policy of the United States respecting the management of its relations with foreign governments was the Treaty of Washington, more familiarly known as the Clayton and Bulwer treaty. The proceedings of the Senate (of which Mr. Douglas was then a member) upon this treaty were, of course, secret, and the record since made public presents the statement of the votes of senators, and the resolutions of the Senate. Involved in this treaty was the policy of the United States respecting the states of Central America, and the enforcement of what is known historically as the Monroe Doctrine.

In March, 1849, General Taylor succeeded Mr. Polk in the presidency. The Hon. John M. Clayton succeeded Mr. Buchanan as secretary of state. During the summer and winter following the administration undertook to establish some fixed relations respecting affairs in Central America. The result was the Clayton and Bulwer treaty. This convention was communicated to the Senate by a special message on the 22d of April, 1850. On the 22d of May following it was ratified by that body by the following vote:

Yeas — F. Badger of North Carolina, Baldwin of Connecticut, Bell of Tennessee, Berrien of Georgia, Butler of South Carolina, Cass of Michigan, Chase of Ohio, Clarke of Rhode Island, Clay of Kentucky, Cooper of Pennsylvania, Corwin of Ohio, Davis of Massachusetts, Dawson of Georgia, Dayton of New Jersey, Dodge of Wisconsin, Dodge of Iowa, Downs of Louisiana, Felch of Michigan, Foote of Mississippi, Green of Rhode Island, Hale of New Hampshire, Houston of Texas, Hunter of Virginia, Jones of Iowa, King of Alabama, Mangum of North Carolina, Mason of Virginia, Miller of New Jersey, Morton of Florida, Norris of New Hampshire, Pearce of Maryland, Pratt of Maryland, Sebastian of Arkansas, Seward of New York, Shields of Illinois, Smith of Connecticut, Soule of Louisiana, Spruance of Delaware, Sturgeon of Pennsylvania, Underwood of Kentucky, Wales of Delaware, and Webster of Massachusetts—42.

Nays — Atchison of Missouri, Borland of Arkansas, Bright of Indiana, Clemens of Alabama, Davis of Mississippi, Dickinson of New York, Douglas of Illinois, Turney of Tennessee, Walker of Wisconsin, Whitcomb of Indiana, and Yulee of Florida—11.

The very interesting debates were not published, though it was well known at the time that Mr. Douglas had taken an active part in opposition to the ratification of the treaty.

At the session of 1852–3, General Cass called the attention of the Senate to certain alleged misunderstandings between the two governments respecting the meaning of certain stipulations in the treaty. A debate of deep interest sprung up, and for several days the entire subject of the treaty was discussed. Mr. Clayton was then at his residence in Delaware. So deeply did he consider himself involved in the matters agitated before the Senate, that he addressed a long letter by telegraph to the National Intelligencer. The Legislature of Delaware shortly after elected him to a seat in the Senate. On the 3d of March Congress adjourned; but, as is usual upon the incoming of a new administration, the retiring President called a special session of the Senate to consider such executive

business as might be laid before them. Mr. Clayton took his
seat at this special session, and, by way of a resolution calling
for information, he renewed the controversy. Upon this resolution, the whole subject of the Clayton-Bulwer treaty and
Central American affairs was discussed in a debate which was
protracted until late in April. As Mr. Douglas bore a conspicuous part in the debate in February, as well as at the special session, his speeches on these occasions are quoted from
largely, as presenting in a clear and comprehensive form his
views and opinions upon the important subjects embraced in
the debates.

On the 14th of February, in the Senate, Mr. Douglas said:

Thirty years ago, Mr. Monroe, in his message to Congress, made a memorable declaration with respect to European colonization upon this continent.
That declaration has ever since been a favorite subject of eulogism with orators, politicians, and statesmen. Recently it has assumed the dignified appellation of the "*Monroe doctrine.*" It seems to be the part of patriotism
for all to profess that doctrine, while our government has scarcely ever failed
to repudiate it practically whenever an opportunity for its observance has
been presented. The Oregon treaty is a noted case in point. Prior to that
convention there was no British colony on this continent west of the Rocky
Mountains. The Hudson's Bay Company was confined by its charter to the
shores of the bay, and to the streams flowing into it, and to the country
drained by them. The western boundary of Canada was hundreds of miles
distant; and there was no European colony to be found in all that region
on the Pacific coast stretching from California to the Russian possessions.
We had a treaty of non-occupancy with Great Britain, by the provisions of
which neither party was to be permitted to colonize or assume dominion over
any portion of that territory. We abrogated that treaty of non-occupancy,
and then entered into a convention, by the terms of which the country in
question was divided into two nearly equal parts, by the parallel of the forty-
ninth degree of latitude, and all on the north confirmed to Great Britain,
and that on the south to the United States. By that treaty Great Britain
consented that we might establish territories and states south of the forty-
ninth parallel, and the United States consented that Great Britain might, to
the north of that parallel, establish new European colonies, in open and flagrant violation of the Monroe doctrine. It is unnecessary for me to remind
the country, and especially my own constituents, with what energy and emphasis I protested against that convention, upon the ground that it carried
with it the undisguised repudiation of the Monroe declaration, and the consent of this republic that new British colonies might be established on that
portion of the North American continent where none existed before.

Again: as late as 1850 a convention was entered into between the government of the United States and Great Britain, called the Clayton and Bulwer treaty, every article and provision of which is predicated upon a practical
negation and repudiation of what is known as the Monroe doctrine, as I
shall conclusively establish before I close these remarks. Since the ratification of that treaty and in defiance of its express stipulations, as well as of
the Monroe declaration, Great Britain has planted a new colony in Central
America, known as the colony of the Bay Islands. In view of this fact, and
with the colony of the Bay Islands in his mind's eye, the venerable senator

from Michigan lays upon the table of the Senate, and asks us to affirm by our votes, a resolution in which it is declared that "WHILE EXISTING RIGHTS SHOULD BE RESPECTED, AND WILL BE BY THE UNITED STATES," the American continents "ARE HENCEFORTH *not to be considered as subjects for* FUTURE *colonization by any European power*," and "*that no* FUTURE *European colony or dominion shall, with their consent, be planted or established on any part of the North American continent.*"

Now, sir, before I vote for this resolution, I desire to understand, with clearness and precision, its purport and meaning. Existing rights are to be respected! What is to be the construction of this clause? Is it that all colonies established in America by European powers prior to the passage of this resolution are to be respected by the United States as "existing rights?" Is this resolution to be understood as a formal and official declaration, by the Congress of the United States, of our acquiescence in the seizure of the islands in the Bay of Honduras, and the erection of them into a new British colony? When, in connection with this clause respecting "existing rights," we take into consideration the one preceding it, in which it is declared that "HENCEFORTH" the American continents are not open to European colonization; and the clause immediately succeeding it, which says that "*no future European colony or dominion*" shall, with our consent, be planted on the North American continent, who can doubt that Great Britain will feel herself authorized to construe the resolution into a declaration on our part of unconditional acquiescence in her right to hold all the colonies and dependencies she at this time may possess in America? Is the Senate of the United States prepared to make such a declaration? Is this republic, in view of our professions for the last thirty years, and of our present and prospective position, prepared to submit to such a result? If we are, let us seal our lips, and talk no more about European colonization upon the American continents. What is to redeem our declarations upon this subject in the future from utter contempt, if we fail to vindicate the past, and meekly submit to the humiliation of the present? With an avowed policy, of thirty years' standing, that no future European colonization is to be permitted in America—affirmed when there was no opportunity for enforcing it, and abandoned whenever a case was presented for carrying it into practical effect—is it now proposed to beat another retreat under cover of terrible threats of awful consequences when the offense shall be repeated? "*Henceforth*" no "*future*" European colony is to be planted in America "*with our consent!*" It is gratifying to learn that the United States are never going to "consent" to the repudiation of the Monroe doctrine again. No more Clayton and Bulwer treaties; no more British "alliances" in Central America, New Granada, or Mexico; no more resolutions of oblivion to protect "existing rights!" Let England tremble, and Europe take warning, if the offense is repeated. "Should the attempt be made," says the resolution, "it will leave the United States *free to adopt* such measures as an independent nation may justly adopt in defense of its rights and honor." Are not the United States now *free* to adopt such measures as an independent nation may *justly adopt* in defense of its *rights and honor?* Have we not given the notice? Is not thirty years sufficient notice? And has it not been repeated within the last eight years, and yet the deed is done in contempt of not only the Monroe doctrine, but of solemn treaty stipulations? Will you ever have a better opportunity to establish the doctrine—a clearer right to vindicate, or a more flagrant wrong to redress? If you do not do it now, your "henceforth" resolutions, in respect to "future" attempts, may as well be dispensed with. I have no resolutions to bring forward in relation to our foreign policy. Circumstances have deprived me of the opportunity or disposition to participate actively in the proceedings of the Senate this session. I know not what the present administration has done or is doing in reference to this question; and I am willing to leave the incoming administration free to assume its own position, and to take the initiation unembarrassed by the action of the Senate.

My principal object in addressing the Senate to-day is to avail myself of the opportunity, now for the first time presented by the removal of the injunction of secrecy, of explaining my reasons for opposing the ratification of the Clayton and Bulwer treaty. In order to clearly understand the question in all its bearings, it is necessary to advert to the circumstances under which it was presented. The Oregon boundary had been established, and important interests had grown up in that territory; California had been acquired, and an immense commerce had sprung into existence; lines of steamers had been established from New York and New Orleans to Chagres, and from Panama to California and Oregon; American citizens had acquired the right of way, and were engaged in the construction of a railroad across the Isthmus of Panama, under the protection of treaty stipulations with New Granada; other American citizens had secured the right of way, and were preparing to construct a canal from the Atlantic to the Pacific, through Lake Nicaragua; and still other American citizens had procured the right of way, and were preparing to commence the construction of a railroad, under a grant from Mexico, across the Isthmus of Tehuantepec. Thus the right of transit on all the routes across the isthmus had passed into American hands, and were within the protection and control of the American government.

In view of this state of things, Mr. Hise, who had been appointed chargé d'affaires, under the administration of Mr. Polk, to the Central American States, negotiated a treaty with the State of Nicaragua which secured to the United States forever the exclusive privilege of opening and using all canals, railroads, and other means of communication, from the Atlantic to the Pacific, through the territory of that republic. The rights, privileges, and immunities conceded by that treaty were all that any American could have desired. Its provisions are presumed to be within the knowledge of every senator, and ought to be familiar to the people of this country. The grant was to the United States, or to such companies as should be organized under its authority, or received under its protection. The privileges were exclusive in their terms and perpetual in their tenure. They were to continue forever as inalienable American rights. In addition to the privilege of constructing and using all roads and canals through the territory of Nicaragua, Mr. Hise's treaty also secured to the United States the right to erect and garrison such fortifications as we should deem necessary at the termini of such communication on each ocean, and at intermediate points along the lines of the works, together with a grant of lands three miles square at the termini for the establishment of towns with free ports and free institutions. I do not deem it necessary to detain the Senate by reading the provisions of this treaty. It is published in the document I hold in my hand, and is open to every one who chooses to examine it. It was submitted to the Department of State in Washington on the 15th of September, 1849, but never sent to the Senate for ratification. In the mean time, the administration of General Taylor had superseded Mr. Hise by the appointment of another representative to the Central American States, and instructed him, in procuring a grant for a canal, to "CLAIM NO PECULIAR PRIVILEGE—NO EXCLUSIVE RIGHT—NO MONOPOLY OF COMMERCIAL INTERCOURSE."

After having thus instructed Mr. Squier as to the basis of the treaty which he was to conclude, Mr. Clayton seems to have been apprehensive that Mr. Hise might already have entered into a convention by which the United States had secured the exclusive and perpetual privilege, and in order to guard against such a contingency, he adds, at the conclusion of the same letter of instructions, the following:

"If a charter or grant of the right of way shall have been *incautiously or inconsiderately* made before your arrival in that country, SEEK *to have it properly* MODIFIED TO ANSWER THE ENDS WE HAVE IN VIEW."

In other words, if Mr. Hise shall have made a treaty by which he may have secured all the desired privileges to the United States exclusively, "seek to have it properly modified," so as to form a partnership with England and other monarchical powers of Europe, and thus lay the foundation for an alliance between the New and Old World, by which the right of European powers to intermeddle with the affairs of American states will be established and recognized. With these instructions in his pocket, Mr. Squier arrived in Nicaragua, and before he reached the seat of government, learned, by a "publication in the Gazette of the Isthmus," that Mr. Hise was already negotiating a treaty in respect to the contemplated canal. Without knowing the provisions of the treaty, but taking it for granted that it was in violation of the principles of General Taylor's administration, as set forth in his instructions, Mr. Squier immediately dispatched a notice to the government of Nicaragua, that "Mr. Hise was superseded on the 2d of April last, upon which date I (Mr. Squier) received my commission as his successor;" "that Mr. Hise was not empowered to enter upon any negotiations of the character referred to;" and concluding with the following request:

"*I have, therefore, to request that* NO ACTION *will be taken by the government of Nicaragua upon the inchoate treaty which may have been negotiated at Guatemala, but that the* SAME MAY BE ALLOWED TO PASS AS AN UNOFFICIAL ACT."

On the same day, Mr. Squier, with commendable promptness, sends a letter to Mr. Clayton, informing our government of what he had learned in respect to the probable conclusion of the Hise treaty, and expressing his apprehension that the information may be true, and adds:

"If so, I shall be placed in a situation of some embarrassment, as I conceive that Mr. Hise has no authority for the step he has taken, and *is certainly not informed of the* PRESENT VIEWS AND DESIRES OF OUR GOVERNMENT."

He also adds:

"Under these circumstances, I have addressed a note [B] to the government of this republic (Nicaragua), requesting that the treaty made at Guatemala (if any such exists) *may be allowed to pass as an unofficial act, and that new negotiations may be entered upon at the seat of government.*"

Having communicated this important intelligence to his own government, Mr. Squier proceeded on his journey with a patriotic zeal equal to the importance of his mission, and on his arrival upon the theatre of his labors opened negotiations for a new treaty in accordance with the "present views and desires of our government," as contained in his instructions. The new treaty was concluded on the 3d of September, 1849, and transmitted to the government, with a letter explanatory of the negotiation, bearing date the 10th of the same month. Mr. Squier's treaty, so far as I can judge from the published correspondence—for the injunction of secrecy forbids a reference to more authentic sources of information—is in strict accordance with his instructions, and entirely free from any odious provisions which might secure "peculiar privileges or exclusive rights" to the United States.

These two treaties—the one negotiated by Mr. Hise and the other by Mr. Squier—were in the State Department in this city when Congress met in December, 1849. The administration of General Taylor was at liberty to choose between them, and submit the one or the other to the Senate for ratification. The Hise treaty was suppressed, without giving the Senate an opportunity of ratifying it or advising its rejection. I am aware that a single letter published in this document of correspondence (House of Representatives, Executive Document, No. 75) gives an apparent excuse—a mere pretext—for withholding it from the Senate. I allude to the letter of Mr. Carache, chargé d'affaires from Nicaragua, to Mr. Clayton, dated Washington, December 31, 1849, that the Hise treaty "has been, as is publicly and universally known, disapproved by my government, and that my government desires the ratification of the treaty signed by Mr. Squier on the 3d of September last." And I am also aware that Mr. Clayton, in reply to this letter, stated to Mr. Carache that "if, however, as you state, that convention has not been approved by your government, there is no necessity for its farther consideration by the government of the United States." From this it would seem that Mr. Clayton desires to have it understood that the failure of the government of Nicaragua to approve the Hise treaty was the reason he suppressed it, and refused to allow the Senate an opportunity of ratifying it. Is that the true reason? Why did the government of Nicaragua fail to approve the Hise treaty? I have already shown conclusively that the failure to approve on the part of the government of Nicaragua was produced by the representative of General Taylor's administration in Central America, acting in obedience to the imperative instruction of the State Department of this city, over the signature of Mr. Clayton himself. Mr. Clayton had instructed Mr. Squier, in advance, that in the event Mr. Hise should have made a treaty before his arrival in the country, he (Mr. Squier) must "*seek to have it properly modified to* ANSWER THE ENDS WE HAVE IN VIEW." Mr. Squier did "seek" to have it so "modified," and with great difficulty, as the correspondence proves, succeeded in the effort. The government and people of Nicaragua were anxious to grant the exclusive and perpetual privilege to the United States, and to prevent the consummation of the grand European alliance and partnership. Mr. Squier, in his letter of September 10, 1849, communicating to Mr. Clayton the joyous news that his efforts had been crowned with complete success, says:

"SIR: *I have the satisfaction of informing the department that I have succeeded in accomplishing* THE OBJECT OF MY MISSION TO THIS REPUBLIC."

Then, after giving an exposition of the main provisions of his treaty, he details the embarrassment he was compelled to encounter before he could bring the government of Nicaragua to terms. Hear him, and then judge whether the failure of the government of Nicaragua to approve the Hise treaty was the reason why Mr. Clayton refused to submit it to the Senate for ratification!

"THE PRINCIPAL SOURCE OF EMBARRASSMENT WAS MR. HISE'S SPECIAL CONVENTION, which had raised extravagant hopes of a relation between the United States, amounting to something closer than exists between the states of our confederacy. However, as matters have been finally arranged, they are all the better for this republic, and quite as favorable to the United States."

So it seems that the Hise treaty was "the principal source of embarrassment" to the consummation of the European partnership. It "had raised extravagant hopes" on the part of the government and people of Nicaragua of a "closer" relation to the United States, which it was difficult to induce them to relinquish. It required all the zeal, skill, and tact of Mr. Squier to accomplish so great a feat. "Finally" the matter was "arranged," and the result communicated to the department with "satisfaction," in these memorable words, which must have carried great joy to Mr. Clayton's heart: "I have succeeded in accomplishing the objects of my mission to this republic." Rejoice, all ye advocates of European intervention in the affairs of the American continent! The Hise treaty is dead! The principal source of embarrassment is removed! Nicaragua has failed to approve the special convention granting peculiar privileges and exclusive rights to the United States! This failure has enabled us "properly to modify the grant, so as to answer the ends we have in view," and, at the same time, relieves Mr. Clayton from the imminent risk of submitting these peculiar privileges to the Senate, where there was great danger of their being accepted. Nicaragua has at last consented! Her appeals to the United States for mediation or protection against British aggression being unheeded—her letters to our government remaining unanswered—their receipt not even acknowledged—her hopes of a closer relation to this Union blasted—the Monroe doctrine abandoned—the Mosquito kingdom, under the British protectorate, rapidly absorbing her territory, she sinks in despair, and yields herself to the European partnership which was about to be established over all Central America by the Clayton and Bulwer treaty !

Now, sir, I repeat that these two treaties—the one negotiated by Mr. Hise and the other by Mr. Squier, the first conceding peculiar privileges and exclusive and perpetual rights to the United States, the second admitting of a partnership in these privileges with European powers, Mr. Clayton suppressed the first, and sent the second to the Senate for ratification, and immediately opened negotiations with the British minister, which resulted in what is known as the Clayton and Bulwer treaty. In stating my objections to this treaty, I shall not become a party to the protracted controversy respecting its true meaning and construction, which has engaged so much of the attention of this session. I leave that in the hands of those who conducted the negotiation and procured its ratification. That is their own quarrel, with which I have no disposition to interfere. Establish which construction you please—that contended for by the secretary of state who signed it, or the one insisted upon by the venerable senator from Michigan, and those who acted in concert with him in ratifying it—neither obviates any one of my objections.

In the first place, I was unwilling to enter into treaty stipulations with Great Britain or any other European power in respect to the American continent, by the terms of which we should pledge the faith of this republic not to do in all coming time that which in the progress of events our interests, duty, and even safety may compel us to do. I have already said, and now repeat, that every article, clause, and provision of that treaty is predicated upon a virtual negation and repudiation of the Monroe declaration in relation to European colonization on this continent. The article inviting any power on earth with which England and the United States are on terms of friendly intercourse to enter into similar stipulations, and which pledges the good offices of each, when requested by the other, to aid in the new negotiations with the other Central American states, and which pledges the good offices of all the nations entering into the "alliance" to settle disputes between the states and governments of Central America, not only recognizes the right of European powers to interfere with the affairs of the American continent, but invites the exercise of such right, and makes it obligatory to do so in certain cases. It establishes, in terms, an alliance between the contracting parties, and invites all other nations to become parties to it. I was opposed also to the clause which stipulates that neither Great Britain nor the United States will ever occupy, colonize, or exercise dominion over any portion of Nicaragua, Costa Rica, the Mosquito Coast, or any part of Central America. I did not desire then, nor do I now, to annex any portion of that country to this Union. I do not know that the time will ever come in my day when I would be willing to do so. Yet I was unwilling to give the pledge that neither we nor our successors ever would. This is an age of rapid movements and great changes. How long is it since those who made this treaty would have told us that the time would never come when we would want California or any portion of the Pacific coast? California being a state of the Union, who is authorized to say that the time will not arrive when our interests and safety may require us to possess some portion of Central America, which lies half way between our Atlantic and Pacific possessions, and embraces the great water lines of commerce between the two oceans? I think it the wiser and safer policy to hold the control of our own action, and leave those who are to come after us untrammeled and free to do whatever they may deem their duty, when the time shall arrive. They will have a better right to determine for themselves when the necessity for action may arise, than we have now to prescribe the line of duty for them. I was equally opposed to that other clause in the same article, which stipulates that neither party will ever fortify any portion of Central America, or any place commanding the entrance to the canal, or in the vicinity thereof. It is not reciprocal, for the reason that it leaves the island of Jamaica, a British colony, strongly fortified, the nearest military and naval station to the line of the canal. It is, therefore, equivalent to a stipulation that the United States shall never have or maintain any fortification in the vicinity of, or commanding the line of navigation and commerce through said canal, while England may keep and maintain those she now has.

I was not satisfied with the clause in relation to the British protectorate over the Mosquito Coast. It is equivocal in terms, and no man can say with certainty whether the true construction excludes the protectorate from the continent or recognizes its rightful existence, and imposes restraints upon its use and exercise. Equivocal terms in treaties are easily understood where the stipulations are between a strong power on the one hand and a feeble one on the other. The stronger enforces its own construction, and the weaker has no alternative but reluctant acquiescence. In this case neither party may be willing to recognize the potential right of the other to prescribe and enforce a construction of the equivocal terms which shall enable it to appropriate to itself all the advantages in question. It would seem that our own government have not ventured to insist upon a rigid enforcement of the provisions of the treaty in relation to the British protectorate over the Mosquito Coast, in the sense in which it was explained and understood when submitted to the Senate for ratification. Has the British protectorate disappeared from Central America? I am not referring to the matters in controversy between certain senators who supported the treaty and Mr. Clayton, in respect to the Balize settlement. I allude to the Mosquito Coast, which, by name and in terms, is expressly made subject to the provisions of the treaty. Has the British protectorate disappeared from that part of Central America? Have the British authorities retired from the port of San Juan, and thereby recognized the right of American citizens and vessels to arrive and depart free of hinderance and molestation? Is it not well known that the protectorate is continued and maintained with increased vigor and boldness? Is not the British consul at San Juan now actively engaged in disposing of the soil, conveying town lots and lands, and exercising the highest functions of sovereignty under the pretext of protecting the rights of the Mosquito king? These things are being done openly and without disguise, and are well known to the world. Can any senator inform me whether this government has taken the slightest notice of these transactions? Has our government entered its protest against these infractions of the treaty, or demanded a specific compliance with our understanding of its terms? How long are we to wait for Great Britain to abandon her occupancy and withdraw her machinery of government? Nearly three years have elapsed since we were boastingly told that by the provisions of the Clayton and Bulwer treaty Great Britain was expelled from Central America. Shall we wait patiently until our silence shall be construed into acquiescence in her right to remain and maintain her possessions?

But there was another insuperable objection to the Clayton and Bulwer treaty which increases, enlarges, and extends the force of all the obnoxious provisions I have pointed out. I allude to the article in which it is provided that

"The government of the United States and Great Britain, *having not only desired to accomplish a particular object*, BUT ALSO TO ESTABLISH A GENERAL PRINCIPLE, THEY HEREBY AGREE TO EXTEND THEIR PROTECTION, BY TREATY STIPULATIONS, TO ANY OTHER PRACTICABLE COMMUNICATIONS, *whether by canal or railway, across the isthmus which connects North and South America, and especially to the interoceanic communications, should the same prove to be practicable, whether by canal or railway, which are now proposed to be established by the way of* TEHUANTEPEC OR PANAMA."

The "particular object" which the parties had in view being thus accomplished—the Hise treaty defeated, the exclusive privilege to the United States surrendered and abandoned, and the European partnership established—yet they were not satisfied. They were not content to "accomplish a particular object," but desired to "ESTABLISH A GENERAL PRINCIPLE!" That which, by the terms of the treaty, was particular and local to the five states of Central America, is, in this article, extended to Mexico on the north, and to New Granada on the south, and declared to be a general principle by which any and all other practicable routes of communication across the isthmus between North and South America are to be governed and protected by the allied powers. New and additional treaty stipulations are to be entered into for this purpose, and the net-work which had been prepared and spread over all Central America is to be extended far enough into Mexico and New Granada to cover all the lines of communication, whether by railway or canal, and especially to include Tehuantepec and Panama. When it is remembered that the treaty in terms establishes an alliance between the United States and Great Britain, and engages to invite all other powers, with which either is on terms of friendly intercourse, to become parties to its provisions, it will be seen that this article seeks to make the principles of the Clayton and Bulwer treaty the law of nations in respect to American affairs. The general principle is established; the right of European powers to intervene in the affairs of American states is recognized; the propriety of the exercise of that right is acknowledged; and the extent to which the allied powers shall carry their protection, and the limits within which they shall confine their operations, are subject to treaty stipulations in the future.

When the American continent shall have passed under the protectorate of the allied powers, and her future made dependent upon treaty stipulations for carrying into effect the object of the alliance, Europe will no longer have cause for serious apprehensions at the rapid growth, expansion, and development of our federal Union. She will then console herself that limits have been set and barriers erected beyond which the territories of this republic can never extend, nor its principles prevail. In confirmation of this view, she will find additional cause for congratulation when she looks into the treaty of peace with Mexico, and there sees the sacred honor of this republic irrevocably pledged that we will never, in all coming time, annex any more Mexican territory in the mode in which Texas was acquired. The fifth article contains the following extraordinary provision :

"The boundary-line established by this article shall be religiously respected by each of the two republics, and no change shall ever be made therein except by the express and free consent of both nations, lawfully given by the general government of each, in conformity with its own Constitution."

One would naturally suppose that, for all the ordinary purposes of a treaty of peace, the first clause of the paragraph would have been entirely sufficient. It declares that "the boundary-line established by this article shall be religiously respected by each of the two republics." Why depart from the usual course of proceeding in such cases, and add, that "*no change shall ever be made therein, except by the express and free consent of both nations,* LAWFULLY *given by the* GENERAL *government of each, in conformity with its* OWN CONSTI-TUTION." What is the meaning of this peculiar phraseology? The history of Texas furnishes the key by which the hidden meaning can be unlocked. The Sabine was once the boundary between the republics of the United States and Mexico. By the revolt of Texas and the establishment of her independence, and the acknowledgment thereof by the great powers of the world, and her annexation to the United States, the boundary between the two republics was "changed" from the Sabine to the Rio Grande *without* "the express and free consent of both nations, *lawfully* given by the *general government* of each, in conformity with its own Constitution." Mexico regarded that change a just cause of war, and accordingly invaded Texas with a view to the recovery of the lost territory. A protracted war ensued, in which thousands of lives were lost, and millions of money expended, when peace is concluded upon the express condition that the treaty should contain an open and frank avowal that the United States has been wrong in the causes of the war, by the pledge of her honor never to repeat the act which led to hostilities.

Wherever you turn your eye, whether to your own record, to the statute-books, to the history of this country or of Mexico, or to the diplomatic history of the world, this humiliating and degrading acknowledgment stares you in the face, as a monument of your own creation, to the dishonor of our common country. Well do I remember the determined and protracted efforts of the minority to expunge this odious clause from the treaty before its ratification, and how, on the 4th of March, 1848, we were voted down by forty-two to eleven. The stain which that clause fastened upon the history of our country was not the only objection I urged to its retention in the treaty. It violated a great principle of public policy in relation to this continent. It pledges the faith of this republic that our successors shall not do that which duty to the interests and honor of the country, in the progress of events, may compel them to do. I do not meditate or look with favor upon any aggression upon Mexico. I do not desire, at this time, to annex any portion of her territory to this Union; nor am I prepared to say that the time will ever come, in my day, when I would be willing to sanction such a proposition. But who can say that, amid the general wreck and demoralization in Mexico, a state of things may not arise in which a just regard for our own rights and safety, and for the sake of humanity and civilization, may render it imperative for us to do that which was done in the case of Texas, and thereby change the boundary between the two republics, without the free consent of the general government of Mexico, lawfully given in conformity with her Constitution? Recent events in Sonora, Chihuahua, and Tamaulipas do not establish the wisdom and propriety of that line of policy which ties our hands in advance, and deprives the government of the right, in the future, of doing whatever duty and honor may require, when the necessity for action may arrive.

Mr. President, one of the resolutions under consideration makes a declaration in relation to the island of Cuba, which requires a passing notice. It is in the following words:

"That, while the United States disclaim any designs upon the island of Cuba, inconsistent with the laws of nations and with their duties to Spain, they consider it due to the vast importance of the subject to make known, in this solemn manner, that they should view all efforts on the part of any other power to procure possession, whether peaceably or forcibly, of that island, which, as a naval or military position, must, under circumstances easy to be foreseen, become dangerous to their southern coast, to the Gulf of Mexico, and to the mouth of the Mississippi, as unfriendly acts, directed against them, to be resisted by all the means in their power."

That we would resist any attempt to transfer the island of Cuba to any European power, either with or without the consent of Spain, there is, I trust, no question in the mind of any American, and the fact is as well known to Europe as it is to our own country. That the United States do not meditate any designs upon the island inconsistent with the laws of nations, and with their duties to Spain, has been demonstrated to the world in a manner that forbids the necessity for a disclaimer of unworthy and perfidious purposes on our part. The resolutions convey, beneath this disclaimer, the implication that our character is subject to suspicion upon that point. Shall we let the presumption go abroad that a disclaimer of an act of dishonesty, and perfidy, and infamy has become necessary upon our part? Sir, is there any thing in the history of our relations with foreign nations, or in respect to Cuba, that should subject our country to such injurious imputations? When has our government failed to perform its whole duty as a neutral power in respect to Cuba? The only complaint has been, that in its great anxiety to preserve in good faith its neutral relations, it has permitted treaty stipulations with Spain, providing for the protection of our citizens, to be wantonly and flagrantly violated. No suspicion that this government has been wanting in energy and fidelity in the enforcement of our laws has been entertained in any quarter. It was the excessive energy and severity with which the duty was performed that has provoked the disapprobation of some portion of the American people.

Sir, what right has Great Britain to call upon the United States, as she did in a late application, to enter into a negotiation to guarantee Cuba to Spain? Such a step might have been necessary on the part of England in order to satisfy Spain that she has abandoned the policy which for centuries has marked her colonial history with plunder and rapine. Why does not England first restore to Spain the island of Jamaica, by the seizure and possession of which she is enabled to overlook Cuba, while it gives her the command of the entrance of the proposed Nicaragua canal? Why does she not restore to old Spain Gibraltar, which, from proximity and geographical position, naturally belongs to her, and is essential to her safety? Why does she not restore the colonial possessions which she has stretched all over the world, commanding every important military and naval station, both upon land and water? Why does she not restore them to their original owners, from whom she obtained them by fraud and violence? Why does she not do these things before she calls upon us to enter into stipulations that we will not rob Spain of the island of Cuba?

The whole system of European colonization rests upon seizure, violence, and fraud. European powers hold nearly all their colonies by the one or the other of these tenures. They can show no other evidence, no other muniment of title. What is there in the history of the United States that requires us to make any such disclaimer? We have never acquired one inch of territory, except by honest purchase and full payment of the consideration. We have never seized any Spanish or other European colony. We have never invaded the rights of other nations. We do not hold in our hand the results of rapine, violence, war, and fraud for centuries, and then prate about honesty, and propose to honest people to enter into guarantees that they will not rob their neighbors. * * * *

I confess I have not formed a very high appreciation of the value of these disclaimers of all intention of committing crimes against our neighbors. I do not think I should deem my house any more secure in the night in consequence of the thief having pledged his honor not to steal my property. If I am surrounded by honest men, there is no necessity for the "friendly assurance;" and if by rogues, it would not relieve my apprehensions or afford much security to my rights. I am unwilling, therefore, to make any disclaimer as to our purposes upon Cuba, or to give any pledge in respect to existing rights upon this continent. The nations of Europe have no right to call upon us for a disclaimer of the one, or for a pledge to protect the other. It is true, British newspapers are in the habit of calumniating the people of the United States as a set of marauders upon the territorial rights of our neighbors. It is also true that, for party purposes, some portion of the press of this country is in the habit of attributing such sentiments to some of our public men; but it is not true, so far as I know, that any one man in either house of Congress does entertain, or has ever entertained or avowed, a sentiment that justifies such an imputation. I am unwilling, therefore, to countenance the vile slander by voting for a resolution which by imputation contains so base an insinuation. Perhaps I may as well speak plainly. I feel that there may be a lurking insinuation in these two clauses, having a little bearing toward an individual of about my proportions. It is the vocation of some partisan presses and personal organs to denounce and stigmatize a certain class of politicians, by attributing to them unworthy and disreputable purposes, under the cognomen of "Young America." It is their amiable custom, I believe, when they come to individualize, to point to me as the one most worthy to bear the appellation. I have never either assumed or disclaimed it. I have never before alluded to it, and should not on the present occasion, had it not been introduced into the discussions of the Senate in such a manner as to leave the impression that I evaded it if I failed to notice it. I am aware that the senator who the other day directed so large a portion of his speech against the supposed doctrines of "YOUNG AMERICA" had no reference to myself in that part of his speech, and that the only allusion he made to me was kind and complimentary. So far as I am concerned, and those who harmonize with me in sentiment and action, the votes to which I have referred, and the reasons I have given in support of them, constitute the only profession of faith I deem it necessary to make on this subject. I am willing to compare votes and acts, principles and professions, with any senator who chooses to assail me. I yield to none in strict observance of the laws of nations and treaty stipulations. I may not have been willing blindly or recklessly to pledge the faith of the republic for all time on points where, in the nature of things, it was not reasonable to suppose that the pledge could be preserved. I may have deemed it wise and prudent to hold the control of our own nation, and leave our successors free, according to their own sense of duty under the circumstances which may then exist.

CUBA.

Now, sir, a few words with regard to the island of Cuba. If any man desires my opinions upon that question, he can learn them very easily. They have been proclaimed frequently for the last nine years, and still remain unchanged. I have often said, and now repeat that, so long as the island of Cuba is content to remain loyal to the crown of Spain, be it so. I have no desire, no wish to disturb that relation. I have always said, and now repeat that, whenever the people of the island of Cuba shall show themselves worthy of freedom by asserting and maintaining their independence and establishing republican institutions, my heart, my sympathies, my prayers are with them for the accomplishment of the object. I have often said, and now repeat that, when that independence shall have been established, if it shall be necessary to their interest or safety to apply as Texas did for annexation, I shall be ready to do by them as we did by Texas, and receive them into the Union. I have said, and now repeat that, whenever Spain shall come to the conclusion that she can not much longer maintain her dominion over the island, and that it is better for her to transfer it to us upon fair and reasonable terms, I am one of those who would be ready to accept the transfer. I have said, and now repeat that, whenever Spain shall refuse to make such transfer to us, and shall make it to England or any other European power, I would be among those who would be in favor of taking possession of the island, and resisting such transfer at all hazards.

Thus far I have often gone; thus far I now go. These are my individual opinions; not of much consequence, I admit, but any one who desires to know them is welcome to them. But it is one thing for me to entertain these individual sentiments, and it is another and very different thing to pledge forever and unalterably the policy of this government in a particular channel, in defiance of any change in the circumstances that may hereafter take place. I do not deem it necessary to affirm by a resolution, in the name of the republic, every opinion that I may entertain and be willing to act upon as the representative of a local constituency. I am not, therefore, prepared to say that it is wise policy to make any declaration upon the subject of the island of Cuba. Circumstances not within our control, and originating in causes beyond our reach, may precipitate a state of things that would change our action and reverse our whole line of policy. Cuba, in the existing position of affairs, does not present a practical issue. All that we may say or do is merely speculative, and dependent upon contingencies that may never happen.

CHAPTER VII.

TERRITORIAL EXPANSION.—FOREIGN AGGRESSIONS.

THE Senate reassembled on the 4th of March. Mr. Clayton submitted resolutions calling for certain information respecting negotiations with Costa Rica, Honduras, etc. On the 8th and 9th of March he addressed the Senate on the general subject of Central American affairs, and criticised with severity the remarks made by Senators Mason, Cass, and Douglas during the debate in February. On the 10th of March Mr. Douglas replied in an argument of rare ability and searching power. He reviewed the entire history of the negotiations respecting Central American affairs during the Taylor administration. A few extracts from the closing portion of his speech will furnish most clearly his views upon the great question of extending the territorial limits of the United States. His views upon that point are stated with great precision and force. He said:

"But, sir, I do not wish to detain the Senate upon this point, or to prolong the discussion. I have a word or two to say in reply to the remarks of the senator from Delaware upon so much of my speech as related to the pledge in the Clayton and Bulwer treaty never to annex any portion of that country. I objected to that clause in the treaty upon the ground that I was unwilling to enter into a treaty stipulation with any European power in respect to this continent, that we would not do, in the future, whatever our duty, interest, honor, and safety might require in the course of events. The senator infers that I desire to annex Central America because I was unwilling to give a pledge **that we never would do it.** He reminded me that there was a clause in the treaty with Mexico containing the stipulation that, in certain contingencies, we would never annex any portion of that country. Sir, it was unnecessary that he should remind me of that provision. He has not forgotten how hard I struggled to get that clause out of the treaty, where it was retained in opposition to my vote. Had the senator given me his aid then to defeat that provision in the Mexican treaty, I would be better satisfied now with his excuse for having inserted a still stronger pledge in his treaty. But, having advocated that pledge then, he should not attempt to avoid the responsibility of his own act by citing it as a precedent. I was unwilling to bind ourselves by treaty for all time to come never to annex any more territory. I am content for the present with the territory we have. I do not wish to annex any portion of Mexico now. I did not wish to annex any part of Central America then, nor do I at this time.

"But I can not close my eyes to the history of this country for the last half century. Fifty years ago the question was being debated in this Senate whether it was wise or not to acquire any territory on the west bank of the Mississippi, and it was then contended that we could never, with safety, extend beyond that river. It was at that time seriously considered whether the Alleghany Mountains should not be the barrier beyond which we should never pass. At a subsequent date, after we had acquired Louisiana and Florida, more liberal views began to prevail, and it was thought that perhaps we might venture to establish one tier of states west of the Mississippi; but, in order to prevent the sad calamity of an undue expansion of our territory, the policy was adopted of establishing an Indian Territory, with titles in perpetuity, all along the western borders of those states, so that no more new states could possibly be created in that direction. That barrier could not arrest the onward progress of our people. They burst through it, and passed the Rocky Mountains, and were only arrested by the waters of the Pacific. Who, then, is prepared to say that in the progress of events, having met with the barrier of the ocean in our western course, we may not be compelled to turn to the north and to the south for an outlet?"   *   *   *   *

"You may make as many treaties as you please to fetter the limbs of this giant republic, and she will burst them all from her, and her course will be onward to a limit which I will not venture to prescribe. Why the necessity of pledging your faith that you will never annex any more of Mexico? Do you not know that you will be compelled to do it; that you can not help it; that your treaty will not prevent it, and that the only effect it will have will be to enable European powers to accuse us of bad faith when the act is done, and associate American faith and Punic faith as synonymous terms? What is the use of your guarantee that you will never erect any fortifications in Central America; never annex, occupy, or colonize any portion of that country? How do you know that you can avoid doing it? If you make the canal, I ask you if American citizens will not settle along its line; whether they will not build up towns at each terminus; whether they will not spread over that country, and convert it into an American state; whether American principles and American institutions will not be firmly planted there? And I ask you how many years you think will pass away before you will find the same necessity to extend your laws over your own kindred that you found in the case of Texas? How long will it be before that day arrives? It may not occur in the senator's day, nor mine. But, so certain as this republic exists, so certain as we remain a united people, so certain as the laws of progress which have raised us from a mere handful to a mighty nation shall continue to govern our action, just so certain are these events to be worked out, and you will be compelled to extend your protection in that direction.

"Sir, I am not desirous of hastening the day. I am not impatient of the time when it shall be realized. I do not wish to give any additional impulse to our progress. We are going fast enough. But I wish our policy, our laws, our institutions, should keep up with the advance in science, in the mechanic arts, in agriculture, and in every thing that tends to make us a great and powerful nation. Let us look the future in-the face, and let us prepare to meet that which can not be avoided. Hence I was unwilling to adopt that clause in the treaty guaranteeing that neither party would ever annex, colonize, or occupy any portion of Central America. I was opposed to it for another reason. It was not reciprocal. Great Britain had possession of the island of Jamaica. Jamaica was the nearest armed and fortified point to the terminus of the canal. Jamaica at present commands the entrance of the canal; and all that Great Britain desired was, inasmuch as she had possession of the only place commanding the canal, to procure a stipulation that no other power would ever erect a fortification nearer its terminus. That stipulation is equivalent to an agreement that England may fortify, but that we never shall. Sir, when you look at the whole history of that question, you will see that England, with her far-seeing, sagacious policy, has attempted to circumscribe, and restrict, and restrain the free action of this government. When was it that Great Britain seized the possession of the terminus of this canal? Just six days after the signing of the treaty which secured to us California! The moment England saw that, by the pending negotiations with Mexico, California was to be acquired, she collected her fleets and made preparations for the seizure of the port of San Juan, in order that she might be gate-keeper on the public highway to our new possessions on the Pacific. Within six days from the time we signed the treaty, England seized by force and violence the very point now in controversy. Is not this fact indicative of her motives? Is it not clear that her object was to obstruct our passage to our new possessions? Hence I do not sympathize with that feeling which the senator expressed yesterday, that it was a pity to have a difference with a nation SO FRIENDLY TO US AS ENGLAND. Sir, I do not see the evidence of her friendship. It is not in the nature of things that she can be our friend. It is impossible she can love us. I do not blame her for not loving us. Sir, we have wounded her vanity and humbled her pride. She can never forgive us. But for us, she would be the first power on the face of the earth. But for us, she would have the prospect of maintaining that proud position which she held for so long a period. We are in her way. She is jealous of us, and jealousy forbids the idea of friendship. England does not love us; she can not love us; and we do not love her either. We have some things in the past to remember that are not agreeable. She has more in the present to humiliate her that she can not forgive.

"I do not wish to administer to the feeling of jealousy and rivalry that exists between us and England. I wish to soften and allay it as much as possible; but why close our eyes to the fact that friendship is impossible while jealousy exists? Hence England seizes every island in the sea and rock upon our coast where she can plant a gun to intimidate us or to annoy our commerce. Her policy has been to seize every military and naval station the world over. Why does she pay such enormous sums to keep her post at Gibraltar, except to hold it '*in terrorem*' over the commerce of the Mediterranean? Why her enormous expense to maintain a garrison at the Cape of Good Hope, except to command the great passage on the way to the Indies? Why is she at the expense to keep her position on the little barren islands Bermuda and the miserable Bahamas, and all the other islands along our coast, except as sentinels upon our actions? Does England hold Bermuda because of any profit-it is to her? Has she any other motive for retaining it except jealousy which stimulates hostility to us? Is it not the case with all her possessions along our coast? Why, then, talk about the friendly bearing of England toward us when she is extending that policy every day? New treaties of friendship, seizure of islands, and erection of new colonies in violation of her treaties, seem to be the order of the day. In view of this state of things, I am in favor of meeting England as we meet a rival; meet her boldly, treat her justly and fairly, but make no humiliating concession even for the sake of peace. She has as much reason to make concessions to us as we have to make them to her. I would not willingly disturb the peace of the world, but, sir, the Bay Island colony must be discontinued. *It violates the treaty.*"

At a subsequent part of the debate he quoted the letter of Mr. Everett (secretary of state under Mr. Fillmore) declining, on the part of the United States government, the agreement proposed by England and France, that neither nation should ever annex or take possession of Cuba. Mr. Everett, in declining that proposition, said:

"But, whatever may be thought of these last suggestions, it would seem impossible for any one who reflects upon the events glanced at in this note to mistake the law of American growth and progress, or think it can be ultimately arrested by a convention like that proposed. In the judgment of the President, it would be as easy to throw a dam from Cape Florida to Cuba, in the hope of stopping the flow of the Gulf Stream, as to attempt, by a compact like this, to fix the fortunes of Cuba, now and for hereafter, or, as is expressed in the French text of the convention, 'pour le present comme pour l'avenir'—that is, for all coming time."

Mr. Douglas, in commenting upon this, said:

"There the senator is told that such a stipulation (to annex no more territory) might be applicable to European politics, but would be unsuited and unfitted to American affairs; that he has mistaken entirely the system of policy which should be applied to our own country; that he has predicated his action upon those old antiquated notions which belong to the stationary and retrograde movements of the Old World, and find no sympathy in the youthful, uprising aspirations of the American heart. I endorse fully the sentiment. I insist that there is a difference, a wide difference, between the system of policy which should be pursued in America and that which would be applicable to Europe. Europe is antiquated, decrepit, tottering on the verge of dissolution. When you visit her, the objects which enlist your highest admiration are the relics of past greatness; the broken columns erected to departed power. It is one vast grave-yard, where you find here a tomb indicating the burial of the arts; there a monument marking the spot where liberty expired; another to the memory of a great man whose place has never been filled. The choicest products of her classic soil consist in relics, which remain as sad memorials of departed glory and fallen greatness! They bring up the memories of the dead, but inspire no hope for the living! Here every thing is fresh, blooming, expanding, and advancing. We wish a wise, practical policy adapted to our condition and position. Sir, the statesman who would shape the policy of America by European models, has failed to perceive the antagonism which exists in the relative position, history, institutions—in every thing pertaining to the Old and the New World."

THE FRIENDSHIP OF ENGLAND.

In reply to a remark, in the same debate, by Mr. Butler, he said:

acter, when we shall be silent in regard to British outrages, and avenge ourselves by punishing the weaker powers instead of grappling with the stronger.
I never did fancy that policy nor admire that chivalry which induced a man,
when insulted by a strong man of his own size, to say that he would whip
the first boy he found in the street in order to vindicate his honor, or, as is
suggested by a gentleman behind me, that he would go home and whip his
wife [laughter] in order to show his courage, inasmuch as he was afraid to
tackle the full-grown man who had committed the aggression.   Sir, these
outrages can not be concealed; they can not have the go-by; we must meet
them face to face.   Now is the time when England must give up her claim
to search American vessels, or we must be silent in our protests, and resolutions, and valorous speeches against that claim.   It will not do to raise a
navy for the Chinese seas, nor for Puget's Sound, nor for Mexico, nor for the
South American republics.   It may be used for those purposes, but England
must first be dealt with.   Sir, we shall be looked upon as showing the white
feather if we strike a blow at any feeble power until these English aggressions and insults are first punished, and security is obtained that they are not
to be repeated."

After referring to the unanimous action of Congress in 1839
investing Mr. Van Buren with power and means to resist aggressions during the controversy respecting the northeastern
boundary, he said:

"The vote in the Senate was unanimous, and in the House of Representatives it was one hundred and ninety-seven against six.   This unanimity
among the American people, as manifested by their representatives, saved
the two countries from war, and preserved peace between England and the
United States upon that question.   If the Senate had been nearly equally divided in 1839, if there had been but half a dozen majority for the passage of
the measure, if the vote had been nearly divided in the House of Representatives, England would have taken courage from the divisions in our own councils, she would have pressed her claim to a point that would have been utterly inadmissible and incompatible with our honor, and war would have been
the inevitable consequence.

"I tell you, sir, the true peace measure is that which resents the insult and
redresses the wrong promptly upon the spot, with a unanimity that shows the
nation can not be divided."

He thus closed his remarks:

"Besides, sir, as has been intimated by the senator from Massachusetts,
England has given pledges for her good behavior on this continent.   She is
bound over to keep the peace.   She has large possessions upon this continent
of which she could be deprived in ninety days after war existed; and she
knows that, the moment she engages in war with us, that moment her power
upon the American continent and upon the adjacent islands ceases to exist.
While I am opposed to war—while I have no idea of any breach of the peace
with England, yet I confess to you, sir, if war should come by her act and not
ours—by her invasion of our right and our vindication of the same, I would
administer to every citizen and every child Hannibal's oath of eternal hostility as long as the English flag waved or their government claimed a foot of
land upon the American continent or the adjacent islands.   Sir, I would
make it a war that would settle our disputes forever, not only of the right of
search upon the seas, but the right to tread with a hostile foot upon the soil
of the American continent or its appendages.   England sees that these consequences would result.   Her statesmen understand these results as well as

we, and much better. Her statesmen have more respect for us in this particular than we have for ourselves. They will never push this question to the point of war. They will look you in the eye, march to you steadily, as long as they find it is prudent. If you cast the eye down she will rush upon you. If you look her in the eye steadily, she will shake hands with you as friends, and have respect for you.

"*Mr. Hammond.* Suppose she does not?

"*Mr. Douglas.* Suppose she does not, my friend from South Carolina asks me. If she does not, then we will appeal to the God of battles—we will arouse the patriotism of the American nation—we will blot out all distinctions of party, the voice of faction will be hushed, the American people will be a unit; none but the voice of patriotism will be heard, and from the north and the south, from the east and the west, we will come up as a band of brothers, animated by a common spirit and a common patriotism, as were our fathers of the Revolution, to repel the foreign enemy, and afterward differ as we please, and discuss at our leisure matters of domestic dispute. Sir, I am willing to suppose the case which is suggested by the senator from South Carolina: suppose England does not respect our rights? To fight her now—

"*Mr. Hammond.* I said, suppose England would not submit to be bullied.

"*Mr. Douglas.* Who proposes to bully England?

"*Mr. Hammond.* I understood the senator to say that if we looked down she would rush on us, but if we looked up she would give way. I consider that bullying.

"*Mr. Douglas.* Precisely; that is the case of a bully always. He will fix his eye on his antagonist's, and see if it is steady. If it is not, he will approach a little nearer. If it is, he stops; but if his eye sinks, he rushes on him; and that is the parallel in which I put England, playing the bully with us. The question is, whether we will look her steadily in the eye, and maintain our rights against her aggressions. We do not wish to bully England. She is resisting no claim of ours. She sets up the claim to search our vessels, stop them on the high seas, invade our rights, and we say to her that we will not submit to that aggression. I would ask to have the United States act upon the defensive in all things—make no threat, indulge in no bullying, but simply assert our right; then maintain the assertion with whatever power may be necessary, and the God of our fathers may have imparted to us for maintaining it—that is all. I believe that is the true course to peace. I repeat that, if war with England comes, it will result from our vacillation, our division, our hesitation, our apprehensions lest we might be whipped in the fight. Perhaps we might. I do not believe it. I believe the moment England declares war against the United States, the prestige of her power is gone. It will unite our own people; it will give us the sympathy of the world; it will destroy her commerce and her manufactures, while it will extend our own. It will sink her to a second-rate power upon the face of the globe, and leave us without a rival who can dispute our supremacy. We shall, however, come to that point early through the paths of peace. Such is the tendency of things now. I would rather approach it by peaceable, quiet means, by the arts and sciences, by agriculture, by commerce, by immigration, by natural growth and expansion, than by warfare. But if England is impatient of our rising power, if she desires to hasten it, and should force war upon us, she will seal her doom now; whereas Providence might extend to her, if not a pardon, at least a reprieve for a few short years to come."

FILIBUSTERISM.

On the 7th of January, 1858, President Buchanan communicated to the Senate, in obedience to a resolution of that body, copies of the orders, instructions, and correspondence with reference to the arrest of William Walker on the coast of Central America.   On the motion to refer these documents, a debate took place involving the propriety of Commodore Paulding's conduct, and the course of the President in relation thereto, and also as to the views expressed by him in his communication accompanying the papers.   In this debate, Messrs. Davis and Brown of Mississippi, Pugh of Ohio, and Toombs of Georgia, sharply criticised the message, and repudiated the existence of the power claimed by the President in his message. The President was ably defended, and with much warmth, by Mr. Seward, and by Mr. Doolittle of Wisconsin.   During this debate Mr. Douglas expressed his views upon the affair, and upon filibusterism generally, in the following terms:

Mr. Douglas. I do not rise to prolong the debate, but to return the compliment which my friend from Mississippi [Mr. Brown] paid me when he said he admired my pluck in speaking my sentiments freely, without fear, when I differed from the President of the United States.   He has shown his pluck, and various others have shown theirs, on the present occasion.   According to the doctrine announced the other day, each senator who has done so has read himself out of the party.   I find that I am getting into good company; I have numerous associates; I am beating up recruits a little faster than General Walker is at this time.   [Laughter.]   I think, however, it will be found, after a while, that we are all in the party, intending to do our duty, expressing our opinions freely and fearlessly, without any apprehension of being excommunicated, or having any penalties inflicted on us for thinking and speaking as we choose.   If my friend from Louisiana [Mr. Slidell] were in his seat, I should say to him, inasmuch as he declared in his Tammany Hall letter that he was going to fill by recruits from the Republicans all the vacancies caused by desertions in the Democratic party on account of differences with the President in opinion, that he seems to have been very successful to-day in getting leading Republicans on his side, and recruiting his ranks just about as rapidly as there are desertions on this side of the house. [Laughter.]   The senator from New York, I believe, has the command of the new recruits.   Well, sir, strange things occur in these days.   Men rapidly find themselves in line and out of line, in the party and out of the party.

Mr. Seward. Will the honorable senator allow me to interrupt him?

Mr. Douglas. Certainly.

Mr. Seward. I have an inducement on this occasion which is new and peculiarly gratifying to me, which will excuse me for being found on the side of the administration.   The message announces that, in the judgment of the President, this expedition of Mr. Walker was in violation of the laws of the land, and therefore to be condemned.   So far I agree with him; but he goes further, and pronounces it to be in violation of "the higher law;" and I am sure I should be recreant to my sense of "the higher law" itself if I did not come to his support on such an occasion.   [Laughter.]

Mr. Douglas. I perceive the consistency of the senator from New York in the ground on which he bases his support of this message.   Now, sir, so far as the President pronounces this arrest of General Walker to have been a violation of the law of the land, I concur with him.   As to the allusion to "the higher law," I think that is well enough in its place, but it is not exactly appropriate in the execution of the neutrality laws of the United States. I would rather look into the statutes of the United States for the authority of the President to use the army and navy in enforcing the neutrality laws. By the statute of 1818 he has ample authority within the jurisdiction of the United States, and that jurisdiction is defined to extend as far as one marine league from the coast. If an arrest be made within that distance, the courts of the United States have jurisdiction, but there is no authority to arrest beyond that distance. The authority given in the eighth section of the act, to which reference is made, but which is not quoted in the message, is confined in terms to cases within the jurisdiction of the United States as defined in the act. How defined? Defined in the previous sections as being within one marine league of the coast. It thus appears that the whole extent of the President's power to use the army and navy under the act of 1818 is within our own waters, and one marine league from the coast.

I did suppose that the President himself put that construction on his authority, for I understood him to ask for further and additional authority from Congress to enable him to put down filibustering expeditions. What further authority could he want, if the existing laws allowed him to roam over the high seas, and sail around the world, and go within one marine league of every nation on the earth? It might be supposed that his authority was extensive enough to employ his entire navy, and that, certainly, he would not ask for power to invade other nations.

For these reasons I supposed that the President, on reflection and examination, had come to the conclusion that his authority was full and ample within one marine league of our coast, and ceased the moment you passed beyond that on the high seas. That has been my construction of the neutrality laws. I believe it is the fair construction. I am in favor of giving those neutrality laws a fair, faithful, and vigorous execution. I believe the laws of the land should be vigorously and faithfully executed. There may be public sentiment in certain localities unfavorable to the operation of the law, but prejudice should not be allowed to deter us from its execution. This is a government of law. Let us stand by the laws so long as they stand upon the statute-book, and execute them faithfully, whether we like or dislike them.

Sir, I have no fancy for this system of filibustering. I believe its tendency is to defeat the very object they have in view, to wit, the extension of the area of freedom and the American flag. The President avows that his opposition to it is because it prevents him from carrying out a line of policy that would absorb Nicaragua and the countries against which these expeditions are fitted out. I do not know that I should dissent from the President in that object. I would like to see the boundaries of this republic extended gradually and steadily, as fast as we can Americanize the countries we acquire, and make their inhabitants loyal American citizens when we get them. Faster than that I would not desire to go. My opposition to the Clayton-Bulwer treaty, which pledges the faith of this nation never to annex Central America, or colonize it, or exercise dominion over it, was not based on the ground that I desired then to acquire the country; but inasmuch as I saw that the time might come when Nicaragua would not be too far off to be embraced within our republic, being just half way to California, and on the main road there, I was unwilling to pledge the faith of this nation that in all time we never would do that which I believed our interest and our safety would compel us to do. I have no objection to this gradual and steady expansion as fast as we can Americanize the countries. I believe the interests of commerce, of civilization, every interest which civilized nations hold dear, would be benefited by expansion; but still I desire to see it done regularly and lawfully, and I apprehend that these expeditions have a tendency to check it. To that extent I have sympathized with the reasons which the President has assigned in his message for his opposition to them; but I desire that his opposition shall be conducted lawfully; for I am no more willing to allow him unlawfully to break them up than I am to permit them unlawfully to fit them out. I am not willing to send out naval officers with vague instructions, and set them to filibustering all over the high seas and in the ports of foreign countries under the pretext of putting down filibustering. Let us hold the navy clearly within the law. Let the instructions that are given to our officers be clear and specific; and if they do not obey the law, cashier them, or, by other punishment, reduce them to obedience to the law.

But in this case it is a very strange fact that Captain Chatard is degraded and brought home for not arresting Walker on the identical spot where Commodore Paulding did arrest him. Paulding and Chatard are thus placed in a peculiar position. Paulding arrests him, we are told, in violation of law. Chatard is degraded for not arresting him in violation of law. This shows that the moment we depart from the path of duty, as defined by law, we get into difficulty every step we take. All the difficulties and embarrassments connected with the conduct of Paulding and Chatard arise from the fact that in our anxiety to preserve the good opinion of other nations, by putting a stop to filibustering, we have gone beyond the authority of law. I think it will be better for us to confine ourselves to the faithful execution of the neutrality laws as they stand, and stop these expeditions, if we can, before they are fitted out. If, notwithstanding our efforts, they escape, we are not responsible for them. I do not hold that every three men that leave this country with guns upon their shoulders are necessarily fitting out a military expedition against countries with which we are at peace. Each citizen of the United States has the same right under the Constitution to expatriate himself that a man of foreign birth has to naturalize himself under our laws. When the Constitution of the United States declares that foreigners coming here may be naturalized, it recognizes the universal principle that all men have a right to expatriate themselves and become naturalized in other countries. Walker had a right, under the Constitution of the United States, to become a naturalized citizen of Nicaragua. Nicaragua had the same right to make him a citizen of that country that we have to make a German or an Irishman a citizen of this. When Walker went from California, on his first expedition to Nicaragua, and became naturalized there, he was from that moment a citizen of Nicaragua, and not a citizen of the United States. You have no more right to treat Walker as a citizen of the United States than Great Britain has to follow an Irishman to this country, and claim that he is a British subject after he has been naturalized here. You have no more right to put your hands on Walker, after his naturalization by Nicaragua, than Austria or Prussia has to follow their former subjects here and arrest them on the ground that they were once Germans. Walker is a Nicaraguan, and not an American. Since he has been President of that republic, recognized as such, it is too late for us to deny that he is a citizen of that country, or to claim that he is an American citizen. We are not responsible for his action when he is once beyond our jurisdiction. If he violated our laws here, we can punish him; but we have no right to punish him for any violation of the laws of Nicaragua. If he invites men to join him, and they get their necks in the halter, they must not call upon us to untie the noose after they have expatriated themselves.

It is a modern doctrine that no citizen can leave our shores to engage in a foreign war. We filled the Russian regiments, during the Crimean war, with American surgeons, and only lately the Emperor of Russia has been delivering medals and acknowledgments of knighthood to these very men. We also allowed our men to go and join the Turks, the English, and the French, and

F

fight against the Russians. American senators were in the habit of giving to their friends letters to the Russian minister, in order to enable them to obtain from him commissions in the Russian army during the Crimean war. Did we suppose that we were violating the neutrality laws? We knew that each person that went on that service went on his own responsbility. If he got a leg shot off, he could not call upon us to protect him, or to punish the man who shot the gun. So it is with those who choose to go to Nicaragua and try their fortunes there.

I had hoped that the feverish excitement in favor of these expeditions would have ceased long ago, and that we should be enabled to acquire whatever interest we desired in Central America in a regular, lawful manner, through negotiation rather than through these expeditions. But, sir, when I am called upon to express an opinion in regard to the legality of these movements, I must say that in my judgment the arrest of Walker was an act in violation of the law of nations and unauthorized by our own neutrality laws. To this extent, like the gentlemen around me who have spoken, I dissent from the President of the United States. I do so with deep regret, with great pain. My anxiety to act with that distinguished gentleman, and conform to his recommendations as far as possible, will induce me to give the benefit of all doubts in his favor; but where my judgment is clear, like my friend from Mississippi [Mr. Brown], I must take it upon myself to speak my own opinions and abide the consequences.

THE ACQUISITION OF CUBA.

In December, 1858, after the election of that year in Illinois, Mr. Douglas visited the city of New Orleans. He was about closing his speech in explanation of his course upon Lecomptonism, when there were loud cries of "Cuba! Cuba!" from the audience. In response to these calls, Mr. Douglas said:

"It is our destiny to have Cuba, and it is folly to debate the question. It naturally belongs to the American continent. It guards the mouth of the Mississippi River, which is the heart of the American continent, and the body of the American nation. Its acquisition is a matter of time only. Our government should adopt the policy of receiving Cuba as soon as a fair and just opportunity shall be presented. Whether that opportunity occur next year or the year after, whenever the occasion arises and the opportunity presents itself, it should be embraced.

"The same is true of Central America and Mexico. It will not do to say we have territory enough. When the Constitution was formed there was enough, yet in a few years afterward we needed more. We acquired Louisiana and Florida, Texas and California, just as the increase in our population and our interests demanded. When, in 1850, the Clayton-Bulwer treaty was sent to the Senate for ratification, I fought it to the end. They then asked what I wanted with Central America. I told them I did not want it then, but the time would come when we must have it. They then asked what my objection to the treaty was. I told them I objected to that, among other clauses of it, which said that neither Great Britain nor the United States should ever buy, annex, colonize, or acquire any portion of Central America. I said I would never consent to a treaty with any foreign power pledging ourselves not to do in the future whatever interest or necessity might compel us to do. I was then told by veteran senators, as my distinguished friend well knows (looking toward Mr. Soulé), that Central America was so far off that we should never want it. I told them then, "Yes; a good way off—half way to California, and on the direct road to it.' I said it was our right and duty to open all the highways between the Atlantic and the Gulf States and our possessions on the Pacific, and that I would enter into no treaty with Great Britain or any other government concerning the affairs of the American continent. And here, without a breach of confidence, I may be permitted to state a conversation which took place at that time between myself and the British minister, Sir Henry Lytton Bulwer, on that point. He took occasion to remonstrate with me that my position with regard to the treaty was unjust and untenable; that the treaty was fair because it was reciprocal, and it was reciprocal because it pledged that neither Great Britain nor the United States should ever purchase, colonize, or acquire any territory in Central America. I told him that it would be fair if they would add one word to the treaty, so that it would read that neither Great Britain nor the United States should ever occupy or hold dominion over Central America or Asia. But he said, 'You have no interests in Asia.' 'No,' answered I, 'and you have none in Central America.'

" 'But,' said he, 'you can never establish any rights in Asia.' 'No,' said I, 'and we don't mean that you shall ever establish any in America.' I told him it would be just as respectful for us to ask that pledge in reference to Asia, as it was for Great Britain to ask it from us in reference to Central America.

"If experience shall continue to prove, what the past may be considered to have demonstrated, that those little Central American powers can not maintain self-government, the interests of Christendom require that some power should preserve order for them. Hence I maintain that we should adopt and observe a line of policy in unison with our own interests and our destiny. I do not wish to force things. We live in a rapid age. Events crowd upon each other with marvelous rapidity. I do not want territory any faster than we can occupy, Americanize, and civilize it. I am no filibuster. I am opposed to unlawful expeditions. But, on the other hand, I am opposed to this country acting as a miserable constabulary for France and England.

"I am in favor of expansion as fast as consistent with our interest and the increase and development of our population and resources; but I am not in favor of that policy unless the great principle of non-intervention and the right of the people to decide the question of slavery and all other domestic questions for themselves shall be maintained. If that principle prevail, we have a future before us more glorious than that of any other people that ever existed. Our republic will endure for thousands of years. Progress will be the law of its destiny. It will gain new strength with every state brought into the confederacy. Then there will be peace and harmony between the free states and the slave states. The more degrees of latitude and longitude embraced beneath our Constitution, the better. The greater the variety of productions, the better; for then we shall have the principles of free trade apply to the important staples of the world, making us the greatest planting as well as the greatest manufacturing, the greatest commercial as well as the greatest agricultural power on the globe."

CHAPTER VIII.

THE COMPROMISE OF 1850.

Mr. Douglas took an active part in the proceedings which resulted in the measures of legislation known as the "Compromise of 1850." The general history of that compromise is well known to the American people. It has for a number of years been so thoroughly and so frequently discussed, that its history, as well as its provisions, have become familiar to all who take an interest in political matters.

A brief synopsis of the events preceding and attending the adoption of that compromise will not be uninteresting, at least to those whose interest in the history of Mr. Douglas's career has induced them to read thus far in these pages. By the treaty of Guadalupe Hidalgo (voted against by Mr. Douglas), the United States acquired the territory of California, Utah, and New Mexico. That treaty was ratified in 1848, and Congress shortly after adjourned without making any provision for the government of the newly-acquired country. During the short session of 1848–'9 several efforts were made, the most prominent of which was the Clayton Compromise, and the amendment of Mr. Walker of Wisconsin, which, though they both passed the Senate, failed to meet the approval of the House of Representatives. The struggle was between the friends and the opponents of the Wilmot Proviso. Congress adjourned on the 4th of March, 1849, without having made any provision for the government of the new territories. In the mean time the discovery of gold in California had drawn thousands to that state; a civil government was absolutely necessary. The only government there was that of General Riley, who, by virtue of his office as commander of the American forces, exercised to a limited extent the functions of a civil governor. During the summer of 1849, the people of California, aided by General Riley, who acted under instructions from Washington, called a convention, formed a state Constitution, elected state officers, put their state government in operation, elected two United States senators and two members of the

House of Representatives. The Constitution of the new state prohibited slavery. These proceedings in California had greatly added to the excitement upon the pending issue of a congressional prohibition of slavery in the territories. Those who had opposed any action of Congress which applied a prohibition of slavery to any part of the new territory denounced the action of the people of California. They demanded that the usurpation by the squatters on the Pacific should be rebuked by Congress. It was held by many that the action of California was a "snap judgment" upon the South; that, taking advantage of the non-action by Congress, the people of California had been induced to do that, by the proceeding of establishing a state government and the adoption of a Constitution prohibiting slavery, which Congress had positively refused to do, and which Congress had not the power to do. To admit California as a state, to recognize the "usurpation" of sovereign powers by her people, and to recognize her broad, emphatic, and sweeping prohibition of slavery, by which the people of one half the states of the Union were to be forever denied the privilege and right of remaining with their property upon the common territory of all the states, was to do indirectly that which Congress could not do directly without giving good cause for a withdrawal from the Union by those states thus placed upon an inequality of right in the territories. This was the argument against the admission of California as far as the Slavery question was involved. But that was only one point in the great controversy. The majority of the Northern members elected to Congress were pledged to vote for the application of the Wilmot Proviso to all the territories of the United States. The Texas Boundary question was another vexed and exciting question. Texas claimed, as part of her territory, a vast region now embraced in the territorial limits of New Mexico. Texas was a slaveholding state. To admit her claims was to deliver up a large portion of "free soil" to the "slave power." In the general excitement, the subjects of the local traffic in slaves and the continuance of slavery in the District of Columbia were agitated; and last, but not least, was the no less exciting, and, even to this day, hotly contested claim for a sufficient law to enforce the constitutional mandate for the rendition of fugitive slaves. Both sides had demands, and both sides were determined to resist the demands of each other. The Supreme Court having decided that it was not obligatory on the part of the states to provide by their laws for the enforcement of the rights of claimants of fugitive slaves, the existing law of Congress on that subject was clearly insufficient. Following this decision, many of the states abolished all laws intended to aid in the rendition of fugitives from service; others passed laws prohibiting their officers from aiding in any such cause.

The North—and, when we use the terms North and South in this matter, we mean the representatives in Congress of the extreme sentiments of both sections—the North required,

1. The establishment of governments for all the territories of the United States, with a prohibition of slavery.

2. The admission of California.

3. The abolition of the local slave-trade in the District of Columbia.

4. The abolition of slavery in the District of Columbia.

The South claimed:

1. An efficient fugitive slave act.

2. The establishment of territorial governments for all the territories, including California, but without a prohibition of slavery.

The Texas Boundary question was one on which the several parties divided, the South supporting the claims of Texas, and the North insisting that the disputed territory formed part of New Mexico.

State Legislatures had passed various resolutions during the controversy, taking strong grounds upon these several subjects. Most of the Northern states had instructed their senators to vote for the Wilmot Proviso, and one of these states so instructing was Illinois.

When Congress met in December, 1849, these exciting questions were fully before the people. General Taylor had been elected President by the votes of the most ultra anti-slavery states, and by the votes of the most ultra Southern states. The two extremes had rejected the wise, and safe, and only practicable principle of General Cass, as avowed in his Nicholson Letter, and had put their confidence in a man whose views were, to speak most kindly, unknown. Massachusetts and Vermont had voted with Georgia and Tennessee; both extremes were sure that the candidate represented their respective views. Somebody was to be undeceived.

Happily for the country, and happily for the peace and harmony of the Union which he had so long and so nobly served, and upon every page of whose history for half a century his name and deeds will ever stand as bright as the brightest and as pure as the purest, HENRY CLAY had come forth from his retirement, had quit the peaceful shades of Ashland, once more to mingle in the strife of contending sections, and once more by his magic voice to quell the storm, and guide the hostile factions into one common path of peace and safety. At that time the Senate was in its zenith. It numbered among its members men whose names were historical—Webster, Phelps, Calhoun, Benton, Berrien, King (we name only those who are no longer living), each was in himself a host, whose loss can best be appreciated by stating that a Sumner now represents Massachusetts, and an Iverson holds the seat of Berrien. The list of senators of that session will compare, in all the elements of true greatness, with that of the same number of men in any country in any age. The House of Representatives failed for several weeks in organizing. At last, by the adoption of the plurality rule, on the 22d of December, Mr. Cobb was elected speaker. A portion of the North would not vote for Mr. Winthrop because he was not sufficiently ultra as an anti-slavery man, and a portion of the South refused to vote for Mr. Cobb because he was not ultra enough on the other extreme.

The President's message was received a few days later, and the country were advised for the first time as to the views of the administration upon the Territorial question. The President recommended to the favorable consideration of Congress the action taken by the people of California for admission into the Union. He also recommended that Congress should abstain from any action with respect to the Territory of New Mexico, as the people there would, at no distant period, present themselves for admission into the Union. This message was not calculated to quiet the storm. The administration was charged with having instigated the proceedings in California, and resolutions calling for information were introduced into both houses. These, after warm discussion, were adopted.

The questions at issue were soon brought before the Senate in a variety of forms. On the 14th of January, Mr. Houston submitted a series of resolutions covering most of the subjects. On the 16th Mr. Benton introduced a bill proposing to Texas a reduction of her limits, and to pay her fifteen millions of dollars. On the same day Mr. Foote introduced a bill establishing territorial governments for California, Deseret, New Mexico, and to enable the people of San Jacinto (a new state to be formed out of Texas) to form a state government. And Mr. Butler, from the Committee on the Judiciary, reported a Fugitive Slave Bill. On the 8th of January the resolutions of the State of Vermont upon the subject of slavery were presented, and the motion to print them was objected to. In December a resolution tendering the apostle of temperance, Father Mathew, the privilege of the floor, was introduced, was debated—the debate turning exclusively upon the anti-slavery views of that gentleman.

On the 29th of January Mr. Clay submitted his famous series of resolutions proposing a plan of settlement of all the distracting questions. They were promptly discussed.

On February 5th and 6th Mr. Clay addressed the Senate upon the subjects embraced in his resolutions. On the 13th of the same month the President communicated to the Senate the Constitution of the State of California. Mr. Benton suggested its reference to a select committee. Mr. Foote suggested that it be referred to a select committee of fifteen, to be instructed to consider all the questions relating to slavery in the territories, etc. Mr. Douglas moved to refer it to the Committee on Territories, of which he was chairman.

On February 25th Mr. Foote offered his resolution to refer all the pending resolutions, etc., upon the subject of the Territories, Texas Boundary, California, etc., to a select committee of thirteen. He stated that it was his wish that this committee should be constituted as follows: Mr. Clay, Chairman; three Northern Whigs, three Northern Democrats, three Southern Whigs, and three Southern Democrats. On the 28th of February Mr. Bell submitted a series of resolutions embracing a plan of compromise.

In the mean time, from the first day the Senate had proceeded to legislative business, Mr. Hale had from time to time presented petitions praying the prohibition of slavery in the Territories, others praying its abolition in the District of Columbia, others remonstrating against the admission of slave states, etc., etc. The presentation of these petitions frequently led to very exciting discussions, sometimes consuming the entire day's sitting. They were generally stopped by an objection to their reception, and then by an affirmative vote upon laying the motion to receive on the table. The debates on all these propositions embraced all the questions involved in the complicated series. On the 7th of February Mr. Hale presented a memorial praying the dissolution of the Union. A debate upon its reception took place, in which Mr. Douglas defined his position upon the subject of the duty of Congress to receive petitions generally, and particularly upon the reception of petitions relating to slavery. The debate on this question was continued several hours on several successive days. Mr. Douglas's remarks will be found elsewhere in this volume.

Mr. Benton having moved to amend Mr. Douglas's motion to refer the President's message and the California Constitution to the Committee on Territories, by adding that said committee be instructed to report a bill for the admission of California, disconnected with any other subject of legislation, and this amendment having opened up on that motion a debate upon the general subject of slavery and the propriety of passing a compromise in one omnibus bill, Mr. Douglas, on the 22d of January, moved to take up from the table the memorial of the people of Deseret asking a state or territorial government, and refer it to his committee. An animated debate took place —the South generally urging the reference to the Judiciary Committee. The motion, however, was agreed to—yeas 30, nays 20. He then moved to refer the bill introduced by Mr. Foote to the same committee, and this motion was also agreed to—yeas 25, nays 22. The committee now had the entire subject before them. The debates on the general subject continued. On the 4th of March, Mr. Calhoun, who had been in failing health for some time, appeared in the Senate, and his last great speech was read to a crowded chamber by Mr. Mason. Three days later, on March 7th, Webster made his famous speech, and the spectre of the Wilmot Proviso was banished. From that day forth it lost its terrors, and a better feeling prevailed. There were no longer any fears of its adoption, and the attention was then directed to some broad, national, and just principle which should be adopted as a final rule in all like cases. On March 14th and 15th Mr. Douglas addressed the Senate upon the subject of the admission of California—a speech which, for argument and power, will compare favorably with any delivered in Congress upon that question.

On March 25th, Mr. Douglas, from the Committee on Territories, reported bills as follows:

" A bill for the admission of the State of California into the Union ;"

" A bill to establish the territorial governments of Utah and New Mexico, and for other purposes ;" which bills were read, ordered to a second reading, and ordered to be printed.

In addition to all the resolutions and propositions before the Senate, the three leading questions of the compromise were now before the body in the shape of bills ready for legislative action. The struggle in the Senate for the select committee of thirteen was animated and protracted. For a long time it hung in doubtful balance. The friends of that measure desired to pass all the subjects embraced in one bill. To this there were many objections. Mr. Benton was particularly strenuous in his opposition to any proposition having for its object the connection of the admission of California with any other subject. He declared it an indignity to couple her admission with any other measure. At every stage of the motion to raise the committee of thirteen, he presented his motion to except from the matters referred to said committee the question of the admission of California. When his amendments were voted down in one form he proposed them in another. Mr. Douglas was one of those who had doubted the expediency of uniting the several measures in one bill. But, having succeeded in getting the matters before the Senate in separate bills, and as nothing could be done with either bill as long as a majority of the Senate desired a report from a select committee, he urged the friends of the California Bill to allow the committee to be raised, to abandon a struggle which could result only in a delay of action. Pending these measures, on the 31st of March Mr. Calhoun's death took place. It was not until the 18th of April that the Senate came to a vote upon the motion to raise the select committee of thirteen, and before that time the several memorable scenes between Foote and Benton took place. The vote on raising the committee was, yeas 30, nays 18. On the 19th of April the Senate proceeded to ballot for the members of the committee, and the following senators were elected:

Mr. Clay, chairman; Messrs. Cass, Dickinson, Bright, Webster, Phelps, Cooper, King, Mason, Downs, Mangum, Bell, Berrien.

As soon as the committee was raised, Mr. Douglas persistently presented his motion to take up the bill for the admission of California. On the day the committee was elected he made the motion making that bill the special order. He was sustained by Mr. Clay; but a committee of six senators having been appointed to accompany the remains of Mr. Calhoun to South Carolina, Mr. Clay said that he "wished some understanding on the subject of taking up this California Bill with the senator from Illinois and the Senate." He then stated that the committee of six were about leaving the city, and he wished some understanding that the bill, during the absence of these six members, should not be pressed to a vote. Mr. Douglas promptly responded that he would not feel authorized to ask a vote in the absence of the committee on a duty like that. His only object was to have the bill considered, and, when the Senate had arrived at the point for a test vote, he would defer that vote until the committee should return. To this Mr. Clay said:

"*Mr. Clay.* That is exactly in conformity with the liberal, manly course of the senator, and, with that understanding, I hope the bill will be taken up."

Mr. Clay gave notice on that same day that he would, while the bill was under consideration, move to add to it provisions for territorial governments and for the adjustment of the Texas Boundary; and, in explanation, stated that the amendments he proposed to offer were "the bills reported by the senator from Illinois, and which have already been printed." Mr. Benton gave notice that he would resist all such amendments; and on the 22d, his resolution "that the said committee (of thirteen) be instructed to report separately upon each different subject referred to it, and that the said committee tack no two bills of different natures together, nor join in the same bill any two or more subjects which are in their nature foreign, incoherent, or incongruous to each other," was taken up and debated. In the course of that debate, Mr. Cass, a member of the committee, said:

"Now, sir, I think it quite possible, yea, even probable, that the committee will not report any bill at all. The senator (Mr. Benton), then, is presupposing a state of things which may never occur at all, and which it will be quite time enough to discuss when it does. * * *

" It is perhaps necessary that I should explain what I said a moment ago. I merely meant that, instead of reporting a specific bill or bills, it was quite possible that the committee may propose amendments to, or recommend the passage of bills now before the Senate."

The probable course of the committee, as suggested by Mr. Cass, was the one favored by the distinguished chairman of that committee. It was not his intention then, and not until after his report was written, to report a bill that would include the admission of California or governments for the Territories. Whoever will turn to the report of the select committee will see that it recommends the passage of the bill reported from the Committee on Territories for that purpose, and that the bill reported from the same committee, establishing territorial governments for New Mexico and Utah, making proposals to Texas for the settlement of her boundaries, should be added by the Senate to the California Bill, and all passed as one measure. In the report no mention is made of any bill agreed upon by the committee, except one to abolish the slave-trade in the District of Columbia.

How Mr. Clay came to change his determination in this respect may possibly be explained by stating the substance of a conversation between him and Mr. Douglas. Mr. Clay made his report on Wednesday, the 8th of May. On Tuesday, the 7th, Mr. Clay and Mr. Douglas met in the Senate Chamber, and, after an exchange of friendly greetings and some conversation on indifferent subjects, Mr. Douglas inquired of Mr. Clay when he would report his Compromise Bill. Mr. Clay said that he should present an elaborate report upon all the subjects before the committee, in which would be recommended that the Senate should unite the two bills, California and Territorial, which Mr. Douglas had previously reported from the Committee on Territories, and pass them in one act; but he should report no bill on those subjects from his committee. Mr. Douglas asked why Mr. Clay did not himself unite the two bills and report them from the select committee as their bill; to which Mr. Clay promptly answered, that such a course would not be just or fair toward Mr. Douglas, the author of those bills, particularly after having had all the labor, and having prepared them in a form so perfect that he (Mr. Clay) could not change them in any particular for the better; hence, continued Mr. Clay, as a matter of justice toward Mr. Douglas, he intended to recommend to the Senate to take up the bills as they stood, and, after uniting them, pass them without change.

Mr. Douglas at once stated that he had no such pride in the mere authorship of the measures as to induce him to desire that the select committee, out of regard to him, should omit adopting that course which would or might possibly best accomplish the great object in view. Moreover, there was another reason, which he regarded as of the very highest importance, why the select committee should report to the Senate the bills united into one. It was his opinion they could never pass the two houses of Congress as a joint measure, because the union of them would unite the Opposition to the several measures without uniting their respective friends; the bill for the admission of California, as a separate measure, would receive all the votes from the North, and enough from the South to secure its passage; while the Territorial Bills, if not connected with the California Bill, could receive nearly all the Southern votes, with a sufficient number from the North to secure their passage through both houses of Congress. For this reason, he urged that, if the bills were to be united at all, they should be united by the select committee, and in that form reported to the Senate as the action of that committee. If that course were adopted by the select committee, the Senate would have the several measures before them in two forms —one as separate measures, and the other as a joint measure, and thus all the chances of success would be secured; for, in the event of the defeat of the joint measure, the friends of the Compromise could fall back upon the bills separately. If united in the Senate, and then defeated, all would be defeated.

Mr. Clay acknowledged the full force of this reasoning, but repeated that to take the bills of Mr. Douglas and report them as the great Compromise Bill, prepared by the select committee, would be unjust to their author, who was entitled to all the honor of preparing them.

Mr. Douglas then said: "I respectfully ask you, Mr. Clay, what right have you, to whom the country looks for so much, and as an eminent statesman having charge of a great measure for the pacification of a distracted country, to sacrifice to any

extent the chances of success on a mere punctilio as to whom
the credit may belong of having first written the bills? I, sir,
waive all claim and personal consideration in this matter, and
insist that the committee shall pursue that course which they
may deem best calculated to accomplish the great end we all
have in view, without regard to any interest merely personal
to me."

Mr. Clay (extending his hand to Mr. Douglas). "You are
the most generous man living. I *will* unite the bills and report them; but justice shall nevertheless be done to you as
the real author of the measures."

The next morning Mr. Clay presented his report, and also
reported the bill subsequently known as the "Omnibus Bill,"
being a bill consisting of Mr. Douglas's two bills attached together by a wafer. Extracts from subsequent debates will
be found in this volume, and will show, to the satisfaction
of all, who was the author of the compromise acts of 1850 relating to territorial questions. True to his promise, Mr. Clay
subsequently bore honorable testimony to the ability, fairness,
and patriotism displayed by Mr. Douglas throughout that long
and memorable session.

The only change made by the select committee in the Territorial Bill was to insert in the sections defining the powers
of the Territorial Legislature the words "nor in respect to African slavery." The effect of this amendment was to deny to
the Legislature of the Territories the privilege or authority to
legislate upon the subject of African slavery.

On May 13th Mr. Clay addressed the Senate in support of
the bill. On the 15th, Mr. Douglas, with a view of saving
time, by ascertaining at once the sense of the Senate as to
whether the questions involved in controversy should be considered upon the Omnibus Bill or upon the separate bills,
moved, as a test question on that point, to lay Mr. Clay's bill
on the table. The motion was rejected—yeas 24, nays 28.
The Senate having thus decided to consider the general bill in
preference to the separate measures, the former thenceforth,
and until its fate was accomplished, occupied the consideration
of the Senate to the exclusion of the bills of the Committee on
Territories.

Mr. Jefferson Davis moved to amend the bill so as to restrain the Legislature from interfering "with those rights of

property growing out of the institution of African slavery as it exists in any of the states of the Union."

This amendment provoked considerable discussion. It was originally proposed on the 15th of May; on the next day it was modified so as to leave in the section the prohibition of any legislation in respect to African slavery, but declaring that nothing in the bill should be construed as preventing the Territorial Legislature from passing such laws or providing such remedies as may protect the owners of African slaves in said Territory in the enjoyment of their property, etc. On the 22d of May, at the suggestion of Mr. Pratt, Mr. Davis farther modified his proposed amendment so as to declare that the Territorial Legislature shall not pass any law " to introduce or exclude African slavery;" providing also that nothing in the act contained should prevent the Territorial Legislature from " passing such laws as may be necessary for the protection of the rights of property of any kind which may have been, or may be hereafter, lawfully introduced into said Territory."

On the 3d of June the amendment was warmly debated; but, as the question involved was renewed some weeks later, the extracts from the speeches made upon the question of the power of the Territorial Legislature to legislate upon the subject of African slavery, both at this as well as the later period of the debate, will be found grouped together on a subsequent page. On the 5th of June, the amendment of Mr. Davis, which prohibited the Legislature from introducing or excluding slavery, but authorized them to pass laws to protect slave property there, was rejected—yeas 25, nays 30. The bill stood as reported by the committee of thirteen, including the words " nor in respect to African slavery."

Mr. Berrien moved to amend by making the clause read, " But no law shall be passed interfering with the primary disposition of the soil, nor establishing or prohibiting African slavery." And that amendment was agreed to — yeas 30, nays 27.

Mr. Douglas then moved to strike out the words " nor establishing or prohibiting African slavery." And the motion was rejected—yeas 21, nays 33, as follows:

Yeas—Bradbury, Cass, Chase, Clarke, Clay, Cooper, Corwin, Dickinson, Dodge of Iowa, Douglas, Felch, Greene, Hamlin, Jones, Miller, Norris, Seward, Shields, Sturgeon, Underwood, and Upham.

Nays—Atchison, Badger, Baldwin, Bell, Benton, Berrien, Borland, Bright, Butler, Clemens, Davis of Mississippi, Dawson, Dodge of Wisconsin, Downs, Foote, Hale, Houston, Hunter, King, Mangum, Mason, Morton, Pearce, Pratt, Rusk, Sebastian, Soulé, Spruance, Turney, Walker, Webster, Whitcomb, Yulee.

So the bill stood with the prohibition on the powers of the Territorial Legislature.

In the mean time the Wilmot Proviso, in every imaginable shape, was offered as an amendment to the bill, and always voted down. If every motion to insert it be not mentioned, the reader will not understand by the omission that it was not submitted on every possible occasion by its advocates and friends. Mr. Douglas, for reasons stated on a subsequent page, voted for these amendments whenever offered.

The debate progressed. On the 14th of June, Mr. Turney, of Tennessee, moved to strike out all that part of the bill relating to the Texas Boundary. Lost—yeas 24, nays 27, the senators from Texas voting in the negative. On the 15th of June Mr. Soulé moved to insert the following clause in that part of the bill relating to Utah:

"And when the said Territory, or any portion of the same, shall be admitted as a state, it shall be received into the Union with or without slavery, as their Constitution may prescribe at the time of their admission."

This amendment was debated for three days, and on the 17th it was adopted by the following vote:

Yeas—Atchison, Badger, Bell, Benton, Berrien, Bright, Butler, Cass, Clay, Clemens, Cooper, Davis of Mississippi, Dawson, Dodge of Iowa, Douglas, Downs, Foote, Houston, Hunter, Jones, King, Mason, Morton, Norris, Pearce, Pratt, Rusk, Sebastian, Shields, Soulé, Spruance, Sturgeon, Turney, Underwood, Wales, Webster, Whitcomb, Yulee—38.

Nays—Baldwin of Connecticut, Chase of Ohio, Clarke of Rhode Island, Davis of Massachusetts, Dayton of New Jersey, Dodge of Wisconsin, Greene of Rhode Island, Hale of New Hampshire, Miller of New Jersey, Smith of Connecticut, Upham of Vermont, Walker of Wisconsin—12.

Pending this amendment, Mr. Douglas stated why a provision of that kind had not originally been placed in the bill, and also the reasons why he had voted on several previous occasions for the Wilmot Proviso.

He said:

"I shall vote for this amendment, not because I believe it confers any new right upon the people of the Territories, or modifies the terms of any old right which they possess. I shall vote for it as the assertion of a principle which is already in the Constitution, and which I believe would be implied, and be equally valid, if not here expressed. I would not deem it necessary to express it again but for the fact that the amendment has been offered, and but for the farther fact that I have heard, to my surprise, the doctrine that the people, when they come to form a state government, have a right to do as they please in moulding their domestic institutions questioned in some quarters.

"If it is questioned, I see no reason why we should not express, when it comes in our way, what we believe to be the true constitutional doctrine. I believe the people have a right to do as they please when they form their Constitution, and, no matter what domestic regulations they may make, they have a right to come into the Union, provided there is nothing in their Constitution which violates the Constitution of the United States. Believing that, I shall vote for the amendment, in order that the Senate may express its opinion in this bill. I have always held that the people have a right to settle these questions as they choose, not only when they come into the Union as a state, BUT THAT THEY SHOULD BE PERMITTED TO DO SO WHILE A TERRITORY.

"If I have ever recorded a vote contrary to that principle, even as applicable to Territories, it was done under the influence of the pressure of an authority higher than my own will. Each and every vote that I have given contrary to that principle is the vote of those who sent me here, and not my own. I have faithfully obeyed my instructions, in letter and in spirit, to the fullest extent. They were confined to the prohibition of slavery in the Territories while they remained Territories, and leaving the people to do as they please when they shall be admitted into the Union as states. The vote which I am now about to give is entirely consistent with those instructions. I repeat that, according to my view of this subject, all these vexed questions ought to be left to the people of the States and Territories interested, and that any vote which I have given, or may give, inconsistent with this principle, will be the vote of those who gave the instructions, and not my own."

The part of the bill proposing terms to Texas for the adjustment of the boundaries between that state and the Territory of New Mexico was the most embarrassing and perplexing. It was debated almost every day. As Mr. Rusk said, it was the first thing discussed each morning, and the last at night. Mr. Clay had left a blank in the bill for the amount of money to be paid to Texas, and he was questioned and assailed in every way to name the sum with which he intended to fill that blank. He parried all efforts to draw him out on that subject, declaring that, when the bill had reached its last stage, he would move to fill the blank. As a matter of history, it may be here stated that the proper time never arrived, and the "omnibus broke down" with that blank unfilled. On the 19th of June Mr. Underwood moved to strike out all the sections of the bill relating to the Texas Boundary, and to insert a provision authorizing the determination of the boundary by a suit in the Supreme Court. This was eventually rejected. On the 20th Mr. Berrien moved to limit the representation of California in the House of Representatives to one member, and providing that that representative, as well as the senators, should be chosen after the passage of the bill. Upon this proposition Mr. Douglas vindicated the justice of allowing California her two members in the House, and of admitting them at once to their seats upon the passage of the bill. The motion was lost—yeas 12, nays 28.

On June 24th and 25th Mr. Soulé advocated with great power and eloquence an amendment postponing the admission of California until that state had by an ordinance relinquished all title or claim to tax, dispose of, or interfere with the primary disposal of the public domain by the United States within her limits; that she would not interfere with the United States in the control of the mining regions, etc.; that the navigable waters should be open and free to all citizens of the United States; and that the southern boundary of the state shall be restricted to the line of 36° 30′ north latitude.

On the 26th, and again on the 28th, Mr. Douglas replied to this speech of Mr. Soulé, demonstrating that the argument that, unless this ordinance was adopted by California previous to her admission, the public lands and mines would escheat to that state, was wholly unsound. His speech was thorough and complete. It reviewed the entire history of the policy, as well as the possessory right of the government of the United States to the public domain, wherever situated, whether in state or territory. The limits of this work will not admit the publication here of this speech in full, and to abbreviate it would destroy its force. The speech was deemed so conclusive upon the points embraced in it that it was printed in pamphlet, and thousands of copies of it were circulated, particularly in California.

The amendment was rejected—yeas 19, nays 36.

Mr. Jefferson Davis about this period offered an amendment proposing to repeal or annul all the Mexican laws, customs, etc., which, existing previous to the acquisition of the territory, prohibited or abolished slavery. This was rejected—yeas 18, nays 30; every northern Democrat who voted voting in the negative.

On the 9th of July—the intervening time having been occupied in speeches mainly against the bill—Mr. Butler was addressing the Senate, when he was interrupted by Mr. Webster, who, in appropriate terms, announced the dying condition of

President Taylor.   The Senate adjourned, and the consideration of the Compromise Bill was not resumed until the 15th of
July.   On that day it was taken out of Committee of the
Whole and reported to the Senate, and the amendments were
concurred in.   Mr. Benton then commenced an active war upon
the bill by proposing amendments, particularly to that part relating to the adjustment of the boundary of Texas.   On July
17 Mr. Webster made an elaborate speech in favor of the bill
—the last speech delivered by him in the Senate.   On the 22d
the Senate was notified of the resignations of Messrs. Webster
and Corwin, who had accepted places in Mr. Fillmore's cabinet.   They were soon succeeded by Messrs. Winthrop and
Ewing, both opponents of the bill.

Mr. King, of Alabama, moved to amend the bill by making
the admission of California conditional with the establishment
of her southern boundary on the line of 35° 30′ north latitude.
Mr. Jefferson Davis moved to make the line 36° 30′.

Both propositions were rejected—36° 30′ by a vote of 32 to
23, and 35° 30′ by a vote of 37 to 20.

Mr. Bradbury, of Maine, on the 23d of July moved to strike
out of the bill all relating to the adjustment of the Texas boundary, and to insert a section providing for the appointment of
commissioners by the United States and by Texas, who were
to ascertain and agree upon a boundary, and report the same,
which, if agreed to by the United States and by Texas, was to
be binding upon both parties.

Mr. Benton and other senators proposed various amendments to Mr. Bradbury's proposition, all of which were rejected, and finally that proposition, on the 29th of July, was rejected—yeas 29, nays 29; both senators from Texas voting in the
negative.

Mr. Seward submitted an amendment admitting New Mexico as a state, and supported it in a long speech which provoked
an angry and excited debate.   This was rejected—yeas 1,
nays 42.

Mr. Bradbury then renewed his amendment, having slightly
modified it.   The debate was renewed, and proceeded with
great feeling, the bill evidently having approached a crisis.
Mr. Walker moved, on the 30th, that the bill be laid on the table; lost—yeas 25, nays 32.   Mr. Dawson moved to amend
the proposition of Mr. Bradbury by providing that during the

proceedings of the Boundary Commission the territorial government provided in the bill should not go into operation in that part of the Territory lying east of the Rio Grande, being the territory in dispute.

This proviso was agreed to, and Mr. Bradbury's proposition, as amended, was then inserted in lieu of the sections of the bill containing the proposals to Texas for the adjustment of her boundary—yeas 30, nays 28.

POWER OF THE TERRITORIAL LEGISLATURES—AGAIN.

At this stage of the bill Mr. Norris moved to strike out the words which prohibited the Territorial Legislature from passing any law "establishing or prohibiting African slavery," the object of the amendment being to leave the Territorial Legislature as free to pass laws upon that question as upon any other "rightful subject of legislation." In order to show that the object in placing in the bill the restriction was to deny the power and the authority of the Territorial Legislature to legislate upon that matter, and the object in moving to strike it out was to recognize and admit such a power and authority in the Legislature, and that these objects were fully understood by all parties, and also to show what was the final decision of the Senate upon this point, which has become so important in the political discussions of the present day, extracts from some of the speeches delivered upon the subject are here inserted.

FROM THE DEBATE ON MR. DAVIS'S AMENDMENT—MR. DOUGLAS, OF ILLINOIS.

I wish to say one word before this part of the bill is voted upon. I must confess that I rather regretted that a clause had been introduced into this bill providing that the territorial governments should not legislate in respect to African slavery. The position that I have ever taken has been, that this and all other questions relating to the domestic affairs and domestic policy of the Territories ought to be left to the decision of the people themselves, and that we ought to be content with whatever way they may decide the question, because they have a much deeper interest in these matters than we have, and know much better what institutions suit them than we, who have never been there, can decide for them. I would, therefore, have much preferred that that portion of the bill should have remained as it was reported from the Committee on Territories, with no provision on the subject of slavery the one way or the other; and I do hope yet that that clause in the bill will be stricken out. I am satisfied, sir, that it gives no strength to the bill; I am satisfied, even if it did give strength to it, that it ought not to be there, because it is a violation of principle—A VIOLATION OF THAT PRINCIPLE UPON WHICH WE HAVE ALL RESTED OUR DEFENSE OF THE COURSE WE HAVE

TAKEN ON THIS QUESTION. I do not see how those of us who have taken the position which we have taken (that of non-interference), and have argued in favor of the right of the people to legislate for themselves on this question, can support such a provision without abandoning all the arguments which we urged in the presidential campaign in the year 1848, and the principles set forth by the honorable senator from Michigan in that letter which is known as the "Nicholson Letter." We are required to abandon that platform; we are required to abandon those principles, and to stultify ourselves, and to adopt the opposite doctrine, and what for? In order to say that the people of the Territories shall not have such institutions as they shall deem adapted to their condition and their wants. I do not see, sir, how such a provision as that can be acceptable either to the people of the North or South. Besides, it settles nothing; it leaves it a matter of doubt and uncertainty what is to be the condition of things under the bill; and, whatever shall be ascertained to be the condition in respect to slavery, it may turn out that, while the law is held to be one way, the people of the Territory are unanimous the other way. And, sir, is an institution to be fixed upon a people in opposition to their unanimous opinion? Or are the people, by our action here, to be deprived of a law which they unanimously desire, and yet have no power to remedy the evil? I, for one, think that such ought not to be the case. In my own opinion, I have no doubt as to what the law would be under that provision; but if I were left to the exercise of my own judgment and to carry out my own principles, I desire no provision whatever in respect to the institution of slavery in the Territories. I wish to leave the people of the Territories free to enact just such laws as they please in respect to this institution. On this one point I am not left to follow my own judgment nor my own desire. I am to express the will of my constituents which has been solemnly pronounced. My vote, sir, will be in accordance with their instructions; but I desire that that vote shall be given upon the direct question; to come fairly up to these instructions, and not to this indirect mode, which settles nothing, whether it is adopted or rejected.

MR. DAVIS, OF MISSISSIPPI.

*   *   *   *   *   *   *   *

A word now to the senator from Illinois (Mr. Douglas). It is to his argument that I address myself. The difference between that senator and myself consists in who are a people. The senator says that the inhabitants of a Territory have a right to decide what their institutions shall be. When? By what authority? How many of them? Does the senator tell me, as he said once before, from the authority of God? Then one man goes into a Territory and establishes the fundamental law for all time to come. It would then be unquestionably the unanimous opinion of what that law should be; and are all the citizens of the United States, joint owners of that Territory, to be excluded because one man chooses to exclude all others who might come there? That is the doctrine carried out to its fullest extent. I claim that a people having sovereignty over a Territory should have power to decide what their institutions shall be. That is the Democratic doctrine, as I have always understood it, and under our Constitution the inhabitants of the Territories acquire that right whenever the United States surrender the sovereignty to them by consenting that they shall become states of the Union, and they have no such right before. *The difference, then, between the senator from Illinois and myself is the point at which the people do possess and may assert this right.* It is not the inhabitants of the Territory, but the people as a political body—the people organized—who have the right; and on becoming a state, by the authority of the United States, exercising sovereignty over the Territory, they may establish a fundamental law for all time to come. Then, again, the senator states what, during the last presidential canvass, was his position in relation to the doctrine of non-intervention. I am sorry to hear him state it as he has. If non-intervention means that the government shall refuse protection to property, then, sir, upon what basis rests the right of taxation; whence arises the claim to personal service of citizens? There must be mutual obligations—support from one, protection to the other. Whatever section has its property excluded from this protection by the government has a right, from that day forth, to withhold all farther support. What claim, sir, has the government to the assistance and support of the citizens if it refuses them protection? And what are all the great principles of our Constitution if they are transferred to a government without power to use them? If this federal government, to which the states have transferred their authority over the property belonging to them in the Territories of the United States, is stopped by such a principle as is here declared by the senator from Illinois from exercising that authority, I would ask what is the value of the trust? It stands at the mercy of every group of men who may find themselves conglomerated in any Territory of the United States, and is rendered unable to discharge the trust which has been conferred upon it. Willing or unwilling, as the case may be, to render that justice to one part of the owners of the public domain which another receives, and all have an equal right to demand.

Mr. Douglas. The senator from Mississippi puts a question to me as to what number of people there must be in a Territory before this right to govern themselves accrues. Without determining the precise number, I will assume that the right ought to accrue to the people at the moment they have enough to constitute a government; and, sir, the bill assumes that there are people enough there to require a government, and enough to authorize the people to govern themselves. If, sir, there are enough to require a government, and to authorize you to allow them to govern themselves, there are enough to govern themselves upon the subject of negroes as well as concerning other species of property and other descriptions of institutions. Your bill concedes that government is necessary. Your bill concedes that a representative government is necessary—a government founded upon principles of popular sovereignty, and the right of the people to enact their own laws; and for this reason you give them a Legislature constituted of two branches, like the Legislatures of the different states and territories of the Union; you confer upon them the right to legislate upon all rightful subjects of legislation except negroes. Why except negroes? Why except African slavery? If the inhabitants are competent to govern themselves upon all other subjects, and in reference to all other descriptions of property—if they are competent to regulate the laws in reference to master and servant, and parent and child, and commercial laws affecting the rights and property of citizens, they are competent also to enact laws to govern themselves in regard to slavery and negroes. Why, when you concede the fact that they are entitled to any government at all, you concede the points that are contended for here. But the senator from Mississippi says that he is contending for a principle that requires Congress to protect property, and that I am contending against it. Not at all, sir; I desire to give them such a government as will enable them to protect property of every kind and description. I wish to make no exception. He desires to make an exception.

Mr. Davis. Not at all.

Mr. Douglas. The government contended for authorizes them to protect property in horses, in cattle, in merchandise, and property of every kind and description, real and personal; but the senator from Mississippi says that you must exclude African slavery.

Mr. Davis. No, sir, he said no such thing.

Mr. Douglas. He excepted—

Mr. Davis, of Mississippi. With the senator's permission, I will explain. He is attacking the bill, but I had nothing to do with the bill except to try and better it.

Mr. Douglas. I begin to discover my error. I am holding the senator responsible for the work of the committee of thirteen.

Mr. Davis (in his seat). It was a very grave error.

Mr. Douglas. I was making war upon him by mistake. I must pay my respects to the committee of thirteen. They make the distinction that the people of the Territory are to govern themselves in respect to the right in all kinds of property but African slaves. I want to know why this exception? Upon what principle is it made? What is the necessity for it? Is it not as important as any other right in property? Why, then, should it be excepted and reserved? And, sir, if you reserve it, to this Congress? No, sir; you deny it to the people, and you deny it to the government here; and here is to be one species of property, one description of institution—

Mr. Downs. Will the senator allow me to ask him a question?

Mr. Douglas. Certainly; I yield the floor.

Mr. Downs. I ask the senator whether he did not vote for and approve of the Clayton Compromise Bill?

Mr. Douglas. That would not prove a great deal. I suppose if I did that it would not prove that this was right or wrong; but I will answer the senator's question. I struggled then as I do now for the principle that I am contending for. That bill was hatched up in my absence, from a necessity which all will acknowledge. I got back here just time enough to vote on the question, and, after all other things had failed—after the principle I contended for had failed, I did vote for that bill rather than to have no government at all. I preferred that bill to leaving the people, as they have been left, without a government. But, sir, while that was the case, I did not approve then of that principle, and I do not approve of it now; and I put the question to the senator from Louisiana (Mr. Downs), whether he can not give me a better answer, for this exception as to the rights of the people, than that I had from necessity, when forced upon me by others, voted for a bill containing such a clause, rather than to leave the people without a government, and have the country kept in a state of strife and agitation.

Mr. Downs. I merely wish to say, in reply to the senator, that the reasons why I think this exception ought to be made were contained in the remarks which I made the other day. He will find all I have to say on the subject there.

Mr. Douglas. Now, Mr. President, I have a word to say to the honorable senator from Mississippi (Mr. Davis). He insists that I am not in favor of protecting property, and that his amendment is offered for the purpose of protecting property under the Constitution. Now, sir, I ask you what authority he has for assuming that? Do I not desire to protect property because I wish to allow these people to pass such laws as they deem proper respecting their rights in property without any exception? He might just as well say that I am opposed to protecting property in merchandise, in steam-boats, in cattle, in real estate, as to say that I am opposed to protecting property of any other description; for I desire to put them all on an equality, and allow the people to make their own laws in respect to the whole of them. But the difference is this: he desires an amendment which he thinks will recognize the institution of slavery in the territories as now existing in this country. I do not believe it exists there now by law. I believe it is prohibited there by law at this time, and the effect, if not the object of his amendment, would be to introduce slavery by law into a country from which I think a large majority of this Senate are of opinion it is now excluded, and he calls upon us to vote to introduce it there. The senator from Kentucky, who brought forward this Compromise, tells us that he can never give a vote by which he will introduce slavery where it does not exist. Other senators have declared the same thing, to an extent which authorizes us to assume that the majority of this Senate will never extend slavery by law into territory now free. What, then, must be the effect of the adoption of the provision offered by the senator from Mississippi? It would be the insertion of a provision that must infallibly defeat the bill, deprive the people of the Territories of government, leave them in a state of anarchy, and keep up excitement and agitation in this country. I do not say, nor would I intimate, that such is the object of the senator from Mississippi. I know that he has another and a different object—an object which he avows. That object is to extend the institution of slavery to this Territory; or, rather, as he believes it to be already carried there by law, to continue its legal existence in the Territory.

After discussing the question of the power of Congress to prohibit slavery in the Territories, Mr. Douglas continued:

But I do say that, if left to myself to carry out my own opinions, I would leave the whole subject to the people of the Territories themselves, and allow them to introduce or to exclude slavery, as they may see proper. I believe that that is the principle upon which our institutions rest. I believe it is one of those rights to be conceded to the Territories the moment they have governments and Legislatures established for them; because, by establishing a government and giving them power to form a Legislature, you admit that they are competent to govern themselves; otherwise they would not be authorized to establish a Legislature and confide all their rights to it, with the exception of this one of the institution of slavery. For these reasons, and others which I will not enlarge upon, I am opposed to any provision in this bill prohibiting the people of the Territory from legislating in respect to African slavery. I would desire to see it stricken out; and I repeat that I can not conceive how the senator from Michigan (Mr. Cass), and those who think with him, and acted with him during the last campaign, can go for a provision of this kind without abandoning the position which they assumed; and upon that point I have the senator from Mississippi with me. I recollect that early in the session he made a speech here, in which he declared that he put that construction on the letter of the senator from Michigan (Mr. Cass) during the campaign, and that it made him a little lukewarm in his support of that gentleman. I do not believe, sir, that the Senate can agree upon any principle by which a bill can pass giving governments to the Territories in which the word "slavery" is mentioned. If you prohibit—if you establish—if you recognize—if you control—if you touch the question of slavery, your bill can not, in my opinion, pass this body. But the bill that you can pass is one that is open upon these questions, that says nothing upon the subject, but leaves the people to do just as they please, and to shape their institutions according to what they may conceive to be their interests both for the present and the future.

MR. KING, OF ALABAMA (AFTERWARD VICE-PRESIDENT).

*　*　*　*　*　*　*　*　*　*　*　*

Sir, I do not think there is a solitary gentleman on the other side, belonging to a particular party, that would be in favor of giving to these Territorial Legislatures this full power to pass laws either for the prohibition or the introduction of slavery. They would be afraid of its introduction; and the probability is that their fears would not be entirely groundless. I, sir, am opposed to giving to the Territorial Legislatures any power either to prohibit or to introduce it. I believe that the power does not exist on the part of Congress, and, in that respect, I differ with the senator from Illinois in toto. Sir, his argument is a Free-soil speech; it is the Wilmot Proviso, so far as the argument goes, as to giving to the Congress of the United States the power of regulating every description of property which the citizens of the country possess who choose to emigrate there. The senator went vastly beyond what I have heard before, because it was then confined to slavery. But he would prohibit all property, because, forsooth, the government of the United States prevented traders from going into the Indian country and selling certain articles to these unfortunate beings. Sir, the first territorial governments which we established were simply for the protection of persons and property, and consisted of a governor and council. And are senators prepared to say that this governor and his council, if governments should be ordained for these Territories, should have the power of regulating property entirely? Sir, I never did agree with my friend from Michigan in regard to what is supposed to be the construction of the Nicholson Letter. I never did believe that a Territorial Legislature possessed any power whatever but such as is delegated to it by the Congress of the United States; and the power which it did possess simply related to the protection of persons and property, and the punishment of crime. Sir, what do you require of them? That they shall pass no law that is not to be submitted to Congress for its approbation, leaving them strictly to the control of the Congress of the United States in every act that they may pass. And yet gentlemen get up at this day, and advocate on the floor of the Senate the monstrous doctrine that these Territorial Legislatures, consisting of a mere handful of men, should make laws to affect every description of property. I would greatly prefer that my friend would leave out this provision, which by some is considered unnecessary. The section, it appears to me, effects every thing that ought to be desired, and it leaves no idea that any thing is covered up in it which ought not to be there.

Mr. Douglas. I must say, Mr. President, that it appears to me that my friend from Alabama has not shown his usual courtesy in the remarks he has just made. He has been pleased to say that my speech was a Free-soil speech, and a Wilmot Proviso speech. And why? because I made an argument in favor of the Territorial Bill in the Senate, neither adopting nor rejecting any provision in relation to slavery in the Territories. In other words, I made an argument in favor of the doctrine advocated by my friend from Michigan (Mr. Cass), so far as the territorial governments were concerned. The senator from Alabama says that he never agreed with my friend from Michigan on this point, and that my argument is Free-soilism and Wilmot Provisoism. He then changes his position with his eyes open, having advocated the Wilmot Proviso at the last presidential election, and he became an advocate of it with his eyes open on that subject.

Mr. King. I suppose the senator, in making this statement, means nothing personal.

Mr. Douglas. Not at all.

Mr. King. I said nothing about the argument as to the power of the Territorial Legislature to pass such laws. The portion to which I referred was that portion in which he contended that Congress had all power over the Territories—to exclude from, or admit into, or control property in those Territories.

Mr. Douglas. Now, sir, we will turn to that point. My argument was in favor of passing a Territorial Bill without any provision on the subject of slavery. I undertake to say that three months ago the senator from Alabama was in favor of—

G

The *Vice-President*. It is not in order to make any personal allusions.

Mr. Douglas. It can not be out of order to tell the truth in a respectful manner.

Mr. King. I am still in favor of establishing territorial governments without saying any thing on the subject of slavery, so far as the introduction of it into or the exclusion of it from the Territories is concerned. That is what I was in favor of three months ago, and is what I am in favor of still.

Mr. Douglas. I stated that that has been a doctrine unanimously entertained, so far as I have understood it—that territorial bills were to be passed silent upon the subject of slavery, and that no provision was to be made upon the subject. I understand that that has been the unanimous doctrine; that is what I now advocate; that is what I made an argument in favor of. I did not propose to say in the bill that the Territorial Legislature should have the power to legislate on the subject of slavery, or that Congress should have power to prohibit or establish it in the Territories. I proposed to strike out that prohibition of the Territorial Legislature on the subject, and, that being done, it would read that territorial legislation should extend to all rightful subject of legislation within their boundaries. I proposed to make it an open question, so that the people themselves could do with it as they pleased. Now, sir, let me compare notes with the senator, and see who is in favor of the Wilmot Proviso and Free-soil doctrine on this point. He desires a prohibition on the part of Congress that the Territorial Legislatures shall not legislate in respect to slavery. Why, sir, the laws of Mexico prohibited slavery in those territories when we acquired them from that country, and, according to the law of nations, the laws of Mexico are still in force. And what is it that the senator proposes? why, it is to continue those laws in force, and to prevent the people themselves from repealing them. And that is the very doctrine of the senator from Wisconsin, which he wants to continue and retain in the bill. That was the reason it was voted into the bill by the committee of thirteen, the senator from Vermont giving the casting vote to put it in, because it was a perpetuation of the prohibition of slavery forever. Sir, I wish to strike it out, because I do not wish to perpetuate any institution against the will of the people. I wish to leave them free to regulate their own institutions in their own way, without compelling them to establish an institution there, on the one hand, if they do not wish, nor preventing them, on the other, from establishing it if they do wish it. Sir, I only made those remarks which I thought were courteous. I had made a speech in favor of the doctrines I have always held, and I did not expect to see the senator from Alabama show that irritability of temper, and to hear him use epithets instead of attempting to reply to an argument which he knew to be frankly and candidly made. I made no uncourteous remark. Now, sir, I admit that I would rather take the doctrine as it is to be found in the bill of the senator from Kentucky, than one which would stultify the whole Democratic party. It is now clear that the object is to stultify the whole Democratic party of 1848. It is now intended to rebuke the doctrine we advocated at that time. The senator from Mississippi said he was opposed to it, the senator from Alabama says he too is opposed to it; the doctrines of the senator from Michigan are to be abandoned, new doctrines are to be raised, and the supporters of the doctrines enunciated in 1848 are to be smoothed down and required to vote for a measure which is intended to stultify and disgrace the whole Democratic party. That, sir, is the question which we are to meet, and, if we must meet it, let us meet it openly and like men. The senator from Kentucky was manly enough to say that he was opposed to this measure; he was manly enough to rise above all political rivalries, and to say that it was wrong to put the question on such a basis. We can stand where we stood in 1848, and where we have ever stood upon this question. But, sir, when we are required to retrace our steps and renounce what we have alleged to be our principles, that becomes quite a different question.

MR. CASS, OF MICHIGAN.

*   *   *   *   *   *   *

Now, with respect to the amendments. I shall vote against them both; and then I shall vote in favor of striking out the restriction in the bill upon the power of the territorial governments. I shall do so upon this ground. I was opposed, as the honorable senator from Kentucky has declared he was, to the insertion of this prohibition by the committee. I consider it inexpedient and unconstitutional. I have already stated my belief that the rightful power of internal legislation in the Territories belongs to the people. You have the right to govern, but not to legislate for them—the doctrine for which our fathers contended, and which brought about our separation from England. But, sir, how is it possible to vote for this interdict without conceding the constitutional right of Congress to pass the Wilmot Proviso? Congress can only insert this clause upon the assumption that they have full power over the Territories—power to admit, power to exclude, as well as power to say that the Territorial Legislature may do one or the other, for neither can be exercised but by virtue of full jurisdiction.

The action of the Senate upon the pending proposition has already been stated—the restriction upon the powers of the Territorial Legislature was voted in.

FROM THE DEBATE ON MR. MORRIS'S MOTION TO STRIKE OUT —MR. PHELPS, OF VERMONT.

I had determined, Mr. President, not to open my mouth in the course of this debate, and I should not do so now were it not for the allusion just made to me by the senator from Mississippi. It is very true that the provision in the Clayton Bill, as it has been termed—the same proposed now to be stricken out of this bill—originated in the committee with me. But, after what has fallen from the senator from Mississippi, I deem it due to myself to explain the reasons why I shall now vote against the proposition to keep that in the bill which, on that occasion, I advocated.   *   *   *

But the bill now before us presents the subject in a very different light. We propose now to create a Legislature to be elected by the people of the Territory, representing the wishes and feelings of that people, and responsible to that people for their legislative course. Under these circumstances, Mr. President, the subject assumes, in my judgment, a very different aspect. It is no longer a question whether the appointees of the President are to be left to regulate this important subject, but it becomes a question whether the Legislature of the Territory, elected by the people of that Territory, shall have the control over it. This distinction is, in my judgment, material; and, therefore, if the proposition were now to erect such a government as was contemplated by that bill in 1848, I would retain the position I then occupied. But I feel bound now to say that I can not take from a Legislature, elected by the people of these Territories, the control over their domestic relations. It is wrong in principle. It so happens that those of us at the North who have heretofore insisted upon the exercise of the power of Congress over this subject to exclude slavery from these Territories are now in a position to permit the people of the Territories to have their own way, and regulate the subject as may suit themselves. It is unnecessary for me to explain how this change of position has been produced. It is enough for me to say now that I regard this subject of the question of the prohibition of slavery as a fit subject of local legislation, and one which should be given exclusively to the local Legislatures.

When it is proposed to-day to deny to the people in these Territories, or their immediate representatives, elected by themselves, the control over the subject, I must say I can not sustain the proposition.

* * * I do not know but that it is necessary for me to ask pardon for having addressed the Senate at this time. I did not intend to express my opinion at all ; but, after the allusion made to me by the senator from Mississippi, it became necessary ; because, on the occasion referred to by him, I submitted this very proposition to prevent the Territorial Legislature from acting on this subject, and on the present occasion I am against the proposition. The reason why I have changed my position is simply the fact that the restriction in 1848 was upon a government created by the executive of the United States, and not by the people of the Territory. The restriction now proposed is upon the immediate representatives of that people.

MR. PRATT, OF MARYLAND.

Mr. President: As this amendment is up, I hope I may be allowed to say a few words, so that my constituents can understand my position.

The great doctrine of the South, as I understand it, and the only true ground upon which the South can stand, is the doctrine of non-intervention. Now what I understand by non-intervention is the denial to the executive and legislative authority of the federal government of all power over the subject of slavery any where and every where. That is the non-intervention upon which I have been taught to rest the rights of the South ; that is the non-intervention upon which I am now willing to rest them—that neither the executive nor legislative branches of the federal government have the power, in any way whatever, to interfere with the subject of domestic slavery any where. And I am therefore perfectly willing that the amendment which was originally adopted should be stricken out, as proposed by my friend from New Hampshire (Mr. Norris). But there is another reason which, it seems to me, must render this provision, in the eyes of every one, inoperative, if it continue in the bill. You have this morning adopted an amendment by which the Territorial government established by the bill is not to operate, in præsenti, within the larger portion of the territory claimed as New Mexico. Therefore, in consequence of that restriction, there could be no legislation in reference to the subject of slavery within that Territory at the present time.

With regard to the other Territory, Utah, slaves are already held there ; and if you give to the people of that Territory power to regulate it—which they would have if this clause is stricken out—they would legislate in favor of that Southern institution in which we are interested. I therefore, for one, as a Southern man, standing up for the rights of the South as much as any man here, am willing that this clause should be stricken out, more particularly when it will gain some votes for the bill.

MR. TURNEY, OF TENNESSEE.

* * * * * * * * *

Sir, if the pending motion prevails, the people of New Mexico will have the power to exclude the Southern people from the territory to be acquired from Texas, and to spread over it the Wilmot Proviso. I would as soon vote for that proviso here. I believe it would be more magnanimous to vote for it here than to fight behind the bush in this way.

Now what was fair two years ago, when we had a Southern President— what was then sound policy, just and equitable to all sections—seems now, according to some gentlemen, to be unfair, unjust, unsound. There is a change of circumstances. A different set of officers will be sent there. A set of officers, entertaining very different opinions to vhat would have been sent two years ago, are now to be sent by the present executive, who will most heartily desire to exclude Southern men. If this bill is to pass they will be excluded, especially if this motion shall prevail. They will be excluded in less than six months after the law shall become final and go into operation.

The first Territorial Legislature, considering the public sentiment there, will exclude the South forever. For these reasons, I can not vote for the amendment of the gentleman from New Hampshire.

MR. BERRIEN, OF GEORGIA.

I wish the Senate to understand that the direct effect of sanctioning this amendment will be to invest the Territorial Legislature of New Mexico with the power to allow or prohibit slavery—to allow if they exist, or to re-enact if they do not, the Mexican laws.

MR. CLAY, OF KENTUCKY.

I heard with great pleasure the senator from Vermont (Mr. Phelps). I regret that he has not favored the Senate with saying more than he has done upon this subject. One of the most interesting speeches that I have read was pronounced by that senator two years ago, and which really gave me more information upon this subject than I have derived from any thing which I have heard during this session. But, sir, I have not risen to detain the Senate. I have risen to say a few words only on the proposition before the Senate; and I do think that, if my Southern friends, and my Northern friends too, will only listen, if I am not entirely incorrect in the views I propose to present, they will concur in the motion made by the senator from New Hampshire to strike out this clause. The clause is an interdiction imposed by Congress upon the local Legislature either to introduce or to exclude slavery. Now, sir, it appears to me to be perfectly clear that Congress has no such power according to the Southern doctrine. That doctrine is one of clear and clean non-intervention. The amendment in the bill, on the contrary, assumes the power to exist in Congress, which is denied; for, if Congress possesses the power to impose this interdiction, Congress has the power to impose the Wilmot Proviso. The only difference is, that the action of Congress in the one case is direct, and that the action of Congress in the other case is indirect. It appears to me, therefore, that upon the great principle upon which Southern gentlemen have rested the support of their rights, they ought to oppose the exercise of this power by Congress to interdict the local Legislature. Sir, it is a little remarkable that, by the one side of the Union, whose interest it should be to preserve the clause, the amendment is opposed; and that the other side of the Union, whose principles, according to my humble conception, should lead them to oppose the clause which is proposed to be stricken out, are in favor of it. In point of interest, the North should be for retaining the clause, because if, as they suppose, and as I believe, there is at this moment an abolition of slavery in the Territories, this clause serves to continue that abolition of slavery; therefore it is to their interest to retain this clause, because it would give an additional security to the exclusion of slavery, which they desire. I know that my Northern friends who are anxious to exclude this clause by the adoption of this amendment, go upon a higher principle than mere interest. They go upon the very principle which the South has contended for. They say—for upon this subject I have conversed with them freely—that they are aware of the advantage to their interest which might result from the retention of the clause, but that it is in contravention of the principle for which they have contended on behalf of Southern interests, and that is the principle of non-intervention on the subject of slavery. They will sacrifice their interests for the preservation of the great principle upon which they are willing to stand with their Southern friends—the principle of non-intervention; and which, if the amendment prevails, is the principle which pervades the entire bill, running through it from first to last. I know, sir, that another principle has been contended for by Southern gentlemen of great eminence, and that principle is, that the Constitution of the United States confers upon the slaveholder the right to carry his slaves into these Territories. If so, where is the necessity of this interdiction? The Constitution is paramount and supreme; and if the Legislature of the Territory were to pass any law in violation of the Constitution, that law unquestionably would be null and void from the moment of its passage; and, as suggested by the senator from Maryland, there is a suspension of the operations of this bill in reference to the only Territory in contest—New Mexico—this side of the Rio Grande, until this effort at compromise shall be successful, or thwarted and defeated. It appears to me, therefore, that upon the very principle for which Southern gentlemen have stood up, they should strike out this clause from the bill, and leave it a clear and indisputable bill of non-intervention, from the enacting clause to the end.

MR. CASS, OF MICHIGAN.

But, quitting the subject of legislative inconsistency, and adverting to the immediate proposition, let me ask what you are doing. What? You are passing a law for the organization of a government for the people of New Mexico, not for the regulation of their own domestic concerns—those relations of life which belong essentially to every free community. You do not undertake to tax them. It would be a monstrous assumption, at which every American would revolt. You do not undertake to regulate the relations of husband and wife, or parent and child, or guardian and ward, nor to pronounce upon the other internal questions which belong to them. We should all revolt also at such an attempt. Well, sir, it is not in the power of the most acute political casuistry to point to any difference in principle between the exercise of these powers and the attempt to take from the people the right to regulate at their pleasure the relation of master and servant, including the condition of slavery. The senator from Georgia (Mr. Berrien) has advanced views which certainly struck me with surprise, in this country and in this age of the world. He said that the Territorial Legislature were the agents of this government, and that we had a right to do any thing here which they could do there. Mr. President, such a proposition as that strikes at the very root of human liberty. It is far better suited to the meridian of Constantinople than to that of Washington. It assumes for us full power to do as we please with the people of a remote community, without representation, with separate interests, and of whose concerns we are wholly ignorant. Why, this is the very pretension which led to our Revolution—the very pretension which Lord North advanced, and which our fathers resisted. The claim was, and it was embodied in a memorable act of Parliament, that "his majesty in Parliament had the right to bind the colonies in all cases whatsoever;" and here, in the American Senate, the whole doctrine of our revolutionary struggle is cast aside, and the very power assumed for a republican Legislature which was denied to a monarchical one—the power to bind the Territories in all cases whatsoever. I will not argue such a doctrine as that. I appeal to our whole history for its refutation. The Territorial Legislatures our agents! and who made them so? What law of God or man has so dealt with human rights as to authorize such a pretense? What said our fathers upon this general subject? Why, they acknowledged the right of the British government to institute governments for the colonies, to establish the general outlines, but not to regulate their internal domestic concerns. Such a claim, where there is no representation, change the terms as we may, is the very essence of tyranny. It was for this right of self-government that the patriots of the Revolution entered into a fearful contest with the mightiest nation on the face of the earth, and out of which, by the blessing of God and by their undaunted firmness, they came triumphantly, securing their own liberties, and ours too, so long as we have wisdom and patriotism to maintain them. And I must confess that nothing has astonished me more, in all the discussions that have grown out of this controversy, than the coolness with which gentlemen rise here and maintain the right of Congress to legislate for these distant Territories in all cases whatsoever, annihilating human freedom, and establishing arbitrary power by the same pretension. If this is not tyranny, tell me what it is. Is your claim founded on the Constitution? Put your finger on the place and show it. There is not the first word which, expressly or by implication, gives it to you. Even the right to organize governments is not there. But if you assume that as a matter of necessity, what necessity is there for you, not to govern these distant people, but to legislate for them, and to take from them the very first attribute of freedom? Do you found this claim upon your superior wisdom—upon your capacity to judge what is suited to the people better than they can judge for themselves? I ask you where ever there was an arbitrary government which had not the same self-sufficient opinion of its own wisdom, and of the ignorance of the people? Lord North thought so and said so. The sultan thinks so; and at Vienna and Petersburgh to doubt such a clear proposition is to insure a residence in Siberia, or to exhaust life in Austrian dungeons.

Pending the decision of the Senate on these bills, the senators elect from the State of California were in daily attendance in the lobby of the Senate. They heard all these debates —debates upon a bill so deeply important to their state, and upon the passage of which, it was believed, depended their admission as senators of the United States. The senator from Illinois had the California Bill under his especial charge. He was its friend and advocate—its champion and defender. He proclaimed his views in a tone of voice that would enable a deaf man to hear them, and in language so plain that a simpleton could understand him. His speeches were published daily, and were read by all. The senators from California were not deaf, nor were they simpletons; they read the papers, and read and understood the sentiments of every man in the Senate upon the Territorial question. Yet, nine years later, one of those senators, who had heard Douglas make the speeches we have quoted above, told the people of California that he had voted to remove Judge Douglas from the committee where he had matured the bill for the admission of California, because, in a speech delivered in 1858, that man Douglas had declared that he was in favor of allowing the people of a Territory, through their own Legislature, to exclude slavery if they did not desire it in the Territory! Wonderful awakening to the cause of justice! In 1859, WILLIAM M. GWIN, senator from the State of California, declared Stephen A. Douglas to be a political outcast, who had been displaced from the chairmanship of a committee because he had expressed an opinion that the people of a Territory might exclude slavery by the action of their Territorial Legislature; and in 1850 the same WILLIAM M. GWIN selected from the sixty members of the United States Senate the same Stephen A. Douglas as the most appropriate person to present his credentials to the United States Senate, notwithstanding he had, in the hearing of said Gwin, a few weeks previously, in the speeches we have quoted, expressed the same opinions most unequivocally, broadly, and distinctly. Wonderful change of opinion! Remarkable falling of the scales!

THE DESTRUCTION OF "THE OMNIBUS."

On the 31st of July, after the adoption of Mr. Norris's motion, Mr. Pearce, of Maryland, desiring to get rid of the proviso of Mr. Dawson, attached to the proposition of Mr. Bradbury, moved to strike out all those sections of the bill relating to the establishment of a territorial government for New Mexico, intending, when that motion was agreed to, to move to reinsert all of them again except the Dawson amendment, in lieu of which he said he would offer a proviso to the effect that the territorial government provided for New Mexico by the bill should not go into effect until March, 1851. Under this proposition, if the Texas Boundary was not settled by March, '51, the government of New Mexico would go into operation on both sides of the Rio Grande, extending over, of course, the territory claimed by Texas. The motion to strike out was agreed to—yeas 33, nays 22. Mr. Pearce then moved to insert as above stated. A motion to postpone the bill indefinitely was made and lost—yeas 27, nays 32. A long debate ensued, and another motion to postpone indefinitely resulted—yeas 29, nays 30; the senators from Texas voting in the affirmative.

Mr. Yulee, of Florida, moved to strike out of Mr. Pearce's amendment all that related to Texas, being the Bradbury proposition, and this motion was agreed to—yeas 29, nays 28. A motion to indefinitely postpone was again made, and lost by a majority of one.

The question was, after much debate and many rejected motions to adjourn, etc., taken on Mr. Pearce's motion to restore the sections of the bill relating to New Mexico, and was decided in the negative—yeas 25, nays 29. So Texas and New Mexico were both put out of the omnibus.

Mr. Walker moved to strike out all relating to Utah, leaving California alone in the bill, but that motion failed.

Mr. Atchison then moved to strike out all of the bill relating to California, or, as he expressed it, "to turn her out of the omnibus." This was rejected by a tie vote, 29 to 29.

Motions to adjourn, to postpone indefinitely, etc., etc., were made in rapid succession, but all failed; the Senate was determined to finish the bill that night.

At last the Senate reconsidered the vote rejecting Mr. Atchison's motion, and then, by a vote of 34 to 25, struck out all that related to California. And Utah was the only passenger left in the omnibus!

An incident took place at this time which has derived a peculiar significance from events that have occurred in the legislative history of Congress since that time. It being necessary to alter the proposed boundaries of Utah, in order to include some settlement whose exact locality had to some extent been more definitely ascertained since the original framing of the bill, Mr. Douglas moved to fix the southern boundary upon the line of 37° north latitude.

Mr. Davis, of Mississippi, moved to insert 36° 30' in lieu of 37°.

Mr. Douglas accepted the amendment as a modification of his own.

Mr. Hale, of New Hampshire, said: "I wish to say a word as a reason why I shall vote against the amendment. I shall vote against 36° 30' because I think there is an implication in it. (Laughter.) I will vote for 37°, or 36° either, just as it is convenient, but it is idle to shut our eyes to the fact that here is an attempt in this bill—I will not say it is the intention of the mover—*to pledge this Senate and Congress to the imaginary line of* 36° 30', because there are some historical recollections connected with it in regard to this controversy about slavery. I will content myself with saying that I never will, by vote or speech, admit or submit to any thing that may bind the action of our legislation here, to make the parallel of 36°

30′ the boundary-line between slave and free territory. And when I say that, I explain the reason why I go against the amendment.”

The amendment of Mr. Douglas was rejected, yeas 26, nays 27, and among those voting in the negative—voting never to admit or submit to any thing that might bind the action of Congress to make the Missouri Compromise line of 36° 30′ the boundary between slave and free territory—were Chase of Ohio, Dayton of New Jersey, Hale of New Hampshire, Hamlin of Maine, and Seward of New York, who, five years thereafter, denounced the repeal or removal of that “imaginary line” when proposed by the same senator who now moved its recognition! In 1850 these abolitionists refused to vote to make it the southern boundary of a territory, lest doing so might, by implication, be an admission of the “historical recollections” of that line. In 1854, no men were more loud or more vehement than these same men in glorifying the “historical recollections” of the “sacred compact” and “time-honored compromise!”

The amendment having been rejected, the following remarks were made:

Mr. Douglas. “It is necessary to make some change of boundary in order to include the Mormon settlements. Thirty-seven degrees will include them as well as 36° 30′. I move to insert ‘37°.’ ”

Mr. Hale. “Agreed. I have no objection.”

Mr. Mason. “I move to amend the amendment of the senator from Illinois by inserting ‘36°’ instead of ‘37°.’ ”

Mr. Hale. “I have no objection.”

Mr. Mason’s amendment was rejected, and “37°,” as proposed by Mr. Douglas, was adopted.

The struggle to defeat the bill was protracted some time longer, but at last the question was put on ordering it to a third reading, and the yeas and nays stood as follows:

Yeas—Atchison of Missouri, Badger of North Carolina, Benton of Missouri, Berrien of Georgia, Bradbury of Maine, Bright of Indiana, Butler of South Carolina, Cass of Michigan, Davis of Mississippi, Dawson of Georgia, Dickinson of New York, Dodge of Iowa, Douglas of Illinois, Downs of Louisiana, Felch of Michigan, Houston of Texas, Hunter of Virginia, Jones of Iowa, King of Alabama, Mason of Virginia, Morton of Florida, Norris of New Hampshire, Pratt of Maryland, Sebastian of Arkansas, Shields of Illinois, Soulé of Louisiana, Spruance of Delaware, Sturgeon of Pennsylvania,

Turney of Tennessee, Underwood of Kentucky, Wales of Delaware, Yulee of Florida—Total, 32.

Nays—Baldwin of Connecticut, Bell of Tennessee, Chase of Ohio, Clarke of Rhode Island, Davis of Massachusetts, Dayton of New Jersey, Dodge of Wisconsin, Ewing of Ohio, Greene of Rhode Island, Hale of New Hampshire, Hamlin of Maine, Miller of New Jersey, Pearce of Maryland, Seward of New York, Smith of Connecticut, Upham of Vermont, Walker of Wisconsin, Winthrop of Massachusetts—Total, 18.

The next day the bill was passed without a division. The title was amended to read, "A Bill to establish a Territorial Government for the Territory of Utah;" and the bill was sent to the House.

CHAPTER IX.

WHAT BECAME OF THE COMPROMISE.

On the 1st of August, the Senate, on motion of Mr. Douglas, after debate, proceeded to the consideration of the bill and amendment reported by him for the admission of California. An amendment was proposed to limit her southern boundary by the line of 36° 30', which was rejected. The bill was debated daily until the 12th, when it was ordered to a third reading, and on the next day was passed—yeas 34, nays 18.

On August 7th Mr. Pearce introduced a bill making proposals to Texas for the establishment of her northern and western boundaries, its general features and objects being the same as those contained in that part of the Omnibus Bill relating to this question; and, after discussion and amendment, the bill, on August 9th, passed the Senate by yeas 30, nays 20.

As soon as the bill for the admission of California had passed, Mr. Douglas moved to take up the bill to establish a Territorial Government for New Mexico. The motion prevailed, and that bill was considered by the Senate, and on the 15th of August was read a third time and passed—yeas 27, nays 10.

The Fugitive Slave Bill was taken up on August 15th; was ordered to a third reading on the 23d by a vote of yeas 27, nays 12, and passed on the 26th without a division.

On the 28th of August the Bill to Suppress the Slave-trade in the District of Columbia, being the last of the series of measures recommended by Mr. Clay's committee of thirteen, was taken up in the Senate. During its consideration Mr. Seward moved as a substitute a bill abolishing slavery in the

District of Columbia, which proposition was debated at great length. The amendment was rejected, but five senators voting for it, viz., Chase, Dodge of Wisconsin, Hale, Seward, and Upham.

THE EXCLUSION OF FREE NEGROES BY THE STATES.

During this debate, the powers and authority of South Carolina and Louisiana to prohibit immigration and residence of negroes within their respective limits was elaborately discussed, the debate at times becoming animated, and frequently very personal. Upon that point Mr. Douglas said:

"My own state has been frequently referred to in this debate as containing a provision in her Constitution similar to the one complained of in South Carolina, Louisiana, and other states. Illinois has a provision in her Constitution making it the duty of the Legislature to provide efficient means for keeping all negroes from coming into the state who were not natives of or residents in the state at the time of the adoption of that instrument. Here, then, is a clear case of legislation of this description in a free state. We, too, have a constitutional provision upon this subject; and, before that constitutional provision was adopted by an overwhelming majority of our people—it having been submitted to the people separately, and independent of the balance of the Constitution, so as to get an expression of the popular voice on the subject—even before that provision was adopted, our laws provided that if a negro came into the state he was required to procure a white man to go his security for good behavior, and in the event of his failing to give the security he was hired out to service for one year; if, at the end of the year, he still failed to give it, he was hired out for another year; and so on until he could find some white person to go security for his good behavior, and that he would not become a charge upon the public. Such has been the legislation of my own state from the time she was first admitted into the Union, and I presume it has been the same in other free states. Those provisions were rigidly enforced; and now, when I hear that Massachusetts can not get a trial of the constitutional question involved in that legislation, I will assure the senators from that state that, if they will come to Illinois, we will furnish them all the facilities to test the constitutional question. We are willing to have the right tested so far as we are concerned. The trial, then, can take place between two free states of the Union, where there will be no sectional prejudices, no hostile feelings incited, and where we can have a fair trial upon the constitutional questions involved. We believe that we have a right to pass all those laws that we deem necessary to the quiet and peace of our own community. These laws are passed among us as police regulations; they are executed as such. There is no difficulty in having a trial there, and an appeal to the Supreme Court of the United States; and then we can see whether we have the right or not. We believe that we have the right. We border upon slave states upon two sides. We do not wish to make our state an asylum for all the old, and decrepit, and broken down negroes that may be sent to it. We desire every other state to take care of her own negroes, whether free or slave, and we will take care of ours. That law was adopted for the purpose of preventing other states inundating and colonizing Illinois with free negroes. We do not believe it to be wise and politic to hold out inducements for that class of people to come and live among us. Those who have been born in the state, or who were resident there at the time of the enactment of these laws, are protected in the enjoyment of all their civil rights, but they are not placed upon an equality with the whites. They are not permitted to serve on juries, or in the militia, or to vote at elections, or to exercise any other political rights. They are recognized as inhabitants, and protected as such in all their rights of person and property. While we protect those who are there, and their posterity, we do not intend to be inundated by colonies of negroes from other states, sent to us in order to get rid of the trouble of them at home.

It is for this reason that Illinois has adopted this system of legislation, and, having adopted it, we do not desire to insist on it unless it is consistent with the Constitution of the United States. We are willing to have that question tested. We invite any gentleman who deems it right to oppose these laws to bring his suit. We will furnish him all facilities for having the question decided, and then we shall know whether the right exists or not. I would much have preferred this question should have arisen between two of the free states of the Union, when there would have been no prejudices or sectional jealousies, or other improper motives to enter into it to bias our judgment and excite our passions, than to see it arrayed here as one of the sectional questions between the North and the South."

On the 16th of September this bill was passed—yeas 33, nays 19. All these bills were acted upon favorably by the House, and were approved by the President.

Pending the question on the passage of this last bill, the following remarks were made in the debate:

Mr. Benton. I wish this morning to make a remark which is called for by what has taken place. I am one of those who insisted, both as a matter of right and as a matter of expediency, that certain bills, commonly called the Omnibus, should be separated, and treated on their own merits. I was answered by arguments of expediency, that the bills would pass sooner all together, and that thereby a better effect would be produced in settling the public mind. I disagreed with those arguments, and I then brought upon myself a great deal of censure in some parts of the country, and especially in my own state. The thing is now over; the votes have been taken, and the results tell what history will tell, that I was right in every thing that I said. We have had votes upon every subject, and, when separated, every subject passed—passed quickly, without a struggle, and by a great majority; and the effect on the public mind has been just as sedative as if the whole dose had been taken at once; and, sir, when we come to look into the yeas and nays on the four leading measures, the admission of California, the Territorial government for Utah and New Mexico, and the settlement of the Texan Boundary question, we find that the yeas who voted for all the four measures amount to just seventeen! and, counting in one who was absent (Mr. Clay), they would have been just eighteen—eighteen out of sixty. That there may be no mistake about it, I will read the names, so that, if I am wrong in any particular, I may be corrected. Those who voted for all the measures are Messrs. Bradbury, Bright, Cass, Cooper, Dodge, Dickinson, Douglas, Felch, Houston, Jones, Mangum, Norris, Shields, Spruance, Sturgeon, Wales, and Whitcomb—just seventeen, and the one absent would make eighteen. And that I hold to be the true strength of the Omnibus Bill, as proved by the result when every member was at liberty to vote precisely as he thought right, uninfluenced by any other consideration than what belonged to the bill itself. Then, with respect to the committee of thirteen, I find there were only five of them voting for the whole of these measures; and I will read their names, so that, if there be any mistake, I may be corrected: they were Messrs. Bright, Cass, Cooper, Dickinson, and Dodge of Iowa. So that there were only five of the committee out of thirteen who voted for all of these bills; one of them (Mr. Webster) being absent by reason of accepting a cabinet appointment, and another for his health. Now, sir, the majority by which these bills passed severally were these: Utah by a majority of eighteen; Texas Boundary by a majority of ten; California by a majority of sixteen; and New Mexico by a majority of seventeen. I give these results for the purpose of justifying myself in standing out for what I considered to be a parliamentary law in originally wishing to separate all these bills, and I now say that the result has confirmed every thing I said upon this floor.

Mr. Dodge of Iowa. I rise for the purpose of correcting the senator from Missouri. I wish to say, as a historical fact, that I was not one of the committee of thirteen.

Mr. Benton. Ah! then that makes my position so much the stronger, and reduces the number to four out of the whole thirteen.

Mr. Davis of Mississippi. While gentlemen are dividing the honors that result from the passage of these bills, either in a joint or separate form, I have only to say that, so far as I am concerned, they are welcome to the whole. I do not represent that public opinion which required the passage of them, either jointly or separately. If any man has a right to be proud of the success of these measures, it is the senator from Illinois (Mr. Douglas). They were brought before the Senate by the committee, which it is claimed has done so much for the honor of the Senate and the peace of the country, merely stuck together—the work of other men, save and except the little bill to suppress the slave-trade in the District of Columbia. I merely wish to say that, so far as the public opinion of the community which I represent has been shadowed forth in public meetings and in the public press, it has been wholly adverse to the great body of these measures. I voted for one—that which the senator from Virginia originated, and which was modified in the Senate till I thought, as far as we could make it so, it became efficient for the protection of our rights. That was the only one which met my approval.

MR. DOUGLAS ON THE COMPROMISE AFTER ITS ADOPTION.

During the summer and fall of 1851 an animated contest for governor had taken place in Mississippi; Mr. Foote had been the candidate of those who in that state approved those measures, and he had been elected. His duties as governor did not commence until January; he therefore appeared in the Senate at the opening of the session in 1851–'2, and on the 4th of that month submitted a resolution declaring that, in the opinion of Congress, the measures of adjustment adopted in 1850 were a settlement of the questions embraced in them, and which ought to be respected and acquiesced in, etc.

Immediately after the adjournment of Congress after the passage of the compromise measures in 1850, Mr. Douglas returned to Illinois. The Northern country had been greatly agitated and excited by the misrepresentations of the terms, character, and requirements of the Fugitive Slave Act. It was vehemently denounced, and had but few willing or competent defenders. When he arrived in Chicago, that city was in a tempest of abolition fury. The excitement was general, and the vast majority of the people had been led to believe that the act was really and truly of the infamous character that was represented by the abolitionists. The city council, yielding to the storm, had passed resolutions denouncing the act as a violation of the Constitution of the United States and of the law of God, and those senators and representatives who voted for it, and also those who were absent, and, consequently, did not vote against it, as traitors, Benedict Arnolds, and Judas Iscariots. The council also released the " citizens, officers, and police of the city" from all obligation to assist or participate in the execution of the law, and declared that "it ought not to be respected by any intelligent community." On the next night a mass meeting of the citizens was held for the purpose of approving and sanctioning the action of the Common Council, and organizing violent and successful resistance to the execution of the law. A committee reported to this meeting a series of resolutions more revolutionary in their character, and going to a greater extent in resisting the authority of the federal government than even those of the Common Council. Numerous speeches in support of the resolutions were received with boisterous and furious applause, pledging their authors to resist even unto " the dungeon and the grave."

Mr. Douglas appeared upon the stand, and stated that, in consequence of the action of the Common Council and the phrensied excitement which seemed to rage all around him, he desired to be heard before the assembled people of the city in vindication of all the measures of adjustment, and especially of the Fugitive Slave Law. He said he would not make a speech that night, because the call for the meeting was not sufficiently broad to authorize a speech in *defense* of those measures ; but he would avail himself of that opportunity to give notice that on the next night he would address the people of Chicago upon these subjects. He invited men of all parties and shades of opinion to attend and participate in the proceedings, and assured them that he would answer every objection made, and every question which should be propounded, touching the measures of adjustment, and especially the Fugitive Bill. After farther discussion, and much confusion

and opposition, the meeting was induced to adjourn, and hear
Mr. Douglas's defense before they would condemn him. In
the mean time, the excitement continued to increase, and the
next night (October 23) a tremendous concourse of people assembled—by far the largest meeting ever held in the city—and
Mr. Douglas delivered a speech in defense of the Fugitive Slave
Act and other measures. The meeting then resolved *unanimously* to faithfully carry into effect the provisions of the Fugitive Slave Law, and to perform every other duty and obligation under the Constitution of the United States. The meeting
also adopted, with only eight or ten dissenting voices, a resolution repudiating the action of the Common Council, and then
adjourned with nine cheers—three for Douglas, three for the
Constitution, and three for the Union.

In the debate on the resolution of Mr. Foote, Judge Douglas entered into an explanation of the causes which produced
his absence at the time when the vote was taken on the passage of the Fugitive Slave Law, and also of his votes for the
Wilmot Proviso. Although these explanations were made
more than a year subsequent to his speech before the Chicago
meeting, it is deemed appropriate to include them here, and to
follow them up by the speech which is so frequently referred
to in them. This speech embraces a concise history of his
previous action upon the subject of slavery.

On the 23d of December, 1851, Mr. Foote's resolution being
under consideration, Mr. Douglas addressed the Senate as follows:

WHY HE DID NOT VOTE FOR THE FUGITIVE SLAVE ACT.

The senator from Texas (Mr. Houston), in the course of his speech, took
occasion to say that he was the only senator now holding a seat upon this
floor who voted for all the measures of compromise. That may be so, for
aught I know to the contrary. But the inference drawn from that remark,
and the distinct idea conveyed by it, do great injustice to me, and perhaps to
other senators. I voted, sir, for all the measures of the compromise but one ;
and I undertake to say, in regard to that one, that it was well known to the
Senate before the measure passed, and at the time it passed, and has been
distinctly proclaimed to the country since, that I would have voted for the
Fugitive Slave Law if I could have been in the Senate at the time, and that
I was anxious to be here for the purpose of casting that vote. I say it was
distinctly known, because I had so declared in debate prior to the passage of
that act ; because every senator on both sides of the chamber who conversed
with me knew that I was friendly to the measure ; and because, when I returned home, before my own constituents, I assumed the responsibility of an
affirmative vote upon the bill. Yes, sir, the imputation has been repeatedly
made by implication on this floor, and in express terms by the partisan jour-

nals, that all those whose names are not recorded on the passage of the bill dodged the question! Whatever political sins I may at any time have committed, I think I may safely assert that no senator ever doubted my willingness to assume the full measure of responsibility resulting from my official position. The dodging of votes—the attempt to avoid responsibility—is no part of my system of political tactics. And yet, sir, the special organ of the administration has on several occasions accused me, in connection with the distinguished senator from Michigan, with having dodged the vote on this bill. In order to put this accusation to rest, once for all, now and forever, I have concluded to give a detailed account of the circumstances which occasioned my absence at the time the bill passed, although it may subject me to the mortification of exposing my private and pecuniary affairs to the public view. I had a pecuniary obligation maturing in New York for near four thousand dollars, in payment of property which I had purchased in Chicago. Apprehending that my public duties with reference to these very compromise questions might render it improper to leave the city when the day of payment arrived, I made an arrangement with Mr. Maury, President of the Bank of the Metropolis, to arrange the matter for me temporarily until my official duties would enable me to give it my personal attention. Feeling entirely secure under this arrangement, I thought no more of it until, on the day the debt became due, I received a note from Mr. Maury, expressing his deep regret and mortification that, in consequence of the unexpected absence of a majority of the directors of his bank on that day, he was unable to carry out the arrangement. I thus found myself suddenly placed in the position in which I was compelled to go to New York instantly, or to suffer my note to be protested, and the commercial credit of my endorser to be greatly impaired. I immediately passed around the chamber, and inquired of several senators on each side friendly to the Fugitive Bill whether I could venture to be absent three or four days for the purpose of attending to this item of business, and I received from them the uniform answer that the discussion would continue at least a week, and probably two weeks longer, before the voting could begin. Relying implicitly upon this assurance, I went from the Senate Chamber directly to the cars, and, riding all night, arrived in New York the next day. Meeting several Illinois friends there, I was enabled to meet the obligation, and avoid a protest during the three days' grace allowed me by law. While dining with these friends at the Astor House on the day I had concluded my business, one of them alluded to the fact that the Fugitive Bill had been ordered to be engrossed for a third reading in the Senate. I expressed my surprise, and doubted the correctness of the statement. He then showed me the paper containing the telegraphic announcement, when I immediately rose from the table, and told my friends that I must leave for Washington that afternoon, in order to be able to *vote for the bill on its final passage* the next day. I left New York in the five o'clock train that afternoon, and, after riding all night, on my arrival here the next day, I found that the final vote had been taken the day previous. I immediately consulted with my colleague, now present (Mr. Shields), who authorizes me to say that he distinctly recollects the conversation in which I expressed my deep regret that I could not have arrived here in time to vote for the bill, and that I intended then to ask of the Senate permission to explain the cause of my absence; in reply to which my colleague suggested that such an explanation would be entirely unnecessary, for the reason that it was well known to the Senate and the country that I was in favor of the bill; and for the further reason that in all probability the bill would undergo some amendment in the House of Representatives, which would require its being returned to the Senate for concurrence, when I would have an opportunity not only of speaking, but of voting for the bill. I acquiesced in this suggestion of my colleague, and for that reason made no explanation at that time. A few days afterward, as you well know (Mr. Shields being in the chair), and as many other senators may recollect, I was taken ill, and rendered incapable of being in the Senate but a few times during the residue of the session. I was confined to my bed for several weeks, extending beyond the adjournment, having been rendered a cripple by a surgical operation on one hip. So soon as I was able to be removed, I was taken home under the care and kind attention of one of my colleagues of the House of Representatives. Every where on my route I found the most boisterous and determined opposition to the Fugitive Law; but nowhere was the excitement so fierce and terrific as at Chicago, where I had recently taken up my residence. There the press and the pulpit had joined in the work of misrepresentation and denunciation. A spirit of determined resistance had been incited, and seemed to pervade the whole community. The Common Council of the city, in its official capacity, had passed resolutions denouncing the Fugitive Slave Law as a violation of the law of God and the Constitution of the United States, calling upon the police of the city to disregard it, and the citizens not to obey it. The next night a meeting of 2000 people assembled; and in that meeting, in the midst of the most terrific applause, it was determined to defy "death, the dungeon, and the grave," in resistance to the execution of the law. I walked into that meeting, and from the stand gave notice that on the next night I would appear there and defend every measure of the Compromise, and especially the Fugitive Slave Law, from each and every objection urged to it, and I called upon the entire people of the city to come and hear me. I told that body of men there assembled, in the face of their denunciations and of their threats, that I was right and they were wrong, and if they would come and hear me I would prove it to them.

The next night, in the presence of 4000 people, with the city council and the abolitionists occupying positions in front of the stand, which was partially surrounded in the rear by a large body of armed negroes, including many fugitive slaves, I stood, and made the speech which I now hold in my hand, and which I caused to be laid upon the table of every senator and representative at the opening of the last session of Congress. In that speech, if any senator will take the trouble to read it, he will find that I assumed the responsibility of an affirmative vote on the passage of the law, and made the same explanation of the causes of my absence that I have given to-day, and called upon the gentlemen whose names I have stated to the Senate as having been in New York with me when the vote was taken, and who were in the meeting when the Chicago speech was made, to confirm my statement in regard to my absence, and my wish at that time to vote for the law. You will also find in that speech that I vindicate the law in respect to both its constitutionality and necessity; that I defend it as a whole, and in all its parts; that I answer every objection that has ever been urged against it. The objections relating to the right of trial by jury, to the writ of *habeas corpus*, to records from other states, to the fees of the commissioners, to the pains and penalties, to the "higher law"—every objection which the ingenuity and fanaticism of abolitionism could invent, was fully and conclusively answered in that speech—at least to the satisfaction of that vast assemblage of people. I am extremely reluctant to speak of the effect of my own speeches; but it is a part of the history of that transaction, that the meeting, comprising three fourths of all the legal voters of the city, a majority of whom had the night previously pledged themselves to open and violent resistance, after the speech was concluded, *unanimously adopted a series of resolutions in favor of sustaining and carrying into effect every provision of the Constitution and laws in respect to the surrender of fugitive slaves.* The resolutions were written and submitted to the meeting by myself, and cover the entire ground. I will only detain the Senate while I read one or two of them, and refer to the pamphlet copy of the speech for the whole series. (See *Chicago Speech*.)

It only remains for me to state that the same city council assembled on the next night, and repealed their nullifying resolutions by a vote of twelve to one.

Now, Mr. President, I have given you a detailed account of my course in relation to the Fugitive Law. I have no comments to make upon it. I submit the facts, and leave the Senate and country to draw their own conclusions. These facts are not now submitted for the first time. They are contained in the pamphlet copy of the Chicago speech which I hold in my hand, and which, I repeat, was laid on the table of every senator and representative more than a year ago, and fifty thousand copies were distributed by senators and representatives to every portion of the Union. I may also be permitted to add that, so far as my knowledge or belief extends, this was the first public speech ever made in a free state in defense of the Fugitive Law, and the Chicago meeting was the first public assemblage in any free state that determined to support and sustain it. At Chicago the reaction commenced. There rebellion and treason received their first check, the fanatical and revolutionary spirit was rebuked, and the supremacy of the Constitution and laws asserted and maintained. I claim no credit for the part I acted. I did no more than my duty as a citizen and a senator. I claim to have done my duty, and for that I was entitled to exemption from the repeated charges by the special organ of the administration, and other partisan prints, of having dodged the question. I never dodge a question. I never shrink from any responsibility which my position and duty justly devolve upon me. I never hesitate to give an unpopular vote, or to meet an indignant community, when I know I am right. My political opponents in my own state have never made such a charge against me, and I feel that upon this point I can appeal to the Senate with perfect safety for a unanimous verdict in my favor.

WHY HE VOTED FOR THE WILMOT PROVISO.

Mr. President, while I am engaged in the work of self-defense, I will refer to one other point. I have recently seen it stated in several papers that at some time, and on some occasion, I had been the advocate and supporter of the Wilmot Proviso. This charge, upon investigation, will be found to be as unjust and unfounded as that in regard to the Fugitive Law. In order to put the question to rest and beyond dispute forever, I will take a brief review of my course on the whole slavery agitation, and show clearly and distinctly the principles by which my action upon the subject has always been governed. It is no part of my purpose, on the present occasion, to vindicate the correctness of my views and principles, but simply to show what they are, and what my official acts have been, in order that the public may judge for themselves. I have always opposed the introduction of the subject of slavery into the halls of Congress for any purpose—either for discussion or action—except in the cases specified and enjoined by the Constitution of the United States, as in the case of the reclamation of fugitives from labor. The first important vote I ever gave in the House of Representatives was in favor of the rule excluding abolition petitions, and my vote stands recorded against its repeal at the time it was abolished. My action here since I have been a member of the Senate has been governed by the same principle. Whenever the slavery agitation has been forced upon us, I have always met it fairly, directly, and fearlessly, and endeavored to apply the proper remedy. Whether the remedy proposed by me has always been the wisest and most appropriate is a fair subject of discussion, and will doubtless give rise to a wide diversity of opinion. When the stormy agitation arose in connection with the annexation of Texas, I originated and first brought forward the Missouri Compromise as applicable to that Territory, and had the gratification to see it incorporated in the bill which annexed Texas to the United States. I did not deem it a matter of much moment as applicable to Texas alone, but I did conceive it to be of vast importance in view of the probable acquisition of New Mexico and California. My preference for the Missouri Compromise was predicated on the assumption that the whole people of the United States would be more easily reconciled to that measure than to any other mode of adjustment; and this assumption rested upon the fact that the Missouri Compromise had been the means of an amicable settlement of a fearful controversy in 1821, which had been acquiesced in cheerfully and cordially by the people for more than a quarter of a century, and which all parties and sections of the Union professed to respect and cherish as a fair, just, and honorable adjustment. I could discover no reason for the application of the Missouri line to all the territory owned by the United States in 1821 that would not apply with equal force to its extension to the Rio Grande and also to the Pacific, so soon as we should acquire the country. In accordance with these views, I brought forward the Missouri Compromise at the session of 1844-'45 as applicable to Texas, and had the satisfaction to see it adopted. Subsequently, after the war with Mexico had commenced, and when, in August, 1846, Mr. Wilmot first introduced his proviso, I proposed to extend the Missouri Compromise to the Pacific as a substitute for the Wilmot Proviso. When the proviso was voted into the Two Million Bill in opposition to my vote, I voted against the bill—which I would otherwise have supported—because the proviso was there. Again, in 1847, when the proviso was voted into the Three Million Bill, I voted against the bill for the same reason. The next time I had the opportunity of voting on the proviso was in the spring of 1848, in the Senate, pending the ratification of the treaty of peace with Mexico, when it was offered as an amendment to the treaty, I believe by a senator from Connecticut, now not a member of this body. The record shows that I here again voted against the proviso. This was the last vote ever taken on the Wilmot Proviso—the last that ever could be taken upon it as applicable to the country acquired from Mexico, for the reason that by this treaty we acquired the country without any such condition as that proposed by Mr. Wilmot. It should be borne in mind that the Wilmot Proviso not only proposed to prohibit slavery in the Territories while they remained Territories, but also went farther, and proposed to insert a stipulation in the treaty with a foreign power pledging the faith of the nation that slavery should never exist in the country acquired, either while it remained in the condition of Territories, or after it should have been admitted into the Union as states on an equal footing with the original states. I denounced this proviso as being unwise, improper, and unconstitutional; I never voted for it, and publicly declared that I never would vote for it, even under the pressure of instructions. The Wilmot Proviso being thus disposed of forever, and California and New Mexico having been acquired without any condition or stipulation in respect to slavery, the question arose as to what kind of territorial governments should be established for those countries. A domestic affliction suddenly called me from the capital, and detained me several weeks. On my return I found pending before the Senate the measure known as the Clayton Bill. Its provisions were not such as I would have proposed as chairman of the Territorial Committee had I been present, yet it had the high merit of having been reported with great unanimity by a special committee of the most eminent and distinguished members of the Senate, fairly representing all the different sections and interests of the Union. This fact afforded reason for the hope that the bill might receive

the sanction of both houses of Congress, and thus put an end to the controversy. Under the influence of these considerations, the bill received my cordial support, and passed the Senate by an overwhelming majority, but was
promptly rejected by the House of Representatives. The controversy being
reopened with increased violence, and my position at the head of the Territorial Committee requiring me to take the initiative in some plan of fair and
just settlement, I brought forward my original proposition to extend the Missouri Compromise to the Pacific in the same sense and with the same understanding with which it was originally adopted. This proposition met the
approbation of the Senate, and passed this body by a large majority, but was
instantly rejected in the House of Representatives by a still larger majority.
The day of adjournment having arrived, no farther efforts were made to adjust the difficulty during that session. At the opening of the next session,
upon consultation with the friends of the measure, it was generally conceded
—with, perhaps, here and there an individual exception—that there was no
hope left for the Missouri Compromise, and consequently some other plan of
adjustment must be devised. I was reluctant to give up the Missouri Compromise, having been the first to bring it forward, and having struggled for
it in both houses of Congress for about five years. But public duty demanded that all considerations of pride of character and of opinion should be made
subservient to the public peace and tranquillity. I gave it up—reluctantly,
to be sure—and conceived the idea of a bill to admit California as a state,
leaving the people to form a constitution and settle the question of slavery
afterward to suit themselves. I submitted this bill to the then President of
the United States (Mr. Polk), and have the satisfaction of stating that it received his sanction, and was introduced by me with his approbation. The
great argument in favor of this bill was that it recognized the right of the
people to determine all questions relating to their domestic concerns in their
own way, and authorized them to do so uninfluenced by executive dictation,
or by the apprehension that, unless they decided the slavery question in a
particular way, their application for admission would be rejected by Congress. I do not endorse and never did sanction the charge against the late
administration of having used improper means, or any means to influence the
decision of the people of California upon this question; but I do say that,
had this bill become the law of the land, no such charge would ever have
been made or suspicion entertained. The great misfortune is, that a large
portion of the South really believe that improper influences were used to produce the result in California. They do not deny the right of the people of
California to make that decision, but they insist that the right should have
been exercised freely, and uninfluenced by any act of the agents of the administration, or by the apprehension of an adverse decision by Congress in the
event that they had decided the Slavery question otherwise. But, Mr. President, the Judiciary Committee reported against and the Senate refused to
pass my bill to admit California as a state, leaving the question of slavery
open to be decided afterward by the people, and thus cut off all hope of adjustment in that mode. According to my recollection, the next important
measure which promised the slightest hope of giving peace to the country
was the proposition of the senator from Wisconsin, which is usually known as
the "Walker Amendment." All other plans having failed, as a last hope I
came warmly into the support of that proposition, and struggled for its adoption through that terrible night session, as many senators will recollect.

This brief history brings us down to the commencement of that memorable
long session when the late compromise measures were adopted. Mr. President, I may be permitted here to pause and remark that, during the period
of five years that I was laboring for the adoption of the Missouri Compromise,
my votes on the Oregon question, and upon all incidental questions touching

slavery, were given with reference to a settlement on that basis, and are consistent with it. If, therefore, any gentleman has the curiosity or wish to understand the meaning of any or all the votes I had occasion to give during that period on this question, he has only to bear in mind the Missouri Compromise, and then observe the perfect harmony between each vote and that measure.

Now, sir, I approach the history of the compromise measures. My account will be brief and easily understood. Having again been placed by the Senate at the head of the Territorial Committee, it became my duty to prepare and submit some plan of adjustment. Early in December, within the first two or three weeks of the session, I wrote, and laid before my committee for their examination and approval, two bills—one for the admission of California into the Union, and the other containing three distinct measures : first, for the establishment of a Territorial government for Utah ; second, for the establishment of a Territorial government for New Mexico; and, third, for the settlement of the Texas Boundary. These bills remained before the Committee on Territories from the month of December until the 25th of March before I could obtain the consent of the committee to report them. On that day I reported those bills, each member of the committee reserving the right to oppose any portion of them his judgment should disapprove of, and I being the only member who was responsible for all the provisions of those two bills. Those bills were on my motion ordered to be printed, and laid on the table of each member of both houses of Congress. These printed bills having lain on your table about four weeks, the Senate, on motion of Mr. Foote, appointed a committee of thirteen, with the distinguished senator from Kentucky (Mr. Clay) at its head. That committee took my two printed bills, joined them together with a wafer, and reported them to the Senate as one bill, which is well known to the country as the "Omnibus Bill." If any gentleman has the curiosity to investigate this matter, he can walk to the secretary's table and inspect the original Omnibus Bill. He will find that it consists of two printed bills with a wafer between them, and a black line drawn through the words "Mr. Douglas, from the Committee on Territories," and in lieu of them are inserted these other words : "Mr. CLAY, from the Committee of Thirteen," reported the following bill. The committee had also made some slight and comparatively unimportant amendments, nearly all of which were disagreed to by the Senate. The Committee of Thirteen, therefore, did not originate or write any one measure contained in the omnibus. They availed themselves of the labors of the Committee on Territories, and their distinguished chairman did us the justice so to state at the time he reported the bill. The Committee of Thirteen put a wafer between our bills, and the Senate took out the wafer and passed them separately. I supported the omnibus as a joint measure. I also supported each measure separately. I had no pride of opinion that the bills should be passed in the precise form I had reported them. I desired to see the controversy terminated, and was willing to take the measure jointly or separately, or in any form in which they could pass both houses of Congress. I reported them separately because I had ascertained the fact from actual count that they could pass separately, and could never pass jointly.

Mr. President, I claim no credit for having originated and proposed the measures contained in the omnibus. There was no peculiar or remarkable feature in them. They were merely ordinary measures of legislation, well adapted to the circumstances, and their sole merit consisted in the fact that separately they could pass both houses of Congress. Being responsible for these bills, as they came from the hands of the Committee on Territories, I wish to call the attention of the Senate and of the country to the fact that they contained no prohibition of slavery—no provision upon the subject. And now I come to the main point, which explains the object of the detailed statement which I have just made. The Legislature of Illinois, by a combination of every Whig in each house with a few Free-soil Democrats, had passed a resolution instructing me to vote for a bill for the government of the territory acquired from Mexico which should contain an express prohibition of slavery in said Territory. The instruction did not go to the extent of the Wilmot Proviso by attempting to prohibit slavery in the states as well as the Territories, but the movers of it contented themselves with the provision that slavery should be prohibited in the Territories while they remained such, leaving the people to do as they pleased when they became a state. Yet the instruction was designed and deemed sufficient to compel me to resign my seat and give place to a Free-soiler, for there could have been no expectation of their electing a Whig. They knew my inflexible opposition to the principle asserted in the instructions, at the same time that they knew that the right of instruction was the settled doctrine of both parties in my state, which no man could repudiate with safety. Knowing that this combination of Whigs and Free-soilers flattered themselves that they had succeeded in a party trick which would drive me from the Senate and give place to a Free-soiler who would come here and carry out abolition doctrines, I confess that they would have succeeded in their plot had I been certain that all the measures of the Compromise could have been passed without my vote and in opposition to the vote of an abolitionist in my place. Notwithstanding these instructions, I wrote the bills and reported them from the Committee on Territories without the prohibitions, in order that the record might show what my opinions were; but, lest the trick might fail, a Free-soil senator offered an amendment in the precise language of my instructions. I knew that the amendment could not prevail, even if my colleague and myself recorded the vote of our state in its favor.

But if I resigned my place to an abolitionist, it was almost certain that the bills would fail on their passage. After consulting with my colleague and with many senators friendly to the bills, I came to the conclusion that duty required that I should retain my seat. I was prepared to fight and defy abolitionism in all its forms, but I was not willing to repudiate the settled doctrine of my state in regard to the right of instruction. Before the vote was taken, I made a speech reviewing my course on the Slavery question and defining my position. I denounced the doctrine of the amendment, declared my unalterable opposition to it, and gave notice that any vote which might be recorded in my name seemingly in its favor would be the vote of those who gave the instructions, and not my own. Under this protest, I recorded a vote for this and one or two other amendments embracing the same principle, and then renewed my protest against them, and gave notice that I should not hold myself responsible for them. Immediately on my return home to my constituents, and in that same Chicago speech to which I have referred, I renewed my protest against those votes, and repeated the notice to that excited and infuriated meeting that they were their votes and not mine. I will detain the Senate a moment while I read a passage from that speech. Speaking of the Territorial bills, I say— [Mr. Douglas then quoted from his Chicago speech those portions referring to the powers of the Legislature of the Territories.]

This speech was immediately printed, and circulated all over the state. I at the same time traveled over a good portion of the state, and made many speeches of the same tenor, the last of which was made in the capital of our state. A few weeks afterward the Legislature assembled, and one of their first acts was to repeal the resolutions of instructions to which I have referred, and to pass resolutions approving of the course of my colleague and myself on the compromise measures by a vote of three or four to one. From that day Illinois has stood firm and unwavering in support of the compromise measures and of all the compromises of the Constitution.

THE CHICAGO SPEECH.

The following is a copy of the speech made by Judge Douglas to the excited meeting in Chicago on the 23d of October, 1850. The report was written out next day, and much that was said is omitted. The argument, however, is preserved, and, as a whole, it will not surprise the reader that it produced a powerful effect upon a people who, really and truly loyal to the Constitution, had been misled and induced to acts of folly by the persevering misrepresentations of the abolitionists. Four years later, these fanatics, profiting by their fatal experience in allowing Judge Douglas to defend himself before the people, took care to prevent another conversion of public sentiment, and refused to let him be heard. The following is the speech:

The agitation on the subject of slavery now raging through the breadth of the land presents a most extraordinary spectacle. Congress, after a protracted session of nearly ten months, succeeded in passing a system of measures, which are believed to be just to all parts of the republic, and ought to be satisfactory to the people. The South has not triumphed over the North, nor has the North achieved a victory over the South. Neither party has made any humiliating concessions to the other. Each has preserved its honor, while neither has surrendered an important right, or sacrificed any substantial interest. The measures composing the scheme of adjustment are believed to be in harmony with the principles of justice and the Constitution.

And yet we find that the agitation is reopened in the two extremes of the Union with renewed vigor and increased violence. In some of the Southern States, special sessions of the Legislatures are being called for the purpose of organizing systematic and efficient measures of resistance to the execution of the laws of the land, and for the adoption of disunion as the remedy. In the Northern States, municipal corporations, and other organized bodies of men, are nullifying the acts of Congress, and raising the standard of rebellion against the authority of the federal government.

At the South, the measures of adjustment are denounced as a disgraceful surrender of Southern rights to Northern abolitionism.

At the North, the same measures are denounced with equal violence as a total abandonment of the rights of freemen to conciliate the slave power.

The Southern disunionists repudiate the authority of the highest judicial tribunal on earth upon the ground that it is a pliant and corrupt instrument in the hands of Northern fanaticism.

The Northern nullifiers refuse to submit the points at issue to the same exalted tribunal upon the ground that the Supreme Court of the United States is a corrupt and supple instrument in the hands of the Southern slaveocracy.

For these contradictory reasons the people in both sections of the Union are called upon to resist the laws of the land and the authority of the federal government by violence, even unto death and disunion.

Strange and contradictory positions!

Both can not be true, and I trust in God neither may prove to be. We have fallen on evil times, when passion, and prejudice, and ambition can so blind the judgments and deaden the consciences of men that the truth can not be seen and felt. The people of the North or the South, or both, are acting under a total delusion. Should we not pause and reflect, and consider whether we, as well as they, have not been egregiously deceived upon this subject? It is my purpose this evening to give a candid and impartial exposition of these measures, to the end that the truth may be known. It does not become a free people to rush madly and blindly into violence, and bloodshed, and death, and disunion, without first satisfying our consciences upon whose souls the guilty consequences must rest.

The measures known as the adjustment or compromise scheme are six in number:

1. The admission of California, with her free Constitution.

2. The erection of a Territorial government for Utah, leaving the people to regulate their own domestic institutions.

3. The creation of a Territorial government for New Mexico, with like provisions.

4. The adjustment of the disputed boundary with Texas.

5. The abolition of the slave-trade in the District of Columbia.

6. The Fugitive Slave Bill.

The first three of these measures—California, Utah, and New Mexico—I prepared with my own hands, and reported from the Committee on Territories, as its chairman, in the precise shape in which they now stand on the statute-book, with one or two unimportant amendments, for which I also voted. I therefore hold myself responsible to you, as my constituents, for those measures as they passed. If there is any thing wrong in them, hold me responsible; if there is any thing of merit, give the credit to those who passed the bills. These measures are predicated on the great fundamental principle that every people ought to possess the right of forming and regulating their own internal concerns and domestic institutions in their own way. It was supposed that those of our fellow-citizens who emigrated to the shores of the Pacific and to our other Territories were as capable of self-government as their neighbors and kindred whom they left behind them; and there was no reason for believing that they have lost any of their intelligence or patriotism by the wayside, while crossing the Isthmus or the Plains. It was also believed that, after their arrival in the country, when they had become familiar with its topography, climate, productions, and resources, and had connected their destiny with it, they were fully as competent to judge for themselves what kind of laws and institutions were best adapted to their condition and interests, as we were, who never saw the country, and knew very little about it. To question their competency to do this was to deny their capacity for self-government. If they have the requisite intelligence and honesty to be intrusted with the enactment of laws for the government of white men, I know of no reason why they should not be deemed competent to legislate for the negro. If they are sufficiently enlightened to make laws for the protection of life, liberty, and property—of morals and education—to determine the relation of husband and wife—of parent and child—I am not aware that it requires any higher degree of civilization to regulate the affairs of master and servant. These things are all confided by the Constitution to each state to decide for itself, and I know of no reason why the same principle should not be extended to the Territories. My votes and acts have been in accordance with these views in all cases, except the instances in which I voted under your instructions. Those were your votes, and not mine. I entered my protest against them at the time—before and after they were recorded—and shall never hold myself responsible for them. I believed then, and believe now, that it was better for the cause of freedom, of humanity, and of Republicanism, to leave the people interested to settle all these questions for themselves. They have intellect and consciences as well as we, and have more interest in doing that which is best for themselves and their posterity, than we have as their self-constituted and officious guardians. I deem it fortunate for the peace and harmony of the country that Congress, taking the same view of the subject, rejected the proviso, and passed the bills in the shape in which I originally reported them. So far as slavery is concerned, I am sure that any man who will take the pains to examine the history of this question will come to the conclusion that this is the true policy, as well as the sound Republican doctrine. Mr. Douglas here went into a historical view of the subject, to show that slavery had never been excluded in fact from one inch of the American continent by act of Congress, after which he said:

But let us return to the measures immediately under discussion. It must be conceded that the question of the admission of California was not free from difficulty, independent of the subject of slavery. There were many irregularities in the proceedings; in fact, every step in her application for admission was irregular, when viewed with reference to a literal compliance with the most approved rules and usages in the admission of new states. On the other hand, it should be borne in mind that this resulted from the necessity of the case. Congress had failed to perform its duty—had established no Territorial government, and made no provision for her admission into the Union. She was left without government, and was therefore compelled to provide one for herself. She could not conform to rules which had not been established, nor comply with laws which Congress had failed to enact. The same irregularities had occurred, however, and been waived, in the admission of other states under peculiar circumstances. True, they had not all occurred in the case of any one state; but some had in one, others in another; so that, by looking into the circumstances attending the admission of each of the new states, we find that all of these irregularities, as they are called, had intervened and been waived in the course of our legislative history. Besides, the Territory of California was too extensive for one state (if we are to adopt the old states as a guide in carving out new ones), being about three times the size of New York; and her boundaries were unnatural and unreasonable, disregarding the topography of the country, and embracing the whole mining region and her coast in the limits. Thus it will be seen that the Slavery question was not the only real difficulty that the admission of California presented to the minds of calm and reflecting men, although it can not be denied that it was the exciting cause, which stimulated a large portion of the people in one section to demand her instant admission, and in the other to insist upon her unconditional rejection. Even in this point of view, I humbly conceive that the ultras in each extreme of the republic acted under a misconception of their true interests and real policy. The whole of California— from the very nature of the country, her rocks and sands, elevation above the sea, climate, soil, and productions—was bound to be free territory by the decision of her own people, no matter when admitted or how divided. Hence, if considered with reference to the preponderance of political power between the free and slaveholding states, it was manifestly the true policy of the South to include the whole country in one state, while the same reasons should have induced the North to subdivide it into as many states as the extent of the territory would justify. But, in my opinion, it was not proper for Congress to act upon any such principle. We should know no North, no South, in our legislation, but look to the interests of the whole country. By our action in this case, the rights and privileges of California and the Pacific coast were principally to be affected. By erecting the country into one state instead of three, the people are to be represented in the Senate by two in the place of six senators. If their interests suffer in consequence, they can blame no one but themselves, for Congress only confirmed what they had previously done. The problem in relation to slavery should have been much more easily solved. It was a question which concerned the people of California alone. The other states of the Union had no interest in it, and no right to interfere with it. South Carolina settled that question within her own limits to suit herself; Illinois has decided it in a manner satisfactory to her own people; and upon what principle are we to deprive the people of the State of California of a right which is common to every state in the Union?

The bills establishing Territorial governments for Utah and New Mexico are silent upon the subject of slavery, except the provision that, when they should be admitted into the Union as states, each should decide the question of slavery for itself. This latter provision was not incorporated in my original bills, for the reason that I conceived it to involve a principle so clearly deducible from the Constitution that it was unnecessary to embody it in the form of legal enactment. But when it was offered as an amendment to the bills, I cheerfully voted for it, lest its rejection should be deemed a denial of the principle asserted in it. The abolitionists of the North profess to regard these bills as a total abandonment of the principles of freedom, because they do not contain an express prohibition of slavery, while the ultras of the South denounce the same measures as equivalent to the Wilmot Proviso.

He then explained and defended the Texas Boundary measure, and the Bill for the Suppression of the local Slave-trade in the District of Columbia. He then took up the Fugitive Slave Act, and said:

DEFENSE OF THE FUGITIVE SLAVE LAW.

Before I proceed to the exposition of that bill, I will read the preamble and resolutions passed by the Common Council of this city night before last.

Mr. Douglas then read as follows:

"*Whereas*, The Constitution of the United States provides that the privilege of the writ of habeas corpus shall not be suspended, unless when, in cases of rebellion or invasion, the public safety may require it; and

"*Whereas*, The late act of Congress, purporting to be for the recovery of fugitive slaves, virtually suspends the habeas corpus and abolishes the right of trial by jury, and by its provisions not only fugitive slaves, but white men, "owing service" to another in another state, viz., the apprentice, the mechanic, the farmer, the laborer engaged on contract or otherwise, whose terms of service are unexpired, may be captured and carried off summarily, and without legal resource of any kind; and

"*Whereas*, No law can be legally or morally binding on us which violates the provisions of the Constitution; and

"*Whereas*, Above all, in the responsibilities of human life, and the practice and propagation of Christianity, the laws of God should be held paramount to all human compacts and statutes; Therefore,

"*Resolved*, That the senators and representatives in Congress from the free states, who aided and assisted in the passage of this infamous law, *and those who basely sneaked away from their seats, and thereby evaded the question*, richly merit the reproach of all lovers of freedom, and are fit only to be ranked with the traitors Benedict Arnold and Judas Iscariot, who betrayed his Lord and Master for thirty pieces of silver.

"*And Resolved*, That the citizens, officers, and police of the city be, and they are hereby, requested to abstain from all interference in the capture and delivering up of the fugitive from unrighteous oppression, of whatever nation, name, or color.

"*Resolved*, That the Fugitive Slave Law lately passed by Congress is a cruel and unjust law, and ought not to be respected by any intelligent community, and that this council will not require the city police to render any assistance for the arrest of fugitive slaves.

"*Ayes*—Ald. Milliken, Loyd, Sherwood, Foss, Throop, Sherman, Richards, Brady, and Dodge.

"*Nays*—Ald. Page and Williams."

But for the passage of these resolutions, said Mr. D., I should not have addressed you this evening, nor, indeed, at any time before my return to the Capitol. I have no desire to conceal or withhold my opinions, no wish to avoid the responsibility of a full and frank expression of them, upon this and all other subjects which were embraced in the action of the last session of Congress. My reasons for wishing to avoid public discussion at this time were to be found in the state of my health, and the short time allowed me to remain among you.

Now to the resolutions. I make no criticism upon the language in which they are expressed; that is a matter of taste, and in every thing of that kind I defer to the superior refinement of our city fathers. But it can not be disguised that the polite epithets of "traitors, Benedict Arnold and Judas Iscariot, who betrayed his Lord and Master for thirty pieces of silver," will be understood abroad as having direct personal application to my esteemed colleague, Gen. Shields, and myself. Whatever may have been the intention of those who voted for the resolutions, I will do the members of council the justice to say that I do not believe they intended to make any such application. But their secret intentions are of little consequence when they give their official sanction to a charge of infamy, clothed in such language that every man who reads it must give it a personal application. The whole affair, however, looks strange, and even ludicrous, when contrasted with the cordial reception and public demonstrations of kindness and confidence, and even gratitude for supposed services, extended to my colleague and myself upon our arrival in this city one week ago. Then we were welcomed home as public benefactors, and invited to partake of a public dinner by an invitation numerously signed by men of all parties and shades of opinion. The invitation had no sooner been declined, for reasons which were supposed to be entirely satisfactory, and my colleague started for his home, than the Common Council, who are presumed to speak officially for the whole population of the city, attempted to brand their honored guests with infamy, and denounce them as Benedict Arnolds and Judas Iscariots! I have read somewhere that it was a polite custom, in other countries and a different age, to invite those whom they secretly wished to destroy to a feast, in order to secure a more convenient opportunity of administering the hemlock! I acquit the Common Council of any design of introducing that custom into our hospitable city. But I have done with this subject, so far as it has a personal bearing.

It is a far more important and serious matter, when viewed with reference to the principles involved, and the consequences which may result. The Common Council of the city of Chicago have assumed to themselves the right, and actually exercised the power, of determining the validity of an act of Congress, and have declared it void upon the ground that it violates the Constitution of the United States and the law of God! They have gone further; they declared, by a solemn official act, that a law passed by Congress "ought not to be respected by any intelligent community," and have called upon "the citizens, officers, and police of the city" to abstain from rendering any aid or assistance in its execution! What is this but naked, unmitigated nullification? An act of the American Congress nullified by the Common Council of the city of Chicago! Whence did the council derive their authority? I have been able to find no such provision in the city charter, nor am I aware that the Legislature of Illinois is vested with any rightful power to confer such authority. I have yet to learn that a subordinate municipal corporation is licensed to raise the standard of rebellion, and throw off the authority of the federal government at pleasure! This is a great improvement upon South Carolinian nullification. It dispenses with the trouble, delay, and expense of convening Legislatures and assembling conventions of the people, for the purpose of resolving themselves back into their original elements, preparatory to the contemplated revolution. It has the high merit of marching directly to its object, and by a simple resolution, written and adopted on the same night, relieving the people from their oaths and allegiance, and of putting the nation and its laws at defiance! It has heretofore been supposed, by men of antiquated notions, who have not kept up with the progress of the age, that the Supreme Court of the United States was invested with the power of determining the validity of an act of Congress passed in pursuance of the forms of the Constitution. This was the doctrine of the entire North, and of the nation, when it became necessary to exert the whole power of the government to put down nullification in another portion of the Union. But the spirit of the age is progressive, and is by no means confined to advancement in the arts and physical sciences. The science of politics and of government is also rapidly advancing to maturity and perfection. It is not long since that I heard an eminent lawyer propose an important reform in the admirable judicial system of our state, which, he thought, would render it perfect. It was so simple and eminently practicable that it could not fail to excite the admiration of even the casual inquirer. His proposition was, that our judicial system should be so improved as to allow an appeal, on all constitutional questions, from the Supreme Court of this state to two justices of the peace! When that shall have been effected, but one other reform will be necessary to render our national system perfect, and that is, to change the federal Constitution, so as to authorize an appeal, upon all questions touching the validity of acts of Congress, from the Supreme Court of the United States to the Common Council of the city of Chicago!

So much for the general principles involved in the acts of the council. I will now examine briefly the specific grounds of objection urged by the council against the Fugitive Slave Bill, as reasons why it should not be obeyed.

The objections are two in number: first, that it suspends the writ of habeas corpus in time of peace, in violation of the Constitution; secondly, that it abolishes the right of trial by jury.

How the council obtained the information that these two odious provisions were contained in the law, I am unable to divine. One thing is certain, that the members of the council who voted for these resolutions had never read the law, or they would have discovered their mistake. There is not one word in it in respect to the writ of habeas corpus or the right of trial by jury. Neither of these subjects is mentioned or referred to. The law is entirely silent on these points. Is it to be said that an act of Congress which is silent on the subject ought to be construed to repeal a great constitutional right by implication? Besides, this act is only an amendment—amendatory of the old law—the act of 1793—but does not repeal it. There is no difference between the original act and the amendment in this respect. Both are silent in regard to the writ of habeas corpus and the right of trial by jury. If to be silent is to suspend the one and abolish the other, then the mischief was done by the old law fifty-seven years ago. If this construction be correct, the writ of habeas corpus has been suspended, and trial by a jury abolished, more than half a century, without any body ever discovering the fact, or, if knowing it, without uttering a murmur of complaint.

Mr. Douglas then read the whole of the act of 1793, and compared its provisions with the amendment of last session, for the purpose of showing that the writ of habeas corpus and the right of trial by jury were not alluded to or interfered with by either. But I maintain, said Mr. **D.**, that the writ of habeas corpus is applicable to the case of the arrest of a **fugitive** under this law, in the same sense in which the Constitution intended to confer it, and to the fullest extent for which that case is ever rightfully issued in any case. In this I am fully sustained by the opinion of Mr. Crittenden, the attorney general of the United States. As soon as the bill passed the two houses of Congress, an abolition paper raised the alarm that the habeas corpus had been suspended. The cry was eagerly caught up, and transmitted by lightning upon the wires to every part of the Union by those whose avocation is agitation. The President of the United States, previous to signing the bill, referred it to the attorney general for his opinion upon the point whether any portion of it violated any provision of the Constitution of the United States, and especially whether it could possibly be construed to suspend the writ of habeas corpus. I have the answer of the attorney general before me, in which he gives it as his decided opinion that every part of the law is entirely consistent with the Constitution, and that it does not suspend the writ of habeas corpus. I would commend the argument of the attorney general to the careful perusal of those who have doubts upon the subject. Upon the presentation of this opinion, and with entire confidence in its correctness, President Fillmore signed the bill.

[Here Mr. Douglas was interrupted by a person present, who called his attention to the last clause of the 6th section of the bill, which he read, and asked him what construction he put upon it, if it did not suspend the writ of habeas corpus.]

Mr. Douglas, in reply, expressed his thanks to the gentleman who propounded the inquiry. His object was to meet every point, and remove every doubt that could be possibly raised; and he expressed the hope that every gentleman present would exercise the privilege of asking him questions upon all points upon which he was not fully satisfied. He then proceeded to answer the question which had been propounded. That section of the bill provides for the arrest of the fugitive and the trial before the commissioner; and if the facts of servitude, ownership, and escape be established by competent evidence, the commissioner shall grant a certificate to that effect, which certificate shall be conclusive of the right of the person in whose favor it is issued to remove the fugitive to the state from which he fled. Then comes the clause which is supposed to suspend the habeas corpus : "*And shall prevent all molestation of said person or persons by any process issued by any court, judge, magistrate, or other person whomsoever.*"

The question is asked whether the writ of habeas corpus is not a "PROCESS" within the meaning of this act? I answer that it undoubtedly is such a "process," and that it may be issued by any court or judge having competent authority—not for the purpose of "molesting" a claimant, having a servant in his possession, with such a certificate from the commissioner or judge, but for the purpose of ascertaining the fact whether he has such certificate or not; and if so, whether it be in due form of law; and if not, by what authority he holds the servant in custody. Upon the return of the writ of habeas corpus, the claimant will be required to exhibit to the court his authority for conveying that servant back; and if he produces a "certificate" from the commissioner or judge in due form of law, the court will decide that it has no power to "molest the claimant" in the exercise of his rights under the law and the Constitution. But if the claimant is not able to produce such certificate, or other lawful authority, or produces one which is not in conformity with law, the court will set the alleged servant at liberty, for the very reason that the law has not been complied with. The sole object of the writ of habeas corpus is to ascertain by what authority a person is held in custody; to release him if no such authority be shown; and to refrain from any molestation of the claimant if legal authority be produced. The habeas corpus is necessary, therefore, to carry the Fugitive Slave Law into effect, and, at the same time, to prevent a violation of the rights of freemen under it. It is essential to the security of the claimant, as well as the protection of the rights of those liable to be arrested under it. The reason that the writ of habeas corpus was not mentioned in the bill must be obvious. The object of the new law seems to have been to amend the old one in those particulars wherein experience had proven amendments to be necessary, and in all other respects to leave it as it had stood from the days of Washington. The provisions of the old law have been submitted to the test of long experience—to the scrutiny of the bar and the judgment of the courts. The writ of habeas corpus had been adjudged to exist in all cases under it, and had always been resorted to when a proper case arose. In amending the law there was no necessity for any new provision upon this subject, because nobody desired to change it in this respect.

But why this extraordinary effort, on the part of the professed friends of the fugitive, to force such a construction upon the law, in the absence of any such obnoxious provision, as to deprive him of the benefit of the writ of habeas corpus? The law does not do so in terms; and if it is ever accomplished, it must be done by implication, contrary to the understanding of those who enacted, and in opposition to the practice of the courts, acquiesced in by the people from the foundation of the government. One would naturally suppose that, if there was room for doubt as to what is the true construction, those who claim to be the especial and exclusive friends of the negro would contend for that construction which is most favorable to liberty, justice, and humanity. But not so. Directly the reverse is the fact. They exhaust their learning, and exert all their ingenuity and skill, to deprive the negro of all rights under the law. What can be the motive? Certainly not to protect the rights of the free, or to extend liberty to the oppressed; for they strive to fasten upon the law such a construction as would defeat both of these ends. Can it be a political scheme, to render the law odious, or to excite prejudice against all who voted for it, or were unavoidably absent when it passed? No matter what the motive, the effects would be disastrous to those whose rights they profess to cherish, if their efforts should be successful.

Now, a word or two in regard to the right of trial by jury. The city council, in their resolutions, say that this law abolishes that right. I have already shown you that the council are mistaken—that the law is silent upon the subject, and stands now precisely as it has stood for half a century. If the law is defective on that point, the error was committed by our fathers in 1793, and the people have acquiesced in it ever since, without knowing of its existence or caring to remedy it. The new act neither takes away nor confers the right of trial by jury. It leaves it just where our fathers and the Constitution left it under the old law. That the right of trial by jury exists in this country for all men, black or white, bond or free, guilty or innocent, no man will be disposed to question who understands the subject. The right is of universal application, and exists alike in all the states of the Union; it always has existed, and always will exist, so long as the Constitution of the United States shall be respected and maintained, in spite of the efforts of the abolitionists to take it away by a perversion of the Fugitive Law. The only question is, *where* shall this jury trial take place? Shall the jury trial be had in the state where the arrest is made, or the state from which the fugitive escaped? Upon this point the act of last session says nothing, and, of course, leaves the matter as it stood under the law of '93. The old law was silent on this point, and therefore left the courts to decide it in accordance with the Constitution. The highest judicial tribunals in the land have always held that the jury trial must take place in the state under whose juris-diction the question arose, and whose laws were alleged to have been vio-lated. The same construction has always been given to the law for surren-dering fugitives from justice. It provides also for sending back the fugitive, but says nothing about the jury trial, or where it shall take place. Who ever supposed that that act abolished the right of trial by jury? Every day's practice and observation teach us otherwise. The jury trial is always had in the state from which the fugitive fled. So it is with a fugitive from labor. When he returns, or is surrendered under the law, he is entitled to a trial by jury of his right of freedom, and always has it when he demands it. There is great uniformity in the mode of proceeding in the courts of the Southern States in this respect. When the supposed slave sets up his claim, to the judge or other officer, that he is free, and claims his freedom, it becomes the duty of the court to issue its summons to the master to appear in court with the alleged slave, and there to direct an issue of freedom or servitude to be made and tried by a jury. The master is also required to enter into bonds for his own appearance and that of the alleged slave at the trial of the cause, and that he will not remove the slave from the county or jurisdiction of the court in the mean time. The court is also required to appoint counsel to conduct the cause for the slave, while the master employs his own counsel. All the officers of the court are required by law to render all facilities to the slave for the prosecution of his suit free of charge, such as issuing and serv-ing subpœnas for witnesses, etc. If upon the trial the alleged slave is held to be a free man, the master is required to pay the costs on both sides. If, on the other hand, he is held to be a slave, the state pays the costs. This is the way in which the trial by jury stood under the old law; and the new one makes no change in this respect. If the act of last session be repealed, that will neither benefit nor injure the fugitive, so far as the right of trial by jury is concerned.

For these two reasons—the habeas corpus and the trial by jury—the Com-mon Council have pronounced the law unconstitutional, and declared that it ought not to be respected by an enlightened community. I have shown that neither of the objections are well founded, and that, if they had taken the trouble to read the law before they nullified it, they would have avoided the mistake into which they have fallen. I have spoken of the acts of the city council in general terms, and it may be inferred that the vote was unani-mous. I take pleasure in stating that I learn from the published proceed-ings that there was barely a quorum present, and that Aldermen Page and Williams voted in the negative.

Having disposed of the two reasons assigned by the Common Council for the nullification of the law, I shall be greatly indebted to any gentleman who will point out any other objection to the new law which does not apply with equal force to the old one. My object in drawing the parallel between the new and old law is this: The law of '93 was passed by the patriots and sages who framed our glorious Constitution, and approved by the Father of his Country. I have always been taught to believe that they were men well versed in the science of government, devotedly attached to the cause of free-dom, and capable of construing the Constitution in the spirit in which they made it. That act has been enforced and acquiesced in for more than half a century, without a murmur or word of complaint from any quarter.

I repeat—will any gentleman be kind enough to point out a single objec-tion to the new law which might not be urged with equal propriety to the act of '93?

[Here a gentleman present rose, and called the attention of Mr. Douglas to the penalties in the seventh section of the new law, and desired to know if there were any such obnoxious provisions in the old one.]

Mr. Douglas then read the section referred to, and also the fourth section of the act of '93, and proceeded to draw the parallel between them. Each makes it a criminal offense to resist the due execution of the law; to knowingly and willfully obstruct or hinder the claimant in the arrest of the fugitive; to rescue such fugitive from the claimant when arrested; to harbor or conceal such person after notice that he or she was a fugitive from labor. In this respect the two laws were substantially the same in every important particular. Indeed the one was almost a literal copy of the other. I can conceive of no, act which would be an offense under the one that would not be punishable under the other. In the speeches last night, great importance was given to the clause which makes it an offense to harbor or conceal a fugitive. You were told that you could not clothe the naked, nor feed the hungry, nor exercise the ordinary charity toward suffering humanity, without incurring the penalty of the law. Is this a true construction of that provision? The act does not so read. The law says that you shall not "harbor or conceal such fugitive, *so as to prevent the discovery and arrest* of such person after notice or knowledge of the fact that such person was a fugitive from service or labor as aforesaid." This does not deprive you of the privilege of extending charities to the fugitive. You may feed him, clothe him, may lodge him, provided you do not harbor or conceal him, so as to prevent discovery and arrest, after notice or knowledge that he is a fugitive. The offense consists in preventing the discovery and arrest of the fugitive after knowledge of the fact, and not in extending kindness and charities to him. This is the construction put upon a similar provision in the old law by the highest judicial tribunals in the land. The only difference between the old law and the new one, in respect to obstructing its execution, is to be found in the amount of the penalty, and not in the principle involved.

But it is further objected that the new law provides, in addition to the penalty, for a civil suit for damages, to be recovered by an action of debt by any court having jurisdiction of the cause. This is true; but it is also true that a similar provision is to be found in the old law. The concluding clause in the last section of the act of '93 is as follows:

"Which penalty may be recovered by and for the benefit of such claimant, by action of debt, in any proper court to try the same; *saving, moreover, to the person claiming such labor or service, his right of action for or on account of the said injuries, or either of them.*"

Thus it will be seen that upon this point there is no difference between the new and the old law.

Is there any other provision of this law upon which explanation is desired?

[A gentleman present referred to the 10th section, and desired an explanation of the object and effect of the record from another state therein provided for.]

I am glad, said Mr. D., that my attention has been called to that provision; for I heard a construction given to it in the speeches last night entirely different to the plain reading and object of that section. It is said that this provision authorizes the claimant to go before a court of record of the county and state where he lives, and there establish by ex-parte testimony, in the absence of the fugitive, the facts of servitude, of ownership, and escape; and when a record of these facts shall have been made, containing a minute description of the slave, it shall be conclusive evidence against a person corresponding to that description, arrested in another state, and shall consign the person so arrested to perpetual servitude. The law contemplates no such thing, and authorizes no such result. I have the charity to believe that those who have put this construction upon it have not carefully examined it. The record from another state predicated upon "satisfactory proof to such court or judge" before whom the testimony may be adduced, and the record made, is to be conclusive of two facts only :

1st. That the person named in the record does owe service to the person in whose behalf the record is made.

2d. That such person has escaped from service.

The language of the law is, that "the transcript of the record authenticated," etc., "shall be held and taken to be full and conclusive evidence of the fact of escape, and that the service or labor of such person escaping is due to the party in such record mentioned." The record is conclusive of these two facts so far as to authorize the fugitive to be sent back for trial under the laws of the state whence he fled, *but it is no evidence that the person arrested here is the fugitive named in the record.* The question of *identity* is to be proven here to the satisfaction of the commissioner or judge, before whom the trial is had, by "*by other and further evidence.*" This is the great point in the case. The whole question turns upon it. The man arrested may correspond to the description set forth in the record, and yet not be the same individual. We often meet persons resembling each other to such an extent that the one is frequently mistaken for the other. The identity of the person becomes a matter of proof—a fact to be established by the testimony of competent and disinterested witnesses, and to be decided by the tribunal before whom the trial is had, conscientiously and impartially, according to the evidence in the case. The description in the record, unsupported by other testimony, is not evidence of the identity. It is not inserted for the especial benefit of the claimant, much less to the prejudice of the alleged slave. It is required as a test of truth, a safeguard against fraud, which will often operate favorably to the fugitive, but never to his injury. If the description be accurate and true, no injustice can possibly result from it ; but if it be erroneous or false, the claimant is concluded by it ; and the fugitive, availing himself of the error, defeats the claim, in the same manner as a discrepancy between the allegations and the proof, in any other case, results to the advantage of the defendant. I repeat that, when an arrest is made under a record from another state, the identity of the person must be established by competent testimony. The trial, in this instance, would be precisely the same as in the case of a white man arrested on the charge of being a fugitive from justice. The writ of the governor, predicated upon an indictment, or even an affidavit from another state, containing the charge of crime, would be conclusive evidence of the right to take the fugitive back ; but the identity of the person in that case, as well as a fugitive from labor, must be proven in the state where the arrest is made by competent witnesses before the tribunal provided by law for that purpose. In this respect, therefore, the negro is placed upon a perfect equality with the white man who is so unfortunate as to be charged with an offense in another state, whether the charge be true or false. In some respects, the law guards the rights of the negro charged with being a fugitive from labor more rigidly than it does those of a white man who is alleged to be a fugitive from justice. The record from another state must be predicated upon "proof satisfactory to the court or judge" before whom it is made, and must set forth the "matter proved," before it can be evidence against a fugitive from labor, or for any purpose ; whereas an innocent white man who is so unfortunate as to be falsely charged with a crime in another state by the simple affidavit of an unknown person, without indictment or proof to the satisfaction of any court, is liable to be transported to the most distant portions of this Union for trial.

Here we find the act of last session is a great improvement upon the law of '93 in reference to fugitives, white or black, whether they fled from justice or labor. But it is objected that the testimony before the court making the record is *ex parte*, and therefore in violation of the principles of justice and the Constitution, because it deprives the accused of the privilege of meeting the witnesses face to face, and of cross-examination. Gentlemen forget that all proceedings for the arrest of fugitives are necessarily *ex parte*, from the nature of the case. They have fled beyond the jurisdiction of the court, and the object of the proceeding is that they may be brought back, confront the witnesses, and receive a fair trial according to the Constitution and laws. If they would stay at home in order to attend the trial and cross-examine the witnesses, the record would be unnecessary, and the Fugitive Law inoperative. It is no answer to this proposition to say that slavery is no crime, and therefore the parallel does not hold good. I am not speaking of the guilt or innocence of slavery; I am discussing our obligations under the Constitution of the United States. That sacred instrument says that a fugitive from labor "*shall be delivered up* on the claim of the owner." The same clause of the same instrument provides that fugitives from justice shall be delivered up. We are bound by our oaths to our God to see that claim, as well as every other provision of the Constitution, carried into effect. The moral, religious, and constitutional obligations resting upon us, here and hereafter, are the same in the one case as in the other. As citizens, owing allegiance to the government and duties to society, we have no right to interpose our individual opinions and scruples as excuses for violating the supreme law of the land as our fathers made it, and as we are sworn to support it. The obligation is just as sacred, under the Constitution, to surrender fugitives from labor as fugitives from justice; and the Congress of the United States, according to the decision of the Supreme Court, are as imperatively commanded to provide the necessary legislation for the one as for the other. The act of 1793, to which I have had occasion to refer so frequently, and which has been read to you, provided for these two cases in the same bill. The first half of that act, relating to fugitives from justice, applies, from the nature and necessity of the case, principally to white men; and the other half, for the same reasons, applies exclusively to the negro race. I have shown you, by reading and comparing the two laws in your presence, that there is no constitutional guaranty, or common-law right, or legal or judicial privilege, for the protection of the white man against oppression and injustice, under the law framed in 1793, and now in force, for the surrender of fugitives from justice, that does not apply in all its force in behalf of the negro, when arrested as a fugitive from labor, under the act of the last session. What more can the friends of the negro ask than, in all his civil and legal rights under the Constitution, he shall be placed on an equal footing with the white man? But it is said that the law is susceptible of being abused by perjury and false testimony. To what human enactment does not the same objection lie? You, or I, or any other man, who was never in California in his life, are liable, under the Constitution, to be sent there in chains for trial as a fugitive from justice by means of perjury and fraud. But does this fact prove that the Constitution, and the laws for carrying it into effect, are wrong, and should be resisted, as we were told last night, even unto the dungeon, the gibbet, and the grave? It only demonstrates to us the necessity of providing all the safeguards that the wit of man can devise for the protection of the innocent and the free, at the same time that we religiously enforce, according to its letter and spirit, every provision of the Constitution. I will not say that the act recently passed for the surrender of fugitives from labor accomplishes all this, but I will thank any gentleman to point out any one barrier against abuse in the old law, or in the law for the surrender of white men, as fugitives from justice, that is not secured to the negro under the new law. I pause in order to give any gentleman an opportunity to point out the provision. I invite inquiry and examination. My object is to arrive at the truth—to repel error and dissipate prejudice—and to avoid violence and bloodshed. Will any gentleman point out the provision in the old law for securing and vindicating the rights of the free man that is not secured to him in the act of last session?

[A gentleman present rose and called the attention of Mr. Douglas to the provision for paying out of the Treasury of the United States the expenses of carrying the fugitive back in case of anticipated resistance.]

Ah! said Mr. Douglas, that is a question of dollars and cents, involving no other principle than the costs of the proceeding. I was discussing the question of human rights—the mode of protecting the rights of freemen from invasion, and the obligation to surrender fugitives under the Constitution. Is it possible that this momentous question, which, only forty-eight hours ago, was deemed of sufficient importance to authorize the city council to nullify an act of Congress, and raise the standard of rebellion against the federal government, has dwindled down into a mere petty dispute who shall pay the costs of suit? This is too grave a question for me to discuss on this occasion. I confess my utter inability to do it justice. Yesterday the Constitution of the ocean-bound republic had been overthrown; the privileges of the writ of habeas corpus had been suspended; the right of trial by jury had been abolished; pains and penalties had been imposed upon every humane citizen who should feed the hungry and cover the naked; the law of God had been outraged by an infamous act of a traitorous Congress; and the standard of rebellion, raised by our city fathers, was floating in the breeze, calling on all good citizens to rally under its sacred folds, and resist with fire and sword— the payment of the costs of suit upon the arrest of a fugitive from labor!

I will pass over this point, and inquire whether there is any other provision of this law upon which an explanation is desired? I hope no one will be backward in propounding inquiries, for I have but a few days to remain with you, and desire to make a clean business of this matter on the present occasion. Is there any other objection?

[A gentleman rose, and desired to know why the bill provides for paying ten dollars to the commissioner for his fee in case he decided in favor of the claimant, and only five dollars if he decided against him.]

I presume, said Mr. Douglas, that the reason was that he would have more labor to perform. If, after hearing the testimony, the commissioner decided in favor of the claimant, the law made it his duty to prepare and authenticate the necessary papers to authorize him to carry the fugitive home; but if he decided against him, he had no such labor to perform. The law seems to be based upon the principle that the commissioner should be paid according to the service he should render—five dollars for presiding at the trial, and five dollars for making out the papers in case the testimony should require him to return the fugitive. This provision appears to be exciting considerable attention in the country, and I have been exceedingly gratified at the proceedings of a mass meeting held in a county not far distant, in which it was resolved unanimously that they could not be bribed for the sum of five dollars to consign a freeman to perpetual bondage! This shows an exalted state of moral feeling highly creditable to those who participated in the meeting. I doubt not they will make their influence felt throughout the state, and will instruct their members of the Legislature to reform our criminal code in this respect. Under our laws, as they have stood for many years, and probably from the organization of our state government, in all criminal cases, on the preliminary examination before the magistrates, and in all the higher courts, if the prisoner be convicted, the witnesses, jurors, and officers are entitled to their fees and bills of costs; but if he be acquitted, none of them receive a cent. In order to diffuse the same high moral sense throughout the whole community, would it not be well, at their next meeting, to pass another resolution, that they would not be bribed by the fees and costs of suit in any case, either as witnesses, jurors, magistrates, or in any other capacity, to consign an innocent man to a dismal cell in the penitentiary, or expose him to an ignominious death upon the gallows? Such a resolution might do a great deal of good in elevating the character of our people abroad, at the same time that it might inspire increased confidence in the liberality and conscientiousness of those who adopted it!

Is there any other objection to this law?

[A gentleman rose, and called the attention of Mr. Douglas to the provision vesting the appointment of the commissioners under it in the courts of law, instead of the President and Senate, and asked if that was not a violation of that provision of the Constitution which says that judges of the Supreme Court, and of the inferior courts, should be appointed by the President and Senate.]

I thank the gentleman, said Mr. D., for calling my attention to this point. It was made in the speech of a distinguished lawyer last night, and evidently produced great effect upon the minds of the audience. The gentleman's high professional standing, taken in connection with his laborious preparation for the occasion, as was apparent to all, from his lengthy written brief before him while speaking, inspired implicit confidence in the correctness of his position. My answer to the objection will be found in the Constitution itself, which I will read, so far as it bears upon this question:

"The President shall nominate, and by and with the consent of the Senate shall appoint embassadors, other public ministers, and consuls, judges of the Supreme Court, and all other officers of the United States, whose appointments are not herein otherwise provided for, and which shall be established by law."

Now it will be seen that the words "inferior courts" are not mentioned in the Constitution. The gentleman, in his zeal against the law, and his phrensy to resist it, interpolated these words, and then made a plausible argument upon them. I trust this was all unintentional, or was done with the view of fulfilling the "higher law." But there is another sentence in this same clause of the Constitution which I have not yet read. It is as follows:

"But the Congress may by law vest the appointment of such inferior officers as they think proper in the President alone, in the courts of law, or in the heads of departments."

The practice under this clause has usually been to confer the power of appointing those inferior officers, whose duties were executive or ministerial, upon the President alone, or upon the head of the appropriate department; and in like manner to give to the courts of law the privilege of appointing their subordinates, whose duties were in their nature judicial. What is meant by "inferior courts," whose appointment may be vested in the "courts of law," will be seen by reference to the 8th section of the Constitution, where the powers of Congress are enumerated, and among them is the following:

"To constitute tribunals inferior to the Supreme Court."

Is the tribunal which is to carry the Fugitive Law into effect inferior to the Supreme Court of the United States? If it is, the Constitution expressly provides for vesting the appointment in the courts of law. I will remark, however, that these commissioners are not appointed under the new law, but in obedience to an act of Congress which has stood on the statute-books for many years. If those who denounce and misrepresent the act of last session had condescended to read it before they undertook to enlighten the people upon it, they would have saved themselves the mortification of exposure, as I will show by reading the first section.

Here Mr. Douglas read the law, and proceeded to remark: Thus it will be seen that these commissioners have been in office for years, with their duties prescribed by law, nearly all of which were of a judicial character, and that the new law only imposes additional duties, and authorizes the increase of the number. Why has not this grave constitutional objection been discovered before, and the people informed how their rights have been outraged in violation of the supreme law of the land? Truly, the passage of the Fugitive Bill has thrown a flood of light upon constitutional principles!

Is there any other objection to the new law which does not apply to the act of '93?

[A gentleman rose, and said that he would like to ask another question, which was this: if the new law was so similar to the old one, what was the necessity of passing any at all, since the old one was still in force?]

Mr. Douglas, in reply, said, that is the very question I was anxious some one should propound, because I was desirous of an opportunity of answering it. The old law answered all the purposes for which it was enacted tolerably well until the decision by the Supreme Court of the United States, in the case of Priggs v. the State of Pennsylvania, eight or nine years ago. That decision rendered the law comparatively inoperative, for the reason that there were scarcely any officers left to execute it. It will be recollected that the act of '93 imposed the duty of carrying it into effect upon the magistrates and other officers under the state governments. These officers performed their duties under that law with fidelity for about fifty years, until the Supreme Court, in the case alluded to, decided that they were under no legal obligation to do so, and that Congress had no constitutional power to impose the duty upon them. From that time many of the officers refused to act, and soon afterward the Legislature of Massachusetts, and many other states, passed laws making it criminal for their officers to perform these duties. Hence the old law, although efficient in its provisions, and similar in most respects, and especially in those objected to almost identical with the new law, became comparatively a dead letter for want of officers to carry it into effect. The judges of the United States courts were the only officers left who were authorized to execute it. In this state, for instance, Judge Drummond, whose residence was in the extreme northwest corner of the state, within six miles of Wisconsin and three of Iowa, and in the direction where fugitives were least likely to go, was the only person authorized to try the case.

If a fugitive was arrested at Shawneetown or Alton, three or four hundred miles from the residence of the judge, the master would attempt to take him across the river to his home in Kentucky or Missouri, without first establishing his right to do so. This was calculated to excite uneasiness and doubts in the minds of our citizens as to the propriety of permitting the negro to be carried out of the state, without the fact of his owing service, and having escaped, being first proved, lest it might turn out that the negro was a free man and the claimant a kidnapper. And yet, according to the express terms of the old law, the master was authorized to seize his slave wherever he found him, and to carry him back without process, or trial, or proof of any kind whatsoever. Hence it was necessary to pass the act of last session, in order to carry into effect, in a peaceable and orderly manner, the provisions of the law and the Constitution on the one hand, and to protect the free colored man from being kidnapped and sold into slavery by unprincipled men on the other hand. The purpose of the new law is to accomplish these two objects—to appoint officers to carry the law into effect, in the place of the magistrates relieved from that duty by the decision of the Supreme Court, and to guard against harassing and kidnapping the free blacks, by preventing the claimant from carrying the negro out of the state until he establishes his legal right to do so. The new law, therefore, is a great improvement in this respect upon the old one, and is more favorable to justice and freedom, and better guarded against abuse.

[A person present asked leave to propound another question to Mr. Douglas, which was this: "If the new law is more favorable to freedom than the old one, why did the Southern slaveholders vote for it, and desire its passage?"]

Mr. Douglas said he would answer that question with a great deal of pleasure. The Southern members voted for it for the reason that it was a better law than the old one—better for them, better for us, and better for the free blacks. It places the execution of the law in the hands of responsible officers of the government, instead of leaving every man to take the law into his own hands and to execute it for himself. It affords personal security to the claimant while arresting his servant and taking him back, by providing him with the opportunity of establishing his legal rights, by competent testimony before a tribunal duly authorized to try the case, and thus allay all apprehensions and suspicions, on the part of our citizens, that he is a villain, attempting to steal a free man for the purpose of selling him into slavery. The slaveholder has as strong a desire to protect the rights of the free black man as we have, and much more interest to do so; for he well knows that if outrages should be tolerated under the law, and free men are seized and carried into slavery, from that moment the indignant outcry against it would be so strong here and every where, that even a fugitive from labor could not be returned, lest he also might happen to be free. The interest of the slaveholder, therefore, requires a law which shall protect the rights of all free men, black or white, from any invasion or violation whatever. I ask the question, therefore, whether this law is not better than the old one—better for the North and the South—better for the peace and quiet of the whole country? Let it be remembered that this law is but an amendment to the act of '93, and that the old law still remains in force, except so far as it is modified by this. Every man who voted against this modification thereby voted to leave the old law in force; for I am not aware that any member of either house of Congress ever had the hardihood to propose to repeal the law, and make no provisions to carry the Constitution into effect. But the cry of repeal, as to the new law, has already gone forth. Well, suppose it succeeds; what will those have gained who joined in the shout? Have I not shown that all the material objections they urge against the new law apply with equal force to the old one? What do they gain, therefore, unless they propose to repeal the old law also, and make no provisions for performing our obligations under the Constitution? This must be the object of all men who take that position. To this it must come in the end. The real objection is not to the new law, nor to the old one, but to the Constitution itself. Those of you who hold these opinions do not mean that the fugitive from labor shall be taken back. That is the real point of your objection. You would not care a farthing about the new law or the old law, or any other law, or what provisions it contained, if there was a hole in it big enough for the fugitive to slip through and escape. Habeas corpuses—trials by jury—records from other states—pains and penalties—the whole catalogue of objections, would be all moonshine, if the negro was not required to go back to his master. Tell me frankly, is not this the true character of your objection?

[Here several gentlemen gave an affirmative answer.]

Mr. Douglas said he would answer that objection by reading a portion of the Constitution of the United States. He then read as follows:

"No person held to service or labor in one state, under the laws thereof, escaping into another, shall, in consequence of any law or regulation therein, be discharged from such service or labor, BUT SHALL BE DELIVERED UP on the claim of the party to whom such service or labor may be due."

This, said Mr. D., is the supreme law of the land, speaking to every citizen of the republic. The command is imperative. There is no avoiding—no escaping the obligation, so long as we live under, and claim the protection of, the Constitution. We must yield implicit obedience, or we must take the necessary steps to release ourselves from the obligation to obey. There is no other alternative. We must stand by the Constitution of the Union, with all its compromises, or we must abolish it, and resolve each state back into its original elements. It is, therefore, a question of union or disunion. We can not expect our brethren of other states to remain faithful to the compact, and permit us to be faithless. Are we prepared, therefore, to execute faithfully and honestly the compact our fathers have made for us?

[Here a gentleman rose, and inquired of Mr. Douglas whether the clause in the Constitution providing for the surrender of fugitive slaves was not in violation of the law of God?]

Mr. Douglas in reply—The divine law is appealed to as authority for disregarding our most sacred duties to society. The city council have appealed to it as their excuse for nullifying an act of Congress; and a committee embodied the same principle in their resolutions to the meeting in this hall last night, as applicable both to the Constitution and laws. The general proposition that there is a law paramount to all human enactments—the law of the Supreme Ruler of the Universe—I trust that no civilized and Christian people is prepared to question, much less deny. We should all recognize, respect, and revere the divine law. But we should bear in mind that the law of God, as revealed to us, is intended to operate on our consciences, and insure the performance of our duties as individuals and Christians. The divine law does not prescribe the form of government under which we shall live, and the character of our political and civil institutions. Revelation has not furnished us with a Constitution—a code of international law—and a system of civil and municipal jurisprudence. It has not determined the right of persons and property, much less the peculiar privileges which shall be awarded to each class of persons under any particular form of government. God has created man in his own image, and endowed him with the right of self-government, so soon as he shall evince the requisite intelligence, virtue, and capacity to assert and enjoy the privilege. The history of the world furnishes few examples where any considerable portion of the human race have shown themselves sufficiently enlightened and civilized to exercise the rights and enjoy the blessings of freedom. In Asia and Africa we find nothing but ignorance, superstition, and despotism. Large portions of Europe and America can scarcely lay claim to civilization and Christianity; and a still smaller portion have demonstrated their capacity for self-government. Is all this contrary to the laws of God? And if so, who is responsible? The civilized world have always held that when any race of men have shown themselves so degraded, by ignorance, superstition, cruelty, and barbarism, as to be utterly incapable of governing themselves, they must, in the nature of things, be governed by others, by such laws as are deemed applicable to their condition. It is upon this principle alone that England justifies the form of government she has established in the Indies, and for some of her other colonies—that Russia justifies herself in holding her serfs as slaves, and selling them as a part of the land on which they live—that our Pilgrim Fathers justified themselves in reducing the negro and Indian to servitude, and selling them as property—that we, in Illinois and most of the free states, justify ourselves in denying the negro and the Indian the privilege of voting, and all other political rights—and that many of the states of the Union justify themselves in depriving the white man of the right of the elective franchise, unless he is fortunate enough to own a certain amount of property.

These things certainly violate the principle of absolute equality among men, when considered as component parts of a political society or government, and so do many provisions of the Constitution of the United States, as well as the several states of the Union. In fact, no government ever existed on earth in which there was a perfect equality in all things among those composing it and governed by it. Neither sacred nor profane history furnishes an example. If inequality in the form and principles of government is therefore to be deemed a violation of the laws of God, and punishable as such, who is to escape? Under this principle all Christendom is doomed, and no pagan can hope for mercy! Many of these things are, in my opinion, unwise and unjust, and, of course, subversive of Republican principles; but I am not prepared to say that they are either sanctioned or condemned by the divine law. Who can assert that God has prescribed the form and principles of government, and the character of the political, municipal, and domestic institutions of men on earth? This doctrine would annihilate the fundamental principle upon which our political system rests. Our forefathers held that the people had an inherent right to establish such Constitution and laws for the government of themselves and their posterity as they should deem best calculated to insure the protection of life, liberty, and the pursuit of happiness, and that the same might be altered and changed as experience should satisfy them to be necessary and proper. Upon this principle the Constitution of the United States was formed, and our glorious Union established. All acts of Congress passed in pursuance of the Constitution are declared to be the supreme laws of the land, and the Supreme Court of the United States is charged with expounding the same. All officers and magistrates under the federal and state governments—executive, legislative, judicial, and ministerial—are required to take an oath to support the Constitution before they can enter upon the performance of their respective duties. Any citizen, therefore, who in his conscience believes that the Constitution of the United States is in violation of a "higher law," has no right, as an honest man, to take office under it, or exercise any other function of citizenship conferred by it. Every person born under the Constitution owes allegiance to it, and every naturalized citizen takes an oath to support it. Fidelity to the Constitution is the only passport to the enjoyment of rights under it. When a senator elect presents his credentials, he is not allowed to take his seat until he places his hand upon the Holy Evangelist, and appeals to his God for the sincerity of his vow to support the Constitution. He who does this, with a mental reservation or secret intention to disregard any provision of the Constitution, commits a double crime—is morally guilty of perfidy to his God and treason to his country!

If the Constitution of the United States is to be repudiated upon the ground that it is repugnant to the divine law, where are the friends of freedom and Christianity to look for another and a better? Who is to be the prophet to reveal the will of God, and establish a theocracy for us?

Is he to be found in the ranks of Northern abolitionism or of Southern disunion; or is the Common Council of the city of Chicago to have the distinguished honor of furnishing the chosen one? I will not venture to inquire what are to be the form and principles of the new government, or to whom is to be intrusted the execution of its sacred functions; for when we decide that the wisdom of our Revolutionary fathers was foolishness, and their piety wickedness, and destroy the only system of self-government that has ever realized the hopes of the friends of freedom, and commanded the respect of mankind, it becomes us to wait patiently until the purposes of the Latter-Day Saints shall be revealed unto us.

For my part, I am prepared to maintain and preserve inviolate the Constitution as it is, with all its compromises; to stand or fall by the American Union, clinging with the tenacity of life to all its glorious memories of the past and precious hopes for the future.

Mr. Douglas then explained the circumstances which rendered his absence unavoidable when the vote was taken on the Fugitive Bill in the Senate. He wished to avoid no responsibility on account of that absence, and therefore desired it to be distinctly understood that he should have voted for the bill if he could have been present. He referred to several of our most prominent and respected citizens by name as personally cognizant of the fact that he was anxious at that time to give that vote. He believed the passage of that or some other efficient law a solemn duty, imperatively demanded by the Constitution. In conclusion, Mr. D. made an earnest appeal to our citizens to rally as one man to the defense of the Constitution and laws, and, above all things, and under all circumstances, to put down violence and disorder by maintaining the supremacy of the laws. He referred to our high character for law and order heretofore, and also to the favorable position of our city for commanding the trade between the North and South, through our canals and railroads, to show that our views and principles of action should be broad, liberal, and national, calculated to encourage union and harmony instead of disunion and sectional bitterness. He concluded by remarking that he considered this question of fidelity to the Constitution and supremacy of the laws as so far paramount to all other considerations, that he had prepared some resolutions to cover these points only, which he would submit to the meeting, and take their judgment upon them. If he had consulted his own feelings and views only, he should have embraced in the resolutions a specific approval of all the measures of the compromise; but as the question of rebellion and resistance to the federal government has been distinctly presented, it has been thought advisable to meet that issue on this occasion, distinct and separate from all others.

Mr. Douglas then offered the following resolutions, which were adopted without a dissenting voice:

Resolved, That it is the sacred duty of every friend of the Union to maintain, and preserve inviolate, every provision of our federal Constitution.

Resolved, That any law enacted by Congress, in pursuance of the Constitution, should be respected as such by all good and law-abiding citizens, and should be faithfully carried into effect by the officers charged with its execution.

Resolved, That so long as the Constitution of the United States provides that all persons held to service or labor in one state, escaping into another state, "SHALL BE DELIVERED UP on the claim of the party to whom the service or labor may be due," and so long as members of Congress are required to take an oath to support the Constitution, it is their solemn and religious duty to pass all laws necessary to carry that provision of the Constitution into effect.

Resolved, That if we desire to preserve the Union, and render our great republic inseparable and perpetual, we must perform all our obligations under the Constitution, at the same time that we call upon our brethren in other states to yield implicit obedience to it.

Resolved, That as the lives, property, and safety of ourselves and our families depend upon the observance and protection of the laws, every effort to excite any portion of our population to make resistance to the due execution of the laws of the land should be promptly and emphatically condemned by every good citizen.

Resolved, That we will stand or fall by the American Union and its Constitution, with all its compromises, with its glorious memories of the past and precious hopes of the future.

[The following was offered in addition by B. S. Morris, and also adopted:]

Resolved, That we, the people of Chicago, repudiate the resolutions passed by the Common Council of Chicago upon the subject of the Fugitive Slave Law passed by Congress at its last session.

On the succeeding night the Common Council of the city repealed their nullifying resolution by a vote of 12 to 1.

CHAPTER X.

THE KANSAS-NEBRASKA ACT.

WHATEVER question or doubt may have existed or may now exist as to the authorship of the Compromise Acts of 1850 respecting the Territories, there is not the slightest question as to where the responsibility—the honor or blame, the credit or odium—for the Kansas-Nebraska Act, belongs. No one has denied that to Stephen A. Douglas belongs whatever fame that justly attaches to an act of legislation, which has been more celebrated (for the censure by its enemies, and praise by its friends) than any act of Congress since the foundation of the government. During its pendency it was used as a pretext by the fanatics of the North for the wildest exhibition of ungovernable fury. It drew upon its author the most unbounded abuse and denunciation; while it was pending in Congress a storm, such as has never been known in the political annals of the country was gathering, and it broke with all its force upon his head. Undismayed by threats, he followed the chart that he had laid down, and has lived to see himself the political hero and leader of his own party in all those states where the storm beat fastest and raged the fiercest.

Though Mr. Douglas has gained all the credit and all the opprobrium of the "Nebraska Bill," and to a great extent his name is more prominently associated with that, than with any previous act of public interest, the truth is, that the Kansas-Nebraska Act and its repeal of the Missouri restriction was not an original measure. It was but a second volume in the history of the struggle for popular right, commenced in the contest over the Compromise of 1850; it was but another act in the grand drama which in 1850 had ended with a full recognition of the freedom of the American people, whether in state or territory, to regulate their own domestic relations without interference by Congress. The Kansas-Nebraska Act was nothing more nor less than an act to extend to the people of Kansas and Nebraska the same rights and privileges which, in 1850, by the advice, by the aid and support of the patriot

Henry Clay, had been extended to the people of Utah and New Mexico. Search the bill from one end to the other, examine in detail all its provisions, and it will be found to contain no more and no less than that the free, hardy, white American settlers of Kansas and Nebraska shall have the same right to govern themselves that in 1850 was extended to the semi-civilized and amalgamated races that peopled the newly acquired Territories of New Mexico and Utah.

But, it is said, in passing that bill, Douglas repealed the Missouri restriction—repealed the act of Congress which declared that north of the line of 36° 30′ slavery should not exist, and that south of it, it might exist. It repealed a guaranty and a prohibition—both wrong in principle, unconstitutional, and wholly inconsistent with any sound rule of justice and propriety. The people north of 36° 30′ were as much entitled to have slaves if they desired them as the people south of that line, and the restriction was not upon slavery but upon the freedom and political rights of the people. South of 36° 30′ the people were recognized as capable of self government and as safe depositaries of the power to have or reject the institution of slavery, while those living north of that line were bound with the degrading limitation—that if left to govern themselves they would certainly misuse the power to their own injury. It was a restriction which in terms and effect discriminated against the intelligence and capacity of the northern people.

As has been shown in the brief history, given in these pages, of the Compromise measures of 1850, the struggle in those days was over the question whether the people should be allowed to legislate to the exclusion or introduction of African slavery. The struggle took place on the "Omnibus Bill," and so decisive and complete was the action then, that when that Omnibus broke down, and Mr. Douglas' separate measures came up, the attempt to take that power out of the hands of the people was not renewed, and the bills passed without a question on that point.

In 1854, when it became necessary to establish a territorial government over the western territory—a proposition long pending but never seriously needed until then—Mr. Douglas, as Chairman of the Committee on Territories, regarding the action of the Senate and of Congress upon the Compromise

Acts of 1850, and also the emphatic endorsement of those measures by the people in 1852, as conclusive as to the principles upon which the Territorial question should be governed, so framed his bill as to make it identical in all essential matters with the acts of 1850. On the 4th of January he reported the bill for the establishment of a territorial government for Nebraska, and at the same time made a written report which stated that the bill was designed to carry out in good faith the principle adopted by Congress in the measures of 1850, and the report closed as follows:

From these provisions it is apparent that the compromise measures of 1850 affirm and rest upon the following propositions:

First.—That all questions pertaining to slavery in the territories, and in the new states to be formed therefrom, are to be left to the decision of the people residing therein, by their appropriate representatives, to be chosen by them for that purpose.

Second.—That "all cases involving title to slaves," and "questions of personal freedom," are referred to the adjudication of the local tribunals, with the right of appeal to the Supreme Court of the United States.

Third.—That the provisions of the Constitution of the United States, in respect to fugitives from service, is to be carried into faithful execution in all "the organized territories" the same as in the states. The substitute for the bill which your committee have prepared, and which is commended to the favorable action of the Senate, proposes to carry these propositions and principles into practical operation, in the precise language of the compromise measures of 1850.

It will be seen by the report that the committee did not recommend the repeal, in express terms, of the Missouri restriction, though they declared that the bill, as reported by them, left the question of slavery in the territory "to the decision of the people residing therein, by their appropriate representatives chosen by them for that purpose." Their object was to leave the people of Nebraska and Kansas, as the people of Utah and New Mexico had been left, free to act for themselves in the matter of slavery. That part of the report has been frequently quoted by the enemies of popular right to show that the repeal of the Missouri Compromise was an "after-thought," and agreed upon afterwards at the dictation of the "slave oligarchy." The committee stated distinctly that they designed to leave the people of the territory, through their legislature, all the legislative power over slavery, and all other questions, that was conceded by the legislature of 1850 to the Territories of Utah and New Mexico. The committee evidently supposed and intended that the words of the bill declaring " that the legislative power of said territory shall extend to all rightful subjects of legislation," removed all obstacles to the exercise of that power over the subject of slavery; and that, therefore, the act of Congress interdicting slavery might be left, as was the Mexican law in the other cases, to the courts for a decision as to its authority and legal force. Be that as it may, the committee soon found that a wide difference of opinion prevailed in the Senate as to the effect of the language of the bill. Did it leave the territorial legislature free to act upon the subject of slavery? How could the legislature act when an act of Congress stood in their way prohibiting the existence of slavery north of 36° 30'. It was necessary to make the bill clear and distinct upon this point. Did the Missouri restriction bind the hands of the territorial legislature against the admission of slavery? If it did, then while that restriction existed as a law the people of Nebraska could not be admitted to the enjoyment of the same freedom in legislation that was secured by the acts of 1850 to the people of Utah and New Mexico; and consequently the principle of the Compromise Act could not be applied to the territorial act designed for Nebraska and Kansas. The removal of the Missouri restriction was imperatively necessary if the territorial legislature was to be left free to exercise the power of legislation respecting African slavery. To do that—to remove all obstacles in the way of the free and full exercise of legislative power over that as well as all other subjects of domestic concern—the Missouri restriction was repealed; it was repealed for no other reason, because there *was no other possible reason for repealing it*. It stood in the way of the practical application of the principle established in the acts of 1850. If allowed to stand, it would create the necessity for the organization of territorial governments for Nebraska and Kansas on a principle and theory totally distinct and different from that followed in the cases of Utah and New Mexico. The North, in 1850, had perseveringly and successfully struggled for the recognition of the power and authority of the territorial legislature over the subject of African slavery. The North, by an almost unanimous vote for Scott and Pierce in 1852, had approved and ratified the action of Congress in 1850. Was the North now, in 1854, to change front? Was the North to repudiate the principles it had asserted in 1850, and clamor again for the empty and valueless Congressional prohibition ?

On the first day of the session Mr. Dodge, of Iowa, gave notice of his intention to introduce a bill for the government of the Territory of Nebraska; on the 4th of December he did introduce the bill, which was referred to the Committee on Territories, of which Mr. Douglas was chairman. On the 4th of January Mr. Douglas, as has been stated, reported the bill back with amendments. On the 23d of January the committee made the report already noticed, and reported a further amendment dividing the immense region into two territories, Kansas and Nebraska. This division was made upon the solicitation of the representatives of the people of the territory, and by the advice of the representatives in Congress from Iowa and Missouri.

In the meantime, on the 16th of January, Mr. Dixon, of Kentucky, had given notice that when the bill was taken up for action he would offer as an amendment the following :

"That so much of the eighth section of an act approved March 6, 1820, entitled 'An Act to authorize the people of the Missouri Territory to form a Constitution and state government, and for the admission of such state into the Union on an equal footing with the original states, and to prohibit slavery in certain territories,' as declares 'that in all that territory ceded by France to the United States, under the name of Louisiana, which lies north of thirty-six degrees thirty minutes north latitude, slavery and involuntary servitude, otherwise than as a punishment of crimes whereof the parties shall have been duly convicted, shall be forever prohibited,' shall not be so construed as to apply to the territory contemplated by this act, or to any other territory of the United States; *but that the citizens of the several states or territories shall be at liberty to take and hold their slaves within any of the territories of the United States or of the states to be formed therefrom*, as if the said act, entitled as aforesaid, and approved as aforesaid, had never been passed."

Here was the same proposition which in 1850 had been rejected by Congress, and voted down by the friends of the Compromise. It was a proposition declaring the right of the slaveholder to carry his slaves into the territory. In 1850, those who supported the right of the territorial legislature to legislate on that subject refused to declare by Congressional act the right to take slaves into the territory, because such a provision in an act of Congress would override an act of the territorial legislature. In the bill, as reported on the 23d of January, the committee expressed more clearly what was originally their intention respecting the removal of the Missouri restriction. In the fourteenth section of the Nebraska-Kansas act they provided:

"That the Constitution and all laws of the United States which are not locally inapplicable, shall have the same force and effect within the said territory of Nebraska as elsewhere within the United States; except the eighth section of the act preparatory to the admission of Missouri into the Union, approved March sixth, eighteen hundred and twenty, which was superseded by the principles of the legislation of eighteen hundred and fifty, commonly called the compromise measures, and is hereby declared inoperative."

We doubt whether in the history of legislation any one sentence in a proposed measure ever furnished the pretext for a political agitation equal to that which followed the report of the above.

The necessity for repealing the Missouri restriction, if it was intended to frame the Nebraska bill by the principles of the acts of 1850, had been seen as well by the extremists at the north as by those of the south; and, almost simultaneously with Mr. Dixon's proposition to extend slavery, another was presented by Mr. Sumner, of Massachusetts, that nothing contained in the bill "shall be construed to abrogate or in any way contravene the act of March 6, 1820," in which it was declared that slavery was prohibited in the Louisiana territory north of 36° 30'.

Here was the old contest of 1850 about to be renewed. The Dixon amendment, proposing to recognize an extension of slavery by Congressional enactment; the Sumner amendment proposing a Congressional prohibition of slavery. Both were opposed to and inconsistent with the right of the territorial legislature to regulate that as well as all other domestic relations; which right having been expressly conceded to the people of New Mexico and Utah by the acts of 1850, it was the aim and purpose of Mr. Douglas to secure to the people of Nebraska and Kansas. He rejected both propositions, and adhered to the principle and policy so emphatically sanctioned in 1850 by Congress and subsequently ratified by the people.

On Tuesday, *January* 24, the bill was taken up. Mr. Chase, of Ohio, urged that the Senate had not had an opportunity of examining the bill; he said, "only yesterday the committee changed the form of the bill altogether, and proposed to create two territories instead of one, and also changed materially the provisions upon other questions of very great public interest; and the bill thus having been changed in fact into two bills, has been only laid on the tables of Senators this morning, *and I presume no one has had an opportunity to read it.* It involves very important matters, and I think that when we take it up it should be with a determination to proceed with it until it shall be disposed of." He then urged that it be postponed until the next week.

Mr. Sumner suggested that it be postponed until the 31st of January.

Mr. Douglas acquiesced in the request, and on his motion the bill was postponed to Monday, January 30th.

This request to postpone an important bill for one week may seem to the reader to have been a trivial matter for special notice here, but it subsequently became the subject of a protracted and exciting debate. The request was made on Tuesday, January 24th. On the Monday after, January 30th, the bill was again taken up, and the request of Mr. Chase, with its purposes and aims, were made historical in all their infamy.

As soon as the bill was taken up Mr. Douglas said :

"When I proposed, on Tuesday last, that the Senate should proceed to the consideration of the bill to organize the Territories of Nebraska and Kansas, it was my purpose only to occupy ten or fifteen minutes in explanation of its provisions. I desired to refer to two points—first, to those provisions relating to the Indians, and second, to those which might be supposed to bear upon the question of slavery. * * * *

"Upon the other point—that pertaining to the question of slavery in the territories—it was the intention of the committee to be equally explicit. We took the principles established by the compromise acts of 1850 as our guide, and intended to make each and every provision of the bill accord with these principles. These measures are established and rest upon the great principles of self-government—that the people should be allowed to decide the questions of their domestic institutions for themselves, subject only to such limitations and restrictions as are imposed by the Constitution of the United States, instead of having them determined by an arbitrary or geographical line.

"The original bill reported by the committee as a substitute for the bill introduced by the senator from Iowa (Mr. Dodge), was believed to have accomplished this object. The amendment which was subsequently reported by us was only designed to render that clear and specific which seemed, in the minds of some, to admit of doubt and misconstruction. In some parts of the country the original substitute was deemed and construed to be an annulment or a repeal of what has been known as the Missouri Compromise, while in other parts it was otherwise construed. As the object of the committee was to conform to the principles established by the compromise measures of 1850, and to carry these principles into effect in the territories, we thought it was better to recite in the bill precisely what we understood to have been accomplished by those measures, viz., that the Missouri Compromise, having been superseded by the legislation of 1850, has become, and ought to be declared, inoperative; and hence we propose to leave the ques-

I

tion to the people of the states and the territories, subject only to the limitations and provisions of the Constitution.

"Sir, this is all that I intended to say if the question had been taken up for consideration on Tuesday last, but since that time occurrences have transpired which compel me to go more fully into the discussion. It will be borne in mind that the Senator from Ohio (Mr. Chase), then objected to the consideration of the bill, and asked for its postponement until this day, on the ground that there had not been time to understand and consider its provisions; and the Senator from Massachusetts (Mr. Sumner) suggested that the postponement should be for one week for that purpose. These suggestions seeming to be reasonable in the opinion of senators around me I yielded to their request, and consented to the postponement of the bill until this day.

"Sir, little did I suppose, at the time that I granted that act of courtesy to those two senators, that they had drafted and published to the world a document, over their own signatures, in which they arraigned me as having been guilty of a criminal betrayal of my trust, as having been guilty of an act of bad faith, and as having been engaged in an atrocious plot against the cause of free government. Little did I suppose that those two senators had been guilty of such conduct, when they called upon me to grant that courtesy, to give them an opportunity of investigating the substitute reported by the committee. I have since discovered that on that very morning the *National Era*, the abolition organ in this city, contained an address, signed by certain abolition confederates, to the people, in which the bill is grossly misrepresented, in which the action of the committee is grossly perverted, in which our motives are arraigned and our characters calumniated. And, sir, what is more, I find that there was a postscript added to the address, published that very morning, in which the principal amendment reported by the committee was set out, and then coarse epithets applied to me by name. Sir, had I known those facts at the time I granted that act of indulgence, I should have responded to the request of those senators in such terms as their conduct deserved, so far as the rules of the Senate and a respect for my own character would have permitted me to do. In order to show the character of this document, of which I shall have much to say in the course of my argument, I will read certain passages:

"'We arraign this bill as a gross violation of a sacred pledge; as a criminal betrayal of precious rights; as part and parcel of an atrocious plot to exclude from a vast unoccupied region emigrants from the Old World and free laborers from our own states, and convert it into a dreary region of despotism, inhabited by masters and slaves.'

"*A Senator.* By whom is the address signed?

"*Mr. Douglas.* It is signed 'S. P. Chase, senator from Ohio, Charles Sumner, senator from Massachusetts, J. R. Giddings and Edward Wade, representatives from Ohio, Gerrit Smith, representative from New York, Alexander De Witt, representative from Massachusetts;' including, as I understand, all the abolition party in Congress.

"Then, speaking of the Committee on Territories, these confederates use this language:

"'The *pretences*, therefore, that the territory, covered by the positive prohibition of 1820, sustains a similar relation to slavery with that acquired from Mexico, covered by no prohibition except that of disputed constitutional or Mexican law, and that the Compromises of 1850 require the incorporation of the pro-slavery clause of the Utah and New Mexico bill in the Nebraska act, are mere *inventions, designed to cover up from public reprehension meditated bad faith.*'

"'Mere inventions to cover up bad faith.' Again:

" ' Servile demagogues may tell you that the Union can be maintained only by submitting to the demands of slavery.' "

"Then there is a postscript added, equally offensive to myself, in which I am mentioned by name. The address goes on to make an appeal to the Legislatures of the different states, to public meetings, and to ministers of the gospel in their pulpits, to interpose and arrest the vile proceeding which is about to be consummated by the senators who are thus denounced. That address, sir, bears date Sunday, January 22, 1854. Thus it appears that on the holy Sabbath, while other senators were engaged in divine worship, these abolition confederates were assembled in secret conclave, plotting by what means they should deceive the people of the United States, and prostrate the character of brother senators. This was done on the Sabbath day, and by a set of politicians, to advance their own political and ambitious purposes, in the name of our holy religion.

"But this is not all. It was understood from the newspapers that resolutions were pending before the Legislature of Ohio proposing to express their opinions upon this subject. It was necessary for these confederates to get up some exposition of the question by which they might facilitate the passage of the resolutions through that Legislature. Hence you find that on the same morning that this document appears over the names of these confederates in the abolition organs in this city, the same document appears in the New York papers—certainly in the *Tribune, Times,* and *Evening Post*—in which it stated, on authority, that it is 'signed by the senators and a majority of the representatives from the State of Ohio'—a statement which I have every reason to believe was utterly false, and known to be so at the time that these confederates appended it to the address. It was necessary in order to carry out this work of deception, and to hasten the action of the Ohio Legislature, under a misapprehension of the real facts, to state that it was signed, not only by the abolition confederates, but by the whole Whig representation, and a portion of the Democratic representation in the other House from the State of Ohio.

" *Mr. Chase.* Mr. President—

" *Mr. Douglas.* Mr. President, I do not yield the floor. A senator who has violated all the rules of courtesy and propriety, who showed a consciousness of the character of the act he was doing by concealing from me all knowledge of the fact—who came to me with a smiling face, and the appearance of friendship, even after that document had been uttered—who could get up in the Senate and appeal to my courtesy in order to get time to give the document a wider circulation before its infamy could be exposed—such a senator has no right to my courtesy upon this floor."

Mr. Douglas then, in an argument extended over two hours, discussed the general history of the legislation by Congress upon the subject of slavery in Congress, and in defense of his position that the principle established in the acts of 1850 was inconsistent with a congressional prohibition of slavery, such as was contained in the eighth section of the Missouri Act.

Mr. Chase followed in a lame apology. He ignored the fact that on the 24th he had suggested that no senator had read the bill. He admitted that the address had been published in one New York paper on the 23d, and said that the date prefixed to the document as printed was a typographical error

The representation made that the address bore the signatures of a majority of the Ohio delegates was made under an impression that they would sign it; but as alterations in the document were demanded, which could not be conceded, the address had been sent out in the original form by those whose names had been attached to it. He produced a copy of the address bearing date January 19th, yet even in that copy there was set forth a correct copy of the fourteenth section of the bill as reported by the Committee on Territories on Monday, January 23d. How a copy of that section had been obtained, so as to incorporate it in an address bearing date the 19th, was not explained.

Mr. Sumner declined any explanation. He fell back upon his dignity, and assumed all the responsibility for what he had done.

The trick, so far as it was designed to create a false impression of the character of the bill, and to produce a violent hostility to it, founded upon that false impression, was more successful, perhaps, than any like disreputable act had ever been. The Legislatures of most of the states were then in session; this address reached the members; no explanation of the bill had been made in Congress; its terms and provisions had not been published in the newspapers of the day. The address was sent all over the North. It found its way by hundreds into every village in the Northern states. Petitions and remonstrances were printed and sent abroad for signatures. In the absence of all explanations or counter statements, the language of the address was well calculated to produce alarm and excitement. Its appeals were earnest, and its authors had not hesitated to assert untruths whenever such would serve to make their appeal more forcible or their pathos more sensational.

Here is an extract:

"Take your maps, fellow-citizens, we entreat you, and see what country it is which this bill, gratuitously and recklessly, *proposes to open to slavery.*"

＊　　＊　　＊　　＊　　＊　　＊　　＊　　＊　　＊

"This immense region, occupying the very heart of the North American continent, and larger by thirty-three thousand square miles than all the existing free states, excluding California,—this immense region, well watered and fertile, through which the middle and northern routes, from the Atlantic to the Pacific must pass,—this immense region, embracing all the unorganized territory of the nation, except the comparatively insignificant district of Indian Territory north of Red River, and between Arkansas and Texas, and now for more than thirty years regarded by the common consent of the

American people as consecrated to freedom by statute and compact—this immense region the bill now before the Senate, without reason and without excuse, but in flagrant disregard of sound policy and sacred faith, *purposes to open to slavery.*"   *   *   *   *   *   *

"We confess our total inability properly to delineate the character or describe the consequences of this measure. Language fails to express the sentiments of indignation and abhorrence which it inspires; and no vision less penetrating and comprehensive than that of the All-Seeing can reach its evil issues.

"We appeal to the people. We warn you that the dearest interests of freedom and the Union are in imminent peril.

"We implore Christians and Christian ministers to interpose. Their divine religion requires them to behold in every man a brother, and to labor for the advancement and regeneration of the human race."

Reader, the bill of which these men were writing was one declaring that the free white men of Nebraska and Kansas, like their countrymen in the states and territories, were capable of self-government, and that they were of right entitled to and ought to be allowed the privilege of legislating as freely upon the subject of African slavery as upon any other question of territorial government.

The circulation of this address was promptly followed by every possible effort to prejudice the public mind against the bill. Thousands of the people did get alarmed. They did believe that "the interests of freedom and the Union were in imminent peril." Agitation was incessant; excitement followed agitation and in a few weeks the evil work of misrepresentation and fanaticism had accomplished to a great extent its ends. Christian ministers in all sincerity believed the statements of the address. They never supposed that men holding high position as senators would, under an appeal in the name of Christianity, promulgate the wildest perversions of truth. They thought that an irreparable evil was threatened in the Nebraska bill; they, therefore, hurriedly affixed their names to printed petitions prepared and distributed among them. By the trick described, the conspirators had gained an advantage over the supporters of the bill. Their address had been issued ten days before any explanation of the bill had been made, and when that explanation was made, it was impossible to send it where the address had gone. In the interval, an opposition to the bill, and a prejudice against its author and supporters had been established so immovably that it was almost useless to rely upon any other means than time to vindicate the truth.

The Legislature of Rhode Island was the first to respond to the address. Resolutions denouncing the bill in general terms were promptly introduced and passed both Houses, and were actually presented to Congress on that same 30th of January when the bill was first taken up for consideration.

On the 1st of February, Mr. Sumner presented a memorial from citizens of Pennsylvania remonstrating against the extension of slavery to territory from which it had been excluded by the Missouri Compromise; and thenceforth, day after day until a late period of the session, and long after the passage of the act, petitions and remonstrances, responsive to the address, were presented to both Houses of Congress. It was soon announced and was so stated in debate in Congress, that the great body of the clergy of the North were uniting in a protest against the bill. Though not chronologically in order at this point of the history of the bill, yet, as it formed part, and a leading part, of the great warfare made upon the bill and its author, it may as well be noticed at this time. The form of the remonstrance or protest was the same in all parts of the country. The protest subsequently presented to the Senate by Mr. Everett from the three thousand and fifty clergymen of New England was in the following words:

"*To the Honorable the Senate and House of Representatives in Congress assembled:*

"The undersigned, clergymen of different religious denominations in New England, hereby, in the name of Almighty God, and in his presence, do solemnly protest against the passage of what is known as the Nebraska bill, or any repeal or modification of the existing legal prohibitions of slavery in that part of our national domain which it is proposed to organize into the Territories of Nebraska and Kansas. We protest against it as a great moral wrong, as a breach of faith, eminently unjust to the moral principles of the community and subversive of all confidence in national engagements; as a measure full of danger to the peace and even the existence of our beloved Union, and exposing us to the righteous judgments of the Almighty; and your protestants, as in duty bound, will ever pray.

"*Boston, Massachusetts, March* 1, 1854."

This memorial, or protest, as was explained by Mr. Everett, though dated March 1, had been signed by nearly all the protestants long previous to that day. It had taken weeks to collect and arrange all the signatures, and its date was probably the day on which the roll was completed and forwarded to Washington. It was presented to the Senate by Mr. Everett on March 14—ten days after the bill had passed the Senate.

A debate ensued, and a warm one. The protestants were charged with having assumed an authority which they did not possess; that they presumed to speak to the Senate in the name of the Almighty, and to pronounce his judgments upon the Senate for their conduct in passing the measure. Mr. Douglas bore a conspicuous part in this debate. A similar memorial from clergymen in the northwest was subsequently forwarded to him for presentation, and upon matters growing out of that he expressed his sentiments at large, in speeches and by letter.

On the 27th of March a meeting was held in Chicago, at which twenty-five clergymen were present. They adopted a protest against the Nebraska bill, and passed a series of resolutions denouncing Mr. Douglas and other senators for their remarks upon the protest of the New England clergymen. Printed slips of the proceedings of the meeting and of the protest and resolutions were forwarded to Mr. Douglas. He, under date of April 6, addressed a very elaborate letter to the reverend gentlemen composing the meeting, in which he defended himself and his fellow-senators from unjust accusations set forth in the resolutions.

In replying to the reflections cast upon him by the resolutions, he quoted the protest adopted at the meeting, from the printed slips and newspapers of Chicago sent to him.

On the 8th of May following, Mr. Douglas presented to the Senate a protest which the Rev. A. M. Stewart certified to be a true copy of the protest adopted at the meeting of the twenty-five clergymen at Chicago on the 27th of March. It had been detained until it had received the signatures of 504 clergymen of the northwest. As in his letter he had treated the protest adopted by these gentlemen as identical in terms with that of the New England clergymen, and as the one communicated to him by Mr. Stewart was quite different, inasmuch as that it did not contain the words " in the name of Almighty God," Mr. Douglas explained his action in the matter. He had received from Chicago an envelope containing a printed slip with the proceedings of the meeting; he had also received copies of two of the daily papers—both hostile to him politically, in which the protest and resolutions were set forth over the signatures of the officers of the meeting, precisely as he had quoted them in his letter. He had never doubted the correctness of those published reports of the proceedings, until after the publication of his letter of reply. He then read in one of the Chicago abolition papers a series of letters written by "one of the twenty-five," in which he was accused of having attributed language to the Chicago clergymen which they had not employed, and denounced for having reprimanded them unjustly.

Mr. Douglas in explaining this matter in the Senate, said :

" After seeing the denials to which I have referred, I wrote to Chicago to ascertain how the mistake occurred. My letters inform me that the facts are these : The meeting was held on the day stated, the 27th of March. The proceedings of the meeting were furnished by the secretary to the Chicago *Tribune*, the paper which they have selected as their organ. They were printed at the *Tribune* office ; slips were sent to the other papers ; and the slip sent to me contained the proceedings of that meeting, as furnished by the secretary. But after the publication, and when the community condemned the blasphemy of the protest, and these clergymen found that their own congregations would not submit to it, one of them called upon the editor, took back the proceedings, alleged that there was an error in them, struck out those words, and had the proceedings republished as corrected, but did not send the republication to me, and I never knew of it until I wrote to Chicago for the facts. I do not complain of their withdrawing the expression referred to. I am glad they did so. I am glad they saw the error which they had committed, and corrected it. But, sir, I submit to you whether it was right for men, fair-minded men, whatever their profession, after changing their memorial, to come out and charge me with fraud, because I replied to it in the language in which they sent it to me. I admit their right to make the modification. It was their duty to make that modification. But why persevere in a charge running through five numbers of a newspaper, over the signature of " One of the Twenty-five," endeavoring to fasten fraud upon me, when I have evidence to prove that they published their memorial in the shape in which I answered it ? I received it from them in that shape. I answered it as I found it ; and if they have discovered their error, and corrected it, they ought to acknowledge the fact, instead of charging fraud on me. I make no charge against them ; I am only vindicating myself. But, as far as I can see, the only change was in these words. Now, let me go a little further, and assume that these words, 'in the name of Almighty God,' got into their memorial by mistake ; why did they not call upon the editor of their paper, who published it, to explain how that mistake occurred, instead of charging it upon me ?"

This matter may seem to be unworthy the space it occupies, yet it serves to show how pertinaciously and unjustly he was pursued by those who honestly or otherwise regarded the Nebraska Act as a wrong. For months he was denounced through all the opposition papers of the North with having falsified the protest of the clergy of Chicago in order to write a reply ; and with having attributed to them language which they had never used. Nor was the denunciation confined to that point. As early as the 4th of March, he and the Nebraska Bill had been denounced from a pulpit in Chicago, and the sermon on that occasion had been printed and widely circulated. That was long before the protest of the New England clergy had been presented to or discussed in the Senate.

He had no paper in Chicago to defend the bill or himself. He was exposed to a constant warfare from all quarters, and had no means of defence. All the Chicago papers were open to condemn, none ventured a word in his behalf. It was his home; it was the great city of the northwest. There, in preference to all other places he needed defence, yet there he was left alone to meet the storm which falsehood, private and political malice, disappointed ambition and open knavery, were fast gathering to meet him on his return.

Now to return to the bill before the Senate.

Mr. Chase had the floor to reply to Mr. Douglas, but not being prepared to go on with his argument, he asked, and the Senate granted, a postponement until the Friday following, on that day he made an extended argument. On the 7th of February, the debate having progressed in the meantime, Mr. Douglas moved an amendment to the fourteenth section of the bill, so as that part of the bill would read as follows:

"That the Constitution and laws of the United States, which are not locally inapplicable, shall have the same force and effect within the said Territory of Nebraska as elsewhere within the United States, except the eighth section of the act preparatory to the admission of Missouri into the Union, approved March 6, 1820, which being inconsistent with the principle of non-intervention by Congress with slavery in the states and territories as recognized by the legislation of 1850, (commonly called the Compromise measure) is hereby declared inoperative and void, it being the true intent and meaning of this act not to legislate slavery into any territory or state, nor to exclude it therefrom, but to leave the people thereof perfectly free to form and regulate their domestic institutions in their own way, subject only to the Constitution of the United States."

This amendment was agreed to on the 15th, by a vote of—yeas 35, nays 10.

THE CELEBRATED "CHASE AMENDMENT."

On the 15th of February Mr. Chase proposed to insert immediately after the words above given, as having been put into the bill on the motion of Mr. Douglas, the following:

"Under which (the Constitution of the United States) the people of the territory, through their appropriate representatives, may, if they see fit, prohibit the existence of slavery therein."

As it has of late become a matter of doubt in the minds of some gentlemen who voted for and supported the Nebraska Bill, as to whether any one had ever suggested, while it was pending, that under its provisions the people of the territories, through their Legislature, would have the power to legislate upon the subject of slavery ; and as the action of the Senate upon this amendment of Mr. Chase has been quoted by all the Republican papers, by executive officers and authority, and has even been published in official journals over the signature of an intelligent senator (possibly by others), as conclusive evidence that the Senate *did not* intend to concede any such power in the Territorial Legislature, it is necessary for the sake of truth, if not of justice, and not for the purpose of contradicting the statement or calling in question the veracity of any person, that a somewhat extended notice of what took place on this amendment should be given.

For a more clear understanding of what occurred it should be borne in mind that the bill had been reported with an amendment—the latter in the nature of a substitute for the former. The substitute was the measure which the friends of the bill were maturing. The general question pending was on the adoption of the substitute in lieu of the bill. Pending that question it was in order to amend the substitute, which was of itself a pending amendment. Beyond an amendment to an amendment parliamentary law does not admit a proposal to amend. Consequently Mr. Chase's motion was an amendment to an amendment, and was not of itself open to amendment, unless he voluntarily modified his own motion.

In proposing his amendment Mr. Chase thus stated its " design :"

"Now, I desire to have the sense of the Senate upon the question, whether or not, under the limitations of the Constitution of the United States, the people of the territories can prohibit the existence of slavery."

Mr. Pratt, of Maryland, promptly responded :

" The principle which the senator from Ohio has announced as the principle of his amendment is, that the question shall be left entirely and exclusively to the people of the territories whether they will prohibit slavery or not. Now, for the purpose of testing the sincerity of the senator, and for the purpose of deducing the principle in his amendment correctly, I propose to amend it by inserting after the word 'prohibit' the words 'or introduce' · so that if my amendment be adopted, and the amendment of the senator from Ohio, as so amended, be introduced as part of the bill, the principle which he says he desires to have tested here will be inserted in the bill, that the people of the territories shall have power either to introduce or prohibit slavery as they may think proper. I suppose the question will be first taken on the amendment which I offer to the amendment."

Messrs. Seward and Chase at once raised the question that as an amendment (Chase's) to an amendment (the substitute) was pending, no further amendment was in order; and the Chair necessarily ruled Mr. Pratt's motion out of order. After some debate

Mr. Shields said: If the honorable senator (Mr. Chase) will permit me, I will suggest to him, if he wishes to test that proposition, to put the converse, as suggested by the honorable senator from Maryland, and *then it will be a fair proposition.* Let the senator from Ohio accept the amendment of the senator from Maryland, for the purpose of testing the question.

Mr. Chase: I was about to state why I could not accept the amendment of the senator from Maryland. I have no objection that the vote should be taken upon it, and it is probable that it would receive the sanction of a majority here; but with my views of the Constitution I cannot vote for it. I do not believe that a Territorial Legislature, though it may have the power to protect the people against slavery, is constitutionally competent to introduce it.

* * * * * *

Mr. Badger, of North Carolina, having called for the reading of the amendment, said:

Mr. President: I have understood, I find correctly, the purport of the amendment offered by the honorable senator from Ohio. The purpose of the amendment and the effect of the amendment, if adopted by the Senate and standing as he proposes, are clear and obvious. The effect of the amendment and the design of the amendment are to overrule and subvert the very proposition introduced into the bill upon the motion of the chairman of the Committee on Territories. Is not that clear? The provision as it stands, since the amendment has been adopted, is an unrestricted and unreserved reference to the territorial authorities or the people themselves to determine upon the question of slavery; and therefore by the very terms, as well as by the obvious meaning and legal operation of that amendment, to enable them either to exclude or to introduce or allow slavery.

"If, therefore, the amendment proposed by the senator from Ohio were appended to the bill in the connection in which he introduces it, the necessary and inevitable effect of it would be to control and limit the language which the Senate has just put into the bill, and to give it this construction: that though Congress leaves them to regulate their own domestic institutions as they please, yet, in regard to the subject matter of slavery, the power is confined to the exclusion or prohibition of it. I say this is both the legal effect and the manifest design of the amendment. The legal effect is obvious upon the statement. The design is obvious upon the refusal of the gentleman to incorporate in his amendment what was suggested by my honorable friend from Maryland, the propriety and fairness of which was instantly seen by my friend from Illinois (Mr. Shields). Is it proposed by the senator to test the question whether these people shall expressly have authority to determine for themselves upon the existence of this domestic relation? If so, and the language just put into the bill is not sufficiently explicit, in his estimation, is it not beyond all question that you should put in the words 'or introduce?' Under the bill, as it stands, the people may regulate their domestic relation as they see fit; but, says the amendment of the senator from Ohio, that shall enable them, under the Constitution, to prohibit slavery. What is the effect of that amendment but to modify, reduce, restrain, and bring down the latitude of authority conferred upon them by the previous language just incorporated into the bill." *   *   *

"Now, sir, the true, direct, and manly course to meet this question is that suggested by my honorable friend from Illinois (Mr. Shields). Put in your amendment that the people of the territories shall be at liberty to exclude or introduce, and if there is anything in the Constitution of the United States which disables a territorial government from introducing slavery, if the honorable senator believes that, if he is sincere in that opinion, there sits a tribunal below us who will pass upon the validity and constitutionality of any act that we may pass.

"I have no hesitation, therefore, in saying that I shall vote against the amendment of the senator from Ohio. The clause as it stands is ample. It submits the whole authority to the territory to determine for itself. That, in my judgment, is the place where it ought to be put. If the people of these territories choose to exclude slavery, so far from considering it as a wrong done to me or to my constituents, I shall not complain of it. It is their own business."

The debate then became general, and the Senate adjourned without taking the question.

The debate upon the general character of the bill continued from day to day until the 2d of March, when the amendment proposed by Mr. Chase again was noticed.

Mr. Badger again referring to it used the following strong language:

"The language of the bill, as amended upon the motion of the honorable chairman of the Committee on Territories, is full, complete, and ample, giving the people of these territories, through their governments, the unrestricted and unqualified right to decide upon all their domestic relations, slavery included; and then the honorable senator from Ohio, as if he supposed that either we were so dull that we could not understand, or that the public were so purblind that they could not see, proposes to add, as an amendment explanatory of the previous language, that they shall have power to prohibit slavery. He knows, sir, he means, sir, that that language, so standing, shall have, as in the court below it would have, the necessary effect of controlling, limiting, and restraining the former language, so that the territories should have no right over this subject but to prohibit slavery. If it does not mean this—if he does not intend this—why did he refuse to insert the words which the instinctive candor and openness of my honorable friend from Illinois (Mr. Shields) suggested 'to prohibit or allow slavery?' Sir, no member of this body who is in favor of the bill need be in the least troubled.

"The senator from Ohio feels himself bound, in order to resist the introduction of slavery into any territory, to disavow the obligation of all compacts, to resist the performance of every engagement, to disavow any, however solemn, stipulations. He can never mean but one thing by any amendment which he offers to this bill, and that thing is mischief to the measure."

"*Mr. Cass* said. * * * Well, sir, the honorable senator from Ohio proposes to insert a provision to take from the people the power of allowing slavery."

"*Mr. Chase.* No, sir."

"*Mr. Cass.* Certainly; that is the effect of it. You allow them the power to prohibit slavery by your amendment, but not to establish it. The original provision, as it stands, *gives them both powers,* subject to the limitations of the Constitution. Then the effect of the amendment of the honorable senator from Ohio, if adopted, would be to throw doubts upon the preceding provision. If we give them both powers, and then, afterwards, in clearer language give but one, it is a strong intimation that we destroy the effect of our own previous provision. It casts a doubt upon it. The true view, therefore, is to repeat both, if repetition is necessary."

"*Mr. Mason,* of Virginia, said: I understand the senator from Ohio to say that the object of this amendment, and the object of all the other amendments which he has offered to the bill, was to place the whole subject of legislation, in its most ample form, in the hands of the people of the territories; and yet he offered, I think, as an amendment, a proposition to authorize that people to legislate for the prohibition of slavery, and refused the suggestion which came from a senator on this floor to give the alternative to the same people, in their discretion, to legislate for the admission of slavery. *That thing has been exposed upon this floor over and over again.*"

The discussion again wandered from the amendment to a variety of topics, some of them personal in their nature. At half past six o'clock p. m. the Senate proceeded to vote on the amendment, which was rejected as follows:

Yeas—Messrs. Chase, Dodge, of Wisconsin, Fessenden, Fish, Foot, Hamlin, Seward, Smith, Sumner and Wade, 10.

Nays—Messrs. Adams, Atchison, Badger, Bell, Benjamin, Brodhead, Brown, Butler, Clay, of Alabama, Clayton, Dawson, Dixon, Dodge, of Iowa, Douglas, Evans, Fitzpatrick, Gwin, Houston, Hunter, Johnson, Jones, of Iowa, Jones, of Tennessee, Mason, Morton, Norris, Pettit, Pratt, Rusk, Sebastian, Shields, Slidell, Stuart, Toucey, Walker, Weller, and Williams, 36.

This is the history of the origin, progress, and fate of the Chase amendment. It proposed to allow the people of the territories to " prohibit" slavery, but denied to them the power to "introduce." It was, in effect, a restriction of the powers of the Legislature to a prohibition, when the object of the bill was to leave the Legislature free and unrestricted in the exercise of all constitutional legislation to prohibit or introduce. As General Cass said, it was a proposition to take from the Legislature the power to admit slavery

This amendment has lately been drawn from the records, and paraded before the country as conclusive testimony that the Senate, including Mr. Douglas, in framing the Kansas-

Nebraska Act, were so opposed to any recognition of the power of the Territorial Legislature to prohibit slavery, that a direct proposition to that effect was voted down by a majority of nearly four to one. When the candid reader remembers that the searcher after the history of that amendment had to read the speeches of its mover, and of Messrs. Badger and Cass, as to its purpose, its design and its effect, he will hardly credit the statement that a learned senator, who was a member of the Senate in 1854 when the bill passed, has had the courage in 1859 to present the amendment, and the vote rejecting it, as direct and positive evidence that the Senate, by a vote of thirty-six to ten, decided that the Territorial Legislature should not be permitted to legislate to the exclusion of slavery.

That the readers of this book may judge for themselves how universal was the " unsoundness" of senators upon the subject which Dr. Gwin has recently made his specialty, some extracts have been made from speeches on the Kansas-Nebraska Bill. Before giving these extracts, however, it should be stated that the only object sought to be established by quoting them is— that when the bill was under consideration it was conceded by all its friends, that unless the Constitution of the United States rendered such legislation void, the legislatures of the territories were, by the express terms of the bill, authorized to legislate for the introduction, prohibition, exclusion, protection and encouragement of African slavery within their territorial limits. The members of the Senate were divided into three classes upon the question of power, viz.:

1. Those who denied the power of Congress to legislate to extend slavery, but claimed that Congress had the power to prohibit; and that the Territorial Legislature, deriving all its powers from Congress, could not legislate except to prohibit slavery. This class was represented by Mr. Chase.

2. Those who denied the power of Congress to legislate to prohibit slavery, but claimed that Congress had the power, and should, when necessary, legislate for the protection of slave property, which, being recognized by the Constitution, must under all just considerations of the equality of the States, be admissible to the territories—the common property of all the States; and that the Legislature of the Territory, being the creature of Congress, could not exercise powers or authority

greater than those possessed by the creator. This class was represented by Mr. Brown, of Mississippi.

3. Those who, whether denying or admitting the power of Congress to legislate for the admission, extension, or prohibition of slavery in the territories, claimed for the people of the territories the power and the right, acting through their Legislatures, to admit or exclude, protect or prohibit African slavery. Of this class was Messrs. Cass, Douglas, and, as was understood, all the Northern supporters of the bill, Mr. Badger, and other Whigs from the South. Messrs Butler and Hunter, from whose speeches quotations are given below, both denied the power of Congress or the Territorial Legislature to prohibit slavery, but both conceded that the bill did give, and that it was intended to give, that power, should its exercise be consistent with the Constitution of the United States. Congress by the act did not withhold or deny the power; on the contrary, these gentlemen as well as all other supporters of the bill who made speeches, conceded that unless the legislation was unconstitutional, it was the intent and effect of the bill to grant, recognize and admit the right of the Legislature to exclude or admit slavery.

MR. WELLER, OF CALIFORNIA.

But, sir, if this be a question between slavery and freedom, then the friends of this measure hold the freedom side of the question. We propose that the people, the original source of all power, those who spoke this government into existence, and whose agents we are, shall be allowed to decide for themselves what local institutions shall exist among them. On the other hand the opponents of the measure advocate slavery. They contend that the American people shall not exercise this right; that their minds shall be enslaved, that their hands shall be tied up, and they prevented from a free decision whether slavery shall exist there or not. We occupy the broad ground of freedom. We have an abiding confidence in the honesty and in the intelligence of the people. We are not afraid to trust them with the decision of this question. How stands it with you? I had supposed that you were the agents and the representatives of the people, but it seems that the servant has become wiser than the master. You who are invested with political power are claiming now that you are better judges of what sort of government the people should have than the people themselves. Is this so? Is there that vast amount of intelligence and of patriotism in the American Congress which makes us far better judges of what the people should have than the people themselves? Our whole system is based upon the principle that man is capable of self-government. The moment you violate this principle, that moment you transcend your authority and destroy the vital element of the republic.

We propose that this (slavery), like all other questions, shall be left to the free decision of the people. The opponents of the measure concede to the people the right, when they form a State constitution, to decide for themselves whether slavery shall exist or not; but in the mean time, while it is a territory, they say slavery ought to be excluded. This is like tying a man's hands and legs, and telling him to go where he pleases.

FROM THE SAME SPEECH OF MR. WELLER.

One of these senators from Ohio (Mr. Wade) went so far as to utter this sentiment:

"Sir, in the days of the revolution Major Andre was hung by the neck until he was dead for accepting a proposition not more base than this, which is a gross betrayal of the rights of the whole North."

What an Egyptian darkness must have pervaded the mind of that Senator before he could have arrived at that conclusion! What sad ravages the foul spirit of fanaticism must have made upon his heart before he could have uttered that sentiment! The simple proposition to leave the people of Kansas and Nebraska free and untrammeled to decide on all their local institutions for themselves is, in his judgment, a more dishonorable proposition than that for which Major Andre was hung! I pray that God may enlighten the benighted mind of that senator and soften his heart, and that ere long he will be restored to a proper degree of judgment and reason—I had almost said decency.

MR. TOUCEY, OF CONNECTICUT.

Sir, I find no difficulty with regard to the territorial governments which we have had. They are assented to by the people who live under them, are adopted by the people, and put in operation by the people; and when the assent of the people and the assent of Congress both combine to uphold a government *de facto*, that government is in the possession of power, and it would be very difficult to question its practical validity. And as the people participate in territorial legislation, and, in fact, the laws originate with them, are proposed and adopted by them, these laws have not only the presumed assent of the people, but their express assent also; and having the implied sanction of Congress, if they are consistent with the Constitution, there seems to be no element wanting to render them effective to all intents and purposes whatsoever. But I mean to say that in the exercise of the power over the territories, acquired by the treaty-making power, you are bound to exercise that power in conformity with the principles of the Constitution; and if you do otherwise, although the law may not reach it, and courts of justice may not reach it, yet you are acting unconstitutionally; and if we knowingly and willingly violate the principles of government in exercising the necessary power that arises from the acquisition of territory, we violate the obligation that is upon us to support the Constitution. When, therefore, this principle of non-interference applies to all the states—applies to every state that has come or will come into the Union—when in a very short period sovereign states will occupy every foot of territory within the limits of the United States, and this principle will become universal, are we justified, are we acting in the true spirit of the Constitution, are we not violating the obligations upon us, when we trample this principle under foot, and undertake to control the domestic relations of a people who are, with our consent, in the possession of legislative power, and admitted by us to be capable of exercising it?

*　　　　　*　　　　　*　　　　　*

Why should we undertake in this government here to exercise this power of dictating to them?

What right have we, in these Atlantic States, over the people of the remote territories to dictate law to them? They are American citizens. They have gone into these territories with the full rights of American citizens. Why should we seek to exercise this arbitrary power over them? Why should we assume on our part to govern them at our will and pleasure? It would be as arbitrary and despotic power as exists anywhere in the civilized or uncivilized world. It will be the same arbitrary power which the parliament of Great Britain undertook to exercise over the American colonies when they resisted and revolted. It will be the despotism practiced by the worst governments over the most abject and down-trodden people of Europe, Asia, and Africa. Having no foundation in the consent of the people who are made its slaves, it will be an unmixed evil in our system, pregnant with the worst consequences of tyranny, and worse than anarchy in its worst form.

And am I to be called upon here to participate in exercising any such power? I detest it. I will never participate in it. I will go to the people and I will ask them if they are willing to be instrumental in the exercise of despotic power over their fellow-citizens; because, forsooth, their enterprise has borne them on to the region of the Rocky Mountains? I will ask if these people have ceased to be Americans; if they have become incapable of exercising the right of self-government, because they have encountered the hardships of the wilderness to become the founders of new states; and if they have themselves so soon forgotten the first principles of liberty, the lessons of the Revolution, and the lessons of the revolutionary fathers, that they are willing to wield this despotic power over their children. Sir, I know what the popular response will be. Sir, I know what it will be. The people of this country will be unanimous—ultimately unanimous. Their "sober second thought" will be everywhere; let the people rule; *let them govern themselves in their own way when in the possession of legislative power ;* let this federal government, in wielding the power over what is necessary over the territories, conform it to the principles upon which the Constitution is founded.

MR. HUNTER, OF VIRGINIA,

after detailing the events attending the legislation in 1850, said :

But the South was voted down, and the whole question was so settled that, practically, there is not one square inch of that territory which the South can ever settle or occupy; and, in exchange for it, the South got, first, the declaration on the part of the leading Northern friends of that Compromise—a declaration which seems to have been sustained by the legislation of the country—that it was unconstitutional to pass any law that should prohibit the introduction of slavery into the unoccupied territories of the United States; and secondly, the admission of the principle that the true mode of organizing that unoccupied territory is to give the people of the territory power to legislate over all rightful subjects of legislation which are consistent with the Constitution. That was all the South received in exchange for its just share of that vast territory; and although I believe that it was the almost universal sentiment of the South that they had been wronged in this adjustment, yet they acquiesced and submitted.

It is then surprising that when we come to organize the territorial government of this country, where slavery is prohibited by preceding legislative restriction, the South should say, "Gentlemen, you said it was unconstitutional to pass a legislative prohibition. Here is one; we ask you to remove it. You said that the true way to constitute a territorial government was to give to the people of that territory power to legislate upon all rightful subjects of legislation consistently with the Constitution. We ask you to give that power to the people in these territories in the precise words contained in the bill for the territorial organization of Utah." Was it not then an inevitable consequence of the course of events I have depicted that the South should make this request? Is it not a matter of justice, is it not a matter of constitutional right, that the North should accord it?

Subsequently, Mr. Stuart, of Michigan, stated that senators from the South had denied that under the language of the bill the Legislature of the Territory would have the same authority over slavery as over any other subject—that under the words of the bill the Legislature was restrained in its action upon the subject of slavery. He referred to Mr. Hunter as one of those who had thus questioned the extent and operation of the words of the bill. Mr. Hunter thus clearly and explicitly responded:

Mr. Hunter: If the senator will allow me, I will state that I only desired it because I thought the Constitution prohibits them from so legislating. I believe the bill, as it now stands, gives the people of the territories all the power that any bill could give them, unless there is some power beyond the Constitution which they may exercise. That was the opinion which I expressed—that they would be restricted by the Constitution, and I presume it will restrict them whether we mention it or not.

MR. CASS, OF MICHIGAN.

" The power of the people to legislate for themselves upon all these questions of domestic policy is the inevitable result of the preceding principles and of American institutions. If Congress have no jurisdiction over the subject, the people must have it, or the most important concerns of social and of civil life would be left without security or protection. No one has ever questioned their just claim to regulate, by their immediate representatives, the various questions connected with their civil and social relations, except this relation of master and servant, and this exception cannot stand the test of any reasonable scrutiny. I am aware of the objections which have been urged against the existence of this right of self-government founded on the connection of the people of the territories with the government of the United States, and I have been amazed at the subtle arguments, politico-metaphysical indeed, which have been presented against the enjoyment of one of the most sacred rights which God has given to man.

The inseparable **union** between **representation** and the **regulation** of the domestic affairs of a **community**, including **taxation, is one** of the **cardinal principles of American** political **faith laid down in** our **state papers, taught in our schools,** and **triumphantly asserted and defended on the battle-field—a principle which the Continental Congress, in 1774, declared** in **these words:**

"**The** English colonists are entitled **to a free and exclusive power of legislation in** their several provincial Legislatures, **where their right of representation can** alone be preserved **in all cases of taxation and internal policy, etc. And** strange is it, in the **vacillation of human opinions, that from defenders we are** urged to become **offenders, and, with the practice, to adopt the principle of** Lord North **in this crusade against human rights. For there is scarcely an** argument **which can be urged against this claim of local** legislation **which the** British **Ministry did not urge against the demands of our** fathers **to be allowed** to legislate **on themselves. We have been told with due gravity, and, I have** no doubt, **with due sincerity, that the United States are the 'Sovereign;' and** we have **been asked, 'and how can sovereignty, the ultimate and supreme power** of **the state, be divided?' Sovereignty indeed! and who can find** the **word in the Constitution, or who can deduce any power from its use? It** is **a process of constructive authority which cannot be too severely** reprobated, **at war, as it is, with the fundamental basis of the confederation. Once** established **its operation as the foundation of Congressional action, and other and nearer rights than those of distant, feeble communities, would soon be prostrated before it."**

* * * * * * * *

"**But, sir, whether the government of the** United **States is sovereign or subordinate, supreme or inferior, confederated or consolidated—and consolidated it will become, if some of these doctrines prevail—are questions not worth a moment's consideration in any inquiry into its legitimate power. Neither these nor any other attributes can confer upon it the least jurisdiction. To find what that is, we must go to the Constitution—to the law and the** testimony. **And all these useless, and some of them unintelligible** abstractions, were **urged as reasons why the internal affairs of American citizens, called** freemen, **should be controlled by a distant legislature, not one member of which** entitled **to vote is elected by, or is responsible to them.**

"**His Majesty in Parliament, said the Government of George III.,** has the **right, by statute, to bind the colonies in all cases whatsoever. It took** Lord **North** and **his master George III. seven years to learn the** falsehood of this **assumption, and the lesson cost them an empire. While** history **is the record of human actions, it is the reiteration of human motives** and pretensions. **And now before all the men of the generation which** successfully resisted **this edict of tyranny have passed away, we are called upon practically to declare that our majesty, this government in Congress, has the right by statute to bind the territories in all cases** whatsoever, or, according **to the new** version, **to sell the people into slavery.** This is good **doctrine over the water at** Berlin, **and Vienna, and at** Petersburgh, but I hope **not upon the** Wabash, though **we are told that God has** spared a precious life **upon its fertile** banks in order **to announce and** promulgate **it. The ways of Providence are** often dark to us **blind mortals, but** seldom darker **than in this case, whether** we consider the **messenger or the** message, the prophet **or the prophecy.** He without whose **knowledge** no sparrow falls **to the ground, sometimes** selects strange instruments, **according to our** comprehension, **to accomplish** his wise designs. **It** was so in the days of Balaam, and if a similar wonder has just occurred in our days and in our midst, nothing is left for us but to bow and believe. But whatever may be the nature of this mission, the doctrine itself would sound better within sight of the tomb of Achilles than within sight of the tomb of Washington. But even under the shadow of Islamism, and within the hearing of the muezzin who calls the faithful to prayer, it would not be considered quite orthodox in this day of Turkish reform.

"And why should not the people of the territories legislate for themselves? The senator from New York intimates that they do not know enough, and can not safely be trusted with this incident of self-government—the power to regulate the condition of master and servant—though he is willing to trust them with all the powers of life and death which depend upon the political action of a country—with complete authority over whites, but a limited one over blacks. This plea of the incompetency of the people to manage their own concerns is the old plea of tyranny all the world over, in the contest between power and freedom; and it never was better rebuked than by the author of the Declaration of Independence, when he said 'if the peopel are not fit to govern themselves, have they found angels, in the shape of men, to govern them?'

"Well, sir, the senator from New York has made the discovery, which escaped the penetration of this Patriarch of the Democratic faith, and has found angels in the shape of Congressmen to govern the territories. I do not believe in this new phase of despotism—making slaves of white communities."

At a later stage of the bill, while the amendment proposed by Mr. Clayton, to restrict the right of suffrage to citizens, was under consideration,

Mr. Atchison, of Missouri, said:

"Very well. We will have no difference in relation to that matter; but the objection I have is, that foreigners, men who are not citizens, men who may never become citizens, will mould and form the institutions in these territories, under the provision of the bill as it stands, unless we concur in the amendment.

"*The first legislature may decide the question of slavery forever in these territories*, and decide as to the right of the people of one-half of the States of this Union to go there or not. It is because they have the right of suffrage, and the right to hold office in these territories, when their institutions are first formed and first moulded, that constitutes my chief and principle objection. If the senator would alter and amend his proposition so that, in the year 1857 or 1858, persons who have declared their intention to become citizens may exercise the right of suffrage and hold office, I will waive my objection."

THE BADGER AMENDMENT.

The Chase amendment having been rejected, Mr. Badger then submitted his amendment, which now forms part of the 14th section of the bill, as follows:

"*Provided*, That nothing herein contained shall be construed to revive or put in force any law or regulation which may have existed prior to the act of the 6th of March, 1820, either protecting, establishing, prohibiting, or abolishing slavery."

This was agreed to, yeas 35, nays 6—five senators from the South and Dodge, of Wisconsin, voting against it.

Mr. Douglas then moved to strike out the provision giving the governor the power of absolute veto, and inserting a clause conferring a limited one ; also to strike out the clause declaring that the acts of the Territorial Legislature should be submitted to Congress, and if disapproved should be null and void. These amendments, designed to give greater freedom to the Legislatures of the Territories, were adopted without a division.

THE CLAYTON AMENDMENT.

The bill as it stood admitted to the right of voting all citizens

"And those who shall have declared, on oath, their intentions to become such, and shall have taken an oath to support the Constitution of the United States and the provisions of this act."

Mr. Clayton, of Delaware, moved to strike out these words, so as to deprive all persons not fully naturalized of the privilege of voting. A brief debate ensued, and the amendment was agreed to, yeas 23, nays 21—Mr. Douglas and all the northern friends of the bill, except one, voting in the negative.

After making some further amendments and rejecting several proposed by Mr. Chase, the question was taken on agreeing with the substitute, and agreed to; the bill was then reported to the Senate, and all the amendments made in Committee of the Whole were concurred in without a count, except that known as the Clayton amendment ; upon that, after debate, the question was taken by yeas and nays, and again decided in the affirmative, yeas 22, nays 20. The bill was then ordered to be engrossed for a third reading, yeas 29, nays 12.

On the next day, March 3d, the question pending was, Shall this bill pass? The bill was taken up at an early hour. Mr. Bell, of Tennessee, addressed the Senate, followed by Dawson, of Georgia, Norris, of New Hampshire, Wade, of Ohio, Mr Toucey, Mr. Fessenden, Mr. Weller, and incidentally by others, and at nearly midnight Mr. Douglas obtained the floor. After some further time in discussing as to further speaking after he closed, he proceeded in a speech, which was delivered even at that hour to crowded galleries, and to a Senate fully aroused and gratified by the force of his argument, the impetuosity of his invective, and the clearness and ability with which he defended himself and the great measure. This speech, under all the circumstances, was one of the most remarkable ever delivered. During the preceding six weeks his name had been coupled with every term of reproach that malignity could invent. He had been hung and burnt in effigy in several places in the New England and other states. Every description of obloquy had been heaped upon him. He had been selected as the victim to be sacrificed by popular frenzy. Instead of being dismayed or cast down by the storm which had been so pitilessly directed against him, he on that memorable night seemed to have increased in all those unyielding persevering qualities which have been so severely tested, and which have never failed to carry him through all the momentous difficulties he has had to encounter. The speech will be found in extenso at the close of this chapter.

Mr. Houston followed, and about 5 o'clock, A. M., the Senate proceeded to vote, and the bill passed.

Yeas—Adams, Miss.; Atchison, Mo.; Badger, N. C.; Bayard, Del.; Benjamin, La.; Brodhead, Pa.: Brown, Miss.; Butler, S. C.; Cass, Mich.; Clay, Ala.; Dawson, Geo.; Dixon, Ky.; Dodge, Iowa; Douglas, Ill.; Evans, S. C.; Fitzpatrick, Ala.; Geyer, Mo.; Gwin, Cal.; Hunter, Va.; Johnson, Ark.; Jones, Iowa; Jones, Tenn.; Mason, Va.; Morton, Fla.; Norris, N. H.; Pettit, Ind.; Pratt, Md.; Rusk, Tex.; Sebastian, Ark.; Shields, Ill.; Slidell, La.; Stuart, Mich.; Thompson, Ky.; Thomson, N. J.; Toucey, Conn.; Weller, Cal.; Williams, N. H.—Total, 37.

Nays—Bell, Tenn.; Chase, Ohio; Dodge, Wis.; Fessenden, Me.; Fish, N. Y.; Foot, Vt.; Hamlin, Me.; Houston, Tex.; James, R. I.; Seward, N. Y.; Smith, Conn.; Sumner, Mass.; Wade, Ohio; Walker, Wis.—Total, 14.

THE NEBRASKA BILL IN THE HOUSE.

On the 7th of March the Senate bill was received in the House of Representatives.

On the 31st of January preceding, Mr. Richardson, of Illinois, had reported "a bill to organize the Territories of Nebraska and Kansas"—being similar in all respects to the measure then pending before the Senate, as reported by Mr.

Douglas, and it was referred to the Committee of the Whole on the State of the Union.

Under the rules of the house, members were permitted to discuss in Committee of the Whole, regardless of the immediate subject under consideration, almost any topic that might suit their taste or their interests. Hence, the whole merits of the Kansas and Nebraska bill—the house as well as the Senate bill—were debated for a long time in Committee of the Whole, without either bill being strictly before the house.

On the 21st of March the Senate bill, by a vote of yeas 110 to nays 95, was sent to the Committee of the Whole; the motion, which was considered by the friends of the bill as hostile to its success, was made by Mr. Cutting, of New York, and out of it subsequently grew a controversy between that gentleman and Mr. Breckinridge, of Kentucky, that for a time gave indications of a personal conflict.

Thus matters stood until the 8th of May, when Mr. Richardson moved that the house resolve itself into Committee of the Whole, avowing his purpose, when in committee, to move to lay aside all other bills on the calendar, and take up the house Nebraska Bill. After considerable maneuvering the house was brought to a vote upon the motion, which was agreed to—yeas 109, nays 88. The Speaker having vacated the chair, Mr. Olds (of Ohio) was called to preside over the Committee of the Whole. Mr. Richardson then moved to lay aside the first bill on the calendar, and the motion was agreed to—ayes 103, nays 82. He then moved to lay aside the next bill, and repeated the motion until the Nebraska Bill was reached. That bill being taken up he moved to amend it by striking out all after the enacting clause, and inserting a substitute in the exact words of the bill passed by the Senate, restoring the words which had been stricken out of that bill on motion of Mr. Clayton.

On Thursday, May 11th, the house met at 12 o'clock, M. Mr. Richardson submitted the usual motion for closing debate in committee upon the Nebraska Bill, whereupon the opponents of the bill resorted to the routine of motions for adjournment, call of the house, lay upon the table, etc., etc. The struggle was a protracted one, continuing until a few minutes before 12 o'clock on Friday (12th) night, when, on motion of

Mr. Richardson, the house adjourned, after a continuous session of thirty-six hours. On Saturday, 13th, the business was renewed, but after a few hours a motion to adjourn prevailed. On Monday, 15th, the house resumed the consideration of the motion; but as by the rules any motion to suspend the rules could take priority of the pending proposition, Mr. Richardson, to avoid having his motion crowded out by propositions of that character, modified his motion, or, in fact, moved to suspend the rules, to enable him to offer the following resolution:

Resolved, That debate on House Bill No. 236, to organize the territories of Nebraska and Kansas, shall terminate at 12 o'clock, Saturday, 20th inst., and that the consideration of the special order on bill No. 295, for the Pacific Railroad, be postponed until the 24th inst.

The motion to suspend the rules required a vote of two-thirds; and the house, by a vote of yeas 137, nays 66, suspended the rules, and the resolution was introduced. Prominent among those of the "distinguished" members of the present Republican party who, in this life-struggle for the Nebraska Bill, voted with its friends and placed it within the control of a mere majority, were the Hon. N. P. Banks, of Massachusetts, John Wentworth, of Illinois, and James H. Lane, of Kansas. Without the votes of these "eminent" gentlemen the Kansas-Nebraska Bill would in all probability have never got out of the Committee of the Whole.

The question then recurred on the adoption of the resolution, and resort was again had to parliamentary tactics; the struggle was protracted until six o'clock next morning, when the resolution was adopted.

The next day, 16th, the bill was considered in committee, and each day until Saturday. At noon on that day—the house having met at 9, A. M.—Mr. Richardson closed the general debate. The bill was still open to amendments, upon which five-minute speeches were permitted. On Monday, May 22d, came the last contest in the house upon the measure. The attendance was large—absentees had all paired off. The galleries were crowded, the lobbies filled, and the floor thronged with senators and others privileged upon the floor. The chaplain, the Rev. W. H. Milburn, in his prayer at the opening of the house thus referred to the expected scenes:

"Oh Thou, the high and mighty Ruler of the Universe, devoutly we implore thy blessing to rest upon this house, again about to enter upon one of the most arduous and memorable struggles the country has ever known. Help every member to keep cool, calm, and self-possessed, remembering that the angry man gives his adversary the advantage, and the enraged party compromises its truest interests. Assist every man to co-operate with the Speaker and Chairman in preserving order, recollecting that the eyes of the country are fixed upon this house, and that the deep interests of the country are involved in the deliberations of this Congress. May every man dare to do his duty, and abide the issues of his conscious convictions, we pray, through Jesus Christ."

The motion to go into committee was resisted but prevailed —yeas 105, nays 70. Under the rule allowing speeches upon *pro forma* amendment, the opponents of the bill could keep it in committee and thus delay final action, at their pleasure. But this was brought to a sudden and most unexpected termination. Mr. Stephens moved to amend the bill by striking out the enacting clause. The effect of this motion, which had precedence of any other motion to amend, if adopted, was equivalent to a rejection of the bill; and made it imperative that the bill should be reported to the house, where a vote could be had confirming or setting aside the action in committee. The motion put an end to the expectations of those who looked forward to a protracted campaign in parliamentary warfare. Mr. Chandler, at present representing the United States at one of the European courts, in behalf of the opponents of the measure, denounced the movement as "wicked," and indulged in other warm language of reprobation. When the committee was dividing a member from New York called upon the opposition to "oppose tyranny by revolution." Mr. Stephens' motion was agreed to, and the committee rose and reported its action to the house. The bill was now before the house, and so far its friends had made great progress; but it was Monday, and motions to suspend the rules were by the rules in order as privileged questions. Mr. Richardson moved the previous question with a view to bring the house to a vote upon the bill and pending amendments. Motions to adjourn and to adjourn till Wednesday were made repeatedly and rejected. Motions to suspend the rules were interposed. Finally, the house was brought to a vote upon concurring with the committee in striking out the enacting clause of the bill, and the House refused to concur—yeas 97, nays 117.

Mr. Richardson then moved to amend the bill by striking

K

out all after the enacting clause, and inserting the Senate bill
without the Clayton amendment.   This was agreed to—yeas
115, nays 96.   A motion to lay on the table was rejected—
yeas 100, nays 114.   The bill was ordered to be engrossed
for a third reading—yeas 112, nays 99, and the bill was passed
—yeas 113, nays 100.   The title was then agreed to at half-
past eleven o'clock, P. M., and the house, having disposed of
the bill, adjourned.

On the next day the bill was delivered to the Senate.   It
was read the first time, but Mr. Sumner objecting the second
reading did not take place; on the 24th it was read the
second time and considered.   Mr. Pearce renewed the Clayton amendment.

The bill was debated until a late hour on the 24th, and on
the 25th was resumed.   A warm and at one time very angry
discussion took place between Mr. Bell and the other southern
Whigs.   Mr. Bell had voted to insert in the bill, when it was
before the Senate in February, the clause repealing the Missouri restriction; and yet had voted against the bill because
of that repeal.

The Clayton amendment, as renewed by Mr. Pearce, was
rejected—yeas 7, nays 41.

At one o'clock, on the morning of the 26th of May, Mr.
Douglas closed the debate, and the bill, by a vote of—yeas 35,
nays 13, was ordered to a third reading.   It was then read a
third time and passed without a division.

And thus ended the struggle in Congress upon that much
abused, but the wisest, safest, and most just measure ever
adopted by Congress for the vexed question of slavery in the
territories.

The following is Mr. Douglas' memorable speech of
March 3d:

Mr. Douglas. Mr. President, before I proceed to the general argument upon
the most important branch of this question, I must say a few words in reply
to the senator from Tennessee [Mr. Bell], who has spoken upon the bill to-
day.   He approves of the principles of the bill; he thinks they have great
merit; but he does not see his way entirely clear to vote for the bill, because
of the objections which he has stated, most of which relate to the Indians.

Upon that point I desire to say that it has never been the custom in territorial bills to make regulations concerning the Indians within the limits of
the proposed territories.   All matters relating to them it has been thought
wise to leave to subsequent legislation, to be brought forward by the Committee on Indian Affairs.   I did venture originally in this bill to put in one
or two provisions upon that subject; but, at the suggestion of many sena-

tors on both sides of the chamber, they were stricken out in order to allow the appropriate committee of the Senate to take charge of that subject. I think, therefore, since we have stricken from the bill all those provisions which pertain to the Indians, and reserved the whole subject for the consideration and action of the appropriate committee, we have obviated every possible objection which could reasonably be urged upon that score. We have every reason to hope and trust that the Committee on Indian Affairs will propose such measures as will do entire justice to the Indians, without contravening the objects of Congress in organizing these territories.

But, sir, allusion has been made to certain Indian treaties, and it has been intimated, if not charged in direct terms, that we were violating the stipulations of those treaties in respect to the rights and lands of the Indians. The senator from Texas [Mr. Houston] made a very long and interesting speech on that subject; but it so happened that most of the treaties to which he referred were with Indians not included within the limits of this bill. We have been informed, in the course of the debate to-day, by the chairman of the Committee on Indian Affairs [Mr. Sebastian], that there is but one treaty in existence relating to lands or Indians within the limits of either of the proposed territories, and that is the treaty with the Ottawa Indians, about two hundred persons in number, owning about thirty-four thousand acres of land. Thus it appears that the whole argument of injustice to the red man, which in the course of this debate has called forth so much sympathy and indignation, is confined to two hundred Indians, owning less than two townships of land. Now, sir, is it possible that a country, said to be five hundred thousand square miles in extent, and large enough to make twelve such states as Ohio, is to be consigned to perpetual barbarism merely on account of that small number of Indians, when the bill itself expressly provides that those Indians and their lands are not to be included within the limits of the proposed territories, nor to be subject to their laws or jurisdiction? I would not allow this measure to invade the rights of even one Indian, and hence I inserted in the first section of the bill that none of the tribes with whom we have treaty stipulations should be embraced within either of the territories, unless such Indians shall voluntarily consent to be included therein by treaties hereafter to be made. If any senator can furnish me with language more explicit, or which would prove more effectual in securing the rights of the Indians, I will cheerfully adopt it.

Well, sir, the senator from Tennessee, in a very kind spirit, here raises the objection for me to answer, that this bill includes Indians within the limits of these territories with whom we have no treaties; and he desires to know what we are to do with them. I will say to him, that this is not a matter of inquiry which necessarily or properly arises upon the passage of this bill; that is not a proper inquiry to come before the Committee on Territories. You have in all your territorial bills included Indians within the boundaries of the territories. When you erected the Territory of Minnesota, you had not extinguished the Indian title to one foot of land in that territory west of the Mississippi river, and to the major part of that territory the Indian title remains unextinguished to this day. In addition to those wild tribes, you removed Indians from Wisconsin and located them within Minnesota since the territory was organized. It will be a question for the consideration of the Committee on Indian Affairs, and for the action of Congress, when, in settlement and civilization, it shall become necessary to change the present policy in respect to the Indians. When you erected the territorial government of Oregon, a few years ago, you embraced within it all the Indians living in the territory without their consent, and without any such reservations in their behalf as are contained in this bill. You had not at that time made a treaty with those Indians, nor extinguished their title to an acre of land in that territory, nor indeed have you done so to this day. So it is in the organization of Washington Territory. You ran the lines around the country which you thought ought to be within the limits of the territory, and you embraced all the Indians within those lines; but you made no provision in respect to their rights or lands; you left that matter to the Committee on Indian Affairs, to the Indian laws, and to the proper department, to be arranged afterwards as the public interests might require. The same is true in reference to Utah and New Mexico.

In fact, the policy provided for in this bill, in respect to the Indians, is that which is now in force in every one of the territories. Therefore, any senator who objects to this bill on that score should have objected to and voted against every territorial bill which you have now in existence. Yet my friend from Texas has taken occasion to remind the Senate several times that it was a matter of pride—and it ought to be a matter of patriotic pride with him—that he voted for every measure of the Compromise of 1850, including the Utah and New Mexico territorial bill, embracing all the Indians within their limits. My friend from Tennessee, too, has been very liberal in voting for most of the territorial bills; and I therefore trust that the same patriotic and worthy motives which induced him to vote for the territorial acts of 1850 will enable him to give his support to the present bill, especially as he approves of the great principle of popular sovereignty upon which it rests.

The senator from Tennessee remarked further, that the proposed limits of these two territories were too extensive, that they were large enough to be erected into eight different states; and why, he asked, the necessity of including such a vast amount of country within the limits of these two territories? I must remind the senator that it has always been the practice to include a large extent of country within one territory, and then to subdivide it from time to time as the public interest might require. Such was the case with the the old Northwest Territory. It was all originally included within one territorial government. Afterwards Ohio was cut off; and then Indiana, Michigan, Illinois, and Wisconsin were successively erected into separate territorial governments, and subsequently admitted into the Union as states.

At one period, it will be remembered, the Territory of Wisconsin included the country embraced within the limits of the States of Wisconsin and Iowa, and a part of the State of Michigan, and the Territory of Minnesota. There is country enough within the Territory of Minnesota to make two or three States of the size of New York. Washington Territory embraces about the same area. Oregon is large enough to make three or four States as extensive as Pennsylvania, Utah two or three, and New Mexico four or five of like dimensions. Indeed, the whole country embraced within the proposed Territories of Nebraska and Kansas, together with the States of Arkansas, Missouri, and Iowa, and the larger part of Minnesota, and the whole of the Indian country west of Arkansas, once constituted a territorial government, under the name of the Missouri Territory. In view of this course of legislation upon the subject of territorial organization, commencing before the adoption of the Constitution of the United States, and coming down to the last session of Congress, it surely can not be said that there is any thing unusual or extraordinary in the size of the proposed territory, which should compel a senator to vote against the bill, while he approves of the principle involved in the measure.

It has also been urged in debate that there is no necessity for these territorial organizations; and I have been called upon to point out any public and national considerations which require action at this time. Senators seem to forget that our immense and valuable possessions on the Pacific are separated from the states and organized territories, on this side of the Rocky Mountains, by a vast wilderness, filled by hostile savages; that nearly a hundred thousand emigrants pass through this barbarous wilderness every year, on their way to California and Oregon; that these emigrants are American citizens, our own constituents, who are entitled to the protection of law and government; and that they are left to make their way, as best they may, without the protection or aid of law or government.

The United States mails for New Mexico and Utah, and all official communications between this government and the authorities of those territories, are required to be carried over these wild plains, and through the gorges of the mountains, where you have made no provision for roads bridges, or ferries, to facilitate travel, or forts or other means of safety to protect life. As often as I have brought forward and urged the adoption of measures to remedy these evils, and afford security against the dangers to which our people are constantly exposed, they have been promptly voted down as not being of sufficient importance to command the favorable consideration of Congress. Now, when I propose to organize the territories, and allow the people to do for themselves what you have so often refused to do for them, I am told that there are not white inhabitants enough permanently settled in the country to require and sustain a government. True there is not a very large population there, for the very good reason that your Indian code and intercourse laws exclude the settlers, and forbid their remaining there to cultivate the soil. You refuse to throw the country open to settlers, and then object to the organization of the territories upon the ground that there is not a sufficient number of inhabitants.

The senator from Connecticut (Mr. Smith) has made a long argument to prove that there are no inhabitants in the proposed territories, because nearly all of those who have gone and settled there have done so in violation of certain old acts of Congress which forbid the people to take possession of and settle upon the public lands until after they should be surveyed and brought into market.

I do not propose to discuss the question whether these settlers are technically legal inhabitants or not. It is enough for me that they are a part of our own people; that they are settled on the public domain; that the public interests would be promoted by throwing that public domain open to settlement; and that there is no good reason why the protection of law and the blessings of government should not be extended to them. I must be permitted to remind the senator that the same objection existed in its full force to Minnesota, to Oregon and to Washington, when each of those territories were organized; and that I have no recollection that he deemed it his duty to call the attention of Congress to the objection, or considered it of sufficient importance to justify him in recording his own vote against the organization of either of those territories.

Mr. President, I do not feel called upon to make any reply to the argument which the senator from Connecticut has urged against the passage of this bill upon the scorce of expense in sustaining these territorial governments, for the reason that, if the public interests require the enactment of the law, it follows as a natural consequence that all the expenses necessary to carry it into effect are wise and proper.

I will now proceed to the consideration of the great principle involved in the bill, without omitting, however, to notice some of those extraneous matters which have been brought into this discussion with the view of producing another anti-slavery agitation. We have been told by nearly every senator who has spoken in opposition to this bill, that at the time of its introduction the people were in a state of profound quiet and repose; that the anti-slavery agitation had entirely ceased; and that the whole country was acquiescing cheerfully and cordially in the Compromise measures of 1850 as a final adjustment of this vexed question.

Sir, it is truly refreshing to hear senators, who contested every inch of ground in opposition to those measures when they were under discussion, who predicted all manner of evils and calamities from their adoption, and who raised the cry of repeal, and even resistance, to their execution, after they had become the laws of the land—I say it is really refreshing to hear these same senators now bear their united testimony to the wisdom of those measures, and to the patriotic motives which induced us to pass them in defiance of their threats and resistance, and to their beneficial effects in restoring peace, harmony, and fraternity to a distracted country. These are precious confessions from the lips of those who stand pledged never to assent to the propriety of those measures, and to make war upon them so long as they shall remain upon the statute-book. I well understand that these confessions are now made, not with the view of yielding their assent to the propriety of carrying those enactments into faithful execution, but for the purpose of having a pretext for charging upon me, as the author of this bill, the responsibility of an agitation which they are trying to produce. They say that I, and not they, have revived the agitation. What have I done to render me obnoxious to this charge? They say I wrote and introduced this Nebraska Bill. That is true; but I was not a volunteer in the transaction. The Senate, by a unanimous vote, appointed me chairman of the territorial committee, and associated five intelligent and patriotic senators with me, and thus made it our duty to take charge of all territorial business. In like manner, and with the concurrence of these complaining senators, the Senate referred to us a distinct proposition to organize this Nebraska Territory, and required us to report specifically upon the question. I repeat, then, we were not volunteers in this business. The duty was imposed upon us by the Senate. We were not unmindful of the delicacy and responsibility of the position. We were aware that from 1820 to 1850 the abolition doctrine of congressional interference with slavery in the territories and new states had so far prevailed as to keep up an incessant slavery agitation in Congress and throughout the country, whenever any new territory was to be acquired or organized. We were also aware that, in 1850, the right of the people to decide this question for themselves, subject only to the Constitution, was substituted for the doctrine of congressional intervention. The first question, therefore, which the committee were called upon to decide, and indeed the only question of any material importance, in framing this bill, was this: Shall we adhere to and carry out the principles recognized by the Compromise measures of 1850, or shall we go back to the old exploded doctrine of congressional interference, as established in 1820 in a large portion of the country, and which it was the object of the Wilmont Proviso to give a universal application, not only to all the territory which we then possessed, but all which we might hereafter acquire? There were no other alternatives. We were compelled to frame the bill upon the one or the other of these two principles. The doctrine of 1820 or the doctrine of 1850 must prevail. In the discharge of the duty imposed upon us by the Senate, the committee could not hesitate upon this point, whether we consulted our individual opinions and principles or those which were known to be entertained and boldly avowed by a large majority of the Senate. The two great political parties of the country stood solemnly pledged before the world to adhere to the Compromise measures of 1850, "in principle and substance." A large majority of the Senate, indeed every member of the body, I believe, except the two avowed Abolitionists (Mr. Chase and Mr. Sumner), profess to belong to the one or the other of these parties, and hence was supposed to be under a high moral obligation to carry out the "principle and substance" of those measures in all the new territorial organizations. The report of the committee was in accordance with this obligation. I am arraigned, therefore, for having endeavored to represent the opinions and principles of the Senate truly; for having performed my duty in conformity with the parliamentary law; for having been faithful to the trust reposed in me by the Senate. Let the vote this night determine whether I have thus faithfully represented your opinions. When a majority of the Senate shall have passed the bill; when a majority of the states shall have endorsed it through their representatives upon this floor; when a majority of the South and a majority of the North shall have sanctioned it; when a majority of the Whig party and a majority of the Democratic party shall have voted for it; when each of these propositions shall be demonstrated by the vote this night on the final passage of the bill, I shall be willing to submit the question to the country, whether, as the organ of the committee, I performed my duty in the report and bill which have called down upon my head so much denunciation and abuse.

Mr. President, the opponents of this measure have had much to say about the mutations and modifications which this bill has undergone since it was first introduced by myself, and about the alleged departure of the bill, in its present form, from the principle laid down in the original report of the committee as a rule of action in all future territorial organizations. Fortunately there is no necessity, even if your patience would tolerate such a course of argument at this late hour of the night, for me to examine these speeches in detail, and to reply to each charge separately. Each speaker seems to have followed faithfully in the footsteps of his leader—in the path marked out by the Abolition confederates in their manifesto, which I exposed on a former occasion. You have seen them on their winding way, meandering the narrow and crooked path in Indian file, each treading close upon the heels of the other, and neither venturing to take a step to the right or left, or to occupy one inch of ground which did not bear the foot-print of the Abolition champion. To answer one, therefore, is to answer the whole. The statement to which they seem to attach the most importance, and which they have repeated oftener perhaps than any other, is that, pending the Compromise measures of 1850, no man in or out of Congress ever dreamed of abrogating the Missouri Compromise; that from that period down to the present session nobody supposed that its validity had been impaired, or any thing done which rendered it obligatory upon us to make it inoperative hereafter; that at the time of submitting the report and bill to the Senate, on the 4th of January last, neither I nor any member of the committee ever thought of such a thing; and that we could never be brought up to the point of abrogating the eighth section of the Missouri act until after the senator from Kentucky introduced his amendment to my bill.

Mr. President, before I proceed to expose the many misrepresentations contained in this complicated charge, I must call the attention of the Senate to the false issue which these gentlemen are endeavoring to impose upon the country, for the purpose of diverting public attention from the real issue contained in the bill. They wish to have the people believe that the abrogation of what they call the Missouri Compromise was the main object and aim of the bill, and that the only question involved is, whether the prohibition of slavery north of 36° 30' shall be repealed or not? That which is a mere incident they choose to consider the principal. They make war on the means by which we propose to accomplish an object, instead of openly resisting the object itself. The principle which we propose to carry into effect by the bill is this: That *Congress shall neither legislate slavery into any territories or state, nor out of the same; but the people shall be left free to regulate their domestic concerns in their own way, subject only to the Constitution of the United States.*

In order to carry this principle into practical operation, it becomes necessary to remove whatever legal obstacles might be found in the way of its free exercise. It is only for the purpose of carrying out this great fundamental principle of self-government that the bill renders the eighth section of the Missouri act inoperative and void.

Now, let me ask, will these senators who have arraigned me, or any one of them, have the assurance to rise in his place and declare that this great principle was never thought of or advocated as applicable to territorial bills, in 1850; that, from that session until the present, nobody ever thought of incorporating this principle in all new territorial organizations; that the Committee on Territories did not recommend it in their report; and that it required the amendment of the senator from Kentucky to bring us up to that point? Will any one of my accusers dare to make this issue, and let it be tried by the record? I will begin with the Compromises of 1850. Any senator who will take the trouble to examine our journals will find that on the 25th of March of that year I reported from the Committee on Territories two bills including the following measures: the admission of California, a territorial government for Utah, a territorial government for New Mexico, and the adjustment of the Texas boundary. These bills proposed to leave the people of Utah and New Mexico free to decide the slavery question for themselves, *in the precise language of the Nebraska Bill now under discussion.* A few weeks afterwards, the Committee of Thirteen took those two bills and put a wafer between them, and reported them back to the Senate as one bill, with some slight amendments. One of those amendments was, that the territorial legislatures should not legislate upon the subject of African slavery. I objected to that provision upon the ground that it subverted the great principle of self-government upon which the bill had been originally framed by the Territorial Committee. On the first trial, the Senate refused to strike it out, but subsequently did so, after full debate, in order to establish that principle as the rule of action in territorial organizations.

Mr. Dodge, of Iowa. It was done on your own motion.

Mr. Douglas. Upon this point I trust I will be excused for reading one or two sentences from some remarks I made in the Senate, on the 3d of June, 1850:

"The position that I have ever taken has been that this, the slavery question, and all other questions relating to the domestic affairs and domestic policy of the territories, ought to be left to the decision of the people themselves, and that we ought to be content with whatever way they would decide the question, because they have a much deeper interest in these mattters than we have, and know much better what institutions will suit them, than we, who have never been there, can decide for them."

Again, in the same debate, I said:

"I do not see how those of us who have taken the position which we have taken, (that of non-interference,) and have argued in favor of the right of the people to legislate for themselves on this question, can support such a provision without abandoning all the arguments which we urged in the presidential campaign in the year 1848, and the principles set forth by the honorable senator from Michigan in that letter which is known as the 'Nicholson letter.' We are required to abandon that platform; we are required to abandon those principles, and to stultify ourselves, and to adopt the opposite doctrine; and for what? In order to say that the people of the territories shall not have such institutions as they shall deem adapted to their condition and their wants. I do not see, sir, how such a provision as that can be acceptable either to the people of the North or the South."

Mr. President, I could go on and multiply extract after extract from my speeches in 1850, and prior to that date, to show that this doctrine of leaving the people to decide these questions for themselves is not an "after-thought" with me, seized upon this session for the first time, as my calumniators have so frequently and boldly charged in their speeches during this debate, and in their manifesto to the public. I refused to support the celebrated Omnibus Bill in 1850 until the obnoxious provision was stricken out, and the principle of self-government restored, as it existed in my original bill. No sooner were the Compromise measures of 1850 passed, than the Abolition confederates, who lead the opposition to this bill now, raised the cry of repeal in some sections of the country, and in others forcible resistance to the execution of the law. In order to arrest and suppress the treasonable purposes of these Abolition confederates, and avert the horrors of civil war, it became my duty, on the 23d of October, 1850, to address an excited and frenzied multitude at Chicago, in defence of each and all the Compromise measures of that year. I will read one or two sentences from that speech, to show how those measures were then understood and explained by their advocates:

"*These measures are predicated on the great fundamental principle that every people ought to possess the right of forming and regulating their own internal concerns and domestic institutions in their own way.*"

Again:

"These things are all confided by the Constitution to each State to decide for itself, and I KNOW OF NO REASON WHY THE *same principle should not be confided to the territories.*"

In this speech it will be seen that I lay down a general principle of universal application, and make no distinction between territories North or South of 36° 30'.

I am aware that some of the Abolition confederates have perpetrated a monstrous forgery on that speech, and are now circulating though the Abolition newspapers the statement that I said that I would "cling with the tenacity of life to the Compromise of 1850." This statement, false as it is—a deliberate act of forgery, as it is known to be by all who have ever seen or read the speech referred to—constitutes the staple article out of which most of the Abolition orators at the small anti-Nebraska meetings manufacture the greater part of their speeches. I now declare that there is not a sentence, or a line, nor even a word in that speech, which imposes the slightest limitation on the application of the great principle embraced in this bill in all new territorial organizations, without the least reference to the line of 36° 30'.

At the session of 1850–51, a few weeks after this speech was made at Chicago, and when it had been published in pamphlet form and circulated extensively over the States, the Legislature of Illinois proceeded to revise its action upon the slavery question, and define its position on the Compromise of 1850. After rescinding the resolutions adopted at a previous session, instructing my colleague and myself to vote for a proposition prohibiting slavery in the territories, resolutions were adopted approving the Compromise measures of 1850. I will read one of the resolutions, which was adopted in the House of Representatives, by a vote of 61 yeas to 4 nays:

"*Resolved*, That our liberty and independence are based upon the right of the people to form for themselves such a government as they may choose; that this great privilege—the birthright of freemen, the gift of heaven, secured to us by the blood of our ancestors—ought to be extended to future generations; and no limitation ought to be applied to this power, in the organization of any territory of the United States, of either a territorial government or a State Constitution: *Provided*, the government so established shall be republican, and in conformity with the Constitution."

Another series of resolutions having passed the Senate almost unanimously, embracing the same principle in different language, they were concurred in by the house. Thus was the position of Illinois, upon the slavery question, defined at the first session of the Legislature after the adoption of the Compromise of 1850.

Now, sir, what becomes of the declaration which has been made by nearly every opponent of this bill, that nobody in this whole Union ever dreamed that the principle of the Utah and New Mexican bill was to be incorporated into all future territorial organizations? I have shown that my own State so understood and declared it at the time in the most explicit and solemn manner. Illinois declared that our "liberty and independence" rest upon this "principle;" that the principle "ought to be extended to future generations;" and that "NO LIMITATION OUGHT TO BE APPLIED TO THIS POWER IN THE ORGANIZATION OF ANY TERRITORY OF THE UNITED STATES." No exception is made in regard to Nebraska. No Missouri compromise line; no reservation of the country north of 36° 30′, The principle is declared to be the "birthright of freemen;" the "gift of Heaven," to be "applied without limitation," in Nebraska as well as Utah, North as well as South of 36° 30′.

It may not be out of place here to remark that the Legislature of Illinois, at its recent session, has passed resolutions approving the Nebraska bill; and among the resolutions is one in the precise language of the resolution of 1851, which I have just read to the Senate.

Thus I have shown, Mr. President, that the Legislature and people of Illinois have always understood the Compromise measures of 1850 as establishing certain principles as rules of action in the organization of all new territories, and that no limitation was to be made on either side of the geographical line of 36° 30′.

Neither my time nor your patience will allow me to take up the resolutions of the different states in detail, and show what has been the common understanding of the whole country upon this point. I am now vindicating myself and my own action against the assaults of my calumniators; and, for that purpose, it is sufficient to show that, in the report and bill which I have presented to the Senate, I have only carried out the known principles and solemnly declared will of the state whose representative I am. I will now invite the attention of the Senate to the report of the committee, in order that it may be known how much, or rather how little, truth there is for the allegation which has been so often made and repeated on this floor, that the idea of allowing the people in Nebraska to decide the slavery question for themselves was a "sheer after-thought," conceived since the report was made, and not until the senator from Kentucky proposed his amendment to the bill.

I read from that portion of the report in which the committee lay down the principle by which they proposed to be governed:

"In the judgment of your committee, those measures (Compromise of 1850) were intended to have a far more comprehensive and enduring effect than the mere adjustment of the difficulties arising out of the recent acquisition of Mexican territory. They were designed to establish certain great principles, which would not only furnish adequate remedies for existing evils, but *in all time to come* avoid the perils of a similar agitation, *by withdrawing the question of slavery from the halls of Congress and the political arena, and committing it to the arbitrament of those who were immediately interested in and alone responsible for its consequences.*"

After making a brief argument in defence of this principle, the report proceeds, as follows:

"From these provisions, it is apparent that the Compromise measures of 1850 affirm and rest upon the following propositions:

"First. That all questions pertaining to slavery in the territories and in the new states to be formed therefrom, are to be left to the decision of the people residing therein, by their appropriate representatives, to be chosen by them for that purpose."

And, in conclusion, the report proposes a substitute for the bill introduced by the senator from Iowa, and concludes as follows:

"The substitute for the bill which your committee have prepared, and which is commended to the favorable action of the Senate, proposes to carry these propositions and principles into practical operation, in the precise language of the Compromise measures of 1850."

Mr. President, as there has been so much misrepresentation upon this point, I must be permitted to repeat that the doctrine of the report of the committee, as has been conclusively proved by these extracts, is—

First. That the whole question of slavery should be withdrawn from the halls of Congress, and the political arena, and committed to the arbitrament of those who are immediately interested in and alone responsible for its existence.

Second. The applying this principle to the territories and the new states to be formed therefrom, all questions pertaining to slavery were to be referred to the people residing therein.

Third. That the committee proposed to carry these propositions and principles into effect in the precise language of the Compromise measures of 1850.

Are not these propositions identical with the principles and provisions of the bill on your table? If there is a hair's breadth of discrepancy between the two, I ask any senator to rise in his place and point it out. Both rest upon the great principle, which forms the basis of all our institutions, that the people are to decide the question for themselves, subject only to the Constitution.

But my accusers attempt to raise up a false issue, and thereby divert public attention from the real one, by the cry that the Missouri Compromise is to be repealed or violated by the passage of this bill. Well, if the eighth section of the Missouri Act, which attempted to fix the destinies of future generations in those territories for all time to come, in utter disregard of the rights and wishes of the people when they should be received into the Union as states, be inconsistent with the great principle of self-government and the Constitution of the United States, it ought to be abrogated. The legislation of 1850 abrogated the Missouri Compromise, so far as the country embraced within the limits of Utah and New Mexico was covered by the slavery restriction. It is true, that those acts did not in terms and by name repeal the act of 1820, as originally adopted, or as extended by the resolutions annexing Texas in 1845, any more than the report of the Committee on Territories proposes to repeal the same acts this session. But the acts of 1850 did authorize the people of those territories to exercise "all rightful powers of legislation consistent with the Constitution," not excepting the question of slavery; and did provide that, when those territories should be admitted into the Union, they should be received with or without slavery, as the people thereof might determine at the date of their admission. These provisions were in direct conflict with a clause in a former enactment, declaring that slavery should be forever prohibited in any portion of said territories, and hence rendered such clause inoperative and void to the extent of such conflict. This was an inevitable consequence, resulting from the provisions in those acts which gave the people the right to decide the slavery question for themselves, in conformity with the Constitution. It was not necessary to go further and declare that certain previous enactments, which were incompatible with the exercise of the powers conferred in the bills, "are hereby repealed." The very act of granting those powers and rights has the legal effect of removing all obstructions to the exercise of them by the people, as prescribed in those territorial bills. Following that example, the Committee on Territories did not consider it necessary to declare the eighth section of the Missouri Act repealed. We were content to organize Nebraska in the precise language of the Utah and New Mexican bills.   Our object was to leave the people entirely free to form and regulate their domestic institutions and internal concerns in their own way, under the Constitution; and we deemed it wise to accomplish that object in the exact terms in which the same thing had been done in Utah and New Mexico by the acts of 1850. This was the principle upon which the committee reported; and our bill was supposed, and is now believed, to have been in accordance with it.   When doubts were raised whether the bill did fully carry out the principles laid down in the report, amendments were made, from time to time, in order to avoid all misconstruction, and make the true intent of the act more explicit, The last of these amendments was adopted yesterday, on the motion of the distinguished senator from North Carolina, (Mr. Badger,) in regard to the revival of any laws or regulations which may have existed prior to 1820. That amendment was not intended to change the legal effect of the bill.   Its object was to repel the slander which had been propagated by the enemies of the measure in the North, that the southern supporters of the bill desired to legislate slavery into these territories.   The South denies the right of Congress either to legislate slavery into any territory or state, or out of any territory or state.   Non-intervention by Congress with slavery in the states or territories is the doctrine of the bill, and all the amendments which have been agreed to have been made with the view of removing all doubt and cavil as to the true meaning and object of the measure.

Mr. President, I think I have succeeded in vindicating myself and the action of the committee from the assaults which have been made upon us in consequence of these amendments.   It seems to be the tactics of our opponents to direct their arguments against the unimportant points and incidental questions which are to be affected by carrying out the principle, with the hope of relieving themselves from the necessity of controverting the principle itself.   The senator from Ohio (Mr. Chase) led off gallantly in the charge that the committee, in the report and bill first submitted, did not contemplate the repeal of the Missouri Compromise, and could not be brought to that point until after the senator from Kentucky offered his amendment.   The senator from Connecticut (Mr. Smith) followed his lead, and repeated the same statement.   Then came the other senator from Ohio (Mr. Wade), and the senator from New York (Mr. Seward), and the senator from Massachusetts (Mr. Sumner), all singing the same song, only varying the tune.

Let me ask these senators what they mean by this statement?   Do they wish to be understood as saying that the report and first form of the bill did not provide for leaving the slavery question to the decision of the people in the terms of the Utah bill?   Surely they will not dare to say that, for I have already shown that the two measures were identical in principle and enactment.   Do they mean to say that the adoption of our first bill would not have had the legal effect to have rendered the eighth section of the Missouri Act "inoperative and void," to use the language of the present bill?   If this be not their meaning, will they rise in their places and inform the Senate what their meaning was?   They must have had some object in giving so much prominence to this statement, and in repeating it so often.   I address the question to the senators from Ohio and Massachusetts (Mr. Chase and Mr. Sumner).   I despair in extorting a response from them; for no matter in what way they may answer upon this point, I have in my hand the evidence, over their own signatures, to disprove the truth of their answer.   I allude to their appeal or manifesto to the people of the United States, in which they arraign the bill and report, in coarse and savage terms, as a proposition to repeal the Missouri Compromise, to violate plighted faith, to abrogate a solemn compact, etc., etc. This document was signed by these two senators in their official capacity, and published to the world before any amendments had been offered to the bill.

It was directed against the committee's first bill and report, and against them alone. If the statements in this document be true, that the first bill did repeal the eighth section of the Missouri Act, what are we to think of the statements in their speeches since, that such was not the intention of the commitee, was not the recommendation of the report, and was not the legal effect of the bill? On the contrary, if the statements in the subsequent speeches are true, what apology do those senators propose to make to the Senate and country for having falsified the action of the committee in a document over their own signatures, and thus spread a false alarm among the people, and misled the public mind in respect to our proceedings? These senators cannot avoid the one or the other of these alternatives. Let them seize upon either, and they stand condemned and self-convicted; in the one case by their manifesto, and in the other by their speeches.

In fact, it is clear that they have understood the bill to mean the same thing, and to have the same legal effect in whatever phase it has been presented. When first introduced, they denounced it as a proposition to abrogate the Missouri restriction. When amended, they repeated they same denunciation, and so on each successive amendment. They now object to the passage of the bill for the same reason, thus proving conclusively that they have not the least faith in the correctness of their own statements in respect to the mutations and changes in the bill.

They seem very unwilling to meet the real issue. They do not like to discuss the principle. There seems to be something which strikes them with terror when you invite their attention to that great fundamental principle of popular sovereignty. Hence you find that all the memorials they have presented are against repealing the Missouri Compromise, and in favor of the sanctity of compacts—in favor of preserving plighted faith. The senator from Ohio is cautious to dedicate his speech with some such heading as " Maintain Plighted Faith." The object is to keep the attention of the people as far as possible from the principle of self-government and constitutional rights.

Well, sir, what is this Missouri Compromise, of which we have heard so much of late? It has been read so often that it is not necessary to occupy the time of the Senate in reading it again. It was an act of Congress, passed on the 6th of March, 1820, to authorize the people of Missouri to form a Constitution and a state government, preparatory to the admission of such state into the Union. The first section provided that Missouri should be received into the Union "on an equal footing with the original states in all respects whatsoever." The last and eighth section provided that slavery should be " forever prohibited" in all the territories which had been acquired from France North of 36° 30'', and not included within the limits of the State of Missouri. There is nothing in the terms of the law that purports to be a compact, or indicates that it was any thing more than an ordinary act of legislation. To prove that it was more than it purports to be on its face, gentlemen must produce other evidence, and prove that there was such an understanding as to create a moral obligation in the nature of a compact. Have they shown it?

I have heard but one item of evidence produced during this whole debate, and that was a short paragraph from Niles's Register, published a few days after the passage of the act. But gentlemen aver that it was a solemn compact, which could not be violated or abrogated without dishonor. According to their understanding, the contract was that, in consideration of the admission of Missouri into the Union, on an equal footing with the original states in all respects whatsoever, slavery should be prohibited forever in the territories North of 36° 30'. Now, who were the parties to this alleged compact? They tell us that it was a stipulation between the North and the South. Sir, I know of no such parties under the Constitution. I am unwilling that there shall be any such parties known in our legislation. If there is such a geographical line, it ought to be obliterated forever; and there should be no other parties than those provided for in the Constitution, viz: the States of this Union. These are the only parties capable of contracting under the Constitution of the United States.

Now, if this was a compact, let us see how it was entered into. The bill originated in the House of Representatives, and passed that body without a southern vote in its favor. It is proper to remark, however, that it did not at that time contain the eighth section, prohibiting slavery in the territories; but, in lieu of it, contained a provision prohibiting slavery in the proposed State of Missouri. In the Senate, the clause prohibiting slavery in the state was stricken out, and the eighth section added to the end of the bill, by the terms of which slavery was to be forever prohibited in the territory not embraced in the State of Missouri north of 36° 30′. The vote on adding this section stood, in the Senate, 34 in the affirmative, and 10 in the negative. Of the northern senators, 20 voted for it and 2 against it. On the question of ordering the bill to a third reading as amended, which was the test vote on its passage, the vote stood 24 yeas and 20 nays. Of the northern senators, 4 only voted in the affirmative, and 18 in the negative. Thus it will be seen that, if it was intended to be a compact, the North never agreed to it. The northern senators voted to insert the prohibition of slavery in the territories; and then, in the proportion of more than four to one, voted against the passage of the bill. The North, therefore, never signed the compact, never consented to it, never agreed to be bound by it. This fact becomes very important in vindicating the character of the North for repudiating this alleged compromise a few months afterwards. The act was approved and became a law on the 6th of March, 1820. In the summer of that year, the people of Missouri formed a Constitution and state government preparatory to admission into the Union, in conformity with the act. At the next session of Congress the Senate passed a joint resolution, declaring Missouri to be one of the states of the Union, on an equal footing with the original states. This resolution was sent to the House of Representatives, where it was rejected by northern votes, and thus Missouri was voted out of the Union, instead of being received into the Union under the act of the 6th of March, 1820, now known as the Missouri Compromise. Now, sir, what becomes of our plighted faith, if the act of the 6th of March, 1820, was a solemn compact, as we are now told? They have all rung the changes upon it, that it was a sacred and irrevocable compact, binding in honor, in conscience, and morals, which could not be violated or repudiated without perfidy and dishonor! The two senators from Ohio, [Mr. Chase and Mr. Wade,] the senator from Massachusetts, [Mr. Sumner,] the senator from Connecticut, [Mr. Smith,] the senator from New York, [Mr. Seward,] and perhaps others, have all assumed this position.

Mr. Seward. Will the senator excuse me for a moment?

Mr. Douglas. Certainly.

Mr. Seward. Mr. President, I have foreseen that it would be probable that the honorable senator from Illinois would have occasion to reply to many arguments which have been made by the opponents of this measure; and it would seem, therefore, to create a necessity, on the part of the opponents of the bill, to answer his arguments afterwards. Yet, at the same time, meaning to be fair, and desiring to have no such advantage as the last word, but to leave it to him, to whom it rightly belongs, I had proposed, if agreeable to him, when he should state anything which controverted my own position, to make the answer during his speech, instead of deferring it until afterwards. To me the last word is never of any advantage; but I know that it is to him, and ought to be so regarded by him. I have a word to say here, and I propose to say another word at another time; but if it be at all uncomfortable to the senator, I will reserve what I have to say until after he concludes.

Mr. Douglas. If it will take but a minute, I will yield now; but if the senator is to take considerable time, I prefer to go on myself.

Mr. Seward. No, sir, I make no long speeches anywhere; I never make a long speech, and therefore I would prefer saying what I have to submit now, if the honorable senator prefers it.

Mr. Douglas. Very well.

Mr. Seward. I thought he would. In the first place, I find that the honorable senator is coming upon my own ground in regard to compromises.

Mr. Douglas. That is not a vindication of any point which I have attacked. I hope the honorable senator will state his point.

Mr. Seward. I am going to state the point, or I will state nothing. Whoever will refer to my antecedents will find that in the year 1850 I expressed opinions on the subject of legislative compromises between the North and South, which, at that day, were rejected and repudiated.

Mr. Douglas. If the object of the senator is to go back, and go through all his opinions, I can not yield the floor to him; but if his object is now to show that the North did not violate the Missouri Compromise, I will yield.

Mr. Seward. If the honorable senator will allow me just one minute and a half, without dictating what I shall say within that minute and a half, I shall be satisfied.

Mr. Douglas. Certainly, I will consent to that.

Mr. Seward. I find that the honorable senator from Illinois is standing upon the ground upon which I stood in 1850. I have nothing to say now in favor of that ground. On this occasion, I stand upon the ground, in regard to compromises, which has been adopted by the country. Then, when the senator tells me that the North did not altogether, willingly, and unanimously, consent to the Compromise of 1820, I agree to it; but I have been overborne in the country, on the ground that if one northern man carried with him a majority of Congress he bound the whole North. And so I hold in regard to the Compromise of 1820, that it was carried by a vote which has been held by the South and by the honorable senator from Illinois to bind the North. The South having received their consideration and equivalent, I only hold him, upon his own doctrine and the doctrine of the South, bound to stand to it. That is all I have to say upon that point.

A few words more will cover all that I have to say about what the honorable senator may say hereafter as to the North repudiating this contract. When I was absent, I understood the senator alluded to the fact that my name appeared upon an appeal which was issued by the honorable senator from Ohio, and some other members of Congress, to the people, on the subject of this bill. Upon that point it has been my intention throughout to leave to the honorable senator from Illinois, and those who act with him, whatever there is of merit, and whatever there is of responsibility for the present measure, and for all the agitation and discussion upon it. Therefore, as soon as I found, when I returned to the Capitol, that my name was on that paper, I caused it to be made known and published, as fully and extensively as I could, that I had never been consulted in regard to it; that I know nothing about it; and that the merit of the measure, as well as the responsibility, belonged to the honorable senator from Ohio, and those who coöperated with him; and that I had never seen the paper on which he commented; nor have I in any way addressed the public upon the subject.

Mr. Douglas. I wish to ask the senator from New York a question. If I understood his remarks when he spoke, and if I understand his speech as published, he averred that the Missouri Compromise was a compact between the North and the South; that the North performed it on its part; that it had done so faithfully for thirty years; that the South had received all its benefits, and the moment these benefits had been fully realized, the South disavowed the obligations under which it had received them. Is not that his position?

Mr. Seward. I am not accustomed to answer questions put to me, unless they are entirely categorical, and placed in such a shape that I may know exactly, and have time to consider, their whole extent. The honorable senator from Illinois has put a very broad question. What I mean to say, however, and that will answer his purpose, is, that his position, and that the position of the South is, that this was a compromise; and I say that the North has never repudiated that compromise. Indeed, it has never had the power to do so. Missouri came into the Union, and Arkansas came into the Union, under that compromise; and whatever individuals may have said, whatever individuals, more or less humble than myself, may have contended, the practical effect is, that the South has had all that she could get by that compromise, and that the North is now in the predicament of being obliged to defend what was left to her. I believe that answers the question.

Mr. Douglas. Now, Mr. President, I choose to bring men directly up to this point. The senator from New York has labored in his whole speech to make it appear that this was a compact; that the North had been faithful; and that the South acquiesced until she got all its advantages, and then disavowed and sought to annul it. This he pronounced to be bad faith; and he made appeals about dishonor. The senator from Connecticut [Mr. Smith] did the same thing, and so did the senator from Massachusetts [Mr. Sumner], and the senator from Ohio [Mr. Chase]. That is the great point to which the whole abolition party are now directing all their artillery in this battle. Now, I propose to bring them to the point. If this was a compact, and if what they have said is fair, or just, or true, who was it that repudiated the compact?

Mr. Sumner. Mr. President, the senator from Illinois, I know, does not intend to misstate my position. That position, as announced in the language of the speech which I addressed to the Senate, and which I now hold in my hand, is, "this is an infraction of solemn obligations, assumed beyond recall by the South, on the admission of Missouri into the Union as a slave state;" which was one year after the act of 1820.

Mr. Douglas. Mr. President, I shall come to that; and I wish to see whether this was an obligation which was assumed "beyond recall." If it was a compact between the two parties, and one party has been faithful, it is beyond recall by the other. If, however, one party has been faithless, what shall we think of them, if, while faithless, they ask a performance?

Mr. Seward. Show it.

Mr. Douglas. That is what I am coming to. I have already stated that, at the next session of Congress, Missouri presented a Constitution in conformity with the act of 1820; that the Senate passed a joint resolution to admit her; and that the house refused to admit Missouri in conformity with the alleged compact, and, I think, on three distinct votes, rejected her.

Mr. Seward. I beg my honorable friend, for I desire to call him so, to answer me frankly whether he would rather I should say what I have to say in this desultory way, or whether he would prefer that I should answer him afterwards; because it is with me a rule in the Senate never to interrupt a gentleman, except to help him in his argument.

Mr. Douglas. I would rather hear the senator now.

Mr. Seward. What I have to say now, and I acknowledge the magnanimity of the senator from Illinois in allowing me to say it, is, that the North stood by that compact until Missouri came in with a Constitution, one article of which denied to colored citizens of other States the equality of privileges which were allowed to all other citizens of the United States, and then the

North insisted on the right of colored men to be regarded as citizens, and entitled to the privileges and immunities of citizens. Upon that a new compromise was necessary. I hope I am candid.

Mr. Douglas. The senator is candid, I have no doubt, as he understands the facts; but I undertake to maintain that the North objected to Missouri because she allowed slavery, and not because of the free-negro clause alone.

Mr. Seward. No, sir.

Mr. Douglas. Now I will proceed to prove that the North did not object, solely on account of the free-negro clause; but that, in the House of Representatives at that time, the North objected as well because of slavery as in regard to free negroes. Here is the evidence. In the House of Representatives, on the 12th of February, 1821, Mr. Mallory, of Vermont, moved to amend the Senate joint resolution for the admission of Missouri, as follows:

" To amend the said amendment, by striking out all thereof after the word *respects*, and inserting the following: ' Whenever the people of the said State, by a convention, appointed according to the manner provided by the act to authorize the people of Missouri to form a Constitution and state government, and for the admission of such state into the Union on an equal footing with the original states, and to prohibit slavery in certain territories, approved March 6, 1820, adopt a Constitution conformably to the provisions of said act, and shall, IN ADDITION *to said provision, further provide, in and by said Constitution, that neither slavery nor involuntary servitude shall ever be allowed in said State of Missouri,* unless inflicted as a punishment for crimes committed against the laws of said State, whereof the party accused shall be duly convicted: *Provided,* That the civil condition of those persons who now are held to service in Missouri shall not be affected by this last provision."

Here I show, then, that the proposition was made that Missouri should not come in unless, in addition to complying with the Missouri Compromise, she would go further, and prohibit slavery within the limits of the state.

Mr. Seward. Now, then, for the vote.

Mr. Douglas. The vote was taken by yeas and nays. I hold it in my hand. Sixty-one northern men voted for that amendment, and thirty-three against it. Thus the North, by a vote of nearly two to one, expressly repudiated a solemn compact upon the very matter in controversy, to wit: that slavery should not be prohibited in the State of Missouri.

Mr. Weller. Let the senator from New York answer that.

Mr. Douglas. I should like to hear his answer.

Mr. Seward. I desire, if I shall be obtrusive by speaking in this way, that senators will at once signify, or that any senator will signify, that I am obtrusive. But I make these explanations in this way, for the reason that I desire to give the honorable senator from Illinois the privilege of hearing my answer to him as he goes along. It is simply this: That this doctrine of compromises is, as it has been held, that if so many northern men shall go with so many southern men as to fix the law, then it binds the North and South alike. I therefore have but one answer to make: that the vote for the restriction was less than the northern vote which was given against the whole compromise.

Mr. Douglas. Well, now, we come to this point: We have been told, during this debate, that you must not judge of the North by the minority, but by her majority. You have been told that the minority, who stood by the Constitution and the rights of the South, were dough-faces.

Mr. Seward. I have not said so. I will not say so.

Mr. Douglas. You have all said so in your speeches, and you have asked us to take the majority of the North.

Mr. Seward. I spoke of the practical fact. I never said anything about dough-faces.

Mr. Douglas. You have asked us to take the majority instead of the minority.

Mr. Seward. The majority of the country.

Mr. Douglas. I am talking of the majority of the northern vote.

Mr. Seward. No, sir.

Mr. Douglas. I hope the senator will hear me. I wish to recall him to the issue. I stated that the North in the House of Representatives voted against admitting Missouri into the Union under the act of 1820, and caused the defeat of that measure; and he said that they voted against it on the ground of the free-negro clause in her Constitution, and not upon the ground of slavery. Now, I have shown by the evidence that it was upon the ground of slavery, as well as upon the other ground; and that a majority of the North required not only that Missouri should comply with the compact of 1820, so called, but that she should go further, and give up the whole consideration which the senator says the South received from the North for the Missouri Compromise. The compact, he says, was that in consideration of slavery being permitted in Missouri, it should be prohibited in the territories. After having procured the prohibition in the territories, the North, by a majority of her votes, refused to admit Missouri as a slaveholding state, and, in violation of the alleged compact, required her to prohibit slavery as a further condition of her admission. This repudiation of the alleged compact by the North is recorded by yeas and nays, sixty-one to thirty-three, and entered upon the Journal, as an imperishable evidence of the fact. With this evidence before us, against whom should the charge of perfidy be preferred?

Sir, if this was a compact, what must be thought of those who violated it almost immediately after it was formed? I say it was a calumny upon the North to say that it was a compact. I should feel a flush of shame upon my cheek, as a northern man, if I were to say that it was a compact, and that the section of country to which I belong received the consideration, and then repudiated the obligation in eleven months after it was entered into. I deny that it was a compact in any sense of the term. But if it was, the record proves that faith was not observed; that the contract was never carried into effect; that after the North had procured the passage of the act prohibiting slavery in the territories, with a majority in the house large enough to prevent its repeal, Missouri was refused admission into the Union as a slaveholding state, in conformity with the act of March 6, 1820. If the proposition be correct, as contended for by the opponents of this bill, that there was a solemn compact between the North and South that, in consideration of the prohibition of slavery in the territories, Missouri was to be admitted into the Union in conformity with the act of 1820, that compact was repudiated by the North and rescinded by the joint action of the two parties within twelve months from its date. Missouri was never admitted under the act of the 6th of March, 1820. She was refused admission under that act. She was voted out of the Union by northern votes, notwithstanding the stipulation that she should be received; and, in consequence of these facts, a new compromise was rendered necessary, by the terms of which Missouri was to be admitted into the Union conditionally—admitted on a condition not embraced in the act of 1820, and, in addition, to a full compliance with all the provisions of said act. If, then, the act of 1820, by the eighth section of which slavery was prohibited in the territories, was a compact, it is clear to the comprehension of every fair-minded man that the refusal of the North to admit Missouri, in compliance with its stipulations, and without further conditions, imposes upon us a high moral obligation to remove the prohibition of slavery in the territories, since it has been shown to have been procured upon a condition never performed.

Mr. President, in as much as the senator from New York has taken great pains to impress upon the public mind of the North the conviction that the act of 1820 was a solemn compact, the violation or repudiation of which by either party involves perfidy and dishonor, I wish to call the attention of that senator (Mr. Seward) to the fact that his own state was the first to repudiate the compact and to instruct her senators in Congress not to admit Missouri into the Union in compliance with it, nor unless slavery should be prohibited in the State of Missouri.

Mr. Seward. That is so.

Mr. Douglas. I have the resolutions before me, in the printed Journal of the Senate. The senator from New York is familiar with the fact, and frankly admits it:

"STATE OF NEW YORK, }
"IN ASSEMBLY, *November* 13, 1820. }

"Whereas, the legislature of this state, at the last session, did instruct their senators and request their representatives in Congress to oppose the admission, as a state, into the Union, of any territory not comprised within the original boundaries of the United States, without making the prohibition of slavery therein an indispensable condition of admission; and whereas this legislature is impressed with the correctness of the sentiments so communicated to our senators and representatives: Therefore,

"*Resolved* (if the honorable the Senate concur herein), That this legislature does approve of the principles contained in the resolutions of the last session; and further, if the provisions contained in any proposed Constitution of a new state deny to any citizens of the existing states, the privileges and immunities of citizens of such new state, that such proposed Constitution should not be accepted or confirmed; the same, in the opinion of this legislature, being void by the Constitution of the United States. And that our senators be instructed, and our representatives in Congress be requested, to use their utmost exertions to prevent the acceptance and confirmation of any such Constitution."

It will be seen by these resolutions that at the previous session the New York Legislature had "instructed" the senators from that state "TO OPPOSE THE ADMISSION, AS A STATE, INTO THE UNION OF ANY TERRITORY not comprised within the original boundaries of the United States, WITHOUT MAKING THE PROHIBITION OF SLAVERY THEREIN AN INDISPENSABLE CONDITION OF ADMISSION."

These instructions are not confined to territory North of 36° 30'. They apply, and were intended to apply, to the whole country West of the Mississippi, and to all territory which might hereafter be acquired. They deny the right of Arkansas to admission as a slaveholding state, as well as Missouri. They lay down a general principle to be applied and insisted upon everywhere, and in all cases, and under all circumstances. These resolutions were first adopted prior to the passage of the act of March 6, 1820, which the senator now chooses to call a compact. But they were renewed and repeated on the 13th of November, 1820, a little more than eight months after the adoption of the Missouri Compromise, as instructions to the New York senators to resist the admission of Missouri as a slaveholding state, notwithstanding the stipulations in the alleged compact. Now, let me ask the senator from New York by what authority he declared and published in his speech that the act of 1820 was a compact which could not be violated or repudiated without a sacrifice of honor, justice, and good faith. Perhaps he will shelter himself behind the resolutions of his state, which he presented this session, branding this bill as a violation of plighted faith.

Mr. Seward. Will the senator allow me a word of explanation?

Mr. Douglas. Certainly, with a great deal of pleasure.

Mr. Seward. I wish simply to say that the State of New York, for now thirty years, has refused to make any compact on any terms by which a concession should be made for the extension of slavery. But, by the practical action of the Congress of the United States, compromises have been made, which, it is held by the honorable senator from Illinois and by the South, bind her against her consent and approval. And therefore she stands throughout this whole matter upon the same ground—always refusing to enter into a compromise, always insisting upon the prohibition of slavery within the Territories of the United States. But, on this occasion, we stand here with a contract which has stood for thirty years, notwithstanding our protest and dissent, and in which there is nothing left to be fulfilled except that part which is to be beneficial to us. All the rest has been fulfilled, and we stand here with our old opinions on the whole subject of compromises, demanding fulfillment on the part of the South, which the honorable senator from Illinois on the present occasion represents.

Mr. Douglas. Mr. President, the senator undoubtedly speaks for himself very frankly and very candidly.

Mr. Seward. Certainly I do.

Mr. Douglas. But I deny that on this point he speaks for the State of New York.

Mr. Seward. We shall see.

Mr. Douglas. I will state the reason why I say so. He has presented here resolutions of the State of New York which have been adopted this year, declaring the act of March 6, 1820, to be a " solemn compact."

I read from the second resolution:

" But at the same time duty to themselves and to the other states of the Union demands that when an effort is making to violate a solemn compact, whereby the political power of the state and the privileges as well as the honest sentiments of its citizens will be jeoparded and invaded, they should raise their voice in protest against the threatened infraction of their rights, and declare that the negation or repeal by Congress of the Missouri compromise will be regarded by them as a violation of right and of faith, and destructive of that confidence and regard which should attach to the enactments of the federal legislature."

Mr. President, I cannot let the senator off on the plea that I, for the sake of the argument, in reply to him and other opponents of this bill, have called it a compact; or that the South have called it a compact; or that other friends of Nebraska have called it a compact which has been violated and rendered invalid. He and his abolition confederates have arraigned me for a violation of a compact which, they say, is binding in morals, in conscience, and honor. I have shown that the legislature of New York, at its present session, has declared it to be " a solemn compact," and that its repudiation would " be regarded by them as a violation of right and of faith, and destructive of confidence and regard." I have also shown that if it be such a compact, the State of New York stands self-condemned and self-convicted as the first to repudiate and violate it.

But since the senator has chosen to make an issue with me in respect to the action of New York, with the view of condemning my conduct here, I will invite the attention of the senator to another portion of these resolutions. Referring to the fourteenth section of the Nebraska Bill, the Legislature of New York says:

" That the adoption of this provision would be in derogation of the truth, a gross violation of plighted faith, and an outrage and indignity upon the free states of the Union, whose assent has been yielded to the admission into the Union of Missouri and of Arkansas, with slavery, in reliance upon the faithful observance of the provision (now sought to be abrogated) known as the Missouri compromise, whereby slavery was declared to be " for ever prohibited in all that territory ceded by France to the United States, under the name of Louisiana, which lies North of 36° 30' North latitude, not included within the limits of the State of Missouri."

I have no comments to make upon the courtesy and propriety exhibited in this legislative declaration, that a provision in a bill, reported by a regular committee of the Senate of the United States, and known to be approved by three-fourths of the body, and which has since received the sanction of their votes, is "in derogation of truth, a gross violation of plighted faith, and an outrage and indignity," etc. The opponents of this measure claim a monopoly of all the courtesies and amenities which should be observed among gentlemen, and especially in the performance of official duties; and I am free to say that this is one of the mildest and most respectful forms of expression in which they have indulged. But there is a declaration in this resolution to which I wish to invite the particular attention of the Senate and the country. It is the distinct allegation that "the free states of the Union," including New York, yielded their "assent to the admission into the Union of Missouri and Arkansas, with slavery, in reliance upon the faithful observance of the provision known as the Missouri Compromise."

Now, sir, since the Legislature of New York has gone out of its way to arraign the state on matters of truth, I will demonstrate that this paragraph contains two material statements in direct "derogation of truth." I have already shown, beyond controversy, by the records of the Legislature and by the Journals of the Senate, that New York never did give her assent to the admission of Missouri with slavery! Hence, I must be permitted to say, in the polite language of her own resolutions, that the statement that New York yielded her assent to the admission of Missouri with slavery is in "derogation of truth!" and secondly, the statement that such assent was given "in reliance upon the faithful observance of the Missouri compromise" is equally "in derogation of truth." New York never assented to the admission of Missouri as a slave state, never assented to what she now calls the Missouri Compromise, never observed its stipulations as a compact, never has been willing to carry it out; but, on the contrary, has always resisted it, as I have demonstrated by her own records.

Mr. President, I have before me other journals, records, and instructions, which prove that New York was not the only free state that repudiated the Missouri Compromise of 1820, within twelve months from its date. I will not occupy the time of the Senate at this late hour of the night by referring to them, unless some opponent of the bill renders it necessary. In that event, I may be able to place other senators and their states in the same unenviable position in which the senator from New York has found himself and his state.

I think I have shown, that to call the act of the 6th of March, 1820, a compact, binding in honor, is to charge the northern States of this Union with an act of perfidy unparalelled in the history of legislation or of civilization. I have already adverted to the facts, that in the summer of 1820 Missouri formed her Constitution, in conformity with the act of the 6th of March; that it was presented to Congress at the next session; that the Senate passed a joint resolution declaring her to be one of the states of the Union, on an equal footing with the original states; and that the House of Representatives rejected it, and refused to allow her to come into the Union, because her Constitution did not prohibit slavery.

These facts created the necessity for a new compromise, the old one having failed of its object, which was to bring Missouri into the Union. At this period in the order of events—in February, 1821, when the excitement was almost beyond restraint, and a great fundamental principle, involving the right of the people of the new states to regulate their own domestic institutions, was dividing the Union into two great hostile parties—Henry Clay, of Kentucky, came forward with a new compromise, which had the effect to change the issue, and make the result of the controversy turn upon a different point. He brought in a resolution for the admission of Missouri into the Union, not in pursuance of the act of 1820, not in obedience to the understanding when it was adopted, and not with her Constitution as it had been formed in conformity with that act, but he proposed to admit Missouri into the Union upon a "fundamental condition," which condition was to be in the nature of a solemn compact between the United States on the one part and the State of Missouri on the other part, and to which "fundamental condition" the State of Missouri was required to declare her assent in the form of "a solemn public act." This joint resolution passed, and was approved March 2, 1821, and is known as Mr. Clay's Missouri compromise, in contradistinction to that of 1820, which was introduced into the Senate by Mr. Thomas, of Illinois. In the month of June, 1821, the legislature of Missouri assembled and passed the "solemn public act," and furnished an authenticated copy thereof to the President of the United States, in compliance with Mr. Clay's compromise, or joint resolution. On August 10, 1821, James Monroe, President of the United States, issued his proclamation, in which, after reciting the fact that on the 2d of March, 1821, Congress had passed a joint resolution "providing for the admission of the State of Missouri into the Union, on a certain condition;" and that the general assembly of Missouri, on the 26th of June, having, "by a solemn public act, declared the assent of said State of Missouri to the fundamental condition contained in said joint resolution," and having furnished him with an authenticated copy thereof, he, "*in pursuance of the resolution of Congress aforesaid*," declared the admission of Missouri to be complete.

I do not deem it necessary to discuss the question whether the conditions upon which Missouri was admitted were wise or unwise. It is sufficient for my present purpose to remark, that the "fundamental condition" of her admission related to certain clauses in the Constitution of Missouri in respect to the migration of free negroes into that state; clauses similar to those now in force in the Constitutions of Illinois and Indiana, and perhaps other states; clauses similar to the provisions of law in force at that time in many of the old states of the Union; and, I will add, clauses which, in my opinion, Missouri had a right to adopt under the Constitution of the United States. It is no answer to this position to say, that those clauses in the Constitution of Missouri were in violation of the Constitution. If they did conflict with the Constitution of the United States, they were void; if they were not in conflict, Missouri had a right to put them there, and to pass all laws necessary to carry them into effect. Whether such conflict did exist is a question which, by the Constitution, can only be determined authoritatively by the Supreme Court of the United States. Congress is not the appropriate and competent tribunal to adjudicate and determine questions of conflict between the Constitution of a state and that of the United States. Had Missouri been admitted without any condition or restriction, she would have had an opportunity of vindicating her Constitution and rights in the Supreme Court—the tribunal created by the Constitution for that purpose.

By the condition imposed on Missouri, Congress not only deprived that state of a right which she believed she possessed under the Constitution of the United States, but denied her the privilege of vindicating that right in the appropriate and constitutional tribunals, by compelling her, "by a solemn public act," to give an irrevocable pledge never to exercise or claim the right. Therefore Missouri came under a humiliating condition—a condition not imposed by the Constitution of the United States, and which destroys the principle of equality which should exist, and by the Constitution does exist, between all the States of this Union. This inequality resulted from Mr. Clay's compromise of 1821, and is the principle upon which that compromise was constructed. I own that the act is couched in general terms and vague phrases, and therefore may possibly be so construed as not to deprive the state of any right she might possess under the Constitution. Upon that point I wish only to say, that such a construction makes the "fundamental condition" void, while the opposite construction would demonstrate it to be unconstitutional. I have before me the "solemn public act" of Missouri to this fundamental condition. Whoever will take the trouble to read it will find it the richest specimen of irony and sarcasm that has ever been incorporated into a solemn public act.

Sir, in view of these facts I desire to call the attention of the senator from New York to a statement in his speech, upon which the greater part of his argument rested. His statement was, and it is now being published in every abolition paper, and repeated by the whole tribe of abolition orators and lecturers, that Missouri was admitted as a slaveholding state, under the act of 1820; while I have shown, by the President's proclamation of August 10, 1821, that she was admitted in pursuance of the resolution of March 2, 1821. Thus it is shown that the material point of his speech is contradicted by the highest evidence—the record in the case. The same statement, I believe, was made by the senator from Connecticut, (Mr. Smith,) and the senators from Ohio, (Mr. Chase and Mr. Wade,) and the senator from Massachusetts, (Mr. Sumner.) Each of these senators made and repeated this statement, and upon the strength of this erroneous assertion called upon us to carry into effect the eighth section of the same act. This material fact upon which their arguments rested being overthrown, of course their conclusions are erroneous and deceptive.

Mr. Seward. I hope the senator will yield for a moment, because I have never had so much respect for him as I have to-night.

Mr. Douglas. I see what course I have to pursue in order to command the senator's respect. I know now how to get it. [Laughter.]

Mr. Seward. Any man who meets me boldly commands my respect. I say that Missouri would not have been admitted at all into the Union by the United States except upon the compromise of 1820. When that point was settled about the restriction of slavery, it was settled in this way: that she should come in with slavery, and that all the rest of the Louisiana purchase, which is now known as Nebraska, should be forever free from slavery. Missouri adopted a Constitution, which was thought by the northern states to infringe upon the right of citizenship guaranteed by the Constitution of the United States, which was a new point altogether; and upon that point debate was held, and upon it a new compromise was made, and Missouri came into the Union upon the agreement that, in regard to that question, she submitted to the Constitution of the United States, and so she was admitted into the Union.

Mr. Douglas. Mr. President, I must remind the senator again that I have already proven that he was in error in stating that the North objected to the admission of Missouri merely on account of the free-negro clause in her Constitution. I have proven by the vote that the North objected to her admission because she tolerated slavery; this objection was sustained by the North by a vote of nearly two to one. He cannot shelter himself, therefore, under the free-negro dodge, so long as there is a distinct vote of the North objecting to her admission; because, in addition to complying with the act of 1820, she did not also prohibit slavery, which was the only consideration that the South was to have for agreeing to the prohibition of slavery in the territories. Then, having deprived the senator, by conclusive evidence from the records, of that pretext, what do I drive him to? I compel him to acknowledge that a new compromise was made.

Mr. Seward. Certainly there was.

Mr. Douglas. Then, I ask, why was it made? Because the North would not carry out the first one. And the best evidence that the North did not carry out the first one is the senator's admission that the South was compelled to submit to a new one. Then, if there was a new compromise made, did Missouri come in under the new one or the old one?

Mr. Seward. Under both.

Mr. Douglas. This is the first time, in this debate, it has been intimated that Missouri came in under two acts of Congress. The senator did not allude to the resolution of 1821 in his speech; none of the opponents of this bill have said it. But it is now admitted that she did not come into the Union under the act of 1820 alone. She had been voted out under the first compromise, and this vote compelled her to make a new one, and she came in under the new one; and yet the senator from New York, in his speech, declared to the world that she came in under the first one. This is not an immaterial question. His whole speech rests upon that misapprehension or misstatement of the record.

Mr. Seward. You had better say misapprehension.

Mr. Douglas. Very well. We will call it by that name. His whole argument depends upon that misapprehension. After stating that the act of 1820 was a compact, and that the North performed its part of it in good faith, he arraigns the friends of this bill for proposing to annul the eighth section of the act of 1820 without first turning Missouri out of the Union, in order that slavery may be abolished therein by the act of Congress. He says to us, in substance: "Gentlemen, if you are going to rescind the compact, have respect for that great law of morals, of honesty, and of conscience, which compels you first to surrender the consideration which which you have received 'under the compact.'" I concur with him in regard to the obligation to restore the consideration when a contract is rescinded. And, inasmuch as the prohibition in the territories North of 36° 30′ was obtained, according to his own statement, by an agreement to admit Missouri as a slaveholding state on an equal footing with the original states, "in all respects whatsoever," as specified in the first section of the act of 1820; and, inasmuch as Missouri was refused admission under said act, and was compelled to submit to a new compromise in 1821, and was then received into the Union on a fundamental condition of inequality, I call on him and his abolition confederates to restore the consideration which they have received, in the shape of a prohibition of slavery North of 36° 30′, under a compromise which they repudiated, and refused to carry into effect. I call on them to correct the erroneous statement in respect to the admission of Missouri, and to make a restitution of the consideration by voting for this bill. I repeat that this is not an immaterial statement. It is the point upon which the abolitionists rest their whole argument. They could not get up a show of pretext against the great principles of self-government involved in this bill, if they could not repeat all the time, as the senator from New York did in his speech, that Missouri came into the Union with slavery, in conformity to the compact which was made by the act of 1820, and that the South, having received the consideration, is now trying to cheat the North out of her part of the benefits. I have proven that, after abolitionism had gained its point so far as the eighth section of the act prohibited slavery in the territory, Missouri was denied admission by Northern votes until she entered into a compact by which she was understood to surrender an important right now exercised by several states of the Union.

Mr. President, I did not wish to refer to these things. I did not understand them fully in all their bearings at the time I made my first speech on this subject; and, so far as I was familiar with them, I made as little reference to them as was consistent with my duty; because it was a mortifying reflection to me, as a northern man, that we had not been able, in consequence of the abolition excitement at the time, to avoid the appearance of bad faith in the observance of legislation, which has been denominated a compromise. There were a few men then, as there are now, who had the moral courage to perform their duty to the country and the Constitution, regardless of consequences personal to themselves. There were ten northern men who dared to perform their duty by voting to admit Missouri into the Union an an equal footing with the original states, and with no other restriction than that imposed by the Constitution. I am aware that they were abused and denounced as we are now; that they were branded as dough-faces, traitors to freedom, and to the section of the country whence they come.

Mr. Geyer. They honored Mr. Lanman, of Connecticut, by burning him in effigy.

Mr. Douglas. Yes, sir; these Abolitionists honored Mr. Lanman in Connecticut just as they are honoring me in Boston, and other places, by burning me in effigy.

Mr. Cass. It will do you no harm.

Mr. Douglas. Well, sir, I know it will not; but why this burning in effigy? It is the legitimate consequences of the address which was sent forth to the world by certain senators whom I denominated, on a former occasion, as the abolition confederates. The senator from Ohio presented here the other day a resolution—he says unintentionally, and I take it so—declaring that every senator who advocated this bill was a traitor to his country, to humanity, and to God; and even he seemed to be shocked at the results of his own advice when it was exposed. Yet he did not seem to know that it was, in substance, what he had advised in his address, over his own signature, when he called upon the people to assemble in public meetings and thunder forth their indignation at the criminal betrayal of precious rights; when he appealed to ministers of the gospel to desecrate their holy calling, and attempted to inflame passions, and fanaticism, and prejudice against senators who would not consider themselves very highly complimented by being called his equals? And yet, when the natural consequences of his own action and advice come back upon him, and he presents them here, and is called to an account for the indecency of the act, he professes his profound regret and surprise that anything should have occurred which could possibly be deemed unkind or disrespectful to any member of this body!

Mr. Sumner. I rise merely to correct the senator in a statement in regard to myself, to the effect that I had said that Missouri came into the Union under the act of 1820, instead of the act of 1821. I forbore to designate any particular act under which Missouri came into the Union, but simply asserted, as the result of the long controversy with regard to her admission, and as the end of the whole transaction, that she was received as a slave State; and that on being so received, whether sooner or later, whether under the act of 1820 or 1821, the obligations of the compact were fixed—irrevocably fixed—so far as the South is concerned.

Mr. Douglas. The senator's explanation does not help him at all. He says he did not state under what act Missouri came in; but he did say, as I understood him, that the act of 1820 was a compact, and that, according to that compact, Missouri was to come in with slavery, provided slavery should be prohibited in certain territories, and did come in in pursuance of the compact. He now uses the word "compact." To what compact does he allude? Is it not to the act of 1820? If he did not, what becomes of his conclusion that the eighth section of that act is irrepealable? He will not venture to deny that his reference was to the act of 1820. Did he refer to the joint resolution of 1821, under which Missouri was admitted? If so, we do not propose to repeal it. We admit that it was a compact, and that its obligations

L

are irrevocably fixed. But that joint resolution does not prohibit slavery in the territories. The Nebraska Bill does not propose to repeal it, or impair its obligation in any way. Then, sir, why not take back your correction, and admit that you did mean the act of 1820, when you spoke of irrevocable obligations and compacts? Assuming, then, that the senator meant what he is now unwilling either to admit or deny, even while professing to correct me, that Missouri came in under the act of 1820, I aver that I have proven that she did not come into the Union under that act. I have proven that she was refused admission under that alleged compact. I have, therefore, proven incontestably that the material statement upon which his argument rests is wholly without foundation, and unequivocally contradicted by the record.

Sir, I believe I may say the same of every speech which has been made against the bill, upon the ground that it impaired the obligation of compacts. There has not been an argument against the measure, every word of which in regard to the faith of compacts is not contradicted by the public records. What I complain of is this: The people may think that a senator, having the laws and journals before him, to which he could refer, would not make a statement in contravention of those records. They make the people believe these things, and cause them to do great injustice to others, under the delusion that they have been wronged, and their feelings outraged. Sir, this address did for a time mislead the whole country. It made the Legislature of New York believe that the act of 1820 was a compact which it would be disgraceful to violate; and, acting under that delusion, they framed a series of resolutions, which, if true and just, convict that State of an act of perfidy and treachery unparalleled in the history of free governments. You see, therefore, the consequences of these misstatements. You degrade your own State, and induce the people, under the impression that they have been injured, to get up a violent crusade against those whose fidelity and truthfulness will in the end command their respect and admiration. In consequence of arousing passions and prejudices, I am now to be found in effigy, hanging by the neck, in all the towns where you have the influence to produce such a result. In all these excesses, the people are yielding to an honest impulse, under the impression that a grievous wrong has been perpetrated. You have had your day of triumph. You have succeeded in directing upon the heads of others a torrent of insult and calumny from which even you shrink with horror, when the fact is exposed that you have become the conduits for conveying it into this hall. In your State, sir, [addressing himself to Mr. Chase,] I find that I am burnt in effigy in your abolition towns. All this is done because I have proposed, as it is said, to violate a compact! Now, what will those people think of you when they find out that you have stimulated them to those acts, which are disgraceful to your State, disgraceful to your party, and disgraceful to your cause, under a misrepresentation of the facts, which misrepresentation you ought to have been aware of, and should never have been made?

Mr. Chase. Will the senator from Illinois permit me to say a few words?

Mr. Douglas. Certainly.

Mr. Chase. Mr. President, I certainly regret that any thing has occurred in my state which should be otherwise than in accordance with the disposition which I trust I have ever manifested to treat the senator from Illinois with entire courtesy. I do not wish, however, to be understood here, or elsewhere, as retracting any statement which I have made, or being unwilling to reassert that statement when it is directly impeached. I regard the admission of Missouri, and the facts of the transaction connected with it, as constituting a compact between the two sections of the country, a part of which was fulfilled in the admission of Missouri, another part in the admission of Arkansas, and other parts of which have been fulfilled in the admission of Iowa, and the organization of Minnesota, but which yet remains to be fulfilled in respect to the Territory of Nebraska, and which, in my judgment, will be violated by the repeal of the Missouri prohibition. That is my judgment. I have no quarrel with senators who differ with me; but upon the whole facts of the transaction, however, I have not changed my opinion at all, in consequence of what has been said by the honorable senator from Illinois. I say that the fact of the transaction, taken together, and as understood by the country for more than thirty years, constitute a compact binding in moral force; though, as I have always said, being embodied in a legislative act, it may be repealed by Congress, if Congress see fit.

Mr. Douglas. Mr. President, I am sorry the senator from Ohio has repeated the statement that Missouri came in under the compact which he says was made by the act of 1820. How many times have I to disprove the statement? Does not the vote to which I have referred show that such was not the case? Does not the fact that there was a necessity for a new compromise show it? Have I not proved it three times over? and is it possible that the senator from Ohio will repeat it in the face of the record, with the vote staring him in the face, and with the evidence which I have produced? Does he suppose that he can make his own people believe that his statement ought to be credited in opposition to the solemn record? I am amazed that the senator should repeat the statement again unsustained by the fact, by the record, and by the evidence, and overwhelmed by the whole current and weight of the testimony which I have produced.

The senator says, also, that he never intended to do me injustice, and he is sorry that the people of his state have acted in the manner to which I have referred. Sir, did he not say, in the same document to which I have already alluded, that I was engaged, with others, in "a criminal betrayal of precious rights," in an "atrocious plot?" Did he not say that I and others were guilty of "meditated bad faith?" Are not these his exact words? Did he not say that "servile demagogues" might make the people believe certain things, or attempt to do so? Did he not say every thing calculated to produce and bring upon my head all the insults to which I have been subjected, publicly and privately—not even excepting the insulting letters which I have received from his constituents, rejoicing at my domestic bereavements, and praying that other and similar calamites may befall me? All these have resulted from that address. I expected such consequences when I first saw it. In it he called upon the preachers of the gospel to prostitute the sacred desk in stimulating excesses; and then, for fear that the people would not know who it was that was to be insulted and calumniated, he told them in a postscript, that Mr. Douglas was the author of all this iniquity, and that they ought not to allow their rights to be made the hazard of a presidential game! After having used such language, he says he meant no disrespect—he meant nothing unkind! He was amazed that I said in my opening speech that there was any thing offensive in this address; and he could not suffer himself to use harsh epithets, or to impugn a gentleman's motives! No, not he! After having deliberately written all these insults, impugning motive and character, and calling upon our holy religion to sanctify the calumny, he could not think of losing his dignity by bandying epithets, or using harsh and disrespectful terms!

Mr. President, I expected all that has occurred, and more than has come, as the legitimate result of that address. The things to which I referred are the natural consequences of it. The only revenge I seek is to expose the authors, and leave them to bear, as best they may, the just indignation of an honest community, when the people discover how their sympathies and feelings have been outraged, by making them the instruments in performing such desperate acts.

Sir, even in Boston I have been hung in effigy. I may say that I expected it to occur even there, for the senator from Massachusetts lives there. He signed his name to that address; and for fear the Boston abolitionists would not know that it was he, he signed it "Charles Sumner, senator from Massachusetts." The first outrage was in Ohio, where the address was circulated under the signature of "Salmon P. Chase, senator from Ohio." The next came from Boston—the same Boston, sir, which, under the direction of the same leaders, closed Fanueil Hall to the immortal Webster in 1850, because of his support of the compromise measures of that year, which all now confess have restored peace and harmony to a distracted country. Yes, sir, even Boston, so glorious in her early history—Boston, around whose name so many historical associations cling, to gratify the heart and exalt the pride of every American—could be led astray by abolition misrepresentations so far as to deny a hearing to her own great man, who had shed so much glory upon Massachusetts and her metropolis! I know that Boston now feels humiliated and degraded by the act. And sir, (addressing himself to Mr. Sumner), you will remember that when you came into the Senate, and sought an opportunity to put forth your abolition incendiarism, you appealed to our sense of justice by the sentiment, "Strike, but hear me first." But when Mr. Webster went back in 1850 to speak to his constituents in his own self-defense, to tell the truth, and to expose his slanderers, you would not hear him, but *you struck first!*

Again, sir, even Boston, with her Fanueil Hall consecrated to liberty, was so far led astray by abolitionism that when one of her gallant sons, gallant by his own glorious deeds, inheriting a heroic revolutionary name, had given his life to his country upon the bloody field of Buena Vista, and when his remains were brought home, even that Boston, under abolition guidance and abolition preaching, denied him a decent burial, because he lost his life in vindicating his country's honor upon the southern frontier! Even the name of Lincoln and the deeds of Lincoln could not secure for him a decent interment, because abolitionism follows a patriot beyond the grave. (Applause in the galleries.)

The Presiding Officer (Mr. Mason in the chair.) Order must be preserved.

Mr. Douglas. Mr. President, with these facts before me, how could I hope to escape the fate which had followed these great and good men? While I had no right to hope that I might be honored as they had been under abolition auspices, have I not a right to be proud of the distinction and the association? Mr. President, I regret these digressions. I have not been able to follow the line of argument which I had marked out for myself, because of the many interruptions. I do not complain of them. It is fair that gentlemen should make them, inasmuch as they have not the opportunity of replying; hence I have yielded the floor, and propose to do so cheerfully whenever any senator intimates that justice to him or his position requires him to say anything in reply.

Returning to the point from which I was diverted.

I think I have shown that if the act of 1826, called the Missouri compromise, was a compact, it was violated and repudiated by a solemn vote of the House of Representatives in 1821, within eleven months after it was adopted. It was repudiated by the North by a majority vote, and that repudiation was so complete and successful as to compel Missouri to make a new compromise, and she was brought into the Union under the new compromise of 1821, and not under the act of 1820. This reminds me of another point made in nearly all the speeches against this bill, and, if I recollect right, was alluded to in the abolition manifesto; to which, I regret to say, I had occasion to refer so often. I refer to the significant hint that Mr. Clay was dead before any one dared to bring forward a proposition to undo the greatest work of his hands. The senator from New York (Mr. Seward) has seized upon this insinuation, and elaborated it, perhaps, more fully than his compeers; and now the abolition press suddenly, and, as if by miraculous conversion, teems with eulogies upon Mr. Clay and his Missouri compromise of 1820.

Now, Mr. President, does not each of these senators know that Mr. Clay was not the author of the act of 1820? Do they not know that he disclaimed it in 1850 in this body? Do they not know that the Missouri restriction did not originate in the house, of which he was a member? Do they not know that Mr. Clay never came into the Missouri controversy as a compromiser until after the compromise of 1820 was repudiated, and it became necessary to make another? I dislike to be compelled to repeat what I have conclusively proven, that the compromise which Mr. Clay effected was the act of 1821, under which Missouri came into the Union, and not the act of 1820. Mr. Clay made that compromise after you had repudiated the first one. How, then, dare you call upon the spirit of that great and gallant statesman to sanction your charge of bad faith against the South on this question?

Mr. Seward. Will the senator allow me a moment?

Mr. Douglas. Certainly.

Mr. Seward. In the year 1851 or 1852, I think 1851, a medal was struck in honor of Henry Clay, of gold, which cost a large sum of money, which contained eleven acts of the life of Henry Clay. It was presented to him by a committee of citizens of New York, by whom it had been made. One of the eleven acts of his life which was celebrated on that medal, which he accepted, was the Missouri compromise of 1820. This is my answer.

Mr. Douglas. Are the words 'of 1820' upon it?

Mr. Seward. It commemorates the Missouri compromise.

Mr. Douglas. Exactly. I have seen that medal; and my recollection is that it does not contain the words 'of 1820.' One of the great acts of Mr. Clay was the Missouri compromise, but what Missouri compromise? Of course the one which Henry Clay made, the one which he negotiated, the one which brought Missouri into the Union, and which settled the controversy. That was the act of 1821, and not the act of 1820. It tends to confirm the statement which I have made. History is misread and misquoted, and these statements have been circulated and disseminated broadcast through the country, concealing the truth. Does not the senator know that Henry Clay, when occupying that seat in 1850, (pointing to Mr. Clay's chair,) in his speech of the 6th of February of that year, said that nothing had struck him with so much surprise as the fact that historical circumstances soon passed out of recollection; and he instanced, as a case in point, the error of attributing to him the act of 1820. (Mr. Seward nodded assent.) The senator from New York says that he does remember that Mr. Clay did say so. If so, how is it, then, that he presumes now to rise and quote that medal as evidence that Henry Clay was the author of the act of 1820?

Mr. Seward. I answer the senator in this way: that Henry Clay, while he said he did not disavow or disapprove of that compromise, transferred the merit of it to others who were more active in procuring it than he, while he had enjoyed the praise and the glory which were due from it.

Mr. Douglas. To that I have only to say that it can not be the reason; for Henry Clay, in that same speech, did take to himself the merit of the Compromise of 1821, and hence it could not have been modesty which made him disavow the other. He said that he did not know whether he had voted for the act of 1820 or not; but he supposed that he had done so. He furthermore said that it did not originate in the House of which he was a member, and that he never did approve of its principles; but that he may have voted, and probably did vote for it, under the pressure of the circumstances.

Now, Mr. President, as I have been doing justice to Mr. Clay on this question, perhaps I may as well do justice to another great man, who was associated with him in carrying through the great measures of 1850, which mortified the senator from New York so much, because they defeated his purpose of carrying on the agitation. I allude to Mr. Webster. The authority of his great name has been quoted for the purpose of proving that he regarded the Missouri act as a compact—an irrepealable compact. Evidently the distinguished senator from Massachusetts [Mr. Everett] supposed he was doing Mr. Webster entire justice when he quoted the passage which he read from Mr. Webster's speech of the 7th of March, 1850, when he said that he stood upon the position that every part of the American continent was fixed for freedom or for slavery by irrepealable law.

The senator says that by the expression "irrepealable law," Mr. Webster meant to include the Compromise of 1820. Now, I will show that that was not Mr. Webster's meaning—that he was never guilty of the mistake of saying that the Missouri act of 1820 was an irrepealable law. Mr. Webster said in that speech, that every foot of territory in the United States was fixed as to its character for freedom or slavery by an irrepealable law. He then inquired if it was not so in regard to Texas. He went on to prove that it was; because, he said, there was a compact in express terms between Texas and the United States. He said the parties were capable of contracting, and that there was a valuable consideration; and hence, he contended, that in that case there was a contract binding in honor, and morals, and law; and that it was irrepealable without a breach of faith.

He went on to say:

"Now, as to California and New Mexico, I hold slavery to be excluded from those territories by a law even superior to that which admits and sanctions it in Texas—I mean the law of nature, of physical geography, the law of the formation of the earth."

That was the irrepealable law which he said prohibited slavery in the territories of Utah and New Mexico. He next went on to speak of the prohibition of slavery in Oregon, and he said it was an "entirely useless, and in that connection, senseless proviso."

He went further, and said:

"That the whole territory of the states in the United States, or in the newly-acquired territory of the United States, has a fixed and settled character, now fixed and settled by law, which can not be repealed in the case of Texas without a violation of public faith, and can not be repealed by any human power in regard to California or New Mexico; that, *under one or other of these laws*, every foot of territory in the states, or in the territories, has now received a fixed and decided character."

What irrepealable laws? "One or the other" of those which he had stated. One was the Texas compact, the other the law of nature and physical geography; and he contends that one or the other fixed the character of the whole American continent for freedom or for slavery. He never alluded to the Missouri Compromise, unless it was by the allusion to the Wilmot proviso in the Oregon bill; and there he said it was a useless, and, in that connection, senseless thing. Why was it a useless and a senseless thing? Because it was reenacting the law of God; because slavery had already been prohibited by physical geography. Sir, that was the meaning of Mr. Webster's speech. My distinguished friend from Massachusetts [Mr. Everett], when he reads the speech again, will be utterly amazed to see how he fell into such an egregious error as to suppose that Mr. Webster had so far fallen from his high position as to say that the Missouri act of 1820 was an irrepealable law.

Mr. Everett. Will the gentleman give way for a moment?

Mr. Douglas. With great pleasure.

Mr. Everett. What I said on that subject was, that Mr. Webster, in my opinion, considered the Missouri Compromise as of the nature of a compact. It is true, as the senator from Illinois has just stated, that Mr. Webster made no allusion, in express terms, to the subject of the Missouri restriction. But I thought then, and I think now, that he referred in general terms to that as a final settlement of the question, in the region to which it applied. It was not drawn in question then on either side of the House. Nobody suggested that it was at stake. Nobody intimated that there was a question before the Senate whether that restriction should be repealed or should remain in force. It was not distinctly, and in terms, alluded to, as the gentleman correctly says, by Mr. Webster or anybody else. What he said in reference to Texas, applied to Texas alone. What he said in reference to Utah and New Mexico, applied to them alone; and what he said with regard to Oregon, to that territory alone. But he stated in general terms, and four or five times, in the speech of the 7th of March, 1850, that there was not a foot of land in the United States or its territories the character of which, for freedom or slavery, was not fixed by some irrepealable law; and I did think then, and I think now, that by the "irrepealable law," as far as concerned the territory North of 36° 30', and included in the Louisiana purchase, Mr. Webster had reference to the Missouri restriction, as regarded as of the nature of a compact. That restriction was copied from one of the provisions of the ordinance of 1787, which are declared in that instrument itself to be articles of compact. The Missouri restriction is the article of the ordinance of 1787 applied to the Louisiana purchase. That this is the correct interpretation of Mr. Webster's language, is confirmed by the fact that he said, more than once, and over again, that all the North lost by the arrangement of 1850, was the non-imposition of the Wilmot proviso upon Utah and New Mexico. If, in addition to that, the North had lost the Missouri restriction over the whole of the Louisiana purchase, could he have used language of that kind, and would he not have attempted, in some way or other, to reconcile such a momentous fact with his repeated statements that the measures of 1850 applied only to the territories newly acquired from Mexico?

Mr. Douglas. Mr. President, I will explain that matter very quickly. Mr. Webster's speech was made on the 7th of March, 1850, and the territorial bills and the Texas Boundary Bill were first reported to the Senate by myself on the 25th of the same month. Mr. Webster's speech was made upon Mr. Clay's resolution, when there was no bill pending. Then the Omnibus Bill was formed about the 1st of May subsequently; and hence this explains the reason why Mr. Webster did not refer to the principle involved in these acts, and to the necessary effect of carrying out the principle.

Mr. Everett. The expression of Mr. Webster, which I quoted in my remarks on the 8th of February, was from a speech on Mr. Soulé's amendment, offered, I think, in June. In addition to this, I have before me an extract from a still later speech of Mr. Webster, made quite late in the session, on the 17th of July, 1850, in which he reiterated that statement. In it he said:

"And now, sir, what do Massachusetts and the North, the anti-slavery states, lose by this adjustment? What is it they lose? I put that question to every gentleman here, and to every gentleman in the country. They lose the application of what is called the 'Wilmot Proviso' to these territories, and that is all. There is nothing else. I suppose, that the whole North are not ready to do. They wish to get California into the Union; they wish to quiet New Mexico; they desire to terminate the dispute about the Texan boundary in any reasonable manner, cost what it reasonably may. They make no sacrifice in all that. What they do sacrifice is exactly this: The application of the 'Wilmot Proviso' to the territory of New Mexico and the territory of Utah, *and that is all.*"

Could Mr. Webster have used language like that if he had understood that, at the same time, the non-slaveholding states were losing the Missouri restriction, as applied to the whole vast territory included in the bills now before the Senate?

Mr. Douglas. Of course that was all, and if he regarded the Missouri prohibition in the same light as he did the Oregon prohibition, it was a useless, and, in that connection, a senseless proviso; and hence the North lost nothing by not having that same senseless, useless proviso applied to Utah and New Mexico. Now, to show the senator that he must be mistaken as to Mr. Webster's authority, let me call his attention back to this passage in his 7th of March speech:

"Under *one or other* of these laws, every foot of territory in the states or territories has now received a fixed and decided character."

What laws did he refer to when he spoke of " one or other of these laws ?" He had named but two, the Texas compact, and the law of nature, of climate, and physical geography, which excluded slavery. He had mentioned none other; and yet he says "one or other" prohibited slavery in all the states or territories—thus including Nebraska, as well as Utah and New Mexico.

Mr. Everett. That was not drawn in question at all.

Mr. Douglas. Then, if it was not drawn in question, the speech should not have been quoted in support of the Missouri Compromise. It is just what I complain of, that, if it was not thus drawn in question, that use ought not to have been made of it. Now, Mr. President, it is well known that Mr. Webster supported the Compromise measures of 1850, and the principle involved in them, of leaving the people to do as they pleased upon this subject. I think, therefore, that I have shown that these gentlemen are not authorized to quote the name either of Mr. Webster or Mr. Clay in support of the position which they take, that this bill violates the faith of compacts. Sir, it was because Mr. Webster went for giving the people in the territories the right to do as they pleased upon the subject of slavery, and because he was in favor of carrying out the Constitution in regard to fugitive slaves, that he was not allowed to speak in Faneuil Hall.

Mr. Everett. That was not my fault.

Mr. Douglas. I know it was not; but I say it was because he took that position; it was because he did not go for a prohibitory policy; it was because he advocated the same principles which I now advocate, because he went for the same provisions in the Utah Bill which I now sustain in this bill, that Boston abolitionists turned their back upon him, just as they burnt me in effigy. Sir, if identity of principle, if identity of support as friends, if identity of enemies fix Mr. Webster's position, his authority is certainly with us, and not with the abolitionists. I have a right, therefore, to have the sympathies of his Boston friends with me, as I sympathized with him when the same principle was involved.

Mr. President, I am sorry that I have taken up so much time; but I must notice one or two points more. So much has been said about the Missouri Compromise Act, and about a faithful compliance with it by the North, that I must follow that matter a little further. The senator from Ohio (Mr. Wade) has referred, to-night, to the fact that I went for carrying out the Missouri Compromise in the Texas resolutions of 1845, and in 1848, on several occasions; and he actually proved that I never abandoned it until 1850. He need not have taken the pains to prove that fact; for he got all his information on the subject from my opening speech upon this bill. I told you then that I was willing, as a Northern man, in 1845, when the Texas question arose, to carry the Missouri Compromise line through that state, and in 1848 I offered it as an amendment to the Oregon Bill. Although I did not like the principle involved in that act, yet I was willing, for the sake of harmony, to extend it to the Pacific, and abide by it in good faith, in order to avoid the slavery agitation. The Missouri Compromise was defeated then by the same class of politicians who are now combined in opposition to the Nebraska Bill. It was because we were unable to carry out that Compromise, that a necessity existed for making a new one in 1850. And then we established this great principle of self-government which lies at the foundation of all our institutions. What does his charge amount to? He charges it, as a matter of offense, that I struggled in 1845 and in 1848 to observe good faith; and he and his associates defeated my purpose, and deprived me of the ability to carry out what he now says is the plighted faith of the nation.

Mr. Wade. I did not charge the senator with any thing except with making a very excellent argument on my side of the question, and I wished he would make it again to-night. That was all.

Mr. Douglas. What was the argument which I made? A Southern senator had complained that the Missouri Compromise was a matter of injustice to the South. I told him he ought not to complain of that when his Southern friends were here proposing to accept it; and if we could carry it out, he had no right to make such a complaint. I was anxious to carry it out. It would not have done for a northern man who was opposed to the measure, and unwilling to abide it, to take that position. It would not have become the senator from Ohio, who then denounced the very measure which he now calls a sacred compact, to take that position. But, as one who always been in favor of carrying it out, it was legitimate and proper that I should make that argument in reply.

Sir, as I have said, the South were willing to agree to the Missouri Compromise in 1848. When it was proposed by me to the Oregon Bill, as an amendment, to extend that line to the Pacific, the South agreed to it. The Senate adopted that proposition, and the house voted it down. In 1850, after the Omnibus Bill had broken down, and we proceeded to pass the Compromise measures separately, I proposed, when the Utah Bill was under discussion, to make a slight variation of the boundary of that territory, so as to include the Mormon settlements, and not with reference to any other question; and it was suggested that we should take the line of 36° 30'. That would have accomplished the local objects of the amendment very well. But when I proposed it, what did these Freesoilers say? What did the senator from New Hampshire (Mr. Hale), who was then their leader in this body, say? Here are his words:

"*Mr. Hale.* I wish to say a word as a reason why I shall vote against the amendment. I shall vote against 36° 30° *because I think there is an implication in it.* [Laughter.] I will vote for 37° or 36° either, just as it is convenient; but it is idle to shut our eyes to the fact that here is an attempt in this bill—I will not say it is the intention of the mover—to pledge this Senate and Congress to the imaginary line of 36° 30', because there are some *historical recollections connected with it in regard to this controversy about slavery,* I will content myself with saying that *I never will, by vote or speech, admit or submit to any thing that may bind the action of our legislation here to make the parallel of 36° 30' the boundary line between slave and free territory.* And when I say that, I explain the reason why I go against the amendment."

These remarks of Mr. Hale were not made on a proposition to extend the Missouri Compromise line to the Pacific, but on a proposition to fix 36° 30' as the Southern boundary line of Utah, for local reasons. He was against it because there might be, as he said, an implication growing out of historical recollections in favor of the imaginary line between slavery and freedom. Does that look as if his object was to get an implication in favor of preserving sacred this line, in regard to which gentlemen now say there was a solemn compact? That proposition may illustrate what I wish to say in this connexion upon a point which has been made by the opponents of this bill as to the effect of an amendment inserted on the motion of the senator from Virginia (Mr. Mason) into the Texas boundary bill. The opponents of this measure rely upon that amendment to show that the Texas compact was preserved by the acts of 1850. I have already shown, in my former speech, that the object of the amendment was to guaranty to the state of Texas, with her circumscribed boundaries, the same number of states which she would have had under her larger boundaries, and with the same right to come in with or without slavery, as they please.

We have been told over and over again that there was no such thing intimated in debate as that the country cut off from Texas was to be relieved from the stipulation of that compromise. This has been asserted boldly and unconditionally, as if there could be no doubt about it. The senator from Georgia (Mr. Toombs) in his speech, showed that, in his address to his constituents of that state, he had proclaimed to the world that the object was to establish a principle which would allow the people to decide the question of slavery for themselves, North as well as South of 36° 30'. The line of 36° 30' was voted down as the boundary of Utah, so that there should not be even an implication in favor of an imaginary line to divide freedom and slavery. Subsequently, when the Texas Boundary Bill was under consideration, on the next day after the amendment of the senator from Virginia had been adopted, the record says:

" Mr. Sebastian moved to add to the second article the following :

" ' On the condition that the territory hereby ceded may be, at the proper time, formed into a state, and admitted into the Union, with a Constitution with or without the prohibition of slavery therein, as the people of the said territory may at the time determine.' "

Then the senator from Arkansas did propose that the territory cut off should be relieved from that restriction in express terms, and allowed to come in according to the principles of this bill. What was done ? The debate continued:

" Mr. Foote. Will my friend allow me to appeal to him to move this amendment when the territorial bill for New Mexico shall be up for consideration ? It will certainly be a part of that bill, and I shall then vote for it with pleasure. Now it will only embarrass our action."

Let it be remarked that no one denied the propriety of the provision. All seemed to acquiesce in the principle ; but it was thought better to insert it in the territorial bills, as we are now doing, instead of adding it to the Texas Boundary Bill. The debate proceeded:

" Mr. Sebastian. My only object in offering the amendment is to secure the assertion of this principle beyond a doubt. The principle was acquiesced in without difficulty in regard to the territorial government established for Utah, a part of this acquired territory, and it is proper, in my opinion, that it should be incorporated in this bill.

" Messrs. Cass, Foote, and others. Oh, withdraw it.

" Mr. Sebastian. I think this is the proper place for it. It is uncertain whether it will be incorporated in the other bill referred to, and the bill itself may not pass."

It will be seen that the debate goes upon the supposition that the effect was to release the country North of 36° 30' from the obligation of the prohibition; and the only question was whether the declaration that it should be received into the Union " with or without slavery" should be inserted in the Texas bill or the territorial bill.

The debate was continued, and I will read one or two other passages :

"*Mr. Foote.* I wish to state to the senator a fact of which, I think, he is not observant at this moment ; and that is, that the senator from Virginia has introduced an amendment, which is now a part of the bill, which recognizes the Texas compact of annexation in every respect.

"*Mr. Sebastian.* I was aware of the effect of the amendment of the senator from Virginia. It is in regard to the number of states to be formed out of Texas, and is referred to only in general terms."

Thus it will be seen that the senator from Arkansas then explained the amendment of the senator from Virginia, which had been adopted, in precisely the same way in which I explained it in my opening speech. The senator from Arkansas continued :

" If this amendment be the same as that offered by the senator from Virginia, there can certainly be no harm in reaffirming it in this bill, to which I think it properly belongs."

Thus it will be seen that nobody disputed that the restriction was to be removed ; and the only question was as to the bill in which that declaration would be put. It seems, from the record, that I took part in the debate, and said :

"*Mr. Douglas.* This boundary, as now fixed, would leave New Mexico bounded on the east by the 103° of longitude up to 36° 30', and then east to the 100°; and it leaves a narrow neck of land between 36° 30' and the old boundary of Texas, that would not naturally and properly go to New Mexico when it should become a state. This amendment would compel us to include it in New Mexico, or to form it into another state. When the principle shall come up in the bill for the organization of a territorial government for New Mexico, no doubt the same vote which inserted it in the Omnibus Bill and the Utah bill, will insert it there.

" *Several Senators.* No doubt of it."

Upon that debate the amendment of the senator from Arkansas was voted down, because it was avowed and distinctly understood that the amendment of the senator from Virginia, taken in connection with the remainder of the bill, did release the country ceded by Texas North of 36° 30' from the restriction; and it was agreed that if we did not put it into the Texas boundary bill it should go into the territorial bill. I stated, as a reason why it should not go into the Texas boundary bill, that if it did it would be a compact, and would compel us to put the whole ceded country into one state, when it might be more convenient and natural to make a different boundary. I pledged myself then that it should be put into the territorial bill; and when we considered the territorial bill for New Mexico we put in the same clause, so far as the country ceded by Texas was embraced within that territory, and it passed in that shape. When it went into the house they united the two bills together, and thus this clause passed in the same bill, as the senator from Arkansas desired.

Now, sir, have I not shown conclusively that it was the understanding in that debate that the effect was to release the country North of 36° 30', which formerly belonged to Texas, from the operation of that restriction, and to provide that it should come into the Union with or without slavery, as its people should see proper?

That being the case, I ask the senator from Ohio (Mr. Chase) if he ought not to have been cautious when he charged over and over again that there was not a word or a syllable uttered in debate to that effect? Should he not have been cautious when he said that it was a mere after-thought on my part? Should he not have been cautious when he said that even I never dreamed of it up to the 4th of January of this year? Whereas the record shows that I made a speech to that effect during the pendency of the bills of 1850. The same statement was repeated by nearly every senator who followed him in debate in opposition to this bill; and it is now being circulated over the country, published in every abolition paper, and read on every stump by every abolition orator, in order to get up a prejudice against me and the measure I have introduced. Those gentlemen should not have dared to utter the statement without knowing whether it was correct or not. These records are troublesome things sometimes. It is not proper for a man to charge another with a mere after-thought because he did not know that he had advocated the same principles before. Because he did not know it he should not take it for granted that nobody else did. Let me tell the senators that it is a very unsafe rule for them to rely upon. They ought to have had sufficient respect for a brother senator to have believed, when he came forward with an important proposition, that he had investigated it. They ought to have had sufficient respect for a committee of this body to have assumed that they meant what they said.

When I see such a system of misinterpretation and misrepresentation of views, of laws, of records, of debates, all tending to mislead the public, to excite prejudice, and to propagate error, have I not a right to expose it in very plain terms, without being arraigned for violating the courtesies of the Senate?

Mr. President, frequent reference has been made in debate to the admission of Arkansas as a slaveholding state, as furnishing evidence that the abolitionists and freesoilers, who have recently become so much enamored with the Missouri Compromise, have always been faithful to its stipulations and implications. I will show that the reference is unfortunate for them. When Arkansas applied for admission in 1836, objection was made in consequence of the provisions of her Constitution in respect to slavery. When the abolitionists and freesoilers of that day were arraigned for making that objection, upon the ground that Arkansas was South of 36° 30', they replied that the act of 1820 was never a compromise, much less a compact, imposing any obligation upon the successors of those who passed the act to pay any more respect to its provisions than to any other enactment of ordinary legislation. I have the debates before me, but will occupy the attention of the Senate only to read one or two paragraphs. Mr. Hand, of New York, in opposition to the admission of Arkansas as a slaveholding state, said:

"I am aware it will be, as it has already been contended, that by the Missouri Compromise, as it has been preposterously termed, Congress has parted with its right to prohibit the introduction of slavery into the territory south of 36° 30' north latitude."

He acknowledged that by the Missouri compromise, as he said it was preposterously termed, the North was estopped from denying the right to hold slaves South of that line; but, he added:

"There are, to my mind, insuperable objections to the soundness of that proposition."

Here they are:

"In the first place, there was no compromise or compact whereby Congress surrendered any power, or yielded any jurisdiction; and, in the second place, if it had done so, it was a mere legislative act, that could not bind their successors; it would be subject to a repeal at the will of any succeeding Congress."

I give these passages as specimens of the various speeches made in opposition to the admission of Arkansas by the same class of politicians who now oppose the Nebraska bill, upon the ground that it violates a solemn compact. So much for the speeches. Now for the vote. The journal which

I hold in my hand shows that forty-nine northern votes were recorded against the admission of Arkansas.

Yet, sir, in utter disregard—and charity leads me to hope, in profound ignorance—of all these facts, gentlemen are boasting that the North always observed the contract, never denied its validity, never wished to violate it; and they have even referred to the cases of the admission of Missouri and Arkansas as instances of their good faith.

Now, is it possible that gentlemen could suppose these things could be said and distributed in their speeches without exposure? Did they presume that, inasmuch as their lives were devoted to slavery agitation, whatever they did not know about the history of that question did not exist? I am willing to believe, I hope it may be the fact, that they were profoundly ignorant of all these records, all these debates, all these facts, which overthrow every position they have assumed. I wish the senator from Maine (Mr. Fessenden), who delivered his maiden speech here to-night, and who made a great many sly stabs at me, had informed himself upon the subject before he repeated all these groundless assertions. I can excuse him, for the reason that he has been here but a few days, and, having enlisted under the banner of the abolition confederates, was unwise and simple enough to believe that what they had published could be relied upon as stubborn facts. He may be an innocent victim. I hope he can have the excuse of not having investigated the subject. I am willing to excuse him on the ground that he did not know what he was talking about, and it is the only excuse which I can make for him. I will say, however, that I do not think he was required by his loyalty to the abolitionists to repeat every disreputable insinuation which they made. Why did he throw into his speech that foul inuendo about "a northern man with southern principles," and then quote the senator from Massachusetts (Mr. Sumner) as his authority? Ay, sir, I say that foul insinuation. Did not the senator from Massachusetts who first dragged it into this debate wish to have the public understand that I was known as a northern man with southern principles? Was not that the allusion? If it was, he availed himself of a cant phrase in the public mind, in violation of the truth of history. I know of but one man in this country who ever made it a boast that he was "a northern man with southern principles," and he (turning to Mr. Sumner) was your candidate for the Presidency in 1848. (Applause in the galleries.)

The Presiding Officer (Mr. Mason.) Order, order.

Mr. Douglas. If his sarcasm was intended for Martin Van Buren, it involves a family quarrel, with which I have no disposition to interfere. I will only add that I have been able to discover nothing in the present position or recent history of that distinguished statesman which would lead me to covet the *sobriquet* by which he is known—"a northern man with southern principles."

Mr. President, the senators from Ohio and Massachusetts (Mr. Chase and Mr. Sumner) have taken the liberty to impeach my motives in bringing forward this measure. I desire to know by what right they arraign me, or by what authority they impute to me other and different motives than those which I have assigned. I have shown from the record that I advocated and voted for the same principles and provisions in the compromise acts of 1850 which are embraced in this bill. I have proven that I put the same construction upon those measures immediately after their adoption that is given in the report which I submitted this session from the Committee on Territories. I have shown that the Legislature of Illinois at its first session, after those measures were enacted, passed resolutions approving them, and declaring that the same great principles of self-government should be incorporated into all territorial organizations. Yet, sir, in the face of these facts, these senators have the hardihood to declare that this was all an "after-thought" on my part, conceived for the first time during the present session; and that the measure is offered as a bid for presidential votes! Are they incapable of conceiving that an honest man can do a right thing from worthy motives? I must be permitted to tell those senators that their experience in seeking political preferment does not furnish a safe rule by which to judge the character and principles of other senators!

I must be permitted to tell the senator from Ohio that I did not obtain my seat in this body either by a corrupt bargain or a dishonorable coalition! I must be permitted to remind the senator from Massachusetts that I did not enter into any combinations or arrangements by which my character, my principles, and my honor, were set up at public auction or private sale, in order to procure a seat in the Senate of the United States! I did not come into the Senate by any such means.

Mr. Weller. But there are some men whom I know that did.

Mr. Chase, (to Mr. Weller.) Do you say that I came here by a bargain?

The Presiding Officer, (Mr. Mason.) Order must be preserved in the Senate.

Mr. Weller. I will explain what I mean.

The Presiding Officer. The senator from Illinois is entitled to the floor.

Mr. Dodge, of Iowa. I call both the senator from California and senator from Ohio to order.

Mr. Douglas. I cannot yield the floor until I get through. I say, then, there is nothing which authorized that senator to impugn my motives.

Mr. Chase. Will the senator from Illinois allow me? Does he say that I came into the Senate by a corrupt bargain?

Mr. Douglas. I cannot permit the senator to change the issue. He has arraigned me on the charge of seeking high political station by unworthy means. I tell him there is nothing in my history which would create the suspicion that I came into the Senate by a corrupt bargain or a disgraceful coalition?

Mr. Chase. Whoever says that I came here by a corrupt bargain states what is false.

Mr. Weller. Mr. President——

Mr. Douglas. My friend from California will wait till I get through, if he pleases.

The Presiding Officer. The senator from Illinois is entitled to the floor.

Mr. Douglas. It will not do for the senator from Ohio to return offensive expressions after what I have said and proven. Nor can I permit him to change the issue, and thereby divert public attention from the enormity of his offence, in charging me with unworthy motives, while performing a high public duty, in obedience to the expressed wish and known principles of my state. I choose to maintain my own position, and leave the public to ascertain, if they do not understand, how and by what means he was elected to the Senate.

Mr. Chase. If the senator will allow me, I will say, in reply to the remarks which the senator has just made, that I did not understand him as calling upon me for any explanation of the statement which he said was made in regard to a presidential bid. The exact statement in the address was this—it was a question addressed to the people: "Would they allow their dearest rights to be made the hazards of a presidential game?" That was the exact expression. Now, sir, it is well known that all these great measures in the country are influenced, more or less, by reference to the great public canvasses which are going on from time to time. I certainly did not intend to impute to the senator from Illinois—and I desire always to do justice—in that any improper motive. I do not think it is an unworthy ambition to desire to be a President of the United States. I do not think that the bringing forward of a measure with reference to that object would be an improper thing, if the measure be proper in itself. I differ from the senator in my judgment of the measure. I do not think the measure is a right one. In that I express the judgment which I honestly entertain. I do not condemn his judgment; I do not make, and I do not desire to make, any personal imputations upon him in reference to a great public question.

Mr. Weller. Mr. President——

Mr. Douglas. I cannot allow my friend from California to come into the debate at this time, for this is my peculiar business. I may let him in after awhile. I wish to examine the explanation of the senator from Ohio, and see whether I ought to accept it as satisfactory. He has quoted the language of the address. It is undeniable that that language clearly imputed to me the design of bringing forward this bill with a view of securing my own election to the presidency. Then, by way of excusing himself for imputing to me such a purpose, the senator says that he does not consider it "an unworthy ambition;" and hence he says that, in making the charge, he does not impugn my motives. I must remind him that, in addition to that insinuation, he only said, in the same address, that my bill was a "criminal betrayal of precious rights;" he only said it was "an atrocious plot against freedom and humanity;" he only said that it was "meditated bad faith;" he only spoke significantly of "servile demagogues;" he only called upon the preachers of the Gospel and the people at their public meetings to denounce and resist such a monstrous iniquity. In saying all this, and much of the same sort, he now assures me, in the presence of the Senate, that he did not mean the charge to imply an "unworthy ambition;" that it was not intended as a "personal imputation" upon my motives or character; and that he meant "no personal disrespect" to me as the author of the measure. In reply, I will content myself with the remark, that there is a very wide difference of opinion between the senator from Ohio and myself in respect to the meaning of words, and especially in regard to the line of conduct which, in a public man, does not constitute an unworthy ambition.

Mr. Weller. Now, I ask my friend from Illinois to give way to me for a few moments.

Mr. Douglas. I yield the floor.

A debate then took place between Messrs Weller and Chase, which is omitted here.

Mr. Sumner. Will the senator from Illinois yield the floor to me for a moment?

Mr. Douglas. As I presume it is on the same point, I will hear the testimony.

Mr. Sumner. Mr. President, I shrink always instinctively from any effort to repel a personal assault. I do not recognize the jurisdiction of this body to try my election to the Senate; but I do state, in reply to the senator from Illinois, that if he means to suggest that I came into the body by any waiver of principles; by any abandonment of my principles of any kind; by any effort or activity of my own, in any degree, he states that which cannot be sustained by the facts. I never sought, in any way, the office which I now hold; nor was I a party, in any way, directly or indirectly, to those efforts which placed me here.

Mr. Douglas. I do not complain of my friend from California for interposing in the manner he has; for I see that it was very appropriate in him to do so. But, sir, the senator from Massachusetts comes up with a very bold front, and denies the right of any man to put him on defence for the manner of his election. He says it is contrary to his principles to engage in personal assaults. If he expects to avail himself of the benefit of such a plea, he should act in accordance with his professed principles, and refrain from assaulting the character and impugning the motives of better men than himself. Everybody knows that he came here by a coalition or combination between political parties holding opposite and hostile opinions. But it is not my purpose to go into the morality of the matters involved in his election. The public know the history of that notorious coalition, and have formed its judgment upon it. It will not do for the senator to say that he was not a party to it, for he thereby betrays a consciousness of the immorality of the transaction without acquitting himself of the responsibilities which justly attach to him. As well might the receiver of stolen goods deny any responsibility for the larceny, while luxuriating in the proceeds of the crime, as the senator to avoid the consequences resulting from the mode of his election, while he clings to the office. I must be permitted to remind him of what he certainly can never forget, that when he arrived here to take his seat for the first time, so firmly were senators impressed with the conviction that he had been elected by dishonorable and corrupt means, there were very few who, for a long time, could deem it consistent with personal honor to hold private intercourse with him. So general was that impression, that for a long time he was avoided and shunned as a person unworthy of the association of gentlemen. Gradually, however, these injurious impressions were worn away by his bland manners and amiable deportment; and I regret that the senator should now, by a violation of all the rules of courtesy and propriety, compel me to refresh his mind upon these unwelcome reminiscences.

Mr. Chase. If the senator refers to me, he is stating a fact of which I have no knowledge at all. I came here——

Mr. Douglas. I was not speaking of the senator from Ohio, but of his confederate in slander, the senator from Massachusetts (Mr. Sumner). I have a word now to say to the other senator from Ohio (Mr. Wade). On the day when I exposed this abolition address, so full of slanders and calumnies, he rose and stated that, although his name was signed to it, he had never read it; and so willing was he to endorse an abolition document, that he signed it in blank, without knowing what it contained.

Mr. Wade. I have always found them true.

Mr. Douglas. He stated that from what I had exposed of its contents he did not hesitate to endorse every word. In the same speech he said, that in Ohio a negro was as good as a white man; with the avowal that he did not consider himself any better than a free negro. I have only to say that I should not have noticed it if none but free negroes had signed it!

The senator from New York (Mr. Seward), when I was about to call him to account for this slanderous production, promptly denied that he ever signed the document. Now, I say that it has been circulated with his name attached to it; then I want to know of the senators who sent out the document, who forged the name of the senator from New York?

Mr. Chase. I am glad that the senator has asked that question. I have only to say, in reference to that matter, that I have not the slightest knowledge in regard to the manner in which various names were appended to that document. It was prepared to be signed, and was signed, by the gentlemen here who are known as independent Democrats, and how any other names came to be added to it is more than I can tell.

Mr. Douglas. It is not a satisfactory answer, for those who confess to the preparation and publication of a document filled with insult and calumny, with forged names attached to it for the purpose of imparting to it respectability, to interpose a technical denial that they committed the crime. Somebody did forge other people's names to that document. The senators from

Ohio and Massachusetts (Mr. Chase and Mr Sumner) plead guilty to the authorship and publication; upon them rests the responsibility of showing who committed the forgery.

Mr. President, I have done with these personal matters. I regret the necessity which compelled me to devote so much time to them. All I have done and said has been in the way of self-defense, as the Senate can bear me witness.

Mr. President, I have also occupied a good deal of time in exposing the cant of these gentlemen about the sanctity of the Missouri Compromise, and the dishonor attached to the violation of plighted faith. I have exposed these matters in order to show that the object of these men is to withdraw from public attention the real principle involved in the bill. They well know that the abrogation of the Missouri Compromise is the incident and not the principle of the bill. They well understand that the report of the committee and the bill propose to establish the principle in all territorial organizations, that the question of slavery shall be referred to the people to regulate for themselves, and that such legislation should be had as was necessary to remove all legal obstructions to the free exercise of this right by the people.

The eighth section of the Missouri Act standing in the way of this great principle must be rendered inoperative and void, whether expressly repealed or not, in order to give the people the power of regulating their own domestic institutions in their own way, subject only to the Constitution.

Now, sir, if these gentlemen have entire confidence in the correctness of their own position, why do they not meet the issue boldly and fairly, and controvert the soundness of this great principle of popular sovereignty in obedience to the Constitution? They know full well that this was the principle upon which the colonies separated from the crown of Great Britain, the principle upon which the battles of the Revolution were fought, and the principle upon which our republican system was founded. They can not be ignorant of the fact that the Revolution grew out of the assertion of the right on the part of the imperial government to interfere with the internal affairs and domestic concerns of the colonies. In this connection I will invite attention to a few extracts from the instructions of the different colonies to their delegates in the Continental Congress, with the view of forming such a union as would enable them to make successful resistance to the efforts of the crown to destroy the fundamental principles of all free government by interfering with the domestic affairs of the colonies.

I will begin with Pennsylvania, whose devotion to the principle of human liberty, and the obligations of the Constitution, has acquired for her the proud title of Key-stone in the arch of republican states. In her instructions is contained the following reservation:

"Reserving to the people of this colony the sole and exclusive right of regulating the internal government and police of the same."

And, in a subsequent instruction, in reference to suppressing the British authority in the colonies, Pennsylvania uses the following emphatic language:

"Unanimously declare our willingness to concur in a vote of the Congress declaring the United Colonies free and independent States, provided the forming the government and the regulation of the internal police of this colony be always reserved to the people of the said colony."

Connecticut, in authorizing her delegates to vote for the Declaration of Independence, attached to it the following condition:

"Saving that the administration of government, and the power of forming governments for, and the regulation of the internal concerns and police of each colony, ought to be left and remain to the respective colonial legislatures."

New Hampshire annexed this proviso to her instructions to her delegates to vote for independence :

"Provided the regulation of our internal police be under the direction of our own assembly."

New Jersey imposed the following condition :

"Always observing that, whatever plan of confederacy you enter into, the regulating the internal police of this province is to be reserved to the colonial legislature."

Maryland gave her consent to the Declaration of Independence upon the condition contained in this proviso :

"And that said colony will hold itself bound by the resolutions of a majority of the United colonies in the premises, provided the sole and exclusive right of regulating the internal government and police of that colony be reserved to the people thereof."

Virginia annexed the following condition to her instructions to vote for the Declaration of Independence :

"Provided that the power of forming government for, and the regulations of the internal concerns of the colony, be left to respective colonial legislatures."

I will not weary the Senate in multiplying evidence upon this point. It is apparent that the Declaration of Independence had its origin in the violation of that great fundamental principle which secured to the people of the colonies the right to regulate their own domestic affairs in their own way; and that the Revolution resulted in the triumph of that principle, and the recognition of the right asserted by it.

Abolitionism proposes to destroy the right and extinguish the principle for which our forefathers waged a seven years' bloody war, and upon which our whole system of free government is founded. They not only deny the application of this principle to the territories, but insist upon fastening the prohibition upon all the states to be formed out of those territories. Therefore, the doctrine of the abolitionists—the doctrine of the opponents of the Nebraska and Kansas Bill, and of the advocates of the Missouri restriction—demand congressional interference with slavery, not only in the territories, but in all the new states to be formed therefrom. It is the same doctrine when applied to the territories and new states of this Union, which the British government attempted to enforce by the sword upon the American colonies. It is this fundamental principle of self-government which constitutes the distinguishing feature of the Nebraska Bill. The opponents of the principle are consistent in opposing the bill. I do not blame them for their opposition. I only ask them to meet the issue fairly and openly, by acknowledging that they are opposed to the principle which it is the object of the bill to carry into operation. It seems that there is no power on earth, no intellectual power, no mechanical power that can bring them to a fair discussion of the true issue. If they hope to delude the people, and escape detection for any considerable length of time under the catch-word "Missouri Compromise," and "faith of compacts," they will find that the people of this country have more penetration and intelligence than they have given them credit for.

Mr. President, there is an important fact connected with this slavery resolution which should never be lost sight of. It has always arisen from one and the same cause. Whenever that cause has been removed, the agitation has ceased; and whenever the cause has been renewed, the agitation has sprung into existence. That cause is, and ever has been, the attempt on the part of Congress to interfere with the question of slavery in the territories and new states formed therefrom. Is it not wise, then, to confine our action within the sphere of our legitimate duties, and leave this vexed question to take care of itself in each state and territory, according to the wishes of the people thereof, in conformity to the forms and in subjection to the provisions of the Constitution?

The opponents of the bill tell us that agitation is no part of their policy, that their great desire is peace and harmony; and they complain bitterly that I should have disturbed the repose of the country by the introduction of this measure. Let me ask these professed friends of peace and avowed enemies of agitation, how the issue could have been avoided? They tell me that I should have let the question alone—that is, that I should have left Nebraska unorganized, the people unprotected, and the Indian barrier in existence, until the swelling tide of emigration should burst through, and accomplish by violence what it is the part of wisdom and statesmanship to direct and regulate by law. How long could you have postponed action with safety? How long could you maintain that Indian barrier, and restrain the onward march of civilization, Christianity, and free government by a barbarian wall? Do you suppose that you could keep that vast country a howling wilderness in all time to come, roamed over by hostile savages, cutting off all safe communication between our Atlantic and Pacific possessions? I tell you that the time for action has come, and cannot be postponed. It is a case in which the "let-alone" policy would precipitate a crisis which must inevitably result in violence, anarchy, and strife.

You cannot fix bounds to the onward march of this great and growing country. You cannot fetter the limbs of the young giant. He will burst all your chains. He will expand, and grow, and increase, and extend civilization, Christianity, and liberal principles. Then, sir, if you cannot check the growth of the country in that direction, is it not the part of wisdom to look the danger in the face, and provide for an event which you cannot avoid? I tell you, sir, you must provide for continuous lines of settlement from the Mississippi Valley to the Pacific Ocean. And in making this provision you must decide upon what principles the territories shall be organized; in other words, whether the people shall be allowed to regulate their domestic institutions in their own way, according to the provisions of this bill, or whether the opposite doctrine of congressional interference is to prevail. Postpone it, if you will; but whenever you do act, this question must be met and decided.

The Missouri Compromise was interference; the compromise of 1850 was non-interference, leaving the people to exercise their rights under the Constitution. The Committee on Territories were compelled to act on this subject. I, as their chairman, was bound to meet the question. I choose to take the responsibility, regardless of consequences personal to myself. I should have done the same thing last year, if there had been time; but we know, considering the late period at which the bill then reached us from the house, that there was not sufficient time to consider the question fully, and to prepare a report upon the subject. I was, therefore, persuaded by friends to allow the bill to be reported to the Senate, in order that such action might be taken as should be deemed wise and proper.

The bill was never taken up for action; the last night of the session having been exhausted in debate on the motion to take up the bill. This session the measure was introduced by my friend from Iowa (Mr. Dodge), and referred to the Territorial Committee during the first week of the session. We have abundance of time to consider the subject; it was a matter of pressing necessity, and there was no excuse for not meeting it directly and fairly. We were compelled to take our position upon the doctrine either of intervention or non-intervention. We chose the latter, for two reasons: first, because we believed that the principle was right; and, second, because it was the principle adopted in 1850, to which the two great political parties of the country were solemnly pledged.

There is another reason why I desire to see this principle recognized as a rule of action in all time to come. It will have the effect to destroy all sectional parties and sectional agitations. If, in the language of the report of the committee, you withdraw the slavery question from the halls of Congress and the political arena, and commit it to the arbitrament of those who are immediately interested in and alone responsible for its consequences, there is nothing left out of which sectional parties can be organized. It never was done, and never can be done on the bank, tariff, distribution, or any other party issue which has existed, or may exist, after this slavery question is withdrawn from politics. On every other political question these have always supporters and opponents in every portion of the Union—in each state, county, village, and neighborhood—residing together in harmony and good-fellowship, and combating each other's opinions and correcting each other's errors in a spirit of kindness and friendship. These differences of opinion between neighbors and friends, and the discussions that grow out of them, and the sympathy which each feels with the advocates of his own opinions in every other portion of this wide-spread republic, adds an overwhelming and irresistible moral weight to the strength of the confederacy.

Affection for the Union can never be alienated or diminished by any other party issues than those which are joined upon sectional or geographical lines. When the people of the North shall all be rallied under one banner, and the whole South marshaled under another banner, and each section excited to frenzy and madness by hostility to the institutions of the other, then the patriot may well tremble for the perpetuity of the Union. Withdraw the slavery question from the political arena, and remove it to the states and territories, each to decide for itself, such a catastrophe can never happen. Then you will never be able to tell, by any senator's vote for or against any measure, from what state or section of the Union he comes.

Why, then, can we not withdraw this vexed question from politics? Why can we not adopt the principle of this bill as a rule of action in all new territorial organizations? Why can we not deprive these agitators of their vocation, and render it impossible for senators to come here upon bargains on the slavery question? I believe that the peace, the harmony, and perpetuity of the Union require us to go back to the doctrines of the Revolution, to the principles of the Constitution, to the principles of the compromise of 1850, and leave the people, under the Constitution, to do as they may see proper in respect to their own internal affairs.

Mr. President, I have not brought this question forward as a northern man or as a southern man. I am unwilling to recognize such divisions and distinctions. I have brought it forward as an American senator, representing a state which is true to this principle, and which has approved of my action in respect to the Nebraska Bill. I have brought it forward not as an act of justice to the South more than to the North. I have presented it especially as an act of justice to the people of those territories, and of the states to be formed therefrom, now and in all time to come.

I have nothing to say about northern rights or southern rights. I know of no such divisions or distinctions under the Constitution. The bill does equal and exact justice to the whole Union, and every part of it; it violates the rights of no state or territory, but places each on a perfect equality, and leaves the people thereof to the free enjoyment of all their rights under the Constitution.

Now, sir, I wish to say to our southern friends, that if they desire to see this great principle carried out, now is their time to rally around it, to cherish it, preserve it, make it the rule of action in all future time. If they fail to do it now, and thereby allow the doctrine of interference to prevail, upon their heads the consequence of that interference must rest. To our northern friends, on the other hand, I desire to say, that from this day henceforward, they must rebuke the slander which has been uttered against the South, that they desire to legislate slavery into the territories. The South has vindicated her sincerity, her honor, on that point, by bringing forward a provision, negativing, in express terms, any such effect as a result of this bill. I am rejoiced to know that, while the proposition to abrogate the eighth section of the Missouri act comes from a free state, the proposition to negative the conclusion that slavery is thereby introduced comes from a slaveholding state. Thus, both sides furnish conclusive evidence that they go for the principle, and the principle only, and desire to take no advantage of any possible misconstruction.

Mr. President, I feel that I owe an apology to the Senate for having occupied their attention so long, and a still greater apology for having discussed the question in such an incoherent and desultory manner. But I could not forbear to claim the right of closing this debate. I thought gentlemen would recognize its propriety when they saw the manner in which I was assailed and misrepresented in the course of this discussion, and especially by assaults still more disreputable to some portions of the country. These assaults have had no other effect upon me than to give me courage and energy for a still more resolute discharge of duty. I say frankly that, in my opinion, this measure will be as popular at the North as at the South, when its provisions and principles shall have been fully developed and become well understood. The people at the North are attached to the principles of self-government; and you cannot convince them that that is self-government which deprives a people of the right of legislating for themselves, and compels them to receive laws which are forced upon them by a Legislature in which they are not represented. We are willing to stand upon this great principle of self-government everywhere; and it is to us a proud reflection that, in this whole discussion, no friend of the bill has urged an argument in its favor which could not be used with the same propriety in a free state as in a slave state, and *vice versa*. But no enemy of the bill has used an argument which would bear repetition one mile across Mason and Dixon's line. Our opponents have dealt entirely in sectional appeals. The friends of the bill have discussed a great principle of universal application, which can be sustained by the same reasons, and the same arguments, in every time and in every corner of the Union.

PRESIDENT PIERCE AND THE NEBRASKA BILL.

A strong effort was made at the time the Kansas Nebraska Bill was introduced to withhold from President Pierce the full measure of justice touching his support of that measure, particularly that provision repealing the Missouri restriction. The enemies of the bill sought every means to sow discord among its friends, and the most wretched slanders were industriously circulated. These continued long after the bill had become a law. As late as October 6, 1855, the *New York Post*, speaking of the repeal of the Missouri restriction, repeated a whole series of them, condensed into the following paragraph:

"Douglas was at first hostile to the scheme. He refused, as chairman of the Committee on Territories, to propose Atchison's repealing amendment to the Nebraska Bill. Cass was opposed to it; and when introduced at last by Douglas, who surrendered to Atchison, Cass admitted in his speech, prefatory to his voting for it, that it was dangerous and unnecessary. The President was opposed to it, as was disclosed by the *Union*, which opposed the repeal of the Missouri Compromise when first broached in Douglas' ambiguous bill, although the editor is, and was known at the time to be, zealous for the repeal. His holding back was merely in respect to the President's scruples, who was doubly committed against the resurrection of the slave struggle, first by his inaugural address, and then in his maiden message to Congress."

On the 9th of October, 1855, the *Washington Union* contained the following authentic denial of the slanders, and an equally authoritative exposition of the position of President Pierce :

"This is a total perversion of the history of the Nebraska Bill and of the introduction into it of the clause repealing the Missouri restriction. It is not true that either Senators Douglas or Cass, or President Pierce, was ever opposed to the repeal of the Missouri restriction. These statesmen were the early, the earnest, and the consistent advocates of the principle of congressional non-intervention in the territories, and of necessity were opposed to the recognition by act of Congress of the Missouri restriction, which was in direct conflict with that principle. The only question that presented itself to Senator Douglas, as chairman of the Committee on Territories, was whether the Nebraska Bill should be drawn in the language of the Compromise of 1850, and be a litteral copy of the New Mexico and Utah Bills, so far as the slavery question was concerned, and therefore be *a repeal* of the Missouri restriction *by necessary implication*, or whether, in addition to the language of the Compromise of 1850, there should be a clause *expressly repealing* the Missouri restriction."

*　　　*　　　*　　　*　　　*　　　*

"After the bill was introduced the abolition leaders in Congress denounced it with violence as a violation of the Missouri compact; moreover, doubts were suggested by southern men as to whether the repeal of the Missouri Compromise was so clear as to satisfy slave-owners that they might settle in the territory and risk a judicial decision as to their property with safety. On the other hand it was suggested by northern men that there was no doubt about the repeal of the Missouri Compromise; but there was doubt whether the legal effect thereof was not to revive the Louisiana law of 1803, by which Nebraska was slave territory. To remove all room for doubt, and to free the question of non-intervention in Nebraska from all controversy, Senator Douglas himself brought forward the amendments which placed the bill in the shape in which it passed.

"It is due to the truth of history to state, also, that the amendments were seen and approved by President Pierce and General Cass before they were offered in the Senate by Senator Douglas. These three gentlemen were the earnest and consistent advocates of the Nebraska Bill, from its inception to its final passage, and we are entirely certain that its legal effect in the shape in which it passed is identically that which they attributed to it in the shape in which Mr. Douglas first introduced it. We go further, and affirm, with entire confidence in our ability to maintain the assertion, that the bill as it finally passed does not differ in the slightest degree in principle from the Compromise of 1850."

We have thought this much due to Gen. Pierce. The Nebraska Bill was not forced upon his administration. He was not a man to submit to a wrong, or to acquiesce in a wrong. It was his measure—having his full approval before it was proposed to Congress.

CHAPTER XI.

KNOW-NOTHINGISM AND ANTI-NEBRASKAISM.

WHEN the bill passed Congress, the storm of hostility to its enactment was in full progress. The vote in the House upon its passage was classified as follows:

	For.	Against
Democrats, non-slaveholding states	43	43
" slaveholding states	57	4
Whigs, non-slaveholding states	—	44
" slaveholding states	13	7
Free-soilers	—	4
	113	100

The action upon this bill separated the Northern and Southern Whigs. During the winter and spring there had been organizing, under the powerful appliances of secrecy and mystery, a new party. At first it was known as the "Know-nothing" party, under which style it continued to be known as long as it was successful, after which it adopted the general title of the "American" party.

The Nebraska Bill had a very large number of opponents among the Democracy of the Northern States. The Abolition leaders at the North proposed a union of men of all parties, having for its object the exclusion from Congress of every Northern man who had voted for the bill. Into this unfortunate movement a very large number of Democrats thoughtlessly plunged. The new party was styled the "Anti-Nebraska" or "Fusion" party, being a combination of the Abolitionists, Free-soilers, Anti-Nebraska Democrats, Whigs, and Know-nothings. It was under the deluding misrepresentations of the real terms and objects of the Nebraska Bill, and not because of any affection for the proscriptive doctrines of the Know-nothings, that thousands of Democrats were eventually led on step by step, until they found themselves sworn members of the dark-lantern order. The combination was soon a powerful one. It controlled cities, states, and sections. Every where the new party pledged itself to the most ultra doctrines upon the subject of slavery. The hostility toward Catholics and foreigners was revived in a new and most bitter spirit. It was no longer the open and fearless hostility such as culminated in 1844 in the church-burning riots in Philadelphia. The operations were in secret. Its members were unknown; no man could tell whether his neighbor in the councils of his own party was or was not a member of the secret order. Men and parties were paralyzed. Who would dare encounter the new political monster, whose organization was extended to all parts of the country, and embraced men of all parties? It sprung up rapidly. In May the Know-nothings, aided by the Anti-Nebraska men, elected their candidate for mayor in Philadelphia by six thousand majority. This election demonstrated its political power. Political leaders counseled conciliatory measures; others favored an acquiescence in its rule. The Whig party was swallowed up in the capacious portals of the mysterious lodges. Necessarily acting with it, if not indeed actually enrolled as members, were the Anti-Nebraska Democrats, Abolitionists, and Free-soilers. Who was to encounter this new and formidable political party? It was to be crushed by the Democratic party, or it would soon crush the latter. But who in the Democratic party would undertake the task of denouncing a party of whose principles so little was known, and whose organization and membership were so mysterious? Though Congress was in session, not a speech was made upon the subject. Every day it became more evident that the Democratic party alone would have to encounter the Know-nothing party and its allies, yet there were but few willing or sufficiently posted to open the contest.

Mr. Douglas was at the North on a business visit, and stopped, on his return to Washington, in Philadelphia to pass the 4th of July. It has been an immemorial custom for the Democracy in that city to celebrate the 4th of July by an oration in Independence Square. The committee of arrangements, hearing of Mr. Douglas's presence in the city, called on him with a request to address the meeting. He consented, but frankly told them that if he spoke he would necessarily touch upon the Nebraska Bill and Know-nothingism—the two "delicate questions" which timid men at that day did all in their power to avoid. After some conversation upon this matter, it was agreed that Mr. Douglas should be allowed to speak his own sentiments in his own way. He addressed that meeting that day. It was the first speech ever delivered in the United States by any prominent public man, since the organization of the Know-nothing party, against the proscriptive principles of that party. It was received by the Democracy of Philadelphia with enthusiastic delight. It broke the spell which had apparently hung over the party, and which had closed men's lips and paralyzed their hands respecting the most dangerous and insidious opponents that ever threatened the Democratic party. He spoke out words of condemnation and defiance; and men, taking courage from his bold words, felt relieved, and, giving vent to the feelings so long held in subjection, recognized in the orator the bold and daring statesman who never yet, in any part of his eventful career, paused in defense of the right or condemnation of the wrong to inquire what would be the consequences of his action toward himself personally.

From that day forth Know-nothingism had a stern opponent in the Democratic party, and from that day forth the Democracy never faltered until it had subdued, conquered, and broken up the organization in the Northern States. This speech was printed in pamphlet form and widely circulated. Though that part of it relating to the Kansas-Nebraska Bill is in the main a repetition of sentiments advanced by him in the Senate during the pendency of the bill, it is just that it should be here given. It was the first speech made outside of Congress in defense of the bill; and as it is fashionable in some quarters to say that he then represented that bill as meaning something very different to what he now claims for it, it is but just that his exposition then should be placed alongside of his exposition of the same measure now. He said:

Mr. President and Fellow-citizens:

While I am profoundly grateful for the generous enthusiasm with which you have received the kind remarks of my friend General Dawson, I know not whether I ought to make my acknowledgments to him for having created in your minds expectations which it is impossible for me to fulfill. I feel that it is good for us to be here on this day. The day and the place are consecrated to liberty. It is a hallowed spot. I enter Independence Square—I approach Independence Hall on the Fourth of July with feelings akin to those of the pilgrim when he approaches the holy places. It is the birthplace of American liberty. Here the Declaration of Independence was first promulgated—here the Constitution of the United States was formed. On this very spot were proclaimed in that declaration and embodied in that Constitution those glorious principles of civil and religious freedom which our fathers have transmitted to us as the most precious of all earthly blessings. [Great applause.]

M

In these days, when efforts are being made to stir up sectional strife, and organize political parties on geographical lines—when religious intolerance and persecution are being practiced through the agency of secret associations —and when men in high places sacrilegiously deny all obligation to carry into effect the plain and imperative injunctions of the Constitution which they have sworn to support, it is well for good men and true patriots to assemble on our national birthday, at the birthplace of our liberties, and unite their efforts to preserve our republican institutions by perpetuating the principles upon which they rest. [Applause.]

On the 4th of July, '76, from the place where I now stand, our forefathers declared that these " COLONIES ARE, AND OF RIGHT OUGHT TO BE, FREE AND INDEPENDENT STATES." That was the starting-point. Thirteen British colonies were on that day converted into thirteen independent American states. The language is clear and explicit. The causes which led to the separation, and the instructions which the several colonies gave to their delegates in the Congress, prescribing the conditions upon which the Declaration of Independence was to be made, clearly show why this emphatic language was used. The colonies did not, in the first instance, demand independence. They were willing to acknowledge their allegiance to the British crown, provided they were left free to manage and regulate their own internal affairs and domestic concerns in their own way, without the interference or dictation of the imperial government. *They were willing to recognize the right of Great Britain to grant colonial charters, like the organic laws of our Territorial governments, by which the people of the colonies might make their own laws through their representatives in their local Legislatures;* but they solemnly protested against the right of the imperial Parliament, in which they had no representation, to make laws affecting their persons and property without their consent. Upon this point the separation took place, and the Declaration of Independence which you have just heard read declared the thirteen colonies to be " free and independent states." But, before the declaration was made, the colonies gave instructions to their delegates, prescribing the conditions upon which each would consent to such a declaration. These instructions all prescribe the fundamental condition *that the people of each colony shall have the right to manage their internal affairs and domestic concerns as to them shall seem meet and proper.* [Hearty cheers.]

[Mr. Douglas recapitulated some facts of history, and then proceeded as follows:]

Crime, in any of its forms and shapes, is a very great evil in any state or Territory; yet Congress has never presumed to enact criminal codes for the Territories and new states—to declare what shall and what shall not be deemed criminal—to prescribe the penalty and point out the mode of punishment. These things have always been left, and, I trust, always will be left, to the people of the different states and Territories, to be determined by them through their local Legislatures in accordance with their sense of right and duty. Why should we make an exception of the Slavery question, and apply to it a rule which is admitted to be unsound and subversive of constitutional right when applied to any other matter of local and domestic concern? Are not the people of the Territories capable of self-government? If not, why give them a Legislature at all—why allow them to make laws upon any subject? If they are capable of self-government, does it require any higher degree of intelligence to legislate for the negro than for the white man, or to prescribe the relations of master and servant than those of husband and wife, and parent and child?

But, in order to excuse themselves for so palpable a repudiation of the great principle of self-government, the Abolitionists tell us that slavery is a violation of the law of God, and therefore the people of the Territories and new states should not be intrusted with the decision of the question as provided in the Nebraska Bill. Without stopping to inquire into the sinfulness of slavery as a religious question, I do maintain that the mode provided in the Nebraska Bill for determining the controversy of its existence or exclusion, by referring it to the decision of the people, who are immediately interested and alone responsible, is strictly in accordance with the divine law. When God created man, He placed before him good and evil, and endowed him with the capacity to decide for himself, and held him responsible for the consequences of the choice he might make. [Tremendous applause and cheers.]

This is the divine origin of the great principle of self-government. [Applause.] The Almighty breathed the principle into the nostrils of the first man in the garden of Eden, and empowered him and his descendants in all time to choose their own form of government, and to bear the evils and enjoy the blessings of their own deeds. The principle applies to communities, and Territories, and states, as well as to individual men. The principle applies to Kansas as well as to Pennsylvania—to Nebraska as well as to Virginia. The Constitution of the United States is in perfect accord with this divine principle, leaving each state, and the people thereof, at liberty to govern themselves and reap the harvest of the seed they may sow. [Immense applause—cries, "That is right," "that is right."]

I repeat, therefore, that the Constitution of the United States does not establish slavery, nor abolish it any where; nor does it either enlarge or diminish its area. It recognizes and protects all the institutions of the different states, however dissimilar or whatever their character, provided they are not in conflict with any of its provisions. Wherever slavery exists in any state by virtue of the local law, there the Constitution recognizes and protects the institution; and wherever slavery is prohibited by the local law, the Constitution recognizes and protects the prohibition in such state. The Constitution of the United States is the supreme law of the land, to which all must yield implicit obedience. [Applause.]

It authorizes Congress to legislate upon the subject of slavery in two cases only: first, for the suppression of the foreign slave-trade; and, second, for the surrender of fugitives from service. Congress has exerted in good faith the full measures of its authority in both cases. The Abolitionists avow their willingness to abide by the Constitution and law in the one case, where the introduction of any more slaves into the United States is prohibited, for the reason that the result is in harmony with their views. But in the other case, where the act of Congress was passed for the express purpose of carrying into effect a plain provision of the Constitution, by returning the slave to his master, these same Abolitionists say they will not abide by the law—they will trample upon the Constitution—they will set at defiance the constituted authorities, and bear aloft the standard of rebellion against the federal government, for the reason that this clause of the Constitution and the law for carrying it into effect do not harmonize with their views. Their doctrine is that they will abide by and claim the benefit of the Constitution and laws whenever and wherever they tend to advance their peculiar theories and opinions; and, on the contrary, they will resist both the Constitution and laws, with force and violence, whenever that line of policy is necessary to the accomplishment of their philanthropic views upon the subject of slavery.

KNOW-NOTHINGISM.

Efforts are now being made to organize a new party—a great Northern, sectional party—upon the abolition platform, and carry on an offensive war against the local and domestic institutions of one half of the states of the Union, under a banner which shall proclaim to the world that they claim for themselves the protection of the Constitution which they deny to those upon whose rights they make war—that the Constitution is binding upon their opponents, but not upon themselves—and that they hold themselves at liberty at all times to obey or resist it, as may best suit their purposes. Whatever name shall be given to this new political organization—whether it shall be called Whig, Abolition, Free-soil, or Know-nothing—it will still be the antagonism of the Democratic party. Whatever may be the nature of the contest or the prospects of success, the Democracy of the nation must stand firmly by the Constitution as it is, yielding implicit obedience to all of its obligations, and carrying into faithful execution all of its provisions. [Cheers and continued applause.] We must maintain the supremacy of the laws, put down resistance and violence wherever they may occur, and be ready to punish the traitors whenever the overt act of treason shall be committed. [Tremendous cheers and applause.]

Fellow-citizens, it has been said that in the bosom of this new political organization there is a secret society bound together by the most solemn and terrible oaths— *I know not* its name—[Laughter.] Inquire of whom you may, and the answer will be, " I don't know." [Roars of laughter.] And from all the information I can get, I am inclined to believe that "know-nothings" is their name. [Tremendous roars of laughter.]

I was about to say, and I presume that the facts connected with your recent election in this city have furnished you with sufficient evidence upon the subject—I have been informed that there exists in the bosom of this new political organization a secret political society, bound together by the most terrible oaths, to proscribe every man, whether naturalized or not, or whatever his political or religious sentiments, who had the misfortune to be born in a foreign clime, and, like our ancestors, driven by political or religious persecutions to flee from their native land and seek an asylum in America. Is there such an organization among you? [Cries of " Yes," "yes." "There is," "there is."]

It is also said, and with how much truth you have much better opportunities of knowing than I, for of this *I know nothing* [roars of laughter], that this secret society, which controls the nominations and directs the movements of the allied forces against the Democracy, binds its members by the most solemn obligations to proscribe every man who worships God according to the Roman Catholic faith, no matter to what race he may belong, or where he was born. [Cries "That is it," "They do."] It is also said that your recent city election was controlled by this society; that your city government is now being managed under its auspices, and that the whole patronage of the city is distributed under its direction and *in accordance with its principles of proscription.* [Cries "That is so," "It is," "it is," from all sides.]

This secret society, whose members profess to "know nothing" with the view of concealing their political designs, are said to have their branches and auxiliary societies in every city, town, and village, and to be in alliance with this great northern sectional party, which proclaims open war upon the institutions of one half of the states and upon the Constitution of the United States. It is not surprising that a political society, whose efficient secret organization enables them to conceal their plans while they hold out inducements of power and patronage to persons to assume their proscriptive obligations, with the assurance that they can conceal the hand which strikes the blow, and thus avoid the odium and responsibility of the act, while they revel in the spoils of victory—I say it is not surprising that such a political organization should prove formidable and even irresistible in its first efforts, when the specific objects and principles of the society were unknown to the community, and before the people could be aroused to a just sense of their danger. I speak of the society and of its principles of action here and wherever else they have triumphed in the recent elections; for I am not aware that I am personally acquainted with any one man who has taken upon himself their obligations and enrolled his name upon their books.

No principle of political action could have been devised more hostile to the genius of our institutions, more repugnant to the Constitution than those which are said to form the test of membership in this society of "Know-nothings." To proscribe a man in this country on account of his birthplace or religious faith is subversive of all our ideas and principles of civil and religious freedom. It is revolting to our sense of justice and right. It is derogatory to the character of our forefathers, who were all emigrants from the Old World, some at an earlier and some at a later period. They once bore allegiance to the crowned heads of Europe. They, too, suffered the torments of civil and religious persecution, the fury of which tore them from their native homes, and forced them to seek new ones on the shores of America. Indeed, the settlement of this continent, the development of the thirteen united colonies, the Declaration of Independence, and the establishment of this glorious republic, may all be traced back to the accursed spirit of persecution. The Pilgrim fathers fled before their persecutors from England to Holland, and thence to Plymouth Rock, that they might be permitted to worship God agreeably to their own faith. The same spirit compelled the Quakers to seek refuge in the wilderness under William Penn, whose name they imparted to the country they inhabited, and from which the good old commonwealth of Pennsylvania has arisen in her glory and majesty.

Your own beautiful city of Philadelphia stands a living monument, and I trust it may stand an eternal monument, of their gratitude to God for having removed them from the scenes of their troubles to a quiet and peaceful home on the banks of the Delaware, which, in the fullness of their hearts, and in faith that the spirit of religious persecution would never again reach them nor spring up among them, they called the "CITY OF BROTHERLY LOVE." [Cheers and applause.]

The Catholics, who in turn were oppressed and pursued by those who had felt the rod of their power, found an asylum upon the banks of the Chesapeake, and called their little colony after their favorite Queen Mary, to which circumstance the State of Maryland owes her name and her origin.

The gallant Cavaliers, who, after having persecuted the Pilgrims and driven them from the kingdom under Charles I., were in turn routed and pursued by Cromwell, with his invincible army of Roundheads, until they fled to Virginia, where they established the Church of England.

The Huguenots, who settled in South Carolina, were also refugees from religious persecution. Thus it will be seen that the different colonies were the representatives of the various religious sects in Europe, who had each been persecuted, and had nearly all persecuted each other in turn, until, by the strange vicissitudes of fortune, they were driven from their native land and forced to seek an asylum upon this continent, where each could be protected in the worship of God in accordance with the faith he had embraced. In proportion as they became tolerant and just in matters of religion, they became liberal and enlightened in respect to the true principles of civil government. When the Revolution broke out, in defense of their civil and political rights each and all of these colonies rallied under the banner of their common country. The Revolution established their independence by converting the dependent colonies into distinct sovereign states, yet it was not until the adoption of the Constitution of the United States that their liberties were consolidated and placed on a firm and sure basis. In the Constitution it was provided that "NO RELIGIOUS TEST SHALL EVER BE REQUIRED AS A QUALIFICATION TO ANY OFFICE OR PUBLIC TRUST UNDER THE UNITED STATES." [Immense applause.]

This provision was adopted unanimously.   It was the common ground of justice and equality, upon which all religious denominations could stand in harmony and security.   It expressed in plain language the true principles of religious toleration, the correctness and necessity of which had been thoroughly vindicated in the history and experience of each of the colonies.   It was heartily concurred in by Protestant and Catholic—by Puritan and Cavalier —by Quaker and Huguenot—each and all of the religious sects and denominations agreed upon this great principle as a platform, a common ground upon which they and their descendants in all future time could and would stand in the bonds of brotherly affection. [Applause.]

By another clause of the Constitution no man can hold any office under the government of the United States, or under any of the state governments, until he has subscribed an oath to support the Constitution of the United States.   This oath must be taken, and ought to be kept, not only by presidents, and governors, and judges, but by the mayors of your cities and all their subordinates in office. [Tremendous cheers and applause.]

Now, fellow-citizens, permit me to inquire, in all kindness, how can the members of this political society, called " Know-nothings," take upon themselves a solemn oath by which they shall stand pledged to raise up a religious test as a qualification for office, in the very teeth of the Constitution, by proscribing men on account of their religious faith?   Will they excuse themselves upon the ground that *they did not know* of this clause in the Constitution? [Cheers and laughter.]

Will they tell us that *they did not know* the history of their own country— that *they did not know* of the sufferings and persecutions to which their fathers had been subjected on account of their religious faith—that *they did not know* that the obligations and principles of their society were at war with the genius of our whole republican system and in direct conflict with the principles of the Constitution? [Loud cheering.]

If *they did not know* these things, surely there was wisdom in calling themselves " KNOW-NOTHINGS." [Tremendous cheers and roars of laughter.]

Those who do not know should be made to learn and feel that the Constitution is the supreme law of the land; that all men who live under it, and enjoy its protection, must yield implicit obedience to its requirements, in all its parts and provisions, whether they like them or not. [Cheers and continued applause.]

Their likes or dislikes have nothing to do with the question. We live under a government of laws, and the supremacy of the laws must be maintained, no matter from what quarter or motive the resistance may come. [Great applause.]

The equality of all the states under the Constitution, and the right of the people to decide for themselves what kind of local and domestic institutions they will have, are cardinal principles in the Democratic creed. [Loud and enthusiastic cheers.]

To these fundamental propositions let me add another, which forms the corner-stone in the temple of our liberties.   It is, that all men have an inalienable right to worship God according to the dictates of their own conscience, and under our Constitution no man ought or can be proscribed on account of his birthplace or of his religious faith. [Loud cheers and applause.]

These are the issues which the Democratic party of the nation have to meet and maintain before the people in all the states.   Let no consideration of partisan policy or temporary advantage induce us to swerve a hair's breadth from our principles.   If we meet the questions fairly and directly, and fight the battle boldly, and should even suffer a temporary defeat, yet we will have the proud satisfaction of knowing that we have saved our honor at the same time that a glorious triumph awaits us in the future. [Applause.]

Then, fellow-Democrats, let us stand by our arms and be ready to fight the allied forces of Abolitionism, Whigism, Nativeism, and religious intolerance, under whatever name and on whatever field they may present themselves. [Enthusiastic cheers and tremendous applause.]

And if, after struggling as our forefathers struggled for centuries in their native land against civil and religious persecution, we and our children shall be finally borne down and trampled under the heel of despotism, we can still follow their example—flee to the wilderness, and find an asylum in Nebraska, where the principles of self-government have been firmly established in the organic act which recently passed Congress.

This speech very naturally drew upon Mr. Douglas the enmity of the zealous members of the order. It was the first blow aimed at them. It was the first invocation to the Democracy to stand by their principles and treat the Know-nothings as their political enemies. In the Western States the order made rapid progress. It formed the centre around which all and every description of political interest hostile to the Democratic party rallied. Though the Nebraska Bill had been supported by a majority of the Democrats in Congress, and had been approved by the administration of General Pierce, still no attempt had been made to constitute a support of it a test of Democracy. But those Democrats who were hostile to it, having united with the Abolitionists, Free-soilers, and Know-nothings upon a platform of the proscription of every supporter of the bill, its friends had, as a matter of necessity, to rally to its support and to the support of its Congressional advocates.

THE CHICAGO MOB OF 1854.

Congress adjourned about the first of August. Mr. Douglas left Washington soon after, and reached his home in Chicago about the 25th. In the mean time there had been extensive preparations by the Know-nothings and their allies to prevent any appeal by him to the people, such as he had made in Philadelphia. Some of the reverend gentlemen with whom he had had a controversy about their remonstrance took an active part in the matter. There was a thorough and complete organization established not only in Chicago, but throughout all the northern part of Illinois, to meet him every where with personal insult, and, if possible, to prevent his being heard. After he had been in the city some days, public notice was given that, on the night of the 1st of September, he would address his constituents at North Market Hall. The mayor of the city, the Hon. I. L. Milikin, was invited and consented to preside. The announcement of his intention to speak was received with great excitement. The newspapers warned the public to be there, and not to allow him to deceive the people by his sophistries. One paper, appealing directly to the prejudices of the Know-nothings, announced that Mr. Douglas had selected a body-guard of five hundred Irishmen, who, with arms in their hands, were to be present, and compel the people to silence while he spoke, and thus he would claim that they had, by not objecting, admitted his arguments and defense to be complete. Strange as it may seem that such a statement should obtain credence in an intelligent community, yet the fact is unquestionable. In a day or two after, another paper, hostile to Mr. Douglas, declared that there was a feverish sentiment prevailing in the community indicating a season of violence, and proved its assertion by citing the fact that every revolver and pistol in the stores of the city had been sold, and that there were orders for a large number yet unfilled.

The fact that violence was to take place at the meeting was daily impressed upon the public, but with consummate dexterity it was stated that Douglas intended to overawe the public by an armed demonstration. It is needless to say that this was utterly destitute of truth. All he asked, all he desired, was an orderly meeting, that he might be heard in explanation and defense of the Nebraska Bill.

Under such circumstances as these assembled the meeting on that September evening. During the afternoon the flags of such shipping as was owned by the most bitter of the Fusionists were hung at half-mast; at dusk the bells of numerous churches tolled with all the doleful solemnity that might be supposed appropriate for some impending calamity. As the evening closed in, crowds flocked to the place of meeting. At a quarter before eight o'clock Mr. Douglas commenced to address the multitude. The whole area in front of the building, and the street running east to Dearborn and west to Clark Street, were soon densely packed. The roofs of houses opposite, and windows, balconies, and every available standing-spot, were occupied. He had hardly commenced before he was hailed with a storm of hisses; he paused until silence was comparatively restored, when he told the meeting that he came there to address his constituents, and intended to be heard. He was instantly assailed by all manner of epithets and abuse. He stood his ground firmly, contesting with that maddened and excited crowd. His friends—and he had friends there, warm, devoted, and unyielding Democrats—were indignant, and were disposed to resent some of the most indecent outrages. Mr. Douglas appealed to them to be calm; to leave him to deal with the mob before him. He denounced the violence exhibited as a preconcerted thing, and in defiance of yells, groans, cat-calls, and every insulting menace and threat, he read aloud, so that it was heard above the infernal din, a letter informing him that, if he dared to speak, he would be maltreated.

We never saw such a scene before, and hope never to see the like again. What we have described is a pretty fair description of what took place during that protracted struggle. Until ten o'clock he stood firm and unyielding, bidding the mob defiance, and occasionally getting in a word or two upon the general subject. It was the penalty for his speech in Philadelphia. It was the penalty for having made the first assault upon Know-nothingism. It was the penalty for having dared to assail an order including within its members a vast majority of the allied opposition of the Western States. We have conversed since then with men who were present at that mob; with men who went there as members of the order, pledged to stand by and protect each other; with men who were armed to the teeth in anticipation of a scene of bloody violence, and they have assured us that nothing prevented bloodshed that night but the bold and defiant manner in which Douglas maintained his ground. Had he exhibited fear, he would not have commanded respect; had he been suppliant, he would have been spurned; had he been craven, and retreated, his party would in all probability have been assaulted with missiles, leading to violence in return. But, standing there before that vast mob, presenting a determined front and unyielding purpose, he extorted an involuntary admiration from those of his enemies who had the courage to engage in a personal encounter; and that admiration, while it could not overcome the purpose of preventing his being heard, protected him from personal violence.

The motive, the great ruling reason for refusing him the privilege of being heard, was that, as he had in 1850 carried the judgment of the people captive into an endorsement of the

Fugitive Slave Law, so, if allowed to speak in 1854, he would at least rally all Democrats to his support by his defense of the Nebraska Bill. The combined fanatics of Chicago feared the power and effect of his argument in the presence and hearing of the people. They therefore resolved that he should not be heard.

So far as this occasion was concerned the object was successfully attained, and if there were any doubts as to the fact that the course agreed upon had been previously concerted, the experience of the following few weeks served to remove all question on that subject.

Mr. Douglas announced his intention to speak at several points in the state, there being an election for Congressmen and state treasurer then pending. Every where throughout the northern part of the state he was greeted upon his arrival by every possible indignity that could be offered, short of personal violence. Burning effigies, effigies suspended by ropes, banners with all the vulgar mottoes and inscriptions that passion and prejudice could suggest, were displayed at various points. Whenever he attempted to speak, the noisy demonstrations which had proved so successful in Chicago were attempted, but in no place did they succeed in preventing his being heard. At Galena, Freeport, Waukegan, Woodstock, and other points in the very heart of the Abolition and Know-nothing portion of the state, he made strong, clear, and brilliant addresses in defense of the great measure. He justified the repeal of the Missouri restriction upon the same ground that he had justified the Compromise measures of 1850—that it was neither a Pro-slavery nor an Anti-slavery measure—that it was a surrender and a final abandonment by Congress and the federal government of any authority or claim of authority over the subject of slavery in the Territories; and that it recognized in the people of the Territories, acting through their Legislatures, and through their state conventions, full, exclusive, and complete power to prohibit or introduce, to exclude or protect, African slavery within their respective Territorial limits.

In 1854 he proclaimed that doctrine in the face of an excited Abolition mob, drawing from them the fiercest denunciations. In 1858 he proclaimed the same doctrine in the face of a mass meeting at the same place, and, for the first time in the history of the Nebraska Bill, it was discovered by those who preferred the election of Lincoln that Mr. Douglas was preaching a heresy!

It was not until late in the fall, and not until after he had become a candidate for Congress, that Mr. Lyman Trumbull raised the banner of Anti-Nebraskaism, and put himself in open hostility to the Democratic party. A senatorial election was to take place at the approaching session, General Shields's term expiring March 4th, 1855.

The previous Legislature had been largely Democratic, and the senators holding over, if they continued as Democrats, would, with those Democrats certain to be elected, secure a Democratic senator. The elections in Indiana had gone " Fusion" by forty or fifty thousand majority; in Ohio by a majority reaching eighty thousand; in Michigan and Wisconsin by majorities equally overwhelming.

The candidates in Illinois for state treasurer were, James Miller, Whig, Abolition, Know-nothing, Anti-Nebraska, Fusion, and John Moore, Democrat. In November the election took place, resulting in the election to Congress of Richardson, Harris, Allen, and Marshal, Democrats, and Washburne, Woodworth, Norton, Knox, and Trumbull, by the combination. The Democrats elected their candidate for state treasurer.

In the Legislature the state of parties was not so clearly defined. In the House of Representatives, composed of seventy-five members, T. J. Turner (Fusion) was elected speaker, receiving forty votes. In the Senate, composed of twenty-five members, the Democrats had seventeen members who had been elected as Democrats. Of those three, N. B. Judd, B. C. Cook, and J. M. Palmer, senators holding over, had got " tender-footed"—that is, were Anti-Nebraska Democrats, whose consciences would not allow them to vote for General Shields, or any Nebraska Democrat, and whose notions of political morality revolted at the idea of voting for a Whig.

The Legislature met in joint convention on the 8th of February, 1855, for the purpose of electing a senator of the United States to succeed General Shields, and the first ballot resulted —Shields (Democrat) 41, Ficklin (Dem.) 1, Denning (Dem.) 1, Matteson (Dem.) 1. Total (Dem.), 44. Abraham Lincoln 45, L. Trumbull 5, Ogden (Fusion) 1, Kellogg (Fusion) 1, Koerner (Fusion) 2, Edwards (Fusion) 1. Total, 55—one vacancy. On the seventh vote Lincoln received 38, Matteson

44, Trumbull 9, Shields 1, M'Clernand 1, Koerner 1. On the
ninth Matteson received 47, Lincoln 15, Trumbull 35; and on
the tenth Trumbull was elected, receiving 51 votes, Matteson
47, Williams 1—one Whig, Mr. Waters, refusing to take the
apostate Democrat at the dictation of the men who had sacrificed Lincoln.

Resolutions upon the subject of slavery were introduced
into both branches of the Legislature at that session, though
no series received the concurrent approval of both branches.
Trumbull having been elected to the Senate, his district chose
the Hon. Robert Smith (Dem.) to fill the vacancy.

After the election, Mr. Douglas was invited by his political
friends in Chicago to partake of a public dinner, and he accepted
the invitation. The 9th of November was selected for the time,
and on that evening some two hundred gentlemen sat down
to a dinner at the Tremont House. In response to a complimentary sentiment, Mr. Douglas addressed the company in a
very graceful, eloquent, and finished speech. It is part of the
history of his life, was a noble vindication of his conduct, and
was substantially the address which he would have made to
the people of Chicago in September, had he not been prevented
by the mob. Want of space prevents its insertion here. It
was printed in pamphlet form, and, though it claimed for the
people of the Territories full legislative control over the subject
of slavery within their Territorial limits—a control limited only
by the Constitution—no word of dissent was heard from any
Democratic quarter as to the doctrines therein asserted.

A few days after this festive occasion Mr. Douglas left
Chicago on a visit to Louisiana, and subsequently, when at
Washington City, was invited to address a public meeting at
Richmond, Virginia. At the South there was no opposition
to the Nebraska Bill, but the great majority of the old opponents of the Democracy had united under the new and mysterious command of the Know-nothing order. Mr. Douglas addressed a very large meeting at the "African Church," in Richmond, in defense of Democratic principles and in reprobation
of the intolerant creed of the Know-nothings. Of this speech,
which was remarkable for its general ability, one passage, in
which he addressed a most impressive warning against American citizens rashly and inconsiderately binding themselves in
political matters by solemn oaths, attracted universal attention

by its great applicability. The illustration employed, and the application made of it, has not been surpassed by any thing ever said upon the subject. He cited Herod's rash oath under which he bound himself to the death of John the Baptist. Mr. Douglas applied this with great effect to the hasty, inconsiderate, yet solemn and sweeping obligations assumed by the members of the Know-nothing order.

CHAPTER XII.

THE FEDERAL JUDICIARY.

In January, 1855, the Judiciary Committee of the Senate, having had for some years the subject of affording to the members of the Supreme Court such relief as would enable them to perform fully their high duty as the court of last resort in the Union, reported a bill having in view that end. The bill reported by that committee discharged the justices of the Supreme Court from all circuit duty, allowing them, however, the same jurisdiction and powers now vested in them by law within any of the circuits in which they may reside, in allowing writs of habeas corpus and of error, granting injunctions, and generally all such powers as may be exercised under existing law at chambers and out of term. Instead of one term, there were to be two terms of the Supreme Court annually. The bill continued the existing judicial districts, but provided for their arrangement into eleven circuits—viz.: 1. Maine, New Hampshire, Massachusetts, and Rhode Island; 2. New York, Connecticut, and Vermont; 3. Pennsylvania and New Jersey; 4. Delaware, Maryland, and Virginia; 5. North and South Carolina, Georgia, and Florida; 6. Alabama, Mississippi, and Louisiana; 7. Arkansas and Texas; 8. Tennessee, Kentucky, and Missouri; 9. Ohio, Indiana, and Michigan; 10. Illinois, Wisconsin, and Iowa; 11. California. The bill provided for the appointment of eleven circuit judges, one for each of these circuits, at a salary of $4000 per annum each; the circuit judges to perform the circuit duties now performed by the justices of the Supreme Court.

Mr. Douglas, who had given to the subject considerable attention, proposed, on the 5th of January, when the bill came up, a substitute, involving a new plan, or adapting the existing system to the present exigencies and wants of the country. He opposed most strenuously the separation of the Supreme Court judges from the people—from intercourse with the bar and courts throughout the Union. His plan continued the existing District Courts, and conferred on them all the powers and jurisdiction now possessed by the Circuit Courts. He then proposed to establish nine judicial circuits, as follows: 1. The six New England States; 2. New York, New Jersey, and Pennsylvania; 3. Delaware, Maryland, Virginia, and North Carolina; 4. South Carolina, Georgia, Alabama, and Florida; 5. Mississippi, Louisiana, Arkansas, and Texas; 6. Tennessee, Kentucky, Ohio, and Indiana; 7. Illinois, Michigan, Wisconsin, Iowa, and Minnesota; 8. Missouri, New Mexico, Kansas, and Nebraska; 9. California, Oregon, Washington, and Utah. The district judges within those districts to assemble once in each year, with one judge of the Supreme Court to preside, and to hear all appeals from the several District Courts within that circuit. The several judges of the Supreme Court to attend these circuits once in each year, and to alternate, so as that each judge in turn should attend all the circuits. In the debate on this question, Mr. Douglas explained, in his peculiarly forcible manner, the practical workings of this plan proposed by him. He said:

I have been induced, Mr. President, to offer this substitute from a conviction that the plan proposed by the Judiciary Committee will not answer the purposes which they have in view, and will not remedy the evils which they desire to correct. They propose to make a separate Supreme Court, with no other duties than those which are imposed upon the Supreme Court of the United States sitting at Washington alone. Here I differ in toto with the committee. I think the Supreme Court ought to have other jurisdiction. I think it is for the good of the country, and for the good of that court, that its judges should be required to go into the country, hold courts in different localities, and mingle with the local judges and with the bar. I think that if the judges of that court be released from all duties outside the city of Washington, and stay here the whole year round, they will become, as a senator remarked to me a moment ago, mere paper judges. I think they will lose that weight of authority in the country which they ought to have just in proportion as they lose their knowledge of the local legislation, and of the practice and proceedings of the courts below. I believe, therefore, that the theory of the original plan on which our judiciary system was formed was right. In consequence of the increase of the judicial business of the country, some modification of that plan has become necessary in order to preserve the same principle, and render it applicable to our present condition. The plan which I propose in this substitute is simply this: that there shall be no new judges appointed, but the duties now performed by the District and Circuit Courts of the United States in each state shall hereafter be performed by the district judge in that state. According to it, the district judge will hold the District and the Circuit Courts at the same time. Both will be open at the same time; the record of each will be before him, in the same manner as in a court of law with chancery jurisdiction. As both courts are open at the same time, the judge may take up a case on the law docket or the chancery docket, as may be convenient; so, according to my plan, the district judge could take up a case on the docket of either the District or the Circuit Court, both courts being held by the same judge. Then, having released the judges of the Supreme Court from the necessity of going into every district in each state—and where there are three districts in a state, as in Tennessee and other states, that must be a great labor—the question is, how much of this local duty can we devolve upon them without depriving them of the opportunity of performing all their duties at the seat of government? It occurred to me that this point could be settled in the manner which I have proposed in my amendment; that is, to divide the whole United States into nine judicial circuits, and provide that there shall be held, once a year, in each of those circuits, a Court of Appeals, to be composed of the district judge of each district within the circuit, together with one of the judges of the Supreme Court of the United States, who should preside. By way of illustration, suppose the New England States should be made one of the circuits; there are, in New England, six United States District Courts, and the Court of Appeals would therefore be composed of these six district judges, with one judge of the Supreme Court of the United States presiding, which would make a court of seven judges. I provide for appeals to be taken directly from the District Court to this Court of Appeals, and then from the Court of Appeals to the Supreme Court of the United States, with certain restrictions. This illustration would apply to each of the other nine districts, comprehending all the states and all the Territories of the Union. This system would, it seems to me, have very great advantages, and would remedy several evils which we have known to grow up under our present system. You now find that in one district the rules of practice are one way, and in another district entirely different. One district judge decides a controverted principle in one way, and another in another way. If all the district judges in a circuit could come together once a year to review their own decisions, it would tend to bring about uniformity of thought and uniformity of practice within those districts. To secure this object, my substitute provides that the Court of Appeals in each circuit shall prescribe the rules of practice for the District Courts within the circuit. You thus infuse uniformity into all the District Courts within the same circuit, acting under the same rules, and the consequence would be that very few appeals would be taken from the Court of Appeals to the Supreme Court of the United States. I propose also to allow an appeal from the District Court to the Court of Appeals in every case in which it is now allowed by law from the District to the Circuit Courts; and to allow appeals from the Court of Appeals to the Supreme Court, but to fix a higher sum than is now required to be the amount in controversy to entitle the parties to an appeal from a Circuit Court to the Supreme Court, so that small cases may stop at the Courts of Appeal, and none but cases involving large amounts and important principles be carried to the Supreme Court of the United States. Then, sir, with a view of remedying other evils which may now exist, I have introduced another principle, derived from the judicial system of some of the states of the Union. It is what is known as the rotary principle; that is to say, inasmuch as one of the judges of the Supreme Court is to preside in each of the Courts of Appeals once a year in each circuit throughout the United States, I require them to rotate; so that if the chief justice presides in district No. 1 this year, he may next year go to district No. 2, and next to district No. 3, and so on until he come to district No. 9, at San Francisco. Then, the succeeding year, the next judge highest in commission begins at district No. 1, goes to the second, and the third, and all the other districts. The consequence of this would be that a judge of the Supreme Court would not preside in the same circuit over a Court of Appeals more than once in nine years. In that way the foundation of complaints, which sometimes are gotten up—probably unjustly, but yet none the less mischievous for being unjust—that there is a coterie around the judge when he goes every year to the same circuit, would be destroyed. Again, if a judge goes to the New England circuit one year, to the Middle States the next year, then through the Southern States, then to the Western States, and finally to California, he becomes more familiar with the local judicial system of the whole Union; and inasmuch as the Supreme Court is the final Court of Appeals from all decisions of the lower courts throughout the land, its judges ought to be familiar, so far as it is possible for them to become familiar, with the modes of proceeding in the various sections of the Union, with the local legislation, and the local laws of all parts of the country. Now, sir, without meaning any disrespect to any one, but for the purpose of illustrating the practical operation of the principle, I trust I may be permitted to say that I do not think it would be the slightest injury to Judge Curtis, of Boston, after having practiced law all his life in New England, to hold court for one term in Charleston, South Carolina, and then in New Orleans, and again in Chicago, and then in San Francisco. I think a system which required that would liberalize the mind, elevate the train of thought, and expand the range of knowledge of any judge, no matter how exalted he might be. On the other hand, I do not think it would do the slightest harm to Judge Campbell, of Mobile, to send him to Boston to hold court, and let him mingle with the people of New England, and the New England bar and judiciary, and become acquainted with the New England character and New England jurisprudence. Let him go the round until he gets back, at the end of nine years, to his own circuit where he resides, and I think he would be liberalized, and improved, and benefited by the trip. The same remark would apply to each one of the judges. They would then have a degree of knowledge of the systems in each state, and of the local jurisprudence of each part of the country, which would be very valuable to them. They would thus become acquainted with the bar all over the Union, and with the sentiments and feelings of the bar, operating upon the rules of practice and of the rules of court, and would acquire a knowledge which never could be acquired in any other way. Entertaining these opinions, I believe that the best system we could adopt would be to take the present system as it is, adding no new judges, or at least not more than one, if an additional judge should be necessary, and I doubt whether one is; leave the district judges to perform their own duties in the District and Circuit Courts of the United States; constitute the Court of Appeals which I have proposed, and allow an appeal from them to the Supreme Court of the United States. Thus the whole system is harmonious. This plan would never render it necessary, in any expansion of the country, no matter how great, to increase the number of judges on the bench of the Supreme Court of the United States; but when we bring other states into the Union, or organize other Territories, all we shall have to do will be to attach one of those new states or Territories to one of the existing nine judicial circuits. Then this system is complete. It will adapt itself to any expansion of our country, to any increase of business in all time to come, and I believe it will be harmonious in its action.

I have not been able to look into my proposition since I drew it up, and presented it informally at the last session. I did not expect it to come up to-day, and therefore can not go fully into all its details; but there is a special provision in it which I think I ought to notice. In order to give ample compensation to the judges of the Supreme Court for the extra labor which would be imposed on them by my proposition, in addition to their duties on the Supreme bench, I have proposed to allow them the per diem and mileage of members of Congress while they are absent as presiding judges in the Courts of Appeals. If a judge should go only from here to Boston to hold court, the mileage would be but small. If he should go to New Orleans, it would be a very respectable sum; and if he should go to San Francisco, it would be quite a little fortune. I think such a provision would really improve the health of many of the judges, so that they could take a trip to San Francisco without complaining that they would suffer very much by it, though they might find it very unhealthy if some such provision were not made. I also believe, as a matter of justice, that they should receive mileage in proportion to their travel. I do not say whether or not the present salary is sufficient. If it is not, increase it. But I say, in addition to whatever salary you award to them as judges of the Supreme Court, you should allow them a *per diem* while holding the appellate courts, and the mileage of members of Congress while traveling over the country to reach the sittings of those courts. I propose to apply the same principle to the district judges when they leave their respective districts, and go to a central point in the circuit, to sit in the Court of Appeals. I have thus stated briefly the chief provisions of the substitute which I have offered. It has occurred to me that by this proposition we could avoid many of the evils which we are likely to encounter by the adoption of the system reported by the Committee on the Judiciary. I have great reluctance at any time to make a radical and sudden change in the judiciary of the country. If there is any department of this government for which I have a higher reverence than any other—if there is any department in the purity and stability of which I place higher hopes than any other, it is the judiciary. I would not wish to make any such sudden and radical change in that system as would infuse into it too many new men at one time. I would allow that infusion of new blood and new life to come into it by the course of nature, simply by filling vacancies when they may occur from time to time. Sir, I think it is unwise to make a change by which all the Circuit Courts of the Union shall at once be held by new men, perhaps politicians, perhaps lawyers who have never been upon the bench. It is a thing which ought to be done gradually, so that there shall always be a majority of experienced judges upon each of the benches of the country. These views, sir, have operated on my mind. I have doubted whether the system proposed by the Judiciary Committee could be adopted, and if adopted, I have had still more serious doubts whether it would remedy the evils intended to be remedied by those who have brought it forward. But, sir, not being a member of the Judiciary Committee, I have felt great reluctance in interposing my voice on this question. My duties have been such that I have not been able to give it that consideration which the importance of a subject of this magnitude would require; but still, having these firm convictions on my own mind, I have felt that I owed it to the country, and especially to the bench with which I have been associated for a small portion of my life, to make these suggestions, in order that the Senate may pass their judgment upon them, and make such disposition of the subject as they shall think proper.

Mr. Pratt having asked some explanation:

Mr. Douglas. I am aware that I was, perhaps, somewhat confused in the brief explanation which I gave this morning, as the matter came up unexpectedly, and therefore omitted many points which ought to have been fully explained. I have turned my attention, however, to the points to which the senator from Maryland has adverted. It occurred to me that the duties of the Supreme Court of the United States would be materially lessened by the plan which I have proposed in this respect; I have thought that by having a

Court of Appeals, composed of six or seven judges in the respective circuits, one of the justices of the Supreme Court presiding, there would be a much less number of appeals taken to the Supreme Court of the United States than there is under the present system. Under the existing system, an appeal from a District Court to a Circuit Court of the United States is a mere mockery. I do not speak offensively; but I say, in its practical effect it is a mockery, and for this reason: a case is first tried before the district judge, and then an appeal is taken to the Circuit Court. The Circuit Court is composed of that same *district* judge and one judge of the Supreme Court of the United States. If, when the case comes up for hearing before the Circuit Court, the district judge is of the same opinion that he was before, as he probably would be, and the circuit judge differs from him, there would then be no decision, and the case would be certified to the Supreme Court of the United States to decide between them. If, on the contrary, the circuit judge should agree with the judge below, then there would be a decision, but the appeal would have been useless, for it merely led to the affirmation of the opinion below. The consequence is, that whenever there is a difference of opinion between the circuit judge and the district judge, the case is certified to the Supreme Court, and thus you multiply the causes on the docket of the Supreme Court without having accomplished any benefit by the appeal through the intermediate court. But, according to my plan, instead of appealing from the judge below to himself and one other, you appeal to himself and probably six others, and one of those six a judge of the Supreme Court of the United States. If they should reverse a decision unanimously, the chances are that the matter would stop there. If they should be nearly equally divided on a question involving a new or intricate principle of law, or a vast amount of property, the case would probably be appealed. I think, then, that in the practical operation of this system, there would be very few appeals to the Supreme Court of the United States in comparison to the number there is now. Again, sir, the system I have submitted will diminish the duties of the judges of the Supreme Court in another respect. Judge M'Lean, for example, is the judge assigned to the Northwestern Circuit, in which I reside. He is expected to attend to his duties in the Supreme Court here at Washington, and also to preside twice a year in the Circuit Court in Ohio; twice in Indiana; four times in Illinois, there being two districts there, and twice in Michigan. There are, then, ten terms which he is expected to hold in the courts below in one year, besides attending to his duties in the Supreme Court. I propose, instead of his holding ten terms of the Circuit Courts in each year, he shall attend but one term of the Court of Appeals of a particular circuit. It strikes me that this would materially diminish his duties. If the term of the Court of Appeals should last for three months—and certainly it could hardly be expected to take up that much time—he would still have nine months for attendance on the Supreme Court here. My substitute requires the Court of Appeals to be held in the nine circuits on the same day—say the first Monday in June or the first Monday in May. That being the case, the judges of the Supreme Court would arrange their terms so as to allow them to disperse to their respective circuits at the same time, finish their circuits, and get back here at the same time. I take it for granted, therefore, that, instead of being limited, as they now are, to two or three months every year for their duties here, the judges of the Supreme Court, under my plan, would have at least nine months to be at Washington, after performing all their duties in the different circuits. In this way, by giving them eight, or nine, or ten months to be here, instead of three or four months, for their duties in the Supreme Court, and by diminishing the amount of their circuit labors in the mode I have mentioned, they would be enabled to perform all their duties, and have probably one half the year to themselves.

The bill was debated several days; but there was such a diversity of opinion in the Senate as to the principle of the original bill—to exempt the judges of the Supreme Court from circuit duty—that the friends of the bill abandoned it. Before it was disposed of, however, a vote was taken on Mr. Douglas's amendment, and it was rejected—yeas 19, nays 26. Those voting for it were Atchison, Benjamin, Bright, Cass, Clay, Clayton, Dodge of Wisconsin, Dodge of Iowa, Douglas, Fessenden, Foot, Geyer, Gwin, Jones of Iowa, Sebastian, Shields, Stuart, Thomson of New Jersey, and Wade. The subject has never been acted upon definitely since then.

Perhaps no public man in the Union has labored more earnestly and indefatigably in the Senate, in his written papers, and in his addresses before the people, than Mr. Douglas, to sustain and defend the supreme judicial authority of the federal judiciary. He has had to meet and encounter the misrepresentations of the Dred Scott decision, and has had to labor hard, yet willingly and successfully, to defend that decision to its fullest extent before the people of the Northwest. One of the charges made against him in 1858 was that he had conspired with Judge Taney in having that decision made. While he defended the venerable chief justice from the accusation of conspiracy, Mr. Douglas endorsed and approved that decision without equivocation or reservation. Throughout all his speeches will be found a broad emphatic approval of that decision, and of a purpose on all occasions to submit to and abide by whatever decision that court may make upon questions of construction of the Constitution.

In a speech delivered at Springfield June 12, 1857, Mr. Douglas thus referred to the Supreme Court and the Dred Scott decision:

"That we are steadily and rapidly approaching that result I can not doubt, for the slavery issue has already dwindled down into the narrow limits covered by the decision of the Supreme Court of the United States in the Dred Scott case. The moment that decision was pronounced, and before the opinions of the court could be published and read by the people, the newspaper press, in the interest of a powerful political party in this country, began to pour forth torrents of abuse and misrepresentations not only upon the decision, but upon the character and motives of the venerable chief justice and his illustrious associates on the bench. The character of Chief Justice Taney, and his associate judges who concurred with him, require no eulogy—no vindication from me. They are endeared to the people of the United States by their eminent public services—venerated for their great learning, wisdom, and experience—and beloved for the spotless purity of their characters and their exemplary lives.   The poisonous shafts of partisan malice will fall harmless at their feet, while their judicial decisions will stand in all future time, a proud monument to their greatness, the admiration of the good and wise, and a rebuke to the partisans of faction and lawless violence.   If, unfortunately, any considerable portion of the people of the United States shall so far forget their obligations to society as to allow partisan leaders to array them in violent resistance to the final decision of the highest judicial tribunal on earth, it will become the duty of all the friends of order and constitutional government, without reference to past political differences, to organize themselves and marshal their forces under the glorious banner of the Union, in vindication of the Constitution and the supremacy of the laws over the advocates of faction and the champions of violence.   To preserve the Constitution inviolate, and vindicate the supremacy of the laws, is the first and highest duty of every citizen of a free republic.   The peculiar merit of our form of government over all others consists in the fact that the law, instead of the arbitrary will of a hereditary prince, prescribes, defines, and protects all our rights.   In this country the law is the will of the people, embodied and expressed according to the forms of the Constitution.   The courts are the tribunals prescribed by the Constitution, and created by the authority of the people, to determine, expound, and enforce the law.   Hence, whoever resists the final decision of the highest judicial tribunal aims a deadly blow at our whole republican system of government—a blow which, if successful, would place all our rights and liberties at the mercy of passion, anarchy, and violence.   I repeat, therefore, that if resistance to the decisions of the Supreme Court of the United States—in a matter, like the points decided in the Dred Scott case, clearly within their jurisdiction as defined by the Constitution—shall be forced upon the country as a political issue, it will become a distinct and naked issue between the friends and the enemies of the Constitution—the friends and the enemies of the supremacy of the laws."

CHAPTER XIII.

KANSAS AND HER GOVERNMENTS.

UNDER the operation of the Kansas-Nebraska Act, the governments provided for the two Territories were in due time erected.   That established in Nebraska was put in operation, and has been conducted ever since with as little trouble, as little excitement, as little distraction at home or throughout the Union as would be expected from the organization of a new county in Virginia or Illinois.   Not so with Kansas. From the first day of its establishment down to the present Kansas has been the theatre of fearful strife, involving bloodshed upon her plains, the formation of treasonable operations there and in other places, and to some extent, at times, the substitution of irresponsible anarchy for legal and constitutional government.

The entire history of Kansas difficulties formed a leading

question during the session of Congress commencing in December, 1855, and Mr. Douglas took an active and leading part in the eventful chapter of Congressional action upon her affairs. His reports and speeches at that session contain of themselves the best as well as the most concise written narrative not only of what took place in Congress, but of what happened in the unfortunate Territory.

The House of Representatives having been unable to elect a speaker, the President of the United States, without waiting for the usual notice of the organization of the houses, and their readiness to receive any communication from him, on the 31st of December sent in his usual message. He thus referred to affairs in Kansas:

"In the Territory of Kansas there have been acts prejudicial to good order, but as yet none have occurred under circumstances to justify the interposition of the federal executive. That could only be in case of obstruction to federal law, or of organized resistance to Territorial law, assuming the character of insurrection, which, if it should occur, it would be my duty promptly to overcome and suppress. I cherish the hope, however, that the occurrence of any such untoward event will be prevented by the sound sense of the people of the Territory, who, by its organic law, possessing the right to determine their own domestic institutions, are entitled, while deporting themselves peacefully, to the free exercise of that right, and must be protected in the enjoyment of it, without interference on the part of the citizens of any of the states."

On the 24th of January President Pierce sent a special message to Congress upon Kansas affairs. He thus expressed and defined his construction of the purposes, intents, and effect of the Kansas-Nebraska Act. He said:

"The act to organize the Territories of Nebraska and Kansas was a manifestation of the legislative opinion of Congress on two great points of constitutional construction: one, that the designation of the boundaries of a new Territory, and provision for its political organization, and administration as a Territory, are measures which of right fall within the powers of the general government; and the other, that the inhabitants of any such Territory, considered as an inchoate state, are entitled, in the exercise of self-government, to determine for themselves what shall be their own domestic institutions, subject only to the Constitution and the laws duly enacted by Congress under it, and to the power of the existing states to decide, according to the provisions and principles of the Constitution, at what time the Territory shall be received as a state into the Union. Such are the great political rights which are solemnly declared and affirmed by that act."

The President called attention to the various difficulties that had occurred in Kansas, and also the attempt to put the Topeka state government in operation as the government of Kansas—to override and exclude the existing Territorial government. He recommended the passage of a law authorizing the people of Kansas, whenever they might desire it, and were sufficiently numerous to constitute a state, to elect delegates to a convention for the formation of a state government, preparatory to their admission into the Union as a state. The message was referred to the Committee on Territories.

Mr. Douglas, in the mean time, was detained at Cleveland, where, and at Terre Haute, he had been suffering intensely with a bronchial affection. So protracted was his illness that he was not able to proceed to Washington until February, on the 11th of which month he appeared in the Senate.

On the 18th a large number of documents, called for by a resolution of the Senate, were received and referred to the Territorial Committee.

On the 12th of March Mr. Douglas made his elaborate and celebrated report upon Kansas matters, and upon the powers of Congress over the Territories as political communities. The report, and the speech which he delivered a few days later, are in themselves the most complete and concise history of Kansas affairs up to that time. The report was ordered to be printed, and a motion to print extra copies was referred to the Committee on Printing, it being stated and understood that the debate should take place on the bills when reported during the following week.

However, when the Committee on Printing made their report a day or two after, Mr. Trumbull availed himself of the occasion to deliver a speech in review of the report. Mr. Douglas was absent at the time, but, hearing that his colleague was making a speech, went to the Senate, and at its conclusion a sharp personal debate took place respecting this proceeding by Mr. Trumbull. Mr. Douglas likened it to the proceedings on the part of Messrs. Chase and Sumner in 1854, when a delay was asked in the consideration of the Nebraska Bill, during which those who had asked the delay issued an address misrepresenting the character of the bill and the motives of its authors.

On Monday, March 17th, Mr. Douglas reported " a bill to authorize the people of the Territory of Kansas to form a Constitution and state government preparatory to their admission into the Union when they have the requisite population."

On the 20th he addressed the Senate in support of the bill, and upon the general questions embraced in the report. We select from the report some extracts referring to very important points, particularly that portion wherein the power of Congress to establish Territorial governments is considered as a necessity arising in the exercise of the power to admit new states. The report says:

Your committee deem this an appropriate occasion to state briefly, but distinctly, the principles upon which new states may be admitted and Territories organized under the authority of the Constitution of the United States.

The Constitution (section 3, article 4) provides that "new states may be admitted by the Congress into this Union."

Section 8, article 1: "Congress shall have power to make all laws which shall be necessary and proper for carrying into execution the foregoing powers, and all other powers vested by the Constitution in the government of the United States, or in any department or office thereof."

10th amendment: "The powers not delegated to the United States by the Constitution, nor prohibited by it to the states, are reserved to the states respectively, or to the people."

A state of the federal Union is a sovereign power, limited only by the Constitution of the United States.

The limitations which that instrument has imposed are few, specific, and uniform—applicable alike to all the states, old and new. There is no authority for putting a restriction upon the sovereignty of a new state which the Constitution has not placed on the original states. Indeed, if such a restriction could be imposed on any state, it would instantly cease to be a *state* within the meaning of the federal Constitution, and, in consequence of the inequality, would assimilate to the condition of a province or dependency. Hence equality among all the states of the Union is a fundamental principle in our federative system—a principle embodied in the Constitution, as the basis upon which the American Union rests.

African slavery existed in all the colonies, under the sanction of the British government, prior to the Declaration of Independence. When the Constitution of the United States was adopted, it became the supreme law and bond of union between twelve slaveholding states and one non-slaveholding state; each state reserved the right to decide the question of slavery for itself—to continue it as a domestic institution as long as it pleased, and to abolish it when it chose.

In pursuance of this reserved right, six of the original slaveholding states have since abolished and prohibited slavery within their limits respectively, without consulting Congress or their sister states, while the other six have retained and sustained it as a domestic institution, which, in their opinion, had become so firmly ingrafted on their social systems that the relation between the master and slave could not be dissolved with safety to either. In the mean time, eighteen new states have been admitted into the Union, in obedience to the federal Constitution, on an equal footing with the original states, including, of course, the right of each to decide the question of slavery for itself. In deciding this question, it has so happened that nine of these new states have abolished and prohibited slavery, while the other nine have retained and regulated it. That these new states had at the time of their admission, and still retain, an equal right, under the federal Constitution, with the original states, to decide all questions of domestic policy for themselves, including that of African slavery, ought not to be seriously questioned, and certainly can not be successfully controverted.

They are all subject to the same supreme law, which, by the consent of each, constitutes the only limitation upon their sovereign authority.

Since we find the right to admit new states enumerated among the powers expressly delegated in the Constitution, the question arises, Whence does Congress derive authority to organize temporary governments for the Territories preparatory to their admission into the Union on an equal footing with the original states? Your committee are not prepared to adopt the reasoning which deduces the power from that other clause of the Constitution which says,

"Congress shall have power to dispose of and make all needful rules and regulations respecting the territory or other property belonging to the United States."

The language of this clause is much more appropriate when applied to property than to persons. It would seem to have been employed for the purpose of conferring upon Congress the power of disposing of the public lands and *other property belonging to the United States*, and to make all needful rules and regulations for that purpose, rather than to govern the people who might purchase those lands from the United States and become residents thereon. The word "territory" was an appropriate expression to designate that large area of public lands of which the United States had become the owner by virtue of the Revolution, and the cession by the several states. The additional words, "or other property belonging to the United States," clearly show that the term "territory" was used in its ordinary geographical sense to designate the public domain, and not as descriptive of the whole body of the people, constituting a distinct political community, who have no representation in Congress, and consequently no voice in making the laws upon which all their rights and liberties would depend, if it were conceded that Congress had the general and unlimited power to make all "needful rules and regulations concerning" their internal affairs and domestic concerns. It is under this clause of the Constitution, and from this alone, that Congress derives authority to provide for the surveys of the public lands, for securing pre-emption rights to actual settlers, for the establishment of land-offices in the several states and Territories, for exposing the lands to private and public sale, for issuing patents and confirming titles, and, in short, for making all needful rules and regulations for protecting and disposing of the public domain and other property belonging to the United States.

These needful rules and regulations may be embraced, and usually are found, in general laws applicable alike to states and Territories wherever the United States may be the owner of the lands or other property to be regulated or disposed of. It can make no difference, under this clause of the Constitution, whether the "territory, or other property belonging to the United States," shall be situated in Ohio or Kansas, in Alabama or Minnesota, in California or Oregon; the power of Congress to make needful rules and regulations is the same in the states and Territories, to the extent that the title is vested in the United States. Inasmuch as the right of legislation in such cases rests exclusively upon the fact of ownership, it is obvious it can extend only to the tracts of land to which the United States possess the title, and must cease in respect to each tract the instant it becomes private property by purchase from the United States. It will scarcely be contended that Congress possesses the power to legislate for the people of those states in which public lands may be located, in respect to their internal affairs and domestic concerns, merely because the United States may be so fortunate as to own a portion of the territory and other property within the limits of those states. Yet it should be borne in mind that this clause of the Constitution confers upon Congress the same power to make needful rules and regulations in the states as it does in the Territories, concerning the territory or other property belonging to the United States.

In view of these considerations, your committee are not prepared to affirm that Congress derives authority to institute governments for the people of the Territories from that clause of the Constitution which confers the right to make needful rules and regulations concerning the territory or other property belonging to the United States; much less can we deduce the power from any supposed necessity, arising outside of the Constitution, and not provided for in that instrument. The federal government is one of delegated and limited powers, clothed with no rightful authority which does not result directly and necessarily from the Constitution. Necessity, when experience shall have clearly demonstrated its existence, may furnish satisfactory reasons for enlarging the authority of the federal government, by amendments to the Constitution, in the mode prescribed in that instrument, but can not afford the slightest excuse for the assumption of powers not delegated, and which, by the tenth amendment, are expressly "reserved to the states respectively, or to the people." Hence, before the power can be safely exercised, the right of Congress to organize Territories, by instituting temporary governments, must be traced directly to some provision of the Constitution conferring the authority in express terms, or as a means necessary and proper to carry into effect some one or more of the powers which are specifically delegated. Is not the organization of a Territory eminently necessary and proper as a means of enabling the people thereof to form and mould their local and domestic institutions, and establish a state government under the authority of the Constitution, preparatory to its admission into the Union? If so, the right of Congress to pass the organic act for the temporary government is clearly included in the provision which authorizes the admission of new states. This power, however, being an incident to an express grant, and resulting from it by necessary implication, as an appropriate means for carrying it into effect, must be exercised in harmony with the nature and objects of the grant from which it is deduced. The organic act of the Territory, deriving its validity from the power of Congress to admit new states, must contain no provision or restriction which would destroy or impair the equality of the proposed state with the original states, or impose any limitation upon its sovereignty which the Constitution has not placed on all the states. So far as the organization of a Territory may be necessary and proper as a means of carrying into effect the provision of the Constitution for the admission of new states, and when exercised with reference only to that end, the power of Congress is clear and explicit; but beyond that point the authority can not extend, for the reason that all "powers not delegated to the United States by the Constitution, nor prohibited by it to the states, are reserved to the states respectively, or to the people." In other words, the organic act of the Territory, conforming to the spirit of the grant from which it receives its validity, must leave the people entirely free to form and regulate their domestic institutions and internal concerns in their own way, subject only to the Constitution of the United States, to the end that when they attain the requisite population, and establish a state government in conformity to the federal Constitution, they may be admitted into the Union on an equal footing with the original states in all respects whatsoever.

[He then traced the history of the Massachusetts Emigrant Aid Society, and of the Missouri organizations, and proceeded as follows:]

If the people of any state should become so much enamored with their own peculiar institution as to conceive the philanthropic scheme of forcing so great a blessing on their unwilling neighbors, and with that view should create a mammoth moneyed corporation, for the avowed purpose of sending a sufficient number of their young men into a neighboring state, to remain long enough to acquire the right of voting, with the fixed and paramount object of reversing the settled policy and changing the domestic institutions of such state, would it not be deemed an act of aggression, as offensive and flagrant as if attempted by direct and open violence? It is a well-settled principle of constitutional law in this country, that while all the states of the Union are united in one for certain purposes, yet each state, in respect to every thing which affects its domestic policy and internal concerns, stands in the relation of a foreign power to every other state.

Hence no state has a right to pass any law, or do or authorize any act, with the view to influence or change the domestic policy of any other state or Territory of the Union, more than it would with reference to France or England, or any other foreign state with which we are at peace. Indeed, every state of this Union is under higher obligations to observe a friendly forbearance and generous comity toward each other member of the confederacy than the laws of nations can impose on foreign states. While foreign states are restrained from all acts of aggression and unkindness only by that spirit of comity which the laws of nations enjoin upon all friendly powers, we have assumed the additional obligation to obey the Constitution, which secures to every state the right to control its own internal affairs. If repugnance to domestic slavery can justify Massachusetts in incorporating a mammoth company to influence and control that question in any state or Territory of this Union, the same principle of action would authorize France or England to use the same means to accomplish the same end in Brazil or Cuba, or in fifteen states of this Union; while it would license the United States to interfere with serfdom in Russia, or polygamy in Turkey, or any other obnoxious institution in any part of the world. The same principle of action, when sanctioned by our example, would authorize all the kingdoms, and empires, and despotisms in the world to engage in a common crusade against republicanism in America, as an institution quite as obnoxious to them as domestic slavery is to any portion of the people of the United States.

If our obligations arising under the law of nations are so imperative as to make it our duty to enact neutrality laws, and to exert the whole power and authority of the executive branch of the government, including the army and navy, to enforce them, in restraining our citizens from interfering with the internal concerns of foreign states, can the obligations of each state and Territory of this Union be less imperative under the federal Constitution to observe entire neutrality in respect to the domestic institutions of the several states and Territories? Non-interference with the internal concerns of other states is recognized by all civilized countries as a fundamental principle of the laws of nations, for the reason that the peace of the world could not be maintained for a single day without it. How, then, can we hope to preserve peace and fraternal feelings among the different portions of this republic, unless we yield implicit obedience to a principle which has all the sanction of patriotic duty as well as constitutional obligation?

When the emigrants sent out by the Massachusetts Emigrant Aid Company, and their affiliated societies, passed through the state of Missouri in large numbers on their way to Kansas, the violence of their language, and the unmistakable indications of their determined hostility to the domestic institutions of that state created apprehensions that the object of the company was to abolitionize Kansas as a means of prosecuting a relentless warfare upon the institutions of slavery within the limits of Missouri. These apprehensions increased and spread with the progress of events, until they became the settled convictions of the people of that portion of the state most exposed to the danger by their proximity to the Kansas border. The natural consequence was, that immediate steps were taken by the people of the western counties of Missouri to stimulate, organize, and carry into effect a system of emigration similar to that of the Massachusetts Emigrant Aid Company, for the avowed purpose of counteracting the effects, and protecting themselves and their domestic institutions from the consequences of that company's operations.

The material difference in the character of the two rival and conflicting movements consists in the fact that the one had its origin in an aggressive, and the other in a defensive policy; the one was organized in pursuance of the provisions and claiming to act under the authority of a legislative enactment of a distant state, whose internal prosperity and domestic security did not depend upon the success of the movement; while the other was the spontaneous action of the people living in the immediate vicinity of the theatre of operations, excited, by a sense of common danger, to the necessity of protecting their own firesides from the apprehended horrors of servile insurrection and intestine war. Both parties, conceiving it to be essential to the success of their respective plans that they should be upon the field of operations prior to the first election in the Territory, selected principally young men, persons unencumbered by families, and whose conditions in life enabled them to leave at a moment's warning, and move with great celerity, to go at once, and select and occupy the most eligible sites and favored locations in the Territory, to be held by themselves and their associates who should follow them. For the successful prosecution of such a scheme, the Missourians who lived in the immediate vicinity possessed peculiar advantages over their rivals from the more remote portions of the Union. Each family could send one of its members across the line to mark out his claim, erect a cabin, and put in a small crop, sufficient to give him as valid a right to be deemed an actual settler and qualified voter as those who were being imported by the Emigrant Aid Societies. In an unoccupied Territory, where the lands have not been surveyed, and where there were no marks or lines to indicate the boundaries of sections and quarter sections, and where no legal title could be had until after the surveys should be made, disputes, quarrels, violence, and bloodshed might have been expected as the natural and inevitable consequences of such extraordinary systems of emigration, which divided and arrayed the settlers into two great hostile parties, each having an inducement to claim more than was his right, in order to hold it for some new-comer of his own party, and at the same time prevent persons belonging to the opposite party from settling in the neighborhood. As a result of this state of things, the great mass of emigrants from the Northwest and from other states, who went there on their own account, with no other object, and influence by no other motives than to improve their condition and secure good homes for their families, were compelled to array themselves under the banner of one of these hostile parties, in order to insure protection to themselves and their claims against the aggressions and violence of the other.

[He then traced minutely the history of all the elections held in Kansas, the charges of fraud, etc., and the legality of the existing Territorial Legislature, and proceeded:]

Your committee have not considered it any part of their duty to examine and review each enactment and provision of the large volume of laws adopted by the Legislature of Kansas upon almost every rightful subject of legislation, and affecting nearly every relation and interest in life, with a view either to their approval or their disapproval by Congress, for the reason that local laws, confined in their operation to the internal concerns of the Territory, the control and management of which, by the principles of the federal Constitution, as well as by the very terms of the Kansas-Nebraska Act, are confided to the people of the Territory, to be determined by themselves through their representatives in their local Legislature, and not by the Congress, in which they have no representatives, to give or withhold their assent to the laws upon which their rights and liberties may all depend. Under these laws marriages have taken place, children have been born, deaths have occurred, estates have been distributed, contracts have been made, and rights have accrued which it is not competent for Congress to divest. If there can be a doubt in respect to the validity of these laws, growing out of the alleged irregularity of the election of the members of the Legislature, or the lawfulness of the place where its sessions were held, which it is competent for any tribunal to inquire into, with a view to its decision at this day, and after the series of events which have ensued, it must be a judicial question, over which Congress can have no control, and which can be determined only by the courts of justice, under the protection and sanction of the Constitution.

When it was proposed in the last Congress to annul the acts of the legislative assembly of Minnesota incorporating certain railroad companies, this committee reported against the proposition, and, instead of annulling the local legislation of the Territory, recommended the repeal of that clause of the organic act of Minnesota which reserves to Congress the right to disapprove its laws. That recommendation was based on the theory that the people of the Territory, being citizens of the United States, were entitled to the privilege of self-government in obedience to the Constitution; and if, in the exercise of this right, they had made wise and just laws, they ought to be permitted to enjoy all the advantages resulting from them; while, on the contrary, if they had made unwise and unjust laws, they should abide the consequences of their own acts until they discovered, acknowledged, and corrected their errors.

[The report then reviewed the history and origin of the Topeka revolution, the organization, objects, and purposes of the "Kansas Legion," quoting from the history of all the new states that all movements to establish new states must be in subordination to local law, and having no validity until approved by the action of Congress. Having elaborately discussed these questions, the report concluded as follows:]

These facts and official papers prove conclusively that the proposition to the people of California to hold a convention and organize a state government originated with, and that all the proceedings were had in subordination to, the authority and supremacy of the existing local government of the Territory, under the advice and with the approval of the executive government of the United States. Hence the action of the people of California in forming their Constitution and state government, and of Congress in admitting the state into the Union, can not be cited, with the least show of justice or fairness, in justification or palliation of the revolutionary movements to subvert the government which Congress has established in Kansas.

Nor can the insurgents derive aid or comfort from the position assumed by either party to the unfortunate controversy which arose in the State of Rhode Island a few years ago, when an effort was made to change the organic law, and set up a state government in opposition to the one then in existence under the charter granted by Charles the Second of England. Those who were engaged in that unsuccessful struggle assumed, as fundamental truths in our system of government, that Rhode Island was a sovereign state in all that pertained to her internal affairs; that the right to change her organic law was an essential attribute of sovereignty; that, inasmuch as the charter under which the existing government was organized contained no provision for changing or amending the same, and the people had not delegated that right to the Legislature or any other tribunal, it followed, as a matter of course, that they had retained it, and were at liberty to exercise it in such manner as to them should seem wise, just, and proper.

Without deeming it necessary to express any opinion on this occasion in reference to the merits of that controversy, it is evident that the principles upon which it was conducted are not involved in the revolutionary struggle now going on in Kansas; for the reason, that the sovereignty of a Territory remains in abeyance, suspended in the United States, in trust for the people, until they shall be admitted into the Union as a state. In the mean time they are entitled to enjoy and exercise all the privileges and rights of self-government, in subordination to the Constitution of the United States, and in obedience to their organic law passed by Congress in pursuance of that instrument. These rights and privileges are all derived from the Constitution through the act of Congress, and must be exercised and enjoyed in subjection to all the limitations and restrictions which that Constitution imposes. Hence it is clear that the people of the Territory have no inherent sovereign right under the Constitution of the United States to annul the laws and resist the authority of the Territorial government which Congress has established in obedience to the Constitution.

In tracing, step by step, the origin and history of these Kansas difficulties, your committee have been profoundly impressed with the significant fact that each one has resulted from an attempt to violate or circumvent the principles and provisions of the act of Congress for the organization of Kansas and Nebraska. The leading idea and fundamental principle of the Kansas-Nebraska Act, as expressed in the law itself, was *to leave the actual settlers and bona fide inhabitants of each Territory "perfectly free to form and regulate their domestic institutions in their own way, subject only to the Constitution of the United States."* While this is declared to be "the true intent and meaning of the act," those who were opposed to allowing the people of the Territory, preparatory to their admission into the Union as a state, to decide the Slavery question for themselves, failing to accomplish their purpose in the halls of Congress, and under the authority of the Constitution, immediately resorted in their respective states to unusual and extraordinary means to control the political destinies and shape the domestic institutions of Kansas, in defiance of the wishes and regardless of the rights of the people of that Territory as guaranteed by their organic law. Combinations in one section of the Union to stimulate an unnatural and false system of emigration, with the view of controlling the elections, and forcing the domestic institutions of the Territory to assimilate to those of the non-slaveholding states, were followed, as might have been foreseen, by the use of similar means in the slaveholding states to produce directly the opposite result. To these causes, and to these alone, in the opinion of your committee, may be traced the origin and progress of all the controversies and disturbances with which Kansas is now convulsed.

If these unfortunate troubles have resulted as natural consequences from unauthorized and improper schemes of foreign interference with the internal affairs and domestic concerns of the Territory, it is apparent that the remedy must be sought in a strict adherence to the principles, and rigid enforcement of the provisions of the organic law. In this connection your committee feel sincere satisfaction in commending the messages and proclamation of the President of the United States, in which we have the gratifying assurance that the supremacy of the laws will be maintained; that rebellion will be crushed; that insurrection will be suppressed; that aggressive intrusion for the purpose of deciding elections, or any other purpose, will be repelled; that unauthorized intermeddling in the local concerns of the Territory, both from adjoining and distant states, will be prevented; that the federal and local laws will be vindicated against all attempts of organized resistance; and that the people of the Territory will be protected in the establishment of their own institutions, undisturbed by encroachments from without, and in the full enjoyment of the rights of self-government assured to them by the Constitution and the organic law.

In view of these assurances, given under the conviction that the existing laws confer all the authority necessary to the performance of these important duties, and that the whole available force of the United States will be exerted to the extent required for their performance, your committee repose in entire confidence that peace, and security, and law will prevail in Kansas. If any further evidence were necessary to prove that all the collisions and difficulties in Kansas have been produced by the schemes of foreign interference which have been developed in this report, in violation of the principles and in evasion of the provisions of the Kansas-Nebraska Act, it may be found in the fact that in Nebraska, to which the Emigrant Aid Societies did not extend their operations, and into which the stream of emigration was permitted to flow in its usual and natural channels, nothing has occurred to disturb the peace and harmony of the Territory, while the principle of self-government, in obedience to the Constitution, has had fair play, and is quietly working out its legitimate results.

It now only remains for your committee to respond to the two specific recommendations of the President in his special message. They are as follows:

"This, it seems to me, can be best accomplished by providing that, when the inhabitants of Kansas may desire it, and shall be of sufficient numbers to constitute a state, a convention of delegates, duly elected by the qualified voters, shall assemble to frame a Constitution, and thus prepare, through regular and lawful means, for its admission into the Union as a state. I respectfully recommend the enactment of a law to that effect.

" I recommend, also, that a special appropriation be made to defray any expense which may become requisite in the execution of the laws or the maintenance of public order in the Territory of Kansas."

In compliance with the first recommendation, your committee ask leave to report a bill authorizing the Legislature of the Territory to provide by law for the election of delegates by the people, and the assembling of a convention to form a Constitution and state government preparatory to their admission into the Union on an equal footing with the original states, as soon as it shall appear, by a census to be taken under the direction of the governor, by the authority of the Legislature, that the Territory contains ninety-three thousand four hundred and twenty inhabitants, that being the number required by the present ratio of representation for a member of Congress.

In compliance with the other recommendation, your committee propose to offer to the Appropriation Bill an amendment appropriating such sum as shall be found necessary, by the estimates to be obtained, for the purpose indicated in the recommendation of the President.

All of which is respectfully submitted to the Senate by your committee.

On the 20th of March Mr. Douglas addressed the Senate, in a speech of three hours, in vindication of the principles enunciated in the report of the majority of the committee. In that speech he reviewed the entire troubles of Kansas, and traced them, step by step, to the attempts made to violate the Kansas-Nebraska Act. All the violence, and all the confusion, excitement, and distress, were the natural consequences of efforts made by persons and organizations outside of Kansas to wrest from the people of that Territory the privilege of governing themselves. On the 4th of April—the debate having been continued from time to time—Mr. Collamer, of Vermont, a member of the Committee on Territories, having concluded his speech in opposition to the reasoning and conclusions of the majority report made by Mr. Douglas, the latter gentleman replied to him with great animation. The following was the closing part of his speech:

Mr. President, I have said enough to bring back the points to the position in which I left them in my former speech. I am not going to follow the senator from Vermont through all his criticisms on the majority report. They are not of a character which call for a reply at this time, nor would it be fair to detain the Senate for that purpose at this late hour.

The senator from Vermont has explained what he meant by the word "experiment" in his minority report, the natural, and perhaps unavoidable consequence of which would be violence and bloodshed. He says he alluded to the experiment of the Nebraska Bill, by which the question of Slavery was, for the first time in our history, left to the decision of the people. What is the objection to leaving the decision of that, as well as all other local and domestic questions, to the people who are immediately interested in it?

His objection is that it has a tendency to bring opposing elements and inflammable materials into collision from which violence may be apprehended. Does not the same objection apply to all other questions which involve the interests and excite the passions of men as well as the question of Slavery? Does it not apply to the Maine Liquor Law, to railroad controversies, to taxation, to schools, to the location of county seats, to the division of counties—in short, does it not apply to all questions of legislation which affect the property and enlist the feelings and passions of the community? If the objection be a valid one against the Nebraska Bill in respect to the Slavery question, it applies in a greater or less degree to every other subject of legislation in proportion as it affects the interests and feelings of the people. It is an objection to the fundamental principles upon which all free governments rest, and which, when admitted to be valid, drives us irresistibly to despotism. The argument is that the people should not be permitted to vote upon a question involving their social and domestic systems, lest there might arise a diversity of opinion which might possibly degenerate into quarrels and controversies, and terminate in violence! Hence it would seem to follow that if the people were allowed any voice in making their own laws, it should be confined to those insignificant questions in which they feel no interest, and in regard to which there could be no probability of a diversity of opinion! Precious boon—to allow the people to vote when they feel no interest in the question, and deny them the privilege when they do, for fear they will differ in opinion and become excited about it! This is "the experiment"—"the vice of a mistaken law"—to which the senator from Vermont traces all the difficulties in Kansas! He seems to be under the impression that this "experiment" is now introduced into our legislation for the first time in respect to the Slavery question by the Nebraska Bill! He makes the Nebraska Act a far more important measure—one reflecting infinitely more credit upon its author than I ever claimed for it! I was under the impression that the same principle, or experiment, as he prefers to call it, was involved and affirmed in the compromise measures of 1850, and incorporated into the platforms of the Whig party and of the Democratic party in 1852, as a rule of action by which each party pledged itself to be governed in all future controversies upon the Slavery question. Did not the acts for the organization of the Territories of Utah and New Mexico try the same "experiment?" Were not those acts based on the same principle? Did not those acts "leave the people perfectly free to form and regulate their domestic institutions in their own way, subject only to the Constitution of the United States," with the guarantee that, when admitted into the Union, they should be received "with or without slavery," as their Constitution should provide at the time of admission? Did violence and bloodshed result as the natural, and perhaps unavoidable consequences of this experiment in 1850? Have any such consequences resulted from the same experiment in Nebraska in 1854? If violence and bloodshed are the natural consequences of such an experiment, why have not the same causes produced like effects elsewhere as well as in Kansas? I would like to have this inquiry answered by the senator from Vermont, or by the senator from New York [Mr. Seward], who has endorsed his report and pledged himself to make good its positions. I will give them the benefit of my answer now. There were no Emigrant Aid Societies in 1850. There were no organized systems of foreign interference in either of those Territories. The Emigrant Aid Societies have not extended their operations to Nebraska. The "experiment" of self-government—that "vice of a mistaken law"—has had fair play in Nebraska; hence nothing has occurred in that Territory to disturb the peace and quiet of the inhabitants. On the contrary, in Kansas, where there has been organized foreign interference—where the Emigrant Aid Societies concentrated all their efforts to control the domestic institutions and local legislation of the Territory—violence and bloodshed have resulted as the natural consequences, not of the "vice of a mistaken law," but of their experiment of foreign interference with the domestic concerns of a distant Territory!

But the senator from Vermont has made one concession for which I return him my acknowledgments. He admits that, by the Constitution of the United States, each state has a right to decide the Slavery question for itself, and that this right could have been exercised by the people of Kansas when they should form a Constitution, preparatory to their admission into the Union, even if the Nebraska Bill had not repealed the Missouri Compromise. I thank him for this admission. I hope those with whom he acts will endorse the proposition. Then I would like to have him and them explain what harm the repeal has done, and why they desire to have it restored? If Kansas could have become a slave state before as well as now, what is the use of restoring the Missouri Compromise?

Mr. Seward. The honorable senator will excuse me for calling his attention to a misapprehension under which he labors with regard to the remark of the senator from Vermont, who is now absent, which is the only reason why I interpose.

Mr. Douglas. I yield the floor with pleasure.

Mr. Seward. I heard a large portion of the senator's speech, and I did not understand him to say that a state would have the right to come into the Union with or without slavery, as her people pleased, if the Compromise Act had not been repealed. I understood him to say that, after coming in, it would have the right to establish or prohibit slavery.

Mr. Toombs and several other senators. No, no.

Mr. Douglas. On the contrary, he took the distinct ground that a state, when its people assembled to form a Constitution, preparatory to admission, had the right to come in with or without slavery, even under the Missouri Compromise.

Mr. Seward. I did not hear that.

Mr. Douglas. My colleague came to the same conclusion the other day in his speech. We seem to be making converts to the true doctrine. It is a sound constitutional principle. If we get men to admit that a state has the right, when she forms her Constitution, either to have slavery or not, to adopt or reject it as she pleases, it is a pretty good step toward the doctrine of the Nebraska Bill. When that admission is made, I want to know what you all mean when you talk about a breach of faith in the repeal of the Missouri Compromise? You have all been in the habit of saying on the stump, and wherever else you had the opportunity, that by the Nebraska Bill we have broken a covenant which dedicated Kansas and Nebraska to freedom " FOR-EVER." We are now told that "forever" means " hereafter," and lasts only until there are people enough to form a state, and that no particular number is required for that purpose.

The senator from Vermont attempts to ridicule the Nebraska Bill because it contains a provision declaring the Constitution of the United States to be in force in the Territory. He desires to know who ever doubted that such would be the case without that provision? Who was ever silly enough to suppose that the Constitution could be extended by law over a Territory which it did not reach without such law? I will answer his question. I will tell him the man. It was no less a person than Daniel Webster—New England's great statesman, whom she delighted to call the great expounder of the Constitution. Senators who were then members of this body have not forgotten, and will not soon forget, the debate between Mr. Webster and Mr. Calhoun upon this very point, in which the former contended that the Constitution of the United States did not extend over the Territories without an Act of Congress to that effect; while, on the other hand, the great Carolinian insisted that the Constitution was coextensive with the limits, and covered all the territories pertaining to the republic. Without endorsing the peculiar opinions of Mr. Webster on this point, Mr. Clay did not hesitate, in deference to them, to adopt, in the Compromises of 1850, the identical provision which the senator from Vermont now attempts to ridicule, under the supposition that I introduced it into the Nebraska Act for the first time in our legislation. I copied the provision from the compromise measures of 1850 for the same reasons which induced Mr. Clay to adopt it, although it is but fair to say that I never did concur in the opinion of Mr. Webster that the Constitution did not apply to the Territories without an act of Congress carrying it there.

Mr. President, I have a few words to say to the senator from New York [Mr. Seward] before I close my remarks. On the day I presented to the Senate the report of the Committee on Territories, and immediately after the minority report was read at the secretary's desk, he rose and volunteered the pledge that he would make good every position affirmed by it. As he has the floor for the next speech upon this question, he will be expected to redeem this pledge, or acknowledge his inability to do so. One of these positions is, that the "experiment" of allowing the people to settle the Slavery question for themselves in Territories preparatory to their admission into the Union was introduced into our legislation for the first time in the history of this republic in the Kansas-Nebraska Act; and that, if violence resulted from this experiment as a natural, and perhaps unavoidable consequence, it was the "vice of a mistaken law." I call on the senator from New York to sustain the truth of this allegation. I desire him to answer specifically whether the compromise measures of 1850 did not leave the people of New Mexico and Utah perfectly free to decide the Slavery question for themselves, and guarantee their admission into the Union with or without slavery, as their Constitution should provide at the time of admission? I ask him if he did not oppose the bills for the organization of those Territories at that time for the reason that they did not contain the Wilmot Proviso prohibiting slavery, and for the reason that they did contain the guarantee that they should be admitted with or without slavery, as they should decide for themselves? When he answers this question, I would like to have him explain at the same time whether he did not stand pledged in 1852 to sustain the Whig Baltimore platform, and to support General Scott, standing on that platform, "with the resolutions annexed," to use his emphatic language; and whether those resolutions did not bind General Scott, and the party supporting him, to carry out in good faith the compromise measures of 1850 "in substance and in principle?" I desire a direct answer on these points, in order that the Senate may judge how far he redeems his pledge to make good the positions of the minority report. I would like to have him explain the difference between the "experiment" of the compromise measures of 1850 and of the Kansas-Nebraska Act of 1854, in allowing the people to decide the Slavery question for themselves, and whether that principle in each case was equally the "vice of a mistaken law?" If he shall answer that he did regard both measures in the same light, I should be gratified if he will explain how it was that he united with the Whig party in 1852 to sustain the "vice of that mistaken law," and now calls upon all the odds and ends, fragments and portions of parties and isms, to merge all differences on other points, and form a *fusion* with him on the isolated point of eradicating this "vice of a mistaken law" in the name of freedom and humanity? While he is portraying the beauties of negro freedom and equality, and demonstrating the propriety of sacrificing the political and constitutional rights of 20,000,000 of white people for the benefit of 3,000,000 of negroes, I would be glad if he would point out the advantages which the negro will derive from the admission of Kansas with the Topeka Constitution. That Constitution provides that as long as Kansas shall be a state, as long as water runs and grass grows, no negro, FREE or *slave*, shall ever live or breathe under that Constitution.

Mr. Seward. Does the senator wish me to answer now?

Mr. Douglas. Yes, sir.

Mr. Seward. Then my answer is that, such being the Constitution, he is wrong in the premises that I am desirous to admit the State of Kansas for the benefit of the negro. It must be for the benefit of the white man.

Mr. Douglas. Am I to understand the senator that he has abandoned the cause of the negro upon the ground that his freedom and equality are inconsistent with the rights of the white man? What has become of his professions of sympathy for the poor negro? What are we to think of the sincerity of his professions upon this subject?

Mr. Seward. That is another thing.

Mr. Douglas. That is the very thing. If all other considerations are to be made to yield to the paramount object of prohibiting slavery in Kansas upon the ground that the inequality which it imposes is unjust to the negro, will that injustice be removed by adopting a Constitution which in effect declares that the negro, whether free or slave, shall never tread the soil, nor drink the water, nor breathe the air of Kansas? The senator from New York admits that the Constitution with which he proposes by his bill to admit Kansas contains such a provision. Under the code of laws enacted by the Territorial Legislature of Kansas, which the senator, in common with his party, professes to consider monstrous and barbarous, a negro may go to Kansas and be protected in all his rights, so long as he obeys the laws of the land. In order to get rid of those laws, the senator from New York proposes to give effect to a constitutional provision which is designed to prevent the negro forever from entering the state.

I should like to hear from the senator from Massachusetts on this point. I believe he took particular pains a few years ago to arraign the State of Illinois for inserting a similar clause in her Constitution.

Mr. Sumner. Never.

Mr. Douglas. Well, perhaps it was his predecessor, Mr. Winthrop. Upon reflection, I think it was. I think it once became my duty to vindicate the right of my own state to insert such a clause in her Constitution against the assaults of a Massachusetts senator. Had the present senator been here at that time, and found it necessary to have spoken on the subject, is it assuming too much to venture the opinion that he would have joined in that condemnation?

Mr. Sumner. I should condemn it, certainly.

Mr. Douglas. Then, will the senator approve in the Constitution of Kansas what he condemns in the Constitution of Illinois? I would like to hear the senator's response to this inquiry. If such a provision was wrong in Illinois, is it right in Kansas? Had not the Democratic State of Illinois as good a right to adopt such a provision as the Free-soil party of Kansas? Will the senator from Massachusetts vote for the bill introduced by the senator from New York to admit Kansas, at a time when she has not one third of the requisite population, with such a Constitution?

I do not wish to be misunderstood on this point. I object to the admission of Kansas at this time, and under existing circumstances, on entirely different grounds. I affirm the right of Illinois to put such a clause in her Constitution. The people of Illinois had a right to do as they pleased on that subject. We tried slavery while a Territory, notwithstanding the ordinance of 1787, until we found that in our climate and with our productions it was not good for us to retain it, and for that reason we abolished and prohibited it. When we decided that Illinois should be a free state we also determined that it should be a white state. We did not believe in the equality of the negro with the white man, and hence were opposed to a mixture of the races. The Constitution of Illinois was made by white men for the benefit of white men. The same principle of state rights and state equality which authorized Illinois to abolish slavery secured to each other state the privilege of retaining it if it chose. The same principle which authorized Illinois to exclude the free negro allows each other state to receive him if agreeable to her tastes and consistent with her interests. We are perfectly content with the practical operation of this great principle, which teaches the people of each separate community to mind their own business, and accord the same right to their neighbors. Hence I should have no controversy with the senator from New York, or his political associates, in regard to this particular clause in the Kansas Constitution, did they not claim the right, and insist that it is their duty, to examine the provisions of the Constitution of each state applying for admission, and then either to admit or reject the application, according as they may approve or disapprove the Constitution. It is on this ground that they claim the right to inquire whether the Constitution prohibits or protects slavery, and to vote for a free state and against a slave state. It was on this ground that the Northern States voted against the admission of Missouri in 1821—one year after the adoption of the Missouri Compromise—because the Constitution had a similar provision against free negroes to the one in the Kansas Constitution. Hence I desire to learn from the senator from New York whether he and his sympathizing associates do really approve of a constitutional provision which shall deny to the negro forever not merely the right to enjoy the same liberty accorded to the white man, but also the right to live and breathe within the limits of the proposed State of Kansas.

Mr. Seward. Will the honorable senator allow me to answer now?

Mr. Douglas. Yes, sir.

Mr. Seward. I need scarcely inform the honorable senator that I do not approve of any such provision in any Constitution in the world. I never did, and I never shall, vote to approve or sanction, in any Constitution or in any law, a provision which tends to keep any human being—any member of the human family to which I belong, in a condition of degradation below the position which I occupy myself except for his own fault or crime.

Mr. Douglas. The senator does not approve of this position, and never can, for the reason that it does not put the negro on an equality with himself! Then, will he vote for admitting Kansas in this irregular manner, and without the requisite population, merely because her Constitution has a provision which keeps slaves from going into the Territory, together with another clause "which tends to keep a man—being a member of the human family to which he belongs—in a condition of degradation below the position which he occupies himself?" Yet, if he votes for his own bill to admit Kansas with the Topeka Constitution, according to his own doctrine he does vote to sanction a provision to keep the negro out altogether; he will not allow a negro to come in a condition either below him or above him.

Mr. Seward. You can take it either way—above or below.

Mr. Douglas. Yes; he will exclude the negro absolutely if he is below or above him. He will insist upon having the negro upon a footing of entire and perfect equality with himself. Yet, if his bill passes, and Kansas is admitted with the Constitution which has been formed and presented here, all negroes, both free and slave, are forever prohibited from entering the State of Kansas by the terms of the instrument. He can not escape the responsibility of this result on the plea that he does not vote directly to endorse and sanction the Constitution in all its parts; for his doctrine, and the doctrine of his party, is that they not only have the right, but that it is their duty to examine the Constitution in all its parts, and vote for it or against it, according as they approve or disapprove of its provisions, and especially those provisions which degrade the negro below the level of the white man. He must abandon all the principles to which his life has been devoted; he must abandon the creed of the party of which he is the acknowledged leader before he can vote for his own bill. The Black Republican party was organized and founded on the fundamental principle of perfect and entire equality of rights and privileges between the negro and the white man—an equality secured and guaranteed by a law higher than the Constitution of the United States. In your creed, as proclaimed to the world, you stand pledged against "the admission of any more slave states;"

To repeal the Fugitive Slave Law;

To abolish the slave-trade between the states;

To prohibit slavery in the District of Columbia;

To restore the prohibition on Kansas and Nebraska; and

To acquire no more territory unless slavery shall be first prohibited.

That is your creed, authoritatively proclaimed. I trust there is to be no evading or dodging the issue—no lowering of the flag. Let each party stand by its principles and the issues as you have presented them and we have accepted them. Let us have a fair, bold fight before the people, and then let the verdict be pronounced.

Mr. Seward. You will have it.

Mr. Douglas. I rejoice in this assurance. I trust the senator will be able to bring his troops up to the line, and to hold them there. I trust there is to be no lowering of the flag—no abandonment or change of the issues. There are rumors afloat that you are about to strike your colors; that you propose to surrender each one of these issues, not because you do not profess to be right, but because you can not succeed in the right; that you propose to throw overboard all the bold men who distinguished themselves in your service in fighting the anti-Nebraska fight, and to take a new man, who, in consequence of not being committed to either side, will be enabled to cheat somebody by getting votes from both sides! Rumor says that all your veteran generals who have received scars and wounds in the anti-Nebraska campaign are now considered unfit to command, and are to be laid aside in order to take up some new man who has not antagonized with the great principles of self-government and state equality. Rumor says that, in pursuance of this line of policy, you dare not allow your committees in the House of Representatives to bring in bills to redeem your pledges and carry out your principles; that there is to be no bill passed in your Fusion House to repeal the Kansas-Nebraska Act—none to repeal the Fugitive Slave Law —none to abolish the slave-trade between the states—none to abolish slavery in the District of Columbia—none to redeem any one of your pledges, or carry out any one of your principles, upon which you secured a majority in the House by a fusion with Northern Know-nothingism. Rumor says that your committees were arranged with the view of keeping all these questions in the background until after the presidential election, in order that the agitation may be reopened with better prospects of success when power shall have been obtained under the auspices of a new man, who has not been crippled in the great battle. Would it not be a curious spectacle to see this great Anti-Nebraska or Black Republican party—which, less than eighteen months ago, proclaimed a war of extermination, in which no quarter was to granted or received, and no prisoners to be taken—skirmishing to avoid a pitched battle, and get an opportunity to retreat from the face of those whom they determined to hang, and burn, and torture with all the refinements of cruelty which their vengeance could devise? Are the offices and patronage of government so much more important to you than your principles that you feel it your duty to sacrifice your creed, and the men identified with it, in order to get power? Are you prepared to ignore the material points in issue for fear that they will compromit you in the presidential election?

Mr. Wade. We will whip you then.

Mr. Douglas. That remains to be seen. We are prepared to give you a fair fight on the issues you have tendered and we accepted. Let the presidential contest be one of principle alone; let the principles involved be distinctly stated and boldly met, without any attempts at concealment or equivocation; let the result be a verdict of approval or disapproval so emphatic that it can not be misunderstood. One year ago you promised us a fair fight in the open field upon the principles of the Kansas-Nebraska Act! You then unfurled your banner, and bore it aloft in the hands of your own favorite and tried leaders, with your principles emblazoned upon it. Are you now preparing to lower your flag—to throw overboard all your tried men who have rendered service in your cause—and issue a search-warrant in hopes of finding a new man, who has not antagonized with any body, and whose principles are unknown, for the purpose of cheating somebody by getting votes from all sorts of men? Let us have an open and a fair fight. [Applause in the galleries.]

The Chair. The galleries will be cleared if these demonstrations are renewed.

Mr. Douglas. I will not pursue the subject further.

The debate on the bill proceeded from day to day without any action by the Senate until the 25th of June. In the mean time, Mr. Seward had introduced a bill in the nature of a substitute, proposing to admit Kansas as a state under the Topeka Constitution; and Mr. Trumbull had prepared a bill annexing Kansas to Nebraska, and making it subject to the laws and government in force in that Territory, and abolishing the existing government in Kansas. Other bills had been proposed by Messrs. Clayton, Geyer, and others. On the 25th of June, Mr. Toombs, of Georgia, introduced an amendment in the nature of a substitute for the whole bill, and on that day the pending bill, as well as all the proposed amendments and substitutes, were recommitted to the Committee on Territories. On the 30th of June, Mr. Douglas, from the committee, reported a bill (the Toombs Bill, of which so much was said in Illinois during the election of 1858) in lieu of all the propositions referred to the committee.

In the report accompanying this bill, Mr. Douglas referred to and described the injustice of the several propositions referred to the committee, and closed a comment on the bill to admit Kansas under the Topeka Constitution in the following words—words which he faithfully adhered to subsequently in the Lecompton controversy:

"The question now arises whether a Constitution, made by a political party without the authority of law, and under circumstances which afford no safeguards against fraud, and no guarantee of fairness, and raises no presumptions that it embodies the wishes and sentiments of a majority of the inhabitants, shall be forced, by an act of Congress, upon a whole people as their fundamental law, unalterable for nine years.

"In the opinion of your committee, whenever a Constitution shall be formed in any Territory, preparatory to its admission into the Union as a state, justice, the genius of our institutions, the whole theory of our republican system, imperatively demand that the voice of the people shall be fairly expressed, and their will embodied in that fundamental law, without fraud, or violence, or intimidation, or any other improper or unlawful influence, and subject to no other restrictions than those imposed by the Constitution of the United States."

The debate was renewed on the new bill, and at eight o'clock on the morning of the 3d of July, after a continuous session of twenty hours, the bill was passed—yeas 33, nays 12, as follows:

Yeas—Allen of Rhode Island, Bayard of Delaware, Bell of Tennessee, Benjamin of Louisiana, Biggs of North Carolina, Bigler of Pennsylvania, Bright of Indiana, Brodhead of Pennsylvania, Brown of Mississippi, Cass of Michigan, Clay of Alabama, Crittenden of Kentucky, Douglas of Illinois, Evans of South Carolina, Fitzpatrick of Alabama, Geyer of Missouri, Hunter of Virginia, Iverson of Georgia, Johnson of Arkansas, Jones of Iowa, Mallory of Florida, Pratt of Maryland, Pugh of Ohio, Reid of North Carolina, Sebastian of Arkansas, Slidell of Louisiana, Stuart of Michigan, Thompson of Kentucky, Toombs of Georgia, Toucey of Connecticut, Weller of California, Wright of New Jersey, Yulee of Florida.

Nays—Bell of New Hampshire, Collamer of Vermont, Dodge of Wisconsin, Durkee of Wisconsin, Fessenden of Maine, Foot of Vermont, Foster of Connecticut, Hale of New Hampshire, Seward of New York, Trumbull of Illinois, Wade of Ohio, Wilson of Massachusetts.

Pending this bill, Mr. Seward moved as a substitute for it a proposition to admit Kansas as a state under the Topeka Constitution, and the amendment received 11 votes.

Happy for the peace and tranquillity of Kansas, and of the country, would it have been had this bill passed Congress.

But the fell spirit of fanaticism would not permit a settlement of the question, particularly on the eve of a presidential election, when agitation and excitement was the sole available capital and stock in trade of the party having a majority in the House of Representatives.

While the bill was pending in the Senate, a bill for the admission of Kansas was before the House of Representatives. On the 1st of July the House was brought to a direct vote upon it, and it was rejected—yeas 106, nays 107. A motion to reconsider this vote was made by Mr. Barclay, of Pennsylvania, and on the 3d the motion to reconsider prevailed—yeas 101, nays 93; and on the same day, Thursday, July 3d, the bill passed the House—yeas 99, nays 97.

Both houses adjourned until Monday, the 7th. In the Senate the House bill was referred to the Committee on Territories; in the House the Senate bill was suffered to lie on the speaker's table. On the 8th of July Mr. Douglas reported back the House bill for the admission of Kansas as a state with an amendment—that is, striking out all after the enacting clause, and inserting in lieu of it the provisions of the bill passed by the Senate on the 3d instant. After some debate the amendment was agreed to, and the bill, as amended, passed—yeas 30, nays 13. The Senate bill was therefore before the House in two forms, first as a Senate bill, and, secondly, as an amendment to a House bill.

No action was had in the House on these bills until the 29th of July, when Mr. Dunn, of Indiana, called up a motion he had made in February to reconsider a vote committing a bill to annul certain acts of the Legislative Assembly of Kansas. The House having reconsidered the motion to commit, the bill was before it for action, thereupon Mr. Dunn moved to strike out all after the enacting clause, and insert what is known in legislative history as the " Dunn Bill." He moved the previous question, and under its operation his amendment was agreed to, and the bill, as amended, passed—yeas 88, nays 74. The title was then changed to read, " An Act to reorganize the Territory of Kansas, and for other purposes." The bill, when received in the Senate, was referred to the Committee on Territories.

This last bill received the almost unanimous vote of the Republicans in the House. It was an extraordinary effort at

legislation.   It abolished treaties; invaded New Mexico; re-
enacted the Missouri restriction against slavery; re-enacted the
Fugitive Slave Law; legalized slavery in Kansas, New Mexico,
and Nebraska; and declared that any slave who might have
become entitled to freedom by reason of having been carried
into the Territories, should be remanded to slavery if removed
from the Territory within a given period; and ratified and approved all the laws of the "Border Ruffian" Legislature of
Kansas upon the subject of slavery.   Such an extraordinary
act never before received the approval of either house of Congress, and in voting for it the Republicans voted in direct opposition to their entire code of political professions.   Mr.
Douglas, on the 11th of August, reported this bill back, with a
recommendation that it be laid on the table.   Mr. Douglas
made a written report, in which he dissects the bill, and exposes
with master-hand the absurdities, and, it might almost be said,
the stultifications of those Republicans who had voted for it.
The report says:

The first section of the bill provides, "That all that part of the territory
of the United States which lies between the parallels of thirty-six degrees and
thirty minutes and forty degrees of north latitude, and which is east of the
eastern boundary of the Territory of Utah to the southeast corner thereof,
and east of a line thence due south to the said parallel of thirty-six degrees
thirty minutes north latitude, and is bounded on the east by the western
boundary of the State of Missouri, shall constitute one Territory, and shall be,
and hereby is, constituted and organized into a temporary government by the
name of the Territory of Kansas."

By reference to the map, it will be perceived that, in addition to all the
country embraced within the limits of the present Territory of Kansas, it is
proposed to include in the new Territory all the country between the southern boundary of the Territory, as now defined by law, and the parallel of
36° 30', extending from the western boundary of the State of Missouri across
more than twelve and a half degrees of longitude, and being about thirty-five
miles in width at the eastern, and one hundred and five at the western extremity.   The eastern portion of this strip of country, which it is now proposed to incorporate within, and render subject to the jurisdiction of, the Territory of Kansas, was ceded, with other territory, to the Cherokee Indians by
the treaties of the 6th of May, 1828, April 12th, 1833, and May 23, 1836, for
"*a permanent home, and which shall, under the most solemn guarantee of the
United States, be and remain theirs forever*—A HOME THAT SHALL NEVER, IN
ALL FUTURE TIME, BE EMBARRASSED BY HAVING EXTENDED AROUND IT THE
LINES, OR PLACED OVER IT THE JURISDICTION OF A TERRITORY OR STATE, *nor
be pressed upon by* the extension *in any way of any of the* limits of any existing Territory or state."

In view of this "most solemn guaranty of the United States" to the Cher-
okees, your committee can not refrain from the expression of the hope and
belief that the House of Representatives, in passing a bill to extend around
this Indian country the lines of Kansas, and render it subject to the jurisdiction of that Territory, acted without due consideration, and probably without

a full knowledge of these treaty stipulations. When the organic act of Kansas was passed in 1854, the parallel of thirty-seven was fixed upon as the southern boundary of the Territory instead of the line of thirty-six degrees and thirty minutes, with the view to the preservation of faith on the part of the United States toward these Indians; and, lest injustice might be done to other Indian tribes who held their lands under treaties with the United States, it was expressly provided "that nothing in this act contained shall be construed to impair the rights of persons or property now pertaining to the Indians in said Territory, so long as such rights shall remain unextinguished by treaty between the United States and such Indians, or to include any territory which, by treaty with any Indian tribe, is not, without the consent of said tribe, to be included within the territorial limits or jurisdiction of any state or territory; *but all such territory shall be excepted out of the boundaries, and constitute no part of the Territory of Kansas.*" In these considerations your committee find insuperable objections to that portion of the bill from the House of Representatives which proposes to include within the limits, and render subject to the jurisdiction of the Territory of Kansas, any part of the country which is thus secured to the Indians by solemn treaty stipulations.

Nor are the objections less formidable to incorporating within the limits of Kansas that portion of the Territory of New Mexico which lies north of the line of 36° 30', and east of the Rio Grande, and subjecting it to the operation of the other provisions of the bill. That part of New Mexico, containing about 15,000 square miles, was purchased from Texas by one of the acts known as the compromise measures of 1850, and formed a part of the territory for which the United States paid the State of Texas ten millions of dollars. The second section of the act of Congress which contains the terms and conditions of the compact between the United States and Texas for the purchase of that Territory, incorporates the same in the Territory of New Mexico, with the following guarantee : "*And provided further, that when admitted as a state, the said Territory, or any portion of the same, shall be received into the Union with or without slavery, as their Constitution may prescribe at the time of their admission.*"

After asserting this great principle of state equality as applicable to every portion of New Mexico under the Constitution, and as guaranteed in the compact with Texas by fair intendment, so far as the country was acquired from that state, the seventh section of the same act provides "that the legislative power of the said Territory shall extend to all rightful subjects of legislation, consistent with the Constitution of the United States and the provisions of this act"—thus leaving the people perfectly free to form and regulate their domestic institutions in their own way, subject only to the Constitution. It is now proposed in the bill under consideration to repudiate these guarantees and violate these great fundamental principles by annexing to Kansas all that portion of the country acquired from Texas which lies north of 36° 30', and imposing upon it a prohibition of slavery forever, from and after the first day of January, 1858, regardless of the rights and wishes of the people who may inhabit the Territory.

The twenty-fourth section of the bill is in the following words:

"Sec. 24. *And be it further enacted*, That so much of the fourteenth section, and also so much of the thirty-second section, of the act passed at the first session of the thirty-third Congress, commonly known as the Kansas-Nebraska Act, and reads as follows, to wit: 'Except the eighth section of the act preparatory to the admission of Missouri into the Union, approved March 6, 1820, which, being inconsistent with the principles of non-intervention by Congress with slavery in the states and Territories, as recognized by the legislation of 1850, commonly called the compromise measures, is hereby declared inoperative and void; it being the true intent and meaning of this act not to legislate slavery into any Territory or state, nor to exclude it there-from, but to leave the people thereof perfectly free to form and regulate their domestic institutions in their own way, subject only to the Constitution of the United States: *Provided*, That nothing herein contained shall be construed to revive or put in force any law or regulation which may have existed prior to the act of the 6th of March, 1820, either protecting, establishing, prohibiting, or abolishing slavery,' be and the same is hereby repealed; and the said eighth section of said act of the 6th of March, 1820, is hereby revived and declared to be in full force and effect within the said Territories of Kansas and Nebraska: *Provided, however*, That any person lawfully held to service in either of said Territories shall not be discharged from such service by reason of such repeal and revival of said eighth section, if such person shall be permanently removed from such Territory or Territories prior to the 1st day of January, 1858; and any child or children born in either of said Territories, of any female lawfully held to service, if in like manner removed without said Territories before the expiration of that date, shall not be, by reason of any thing in this act, emancipated from any service it might have owed had this act never been passed: *And provided further*, That any person lawfully held to service in any other state or Territory of the United States, and escaping into either the Territory of Kansas or Nebraska, may be re-claimed and removed to the person or place where such service is due, under any law of the United States which shall be in force upon the subject."

In the opinion of your committee there are various grave and serious objections to this section of the bill. In the first place, it expressly repudiates and condemns the great fundamental principles of self-government and state equality which it was the paramount object of the Kansas-Nebraska Act to maintain and perpetuate, as affirmed in the following provision: "It being the true intent and meaning of this act not to legislate slavery into any Territory or state, nor to exclude it therefrom, but to leave the people thereof perfectly free to form and regulate their domestic institutions in their own way, subject only to the Constitution of the United States."

Not content with repealing this wise and just provision, and condemning the sound constitutional principles asserted in it, the bill proceeds to legalize and establish, for a limited time, hereditary slavery, not only in the Territory of Kansas (where there is no other local or affirmative law protecting it than the enactments of the Kansas Territorial Legislature, which have been alleged to be illegal and void, and which the House of Representatives, by amendments to the appropriation bills, have instructed the President not to enforce), but also in all that part of New Mexico which it is proposed to incorporate in the Territory of Kansas, and where slavery was prohibited by the Mexican law, and it is not pretended that there is any territorial enactment recognizing or establishing it. Having thus asserted and exercised the power of introducing and establishing slavery in the Territories by act of Congress, and declaring children hereafter born therein to be slaves for life and their posterity after them, provided they shall be removed therefrom within a special period, the bill proceeds to affirm and exercise the power of prohibiting slavery in the same Territories forever from and after January 1, 1858, by enacting and putting in force the following provision, being the 8th section of the act passed March 6, 1820, to wit:

"Sec. 8. *And be it further enacted*, That in all that territory ceded by France to the United States, under the name of Louisiana, which lies north of thirty-six degrees and thirty minutes north latitude, not included within the limits of the state contemplated by this act, slavery and involuntary servitude, otherwise than in the punishment of crime, whereof the parties shall have been duly convicted, shall be, and is hereby, forever prohibited: *Provided always*, That any person escaping into the same from whom labor or service is lawfully claimed in any state or Territory of the United States, such fugitive may be lawfully reclaimed and conveyed to the person claiming his or her labor or service as aforesaid."

It will be observed that this 8th section of the Missouri Act (commonly called the Missouri Compromise) by its terms only applied to the territory acquired from France, known as the Louisiana Purchase, the western boundary of which was defined by the treaty with Spain in 1819, and subsequently by treaties with Mexico and Texas, to be the 100th meridian of longitude, while the bill under consideration, under the guise of reviving and restoring that provision, extends it more than seven degrees of longitude farther westward, and applies it to that large extent of territory to which it had no application in its original enactment. Nor can it be said with fairness or truth that this provision was applied to any portion of the territory in question by the "joint resolution for annexing Texas to the United States," for the reason that the whole territory embraced within the limits of the Republic of Texas was admitted into the Union as one state, with the privilege of forming not exceeding four other states out of the State of Texas, "by the consent of said state," with the condition that "in such state or states as should be formed out of said territory, north of said Missouri Compromise line, slavery or involuntary servitude (except for crime) shall be prohibited."

It was left discretionary with Texas to remain forever one state, and to retain the whole of her territory as slave territory, or to consent to a division, in which case the prohibition would take effect, by virtue of the compact, from the date of the formation of a new state within the limits of the Republic of Texas north of 36° 30'. If, on the contrary, Texas should determine to withhold her assent, no such new state could ever be formed, and hence the prohibition would never take effect. All difficulty, however, on this point has been removed by the act of 1850, purchasing from Texas all that portion of her territory lying north of 36° 30', and incorporating it in the Territory of New Mexico, with the guarantee that, "when admitted as a state, the said Territory, or any portion of the same, shall be received into the Union with or without slavery, as their Constitution may prescribe at the time of admission." Hence all the territory, to which it is now proposed to apply the Missouri restriction for the first time, under the plea of restoring the Missouri Compromise of the 6th of March, 1820, is protected from any such invasion of the rights of the inhabitants to form and regulate their own domestic affairs in their own way, by the solemn guaranties contained in the compromise measures of 1850, which blotted out the geographical line as a dividing-line between free territory and slave territory, and substituted for it the cardinal principle of self-government in accordance with the Constitution. But it will also be observed that the bill under consideration does not propose to limit the restriction to the territory acquired from Texas, nor the country on the east side of the Rio Grande, but extend it across that river over a portion of the territory acquired from Mexico, which was never claimed by Texas, nor embraced within the Louisiana Purchase, and to which there is no pretext for asserting that the Missouri Compromise ever applied. If, in the application of the 8th section of the act of the 6th of March, 1820 (commonly called the Missouri Compromise), over so large a district of country to which it never had any previous application, it be the policy of the House of Representatives to return to the "obsolete idea" of a geographical line as a dividing-line in all time to come between slave territory and free territory, a perpetual barrier against the advancement of slavery on the one hand and free institutions on the other, the measure falls short of accomplishing the whole of their object in not extending the line to the Pacific Ocean. Your committee can perceive many weighty considerations founded in policy, although wanting the sanction of sound constitutional principles, which might be urged in favor of such a measure, inasmuch as the barrier once erected from ocean to ocean—permitting slavery on the one side and prohibiting it on the other—if universally acquiesced in and religiously observed as a patriotic offering upon the altar of our common country, would put an end to the controversy forever, and form a bond of peace and brotherhood in the future.   But, unfortunately, when this expedient was proposed by the Senate in 1848, it was indignantly repudiated by the House of Representatives, and, as a consequence, the whole country was plunged into a whirlpool of sectional strife and angry crimination, which alarmed the greatest and purest patriots of the land for the safety of the republic, and was only rescued from the impending perils by the adoption of the compromise measures of 1850, which abandoned the policy of a geographical line, and substituted for it the great principles of self-government and state equality in obedience to the federal Constitution.   In view of the history of the past, your committee can perceive no safety in the future except in a strict and religious fidelity to the true principles of the Constitution as embodied in the adjustment of that unfortunate controversy, and adopted by the whole country as rules of action, to be applied in all future time, when in the progress of events it should be necessary to organize Territories or admit new states. The Kansas-Nebraska Act was the logical sequence of the compromise measures of 1850, and rendered imperatively necessary in order to establish and perpetuate the principles of self-government and state equality in the organization of Territories and admission of new states.   For these reasons your committee can not concur with the House of Representatives in the proposition to blot out from the organic act of Kansas and Nebraska those essential provisions and cardinal principles, the faithful observance of which can alone preserve the just rights of the inhabitants of the Territories, and maintain the peace, unity, and fraternity of the republic.   The great object is to withdraw the Slavery question from the halls of Congress, and remand its decision to the people of the several states and Territories, subject to no other conditions or restrictions than those imposed by the Constitution of the United States. Those provisions of the bill under consideration which introduce and establish slavery, together with those which abolish and prohibit it, are alike obnoxious on the score of principle, inasmuch as they assert and exercise the right of Congress to form and regulate the local affairs and domestic institutions of a distant and distinct people without their consent, and regardless of their rights and wishes.   To avoid all misconstruction, however, upon this point, your committee deem it proper to remark, that their objections do not apply to that part of the bill which extends the provisions of the Fugitive Slave Law to the Territories of Kansas and Nebraska, and provides "that any person lawfully held to service in any other state or Territory, and escaping into either the Territory of Kansas or Nebraska, may be reclaimed and removed to the person or place where such service is due, under any law of the United States which shall be in force upon the subject."   In this clause your committee are rejoiced to find a frank and conscientious acknowledgment of the duty of Congress to provide efficient laws for carrying into faithful execution the provision of the Constitution of the United States which provides for the rendition of fugitive slaves as well as all other obligations imposed by that instrument.

The preservation of our free institutions depends upon a faithful observance of the Constitution in all its parts; and the assurance thus furnished that the representatives of the people are ever ready to provide new and additional guarantees when supposed to be necessary for the faithful performance of that constitutional obligation, which has been the subject of the severest criticism in some portions of the country, can not fail to gratify every true friend of the Union.   In this case, however, no such legislation is necessary, inasmuch

KANSAS AND HER GOVERNMENTS.

as the organic act of Kansas and Nebraska extended the provisions of the Fugitive Slave Law to both of those Territories.

[After quoting the 15th and 16th sections of the bill, the report continues:]

It will be observed that these two sections recognize the validity and binding force of the entire code of laws enacted at the Shawnee Mission, by the Legislature of Kansas Territory, and provide for the faithful execution of all those enactments except the criminal code. All justices of the peace, constables, sheriffs, and all other judicial and ministerial officers now in office, are required to continue to exercise and perform the duties of their respective offices. All these officers, with the exception of the governor, three judges, secretary, and marshal, and district attorney, were elected or appointed under the laws enacted by the Legislature of Kansas, while their powers, functions, and duties are all prescribed by those laws and none others. These officers are all required to continue to perform the duties of their respective offices, by observing and enforcing all the laws enacted at the Shawnee Mission, except the criminal code. "All suits, process, and proceedings, civil and criminal, at law and in chancery, and all indictments and informations which shall be pending and undetermined in the courts of the Territory of Kansas or New Mexico when this act shall take effect, shall remain in said courts where pending, to be held, tried, prosecuted, and determined in such courts AS THOUGH THIS ACT HAD NOT BEEN PASSED." The election laws, and the laws concerning slaves and slavery, and all laws protecting the rights of persons and property, and affecting all the relations of life, are recognized as valid and required to be enforced, EXCEPTING CRIMINAL PROSECUTIONS, BY INFORMATION OR INDICTMENT, for violating or disregarding the laws of the Legislature of Kansas, all such prosecutions are required to be forthwith dismissed, and the prisoners set at liberty, and no new prosecutions are to be commenced for "any violation or disregard of said legislative enactments at any time." Such is the legislation provided for in these two sections of the bill. They recognize the validity of the laws enacted at Shawnee Mission, and provide for the enforcement of all of them except in cases of criminal prosecution. Your committee are unable to perceive how the passage of such a bill would restore peace, quiet, and security to the people of Kansas. It has been alleged that there are in that Territory organized bands of lawless and desperate men, who are in the constant habit of perpetrating deeds of violence—murdering and plundering the inhabitants, stealing their property, burning their houses, and driving peaceable citizens from the polls on election day, and even from the Territory. The remedy proposed in the bill is to grant to the perpetrators of these crimes a general amnesty for the past, and a full license in the future to continue their bloody work.

There is no law in force in Kansas by which murder, robbery, larceny, arson, and other crimes known to the criminal codes of all civilized states, can be punished, except under the code enacted by the Legislature of Kansas at the Shawnee Mission. The provisions of "An Act for the Punishment of Crimes against the United States," approved April 30, 1790, are, by its terms, confined in its application to such crimes as shall be committed "within any fort, arsenal, dock-yard, magazine, or any other place or district of country under the sole and exclusive jurisdiction of the United States," and "upon the high seas and navigable waters out of the jurisdiction of any particular state," but has never been held or construed to apply to the Territories of the United States. The act of the 3d of March, 1817, "to provide for the punishment of crimes and offenses committed within the Indian boundaries," extends the provisions of the said act of 1790 to the Indian country, but expressly restricts its application, as its title imports, to crimes committed "within any town, district, or territory *belonging to any nation or nations, tribe or tribes of Indians.*" Hence, the moment the Indian title is extinguished, and the country placed under the jurisdiction of a Territorial government, it ceases to be "under the sole and exclusive jurisdiction of the United States," and is no longer subject to the provisions of either of the above-cited acts. Thus it will be seen that if the bill from the House of Representatives should become a law with the provisions granting a general amnesty in respect to all past crimes, and unlimited license in the future to perpetrate such outrages as their own bad passions might instigate, there would be no law in force in Kansas to punish the guilty or protect the innocent.

Inasmuch as the House of Representatives, by the passage of the bill under consideration, and the Senate, by its bill for the admission of Kansas into the Union, have each recognized the validity of the laws enacted by the Kansas Legislature at Shawnee Mission, so far as they are consistent with the Constitution and the organic act, and affirmed the propriety and duty of enforcing the same, except in certain specified cases, it becomes important to inquire into the extent of the differences of opinion between the House of Representatives and the Senate, in respect to the particular laws which ought not to be enforced. The Senate has already declared in the bill for the admission of Kansas into the Union that all laws and enactments in said Territory which are repugnant to, or in conflict with, the great principles of liberty and justice, as guaranteed by the Constitution of the United States and the organic act, and embodied in the 18th section of that bill, shall be null and void, and that none such shall ever be enforced or executed in said Territory. * * *

It is true that there is apparently another point of difference between the two houses, arising out of the question whether the people of Kansas shall be authorized to elect delegates to a convention (with proper and satisfactory safeguards against fraud, violence, and illegal voting), and form a Constitution and state government preparatory to their admission into the Union, or whether the Territory shall be reorganized in accordance with the provisions of the bill from the House, and left, for some years to come, in that condition. While the House of Representatives has recently expressed its preference for the latter proposition by the passage of the bill under consideration, your committee are not permitted to assume that they have insuperable objections to the admission of Kansas at this time, for the reason that a few weeks previous they passed a bill to admit that Territory as a state, with the Topeka Constitution. Hence, the change of policy on the part of the House, in abandoning the state movement with the Topeka Constitution, and substituting for it the proposition to reorganize the Territory and leave it in that condition, must be taken only as a strong expression of a decided preference on the part of the House for the bill under consideration, and not as conclusive evidence of insuperable objections to a fair bill, with proper and suitable guarantees against fraud and illegal voting, to authorize the people of Kansas to form a Constitution and state government at this time.

The committee recommended that the bill be laid on the table. The bill was laid on the table in the Senate—yeas 35, nays 12, no one venturing to approve or endorse it in that body.

The House did not act on either of the Senate bills relating to Kansas. In the General Appropriation Bill a clause was inserted providing that no part of the money appropriated thereby to defray the expenses of the Territorial government in Kansas should be drawn from the treasury until all the criminal prosecutions on charges of treason in Kansas, or for violation of the laws of the Territorial Legislature, should be dismissed, and the accused parties discharged.

To the Army Bill the House attached a clause that no part of the military force of the United States should be employed to aid in the enforcement of any act of the Kansas Legislature; requiring the President to disband the armed militia of the Territory, to recall all the United States arms therein distributed, and to "prevent armed men going into the Territory to disturb the peace or to aid in the enforcement or resistance of real or pretended law."

These provisions the Senate struck out of the bills. The House refused to agree to the amendments of the Senate, and the Senate insisted on their action. Finally, the House yielded, except in the case of the Army Bill; and, though various committees of conference were held, no agreement was had, and Congress, on the 18th of August, adjourned without passing the Army Bill.

The President convened Congress next day, and sent a message to both houses urging the necessity for the passage of appropriations for the army. The old Army Appropriation Bill was revived, and a new one was introduced; but the House insisting on its Kansas legislation, both failed under the disagreeing votes of the two houses. At last, on a third bill, on the 30th of August, the House, by a vote of 101 to 98, receded from its position, and the bill passed. Congress adjourned the same day without any legislation for Kansas.

CHAPTER XIV.

THE LECOMPTON CONTROVERSY.

The Lecompton controversy was the most severe and painful that has ever attended Mr. Douglas's public career. It was also one that elicited from him a greater exhibition of his native abilities than any other of the many in which he has been engaged. In 1846 he took the high strong ground of the Democratic party as declared at Baltimore upon the Oregon Boundary question. He sustained the President to the utmost of his ability. President Polk, however, induced by high and patriotic motives, thought proper to yield to the advice of the co-ordinate branch of the treaty-making power, and disposed of that question by abandoning 54° 40' and accepting 49°. Upon the annexation of Texas, Mr. Douglas took ground in favor of extending and renewing the line of 36° 30' as a settlement of the Slavery question. He succeeded. In the fierce controversies on the Oregon Territorial Bill he renewed time and again the proposition to extend the Missouri Compromise line of 36° 30' to the Pacific; his efforts proved unavailing, and that bill passed. In 1850 he had supported and defended the Fugitive Slave Law and the compromise acts of that year —defended them in the presence of an armed and hostile meeting at Chicago, and succeeded. In 1854 he had carried through successfully the Kansas-Nebraska Act, and, through violence and denunciation at home and throughout the North, had maintained with unfaltering nerve the rectitude of his conduct. In 1856 he had canvassed Illinois from one end to the other, urging the election of Mr. Buchanan upon the ground that the Democratic party and its candidates were pledged in the most solemn manner to secure to the people of the Territories the right of having slavery or not, as they of their own free action might determine. In answer to the cry that came up from every Republican orator—and in Illinois the leading men of that party from all parts of the country were on the stump— that the government of Kansas, her officers, and Legislature, were in the hands of the "Border Ruffians," his answer was, that no matter who were placed over the people temporarily, no Constitution could be adopted nor state government erected that was not called into being by the votes of the people in ratifying that Constitution. That the ultimate power of adopting a Constitution was in the hands of the people, and could not be taken from them, was the universal answer made to the charge that under the Nebraska Act Kansas would be made a slave state in defiance of the wishes of the people. On that defense, and on that pledge made every where throughout the campaign, Illinois preserved her ancient credit, and gave her electoral vote to Mr. Buchanan.

After the inauguration of Mr. Buchanan it was deemed advisable to select as governor of Kansas some person of ability, who had also discretion to regulate that ability, and personal character entitling him to the respect of men of all parties, not only in the country generally, but particularly in Kansas.

Such a man was Robert J. Walker. When tendered the office he peremptorily declined it. It was a position in which there was little credit to be gained, and a vast amount of responsibility and vexation. Those who had previously gone there had failed, and failed most miserably; indeed, much of the trouble that had existed might have been traced to the incompetency, personal unfitness, or corruption of those who had been selected as governors. Mr. Douglas was particularly anxious for the appointment of Mr. Walker, and took an active part in inducing him to consent to go to Kansas as governor. After long and serious consideration, Mr. Walker accepted the office; in so doing, he placed a condition on file that he was to be governor with the assurance that he was to tell the people of Kansas that they should have the privilege of voting directly for or against any Constitution that might be prepared for them. He proceeded to Kansas, and in his speeches he repeated this pledge, and in so doing stated that he made it with the knowledge and approval of the President and his cabinet; and that, unless the Constitution was submitted to the people for ratification or rejection, he should endeavor to defeat it before Congress.

Mr. Douglas, in Illinois, by speeches delivered at various parts of the state, referred to Governor Walker's course as a proof that the pledges he had made during the previous year, that Mr. Buchanan would faithfully carry out the spirit of the Kansas-Nebraska Act, were about to be redeemed to their letter.

When the convention met in Kansas, and while it was in session, it became obvious that a large portion of the people, led on by fanatical and turbulent spirits, would not participate in forming a state government. While this was to be regretted, yet no person in Illinois believed that the convention would attempt to adopt a Constitution without providing for its submission to the people. Mr. Calhoun himself was solemnly pledged, in writing, to submit the Constitution to the people. Mr. Douglas had justified the course of Governor Walker and the administration. When Congress met, in December, 1857, the President's Message indicated that, as a matter of peace, the administration would, in the event of the Lecompton Constitution being presented, urge the admission of Kansas under that Constitution.

O

The President's Message was communicated on the 8th of December; after it was read, Mr. Douglas stated that he would take an early opportunity to express his views upon the subject of Kansas, in which he was constrained to say he differed with the President to some extent. On the next day he addressed the Senate in the speech of which some extracts are given as follows:

Mr. President,—When yesterday the President's Message was read at the clerk's desk, I heard it but imperfectly, and I was of the impression that the President of the United States had approved and endorsed the action of the Lecompton Convention in Kansas. Under that impression, I felt it my duty to state that, while I concurred in the general views of the message, yet, so far as it approved or endorsed the action of that convention, I entirely dissented from it, and would avail myself of an early opportunity to state my reasons for my dissent. Upon a more careful and critical examination of the message, I am rejoiced to find that the President of the United States has not recommended that Congress shall pass a law to receive Kansas into the Union under the Constitution formed at Lecompton. It is true that the tone of the message indicates a willingness on the part of the President to sign a bill, if we shall see proper to pass one, receiving Kansas into the Union under that Constitution. But, sir, it is a fact of great significance, and worthy of consideration, that the President has refrained from any endorsement of the convention, and from any recommendation as to the course Congress should pursue with regard to the Constitution there formed.

The message of the President has made an argument—an unanswerable argument, in my opinion—against that Constitution, which shows clearly, whether intended to arrive at the result or not, that, consistently with his views and his principles, he can not accept that Constitution. He has expressed his deep mortification and disappointment that the Constitution itself has not been submitted to the people of Kansas for their acceptance or rejection. He informs us that he has unqualifiedly expressed his opinions on that subject in his instructions to Governor Walker, assuming, as a matter of course, that the Constitution was to be submitted to the people before it could have any vitality or validity. He goes further, and tells us that the example set by Congress in the Minnesota case, by inserting a clause in the enabling act requiring the Constitution to be submitted to the people, ought to become a uniform rule, not to be departed from hereafter in any case. On these various propositions I agree entirely with the President of the United States, and I am prepared now to sustain that uniform rule which he asks us to pursue in all other cases, by taking the Minnesota provision as our example.

I rejoice, on a careful perusal of the message, to find so much less to dissent from than I was under the impression there was, from the hasty reading and imperfect hearing of the message in the first instance. In effect, he refers that document to the Congress of the United States—as the Constitution of the United States refers it—for us to decide upon it under our responsibility. It is proper that he should have thus referred it to us as a matter for Congressional action, and not as an administration or executive measure, for the reason that the Constitution of the United States says that "Congress may admit new states into the Union." Hence we find the Kansas question before us now, not as an administration measure, not as an executive measure, but as a measure coming before us for our free action, without any recommendation or interference, directly or indirectly, by the administration now in possession of the federal government. Sir, I propose to examine this question calmly and fairly, to see whether or not we can properly receive Kansas into the Union with the Constitution formed at Lecompton.

The President, after expressing his regret, and mortification, and disappointment that the Constitution had not been submitted to the people in pursuance of his instructions to Governor Walker, and in pursuance of Governor Walker's assurances to the people, says, however, that by the Kansas-Nebraska Act the Slavery question only was required to be referred to the people, and the remainder of the Constitution was not thus required to be submitted. He acknowledges that, as a general rule, on general principles, the whole Constitution should be submitted; but, according to his understanding of the organic act of Kansas, there was an imperative obligation to submit the Slavery question for their approval or disapproval, but no obligation to submit the entire Constitution. In other words, he regards the organic act, the Nebraska Bill, as having made an exception of the Slavery clause, and provided for the disposition of that question in a mode different from that in which other domestic or local, as contradistinguished from federal questions, should be decided. Sir, permit me to say, with profound respect for the President of the United States, that I conceive that on this point he has committed a fundamental error—an error which lies at the foundation of his whole argument on this matter. I can well understand how that distinguished statesman came to fall into this error. He was not in the country at the time the Nebraska Bill was passed; he was not a party to the controversy and the discussion that took place during its passage. He was then representing the honor and the dignity of the country with great wisdom and distinction at a foreign court. Thus deeply engrossed, his whole energies were absorbed in conducting great diplomatic questions, that diverted his attention from the mere Territorial questions and discussions then going on in the Senate and the House of Representatives, and before the people at home. Under these circumstances, he may well have fallen into an error, radical and fundamental as it is, in regard to the object of the Nebraska Bill and the principle asserted in it.

Now, sir, what was the principle enunciated by the authors and supporters of that bill when it was brought forward? Did we not come before the country and say that we repealed the Missouri restriction for the purpose of substituting and carrying out as a general rule the great principle of self-government, which left the people of each state and each Territory free to form and regulate their domestic institutions in their own way, subject only to the Constitution of the United States? In support of that proposition, it was argued here, and I have argued it wherever I have spoken in various states of the Union, at home and abroad, every where I have endeavored to prove that there was no reason why an exception should be made in regard to the Slavery question. I have appealed to the people, if we did not all agree, men of all parties, that all other local and domestic questions should be submitted to the people. I said to them, "We agree that the people shall decide for themselves what kind of a judiciary system they will have; we agree that the people shall decide what kind of a school system they will establish; we agree that the people shall determine for themselves what kind of a banking system they will have, or whether they will have any banks at all; we agree that the people may decide for themselves what shall be the elective franchise in their respective states; they shall decide for themselves what shall be the rule of taxation and the principles upon which their finance shall be regulated; we agree that they may decide for themselves the relations between husband and wife, parent and child, guardian and ward; and why should we not then allow them to decide for themselves the relations between master and servant? Why make an exception of the Slavery question, by taking it out of that great rule of self-government which applies to all the other relations of life?" The very first proposition in the Nebraska Bill was to show that the Missouri restriction, prohibiting the people from deciding the Slavery question for themselves, constituted an exception to a general rule, in violation of the principle of self-government; and hence that that exception should be repealed, and the Slavery question, like all other questions, submitted to the people, to be decided for themselves.

Sir, that was the principle on which the Nebraska Bill was defended by its friends. Instead of making the Slavery question an exception, it removed an odious exception which before existed. Its whole object was to abolish that odious exception, and make the rule general, universal in its application to all matters which were local and domestic, and not national or federal. For this reason was the language employed which the President has quoted; that the eighth section of the Missouri Act, commonly called the Missouri Compromise, was repealed, because it was repugnant to the principle of non-intervention, established by the compromise measures of 1850, "it being the true intent and meaning of this act, not to legislate slavery into any Territory or state, nor to exclude it therefrom, but to leave the people thereof perfectly free to form and regulate their domestic institutions in their own way, subject only to the Constitution of the United States." We repealed the Missouri restriction because that was confined to slavery. That was the only exception there was to the general principle of self-government. That exception was taken away for the avowed and express purpose of making the rule of self-government general and universal, so that the people should form and regulate all their domestic institutions in their own way.

Sir, what would this boasted principle of popular sovereignty have been worth if it applied only to the negro, and did not extend to the white man? Do you think we could have aroused the sympathies and the patriotism of this broad republic, and have carried the presidential election last year, in the face of a tremendous opposition, on the principle of extending the right of self-government to the Negro question, but denying it as to all the relations affecting white men? No, sir. We aroused the patriotism of the country, and carried the election in defense of that great principle which allowed all white men to form and regulate their domestic institutions to suit themselves—institutions applicable to white men as well as to black men—institutions applicable to freemen as well as to slaves—institutions concerning all the relations of life, and not the mere paltry exception of the Slavery question. Sir, I have spent too much strength and breath, and health too, to establish this great principle in the popular heart, now to see it frittered away by bringing it down to an exception that applies to the negro, and does not extend to the benefit of the white man. As I said before, I can well imagine how the distinguished and eminent patriot and statesman now at the head of the government fell into the error—for error it is, radical, fundamental—and, if persevered in, subversive of that platform upon which he was elevated to the presidency of the United States.

Then, if the President be right in saying that by the Nebraska Bill the Slavery question must be submitted to the people, it follows inevitably that every other clause of the Constitution must also be submitted to the people. The Nebraska Bill said that the people should be left "perfectly free to form and regulate their domestic institutions in their own way"—not the Slavery question, not the Maine Liquor Law question, not the Banking question, not the School question, not the Railroad question, but "their domestic institutions," meaning each and all the questions which are local, not national—state, not federal. I arrive at the conclusion that the principles enunciated so boldly and enforced with so much ability by the President of the United States, require us, out of respect to him and the platform on which he was elec d, to send this whole question back to the people of Kansas, and enable them to say whether or not the Constitution which has been framed, each and every clause of it, meets their approbation.

The President, in his message, has made an unanswerable argument in favor of the principle which requires this question to be sent back. It is stated in the message with more clearness and force than any language which I can command; but I can draw your attention to it, and refer you to the argument in the message, hoping that you will take it as a part of my speech—as expressing my idea more forcibly than I am able to express it. The President says that a question of great interest, like the Slavery question, can not be fairly decided by a convention of delegates, for the reason that the delegates are elected in districts, and in some districts a delegate is elected by a small majority; in others by an overwhelming majority; so that it often happens that a majority of the delegates are one way, while a majority of the people are the other way; and therefore it would be unfair, and inconsistent with the great principle of popular sovereignty, to allow a body of delegates, not representing the popular voice, to establish domestic institutions for the mass of the people. This is the President's argument to show that you can not have a fair and honest decision without submitting it to the popular vote. The same argument is conclusive with regard to every other question, as well as with regard to Slavery.

But, Mr. President, it is intimated in the message that, although it was an unfortunate circumstance, much to be regretted, that the Lecompton Convention did not submit the Constitution to the people, yet perhaps it may be treated as regular, because the convention was called by a Territorial Legislature which had been repeatedly recognized by the Congress of the United States as a legal body. I beg senators not to fall into an error as to the President's meaning on this point. He does not say, he does not mean, that this Convention had ever been recognized by the Congress of the United States as legal or valid. On the contrary, he knows, as we here know, that during last Congress I reported a bill from the Committee on Territories to authorize the people of Kansas to assemble and form a Constitution for themselves. Subsequently, the senator from Georgia [Mr. Toombs] brought forward a substitute for my bill, which, after having been modified by him and myself in consultation, was passed by the Senate. It is known in the country as "the Toombs Bill." It authorized the people of Kansas Territory to assemble in convention and form a Constitution preparatory to their admission into the Union as a state. That bill, it is well known, was defeated in the House of Representatives. It matters not, for the purpose of this argument, what was the reason of its defeat. Whether the reason was a political one; whether it had reference to the then existing contest for the presidency; whether it was to keep open the Slavery question; whether it was a conviction that the bill would not be fairly carried out; whether it was because there were not people enough in Kansas to justify the formation of a state—no matter what the reason was, the House of Representatives refused to pass that bill, and thus denied to the people of Kansas the right to form a Constitution and state government at this time. So far from the Congress of the United States having sanctioned or legalized the convention which assembled at Lecompton, it expressly withheld its assent. The assent has not been given, either in express terms or by implication; and being withheld, this Kansas Constitution has just such validity and just such authority as the Territorial Legislature of Kansas could impart to it without the assent and in opposition to the known will of Congress.

Now, sir, let me ask what is the extent of the authority of a Territorial Legislature as to calling a Constitutional convention without the consent of Congress? Fortunately this is not a new question; it does not now arise for the first time. When the Topeka Constitution was presented to the Senate nearly two years ago, it was referred to the Committee on Territories, with a variety of measures relating to Kansas. The committee made a full report upon the whole subject. That report reviewed all the irregular cases which had occurred in our history in the admission of new states. The committee acted on the supposition that whenever Congress had passed an enabling act authorizing the people of a Territory to form a state Constitution, the convention was regular, and possessed all the authority which Congress had delegated to it; but whenever Congress had failed or refused to pass an enabling act, the proceeding was irregular and void, unless vitality was imparted to it by a subsequent act of Congress, adopting and confirming it. The friends of the Topeka Constitution insisted that, although their proceedings were irregular, they were not so irregular but that Congress could cure the error by admitting Kansas with that Constitution. They cited a variety of cases, among others the Arkansas case. In my report, sanctioned by every member of the Committee on Territories except the senator from Vermont [Mr. Collamer], I reviewed the Arkansas case as well as the others, and affirmed the doctrine established by General Jackson's administration, and enunciated in the opinion of Mr. Attorney General Butler, a part of which opinion was copied into the report and published to the country at the time.

Mr. Douglas then discussed the question in all its aspects, and closed his speech as follows:

The President tells us in his message that the whole party pledged our faith and our honor that the Slavery question should be submitted to the people, without any restriction or qualification whatever. Does this schedule submit it without qualification? It qualifies it by saying, "You may vote on slavery if you will vote for the Constitution, but you shall not do so without doing that." That is a very important qualification—a qualification that controls a man's vote, and his action, and his conscience, if he is an honest man—a qualification confessedly in violation of our platform. We are told by the President that our faith and our honor are pledged that the Slavery clause should be submitted without qualification of any kind whatever; and now am I to be called upon to forfeit my faith and my honor in order to enable a small minority of the people of Kansas to defraud the majority of that people out of their elective franchise? Sir, my honor is pledged; and before it shall be tarnished I will take whatever consequences personal to myself may come; but never ask me to do an act which the President, in his message, has said is a forfeiture of faith, a violation of honor, and that merely for the expediency of saving the party. I will go as far as any of you to save the party. I have as much heart in the great cause that binds us together as any man living. I will sacrifice any thing short of principle and honor for the peace of the party; but if the party will not stand by its principles, its faith, its pledges, I will stand there, and abide whatever consequences may result from the position.

Let me ask you, why force this Constitution down the throats of the people of Kansas in opposition to their wishes and in violation of our pledges? What great object is to be attained? *Cui bono?* What are you to gain by it? Will you sustain the party by violating its principles? Do you propose to keep the party united by forcing a division? Stand by the doctrine that leaves the people perfectly free to form and regulate their institutions for themselves, in their own way, and your party will be united and irresistible in power. Abandon that great principle, and the party is not worth saving, and can not be saved after it shall be violated. I trust we are not to be rushed upon this question. Why shall it be done? Who is to be benefited? Is the South to be the gainer? Is the North to be the gainer? Neither the

North nor the South has the right to gain a sectional advantage by trickery or fraud.

But I am besought to wait until I hear from the election on the 21st of December. I am told that perhaps that will put it all right, and will save the whole difficulty. How can it? Perhaps there may be a large vote. There may be a large vote returned. [Laughter.] But I deny that it is possible to have a fair vote on the Slavery clause; and I say that it is not possible to have any vote on the Constitution. Why wait for the mockery of an election, when it is provided, unalterably, that the people can not vote—when the majority are disfranchised?

But I am told on all sides, "Oh, just wait; the pro-slavery clause will be voted down." That does not obviate any of my objections; it does not diminish any of them. You have no more right to force a free-state Constitution on Kansas than a slave-state Constitution. If Kansas wants a slave-state Constitution, she has a right to it; if she wants a free-state Constitution, she has a right to it. It is none of my business which way the Slavery clause is decided. I care not whether it is voted down or voted up. Do you suppose, after the pledges of my honor that I would go for that principle, and leave the people to vote as they please, that I would now degrade myself by voting one way if the Slavery clause be voted down, and another way if it be voted up? I care not how that vote may stand. I take it for granted that it will be voted out. I think I have seen enough in the last three days to make it certain that it will be returned out, no matter how the vote may stand. [Laughter.]

Sir, I am opposed to that concern, because it looks to me like a system of trickery and jugglery to defeat the fair expression of the will of the people. There is no necessity for crowding this measure, so unfair, so unjust as it is in all its aspects, upon us. Why can we not now do what we proposed to do in the last Congress? We then voted through the Senate an enabling act, called "the Toombs Bill," believed to be just and fair in all its provisions, pronounced to be almost perfect by the senator from New Hampshire [Mr. Hale], only he did not like the man, then President of the United States, who would have to make the appointments. Why can we not take that bill, and, out of compliment to the President, add to it a clause taken from the Minnesota Act, which he thinks should be a general rule, requiring the Constitution to be submitted to the people, and pass that? That unites the party. You all voted with me for that bill at the last Congress. Why not stand by the same bill now? Ignore Lecompton, ignore Topeka; treat both those party movements as irregular and void; pass a fair bill—the one that we framed ourselves when we were acting as a unit; have a fair election—and you will have peace in the Democratic party, and peace throughout the country, in ninety days. The people want a fair vote. They never will be satisfied without it. They never should be satisfied without a fair vote on their Constitution.

If the Toombs Bill does not suit my friends, take the Minnesota Bill of the last session—the one so much commended by the President in his message as a model. Let us pass that as an enabling act, and allow the people of all parties to come together and have a fair vote, and I will go for it. Frame any other bill that secures a fair, honest vote, to men of all parties, and carries out the pledge that the people shall be left free to decide on their domestic institutions for themselves, and I will go with you with pleasure, and with all the energy I may possess. But if this Constitution is to be forced down our throats, in violation of the fundamental principle of free government, under a mode of submission that is a mockery and insult, I will resist it to the last. I have no fear of any party associations being severed. I should regret any social or political estrangement, even temporarily; but if it must be, if I can not act with you and preserve my faith and my honor, I will stand on the great principle of popular sovereignty, which declares the right of all people to be left perfectly free to form and regulate their domestic institutions in their own way. I will follow that principle wherever its logical consequences may take me, and I will endeavor to defend it against assault from any and all quarters. No mortal man shall be responsible for my action but myself. By my action I will compromit no man.

The galleries as well as the hall of the Senate Chamber, and every approach to it, were densely crowded. When he concluded his remarks there was an involuntary burst of applause, surpassing any thing that had ever before violated the dignity and decorum of that body. Some debate ensued as to the propriety of expelling all save the members of the Senate, but the matter eventually dropped without any such action.

Mr. Bigler followed in a brief reply, and Mr. Mason addressed himself to a single point. Mr. Douglas, having responded to Mr. Mason, was about addressing himself to the remarks of Mr. Bigler, when a debate ensued, the importance of which consists solely in the refutation of a charge rather intimated than preferred by the senator from Pennsylvania. What was said is taken from the " Globe," as follows :

Mr. Douglas. Yesterday a speech was read to this body, showing that the President had held that doctrine twenty years ago, and he had never disavowed it since. In that speech the President declared that a Territorial Legislature had no power to create a convention to form a Constitution; and that, if they attempted to exercise such a power, it would be an act of usurpation—a high crime—a crime subject to impeachment. The President has held these doctrines for twenty years. He held them at the same time that General Jackson's administration held them in regard to the Arkansas case. The Democratic party has held them ever since. I have proved to-day that the Democratic party, so far as it is bound by our action one year and a half ago, asserted the same doctrine in the Kansas report which I made from the Committee on Territories. I firmly believed then that that committee was a faithful exponent of the views of the Kansas-Nebraska party. In that report we set forth that doctrine, and, as the senator well knows, we published and circulated during the campaign, in order to elect Mr. Buchanan, three hundred thousand copies of that report as a party document. I paid for one hundred thousand copies of them myself. I never heard it intimated that the doctrine then expounded, and on which the President was elected, was repudiated by any portion of the party, and therefore I said that the President of the United States was with me on this question, so far as his record shows.

Mr. Bigler. I must enter my protest and claim the benefit of the statute of limitation, which is applicable to a shorter period than twenty years. I can not consent that the senator from Illinois shall hold the President to principles which he may have laid down twenty years ago, under entirely different circumstances from those which now exist. It is not half so long since the President of the United States declared that the Missouri line would be the best compromise of the slavery difficulty that could be made. In 1848, the senator from Illinois advocated the extension of the Missouri line to the Pacific Ocean, yet he was the man who proposed and insisted that it ought to be repealed. He was at one time in favor of extending it, and therefore made his principle acceptable to him under the circumstances then existing; he was willing then to take it. Now, would it not be very ungenerous in me to hold to-day that the senator's argument was a fallacy, because he at one time advocated the extension of the Missouri line?

Mr. Douglas. I deny the right of the senator from Pennsylvania to interpose the statute of limitations upon this occasion, on the well-known principle that no one but the authorized attorney of the party can interpose that plea. [Laughter.] As the senator has disavowed the authority to act and speak for the President, he has no right to file the plea. If the President of the United States himself will interpose the plea, I shall admit it. I believe in a statute of limitations in regard to political opinions. I need one very much myself on many points. I am not one of those who boast that they have never changed an opinion. Sir, it is a matter of gratification to me that I feel each year that I am a little wiser than I was the year before; and I do not know that a month has ever passed over my head in which I have not modified some opinion in some degree, but I am always frank enough to avow it. Still, it is fair for any man to hold me to a former opinion until I have expressed a contrary one.

Has the President of the United States ever withdrawn the opinion of which I have spoken, expressed twenty years ago, in regard to the power of the Territorial Legislature? I show that the Democratic party stood by it last year. Is not that rather a short period for the application of the statute of limitations? I hope you are not going to cut off the Cincinnati Convention by that statute. I deny your right to plead the statute against the Cincinnati Convention until after the meeting of the Charleston Convention. The Cincinnati platform is the fundamental, unalterable law of the Democratic party until the meeting of the Charleston Convention. Congressmen have no right to change it. Senators have no right to change it. Cabinets can not alter it; and the President, I know, will not attempt to do so. I deny the senator's right to come in with this plea for the President, implying thereby that he has changed his opinion, when that same opinion was last year the doctrine of the Democratic party, and can not be changed for four years to come by the party organization. I am perfectly at home when you come to the discussion of the question whether a man is inside the party or not. I have been in the habit of discussing these platforms and helping to make them. I stand now where I stood last year; not because I am unwilling to change, but because I believed I was right then, and I believe I am right now.

The senator from Pennsylvania has told me that I actually voted for the Toombs Bill last year. That is true; and, as I said to-day, I am ready to vote for it again. He voted for it last year, and so did the gentlemen around me. Let us vote for it again, and have no quarrels among ourselves. It will not do to taunt me with having voted for a measure last year which I am for now, but which you are not for.

Mr. Bigler. I certainly did not present the case in that spirit at all, nor did I look at it in that point of view. I gave it no such aspect whatever. I presented it in this point of view: the senator, in his speech to-day, had held that it was a great wrong upon the people of Kansas to put a government in operation through the agency of their Territorial laws and a Territorial convention, the whole of which had not been submitted to their approbation; and yet only a short year ago he voted for an enabling act which put a state government into operation without submitting any part of it to the people. That is what I said.

Mr. Douglas. My explanation of that is to be given in the precise language of the explanation of the President of the United States in his message, in which he says that, in his instructions to Governor Walker, he took it for granted that the Constitution was to be submitted to the people under a law that was silent on the subject. The Toombs Bill being silent, I took it for granted too, and I supposed every other man did, that it was to be submitted. I merely adopted the same process of reasoning that the President himself says he adopted, and which he was amazed to find was not carried out. If the President was right in taking that for granted, I do not know why I was not right in taking the same thing for granted.

Again, I will ask the senator to show me an intimation from any one member of the Senate, in the whole debate on the Toombs Bill, and in the Union from any quarter, that the Constitution was not to be submitted to the people. I will venture to say, that on all sides of the chamber it was so understood at the time. If the opponents of the bill had understood it was not, they would have made the point on it; and if they had made it, we should certainly have yielded to it and put in the clause. That is a discovery made since the President found out that it was not safe to take it for granted that that would be done which ought in fairness to have been done.

Mr. Bigler. I do not pretend to know any thing on this subject which may not appear in the Journal of Debates. I shall not hold the senator to any thing that does not appear there; but this I will say, that I was present when that subject was discussed by senators before the bill was introduced, and the question was raised and discussed whether the Constitution, when formed, should be submitted to a vote of the people. It was held by those most intelligent on the subject, that in view of all the difficulties surrounding that Territory, the danger of any experiment at that time of a popular vote, it would be better that there should be no provision in the Toombs Bill; and it was my understanding, in all the intercourse I had, that that convention would make a Constitution and send it here without submitting it to the popular vote.

Mr. Douglas. The senator says he will not undertake to state any thing that did not occur here in debate and appear in the published debates, intimating that he has no right, as an honorable man, to do it. I will not undertake to intimate and insinuate that which, as an honorable man, I am not at liberty to express in the body. If he means to insinuate that I was present at such a debate and sanctioned that doctrine, let him say so. If he is not willing to say it, let him not insinuate that I was present, privately sanctioning a measure that I now publicly am not willing to avow.

Mr. Bigler. If I am constantly at fault in matters of courtesy, it is painful to me. I never have so failed to observe propriety before. Perhaps I have spoken wrongfully on this subject. I have told the senator from Illinois before that I should not in any way attempt to reflect upon him.

Mr. Douglas. I will bring this to a close. I will release the senator from all secrecy, if there is any, and ask if he knows that, directly or indirectly, publicly or privately, any where on the face of the earth, I was ever present at such a consultation, where it was called to my attention, and I agreed to pass it without submission to the people? I now ask him that question, with all secrecy removed.

Mr. Bigler. I shall say distinctly what my recollection is clear about, regardless of any consequences. I remember very well that that question was discussed in the house of the senator. I am not certain that he participated in that discussion, but I know that I did. It was urged—I think more especially by the senator from Georgia [Mr. Toombs], not now in his seat—that, under all the circumstances, there ought not to be a provision inserted requiring the Constitution to be submitted to the people. I do not say that the senator from Illinois participated in the discussion. My recollection is not clear on that point; but it is clear that, in an interview with some three or four members, who were talking about the introduction of that bill, that subject was talked over. I have said that it was always my understanding that that convention would have a right to make a Constitution, and send it here, without submitting it to the people.

Mr. Douglas. I never have insisted that there was a clause in that bill expressly requiring the Constitution to be submitted to the people. The point I have made was, that being silent, it was understood as a matter of course that it was to be submitted. Such a clause was unnecessary. That was the President's construction of the act of the Kansas Legislature. That was my construction of the Toombs Bill. That I may have known there was no such clause is unquestionably true; but that I was a party, either by private conferences at my own house, or otherwise, to a plan to force a Constitution on the people of Kansas without submission, is not true. That the bill was silent on the subject is true, and my attention was called to that about the time it was passed; and I took the fair construction to be, that powers not delegated were reserved, and that, of course, the Constitution would be submitted to the people. The point I made on the senator was that he insinuated that I was a party to such an arrangement privately, which he was not at liberty to tell, and yet he insinuated the very fact that he, as an honorable man, could not tell. If a point of honor has restrained him from telling it, a point of honor should restrain him from insinuating it.

Mr. Bigler. In my anxiety to relieve the feelings of the senator from Illinois, I fear I may have done injustice to myself. Now, sir, I wish to account for the impression which was on my mind, and to make no imputation on him. I had called his attention to the Toombs Bill because it was in derogation of the doctrine he has laid down here to-day. When he says there was no sentiment of that kind declared in the Senate, I say I hold that senator only to the record here—only to the Journal of Debates. What next, sir? I justified myself in what I had said by an allusion to a discussion of that precise question with members of this body. My purpose was to show the senator that I should not have made this allegation without some clear impression on my mind. That impression, I tell the senator from Illinois, was strengthened by other things. It was strengthened by the fact that when he made the preparatory bill for the admission of Minnesota, he provided, in express words, that the Constitution should be submitted. If it is an inference irresistible that a Constitution must be submitted when the enabling act is silent, why insert it in the Minnesota Bill? There it is inserted, and I thought it reasonable—I always believed it—I believed it was wise to put it in that shape, in view of the surroundings in the Territory of Kansas. I do not impugn the senator's integrity, or his patriotism, or his high motive, or his courage, or any thing that pertains to him personally. He has had no more constant admirer than myself—none who has defended him oftener. I thought I was doing justice to myself. On account of what I heard in regard to the Minnesota Bill, I got the impression that unless Congress required the submission of the Constitution to a vote of the people, that course need not be pursued.

Mr. Hale. I rise simply for the purpose of making an inquiry. This matter has been pretty tolerably well elucidated; but the honorable senator from Pennsylvania, if I did not misunderstand him, said that, at a private meeting at the house of the honorable senator from Illinois, there was a talk that, owing to some peculiar circumstances, it was not prudent to submit the Constitution to the people of Kansas. I desire him to state what some of those peculiar circumstances were which rendered it inexpedient and unpatriotic. I have not the slightest controversy with the senator from Illinois on that subject.

Mr. Bigler. The senator from New Hampshire is much more familiar with the surroundings in Kansas than he affects to be to-day.

Mr. Hale. I did not know what you talked of over there.

Mr. Bigler. I had reference (and I think I made that very clear) to the condition of the Territory, the bitter feud that divided the people there, the strife and violence that were likely to interfere with a fair election. I said distinctly that the circumstances rendered a fair exercise of the elective franchise exceedingly difficult. Who has said more on that point than the senator from New Hampshire? Who has talked more about usurpation and violence there, and keeping free-state men from the polls? I had the same impressions then that I have now. In all the votes I gave I was controlled and impelled by nearly the same motive as now, and that was to get Kansas into the Union, whenever she came up in an allowable shape, in order to settle the controversy.

Mr. Douglas. I must ask the senator from Pennsylvania whether he means to intimate that in my house, or any other, these considerations were urged why we should pass the bill without a provision to submit the Constitution to the people? Does he mean to say that I ever was, privately or publicly, in my own house or any other, in favor of a Constitution without its being submitted to the people?

Mr. Bigler. I have made no such allegation.

Mr. Douglas. You have allowed it to be inferred. I do not want a false impression to be inferred because the scene is located in my private parlor. Of what importance is it whether in my house or yours, unless I was a party to an agreement of that kind? If I was, let it be said; if I was not, acquit me of it.

Mr. Bigler. I stated that I had no recollection of the senator participating in that conversation.

Mr. Douglas. Well, if I had nothing to do with it, and was not there, I do not know what my house had to do with it.

Mr. Bigler. What I said was the truth, and that is the only defense I have to make before the Senate, and the country, and my God.

Mr. Douglas's speech was published very extensively. It met a hearty response in the Northwest. An immense mass-meeting was held in Chicago some ten days after, and resolutions of the most unqualified approbation of the doctrines of the speech were enthusiastically adopted. A resolution expressing the "unabated confidence" of the Democracy in Mr. Buchanan's patriotism, and that he would administer the government in accordance with the principles asserted in Mr. Douglas's 9th of December speech, was also adopted. A mass-meeting was also held at Janesville, Wisconsin, on the 30th of December, at which several distinguished men, including the Hon. C. H. Larrabee, now in Congress, took an active part. Meetings were held in almost all the counties of the state, all endorsing Mr. Douglas's course.

On the 10th Mr. Douglas gave notice of a bill to authorize the people of Kansas to form a Constitution, preparatory to their admission into the Union as a state; and on the 19th he introduced said bill, which was referred to the Committee on Territories.

On the 16th, a week after Mr. Douglas's speech on Lecompton, Mr. Allen, of Rhode Island, proposed a list of committees —agreed upon in Democratic caucus. On this list the Committee of Territories was thus named.

Douglas (chairman), Jones (Iowa), Sebastian (Arkansas), Fitzpatrick (Alabama), Green (Missouri), Collamer (Vermont), Wade (Ohio). The list, as proposed, was subsequently adopted, every Democratic senator present having voted for it.

On that same day Mr. Green replied to Mr. Douglas, who rejoined. On the 21st Mr. Bigler made a set speech in reply to Mr. Douglas, who rejoined; and on the 22d Mr. Fitch made a speech in reply to Mr. Douglas, who rejoined. On the 13th of January Mr. Fitch made a personal explanation upon the subject of the resolutions passed by the Indiana Democratic State Convention upon the subject of submitting Constitutions to the people for approval or rejection, and Mr. Douglas rejoined. The debate progressed on the motion to refer the President's message.

On the 2d of February the President transmitted to the Senate the Lecompton Constitution, with a recommendation that Kansas be admitted as a state under it; and on the motion to refer the Constitution and the message to the Committee on Territories, the subject was debated day after day, until the 8th, when the motion to refer was agreed to.

It is not the object or the intention of the writer of this book to go into the details of the Lecompton controversy. In another chapter—that referring to the election in Illinois in 1858, something will be said of the history and events attending that controversy which does not appear on the Congressional record. Another reason is, that the unfortunate and deplorable affair has long since been consigned to a grave from which it is confidently hoped it may never rise again. Those who cherish and preserve the animosities that sprung from it are comparatively few in number, and should be left to the task of nourishing a hatred in which no Democrat has any participation. If the Lecompton question had not served them with a pretext for pursuing Mr. Douglas, they would doubtless have found some other that would have answered their purpose fully as well. We do not speak of those who opposed Mr. Douglas

or denounced his views on Lecompton because of a difference
of opinion upon the question.   Men who differ honestly upon
a question of policy rarely ever indulge in hatred toward those
who oppose them ; but the men who adopted the policy of admitting Kansas under the Lecompton Constitution, not because
they thought it right, but because they wished, on account of
personal griefs, to crush Stephen A. Douglas, when baffled, have
not submitted with a good grace, nor do they relax in their
bitterness toward him.   In these feelings the Democracy, as a
party, have no share, and a charitable consideration for the
weaknesses of poor human nature suggests that the curtain be
dropped upon the sufferings of wounded pride.

The admission of Kansas as a slave state, even against the
ascertained wishes of the people of Kansas, was not asked for
by the South.   It was tendered to the South by a majority
of the Northern Democrats in the executive and legislative
branches of government.   While those Northern Democrats
who did not approve of that policy resisted it, we are not aware
that any of them complained of the South for accepting what
was tendered them by the North.   It was thrust upon them by
the North, and Northern Democrats readily appreciated the
responsibility of Southern men refusing the gift.   On the Lecompton question the Democrats of Illinois had no reproaches
or complaints against the South.   They deprecated the policy
as unjust, as a departure from well-established principles, and
whatever difficulty ensued was a difficulty forced upon them,
not by the South, but by those Northern Democrats who supported Lecompton.   We propose, therefore, to close this branch
of Mr. Douglas's Congressional history by a brief record of
what was done in Congress upon the subject.

On the 11th of January the President sent to Congress the
Constitution of the State of Minnesota, which, on motion of
Mr. Douglas, was referred to the Committee on Territories.
On the 26th he reported a bill for the admission of that state.

On the 18th of February, Mr. Green, as the organ of the
committee, by the direction of a majority of its members, reported a bill for the admission of Kansas into the Union.   Mr.
Douglas made a minority report expressive of his views.   An
additional report, containing an expression of the views of
Messrs. Collamer and Wade, was also made.

On the 1st of March the bill was taken up, Mr. Green entering at large into a discussion of the measure. It was then debated from day to day. On the 15th an attempt was made to force a vote, and the session was protracted until after six o'clock the next morning; but the Senate adjourned without any action on the bill. The debate was continued throughout that week.

On the 23d of March Mr. Crittenden submitted his amendment, subsequently known as the "Crittenden Montgomery" amendment. This proposition substantially provided that Kansas should be admitted as a state into the Union with the Lecompton Constitution; but, as the fact whether the Constitution was fairly made was disputed, the admission of the state was conditional upon that instrument being first submitted to a vote of the people, and assented to by a majority of them. In case the Constitution should be approved, the President was to declare Kansas a state of the Union; in case the Constitution was rejected, the bill authorized the people to elect delegates to a new convention, etc., etc. This amendment was rejected—yeas 24, nays 34. After some amendments in the phraseology of the bill, it was read a third time and passed. The following was the vote on the passage:

Yeas—Allen of Rhode Island, Bayard of Delaware, Benjamin of Louisiana, Biggs of North Carolina, Bigler of Pennsylvania, Bright of Indiana, Brown of Mississippi, Clay of Alabama, Evans of South Carolina, Fitch of Indiana, Fitzpatrick of Alabama, Green of Missouri, Gwin of California, Hammond of South Carolina, Henderson of Texas, Houston of Texas, Hunter of Virginia, Iverson of Georgia, Johnson of Arkansas, Johnson of Tennessee, Jones of Iowa, Kennedy of Maryland, Mallory of Florida, Mason of Virginia, Pearce of Maryland, Polk of Missouri, Sebastian of Arkansas, Slidell of Louisiana, Thompson of Kentucky, Thomson of New Jersey, Toombs of Georgia, Wright of New Jersey, Yulee of Florida—33.

Nays—Bell of Tennessee, Broderick of California, Chandler of Michigan, Clark of New Hampshire, Collamer of Vermont, Crittenden of Kentucky, Dixon of Connecticut, Doolittle of Wisconsin, Douglas of Illinois, Durkee of Wisconsin, Fessenden of Maine, Foot of Vermont, Foster of Connecticut, Hale of New Hampshire, Hamlin of Maine, Harlan of Iowa, King of New York, Pugh of Ohio, Seward of New York, Simmons of Rhode Island, Stuart of Michigan, Sumner of Massachusetts, Trumbull of Illinois, Wade of Ohio, Wilson of Massachusetts—25.

The whole number of senators was 62. Of these, 58 voted as above. Mr. Cameron, of Pennsylvania, had paired off with Mr. Davis, of Mississippi. Mr. Bates, of Delaware, and Mr. Reid, of North Carolina, were both detained from the Senate by illness.

Mr. Douglas had been for some ten days or more confined

to his house and to his bed by severe illness. It was understood that, as the vote would take place on Monday or Tuesday, he would address the Senate upon the bill.

On Monday, March 22d, the Senate met at ten o'clock. From an early hour the galleries and every part of the hall had been crowded. During the forenoon, the antechamber, as well as the passages leading to the Senate or north wing of the Capitol, had been thronged. The Kansas Bill having been taken up, Mr. Stuart, of Michigan, addressed the Senate for three hours; Mr. Bayard, of Delaware, followed; and Mr. Broderick, of California, continued the debate until the hour for taking a recess. Mr. Green then stated that Mr. Douglas would speak at night, and that no vote would be taken till next day. The Senate then adjourned till 7 P.M. During the recess of three hours the crowd held possession of the galleries; many of the ladies present had been there during the entire day. No one who had a seat or even standing-room moved, because to do so was to lose the opportunity so earnestly sought to hear Mr. Douglas. The Senate reassembled at 7 o'clock. At that time it was impossible to approach the entrances to the Senate. When Mr. Douglas entered the chamber he was greeted with a burst of applause from the crowded auditory.

Mr. Gwin at once rose and moved that ladies be admitted to the floor of the Senate, and, no objection being made, the motion was agreed to. Ladies then entered the hall, and occupied such positions, standing or sitting, as they could attain. The members of the House of Representatives were present in large numbers, and filled the aisles. Thus the chamber was filled to its utmost capacity. The pressure in the galleries and upon the stairs was very great, leading several times to great confusion.

Mr. Douglas then addressed the Senate as follows:

Mr. President,—I know not that my strength is sufficient to enable me to present to-night the views which I should like to submit upon the question now under consideration. My sickness for the last two weeks has deprived me of the pleasure of listening to the debates, and of an opportunity of reading the speeches that have been made; hence I shall not be able to perform the duty which might naturally have been expected of me, of replying to any criticisms that may have been presented upon my course, or upon my speeches, or upon my report. I must content myself with presenting my views upon the questions that are naturally brought up by the bill under consideration. I trust, however, that I may be pardoned for referring briefly, in the first instance, to my course upon the Slavery question during the period that I have had a seat in the two houses of Congress.

When I entered Congress in 1843, I found upon the statute-book the evidence of a policy to adjust the Slavery question and avoid sectional agitation by a geographical line drawn across the continent, separating free territory from slave territory. That policy had its origin at the beginning of this government, and had prevailed up to that time. In 1787, while the convention was in session forming the Constitution of the United States, the Congress of the Confederation adopted the ordinance of 1787, prohibiting slavery in all the territory northwest of the Ohio River. The first Congress that assembled under the Constitution extended all the provisions of that ordinance, with the exception of the clause prohibiting slavery, to the territory south of that river, thus making the Ohio River the dividing line between free territory and slave territory, free labor and slave labor.

Subsequently, after the acquisition of Louisiana, when Missouri, a portion of that territory, applied for admission into the Union as a state, the same policy was carried out by adopting the parallel of 36° 30' north latitude, from the western border of Missouri, as far westward as our territory then extended, as the barrier between free territory upon the one side and slave territory upon the other.

Thus the question stood when I first entered the Congress of the United States. I examined the question when the proposition was made for the annexation of Texas in 1845, and, though I was unable to vindicate the policy of a geographical line upon sound political principles, still, finding that it had been in existence from the beginning of the government, had been acquiesced in up to that time by the North and by the South, and that it had its origin in patriotic motives, I was anxious to abide by and perpetuate that policy rather than open the slavery agitation, and create sectional strife and heart-burning by attempting to restore the government to those great principles which seemed to me to be more consistent with the right of self-government, upon which our institutions rest. For this reason I cordially acquiesced, in 1845, in the insertion into the resolutions for the annexation of Texas of a clause extending the Missouri Compromise line through the Republic of Texas so far westward as the new acquisition might reach. I not only acquiesced in and supported the measure then, but I did it with the avowed purpose of continuing that line to the Pacific Ocean so soon as we should acquire the territory. Accordingly, in 1848, when we had acquired New Mexico, Utah, and California from the Republic of Mexico, and the question arose in this body in regard to the kind of government which should be established therein, the Senate, on my motion, adopted a proposition to extend the Missouri Compromise line to the Pacific Ocean, with the same understanding with which it was originally adopted. The Journal of the Senate contains the following entry of that proposition:

"On motion of Mr. Douglas to amend the bill, section fourteen, line one, by inserting after the word 'enacted:' 'That the line of 36° 30' of north latitude, known as the Missouri Compromise line, as defined by the eighth section of an act entitled "An Act to authorize the People of the Missouri Territory to form a Constitution and State Government, and for the Admission of said State into the Union on an equality with the original States, and to prohibit Slavery in certain Territories," approved March 6, 1820, be, and the same is hereby declared to extend to the Pacific Ocean, and the said eighth section, together with the compromise therein effected, is hereby revived, and declared to be in full force and binding for the future organization of the Territories of the United States, in the same sense and with the same understanding with which it was originally adopted.'

"It was determined in the affirmative—yeas 32, nays 21.

"On motion of Mr. Baldwin, the yeas and nays being desired by one fifth of the senators present,

"Those who voted in the affirmative are Messrs. Atchison, Badger, Bell, Benton, Berrien, Borland, Bright, Butler, Calhoun, Cameron, Davis of Mississippi, Dickinson, Douglas, Downs, Fitzgerald, Foote, Hannegan, Houston, Hunter, Johnson of Maryland, Johnson of Louisiana, Johnson of Georgia, King, Lewis, Mangum, Mason, Metcalfe, Pearce, Sebastian, Spruance, Sturgeon, Turney, and Underwood.

"Those who voted in the negative are Messrs. Allen, Atherton, Baldwin, Bradbury, Breese, Clarke, Corwin, Davis of Massachusetts, Dayton, Dix, Dodge, Felch, Green, Hale, Hamlin, Miller, Niles, Phelps, Upham, Walker, and Webster.

"So the proposed amendment was agreed to."

Thus it will be seen that the proposition offered by me to extend the Missouri Compromise line to the Pacific Ocean in the same sense and with the same understanding with which it was originally adopted, was agreed to by the Senate by a majority of twelve. When the bill was sent to the House of Representatives, that provision was stricken out, I think, by thirty-nine majority. By that vote the policy of separating free territory from slave territory by a geographical line was abandoned by the Congress of the United States. It is not my purpose on this occasion to inquire whether the policy was right or wrong; whether its abandonment at that time was wise or unwise; that is a question long since consigned to history, and I leave it to that tribunal to determine. I only refer to it now for the purpose of showing the view which I then took of the question. It will be seen, by reference to the votes in the Senate and House of Representatives, that Southern men in a body voted for the extension of the Missouri Compromise line, and a very large majority of the Northern men voted against it. The argument then made against the policy of a geographical line was one which upon principle it was difficult to answer. It was urged that if slavery was wrong north of the line, it could not be right south of the line; that if it was unwise, impolitic, and injurious on the one side, it could not be wise, politic, and judicious upon the other; that if the people should be left to decide the question for themselves on the one side, they should be entitled to the same privilege on the other. I thought these arguments were difficult to answer upon principle. The only answer urged was, that the policy had its origin in patriotic motives, in fraternal feeling, in that brotherly affection which ought to animate all the citizens of a common country; and that, for the sake of peace, and harmony, and concord, we ought to adhere to and preserve that policy. Under these considerations, I not only voted for it, but moved it, and lamented as much as any man in the country its failure, because that failure precipitated us into a sectional strife and agitation, the like of which had never before been witnessed in the United States, and which alarmed the wisest, the purest, and the best patriots in the land for the safety of the republic.

You all recollect the agitation which raged through this land from 1848 to 1850, and which was only quieted by the compromise measures of the latter year. You all remember how the venerable sage and patriot of Ashland was called forth from his retirement for the sole purpose of being able to contribute, by his wisdom, by his patriotism, by his experience, by the weight of his authority, something to calm the troubled waters and restore peace and harmony to a distracted country. That contest waged fiercely, almost savagely, threatening the peace and existence of the Union, until at last, by the wise counsels of a Clay, a Webster, and a Cass, and the other leading spirits of the country, a new plan of conciliation and settlement was agreed upon, which again restored peace to the Union. The policy of a geographical line separating free territory from slave territory was abandoned by its friends only because they found themselves without the power to adhere to it, and carry it into effect in good faith. If that policy had been continued, if the Missouri line had been extended to the Pacific Ocean, there would have been an end to the slavery agitation forever—for on one side, as far west as the Continent extended, slavery would have been prohibited, while on the other, by legal implication, it would have been taken for granted that the institution of slavery would have existed and continued, and emigration would have sought the one side of the line or the other, as it preferred the one or the other class of domestic and social institutions. I confess, sir, that it was my opinion then, and is my opinion now, that the extension of that line would have been favorable to the South, so far as any sectional advantage would have been obtained, if it be an advantage to any section to extend its peculiar institutions. Southern men seemed so to consider it, for they voted almost unanimously in favor of that policy prohibiting slavery on one side, contented with a silent implication in its favor on the other. Northern representatives and senators seemed to take the same view of the subject, for a large majority of them voted against this geographical policy, and in lieu of it insisted upon a law prohibiting slavery every where within the Territories of the United States, north as well as south of the line; and not only in the Territories, but in the dock-yards, the navy-yards, and all other public places over which the Congress of the United States had exclusive jurisdiction.

Such, sir, was the state of public opinion, as evidenced by the acts of representatives and senators on the question of a geographical line by the extension of the Missouri Compromise, as it is called, from 1848 to 1850, which caused it to be abandoned, and the compromise measures of 1850 to be substituted in its place. Those measures are familiar to the Senate and to the country. They are predicated upon the abandonment of a geographical line, and upon the great principle of self-government in the Territories, and the sovereignty of the states over the question of slavery, as well as over all other matters of local and domestic concern. Inasmuch as the time-honored and venerated policy of a geographical line had been abandoned, the great leaders of the Senate, and the great commoners in the other House of Congress, saw no other remedy but to return to the true principles of the Constitution—to those great principles of self-government and popular sovereignty upon which all free institutions rest, and to leave the people of the Territories and of the states free to decide the Slavery question, as well as all other questions, themselves.

Mr. President, I am one of those who concurred cheerfully and heartily in this new line of policy marked out by the compromise measures of 1850. Having been compelled to abandon the former policy of a geographical line, for want of ability to carry it out, I joined with the great patriots to whom I have alluded to calm and quiet the country by the adoption of a policy more congenial to my views of free institutions, not only for the purpose of healing and harmonizing the strife and controversy which then existed, but for the farther purpose of providing a rule of action in all time to come which would avoid sectional strife and sectional controversy in the future. It was one of the great merits of the compromise measures of 1850—indeed, it was their chief merit—that they furnished a principle, a rule of action which should apply every where—north and south of 36° 30'—not only to the territory which we then had, but to all that we might afterward acquire, and thus, if that principle was adhered to, prevent any strife, any controversy, any sectional agitation in the future. The object was to localize, not to nationalize, the controversy in regard to slavery; to make it a question for each state and each Territory to decide for itself, without any other state, or any other Territory, or the federal government, or any outside power interfering, directly or indirectly, to influence or control the result.

My course upon those measures created at first great excitement, and I may say great indignation, at my own home, so that it became necessary for me to go before the people and vindicate my action. I made a speech at Chicago upon my return home, in which I stated the principles of the compromise measures of 1850 as I have now stated them here, and vindicated them to the best of my ability. It is enough to say that, upon sober reflection, the people of Illinois approved the course which I then pursued; and when the Legislature came together, they passed, with great unanimity, resolutions endorsing emphatically the principle of those measures.

In 1854, when it became necessary to organize the Territories of Kansas and Nebraska, the question arose, What principle was to apply to those Territories? It was true they both lay north of the line of 36° 30'; but it was also true that, four years before, the policy of a geographical line had been abandoned and repudiated by the Congress of the United States, and in lieu of it the plan of leaving each Territory free to decide the question for itself had been adopted. I felt it to be my duty, as a senator from the State of Illinois, and I will say as a member of the Democratic party, to adhere in good faith to the principles of the compromise measures of 1850, and to apply them to Kansas and Nebraska, as well as to the other Territories. To show that I was bound to pursue this course, it is only necessary to refer to the public incidents of those times. In the presidential election of 1852, the great political parties of that day each nominated its candidate for the presidency upon a platform which endorsed the compromise measures of 1850, and both pledged themselves to carry them out in good faith in all future times in the organization of all new Territories. The Whig party adopted that platform at Baltimore, and placed General Scott, their candidate, upon it. The Democratic party adopted a platform identical in principles, so far as this question was concerned, and elected General Pierce President of the United States upon it. Thus the Whig party and the Democratic party each stood pledged to apply this principle in the organization of all new Territories. Not only was I as a Democrat—as a senator who voted for their adoption— bound to apply their principle to this case, but, as a senator from Illinois, I was under an imperative obligation, if I desired to obey the will and carry out the wishes of my constituents, to apply the same principle. To show the views of my Legislature upon that subject, I will read one resolution, which was passed at the session of 1851:

"*Resolved*, That our liberty and independence are based upon the right of the people to form for themselves such a government as they may choose; that this great privilege, the birthright of freemen, the gift of Heaven, secured to us by the blood of our ancestors, ought to be extended to future generations; and that no limitation ought to be applied to this power in the organization of any Territory of the United States, of either a Territorial government or a state Constitution: *Provided*, The government so established shall be republican, and in conformity with the Constitution."

That resolution was adopted by a vote of sixty-one in the affirmative and only four in the negative. I undertake to say that resolution spoke the sentiments of the people of Illinois; and I, as their senator, was only carrying out their sentiments and wishes by applying this principle to the Territories of Kansas and Nebraska. This principle was applied in that bill in the precise language of the compromise measures of 1850, except the addition of a clause removing from the statute-book the eighth section of the Missouri Act, as being inconsistent with that principle, and declaring that it was the true intent and meaning of the act not to legislate slavery into any Territory or state, nor to exclude it therefrom, but to leave the people thereof perfectly free to form and regulate their domestic institutions in their own way, subject only to the Constitution of the United States.

Now, sir, the question arises whether the Lecompton Constitution, which has been presented here for our acceptance, is in accordance with this principle embodied in the compromise measures, and clearly defined in the organic act of Kansas. Have the people of Kansas been left perfectly free to form and regulate their domestic institutions in their own way, subject only to the Constitution? Is the Lecompton Constitution the act and deed of the people of Kansas? Does it embody their will? If not, you have no constitutional right to impose it upon them. If it does embody their will, if it is their act and deed, you have, then, a right to waive any irregularities that may have occurred, and receive the state into the Union. This is the main point, in my estimation, upon which the vote of the Senate and the House of Representatives ought to depend in the decision of the Kansas question. Now, is there a man within the hearing of my voice who believes that the Lecompton Constitution does embody the will of a majority of the *bona fide* inhabitants of Kansas? Where is the evidence that it does embody that will?

We are told that it was made by a convention assembled at Lecompton in September last, and has been submitted to the people for ratification or rejection. How submitted? In a manner that allowed every man to vote for it, but precluded the possibility of any man voting against it. We are told that there is a majority of about five thousand five hundred votes recorded in its favor under these circumstances. I refrain from going into the evidence which has been taken before the commission recently held in Kansas to show what proportion of these votes were fraudulent; but, supposing them all to have been legal, *bona fide* residents, what does that fact prove, when the people on that occasion were allowed only to vote for, and could not vote against, the Constitution? On the other hand, we have a vote of the people in pursuance of law, on the 4th of January last, when this Constitution was submitted by the Legislature to the people for acceptance or rejection, showing a majority of more than ten thousand against it. If you grant that both these elections were valid, if you grant that the votes were legal and fair, yet the majority is about two to one against this Constitution. Here is evidence to my mind conclusive that this Lecompton Constitution is not the embodiment of the popular will of Kansas. How is this evidence to be rebutted? By the assumption that the election on the 21st of December, where the voters were allowed to vote for it, but not against it, was a legal election; and that the election of the 4th of January, where the people were allowed to vote for or against the Constitution as they chose, was not a legal and valid election.

Sir, where do you find your evidence of the legality of the election of the 21st of December? Under what law was that election held? Under no law except the decree of the Lecompton Convention. Did that convention possess legislative power? Did it possess any authority to prescribe an election law? That convention possessed only such power as it derived from the Territorial Legislature in the act authorizing the assembling of the convention; and I submit that the same authority, the same power, existed in the Territorial Legislature to order an election on the 4th of January as existed in the convention to order one on the 21st of December. The Legislature had the same power over the whole subject on the 17th of December, when it passed a law for the submission of the Constitution to the people, that it had on the 19th of February, when it enacted the statute for the assembling of the convention.

The convention assembled under the authority of the Territorial Legislature alone, and hence was bound to conduct all its proceedings in conformity with, and in subordination to, the authority of the Legislature. The moment the convention attempted to put its Constitution into operation against the authority of the Territorial Legislature, it committed an act of rebellion against the government of the United States. But we are told by the President that at the time the Territorial Legislature passed the law submitting the whole Constitution to the people, the Territory had been prepared for admission into the Union as a state. How prepared? By what authority prepared? Not by the authority of any act of Congress—by no other authority than that of the Territorial Legislature; and clearly a convention assembled under that authority could do no act to subvert the Territorial Legislature which brought the convention into existence.

But gentlemen assume that the organic act of the Territory was an enabling act; that it delegated to the Legislature all the power that Congress had to authorize the assembling of a convention. Although I dissent from this doctrine, I am willing, for the sake of the argument, to assume it to be correct; and if it be correct, to what conclusion does it lead us? It only substitutes the Territorial Legislature for the authority of Congress, and gives validity to the convention; and therefore the Legislature would have just the same right that Congress otherwise would have had, and no more, and no less. Suppose, now, that Congress had passed an enabling act, and a convention had been called, and a Constitution framed under it; but three days before that Constitution was to take effect, Congress should pass another act repealing the convention law, and submitting the Constitution to the vote of the people: would it be denied that the act of Congress submitting the Constitution would be a valid act? If Congress would have authority thus to interpose, and submit the Constitution to the vote of the people, it clearly follows that if the Legislature stood in the place of Congress, and was vested with the power which Congress had on the subject, it had the same right to interpose, and submit this Constitution to the people for ratification or rejection.

Therefore, sir, if you judge this Constitution by the technical rules of law, it was voted down by an overwhelming majority of the people of Kansas, and it became null and void; and you are called upon now to give vitality to a void, rejected, repudiated Constitution. If, however, you set aside the technicalities of law, and approach it in the spirit of statesmanship, in the spirit of justice and of fairness, with an eye single to ascertain what is the wish and the will of that people, you are forced to the conclusion that the Lecompton Constitution does not embody that will.

Sir, we have heard the argument over and over again that the Lecompton Convention were justified in withholding this Constitution from submission to the people, for the reason that it would have been voted down if it had been submitted to the people for ratification or rejection. We are told that there was a large majority of free-state men in the Territory, who would have voted down the Constitution if they had got a chance, and that is the excuse for not allowing the people to vote upon it. That is an admission that this Constitution is not the act and deed of the people of Kansas; that it does not embody their will; and yet you are called upon to give it force and vitality; to make it the fundamental law of Kansas with a knowledge that it is not the will of the people, and misrepresents their wishes. I ask you, sir, where is your right, under our principles of government, to force a Constitution upon an unwilling people? You may resort to all the evidence that you can obtain, from every source that you please, and you are driven to the same conclusion. (The confusion created by the large number of persons in the galleries endeavoring to find places where they could see and hear, and others pressing in, was so great that the honorable senator could hardly make himself heard.)

Mr. Stuart. I am aware of the very great difficulty of preserving order; but still I think that, by a suggestion from the chair, gentlemen in the galleries and about the lobbies would do it. They can do it if they will The honorable senator from Illinois speaks with difficulty, at any rate, and I hope there will be sufficient order preserved that he may be heard.

The Vice-President. The chair has observed a good deal of disorder about the central door of the main gallery. It is quite obvious that there are as many persons there as can stand now, and therefore it would be well for gentlemen not to press in. They are respectfully requested to preserve order and decorum.

Mr. Douglas. If further evidence was necessary to show that the Lecompton Constitution is not the will of the people of Kansas, you find it in the action of the Legislature of that Territory. On the first Monday in October an election took place for members of the Territorial Legislature. It was a severe struggle between the two great parties in the Territory. On a fair test, and at the fairest election, as is recorded on all hands, ever held in the Territory, a Legislature was elected. That Legislature came together and remonstrated, by an overwhelming majority, against this Constitution, as not being the act and deed of that people, and not embodying their will. Ask the late governor of the Territory, and he will tell you that it is a mockery to call this the act and deed of the people. Ask the secretary of the Territory, ex-Governor Stanton, and he will tell you the same thing. I will hazard the prediction, that if you ask Governor Denver to-day, he will tell you, if he answers at all, that it is a mockery, nay, a crime, to attempt to enforce this Constitution as an embodiment of the will of that people. Ask, then, your official agents in the Territory; ask the Legislature elected by the people at the last election; consult the poll-books on a fair election held in pursuance of law; consult private citizens from there; consult whatever sources of information you please, and you get the same answer—that this Constitution does not embody the public will, is not the act and deed of the people, does not represent their wishes; and hence I deny your right, your authority, to make it their organic law. If the Lecompton Constitution ever becomes the organic law of the State of Kansas, it will be the act of Congress that makes it so, and not the act or will of the people of Kansas.

But we are told that it is a matter of but small moment whether the Constitution embodies the public will or not, because it can be modified and changed by the people of Kansas at any time as soon as they are admitted into the Union. Sir, it matters not whether it can be changed or can not be changed, so far as the principle involved is concerned. It matters not whether this Constitution is to be the permanent fundamental law of Kansas, or is to last only a day, or a month, or a year; because, if it is not their act and deed, you have no right to force it upon them for a single day. If you have the power to force it upon this people for one day, you may do it for a year, for ten years, or permanently. The principle involved is the same. It is as much a violation of fundamental principle, a violation of popular sovereignty, a violation of the Constitution of the United States, to force a state Constitution on an unwilling people for a day, as it is for a year or for a longer time. When you set the example of violating the fundamental principles of free government, even for a short period, you have made a precedent that will enable unscrupulous men in future times, under high partisan excitement, to subvert all the other great principles upon which our institutions rest.

But, sir, is it true that this Constitution may be changed immediately by the people of Kansas? The President of the United States tells us that the people can make and unmake Constitutions at pleasure; that the people have no right to tie their own hands and prohibit a change of the Constitution until 1864, or any other period; that the right of change always exists, and that the change may be made by the people at any time in their own way, at pleasure, by the consent of the Legislature. I do not agree that the people can not tie their own hands. I hold that a Constitution is a social compact between all the people of the state that adopts it ; between each man in the state, and every other man ; binding upon them all ; and they have a right to say it shall only be changed at a particular time and in a particular manner, and then only after such and such periods of deliberation. Not only have they a right to do this, but it is wise that the fundamental law should have some stability, some permanency, and not be liable to fluctuation and change by every ebullition of passion.

This Constitution provides that after the year 1864 it may be changed by the Legislature by a two thirds vote of each House, submitting to the people the question whether they will hold a convention for the purpose of amending the Constitution. I hold that, when a Constitution provides one time of change, by every rule of interpretation it excludes all other times ; and when it prescribes one mode of change, it excludes all other modes. I hold that it is the fair intendment and interpretation of this Constitution that it is not to be changed until after the year 1864, and then only in the manner prescribed in the instrument. If it were true that this Constitution was the act and deed of the people of Kansas—if it were true that it embodied their will —I hold that such a provision against change for a sufficient length of time to enable the people to test its practical workings would be a wise provision, and not liable to objection. That people are not capable of self-government who can not make a Constitution under which they are willing to live for a period of six years without change. I do not object that this Constitution can not be changed until after 1864, provided you show me that it be the act and deed of the people, and embodies their will now. If it be not their act and deed, you have no right to fix it upon them for a day—not for an hour —not for an instant ; for it is a violation of the great principle of free government to force it upon them.

The President of the United States tells us that he sees no objection to inserting a clause in the act of admission declaratory of the right of the people of Kansas, with the consent of the first Legislature, to change this Constitution, notwithstanding the provision which it contains that it shall not be changed until after the year 1864. Where does Congress get power to intervene and change a provision in the Constitution of a state ? If this Constitution declares, as I insist it does, that it shall not be changed until after 1864, what right has Congress to intervene, to alter, or annul that provision prohibiting alteration ? If you can annul one provision, you may another, and another, and another, until you have destroyed the entire instrument. I deny your right to annul ; I deny your right to change, or even to construe the meaning of a single clause of this Constitution. If it be the act and deed of the people of Kansas, and becomes their fundamental law, it is sacred ; you have no right to touch it, no right to construe it, no right to determine its meaning ; it is theirs, not yours. You must take it as it is, or reject it as a whole ; but put not your sacrilegious hands upon the instrument if it be their act and deed. Whenever this government undertakes to construe state Constitutions and to recognize the right of the people of a state to act in a different manner from that provided in their Constitution ; whenever it undertakes to give a meaning to a clause of a state Constitution, which that state has not given ; whenever it undertakes to do that, and its right is acknowledged, farewell to state rights, farewell to state sovereignty ; your states become mere provinces, dependencies, with no more independence and no more rights than the counties of the different states. This doctrine, that Congress may intervene, and annul, construe, or change a clause in a state Constitution,, subverts the fundamental principles upon which our complex system of government rests.

Upon this point, the Committee on Territories, in the majority report, find themselves constrained to dissent from the doctrine of the President. They see no necessity, and, if I understand the report, no legal authority on the part of Congress to intervene and construe this or any other provision of the Constitution; but the distinguished gentleman who makes the report from the Committee on Territories has, in his own estimation, obviated all objection by finding a clause in the Constitution of Kansas which he thinks remedies the whole evil. It is in the Bill of Rights, and is in these words:

"All political power is inherent in the people, and all free governments are founded on their authority, and instituted for their benefit; and, therefore, they have at all times an inalienable and indefeasible right to alter, reform, or abolish their form of government in such a manner as they may think proper."

The Vice President. The senator from Illinois will pause for a moment. The sergeant-at-arms will go up and close the centre door of the ladies' gallery; shut it, and keep it shut, so as to admit no more persons there.

Mr. Douglas. There appears to be some difficulty at the southern door of the eastern gallery, and I hope the chair will direct that to be closed.

The Vice President. The chair has sent an officer to that door to close it, and preserve quiet there. The senator from Illinois will proceed.

Mr. Douglas. The senator from Missouri, who makes the report of the majority of the committee, is under the impression that this clause in the Bill of Rights overrides and changes the provision in the Lecompton Constitution, which declares that there shall be no change until after 1864, and then only by a two thirds vote of the Legislature. How does he make that override the prohibition? By taking the clause in the Bill of Rights which is intended only to assert abstract rights that may be exercised by the people when driven to the last resort, to wit, to revolution. That is an abstract principle, intended to assert the right in the people of Kansas to change their form of government under the same law, the same authority that our ancestors resisted British power, and overthrew the British authority upon this continent. It was under that principle that our fathers burnt up the stamps, and sent the stamp agents out of the country. It was under that principle that our fathers resorted to arms to maintain the right to change their form of government from a monarchy to a republic—change by revolution, because they arrived at the point where resistance was a less evil than submission. That the people have a right to appeal to the God of arms to overthrow the power that oppresses them, and change their form of government whenever their oppressions are intolerable, and resistance is a less evil than submission, is a great truth that no Republican, no Democrat, no citizen of a free country should ever question. But, sir, that clause was never intended to furnish the lawful mode by which this Constitution could be changed, for the reason that the same instrument points out a different mode than the one therein asserted; and when a specific mode is prescribed, and time is to elapse before that mode can be resorted to, that excludes the idea that it can be done in any other mode, or at a prior time.

But, sir, this article from the Bill of Rights proves entirely too much. The President says you may put into this bill a clause recognizing the right of the people of Kansas to change their Constitution by the consent of the first Legislature. What does the Bill of Rights say? That it is the inalienable and indefeasible right of the people, at all times, to alter, abolish, or reform their form of government in such manner as they may think proper, not in such manner as the Legislature shall prescribe, nor at such time as the legislative authority or the existing government may provide, but in such manner as the people think proper in town meeting, in convention, through the Legislature, in popular assemblages, at the point of the bayonet, in any manner the people themselves may determine. That is the right and the nature of the right authorized by this Bill of Rights. It is the revolutionary remedy, not the lawful mode. There are two modes of changing the Constitution of a state—one lawful, the other revolutionary. The lawful mode is the one prescribed in the instrument. The revolutionary mode is one in violation of the instrument. The revolutionary mode may be peaceful or may be forcible; that depends on whether there is resistance. If a people are unanimous in favor of a change, if nobody opposes it, the revolutionary means may be a peaceful remedy; but if, in the progress of the revolution, while you are making the change, you meet with resistance, then it becomes civil war, treason, rebellion, if you fail, and a successful revolution if you succeed.

I say, then, the mode pointed out in the Bill of Rights is the revolutionary mode, and not the lawful means provided in the instrument; but if the Committee on Territories be right in saying that this is a lawful mode, then the recommendation of the President, that Congress should recognize the right to do it by the first Legislature, violates this Constitution. Why? The President recommends us to recognize their rights through the Legislature, and in that mode alone. The Bill of Rights says the people shall do it in such manner as they please. If the construction given by the Committee on Territories be right, you dare not vote for the President's proposition to recognize the right of the first Legislature to do it, for you give a construction to the instrument in violation of its terms.

Mr. Hammond. Will the senator from Illinois allow me to interrupt him a moment?

Mr. Douglas. With a great deal of pleasure.

Mr. Hammond. I understood the senator to say just now that Congress had no right to look into the Constitution of a state and place a construction upon it. If that be true, I would inquire of the senator from Illinois how is Congress to know whether a Constitution is republican or not? If it be true, I would inquire of him, further, why is he here now discussing and placing a construction upon the Constitution of Kansas?

Mr. Douglas. I will take great pleasure in answering the gentleman from South Carolina. I have a right to look into this Constitution to see whether, in my opinion, it is republican. I have this right to look at it only for the purpose of regulating my vote. The judgment on which I base my vote is one binding on nobody but myself. I am talking now, not on forming a construction by which members of Congress are to govern themselves, but I am speaking of your right to place a construction upon this Constitution binding upon the people and government of Kansas. Give me the power to construe the Constitution of Kansas authoritatively, and then I have the power to change it, to alter it, to annul it, to make it mean what I please, and not what they mean.

Mr. Hammond. I should have thought that the senator would have denounced the attempt to construe the Constitution, and left the matter there, after having asserted that no such power exists; but when he goes on to construe it himself, he is inconsistent with his first proposition that there is no right to construe it.

Mr. Douglas. No, sir; I deny the right of Congress to construe it authoritatively for the people of Kansas. I am not denying the right of the senator from South Carolina to put his own construction upon it. I am not denying the right of each senator here to make up his own mind in regard to it. It is the duty of each senator here to do that for himself; but that is only to satisfy his own judgment and his own conscience in regulating his vote upon the question. The point I am arguing is whether this Congress has any power, by a rule of construction, to change the Constitution of a state, and make its construction binding on the authorities and people of that state. I repeat, if this Congress can exercise that power, there is an end of state rights, an end of state sovereignty; this government becomes a consolidated government, an empire, a central power, with provinces and dependencies, and ceases to be a confederation of sovereign and independent states. I am arguing against the propriety of Congress acceding to the recommendation of the President to strike that fatal blow at the sovereignty of the states of this Union.

But, sir, my friend from Ohio, who can not accede quite to this doctrine of the President any more than the Committee on Territories can, proposes to remedy this matter in a different way. He has offered an amendment, which I ask the clerk to read.

The clerk read the following amendment, intended to be proposed by Mr. Pugh, to the amendment intended to be proposed by Mr. Green to the bill (S., N. 161) "for the admission of the State of Kansas into the Union: At the end thereof add the following section:

"Sec. —. *And be it further enacted*, That the admission of the States of Minnesota and Kansas into the Union, by this act, shall never be so construed as to deny, limit, or otherwise impair the right of the people of the said states, with the assent of their Legislatures, severally, at all times, to alter, reform, or abolish their form of government, in such manner as they may think proper, so that the same be still republican and in accordance with the Constitution of the United States."

Mr. Douglas. I am at a loss to know what object my friend from Ohio expects to accomplish by this proviso, that nothing in the act of admission shall be construed to deny, limit, or otherwise impair the right of the people to change their Constitution. Who ever dreamed that there was any thing in the act of admission which could be so construed? It is not the act of admission to which we are alluding; it is the provision in this Constitution which says it shall not be changed until after 1864.

Nobody pretends that you can put any thing in the act of admission which would limit this right. What I am denying is your right to put any thing in the act of admission either to limit, or extend, or construe the Constitution. Nobody pretends that this act of admission affects this point at all. The objection, if it be an objection, is in the Constitution itself, not in the act of admission.

Then what legal effect would the amendment of the senator from Ohio have if it should be adopted? I presume no one pretends that it would have any legal effect. Is there a senator here who pretends that the adoption of the amendment of the senator from Ohio would confer any power or authority on the people of Kansas to change their Constitution which they would not have without it? I am informed the senator from Ohio said, in his speech in explanation of it, that it did not confer any right which the people would not otherwise have. Then why adopt it? I can conceive of but one motive, and that is to lead the people to infer that they have secured a right by that proviso which they really have not got—to lead them to suppose that they have gained an advantage which in reality they do not possess. Is that the object? Is it the object to obviate an objection, and yet, in fact, to leave the objection in full force? Why, I ask, is it proposed to put that amendment in the bill if it has no legitimate effect—if it does not give the people any right, any privilege, which they would not possess without it? Perhaps I may be asked, on the contrary, what is the objection to putting it in? It may be said it is only the expression of the individual opinion of the members of Congress. I will tell you my objection to putting this clause in the act of admission. I object to inserting any clause in the act of admission that expresses any opinion, one way or the other, in respect to the propriety of any provision in the Constitution. If you may pronounce judgment on the propriety of one clause, although it has no legal effect to change it, you may on the propriety of another clause. Suppose, for instance, the senator from

New York should offer an amendment that nothing contained in this act of admission shall be construed to sanction or tolerate the right to hold property in man; or that nothing herein contained shall be construed to authorize or permit slaveholding in said state; or should propose to insert an opinion that slaveholding was a crime; would Southern men think there was no objection to it because it had no legal effect? Are you willing that Congress shall set the example of inserting, in acts of admission, clauses that pronounce judgment against the domestic institutions of a state? Are you willing that a Congress composed of a majority of free-state men shall put clauses in an act of admission condemning slaveholding? Or, if we were a minority, would we be willing that you should put a clause in an act of admission condemning our free institutions?

Now, sir, I hold that Congress has no right to pronounce its opinion even upon the propriety of any local or domestic institution of any state of this Union. Each state is sovereign, with the unlimited and unrestricted power and right to manage its local and internal concerns to suit itself, subject only to the limitations of the Constitution of the United States. I warn gentlemen that when, in order to catch a little popular favor, they set the example of backing up a vote in favor of this enormous fraud by putting a clause in the bill having no legal effect, but expressing opinions upon the propriety of this or that clause of a state Constitution, they are setting an example that may return upon them in a way that will not be pleasant. I protest against Congress interfering either to annul or construe, or express opinions upon the propriety of this clause or that clause of the Constitution. I repeat, if the Constitution be the act and deed of the people of Kansas, and if its provisions are not in violation of the Constitution of the United States, that people had a right to put them there, and you have no right to touch them or to pronounce judgment upon them.

Mr. President, I come back to the question, Ought we to receive Kansas into the Union with the Lecompton Constitution? Is there satisfactory evidence that it is the act and deed of that people—that it embodies their will? Is the evidence satisfactory that the people of that Territory have been left perfectly free to form and regulate their domestic institutions in their own way? I think not. I do not acknowledge the propriety, or justice, or force of that special pleading which attempts, by technicalities, to fasten a Constitution upon a people which, it is admitted, they would have voted down if they had had a chance to do so, and which does not embody their will. Let me ask gentlemen from the South, if the case had been reversed, would they have taken the same view of the subject? Suppose it were ascertained, beyond doubt or cavil, that three fourths of the people of Kansas were in favor of a slaveholding state, and a convention had been assembled by just such means and under just such circumstances as brought the Lecompton Convention together; and suppose that when it assembled it was ascertained that three fourths of the convention were Free-soilers, while three fourths of the people were in favor of a slaveholding state; suppose an election took place in the Territory during the sitting of the convention, which developed the fact that the convention did not represent the people; suppose that convention of Free-soilers had proceeded to make a Constitution and allowed the people to vote for it, but not against it, and thus forced a Free-soil Constitution upon a slaveholding people against their will—would you, gentlemen from the South, have submitted to the outrage? Would you have come up here and demanded that the Free-soil Constitution, adopted at an election where all the affirmative votes were received, and all the negative votes rejected, for the reason that it would have been voted down if the negative votes had been received, should be accepted? Would you have said that it was fair, that it was honest, to force an Abolition Constitution on a slaveholding people against their will? Would you not have come forward and have said to us that you denied that it was the embodiment of the public will, and demanded that it should be sent back to the people to be voted upon, so as to ascertain the fact? Would you not have said to us that you were willing to live up to the principle of the Nebraska Bill, to leave the people perfectly free to form such institutions as they please; and that, if we would only send that Constitution back and let the people have a fair vote upon it, you would abide the result? Suppose we, being a Northern majority, had said to you, "No; we have secured a sectional advantage, and we intend to hold it; and we will force this Constitution upon an unwilling people merely because we have the power to do it;" would you have said that was fair?

Mr. Hammond. Will the senator allow me to answer him?

Mr. Douglas. Certainly.

Mr. Hammond. As the senator looked toward me in asking his question, I will undertake, though without authority, to answer for the slaveholding community. If, having had the power to establish a slaveholding Constitution, we had refrained from exercising it, and those in favor of a free-state Constitution had established one to that effect, I say that the slaveholders would have submitted to it until, through the forms of constitutional law, they could have altered it.

Mr. Douglas. The senator assumes what I did not certainly intend when he says that I looked at him. I was propounding the question, however, to any senator, and am as willing that the senator from South Carolina should reply as any other. He assumes as true, for the purposes of his answer, the very fact that is denied—that they had the power.

Mr. Hammond. Asserted on all hands, sir.

Mr. Douglas. What?

Mr. Hammond. Asserted that there was a free-state majority when the convention was elected.

Mr. Brown. The senator from Illinois asserted it to-night.

Mr. Douglas. Yes; and I assert now that there was a free-state majority; and I assert, also, that one half the counties of the Territory were disfranchised, and not allowed to vote at the election of delegates. (Applause in the galleries.)

Mr. Hammond. That has been answered over and over again—

The Vice-President. The senator from South Carolina will pause until order is restored.

Mr. Mason. I rise to a question of privilege. If there is again disorder in this chamber, I shall insist upon the galleries being cleared.

Mr. Brown. I hope that order will be enforced. The Senate is not a theatre.

Mr. Toombs. The statement just made by the senator from Illinois is a great mistake, and I shall take issue with him when he sits down. I say it is not true in any sense, and I will answer it.

Mr. Mason. Mr. President—

The Vice-President. The senator from Virginia gives notice that if there be a repetition of the demonstrations in the galleries he will move to clear them.

Mr. Mason. If there is again disorder in the galleries, let it arise from what source it may, I shall ask the chair to enforce the order of the Senate.

The Vice-President. Before the debate commenced, the chair expressed the hope that these demonstrations would not occur. He did not then think that he would have to repeat the expression of that hope. This floor is covered by persons not members of the Senate, admitted by the consent of the body unanimously, and certainly something is due to the courtesy of the Senate.

The chair does not believe these demonstrations will be repeated, and therefore takes no further notice of what has occurred.   The senator from Illinois will proceed.

Mr. Douglas. The interposition of the denial that about one half of the counties were disfranchised, I presume, can have but very little weight on the argument.   It has been proven over and over again.   In my estimation the proof is conclusive as to the fifteen counties, and satisfactory, I think, as to nineteen, being half the counties of the Territory, that there were not such a census and registration as authorized a vote for delegates.   It has been attempted to be proved, however, that there was not a great many votes in those counties.   I believe the president of the convention estimates that there were not more than fifteen hundred or two thousand in those counties. Suppose that was all.   There were only a little over two thousand votes polled at the election of delegates in the other nineteen counties which elected all the delegates.   If the disfranchised counties contained fifteen hundred voters, is it not conclusive that, with the addition of five or six hundred persons in the other counties, they could have changed the result?   Having been disfranchised in one half the counties, the friends of those who were disfranchised may not have voted in the other counties, because they had no hope of overcoming the majority in the other half.   I did not intend to go into the argument on that point again, and I should not have alluded to it now but for the fact that the senator from South Carolina had to assume as true, what I understood not to be true, in order to predicate his answer upon it, that he, as a Southern man, would vote to admit the state if the case had been reversed, and a free-state Constitution was being forced upon an unwilling people, with the knowledge that it did not reflect the sentiments of that people.

Mr. Hammond. Allow me to say that if the slaveholders, under these circumstances, had never had a majority at all, they would, nevertheless, have submitted until they could alter the Constitution, if they could possibly do it.

Mr. Douglas. I can only say, then, that they are a very submissive people.   [Laughter.]

Mr. Hammond. Not at all.

Mr. Douglas. I have never seen the day when I would be willing to submit to the action of a minority forcing a Constitution on an unwilling people against their will because it had got an advantage.   It violates the fundamental principle of government ; it violates the foundations on which all free government rests; it is a proposition in violation of the Democratic creed; in violation of the Republican creed ; in violation of the American creed ; in violation of the creed of every party which professes to be governed by the principles of free institutions and fair elections.

Mr. Hammond. Will the senator allow me to say one word more?   If the slaveholders, under the circumstances that he stated, were a minority, they would have submitted.   If they were a majority, as I assume, they would have submitted until, under the forms of constitutional law, they could have properly asserted their power.

Mr. Douglas. I understood the senator to say that ; I must say to him that I would rather not repeat questions on the same point over and over again. I am very feeble to-night, and shall probably not have strength enough to go through with my remarks.   I only desire to say on that point that I regard the principle involved here as vital and fundamental, as lying at the foundation of all free government, and the violation of it as a death-blow to state rights and state sovereignty.   But, sir, I pass on.   If you admit Kansas with the Lecompton Constitution, you also admit her with the state government which has been brought into existence under it.   Is the evidence satisfactory that that state government has been fairly and honestly elected?   Is the evidence satisfactory that the elections were fairly and honestly held, and fairly and honestly returned? You have all seen the evidence showing the fraudulent voting; the forged returns, from precinct after precinct, changing the result not only upon the legislative ticket, but also upon the ticket for governor and state officers. The false returns in regard to Delaware Crossing, changing the complexion of the Legislature, are admitted. The evidence is equally conclusive as to the Shawnee Precinct, the Oxford Precinct, the Kickapoo Precinct, and many others, making a difference of some three thousand votes in the general aggregate, and changing the whole result of the election. Yet, sir, we are called upon to admit Kansas with the state government thus brought into existence not only by fraudulent voting, but forged returns, sustained by perjury. The Senate well recollects the efforts that I made before the subject was referred to the committee, and since, to ascertain to whom the certificates of election were awarded, that we might know whether they were given to the men honestly elected, or to the men whose elections depended upon forgery and perjury. Can any one tell me now to whom those certificates have been issued, if they have been issued at all? Can any man tell me whether we are installing, by receiving this state government, officers whose sole title depends upon forgery, or those whose title depends upon popular votes? We have been calling for that information for about three months, but we have called in vain. One day the rumor would be that Mr. Calhoun would declare the free-state ticket elected, and next day that he would declare the pro-slavery ticket elected. So it has alternated, like the chills and fever, day after day, until within the last three days, when the action of Congress became a little dubious, when it was doubtful whether Northern men were willing to vote for a state government depending upon forgery and perjury, and then we find that the president of the Lecompton Convention addresses a letter to the editor of the Star, a newspaper in this city, telling what he thinks is the result of the election. He says it is true that he has received no answer to his letters of inquiry to Governor Denver; he has no official information on the subject; but, from rumors and unofficial information, he is now satisfied that the Delaware Crossing return was a fraud; that it will be set aside; and that, accordingly, the result will be that certificates will be issued to the free-state men. I do not mean to deny that Mr. Calhoun may think such will be the result; but, while he may think so, I would rather know how the fact is. His thoughts are not important, but the fact is vital in establishing the honesty or dishonesty of the state government which we are about to recognize. It so happens that Mr. Calhoun has no more power, no more authority over that question now than the senator from Missouri, or any other member of this body. The celebrated Lecompton schedule provides that,

"In case of removal, ABSENCE, or disability of the president of this convention to discharge the duties herein imposed on him, the president *pro tempore* of this convention shall perform said duties; and in case of absence, refusal, or disability of the president *pro tempore*, a committee consisting of seven, or a majority of them, shall discharge the duties required of the president of this convention."

As Mr. Calhoun is absent from the Territory, and, by reason of that absence, is deprived of all authority over the subject-matter, and as the president *pro tempore* has succeeded to his powers, is it satisfactory for the deposed president to address a letter to the editor of the Star announcing his private opinion as to who has been elected? I should like to know who the president *pro tempore* is, and where he is; and if he is in Kansas, whether he has arrived at the same conclusion which the ex-president Calhoun has announced. I should like to know whether that president *pro tempore* has already issued his certificate to the pro-slavery men in Kansas, while Mr. Calhoun expresses the opinion in the Star that the certificates will be issued to the free-state men? If that president *pro tempore* has become a fugitive from justice, and escaped from the Territory, I should like then to know who are the committee of seven that were to take his place; and whether they, or a majority of them, have arrived at the same conclusion to which Mr. Calhoun has come? Inasmuch as this opinion is published to the world just before the vote is to be taken here, and is expected to catch the votes of some green members of one body or the other, I should like to know whether certificates have been issued? and, if so, by whom, and to whom? where the president *pro tempore* is? where the committee of seven may be found? and then we might know who constitute the Legislature, and who constitute the state government which we are to bring into being. We are not only to admit Kansas with a Constitution, but with a state government; with a governor, a Legislature, a judiciary; with executive, legislative, judicial, and ministerial officers. Inasmuch as we are told by the President that the first Legislature may take steps to call a convention to change the Constitution, I should like to know of whom that Legislature is composed? Inasmuch as the governor would have the power to veto an act of the Legislature calling a convention, I should like to know who is governor, so that I may judge whether he would veto such an act? Can not our good friends get the president *pro tempore* of the convention to write a letter to the Star? Can they not procure a letter from the committee of seven? Can they not clear up this mystery, and relieve our suspicious minds of any thing unfair or foul in the arrangement of this matter? Let us know how the fact is.

This publication of itself is calculated to create more apprehension than there was before. As long as Mr. Calhoun took the ground that he would never declare the result until Lecompton was admitted, and that, if it was not admitted, he would never make the decision, there seemed to be some reason in his course; but when, after taking that ground for months, it became understood that Lecompton was dead, or was lingering and languishing, and likely to die, and when a few more votes were necessary, and a pretext was necessary to be given in order to secure them, we find this letter published by the deposed ex-president, giving his opinion when he had no power over the subject; and when it appears by the Constitution itself that another man or another body of men has the decision in their hands, it is calculated to arouse our suspicions as to what the result will be after Lecompton is admitted.

Mr. President, in the course of the debate on this bill, before I was compelled to absent myself from the Senate on account of sickness, and I presume the same has been the case during my absence, much was said on the Slavery question in connection with the admission of Kansas. Many gentlemen have labored to produce the impression that the whole opposition to the admission arises out of the fact that the Lecompton Constitution makes Kansas a slave state. I am sure that no gentleman here will do me the injustice to assert or suppose that my opposition is predicated on that consideration, in view of the fact that my speech against the admission of Kansas under the Lecompton Constitution was made on the 9th of December, two weeks before the vote was taken upon the slavery clause in Kansas, and when the general impression was that the pro-slavery clause would be excluded. I predicated my opposition then, as I do now, upon the ground that it was a violation of the fundamental principles of government, a violation of popular sovereignty, a violation of the Democratic platform, a violation of all party platforms, and a fatal blow to the independence of the new states. I told you then that you had no more right to force a free-state Constitution upon a people against their will than you had to force a slave-state Constitution. Will gentlemen say that, on the other side, slavery has no influence in producing that united, almost unanimous support which we find from gentlemen living in one section of the Union in favor of the Lecompton Constitution? If slavery had nothing to do with it, would there have been so much hesitation about Mr. Calhoun's declaring the result of the election prior to the vote in Congress? I submit, then, whether we ought not to discard the Slavery question altogether, and approach the real question before us fairly, calmly, dispassionately, and decide whether, but for the slavery clause, this Lecompton Constitution could receive a single vote in either house of Congress. Were it not for the slavery clause, would there be any objection to sending it back to the people for a vote? Were it not for the slavery clause, would there be any objection to letting Kansas wait until she had ninety thousand people, instead of coming into the Union with not over forty-five or fifty thousand? Were it not for the Slavery question, would Kansas have occupied any considerable portion of our thoughts? would it have divided and distracted political parties so as to create bitter and acrimonious feelings? I say now to our Southern friends that I will act, on this question on the right of the people to decide for themselves, irrespective of the fact whether they decide for or against slavery, provided it be submitted to a fair vote at a fair election, and with honest returns.

In this connection there is another topic to which I desire to allude. I seldom refer to the course of newspapers, or notice the articles which they publish in regard to myself; but the course of the Washington Union has been so extraordinary for the last two or three months, that I think it well enough to make some allusion to it. It has read me out of the Democratic party every other day, at least, for two or three months, and keeps reading me out (laughter); and, as if it had not succeeded, still continues to read me out, using such terms as "traitor," "renegade," "deserter," and other kind and polite epithets of that nature. Sir, I have no vindication to make of my Democracy against the Washington Union, or any other newspaper. I am willing to allow my history and action for the last twenty years to speak for themselves as to my political principles, and my fidelity to political obligations. The Washington Union has a personal grievance. When its editor was nominated for public printer I declined to vote for him, and stated that at some time I might give my reasons for doing so. Since I declined to give that vote, this scurrilous abuse, these vindictive and constant attacks, have been repeated almost daily on me. Will my friend from Michigan read the article to which I allude?

Mr. Stuart read the following editorial article from the Washington Union of November 17, 1857:

"FREE-SOILISM.—The primary object of all government, in its original institution, is the protection of person and property. It is for this alone that men surrender a portion of their natural rights.

"In order that this object may be fully accomplished, it is necessary that this protection should be equally extended to all classes of free citizens without exception. This, at least, is a fundamental principle of the Constitution of the United States, which is the original compact on which all our institutions are based.

"Slaves were recognized as property in the British colonies of North America by the government of Great Britain, by the colonial laws, and by the Constitution of the United States. Under these sanctions vested rights have accrued to the amount of some sixteen hundred million dollars. It is therefore the duty of Congress and the state Legislatures to protect that property.

"The Constitution declares that 'the citizens of each state shall be entitled to all the privileges and immunities of citizens in the several states.' Every citizen of one state coming into another state has therefore a right to the protection of his person, and that property which is recognized as such by the Constitution of the United States, any law of a state to the contrary notwithstanding. So far from any state having a right to deprive him of this property, it is its bounden duty to protect him in its possession.

"If these views are correct—and we believe it would be difficult to invalidate them—it follows that all state laws, whether organic or otherwise, which prohibit a citizen of one state from settling in another, and bringing his slave property with him, and most especially declaring it forfeited, are direct violations of the original intention of a government which, as before stated, is the protection of person and property, and of the Constitution of the United States, which recognizes property in slaves, and declares that 'the citizens of each state shall be entitled to all the privileges and immunities of citizens in the several states,' among the most essential of which is the protection of person and property.

"What is recognized as property by the Constitution of the United States, by a provision which applies equally to all the states, has an inalienable right to be protected in all the states."   *   *   *   *

"The protection of property being, next to that of person, the most important object of all good government, and property in slaves being recognized by the Constitution of the United States, as well as originally by all the old thirteen states, we have never doubted that the emancipation of slaves in those states where it previously existed, by an arbitrary act of the Legislature, was a gross violation of the rights of property."   *   *   *   *

"*The emancipation of the slaves of the Northern States was then, as previously stated, a gross outrage on the rights of property*, inasmuch as it was not a voluntary relinquishment on the part of the owners. It was an act of coercive legislation."   *   *   *   *

"This measure of emancipation was the parent or the offspring of a doctrine which may be so extended as to place the property of every man in the community at the mercy of rabid fanaticism or political expediency. It is only to substitute scruples of conscience in place of established constitutional principle, and all laws and all constitutions become a dead letter. The rights of persons and property become subservient, not to laws and Constitutions, but to fanatical dogmas, and thus the end and object of all good government is completely frustrated. There is no longer any rule of law nor any constitutional guide; and the people are left to the discretion, or rather the madness, of a school of instructors who can neither comprehend their own dogmas nor make them comprehensible to others."   *   *   *   *

"Where is all this to end? and what security have the free citizens of the United States that their dearest rights may not, one after the other, be offered up at the shrine of the demon of fanaticism, the most dangerous of all the enemies of freedom? If the Constitution is no longer to be our guide and protector, where shall we find barriers to defend us against a system of legislation restrained by no laws and no Constitutions, which creates crimes at pleasure, punishes them at will, and sacrifices the rights of persons and property to a dogma or a scruple of conscience? All this is but the old laws of Puritanism now fermenting and souring in the exhausted beer-barrel of Massachusetts. The descendants of this race of ecclesiastical tyrants, or rather ecclesiastical slaves, have spread over the western part of the State of New York, and throughout all the new states, where they have, to some extent, disseminated their manners, habits, and principles, most especially their blind subserviency to old idols, and their abject subjection to their priests. There is no doubt that they aspire to give tone and character to the whole confederacy, and believe that their dream will be realized? We are pretty well convinced, however, that the people of the United States will never become a nation of fanatical Puritans."

Mr. Douglas. Mr. President, you here find several distinct propositions advanced boldly by the Washington Union editorially and apparently authoritatively, and every man who questions any of them is denounced as an Abolitionist, a Free-soiler, a fanatic. The propositions are, first, that the primary object of all government at its original institution is the protection of person and property; second, that the Constitution of the United States declares that the citizens of each state shall be entitled to all the privileges and immunities of citizens in the several states; and that, therefore, thirdly, all state laws, whether organic or otherwise, which prohibit the citizens of one state from settling in another with their slave property, and especially declaring it forfeited, are direct violations of the original intention of the government and Constitution of the United States; and, fourth, that the emancipation of the slaves of the Northern States was a gross outrage on the rights of property, inasmuch as it was involuntarily done on the part of the owner.

Remember that this article was published in the Union on the 17th of November, and on the 18th appeared the first article giving the adhesion of the Union to the Lecompton Constitution. It was in these words:

"KANSAS AND HER CONSTITUTION.—The vexed question is settled. The problem is solved. The dread point of danger is passed. All serious trouble to Kansas affairs is over and gone,"

and a column nearly of the same sort. Then, when you come to look into the Lecompton Constitution, you find the same doctrine incorporated in it which was put forth editorially in the Union. What is it?

"ARTICLE 7, *Section* 1. The right of property is before and higher than any constitutional sanction; and the right of the owner of a slave to such slave and its increase is the same and as inviolable as the right of the owner of any property whatever."

Then in the schedule is a provision that the Constitution may be amended after 1864 by a two thirds vote,

"But no alteration shall be made to affect the right of property in the ownership of slaves."

It will be seen by these clauses in the Lecompton Constitution that they are identical in spirit with this authoritative article in the Washington Union of the day previous to its endorsement of this Constitution, and every man is branded as a Free-soiler and Abolitionist who does not subscribe to them. The proposition is advanced that the emancipation acts of New York, of New England, of Pennsylvania, and of New Jersey, were unconstitutional, were outrages upon the right of property, were violations of the Constitution of the United States. The proposition is advanced that a Southern man has a right to move from South Carolina, with his negroes, into Illinois, to settle there and hold them there as slaves, any thing in the Constitution and laws of Illinois to the contrary notwithstanding. The proposition is, that a citizen of Virginia has rights in a free state which a citizen of a free state can not himself have. We prohibit ourselves from holding slaves within our own limits, and yet, according to this doctrine, a citizen of Kentucky can move into our state, bring in one hundred slaves with him, and hold them as such in defiance of the Constitution and laws of our own state. If that proposition is true, the creed of the Democratic party is false. The principle of the Kansas-Nebraska Bill is, that "each state and each Territory shall be left perfectly free to form and regulate its domestic institutions in its own way, subject only to the Constitution of the United States." I claim that Illinois has the sovereign right to prohibit slavery, a right as undeniable as that the sovereignty of Virginia may authorize its existence. We have the same right to prohibit it that you have to recognize and protect it. Each state is sovereign within its own sphere of powers, sovereign in respect to its own domestic and local institutions and internal concerns. So long as you regulate your local institutions to suit yourselves, we are content; but when you claim the right to override our laws and our Constitution, and deny our right to form our institutions to suit ourselves, I protest against it. The same doctrine is asserted in this Lecompton Constitution. There it is stated that the right of property in slaves is "before and higher than any constitutional sanction."

Mr. President, I recognize the right of the slaveholding states to regulate their local institutions, to claim the services of their slaves under their own state laws, and I am prepared to perform each and every one of my obligations under the Constitution of the United States in respect to them; but I do not admit, and I do not think they are safe in asserting, that their right of property in slaves is higher than and above constitutional sanction, is independent of constitutional obligations. When you rely upon the Constitution and upon your own laws, you are safe. When you go beyond and above constitutional obligations, I know not where your safety is. If this doctrine be true, that slavery is higher than the Constitution, and above the Constitution, it necessarily follows that a state can not abolish it, can not prohibit it, and the doctrine of the Washington Union, that the emancipation laws were outrages on the rights of property and violations of the Constitution, becomes the law.

When I saw that article in the Union of the 17th of November, followed by the glorification of the Lecompton Constitution on the 18th of November, and this clause in the Constitution asserting the doctrine that no state has a right to prohibit slavery within its limits, I saw that there was a fatal blow being struck at the sovereignty of the states of this Union, a death-blow to state rights, subversive of the Democratic platform and of the principles upon which the Democratic party have ever stood, and upon which I trust they ever will stand. Because of these extraordinary doctrines, I declined to vote for the editor of the Washington Union for public printer, and for that refusal, as I suppose, I have been read out of the party by the editor of the Union at least every other day from that time to this. Sir, I submit the question: Who has deserted the Democratic party and the Democratic platform—he who stands by the sovereign rights of the state to abolish and prohibit slavery as it pleases, or he who attempts to strike down the sovereignty of the states, and combine all power in one central government, and establish an empire instead of a confederacy?

The principles upon which the presidential campaign of 1856 was fought are well known to the country. At least in Illinois I think I am authorized to state that they were with clearness and precision, so far as the Slavery question is concerned. The Democracy of Illinois are prepared to stand on the platform upon which the battle of 1856 was fought. It was,

First. The migration or importation of negroes into the country having been prohibited since 1808, never again to be renewed, each state will take care of its own colored population.

Second. That while negroes are not citizens of the United States, and hence not entitled to political equality with whites, they should enjoy all the rights, privileges, and immunities which they are capable of exercising, consistent with the safety and welfare of the community where they live.

Third. That each state and Territory must judge and determine for itself of the nature and extent of its rights and privileges.

Fourth. That while each free state should and will maintain and protect all the rights of the slaveholding states, they will, each for itself, maintain and defend its sovereign right within its own limits to form and regulate their own domestic institutions in their own way, subject only to the Constitution of the United States.

Fifth. That in the language of Mr. Buchanan's letter of acceptance of the presidential nomination, the Nebraska-Kansas Act does no more than give the form of law to this elementary principle of self-government when it doclares "that the people of a Territory, like those of a state, shall decide for themselves whether slavery shall or shall not exist within their limits."

These were the general propositions on which we maintained the canvass on the Slavery question—the right of each state to decide for itself; that a negro should have such rights as he was capable of enjoying, and could enjoy, consistently with the safety and welfare of society; and that each state should decide for itself the nature, and extent, and description of those rights and privileges. Hence, if you choose in North Carolina to have slaves, it is your business, and not ours. If we choose in Illinois to prohibit slavery, it is our right, and you must not interfere with it. If New York chooses to give privileges to the negro which we withhold, it is her right to extend them, but she must not attempt to force us to do the same thing. Let each state take care of its own affairs, mind its own business, and let its neighbors alone, then there will be peace in the country. Whenever you attempt to enforce uniformity, and, judging that a peculiar institution is good for you, and therefore good for every body else, try to enforce it on every body, you will find that there will be resistance to the demand. Our government was not formed on the idea that there was to be uniformity of local laws or local institutions. It was founded upon the supposition that there must be diversity and variety in the institutions and laws. Our fathers foresaw that the local institutions which would suit the granite hills of New Hampshire would be ill adapted to the rice plantations of South Carolina. They foresaw that the institutions which would be well adapted to the mountains and valleys of Pennsylvania would not suit the plantation interests of Virginia. They foresaw that the great diversity of climate, of production, of interests, would require a corresponding diversity of local laws and local institutions. For this reason they provided for thirteen separate states, each with a separate Legislature, and each state sovereign within its own sphere, with the right to make all its local laws and local institutions to suit itself, on the supposition that they would be as different and as diversified as the number of states themselves. Then the general government was made, with a Congress having limited and specified powers, extending only to those subjects which were national and not local, which were federal and not state.

These were the principles on which our institutions were established. These are the principles on which the Democratic party has ever fought its battles. This attempt now to establish the doctrine that a free state has no power to prohibit slavery, that our emancipation acts were unconstitutional and void, that they were outrages on the rights of property, that slavery is national and not local, that it goes every where under the Constitution of the United States, and yet is higher than the Constitution, above the Constitution, beyond the reach of sovereign power, existing by virtue of that higher law proclaimed by the senator from New York, will not be tolerated. When the doctrine of a higher law, a law above the Constitution, a law overriding the Constitution, and imposing obligations upon public men in defiance of the Constitution, was first proclaimed in the Senate, it was deemed moral treason in this body; but now I am read out of the party three times a week by the Washington Union for disputing this higher law, which is embodied in the Lecompton Constitution, that slavery, the right to slave property, does not depend upon human law nor constitutional sanction, but is above, and beyond, and before all constitutional sanctions and obligations! I feel bound, as a senator from a sovereign state, to repudiate and rebuke this doctrine. I am bound as a Democrat, bound as an American citizen, bound as a senator claiming to represent a sovereign state, to enter my protest, and the protest of my constituency, against such a doctrine. Whenever such a doctrine shall be ingrafted on the policy of this country, you will have revolutionized the government, annihilated the sovereignty of the states, established a consolidated despotism with uniformity of local institutions, and that uniformity being slavery, existing by Divine right, and a higher law beyond the reach of the Constitution and of human authority.

Mr. President, if my protest against this interpolation into the policy of this country or the creed of the Democratic party is to bring me under the ban, I am ready to meet the issue. I am told that this Lecompton Constitution is a party test, a party measure ; that no man is a Democrat who does not sanction it, who does not vote to bring Kansas into the Union with the government established under that Constitution. Sir, who made it a party test? Who made it a party measure? Certainly the party has not assembled in convention to ordain any such thing to be a party measure. I know of but one state convention that has endorsed it. It has not been declared to be a party measure by state conventions, or by a national convention, or by a senatorial caucus, or by a caucus of the Democratic members of the House of Representatives. How, then, came it to be a party measure? The Democratic party laid down its creed at its last national convention. That creed is unalterable for four years, according to the rules and practices of the party. Who has interpolated this Lecompton Constitution into the party platform?

Oh! but we are told it is an administration measure. Because it is an administration measure, does it therefore follow that it is a party measure? Is it the right of an administration to declare what are party measures and what are not? That has been attempted heretofore, and it has failed. When John Tyler prescribed a creed to the Whig party, his right to do so was not respected. When a certain doctrine in regard to the neutrality laws was proclaimed to be a party measure, my friends around me here considered it a "grave error," and it was not respected. When the Army Bill was proclaimed an administration measure, the authority to make it so was put at defiance, and the Senate rejected it by a vote of four to one, and the House of Representatives voted it down by an overwhelming majority. Is the Pacific Railroad Bill a party measure? I should like to see whether the guillotine is to be applied to every recreant Democrat who does not come up to that test. Is the Bankrupt Law a party measure? We shall see, when the vote is taken, how many renegades there will be then. Was the Loan Bill an administration measure or a party measure? Is the guillotine to be applied to every one who does not yield implicit obedience to the behests of an administration in power? There is infinitely more plausibility in declaring each of the measures to which I have just alluded to be an administration measure, than in declaring the Lecompton Constitution to be such. By what right does the administration take cognizance of the Lecompton Constitution?

The Constitution of the United States says that "new states may be admitted into the Union by the Congress"—not by the President, not by the cabinet, not by the administration. The Lecompton Constitution itself says, "This Constitution shall be submitted to the Congress of the United States at its next session ;" not to the President, not to the cabinet, not to the administration. The convention in Kansas did not send it to the administration, did not authorize it to be sent to the President, but directed it to be sent to Congress ; and the President of the United States only got hold of it through the commission of the surveyor general, who was also president of the Lecompton Convention. The Constitution as made was ordered to be sent directly to Congress; Congress having power to admit states, and the President having nothing to do with it. The moment you pass a law admitting a state, it executes itself. It is not a law to be executed by the President or by the administration. It is the last measure on earth that could be rightfully made an administration measure. It is not usual for the

Constitution of a new state to come to Congress through the hand of the President. True, the Minnesota Constitution was sent to the President because the Convention of Minnesota directed it to be so sent, and the President submitted it to us without any recommendation. Because senators and representatives do not yield their judgments and their consciences, and bow in abject obedience to the requirements of an administration in regard to a measure on which the administration are not required to act at all, a system of proscription, of persecution is to be adopted against every man who maintains his self-respect, his own judgment, and his own conscience.

I do not recognize the right of the President or his cabinet, no matter what my respect may be for them, to tell me my duty in the Senate Chamber. The President has his duties to perform under the Constitution, and he is responsible to his constituency. A senator has his duties to perform here under the Constitution and according to his oath, and he is responsible to the sovereign state which he represents as his constituency. A member of the House of Representatives has his duties under the Constitution and his oath, and he is responsible to the people that elected him. The President has no more right to prescribe tests to senators than senators have to the President; the President has no more right to prescribe tests to the representatives than the representatives have to the President. Suppose we here should attempt to prescribe a test of faith to the President of the United States, would he not rebuke our impertinence and impudence as subversive of the fundamental principle of the Constitution? Would he not tell us that the Constitution, and his oath, and his conscience were his guide; that we must perform our duties, and he would perform his, and let each be responsible to his own constituency?

Sir, whenever the time comes that the President of the United States can change the allegiance of the senators from the states to himself, what becomes of the sovereignty of the states? When the time comes that a senator is to account to the executive and not to his state, whom does he represent? If the will of my state is one way and the will of the President is the other, am I to be told that I must obey the executive and betray my state, or else be branded as a traitor to the party, and hunted down by all the newspapers that share the patronage of the government? and every man who holds a petty office in any part of my state to have the question put to him, "Are you Douglas's enemy?" if not, "your head comes off?" Why? "Because he is a recreant senator; because he chooses to follow his judgment and his conscience, and represent his state instead of obeying my executive behest." I should like to know what is the use of Congresses; what is the use of Senates and Houses of Representatives, when their highest duty is to obey the executive in disregard of the wishes, rights, and honor of their constituents? What despotism on earth would be equal to this, if you establish the doctrine that the executive has a right to command the votes, the consciences, the judgment of the senators and of the representatives, instead of their constituents? In old England, whose oppressions we thought intolerable, an administration is hurled from power in an hour when voted down by the representatives of the people upon a government measure. If the rule of old England applied here, this cabinet would have gone out of office when the Army Bill was voted down, the other day, in the House of Representatives. There, in that monarchical country, where they have a queen by divine right, and lords by the grace of God, and where Republicanism is supposed to have but a slight foothold, the representatives of the people can check the throne, restrain the government, change the ministry, and give a new direction to the policy of the government, without being accountable to the king or the queen. There the representatives of the people are responsible to their constituents. Across the Channel, under Louis Napoleon, it may be otherwise; yet I doubt whether it would be so boldly proclaimed there that a man is a traitor for daring to vote according to his sense of duty, according to the will of his state, according to the interests of his constituents.

Suppose the executive should tell the senator from California [Mr. Gwin] to vote against his Pacific Railroad Bill; would he obey? If not, he will be deemed a rebel. Suppose the executive should tell the senator from Virginia [Mr. Mason] to vote for the Pacific Railroad Bill, or the senator from Georgia [Mr. Toombs] to vote for the Army Bill, or the senator from Mississippi [Mr. Brown] to sustain him on the Neutrality Laws, we should have more rebels and more traitors. But it is said a dispensation is granted from the fountain of all power for rebellion on all subjects but one. The President says, in effect, "Do as you please on all questions but one;" that one is Lecompton. On what principle is it that we must not judge for ourselves on this measure, and may on every thing else? I suppose it is on the old adage that a man needs no friends when he knows he is right, and he only wants his friends to stand by him when he is wrong. The President says that he regrets this Constitution was not submitted to the people, although he knows that if it had been submitted it would have been rejected. Hence the President regrets that it was not rejected. Would he regret that it was not submitted and rejected if he did not think it was wrong? And yet he demands our assistance in forcing it on an unwilling people, and threatens vengeance on all who refuse obedience. He recommends the Army Bill; he thinks it necessary to carry on the Mormon war; it is necessary to carry out a measure of the administration, and hence it is an administration measure; but he does not quarrel with any body for voting against it. He thinks every one of the other recommendations to which I have alluded is right, and, therefore, there is no harm in going against them. The only harm is in going against that which the President acknowledges to be wrong; and yet the system of proscription, to subdue men to abject obedience to executive will, is to be pursued.

Is it seriously intended to brand every Democrat in the United States as a traitor who is opposed to the Lecompton Constitution? If so, do your friends in Pennsylvania desire any traitors to vote with them next fall? We are traitors if we vote against Lecompton, our constituents are traitors if they do not think Lecompton is right, and yet you expect those whom you call traitors to vote with and sustain you. Are you to read out of the party every man who thinks it wrong to force a Constitution on a people against their will? If so, what will be the size of the administration party in New York? what will it be in Pennsylvania? how many will it number in Ohio, or in Indiana, or in Illinois, or in any other Northern state? Surely you do not expect the support of those whom you brand as renegades? Would it not be well to allow all freemen freedom of thought, freedom of speech, and freedom of action? Would it not be well to allow each senator and representative to vote according to his judgment, and perform his duty according to his own sense of his obligation to himself, and to his state, and to his God?

For my own part, Mr. President, come what may, I intend to vote, speak, and act according to my own sense of duty so long as I hold a seat in this chamber. I have no defense of my Democracy. I have no professions to make of my fidelity. I have no vindication to make of my course. Let it speak for itself. The insinuation that I am acting with the Republicans or Americans has no terror, and will not drive me from my duty or propriety. It is an argument for which I have no respect. When I saw the senator from Virginia acting with the Republicans on the Neutrality Laws, in support of the President, I did not feel it to be my duty to taunt him with voting with those to whom he happened to be opposed in general politics. When

I saw the senator from Georgia acting with the Republicans on the Army Bill, it did not impair my confidence in his fidelity to principle. When I see senators here every day acting with the Republicans on various questions, it only shows me that they have independence and self-respect enough to go according to their own convictions of duty, without being influenced by the course of others.

I have no professions to make upon any of these points. I intend to perform my duty in accordance with my own convictions. Neither the frowns of power nor the influence of patronage will change my action, or drive me from my principles. I stand firmly, immovably upon those great principles of self-government and state sovereignty upon which the campaign was fought and the election won. I stand by the time-honored principles of the Democratic party, illustrated by Jefferson and Jackson—those principles of state rights, of state sovereignty, of strict construction, on which the great Democratic party has ever stood. I will stand by the Constitution of the United States, with all its compromises, and perform all my obligations under it. I will stand by the American Union as it exists under the Constitution. If, standing firmly by my principles, I shall be driven into private life, it is a fate that has no terrors for me. I prefer private life, preserving my own self-respect and manhood, to abject and servile submission to executive will. If the alternative be private life or servile obedience to executive will, I am prepared to retire. Official position has no charms for me when deprived of that freedom of thought and action which becomes a gentleman and a senator.

Mr. President, I owe an apology to the Senate for the desultory manner in which I have discussed this question. My health has been so feeble for some time past that I have not been able to arrange my thoughts, or the order in which they should be presented. If, in the heat of debate, I have expressed a sentiment which would seem to be unkind or disrespectful to any senator, I shall regret it. While I intend to maintain, firmly and fearlessly, my own views, far be it from me to impugn the motives or question the propriety of the action of any other senator. I take it for granted that each senator will obey the dictates of his own conscience, and will be accountable to his constituents for the course which he may think proper to pursue.

On the 1st of April the bill was taken up in the House. The House refused—yeas 95, nays 137—to reject the bill.

Mr. Montgomery, of Pennsylvania, moved to strike out all after the enacting clause, and to insert the same amendment proposed by Mr. Crittenden in the Senate. That amendment was agreed to—yeas 120, nays 112—and, as amended, the bill was passed by the same vote.

The next day (April 2) the Senate—yeas 32, nays 23—refused to concur in the amendment made by the House. On the 8th the House—yeas 119, nays 111—voted to "adhere" to their amendment. On the 13th the Senate "insisted" on its disagreement, and asked for a committee of conference. On the 14th Mr. Montgomery moved that the House "adhere," and Mr. English, of Indiana, moved that the House appoint a committee of conference. The vote on the last motion was—yeas 108, nays 108; the speaker voting in the affirmative, the motion was agreed to. The committees were appointed—Messrs.

Green, Hunter, and Seward on the part of the Senate, and English, Stephens, and Howard on the part of the House. This committee reported to the House on the 23d what is known as the "English Bill," and on the 4th of May the House, by a vote of yeas 112, nays 103, concurred in the report of the committee of conference, and the Senate, by the vote of all the friends of the original bill, did the same. The English Bill became the law. Its fate before the people of Kansas is well known. Thus ended the Lecompton controversy in Congress. Happy for the best interests of the country would it have been had it been allowed to reach its end without the bitterness that attended its progress. We will notice no farther at this time the assaults upon Mr. Douglas than to refer, as an example of the violence to which excited feelings led some men, to an article—leading editorial—in the Washington Union in the early part of March, in which it was demonstrated to the writer's entire satisfaction that no man of small physical stature could be a true Democrat at heart; and that R. J. Walker and S. A. Douglas were so constructed physically that it was naturally impossible for either of them to be a Democrat! In this struggle Mr. Douglas was heartily sustained and supported to the end by his Democratic colleagues in the House, Messrs. Harris, Marshall, Morris, Shaw, and Smith.

CHAPTER XV.

INTERNAL IMPROVEMENTS.

Mr. Douglas, during his entire political life, has agreed with the Democratic party in resisting any general system of internal improvements by the federal government. That hostility to a general system of internal improvements has been expressed over and over again in the platforms of the Democratic party, and has had no warmer defender than Mr. Douglas. Upon some points, however, such as the improvements of rivers and harbors, he has had opinions somewhat peculiar. He has endeavored throughout to discriminate between those works which were essential to the protection of commerce and the improvement of the navigable waters of the country, and those other works asked for by parties having local interests to serve, and desirous to promote them at the expense of the federal treasury. Mr. Douglas voted pretty generally for all the River and Harbor Appropriation Bills, always protesting against such items as were included in them that did not come up to his idea of justice or propriety. He was thus often compelled to vote for a number of small appropriations for what he deemed inappropriate works, or vote against others that were eminently just and proper. He has uniformly protested against that system of legislation which compelled him thus to vote against what was right, or vote for others that did not meet his approval.

RIVER AND HARBOR IMPROVEMENTS.

His effort has been always to break up this irregular, incomplete, and unsatisfactory mode of legislating upon this important subject. The appropriations even for the most needful works had been so irregular and so often interrupted that the works constructed in one season under a partial appropriation would frequently be destroyed or rendered valueless before the additional sum was appropriated. To remedy these evils, he has always urged that Congress would adopt some regular system under which these works could be safely, intelligently, and profitably carried on. All efforts of that kind, however, failed in Congress, where local interests could not be reconciled to any plan that did not include them.

In 1852, when the River and Harbor Bill was under consideration in the Senate, Mr. Douglas, who supported the bill, proposed to add to it three sections, having for their object the recognition and establishment of such works as the business and interests of the country would demand. His amendment proposed to grant the consent of Congress to all the states, and that the several states might authorize the authorities of any city or town within their respective limits, which might be situated on the Atlantic or Pacific coasts, or on the Gulf of Mexico, or on the banks of any bay or arm of the sea connecting therewith, or on the shores of Lakes Champlain, Ontario, Erie, St. Clair, Huron, Michigan, or Superior, or on the banks of any bay or arm of the lake connecting with either of said lakes, to levy duties of tonnage, not exceeding ten cents per ton, upon boats and vessels of every description entering the harbor or waters within the limits of such city or town, the funds to be derived from said duties to be expended exclusively in constructing, enlarging, deepening, improving, and securing safe and commodious harbors and entrances thereto at such cities and towns; the duties thus levied and collected not to exceed the amount necessary for the purpose for which they were levied. It also granted the consent of Congress that, where several states bordered on a lake, such states might enter into an agreement by which a portion of the fund raised by tonnage duties in all the cities and towns within their limits might be applied to such works as should be deemed necessary to improve and render safe and convenient the navigation of the lakes, and of the rivers and channels connecting them together; these works to be the deepening of the channels, or artificial channels to be constructed for that purpose. When canals or artificial channels should be thus constructed, only such tolls should be levied as would be necessary to keep them in repair. His amendment farther granted the consent of Congress that, in all cases where any navigable river or water might be situated, wholly or in part, within the limits of any state, the Legislature of such state might provide for the improvement of the navigation of such river within its own limits, by the collection of a tonnage duty upon all boats and vessels navigating the same. And where a navigable river or water might form the boundary of any two or more states, such states might, by joint action and agreement, provide for the collection of tonnage duties, to be applied exclusively to the improvement of the navigation of such river or navigable water.

This was substantially the proposition of Mr. Douglas. It was offered, not as a substitute for the pending Appropriation Bill, but as an addition thereto. It was intended as a consent on the part of Congress that each state that felt disposed to do so might go on at once and provide the means for putting her harbors in good order, her streams in proper condition, and her channels in a safe and proper state. It was to throw open to the enterprise and public spirit of each community the commerce of the country. Instead of subjecting each city on the lake to the most uncertain chances in the lottery of Congressional appropriations for harbor improvements, it proposed to give the assent of Congress, as required by the Constitution, to each city to go on and make her own harbor. If two cities on the lake, having equal chances for a good lake traffic, should both have their harbors improved by the federal government, there would be no cause of complaint. If, however, Congress interfered, and gave the money to improve one harbor and refused it for the other, it was a discrimination in favor of the one city and against the other that would be most unjust and oppressive. It would be the interference by the federal government to build up one city and break down the other, out of a treasury upon which both had an equality of claim. If this policy would have been so unjust where there were only two cities, how much more so was it unjust when Congress would select one or two harbors on a lake, appropriate money for their improvement, and leave a score of others, equally needy, wholly unprovided for. Such has been and such must ever be the practical operation of the existing system.

Mr. Douglas proposed to throw open the doors in the manner provided in the Constitution, and allow each community to improve its own harbor; to let competition and commercial enterprise decide the question of commercial consequence. If one town made a good harbor, and drew to it a commerce that might have gone elsewhere had the harbor not been put in proper order, then that was an advantage and a success to which such town was entitled, and which its commercial spirit fairly merited. If another town failed to improve its harbor, and thus lost a trade and commerce that it would have otherwise enjoyed, it was a consequence fairly following its omission to do its duty. Why should the federal treasury be employed to build up the commerce of one point and not the other? Why should the federal government interpose its weight and its money for one city in its contest with a rival city? The strongest, and, indeed, only plausible argument urged against this proposal was that it imposed a tax upon the navigating interest. The objection is only plausible—it has no value in reality. All duties, whether upon imports, port duties, tolls, freights, insurance, or otherwise, are a tax: not a tax upon the importer or shipper, manufacturer or producer, but upon the consumer. The consumer eventually pays all the tax imposed upon articles of merchandise. If the tax upon a barrel of flour from Chicago to New York be fifty cents or two dollars, the tax is eventually paid by the consumer. If a tax of five cents per ton be levied upon all vessels passing the St. Clair River, that tax must eventually be added to the cost of the merchandise carried in said vessels. The amount now paid for insurance upon vessels and merchandise passing that river is a tax imposed upon the articles shipped for the trip. If, instead of paying that tax in the shape of extra insurance because of the wretched condition of that great commercial highway, it was applied to the deepening and improvement of the river, it is doubtful, very doubtful, whether in five years the public would be subjected to an aggregate tax equal to that to which they are now subjected in the shape of extra insurance, loss of property, delay in receipt of goods, and all the other innumerable delays resulting from the dangerous and often impassable condition of that stream. The money expended now by the general government for purposes of river and harbor improvement is a tax—a tax mainly collected from the consumers of foreign imports. The same amount of money collected from those communities benefited by the work, and applied under their own direction, would accomplish ten-fold the good now accomplished. If this system were made general, people on the lakes would not be taxed for the improvement of harbors and rivers on the Atlantic, and the friends of the Savannah and Cape Fear River improvements might do all that they desire, and have no cause of complaint on account of the money lavished upon lake harbors and river improvements in the West.

Mr. Douglas supported his proposition in a very earnest speech, in which he argued the constitutional question, and the legislative history of river and harbor appropriations. It met with decided opposition in debate; and as it was intended at that time merely as an index of what he should propose when Congress would eventually, as he supposed, be forced to adopt some plan or system upon the subject, he did not press it, but allowed it to drop.

Subsequently, in January, 1854, he addressed a letter to the Governor of Illinois upon the subject, which letter embodies in a brief form some of the reasons inducing him to favor that plan of providing for the improvement of rivers and harbors. The following is his

LETTER TO GOVERNOR MATTESON.

Washington, January 2d, 1854.

SIR,—I learn from the public press that you have under consideration the proposition to convene the Legislature in special session. In the event such a step shall be demanded by the public voice and necessities, I desire to invite your attention to a subject of great interest to our people, which may require legislative action. I refer to the establishment of some efficient and permanent system for river and harbor improvements. Those portions of the Union most deeply interested in internal navigation naturally feel that their interests have been neglected, if not paralyzed, by an uncertain, vacillating, and partial policy. Those who reside upon the banks of the Mississippi, or on the shores of the great Northern Lakes, and whose lives and property are frequently exposed to the mercy of the elements for want of harbors of refuge and means of safety, have never been able to comprehend the force of that distinction between fresh and salt water, which affirms the power and duty of Congress, under the Constitution, to provide security to navigation so far as the tide ebbs and flows, and denies the existence of the right beyond the tidal mark. Our lawyers may have read in English books that, by the common law, all waters were deemed navigable so far as the tide extended and no farther; but they should also have learned from the same authority that the law was founded upon reason, and where the reason failed the rule ceased to exist. In England, where they have neither lake nor river, nor other water which is, in fact, navigable, except where the tide rolls its briny wave, it was natural that the law should conform to the fact, and establish that as a rule which the experience of all men proved to be founded in truth and reason. But it may well be questioned whether, if the common law had originated on the shores of Lake Michigan—a vast inland sea with an average depth of six hundred feet—it would have been deemed " not navigable," merely because the tide did not flow, and the water was fresh and well adapted to the uses and necessities of man. We therefore feel authorized to repudiate, as unreasonable and unjust, all injurious discrimination predicated upon salt water and tidal arguments, and to insist that if the power of Congress to protect navigation has any existence in the Constitution, it reaches every portion of this Union where the water is in fact navigable, and only ceases where the fact fails to exist. This power has been affirmed in some form, and exercised to a greater or less extent, by each successive Congress and every administration since the adoption of the federal Constitution. All acts of Congress providing for the erection of lighthouses, the placing of buoys, the construction of piers, the removal of snags, the dredging of channels, the inspection of steam-boat boilers, the carrying of life-boats—in short, all enactments for the security of navigation, and the safety of life and property within our navigable waters, assert the existence of this power and the propriety of its exercise in some form.

The great and growing interest of navigation is too important to be overlooked or disregarded. Mere negative action will not answer. The irregular and vacillating policy which has marked our legislation upon this subject is ruinous. Whenever appropriations have been proposed for river and harbor improvements, and especially on the Northern lakes and the Western rivers, there has usually been a death-struggle and a doubtful issue. We have generally succeeded with an appropriation once in four or five years; in other words, we have, upon an average, been beaten about four times out of five in one house of Congress or the other, or both, or by the presidential veto. When we did succeed, a large portion of the appropriation was expended in providing dredging-machines and snag-boats, and other necessary machinery and implements; and by the time the work was fairly begun, the appropriation was exhausted, and farther operations suspended. Failing to procure an additional appropriation at the next session, and perhaps for two, three, or four successive sessions, the administration has construed the refusal of Congress to provide the funds for the prosecution of the works into an abandonment of the system, and has accordingly deemed it a duty to sell, at public auction, the dredging-machines and snag-boats, implements and materials on hand, for whatever they would bring. Soon the country was again startled by the frightful accounts of wrecks and explosions, fires and snags upon the rivers, the lakes, and the sea-coast. The responsibility of these appalling sacrifices of life and property were charged upon those who defeated the appropriations for the prosecution of the works. Sympathy was excited, and a concerted plan of agitation and organization formed by the interested sections and parties to bring their combined influence to bear upon Congress in favor of the re-establishment of the system on an enlarged scale, sufficiently comprehensive to embrace the local interests and influences in a majority of the Congressional districts of the Union. A legislative omnibus was formed, in which all sorts of works were crowded together, good and bad, wise and foolish, national and local, all crammed into one bill, and forced through Congress by the power of an organized majority, after the fearful and exhausting struggle of a night session. The bill would receive the votes of a majority in each house, not because any one senator or representative approved all the items contained in it, but for the reason that humanity, as well as the stern demands of an injured and suffering constituency, required that they should make every needful sacrifice of money to diminish the terrible loss of human life by the perils of navigation. The result was a simple re-enactment of the former scenes. Machinery, implements, and materials purchased, the works recommenced—the money exhausted—subsequent appropriations withheld—and the operations suspended, without completing the improvements, or contributing materially to the safety of navigation. Indeed, it may well be questioned whether, as a general rule, the money has been wisely and economically applied, and in many cases whether the expenditure has been productive of any useful results beyond the mere distribution of so much money among contractors, laborers, and superintendents in the favored localities ; and in others, whether it has not been of positive detriment to the navigating interest.

Far be it from my purpose to call in question the integrity, science, or skill of those whose professional duty it was to devise the plan and superintend the construction of the works. But I do insist that from the nature of their profession and their habits of life they could not be expected to possess that local knowledge—that knowledge of currents and tides—the effects of storms, floods, and ice, always different and ever changing—in each locality of this widely-extended country, which is essential in determining upon the proper site and plan for an improvement to the navigation. Without depreciating the value of science or disregarding its precepts, I have no hesitation in saying that the opinion of an intelligent captain or pilot, who for a long series of years had sailed out of and into a given port in fair weather and foul, and who had carefully and daily watched the changes produced in the channel by the currents and storms, wrecks and other obstructions, would inspire me with more confidence than that of the most eminent professional gentleman, whose knowledge and science in the line of his profession were only equaled by his profound ignorance of all those local and practical questions which ought to determine the site and plan of the proposed improvement. To me, therefore, it is no longer a matter of surprise that errors and blunders occur in the mode of constructing the works, and that follies and extravagance every where appear in the expenditure of the money. These evils seem to be inherent in the system; at least, they have thus far proven unavoidable, and have become so palpable and notorious that it is worse than folly to close our eyes to their existence.

In addition to these facts, it should be borne in mind that a large and intelligent portion of the American people, comprising, perhaps, a majority of the Democratic party, are in the habit of considering these works as constituting a general system of internal improvements by the federal government, and therefore in violation of the creed of the Democratic party and of the Constitution of the United States. These two-fold objections—the one denying the constitutional power, and the other the expediency of appropriations from the national treasury—seem to acquire additional strength and force in proportion as the importance of the subject is enhanced, and the necessity for more numerous and extensive improvements is created by the extension of our territory, the expansion of our settlements, and the development of the resources of the country. As a friend to the navigating interest, and especially identified by all the ties of affection, gratitude, and interest with that section of the republic which is the most deeply interested in internal navigation, I see no hope for any more favorable results from national appropriations than we have heretofore realized. If, then, we are to judge the system by its results, taking the past as a fair indication of what might reasonably be expected in the future, those of us who have struggled hardest to render it efficient and useful are compelled to confess that it has proven a miserable failure. It is even worse than a failure, because, while it has failed to accomplish the desired objects, it has had the effect to prevent local and private enterprise from making the improvements under state authority, by holding out the expectation that the federal government was about to make them.

By way of illustration, let us suppose that twenty-five years ago, when we first began to talk about the construction of railroads in this country, the federal government had assumed to itself jurisdiction of all works of that description to the exclusion of state authority and individual enterprise. In that event, does any one believe we would now have in the United States fourteen thousand miles of railroad completed, and fifteen thousand miles in addition under contract. Is it to be presumed that, if our own state had prostrated itself in humble supplication at the feet of the federal government, and with folded arms had waited for appropriations from the national treasury, instead of exerting state authority, and stimulating and combining individual enterprise, we should now have in Illinois three thousand miles of railroad in process of construction? Let the history of internal improvements by the federal government be fairly written, and it will furnish conclusive answers to these interrogatories. For more than a quarter of a century the energies of the national government, together with all the spare funds in the treasury, were directed to the construction of a Macadamized road from Cumberland, in the State of Maryland, to Jefferson City, in the State of Missouri, without being able to complete one third of the work. If the government were unable to make three hundred miles of turnpike road in twenty-five years, how long would it take to construct a railroad to the Pacific Ocean, and to make all the harbor and river improvements necessary to protect our widely-extended and rapidly-increasing commerce on a sea-coast so extensive that in forty years we have not been able to complete even the survey of one half of it, and on a lake and river navigation more than four times as extensive as that sea-coast? These questions are worthy of the serious consideration of those who think that improvements should be made for the benefit of the present generation as well as for our remote posterity; for I am not aware that the federal government ever completed any work of internal improvement commenced under its auspices.

The operations of the government have not been sufficiently rapid to keep pace with the spirit of the age. The Cumberland Road, when commenced, may have been well adapted for the purposes for which it was designed; but after the lapse of a quarter of a century, and before any considerable portion of it could be finished, the whole was superseded and rendered useless by the introduction of the railroad system. One reason, and perhaps the principal cause, of the slow progress of all government improvements, consists in the fact that the appropriation for any one object is usually too small to be of material service. It may be sufficient for the commencement of the work, but before it can be completed, or even so far advanced as to withstand the effects of storms, and floods, and the elements, the appropriation is exhausted, and a large portion of the work swept away before funds can be obtained for finishing it, or even protecting that which has been done. The ruinous consequences of these small appropriations are well understood and seriously deprecated, but they arise from the necessity of the case, and constitute some of the evils inseparable from the policy. All experience proves that the numberless items of a river and harbor, or internal improvement bill, can not pass, each by itself, and upon its own merits, and that the friends of particular works will not allow appropriations to be made for the completion of others which are supposed to be of paramount importance unless theirs are embraced in the same bill. Each member seems to think the work in his own district to be of the sternest necessity and highest importance, and hence feels constrained to give his own the preference, or to defeat any bill which does not include it. The result is a legislative omnibus, in which all manner of objects are crowded together indiscriminately; and as there never is and never can be money enough in the treasury to make adequate appropriations for the whole, and as the bill can not pass unless each has something, of course the amount for each item must be reduced so low as to make it of little or no service, and thus render the whole bill almost a total loss. In this manner a large portion of our people have been kept in a state of suspense and anxiety for more than half a century, with their hopes always excited and their expectations never realized.

I repeat that the policy heretofore pursued has proved worse than a failure. If we expect to provide facilities and securities for our navigating interests, we must adopt a system commensurate with our wants—one which will be just and equal in its operations upon lake, river, and ocean, wherever the water is navigable, fresh or salt, tide or no tide—a system which will not depend for its success upon the dubious and fluctuating issues of political campaigns and Congressional combinations—one which will be certain, uniform, and unvarying in its results. I know of no system better calculated to accomplish these objects than that which commanded the approbation of the founders of the republic, was successively adopted on various occasions since that period, and directly referred to in the message of the President. It is evidently the system contemplated by the framers of the Constitution when they incorporated into that instrument the clause in relation to tonnage duties by the states with the assent of Congress. The debates show that this provision was inserted for the express purpose of enabling the states to levy duties of tonnage to make harbor and other improvements for the benefit of navigation. It was objected that the power to regulate commerce having already been vested exclusively in Congress, the jurisdiction of the states over harbor and river improvements, without the consent or supervision of the federal government, might be so exercised as to conflict with the Congressional regulations in respect to commerce. In order to avoid this objection, and at the same time reserve to the states the power of making the necessary improvements, consistent with such rules as should be prescribed by Congress for the regulation of commerce, the provision was modified and adopted in the form in which we now find it in the Constitution, to wit: "*no state shall lay duties of tonnage except by the consent of Congress.*" It is evident from the debates that the framers of the Constitution looked to tonnage duties as the source from which funds were to be derived for improvements in navigation. The only diversity of opinion among them arose upon the point whether those duties should be levied and the works constructed by the federal government or under state authority. These doubts were solved by the clause quoted, providing, in effect, that while the power was reserved to the states, it should not be exercised except by the consent of Congress, in order that the local legislation for the improvement of navigation might not conflict with the general enactments for the regulation of commerce. Yet the first Congress which assembled under the Constitution commenced that series of contradictory and partial enactments which has continued to the present time, and proven the fruitful source of conflict and dissension.

The first of these acts provided that all expenses for the support of lighthouses, beacons, buoys, and public piers, should be paid out of the national treasury, on the condition that the states in which the same should be situated respectively should cede to the United States the said works, "together with the lands and tenements thereunto belonging, and together with the jurisdiction of the same." A few months afterward the same Congress passed an act consenting that the States of Rhode Island, Maryland, and Georgia might levy tonnage duties for the purpose of improving certain harbors and rivers within their respective limits. This contradictory legislation upon a subject of great national importance, although commenced by the first Congress, and frequently suspended and renewed at uncertain and irregular periods, seems never to have been entirely abandoned. While appropriations from the national treasury have been partial and irregular—sometimes granted and at others withheld—stimulating hopes only to be succeeded by disappointments, tonnage duties have also been collected by the consent of Congress, at various times and for limited periods, in Pennsylvania, Maryland, Virginia, North Carolina, South Carolina, Georgia, Alabama, Massachusetts, Rhode Island, and perhaps other states. Indeed, there has never been a time, since the declaration of Independence, when tonnage duties have not been collected under state authority for the improvement of rivers or harbors, or both. The last act giving the consent of Congress to the collection of these duties was passed for the benefit of the port of Baltimore in 1850, and will not expire until 1861.

Thus it will be seen that the proposition to pass a general law giving the consent of Congress to the imposition of tonnage duties according to a uniform rule, and upon equal terms in all the states and Territories of the Union, does not contemplate the introduction of a new principle into our legislation upon this subject. It only proposes to convert a partial and fluctuating policy into a permanent and efficient system.

If this proposition should receive the sanction of Congress, and be carried into successful operation by the states, it would withdraw river and harbor improvements from the perils of the political arena, and commit them to the fostering care of the local authorities, with a steady and unceasing source of revenue for their prosecution. The system would be plain, direct, and simple in respect to harbor improvements. Each town and city would have charge of the improvement of its own harbor, and would be authorized to tax its own commerce to the extent necessary for its construction. The money could be applied to no other object than the improvement of the harbor, and no higher duties could be levied than were necessary for that purpose. There would seem to be no danger of the power being abused; for, in addition to the restrictions, limitations, and conditions which should be embraced in the laws conferring the consent of Congress, self-interest will furnish adequate and ample assurances and motives for the faithful execution of the trusts. If any town whose harbor needs improvement should fail to impose the duties and make the necessary works, such neglect would inevitably tend to drive the commerce to some rival port, which would use all the means in its power to render its harbor safe and commodious, and afford all necessary protection and facilities to navigation and trade. If, on the other hand, any place should attempt to impose higher duties than will be absolutely necessary for the construction of the requisite improvements, this line of policy, to the extent of the excess, would have the same deleterious effects upon its prosperity. The same injurious influences would result from errors and blunders in the plan of the work, or from extravagance and corruption in the expenditure of the money. Hence each locality, and every citizen and person interested therein, would have a direct and personal interest in the adoption of a wise plan, and in securing strict economy and entire fidelity in the expenditure of the money. While upon the rivers the plan of operations would not be so direct and simple as in the improvement of harbors, yet even there it is not perceived that any serious inconvenience or obstacle would arise to the success of the system. It would be necessary that the law, which shall grant the consent of Congress to the imposition of the duties, shall also give a like consent in conformity with the same provision of the Constitution, that where the river to be improved shall form the boundary of, or be situated in two or more states, such states may enter into compacts with each other, by which they may, under their joint authority, levy the duties and improve the navigation.

In this manner Pennsylvania, Delaware, and New Jersey could enter into a compact for the improvement of the Delaware River, by which each would appoint one commissioner, and the three commissioners constitute a board, which would levy the duties, prescribe the mode of their collection, devise the plan of the improvement, and superintend the expenditure of the money. The six states bordering on the Ohio River, in like manner, could each appoint a commissioner, and the six constitute a board for the improvement of the navigation of that river from Pittsburg to the Mississippi. The same plan could be applied to the Mississippi, by which the nine states bordering upon that stream could each appoint one commissioner, and the nine form a board for the removal of snags and other obstructions in the channel from the Falls of St. Anthony to the Gulf of Mexico. There seems to be no difficulty, therefore, in the execution of the plan where the water-course lies in two or more states, or forms the boundary thereof in whole or in part; and where the river is entirely within the limits of any one state, like the Illinois or Alabama, it may be improved in such manner as the Legislature may prescribe, subject only to such conditions and limitations as may be contained in the act of Congress giving its consent. All the necessities and difficulties upon this subject seem to have been foreseen and provided for in the same clause of the Constitution, wherein it is declared, in effect, that, with the consent of Congress, tonnage duties may be levied for the improvement of rivers and harbors, and that the several states may enter into compacts with each other for that purpose whenever it shall become necessary, subject only to such rules as Congress shall prescribe for the regulation of commerce.

It only remains for me to notice some of the objections which have been urged to this system. It has been said that tonnage duties are taxes upon the commerce of the country, which must be paid in the end by the consumers of the articles bearing the burden. I do not feel disposed to question the soundness of this proposition. I presume the same is true of all the duties, tolls, and charges upon all public works, whether constructed by government or individuals. The State of New York derives a revenue of more than two millions of dollars a year from her canals. Of course this is a tax upon the commerce of the country, and is borne by those who are interested in and benefited by it. This tax is a blessing or a burden, dependent upon the fact whether it has the effect to diminish or increase the cost of transportation. If we could not have enjoyed the benefit of the canal without the payment of the tolls, and if, by its construction and the payment, the cost of transportation has been reduced to one tenth the sum which we would have been compelled to have paid without it, who would not be willing to make a still further contribution to the security and facilities of navigation, if thereby the price of freights are to be reduced in a still greater ratio? The tolls upon our own canal are a tax upon commerce, yet we cheerfully submit to the payment for the reason that they were indispensable to the construction of a great work, which has had the effect to reduce the cost of transportation between the Lakes and the Mississippi far below what it would have been if the canal had not been made. All the charges on the fourteen thousand miles of railroad now in operation in the different states of this Union are just so many taxes upon commerce and travel, yet we do not repudiate the whole railroad system on that account, nor object to the payment of such reasonable charges as are necessary to defray the expenses of constructing and operating them. But it may be said that if all the railroads and canals were built with funds from the national treasury, and were then thrown open to the uses of commerce and travel free of charge, the rates of transportation would be less than they now are. It may be that the rates of transportation would be less, but would our taxes be reduced thereby? No matter who is intrusted with the construction of the works, somebody must foot the bill. If the federal government undertake to make railroads and canals, and river and harbor improvements, somebody must pay the expenses. In order to meet this enlarged expenditure, it would be necessary to augment the revenue by increased taxes upon the commerce of the country. The whole volume of revenue which now fills and overflows the national treasury, with the exception of the small item resulting from the sales of public lands, is derived from a system of taxes imposed upon commerce and collected through the machinery of the customhouses. No matter, therefore, whether these works are made by the federal government, or by stimulating and combining local and individual enterprise under state authority; in any event, they remain a tax upon commerce to the extent of the expenditure.

That system which will insure the construction of the improvements upon the best plan and at the smallest cost will prove the least oppressive to the tax-payer and the most useful to commerce. It requires no argument to prove—for every day's experience teaches us—that public works of every description can be made at a much smaller cost by private enterprise, or by the local authorities directly interested in the improvement, than when constructed by the federal government. Hence, inasmuch as the expenses of constructing river and harbor improvements must, under either plan, be defrayed by a tax upon commerce in the first instance, and finally upon the whole people interested in that commerce, I am of the opinion that the burdens would be less under this system referred to in the message than by appropriations from the federal treasury. Those who seem not to have understood the difference have attempted to excite prejudice against this plan for the improvement of navigations by comparing it to the burdens imposed upon the navigation of the Rhine, the Elbe, the Oder, and other rivers running through the German states. The people residing upon these rivers did not complain that they were required to pay duties for the improvement of their navigation. Such was not the fact. No duties were imposed for any such purpose. No improvements in the navigation were ever made or contemplated by those who exacted the tolls. Taxes were extorted from the navigating interest by the petty sovereigns through whose dominions the rivers run, for the purpose of defraying the expenses of the pomp, and ceremonies, and follies of vicious and corrupt courts. The complaint was, that grievous and unnecessary burdens were imposed on navigation without expending any portion of the money for its protection and improvement. Their complaints were just. They should have protested, if they had lived under a government where the voice of the people could be heard, against the payment of any more or higher tolls than were necessary for the improvement of the navigation, and have insisted that the funds collected should be applied to that purpose and none other.   In short, a plan similar to the one now proposed would have been a full and complete redress of all their grievances upon this subject.

In conclusion, I will state that my object in addressing you this communication is to invite your special attention to so much of the President's Message as relates to river and harbor improvements, with the view that when the Legislature shall assemble, either in special or general session, the subject may be distinctly submitted to their consideration for such action as the great interests of commerce may demand.

I have the honor to be, very respectfully, your friend and fellow-citizen,

S. A. DOUGLAS.

JOEL A. MATTESON, Governor of the State of Illinois.

THE ILLINOIS CENTRAL RAILROAD GRANT.

In 1843 Mr. Douglas entered Congress, and for over seven years he supported and struggled to obtain that magnificent grant of land which led to the construction of the Illinois Central Railroad, and eventually to the establishment of the grand web of railroads which is now spread out all over the Northwestern States.   The construction of a great railroad from the junction of the Ohio and Mississippi Rivers through the state to a point on the Illinois River, and thence north to Galena, had for many years been one of the leading topics in Illinois. It was regarded then and very justly as the one great thing needed to develop the resources of the state, and attract to its fruitful soil the tide of emigration.   When the Internal Improvement System broke down so irretrievably in the state, the attention of the people was directed to Congress and to the public lands as the only reliable resources from whence the necessary aid to construct the desired work could be expected.

When Mr. Douglas entered Congress there was in existence in Illinois a company possessing certain rights to construct a railroad from Cairo to the north.   This company was generally known as the " Cairo Company ;" it had petitioned Congress for permission to enter as pre-emptions a certain quantity of land along the line of the proposed road.   The title of the company was the " Great Western Railway Company." A Mr. Holbrook was the active operator in its affairs.

In the Senate, at the session of '43,–'4, a bill was introduced and reported upon favorably, granting to Holbrook's company the right of way through the public lands for a railway, and entitling them to enter as pre-emptors the public lands along the route, they to pay the government eventually one dollar and twenty-five cents per acre. Mr. Douglas, who was, as we have stated, a member of the House, was strongly opposed to this measure. He insisted that, if any grant was made, it should be made to the state of Illinois, and not to any private corporation. He had no faith in Holbrook or his associates, and had no idea that they would ever construct the road. He believed that the object of the operators was to obtain the pre-emption privilege, and then sell their charter with it in Europe, and thus get out of the matter. He urged that a failure to carry out in good faith the object in consideration of which the grant was made would have the effect to prevent a like application thereafter, would suspend the land sales for several years, would retard the settlement of the state, and give a very unjust impression abroad as to the prospects of Illinois as an improving and flourishing community. He urged that the scheme proposed should be abandoned, and that Congress should be asked for a direct grant of land to the state to aid it in constructing the proposed railroad. In these objections he was sustained generally by his colleagues in the House. The bill as introduced was persisted in, and passed the Senate, and no action was had upon it in the House. At the next session a bill was introduced into the Senate the same as that of last session, with the exception that the "State of Illinois" was named as the grantee of the right of pre-emption instead of the "Great Western Railway Company." That bill was never taken up. At the session of '45–'6 a bill was introduced into the Senate, granting "to the State of Illinois alternate sections of the public land to aid in the construction of the Northern Cross and Central Railroads in said state." This bill was never taken up during that session. At the session of 1846–'7 a bill was introduced into the Senate granting the right of way and a pre-emption privilege, but containing no grant of land. This bill also was suffered to sleep, and no action was had upon it.

In the winter of 1846–'7 Mr. Douglas was elected to the Senate. During the summer of 1847 he traveled over a large portion of the state, and, wherever he made speeches, he discussed the question of the Illinois Central Railroad. He took the position that whatever grant was obtained should be obtained for the state, and not for private individuals; that the state ought not to take a mere grant of pre-emption privilege

—a privilege of buying the government land for one dollar and a quarter per acre upon the condition of constructing a railroad through them; and told the people he would apply for a grant of alternate sections of land to be given to the state gratuitously on condition that the road was constructed. He expressed a confident hope that that measure would receive an undivided support in Illinois, in which case he had no doubt as to its ultimate success. He urged the propriety of holding public meetings and the signing of memorials having the obtaining of such a grant in view.

The old bills contemplated but one road—that upon the line of the one projected by the state in '36, having its northern terminus at Galena, and carefully avoiding Chicago and the country lying between that city and the Illinois River. He stated his determination to include in the measure a road connecting with the lakes, thus securing for it friends in the Northeastern and Middle States, who did not like a proposition having for its natural tendency the diversion of all trade and traffic from the upper Mississippi toward New Orleans instead of toward the Atlantic sea-board. By making an additional road to the lakes at Chicago, a direct route would be made from the Southwest through to Philadelphia, Baltimore, and New York; would connect the lower Mississippi with the lakes, the lakes and the Eastern States with the Southwest, and give to the vast region north and west of Illinois a communication both east and south.

When Congress met in December, 1847, Mr. Douglas took his seat in the Senate. In a few weeks the old and familiar "Pre-emption" Bill was introduced and referred. In January Mr. Douglas introduced his bill granting alternate sections of the public land to the State of Illinois to aid in the construction of a railroad from Cairo to Galena, with a branch from some appropriate point on the road to Chicago. It also embraced a proposition for a road crossing the state from Indiana to the Mississippi River. Both bills were reported from the Senate Committee on public lands, of which the Hon. Sidney Breese of Illinois was chairman. The latter bill—the one proposed by Mr. Douglas—was subsequently taken up, and early in May was passed by the Senate. The other bill was not acted upon.

The representatives in the House from Illinois all gave to

the measure their cordial support. Toward the close of the session, however, it was laid on the table by a small majority. At the next session, '48–9, Mr. Douglas introduced his bill in the Senate again; but, before any action was had in that body, the Illinois representatives in the House had succeeded in having the bill of the last session restored to its place on the calendar, but Congress adjourned without any farther action on the bill by the House.

In December, 1849, Mr. Douglas, with his colleague, General Shields, who had succeeded Mr. Breese, and the Illinois delegation in the House, matured a bill having but one road in contemplation, and that the Illinois Central and its Chicago branch. That bill, in which all the Illinois members had a part in framing, was introduced into the Senate by Mr. Douglas in January, 1850. The Compromise Measures of that year, and the question of Slavery generally, engrossed nearly all the time and discussions of the Senate. That subject came up almost every morning, and frequently was considered several days in succession, to the exclusion of all other business. There was, however, another reason for delay. When it had become certain that the only act that would be seriously pressed by the Illinois representatives would be one making a grant of land to the State of Illinois, the parties interested in the Cairo Company saw at once an end to their schemes unless they could in some manner circumvent that policy. They therefore proceeded to the Legislature of Illinois, and after a siege, and by the most dexterous management, the Legislature was induced to pass a measure ceding to Holbrook and his associates all lands that might at any time be granted by Congress to the state for the purpose, or in aid of the construction of the Illinois Central Railroad. Here, then, was a new and dangerous pitfall prepared for the great measure. If Congress should grant land to the company, the state would be at the mercy of an irresponsible band of speculators; to prevent this the policy had been changed, so as to secure the grant directly to the state, leaving the latter full power and control over the entire matter, and free to act with whoever would offer the best terms. But Holbrook had effectually headed off this policy by the amendment which he had obtained to his charter. He came to Washington and importuned for the passage of the bill in the shape in which it had been introduced some years before, or he would take the bill then pending. He proposed to be on intimate terms with Mr. Douglas, but the latter declined the association.

At length, when fully informed of all the facts, Mr. Douglas sent for Holbrook, and told him that no bill of any kind would be suffered to pass unless the grant was made directly to the state, and to be held and disposed of by the state freely, and unlimited by any previous charter either to Holbrook or any one else. If Holbrook persisted in the right obtained under his charter and the subsequent legislation of Illinois, he, Mr. Douglas, would expose and denounce the whole scheme as one intended to use the name of the state to obtain an immense property for irresponsible and dishonest men to speculate and grow rich upon. He refused to move in the matter in Congress unless Holbrook would first sign and execute a good and valid release of every right, claim, and demand to any lands that might be granted by Congress to the state for railroad or other purposes. If Holbrook would not sign such a release, and attempted to have any bill passed, Mr. Douglas notified him that he would denounce and expose the whole game. It was a serious matter to the state, and equally so to Holbrook. It was total loss to one or the other. If the law passed as matters then stood, Holbrook's company got all, the state nothing. If Holbrook's company surrendered, as demanded by Mr. Douglas, then the state got all, and the company nothing. If Holbrook refused to surrender, Douglas stood in his way of obtaining any grant of any kind. The alternatives were not inviting to Mr. Holbrook; but at length he yielded; he signed and delivered the demanded release to the state, which release was forwarded to Springfield, and filed in the archives of the State of Illinois. Thus was it that the grant was received by the state unfettered and unimpaired by any of the adroit schemes of the wily speculators upon the public welfare. Having relieved the state of the Holbrook Company's claim, Mr. Douglas at once undertook to get the bill considered.

It was not until April 29 that he could induce the Senate to consider the bill, and then only after a most spirited and fervent appeal. Having once got the bill before the Senate, he pressed it day after day until the 2d of May, when, notwithstanding the covert hostility of some Western senators, the bill passed—yeas 26, nays 14.

The bill was taken to the House, and there, by the skill, good management, and unity of action of the representatives of the state, the House was eventually brought to a vote, and the act making the donation of public land to the State of Illinois, to aid in the construction of the Illinois Central Railroad and its branch to Chicago, became a law.

On his return to Illinois at the close of the session, Mr. Douglas and General Shields were tendered a public dinner by the citizens of Chicago, in consideration of their services in obtaining the passage of this act. The two senators, in declining the honor, took the occasion to award to their colleagues in the House the full measure of credit for the successful carrying of the bill through the intricate parliamentary mazes that surrounded its pathway to completion.

The great Central Railroad of Illinois, the beginning of a system of great works, is now completed. The benefits it has produced to the state can not be calculated. During the five years immediately following the passage of the bill the population of Illinois increased from 850,000 to over 1,300,000. Other railroads have been constructed, and to day the Illinois Central Railroad is but a trunk to which and from which the travel and transportation of the Valley of the Mississippi bend their way by roads from every quarter of the country. The people of Illinois and of the Northwest will never be indifferent to the great benefits resulting from the passage of the Illinois Central Railroad land grant, nor will the men who were instrumental in achieving the great work be forgotten by a grateful people.

Mr. Douglas has always supported and voted for the bills making grants for similar purposes to the states of Alabama, Mississippi, Louisiana, Arkansas, Missouri, Iowa, Michigan, Wisconsin, Minnesota, and perhaps other states.

THE PACIFIC RAILROAD.

Mr. Douglas has been a friend and supporter of what he has himself styled "the great measure of the age"—the construction of a railroad to the Pacific Ocean. He has repeatedly introduced bills for that end, and has as repeatedly been chosen on select committees having that subject in charge. By vote and by speech he has exhibited the sincerity of his interest in this great national work, and has suffered no occasion to pass without appealing to the friends of the road to drop all controversy as to the details, and secure the substance, the main thing, the road itself. He was originally in favor of authorizing the construction of three roads—one at the north, one at the centre, and the other at the south, leaving to the contractors the choice of such route as private interest and enterprise would select as the most promising of success. He has always opposed an arbitrary declaration by Congress of the route to be taken, preferring to fix only the termini, and leave to those interested in the construction of the road to determine the route between the given points, by such considerations as time and experience might suggest.

Bills for the construction of the Pacific railroad have been before Congress for several years, and they have always received the support of Mr. Douglas. If no act has passed for that work, no part of the serious responsibility for the omission of duty can rest upon him. He has never failed in his duty toward this important national work.

When the bill was under consideration in the Senate in 1858, Mr. Douglas, on the 17th of April, thus stated his views:

Mr. President,—I have witnessed with deep regret the indications that this measure is to be defeated at the present session of Congress. I had hoped that this Congress would signalize itself by inaugurating the great measure of connecting the Mississippi Valley with the Pacific Ocean by a railroad. I had supposed that the people of the United States had decided the question at the last presidential election in a manner so emphatic as to leave no doubt that their will was to be carried into effect. I believe that all the presidential candidates at the last election were committed to the measure. All the presidential platforms sanctioned it as a part of their creed. I believe it is about the only measure on which there was entire unanimity; and it is a very curious fact that the measure which commanded universal approbation—the measure upon which all parties united—a measure against which no man could be found, previous to the election, to raise his voice—should be the one that can receive no support, nor the co-operation of any one party, while disputed measures can occupy the whole time of Congress, and can be carried through successfully. I make no complaint of any political party, nor of any gentleman who opposes this bill; but it did strike me that it was a fact to be noticed, that a measure of this description, so long before the country, so well understood by the people, and receiving such universal sanction from them, should not be carried into effect. If the bill which has been devised by the committee is not the best that can be framed, let it be amended and modified until its objectionable features shall be removed. Let us not make a test question of this particular form of bill or that particular form; of this particular route or that particular route ; of the benefits to this section or that section. If there is any thing wrong in the details, in the form, in the construction of the bill, let the objectionable features be removed, and carry out the great object of a railroad communication between the Mississippi Valley and the Pacific Ocean.

Various objections have been raised to this bill, some referring to the route, involving sectional consideration; others to the form of the bill; others to the present time as inauspicious for the construction of such a railroad under any circumstances. Sir, I have examined this bill very carefully. I was a member of the committee that framed it, and I gave my cordial assent to the report. I am free to say that I think it is the best bill that has ever been reported to the Senate of the United States for the construction of a Pacific railroad. I say this with entire disinterestedness, for I have heretofore reported several myself, and I believe I have invariably been a member of the committees that have reported such bills. I am glad to find that we have progressed to such an extent as to be able to improve on the former bills that have, from time to time, been brought before the Senate of the United States. This may not be perfect. It is difficult to make human legislation entirely perfect; at any rate, to so construct it as to bring about an entire unanimity of opinion upon a question that involves, to some extent, selfish, sectional, and partisan considerations. But, sir, I think this bill is fair. First, it is fair in the location of the route, as between the different sections. The termini are fixed. Then the route between the termini is to be left to the contractors and owners of the road, who are to put their capital into it, and, for weal or for woe, are to be responsible for its management.

What is the objection to these termini? San Francisco, upon the Pacific, is not only central, but it is the great commercial mart, the great concentrating point, the great entrepôt for the commerce of the Pacific, not only in the present, but in the future. That point was selected as the western terminus for the reason that there seemed to be a unanimous sentiment that whatever might be the starting-point on the east, the system would not be complete until it should reach the city of San Francisco on the west. I suggested myself, in the committee, the selection of that very point; not that I had any objection to other points; not that I was any more friendly to San Francisco and her inhabitants than to any other port on the Pacific; but because I believe that to be the commanding port, the large city where trade concentrates, and its position indicated it as the proper terminus on the Pacific Ocean.

Then, in regard to the eastern terminus, a point on the Missouri River is selected for various reasons. One is, that it is central as between the North and South—as nearly central as could be selected. It was necessary to commence on the Missouri River, if you were going to take a central route, in order that the starting-point might connect with navigation, so that you might reach it by boats in carrying your iron, your supplies, and your materials for the commencement and the construction of the road. It was essential that you should commence at a point of navigation so that you could connect with the sea-board. If you start it at a point back in the interior five hundred or a thousand miles, as it is proposed, at El Paso, from the navigable waters of the Mississippi, it would cost you more money to carry the iron, provisions, supplies, and men to that starting-point, than it would to make a road from the Mississippi to the starting-point, in order to begin the work. In that case it would be a matter of economy to make a road to your starting-point in order to begin. Hence, in my opinion, it would be an act of folly to think of starting a railroad to the Pacific at a point eight hundred or a thousand miles in the interior, away from any connection with navigable water, or with other railroads already in existence.

For these reasons, we agreed in the bill to commence on the Missouri River. When you indicate that river, a little diversity of opinion arises as to what point on the river shall be selected. There are various respectable, thriving towns on either bank of the river, each of which thinks it is the exact position where the road ought to commence. I suppose that Kansas City,

Wyandott, Weston, Leavenworth, Atchison, **Platte's Mouth City,** Omaha, De Soto, Sioux City, and various other towns whose names have not become familiar to us, and have found no resting-place on the map, each thinks that it has the exact place where the road should begin. Well, sir, I do not desire to show any preference between these towns; either of them would suit me very well; and we leave it to the contractors to say which shall be the one. We leave the exact eastern terminus open for the reason that the public interests will be substantially as well served by the selection of the one as the other. It is not so at the western terminus. San Francisco does not occupy that relation to the towns on the Pacific coast that these little towns on the Missouri River do to the country east of the Missouri. The public have no material interest in the question whether it shall start at the mouth of the Kansas, at Weston, at Leavenworth, at St. Joseph, at Platte's Mouth, or at Sioux City. Either connects with the great lines; either would be substantially central as between North and South. So far as I am concerned, I should not care a sixpence which of those towns was selected as the starting-point, because they start there upon a plain that stretches for eight hundred miles, and can connect with the whole railroad system of the country. You can go directly west. You can bend to the north and connect with the northern roads, or bend to the south and connect with the southern roads.

The senator from Georgia (Mr. Iverson) would be satisfied, as I understand, with the termini, if we had selected one intermediate point, so as to indicate the route that should be taken between the termini. I understand that he would be satisfied if we should indicate that it should go south of Santa Fé, so as to include as the probable line the Albuquerque route, or the one on the thirty-fifth parallel, or the one south of it. Sir, I am free to say that, individually, I should have no objection to the route indicated by the senator from Georgia. I have great faith that the Albuquerque route is an exceedingly favorable one; favorable in its grades, in the shortness of its distances, in its climate, the absence of deep snow, and in the topography of the country. While it avoids very steep grades, it furnishes, perhaps, as much of grass, of timber, of water, of materials necessary for the construction and repair of the road, if not more, than any other route. As a Northern man, living upon the great line of the lakes, you can not indicate a route that I think would subserve our interests, and the great interests of this country, better than that; yet, if I expressed the opinion that the line ought to go on that route between the termini, some other man would say it ought to go on Governor Stevens's extreme northern route; some one else would say it ought to go on the South Pass route; and we should divide the friends of the measure as to the point at which the road should pass the mountains—whether at the extreme north, at the centre, the Albuquerque route, or the further southern one down in Arizona—and we should be unable to decide between ourselves which was best.

I have sometimes thought that the extreme northern route, known as the Stevens' route, was the best, as furnishing better grass, more timber, more water, more of those elements necessary in constructing, repairing, operating, and maintaining a road, than any other. I think now that the preference, merely upon routes, is between the northern or Stevens's route on the one side, and the Albuquerque route on the other. Still, as I never expect to put a dollar of money into the road, as I never expect to have any agency or connection with or interest in it, I am willing to leave the selection of the route between the termini to those who are to put their fortunes and connect their character with the road, and to be responsible, in the most tender of all points, if they make a mistake in the selection. But for these considerations, I should have cheerfully yielded to the suggestion of the senator from Georgia to fix the crossing-point on the Rio Grande River.

But, sir, I am unwilling to lose this great measure merely because of a difference of opinion as to what shall be the pass selected in the Rocky Mountains through which the road shall run. I believe it is a great national measure. I believe it is the greatest practical measure now pending before the country. I believe that we have arrived at that period in our history when our great substantial interests require it. The interests of commerce, the great interests of travel and communication—those still greater interests that bind the Union together, and are to make and preserve the continent as one and indivisible—all demand that this road shall be commenced, prosecuted, and completed at the earliest practicable moment.

I am unwilling to postpone the bill until next December. I have seen these postponements from session to session for the last eight or ten years, with the confident assurance every year that at the next session we should have abundance of time to take up the bill and act upon it. Sir, will you be better prepared at the next session than now? We have now the whole summer before us, drawing our pay, and proposing to perform no service. Next December you will have but ninety days, with all the unfinished business left over, your appropriation bills on hand, and not only the regular bills, but the new deficiency bill; and you will postpone this measure again for the want of time to consider it then. I think, sir, we had better grapple with the difficulties that surround this question now, when it is fairly before us, when we have time to consider it, and when I think we can act upon it as dispassionately, as calmly, as wisely, as we shall ever be able to do.

I have regretted to see the question of sectional advantages brought into this discussion. If you are to have but one road, fairness and justice would plainly indicate that that one should be located as near the centre as practicable. The Missouri River is as near the centre and the line of this road is as near as it can be made; and if there is but one to be made, the route now indicated, in my opinion, is fair, is just, and ought to be taken. I have heretofore been of the opinion that we ought to have three roads: one in the centre, one in the extreme south, and one in the extreme north. If I thought we could carry the three, and could execute them in any reasonable time, I would now adhere to that policy and prefer it; but I have seen enough here during this session of Congress to satisfy me that but one can pass, and to ask for three at this time is to lose the whole. Believing that that is the temper, that that is the feeling, and, I will say, the judgment of the members of both houses of Congress, I prefer to take one road rather than to lose all in the vain attempt to get three. If there were to be three, of course the one indicated in this bill would be the central; one would be north of it, and another south of it. But if there is to be but one, the central one should be taken; for the north, by bending a little down south, can join it; and the south, by leaning a little to the north, can unite with it too; and our Southern friends ought to be able to bend and lean a little, as well as to require us to bend and lean all the time, in order to join them. The central position is the just one, if there is to be but one road. The concession should be as much on the one side as on the other. I am ready to meet gentlemen half way on every question that does not violate principle, and they ought not to ask us to meet them more than half way where there is no principle involved, and nothing but expediency.

Then, sir, why not unite upon this bill? We are told it is going to involve the government of the United States in countless millions of expenditure. How is that? Certainly not under this bill, not by authority of this bill, not without violating this bill. The bill under consideration provides that when a section of the road shall be made, the government may advance a portion of the lands, and $12,500 per mile in bonds on the section thus made, in order to aid in the construction of the next, holding a lien upon the road for the refunding of the money thus advanced.   Under this bill it is not possible that the contractors can ever obtain more than $12,500 per mile on each mile of the road that is completed.   It is, therefore, very easy to compute the cost to the government.   Take the length of the road in miles, and multiply it by $12,500, and you have the cost.   If you make the computation, you will find it will come to a fraction over $20,000,000.   The limitation in the bill is, that in no event shall it exceed $25,000,000.   Therefore, by the terms of the bill, the undertaking of the government is confined to $25,000,000; and, by the calculation, it will be less than that sum.   Is that a sum that would bankrupt the Treasury of the United States?

I predict to you now, sir, that the Mormon campaign has cost, and has led to engagements and undertakings that, when redeemed, will cost more than $25,000,000, if not double that sum.   During the last six months, on account of the Mormon rebellion, expenses have been paid and undertakings have been assumed which will cost this government more than the total expenditure which can possibly be made in conformity with the provisions of this bill.   If you had had this railroad made you would have saved the whole cost which the government is to advance in this little Mormon war alone. If you have a general Indian war in the mountains, it will cost you twice the amount called for by this bill.   If you should have a war with a European power, the construction of this road would save many fold its cost in the transportation of troops and munitions of war to the Pacific Ocean, in carrying on your operations.

In an economical point of view I look upon it as a wise measure.   It is one of economy as a war measure alone, or as a peace measure for the purpose of preventing a war.   Whether viewed as a war measure, to enable you to check rebellion in a Territory, or hostilities with the Indians, or to carry on vigorously a war with a European power, or viewed as a peace measure, it is a wise policy, dictated by every consideration of convenience and public good.

Again, sir, in carrying the mails, it is an economical measure.   As the senator from Georgia has demonstrated, the cost of carrying the mails alone to the Pacific Ocean for thirty years, under the present contracts, is double the amount of the whole expenditure under this bill for the same time in the construction and working of the road.   In the transportation of mails, then, it would save twice its cost.   The transportation of army and navy supplies would swell the amount to three or four fold.   How many years will it be before the government will receive back, in transportation, the whole cost of this advance of aid in the construction of the road?

But, sir, some gentlemen think it is an unsound policy, leading to the doctrine of internal improvements by the federal government within the different states of the Union.   We are told we must continue the road to the limits of the Territories, and not extend it into the states, because it is supposed that entering a state with this contract violates some great principle of state-rights.   Mr. President, the committee considered that proposition, and they avoided that objection in the estimation of the most strict, rigid, tight-laced State-rights men that we have in the body.   We struck out the provision in the bill first drawn, that the President should contract for the construction of a railroad from the Missouri River to the Pacific Ocean, and followed an example that we found on the statute-book for carrying the mails from Alexandria to Richmond, Virginia—an act passed about the time when the resolutions of 1798 were adopted, and the report of 1799 was made—an act that we thought came exactly within the spirit of those resolutions.   That act, according to my recollection, was, that the Department be authorized to contract for the transportation of the United States mail by four-horse post-coaches, with closed backs, so as to protect it from the weather and rain, from Alexandria to Richmond, in the State of Virginia. It occurred to this committee that if it had been the custom, from the beginning of this government to this day, to make contracts for the transportation of the mails in four-horse post-coaches, built in a particular manner, and the contractor left to furnish his own coaches and his own horses, and his own means of transportation, we might make a similar contract for the transportation of the mails by railroad from one point to another, leaving the contractor to make his own railroad, and furnish his own cars, and comply with the terms of the contract.

There is nothing in this bill that violates any one principle which has prevailed in every mail contract that has been made, from the days of Dr. Franklin down to the elevation of James Buchanan to the presidency. Every contract for carrying the mail by horse, from such a point to such a point, in saddle-bags, involves the same principle. Every contract for carrying it from such a point to such a point in two-horse hacks, with a covering to protect it from the storm, involves the same principle. Every contract to carry it from such a point to such a point in four-horse coaches of a particular description, involves the same principle. You contracted to carry the mails from New York to Liverpool in ships of two thousand tons each, to be constructed according to a model prescribed by the Navy Department, leaving the contractor to furnish his own ships, and receive so much pay. That involves the same principle.

You have, therefore, carried out the principle of this bill in every contract you have ever had for mails, whether it be upon the land or upon the water. In every mail contract you have had, you have carried out the identical principle involved in this bill—simply the right to contract for the transportation of the United States mails, troops, munitions of war, army and navy supplies, at fair prices, in the manner you prescribed, leaving the contracting party to furnish the mode and means of transportation. That is all there is in it. I do not see how it can violate any party creed; how it can violate any principle of state-rights; how it can interfere with any man's conscientious scruples. Then, sir, where is the objection?

If you look on this as a measure of economy and a commercial measure, the argument is all in favor of the bill. It is true, the senator from Massachusetts has suggested that it is idle to suppose that the trade of China is to centre in San Francisco, and then pay sixty dollars a ton for transportation across the continent by a railroad to Boston. It was very natural that he should indicate Boston, as my friend from Georgia might, perhaps, have thought of Savannah, or my friend from South Carolina might have indicated Charleston, or the senator from Louisiana might have indicated New Orleans. But I, living at the head of the great lakes, would have made the computation from Chicago, and my friend from Missouri would have thought it would have been very well, perhaps, to take it from St. Louis. When you are making this computation, I respectfully submit you must make the calculation from the sea-board to the centre of the continent, and not charge transportation all the way from the Atlantic to the Pacific; for suppose you do not construct this road, and these goods come by ship to Boston, it will cost something to take them by railroad to Chicago, and a little more to take them by railroad to the Missouri River, half way back to San Francisco again. If you select the centre of the continent, the great heart and centre of the Republic—the Mississippi Valley—as the point at which you are to concentrate your trade, and from which it is to diverge, you will find that the transportation of it by railroad would not be much greater from San Francisco than from Boston. It would be nearly the same from the Pacific that it is from the Atlantic; and the calculation must be made in that point of view. There is the centre of consumption, and the centre of those great products that are sent abroad in all quarters to pay for articles imported. The centre of production, the centre of consumption, the future centre of the population of the continent, is the point to which, and from which, your calculation should be made.

Then, sir, if it costs sixty dollars per ton for transportation from San Francisco to Boston by railroad, half way you may say it will cost thirty dollars a ton. The result, then, of coming from San Francisco to the centre by railroad would be to save transportation by ship from San Francisco to Boston, in addition to the railroad transportation into the interior.

But, sir, I dissent from a portion of the gentleman's argument, so far as it relates to the transportation even from San Francisco to Boston. I admit that heavy articles of cheap value and great bulk would go by ship, that being the cheapest mode of communication; but light articles, costly articles, expensive articles, those demanded immediately, and subject to decay from long voyages and delays, would come directly across by railroad, and what you would save in time would be more than the extra expense of the transportation. You must add to that the risk of the tropics, which destroys many articles, and the process which is necessary to be gone through with to prepare articles for the sea-voyage is to be taken into the account. I have had occasion to witness that evil in one article of beverage very familiar to you all. Let any man take one cup of tea that came from China to Russia overland, without passing twice under the equator, and he will never be reconciled to a cup of tea that has passed under the equator. The genuine article, that has not been manipulated and prepared to pass under the equator, is worth tenfold more than that which we receive here. Preparation is necessary to enable it to pass the tropics, and the long, damp voyage makes as much difference in the article of tea as the difference between a green apple and a dried apple, green corn and dried corn, sent abroad. So you will find it to be with fruits; so it will be with all the expensive and precious articles, and especially those liable to decay and to injury, either by exposure to a tropical climate or to the moisture of a long sea-voyage.

Then, sir, in a commercial point of view, this road will be of vast importance. There is another consideration that I will allude to for a moment. It will extend our trade more than any other measure that you can devise, certainly more than any one that you now have in contemplation. The people are all anxious for the annexation of Cuba as soon as it can be obtained on fair and honorable terms—and why? In order to get the small, pitiful trade of that island. We all talk about the great importance of Central America in order to extend our commerce; it is valuable to the extent it goes. But Cuba, Central America, and all the islands surrounding them put together, are not a thousandth part of the value of the great East India trade that would be drawn first to our western coast, and then across to the Valley of the Mississippi, if this railroad be constructed. Sir, if we intend to extend our commerce—if we intend to make the great ports of the world tributary to our wealth, we must prosecute our trade eastward or westward, as you please; we must penetrate the Pacific, its islands, and its continent, where the great mass of the human family reside—where the articles that have built up the powerful nations of the world have always come from. That is the direction in which we should look for the expansion of our commerce and of our trade. That is the direction our public policy should take—a direction that is facilitated by the great work now proposed to be made.

I care not whether you look at it in a commercial point of view, as a matter of administrative economy at home, as a question of military defense, or in reference to the building up of the national wealth, and power, and glory; it is the great measure of the age—a measure that in my opinion has been postponed too long—and I frankly confess to you that I regard the postponement to next December to mean till after the next presidential election. No man hopes or expects, when you have not time to pass it in the early spring, at the long session, that you are going to consider it at the short session. When you come here at the next session, the objection will be that you must not bring forward a measure of this magnitude, because it will affect the political relations of parties, and it will be postponed then, as it was two years ago, to give the glory to the incoming administration, each party probably thinking that it would have the honor of carrying out the measure. Hence, sir, I regard the proposition of postponement till December to mean till after the election of 1860.

I desire to see all the pledges made in the last contest redeemed during this term, and let the next president, and the parties under him, redeem the pledges and obligations assumed during the next campaign. The people of all parties at the last presidential election decreed that this road was to be made. The question is now before us. We have time to consider it. We have all the means necessary, as much now as we can have at any other time. The senator from Massachusetts intimates that, the treasury being bankrupt now, we can not afford the money. That senator also remarked that we were just emerging from a severe commercial crisis—a great commercial revulsion—which had carried bankruptcy in its train. If we have just emerged from it, if we have passed it, this is the very time of all others when a great enterprise should be begun. It might have been argued when we saw that crisis coming, before it reached us, that we should furl our sails and trim our ship for the approaching storm; but when it has exhausted its rage, when all the mischief has been done that could be inflicted, when the bright sun of day is breaking forth, when the sea is becoming calm, and there is but little visible of the past tempest, when the nausea of sea-sickness is succeeded by joyous exhilaration, inspired by the hope of a fair voyage, let men feel elated and be ready to commence a great work like this, so as to complete it before another commercial crisis or revulsion shall come upon us.

Sir, if you pass this bill, no money can be expended under it until one section of the road has been made. The surveys must be completed, the route must be located, the land set aside and surveyed, and a section of the road made, before a dollar can be drawn from the treasury. If you can pass the bill now, it can not make any drain on the treasury for at least two years to come; and who doubts that all the effects of the late crisis will have passed away before the expiration of those two years.

Mr. President, this is the auspicious time, either with a view to the interests of the country, or to that stagnation which exists between political parties, which is calculated to make it a measure of the country rather than a partisan measure, or to the commercial and monetary affairs of the nation, or with reference to the future. Look upon it in any point of view, now is the time; and I am glad that the senator from Louisiana has indicated, as I am told he has, that the motion for postponement is a test question; for I confess I shall regard it as a test vote on a Pacific railroad during this term, whatever it may be in the future. I hope that we shall pass the bill now.

CHAPTER XVI.

THE CAMPAIGN OF 1858.

THE reader who has given attention to those pages of this book relating to the Lecompton controversy in Congress will of course be informed of many of the events connected with and leading to the most memorable election held in the State of Illinois during the year 1858. To many persons, however, it will be serviceable that, before entering upon the description of the contest of that year, a brief repetition of some leading facts, and a detailed history of others, should be given now.

When the announcement was made by telegraph from St. Louis that Mr. John Calhoun and his associates in the Lecompton Convention had, for the purpose of securing for their monstrosity a legal substance which it could never obtain at the hands of the people, wantonly and wickedly resolved to declare the Lecompton Constitution as already made, and waiting only the sanction of Congress to erect it as the government of the people of the unfortunate Territory, there was in all Illinois a universal expression of indignation. Calhoun had for many years been an active Democrat in the central part of the state, and he was believed to be a man who, whatever other failings and imperfections he might have, would never consent, under any circumstances, to embarrass or injure his party friends by rash or unjustifiable political action. In short, he was esteemed by all as a "safe and reliable" man, who could not be seduced, under any state of things, to do political acts, the effect of which was to destroy, or, to say the least, embarrass and place his party in a most unenviable position before the country. For many days those who had a personal acquaintance with the "Lord President," as he was subsequently styled by the papers of the state, declined giving credit to the reports of the action of the convention, but these doubts were but of short duration; letters from a number of persons in the Territory, and from Calhoun himself, soon removed all question, not only as to the action of the convention, but also as to the full participation of Calhoun in the iniquitous proceedings.

From one end of the state to the other, the Democratic newspaper press immediately and determinedly denounced the action of the convention, and of the daring attempt by Calhoun and his associates to defraud the people of Kansas of a sacred right; to violate the entire spirit of the Kansas-Nebraska Act; to repudiate the saving and most peculiar principle of the Cincinnati platform; to disregard and contemptuously set aside the peremptory and pointed instructions of Mr. Buchanan, and the earnest advice and appeals of Governor Walker. In the very expressive language of Mr. Buchanan, no Democrat in Illinois "had any serious doubt" but that the convention would submit the Constitution to the people, and each Democrat in the state felt that the convention, in utterly scorning and repudiating the instructions of Mr. Buchanan to Governor Walker, had sought, through pure wantonness, to treat the instructions of the venerable President as the "fogyism" of old age. The Chicago *Times*, Springfield *Register*, Quincy *Herald*, Galena *Courier*, Peoria *News*, and Alton *Democrat*—the daily Democratic papers of the state—without any previous consultation or understanding, simultaneously, and with all their power, proclaimed the indignant feeling of the Democracy in their respective localities, and called upon the party to take immediate action, by meetings and resolutions, to sustain Mr. Buchanan and the Cincinnati platform against the cowardly and insolent attempt on the part of the Lecompton Convention to treat both with sovereign contempt. The weekly Democratic press of the state followed with great unanimity, and within ten days from the receipt of the first intelligence of the action of the Lecompton Convention, Illinois, speaking through the Democratic press, had become unanimously pledged to the support and defense of the President in his efforts to preserve the Cincinnati platform pure and inviolate. No Democrat in Illinois believed the silly slander of a Northern senator, that "the administration was a little weak in the knees;" and all relied implicitly that the policy of the government, so clearly and emphatically enunciated in the speeches of Governor Walker and in his instructions from the hand of General Cass, would be carried out to the last extremity, thereby vindicating the power and majesty of the great principle embraced in the Kansas-Nebraska Act, so cordially and unanimously ratified and adopted by the Democracy at Cincinnati.

There was not one Democratic newspaper in all Illinois that did not, with all its power, sustain the President and Governor Walker against the unfortunate and ill-judged action of John Calhoun and his associates at Lecompton.

Judge Douglas was at that time in Chicago; though no public meeting was held at which he could offer his views, there was no doubt entertained by any one, Democrat or Republican, as to his determination to sustain the President in the policy so recently declared by the administration. In a few days Democratic newspapers in other states came into Illinois sustaining the administration and denouncing the Lecomptonites. From the entire Northwest there was not a Democratic paper which opposed the administration by sustaining Calhoun. The papers of New York gave to the Democracy of Illinois the most unbounded assurance that the Democracy of that state would unite with their Western brethren in a vigorous support of the President. Some weeks later, the Washington Union, which, since the action of the Kansas Convention, had remained silent, appeared with an elaborate editorial, claiming in behalf of the slaveholder the constitutional right to carry his slaves into any state or Territory of the United States, and hold them in such state or Territory by virtue of a constitutional right, in defiance of the laws of such state or Territory. As this matter has been treated of in one of Mr. Douglas's speeches, it is unnecessary to do more here than to repeat that this article of the Union was the first indication that the Democracy of Illinois had that any change was contemplated in the policy of the administration; and following immediately upon this strange declaration of the most unsound and untenable propositions was a quasi endorsement of the Lecompton fraud, and a suggestion that the best course to pursue was to acquiesce in it, and thus get rid of a "distracting question." Still, so complete had been Mr. Buchanan's committal to the principles of the Kansas-Nebraska Act; so acknowledged and boasted of General Cass's devotion to unrestrained squatter sovereignty; so well known Mr. Cobb's liberal views, proclaimed so eloquently upon the hills and in the valleys of Pennsylvania during 1856; so emphatic had been Mr. Toucey's endorsement of the right of self-government, that human intellect refused to understand how, in one moment, and without any rational pretense or occasion, an administration could thus suddenly give the negative to its past history and official acts, and render ridiculous at least a majority of its members by making them active supporters of proceedings planned and perpetrated in positive conflict with their opinions and speeches during a long, excited, and severe political contest of but very recent date.

Up to the appearance of these articles in the Washington Union, the Republican party had been panic-stricken. The only hope that that party could have had of perpetuating its existence in the Northwest was a want of fidelity on the part of the Democracy to the Cincinnati platform; and when the Democracy of the Northwest, without a dissenting voice, united in sustaining the administration in its Kansas policy and in repudiating the action of the Lecompton Convention, because it violated the Cincinnati platform, that party saw its own extinction as plainly as it could be written. Its first hope was that Douglas, with a view of being considered the peculiar friend of the South, would sustain the Lecompton Convention. That hope being dissipated, the Republican party was preparing for its demise, when, from a quarter most unexpected, came words of cheering consolation, of hope, and of future glory. There is no use in disguising the fact, even were it possible to do so, that, had the administration, in December, 1857, remained true to its previously maintained policy, and urged upon Congress the duty of disregarding any and all propositions for the admission of Kansas tainted with fraud, and not approved by the free and deliberate choice of the people, the Republican party would have virtually ceased to exist as an organization in the Northwestern States. It would have at once been reduced to a mere handful of abolition fanatics, who by education, as well as natural tastes, habits, and associations, will always cling to the theory that the only way of elevating the negro is by removing every law, custom, or other hinderance to the degradation of the white man to the level of the negro. The thousands who had by their votes, during the previous three years, given a consequence and a power to the Republican party, because of a sincere belief that the policy of the Democratic party had been and would continue to be shaped and changed to promote the ends and purposes of the South as opposed to those of the North, upon the official declaration by the President that he would not sanction or approve of fraud, nor consent to a violation of the leading principle to which he owed his own election, even to secure the admission of another slave state, would have abandoned the Republican party and rallied under the Democratic flag, having no longer any doubt of the honesty of their party. But no such course was pursued by the President. He did give his official approval to the result of fraud ; he did give his executive recommendation to the completion of the violation of the Cincinnati platform by the admission of a state under a Constitution to which the people were not only no party, but which had been kept from them because it was known they would repudiate it. Hence these men, instead of being restored to the Democratic party by a prompt vindication of its honesty and devotion to principle, were repelled, and confirmed in their impression that the Democratic party had but one principle, and that was to promote the ends of slavery. The golden opportunity of putting an end to an organization which, in the hands of the unprincipled managers who have heretofore and ever will control its movements, must be dangerous to the peace and prosperity of the nation and to the supremacy of the Constitution, was neglected and lost. The subsequent action of Congress, of the executive and his cabinet, and of some of the Northern representatives of the Democracy, supplied the Republicans with sufficient proof to enable them to argue with plausibility that the Democratic party was one devoted to the interests of the slaveholding population of the Southern States.

The annual message of Mr. Buchanan, in which he formally proclaimed his approval of Lecomptonism, was received with a most depressing effect upon the party in Illinois. Though he had never been the choice of the party in Illinois, yet, on account of his advanced age, and the fact that he must have felt how many risks the party had always undertaken in advancing him from one high position to another, despite the absence of all personal popularity on his part, and want of striking qualities in his character, Democrats in the West entertained that respect for him which years and long service always excite in the breasts of an intelligent and refined people. While they deplored what they could not but regard as a great error, viewed as a matter of governmental as well as party policy, yet no word of unkindness or reproach was uttered. The message was published in all the papers of the state ; and while the

Republicans were jubilant over it, the Democratic papers published it silently—one only, a weekly paper, edited by a federal office-holder, venturing very slight approval of it. The subsequent messages of the President, both by their manner as well as by their language—the very stupid exhibition of ill-concealed venom by Mr. Bigler, in his speech, which was represented as being an authorized expression of the views of the administration, and the Quixotical effort of Dr. Fitch to read Douglas and all who thought with him out of the party—could not fail to modify very greatly the personal interest previously entertained by the Democracy in the venerable President. The debates in Congress and the proceedings there have already been spoken of in these pages, and it will only be necessary to refer to them now as explaining proceedings in the state. On a previous page will be found some notice of a meeting held in Chicago in December responsive to the speech of Douglas in the Senate on the 9th of December. The names mentioned in those proceedings are of some moment, not because of any consequence attaching personally to the individuals, but as illustrating the depths to which rancorous enmity stooped for the selection of fitting instruments to accomplish its ends.

The resolutions of that meeting were reported by a committee consisting of the following persons: Thomas Hoyne, ex-United States Attorney; Iram Nye, ex-United States Marshal; Isaac Cook, ex-United States Postmaster; Brock M'Vickar, Surgeon United States Marine Hospital; William Price, postmaster; Thomas Dyer, B. F. Bradley, and H. D. Colvin.

The chairman of the meeting was Dr. Daniel Brainard, ex-Surgeon to the United States Marine Hospital, who appointed this committee, and who gave as his reason for placing upon it the federal officers appointed by Mr. Buchanan, as well as those who had been removed, that it was right that the administration should know and be made to feel that no Democrat in Chicago, in office or out of it, could permit so gross a violation of the principles of the party to pass without expressing in the strongest terms a reprobation of the act. The meeting was addressed by Dr. Brainard and others; their speeches were not published, because the friends of Mr. Douglas and those who really desired harmony in the party thought that, if peace and harmony were to be restored, it could be better accomplished by suppressing the fierce invectives employed, and

R

sweeping denunciations, not only of Lecomptonism, but of its supporters. Had these speeches been preserved, it would be refreshing at this time to read how Mr. Bigler was denounced as an overgrown dunce, and Dr. Fitch as a bogus senator whose Pomeroy Letter* ought to have consigned him to a political oblivion so profound that not even a Lecompton Convention could resuscitate his memory.

The President subsequently appointed Messrs. Hoyne, Nye, Brainard, and Cook to office, they having become opponents of Douglas and supporters of Lecomptonism.

In February, Cook, one of the above-named committee, proceeded to Washington, and was nominated to the Senate as postmaster; he was then a defaulter to the government in a

---

* As Dr. Fitch, of Indiana, was one of the "foreign" disturbers in the Illinois contest, and as he was generally styled on the stump "Pomeroy Fitch," it may not be out of place to state why he was so called. At one time he was nominated for Congress in Indiana by the Democracy, whose platform was the Nicholson Letter. Just previous to the election, some Abolitionists in the district, not satisfied with the Whig nominee, addressed a letter to Fitch, propounding questions to him, to which Fitch replied: his reply secured the Abolition vote. The correspondence was secret, and not known to the Democracy until too late to take action upon it. The correspondence on the part of the Abolitionists was conducted by Mr. Pomeroy. We give the letters without comment, except to say that Dr. Fitch very honorably kept all his pledges to Mr. Pomeroy, as will be seen by reference to the journals of the House of Representatives at the time.

"Plymouth, August 4, 1849.

"SIR,—As there are a few who think you have not been quite definite enough on some of the questions involved in the present canvass, I wish you to answer the following questions, to wit:

"1. Will you, if elected, vote for the unconditional repeal of slavery in the District of Columbia?

"2. Will you vote for the abolition of the inter-state slave-trade?

"3. Will you vote for the Wilmot Proviso being extended over the Territories of California and New Mexico, and against any law authorizing slaves to be taken there as property?

"Please answer the above questions yes or no, without comment.

"GROVE POMEROY."

The Answer.

"With pleasure I answer 'YES' to the above questions.

"Entertaining the views indicated in my answer above, I shall not only vote 'yes' on these measures, but if no older or abler member, whose influence would be greater than mine, introduce them into Congress, I shall do it myself, if I have the honor of holding a seat there.

"G. N. FITCH."

very large sum, but nevertheless his confirmation was forced through the Senate—senators of honorable name and distinction uniting in the action. The nomination was not confirmed without opposition, and that, too, of the most determined character; the result was that Cook was not confirmed until after the first of March. In the mean time, while this unheard-of proscription was going on at Washington, letters from cabinet officers and senators were flooding the mails, all tendering office, profit, and honors to such of the gallant Democracy of Illinois as would abandon the principles of the party and take up the banner of hostility to Douglas. In more than one letter, and by more than one of these men who thus wrote in behalf of the President, it was suggested that as the President was too old to attend to business personally, particularly the distribution of patronage, the rewarding of friends would be the especial duty of the gentlemen to whom had been committed that business. It need not be stated that these letters were from presidential aspirants, some in Congress and some in the cabinet. It is with no pleasure that these, as well as other equally disgraceful proceedings on the part of "distinguished" men in the councils of the nation, are recorded here. We have abstained from giving names, because to do so would be to single out individuals and hold them up to scorn and contempt, when, in truth and in fact, they acted, so far as the attempt to corrupt the people, as the authorized exponents of a new and fatal policy which had been adopted for the purpose of defeating Stephen A. Douglas. The result of this species of attempted corruption was soon apparent. A prominent individual residing in Illinois, who perhaps had just received a letter from a member of the cabinet suggesting the importance of sustaining the administration and of defeating Douglas, and intimating that the administration would cheerfully bestow its best offices upon those who would aid in accomplishing these ends, while the writer, who already had the confident assurances of a majority in the Charleston Convention, would not fail to have a particular regard now and hereafter for the person who would publicly avow a hostility to Douglas, would be startled by receiving next day a letter of the same import from a senator, and, before the week was out, would possibly have on his table four or five letters from as many "distinguished Democrats," all praying the defeat of Douglas, and each concluding with the suggestion that the writer had already received promises sufficient to justify him in expecting the nomination at Charleston! The effect of such a course of action on the part of those who had taken the cause of the administration in hand was, as might be expected, entirely fatal. The work was overdone. There were too many engaged in it. No intelligent man who received such letters could have the slightest respect for the writers, or could place the least faith in any thing they said.

Before Cook's confirmation, the Illinois Democratic State Central Committee issued the call for the Democratic State Convention to nominate state officers. The call was signed by the Hon. ALEXANDER STARNE, of Pike County, as chairman, and was approved by all the members of the committee. It apportioned the number of votes which each county would be entitled to in convention, the number being based, according to custom, upon the Democratic vote at the previous presidential election. Counties were authorized, of course, to send as many delegates as they chose, but the number of votes which each county would be entitled to was fixed. The convention was called to meet at Springfield, in the State-house, at ten o'clock A.M., April 21st. It has been stated that this convention was called at an unusually early day; but, by reference to a table published elsewhere in this volume, it will be seen that, with one exception, it was held later than any preceding Democratic State Convention ever held in Illinois. The exception was in 1856, when the convention was held on the first of May. The day after copies of this call reached Washington, Cook's nomination was confirmed; longer delay was thought dangerous to the score of embryo presidents to whom had been pledged the eleven votes of Illinois at the Charleston Convention. He hurried home, and on the 17th of March assumed the duties of postmaster. He immediately turned out a number of competent, worthy men, and filled their places with individuals who had recommendations signed by Fitch, Bright, Cobb, Slidell, and other very excellent statesmen of that class. The best comment upon these appointments is the one furnished by time; two or three of them have since been sent to the Penitentiary, a few others are fugitives from justice, others have been removed by order of the Department, and others have sought safety and peace by voluntary resignation.

The administration had now a representative in Illinois, and if there was a disposition on the part of any one to reflect disrespectfully upon the Chicago postmaster or the policy of the administration, it might be said with great truth that that policy and its representative were eminently worthy of each other. This representative of the administration, being himself illiterate, selected from a brothel in Chicago a clerk, through whose penmanship the Chicago postmaster undertook, in the name and by the authority of the President of the United States, and of several members of his cabinet, to corrupt the Democracy of the state. As the personal and official character of the postmaster of Chicago is of itself not of sufficient importance to require more than a passing notice, even of its infamy, yet as, with a full knowledge of the man, the administration chose to place its character and fortunes in Illinois in his hands, there is no escape from the disagreeable task of recording a few particulars of the joint movements of principal and agent at that time. At Chatham, in Sangamon County, one N. S. Wright had been postmaster, and, up to the period of Cook's appointment to office, had been an ardent supporter of Douglas. By some means—possibly at a personal interview—this man, Wright's, ambition or cupidity had been excited by a suggestion that he ought to be the postmaster at Springfield. That he had been in correspondence with Cook upon the subject is evident, for upon the eighth of April Cook addressed him a letter, warning him that it was the intention of the friends of Mr. Buchanan to get up a new organization in the state; that he, Wright, was expected to secure the election of anti-Douglas delegates to the state convention, but, if defeated in that, he was, by all means, to get up a new delegation. The letter closed with a suggestion that the business of appointing a new postmaster at Springfield would be settled at the meeting of the convention.

It will be seen by the above letter that the administration, through its agent, declared, in advance of the state convention, the purpose of reorganizing the Democracy of Illinois, and instructed the federal officer in that quarter that if he, the federal officer, was beaten in the choice of delegates at the regular Democratic county convention, "by all means to get up another delegation." This letter, owing to the stupidity of some one connected with the Chicago Post-office, never got into the mail, but reached Mr. Wright through the columns of the newspapers, into which it found its way.   Mr. Wright was beaten at the county convention, he being at that time the solitary Lecomptonite in the county; but he "got up a new delegation" on paper by putting down the names of twelve postmasters who would not, as he supposed, dare to say nay to any act done by order of the administration.   Similar letters were sent all over the state; and the efforts of politicians in other states to sow discord and promote differences were unremitting.   There were one hundred counties in the state; in ninety-eight of these the county conventions passed resolutions sustaining the course of Douglas, Harris, Marshall, Morris, Shaw, and Smith, the Democratic delegation in Congress.   In one county resolutions approving of the proposed admission of Kansas under the Lecompton Constitution were passed.   In the other county, the call for a meeting of the county convention was never published, but a few days before the time fixed for the state convention the chairman of the county committee held a private meeting in his own office, and appointed himself and some friends as delegates to the state convention.   In Lake County there were two or three candidates for the Waukegan Post-office : these candidates had been incited "to defeat Douglas" as the surest road to federal profit and honor.   When the county convention met the attendance was full, every township being represented.   The candidates for the post-office were on hand with their resolutions; but the incumbent of the post-office entered the convention, and, in person or by another, submitted anti-Lecompton resolutions.   Such doctrines, coming from such a quarter, were hailed by the Democracy with delight; the candidates for the post-office were voted down almost unanimously, and the Waukegan postmaster had every thing his own way.   In the midst of the enthusiasm he proposed a list of delegates, he being one; the convention adopted the list without question, and adjourned with cheers for Douglas, and Harris, and their Illinois associates in Congress.   The Waukegan postmaster had outwitted his rivals and cheated the convention. In Cook County the Democratic county convention met, and appointed its delegates, at the head of whom was Dr. Daniel Brainard; the resolutions of the convention were strong and decided.   The Chicago postmaster did not even attempt to compete at the convention for the delegation, but called a convention of his own, and appointed "a new delegation."

On the 21st of April Springfield was filled with delegates. Never before in the history of the Democratic party had there been the slightest attempt to get up division; the subject of contested seats on an extensive scale was a new one in an Illinois state convention. For more than twenty years these conventions had been held with the greatest harmony. Now, for the first time, there was an appearance of a storm. The Cook County (Chicago) delegation, the largest in the state, having thirty-six votes, were called together early in the morning to take preliminary steps to meet the contestants before the state convention; Dr. Brainard was, at his own suggestion, appointed to argue and defend the right of the "regulars" to seats in the convention, and to expose the utter illegality and absurdity of whatever pretense Cook and his associates might set up to membership. As the hour approached for the meeting of the convention, the representative hall became crowded. Delegation after delegation entered and took the seats assigned them by the state committee; the hands on the clock pointed to five minutes before ten, and still not one of the men who were to contest the seats in the convention had made his appearance. As the clock struck ten, Mr. Starne, chairman of the state committee, called the convention to order, and, on motion, the Hon. JOHN MOORE was appointed temporary chairman. The convention was further temporarily organized by the appointment of secretaries.

The Hon. Samuel Holmes, of Adams, moved the appointment of a committee to examine the credentials of delegates, and to report to the convention a list of the legally elected delegates, and that said committee consist of one member from each congressional district and two from the state at large.

Hon. John A. M'Clernand requested the gentleman from Adams to modify his motion so as that it would be in the following form:

Whereas, it is understood that there are contesting delegates from one or more counties to this convention, and whereas practice and fairness require that all questions affecting the titles of claimants to seats in this convention should be settled before the convention proceeds to effect a permanent organization; therefore,

Resolved, That the temporary chairman of the convention appoint a committee of eleven on the credentials of members that are contested, and that the members will entertain no proposition and do no business until the report of said committee shall have been acted upon by the convention; and that, until otherwise ordered, the rules of the last House of Representatives of this state be the rules for the government of this convention.

Mr. Holmes accepting this as a substitute for his motion, the preamble and resolution were adopted.

The president appointed as the committee the following persons: Hon. Sam. Holmes, of Adams; Hon. James Mitchell, of Stephenson; Hon. S. S. Hayes, of Cook; Hon. John A. M'Clernand, of Sangamon; Hon. W. C. Gondy, of Fulton; Hon. U. F. Linder, of Coles; Hon. Zadoc Casey, of Jefferson; Hon. W. J. Allen, of Williamson; Hon. W. H. Roosevelt, of Hancock; Gov. J. A. Matteson, of Sangamon; and F. Goodspeed, Esq., of Will.

The secretary called the list of counties in alphabetical order, and it was found that all the counties in the state except Lake and Union were represented, and represented each by one delegation. When all the credentials had been handed in, and the Committee on Credentials were about to retire, Mr. HOLMES rose and said:

"The Committee on Credentials are about to retire to the adjoining room to examine the certificates of all persons claiming seats in the Illinois Democratic State Convention of 1858, and if there are any persons claiming seats in such convention who have not yet presented their claims, they are hereby notified to make known their claims without delay, or hold their peace forever."

Not a contestant appeared then or at any time during the session of the convention. In fact, so bald and fabulous was the pretense of the new delegation, "got up" under the instructions of the administration, that not even a federal office-holder could command sufficient impudence to lay claim to a seat in the convention. The entire number of persons present at Springfield whose names were used by the administration as delegates to a "National Democratic State Convention" was *thirty-nine,* of which some twenty-three were from Chicago. These met in the Senate Chamber, and never claimed seats in the state convention, but declared themselves a convention under the new organization mentioned in Cook's letter to Wright. This meeting of the "new delegations" of the administration, or, as they were at the time jocularly styled, the "Thirty-nine Articles" of Lecomptonism, having no instructions from Washington as to what they should do, except the general one to "defeat Douglas," passed some resolutions declaring that the state convention had been held too soon, and adjourned till June, in order "to give the Democracy time to turn out."

The state convention was in many respects the greatest ever held in the State of Illinois. The names of many of the delegates had long previously been familiar to the party and to the country.

The Committee on Resolutions consisted of the following persons, one being selected from each congressional district and two from the state at large: Gov. Joel A. Matteson; John D. Crouch, of Jo Daviess; Richard T. Merrick, of Cook; John Hise, of La Salle; John M'Donald, of Peoria; James M. Campbell, of M'Donough; John A. M'Clernand, of Sangamon; Zadoc Casey, of Jefferson; J. S. Post, of Macon; S. A. Buckmaster, of Madison; J. S. Robinson, of White.

An abler committee never was appointed by any state convention. The members were all men of standing, and most of them had occupied positions under the state and federal governments. Mr. M'Clernand had represented one of the districts in Congress during many years, and until he declined a re-election. John Hise was known all over the state for his long and able services in the Legislature. Mr. Casey had been lieutenant governor and member of Congress for many years. Messrs. Crouch and M'Donald were experienced editors; Buckmaster, Campbell, and Post were men of sterling Democracy, and known to the central portions of the state as unfaltering supporters of Democratic principles. Mr. Merrick had been an Old Line Whig, who, in the disruption of that party, had united in 1856 with the Democracy, and had rendered earnest and vigorous aid in the election of Mr. Buchanan.

The convention nominated W. B. Fondey and Hon. A. C. French, the former for state treasurer, and the latter for superintendent of public instruction.

The committee on resolutions, through the Hon. JOHN A. M'CLERNAND, reported the following resolutions, which were

R 2

read, and the question having been taken upon each resolution
as it was read, and then upon the whole, they were adopted
without one dissenting voice, and with an enthusiasm that was
extraordinary even in conventions of the Democracy of Illinois.

Resolved, That the Democratic party of the State of Illinois, through their
delegates in general convention assembled, do reassert and declare the principles avowed by them as when, on former occasions, they have presented
their candidates for popular suffrage.

Resolved, That they are unalterably attached to, and will maintain inviolate, the principles declared by the National Convention at Cincinnati in
June, 1856.

Resolved, That they avow, with renewed energy, their devotion to the federal Union of the United States, their earnest desire to avert sectional strife,
their determination to maintain the sovereignty of the states, and to protect
every state, and the people thereof, in all their constitutional rights.

Resolved, That the platform of principles established by the National
Democratic Convention at Cincinnati is the only authoritative exposition of
Democratic doctrine, and they deny the right of any power on earth, except
a like body, to change or interpolate that platform, or to prescribe new or
different tests; that they will neither do it themselves, nor permit it to be
done by others, but will recognize all men as Democrats who stand by and
uphold Democratic principles.

Resolved, That in the organization of states, the people have a right to decide at the polls upon the character of their fundamental law, and that the
experience of the past year has conclusively demonstrated the wisdom and
propriety of the principle that the fundamental law under which a Territory
seeks admission into the Union should be submitted to the people of such
Territory for their ratification or rejection at a fair election, to be held for
that purpose; and that before such Territory is admitted as a state, such
fundamental law should receive a majority of the legal votes cast at such election; and they deny the right and condemn the attempt of any convention
called for the purpose of framing a Constitution, to impose the instrument
formed by them upon the people against their will.

Resolved, That a fair application of these principles requires that the Lecompton Constitution should be submitted to a direct vote of the actual inhabitants of Kansas, so that they may vote for or against that instrument before Kansas shall be declared one of the states of this Union; and until it
shall be ratified by the people of Kansas at a fair election held for that purpose, the Illinois Democracy are unalterably opposed to the admission of
Kansas under that Constitution.

Resolved, That we heartily approve and sustain the manly, firm, patriotic,
and Democratic position of Stephen A. Douglas, Isaac N. Morris, Thomas
L. Harris, Aaron Shaw, Robert Smith, and Samuel S. Marshall, the Democratic delegation of Illinois in Congress, upon the question of the admission
of Kansas under the Lecompton Constitution; and that by their firm and
uncompromising devotion to the Democratic principles, and to the cause of
justice, right, and the people, they have deserved our admiration, increased,
if possible, our confidence in their integrity and patriotism, and merited our
warm approbation, our sincere and hearty thanks, and shall receive our earnest support.

Resolved, That in all things wherein the national administration sustain
and carry out the principles of the Democratic party as expressed in the Cincinnati platform and affirmed in these resolutions, it is entitled to and will
receive our hearty support.

The probability of the reassembling of the Danite meeting was a subject of much discussion. Hundreds of Democrats who had agreed with Mr. Buchanan upon the subject of Lecompton expressed the earnest hope that the ill-advised movement to divide the Democracy would receive no farther countenance from the President. At this time, too, the House of Representatives adopted the English amendment, and in a few days thereafter the Senate concurred. Lecomptonism was at an end. The question of the admission of Kansas with the Lecompton Constitution was referred to the people of Kansas. The struggle was over. Both sides claimed a victory. The advocates of the admission of Kansas with the Lecompton Constitution had all voted to remand the issue of the admission of the state with that Constitution to the people of Kansas for their decision at the polls. It is true they did not submit the approval or disapproval of the Constitution directly to a vote of the people, but they did submit to the people of Kansas a question, in voting on which they were practically to decide whether they were willing to be admitted as a state with Lecompton, or remain a Territory without it.

Many of the opponents of the admission of Kansas with the Lecompton Constitution voted for the English Bill, because they thought it accomplished the same result that would have been accomplished had the Constitution been submitted directly to the people for ratification or rejection. Those Anti-Lecompton men who voted against the English Bill claimed a practical victory, though they could not consistently vote to admit Kansas with that Constitution without a direct vote approving it. There was really, then, not the slightest justification for continuing the proscription of Democrats for having agreed with Judge Douglas. But the official axe was not idle. It was wielded in all the departments of the government. Nor was it confined to Illinois. Postmasters were cut down with a suddenness that was intended to be terrifying; mail agents were dismissed a service that was thereafter to be devoted to the especial aid of Republicanism.

The secretary of the treasury struck down the venerable Jacob Fry, collector of Chicago, who for forty years had been an active Democrat, and had never sullied his own name, nor that of his party, by any act, personal or official, that was unworthy a gentleman. The same secretary continued in office a man who had violated every law recognized by the government or by society for the regulation of official or personal honesty.

The war was continued. Francis J. Grund, "the basest Hessian of them all," was dispatched to Chicago. He was the mouthpiece—and a fitting one—through which despotism spoke its decrees to its cringing servitors in Illinois. The Danite Convention was officially called to meet again at Springfield. Grund was a delegate. Dr. Brainard, having in the mean time made arrangements with Grund for the place of surgeon to the Marine Hospital, was also made a delegate. O. C. Skinner, who had been an active member of the Democratic State Convention, and who had moved the adoption of the resolutions without the change of a word, was also a delegate. The promises of office had been cast far and wide over the state, and, strange to relate, almost every man who had abandoned General Cass and supported the Buffalo platform in 1848 now rallied at the Danite call to defeat Douglas on a suspicion of Free-soilism! The convention was held. The proceedings were boisterous. The principal operators were Grund, Lieb, Carpenter, and Pine; the resolutions, which were of the most denunciatory character, were reported by Carpenter. What has become of those men can be ascertained upon application to Howell Cobb or Attorney General Black. With the exception of Lieb, who is now a Republican, they have all left the State of Illinois. Why they have done so let the government that clothed them with official patronage and power answer.

The effort to compel the attendance of postmasters by threats of removal failed. It is true that the names of many postmasters were published as delegates, but not one in a hundred paid the slightest attention to the matter. The "delegates" consisted principally of men who hoped for office. Nine of the "most eminent" men in the convention subsequently were candidates for Congress in their respective districts, and the manner in which their eminent abilities and their perfidy to the Democratic party were appreciated can be seen by the record of the votes at the election. At this time more than one member of the cabinet was at work denouncing Douglas and urging his defeat. The issue was well known. It was Douglas or Lincoln—a Democrat or a Republican. Yet the defeat of

Douglas was demanded. The Danite convention adjourned on the 9th of June, having nominated John Dougherty and John Reynolds in opposition to Fondey and French. Let it always be remembered that this proceeding took place at the express desire of the administration, and after the passage of the English Bill, and before Mr. Douglas's return to Illinois from Congress. It was designed deliberately to defeat the Democratic state ticket, and to defeat all the Democratic nominees for Congress and for the Legislature.

On the 16th of June the Republican state convention assembled at Springfield, and put in nomination Abraham Lincoln for the United States Senate, and on the same day Dr. Fitch telegraphed to the faithful at Chicago that the removal of the venerable General Fry had been consummated by the confirmation of Mr. Strother as collector of Chicago.

On the same day the special session of the Senate closed its business and adjourned. A few days thereafter, Senator Douglas, accompanied by his family, left Washington *via* Philadelphia and New York for Chicago.

From a list prepared at that time of the Democratic papers published in Illinois, it was found that there were sixty-nine supporting the regular party organization, and five supporting the Danite ticket. Of these five, two were new papers commenced after the entanglement. One other was published by a postmaster, who, as late as January preceding, had " dared" the administration to remove him for denouncing " Lecompton as a fraud," or for supporting Douglas ; but, having become a defaulter as postmaster, was then confidently expecting a higher office, which he ultimately attained, but which he has since vacated *for cause.* Another had changed its politics in consideration of a post-office advertisement for which the government paid $417. The other, edited by a postmaster, had always been Lecompton. Any one not blinded by hatred would have been able to judge by these indications the tide of Democratic sentiment in Illinois. In vain were the facts presented to the administration. They would listen to no reason. It seemed as if the whole power of the administration had been surrendered to the control of those presidential aspirants, who sought in the defeat of Douglas the removal of what they regarded the only person standing between them and the object of their ambition.

On the 9th of July Senator Douglas arrived in Chicago. The circumstances attending his arrival were of such a character as to deserve more than a passing notice. It was an era in his history. It was the third occasion of his return to the city after having taken part in exciting national controversies in Congress. In 1850, after the passage of the compromise measures, he was met by a violent armed mob; but, by the power of a single speech, he had conquered and subdued that mob. In 1854, after the passage of the Nebraska Bill, he was again met by an armed mob, who, remembering the result in 1850 of allowing him to speak to the people, refused to let him be heard, and, after several hours' struggle, forced him to leave the meeting.

And now, after another interval of four years, he again returned to Chicago, from a session during which he had been the object of an assault more fearful than he had ever before encountered. The events of that night were so remarkable that an account of them, published in the Chicago Times the morning after, will not prove uninteresting:

"Yesterday Senator Douglas was received in Chicago, and the occasion, as well as the manner of that reception, was of the most magnificent character. Some few days ago it was heard that he was at Cleveland, and forthwith arrangements were hastily made to give him a reception worthy of his great services. With that view it was determined to appoint a committee to meet him at Michigan City, and escort him to the city. The committee was appointed.

DEPARTURE OF THE COMMITTEE.

"As per announcement in the programme of the reception of Hon. STE-PHEN A. DOUGLAS, published by authority of the Committee of Arrangements, an extra train of cars was ready at 1 o'clock yesterday to convey the Committee of Reception to Michigan City, distant from Chicago sixty miles, at which place Senator Douglas was to take the Michigan Central road on the return trip. It was not contemplated, either by the committee or any one else, that many persons, besides such as were on the committee, would desire to go that distance in the middle of an intensely hot day, over a sandy and exposed road, and accordingly no effort was made to make up a long train. But full half an hour before the time of starting, hundreds of citizens, many of whom came from remote parts of the state, had collected at the depôt. We noticed several stanch Democrats who had come up from the extreme southern section—from Egypt—and still others from the central sections ; indeed, there were delegations here from almost every county in Illinois. While the crowd was gathering, fine bands of music were employed, which, by their inspiriting strains, helped to awaken the most general and intense enthusiasm. In the mean time, also, a great number of large national flags were elevated at conspicuous points near the depôt and elsewhere, and banners of different shapes and colors, besides streamers, pendents, etc., were disposed in all directions. A grand sight it was! All present partook largely of the spirit which inspired to the work of love and patriotism. It was the deliberate preparation of the Democratic citizens of Chicago for the brilliant reception of STEPHEN A. DOUGLAS—of the man, the noble, devoted man, who has at this time more of the confidence and affection of the people of Illinois and of the Union than any other man who can be named.

"It was now 1 o'clock. The train was to start at that hour, and all things being ready, the cars moved off amid shouts from the outside, and answering shouts and music from within. In all, the company numbered four hundred. A splendid banner, that of the Young Men's Democratic Club, was carried upon the locomotive.

"Was there ever in this country, whose people are proverbially parsimonious of public attention, a greater tribute given to any man? Four hundred strong, leading citizens of the state going sixty miles in a melting day to meet a fellow-citizen! And it should be observed that many of this great company came from places distant, some fifty, others one hundred, and still others one hundred and fifty, and even two hundred miles. They came to meet Senator Douglas, to take his true hand in theirs, and to tell him that they and the masses of people in Illinois confide in his great ability, admire the brave consistency of his course, and will sustain him at the ballot-boxes.

"The train proceeded to Michigan City, where it was met by a host of gallant Indianians, who accompanied the judge from Laporte to Michigan City. Some malicious person having secretly spiked the only gun of the town, the Democracy obtained a large anvil, and placing it in the middle of the principal street, made the welkin echo with its repeated discharges.

"The delegation from Chicago, including Democrats from Logan, Peoria, Tazewell, La Salle, Marshall, M'Henry, Knox, Will, Boone, Kankakee, Champaign, Stephenson, Kane, De Kalb, Du Page, and other counties of the state, formed into line, and, preceded by a band of music, marched to the Tremont House, where they met Senator Douglas. After exchanging personal salutations with his friends, Judge Douglas returned, in a few happy remarks, his thanks for this marked expression of their continued friendship.

THE RETURN TO THE CITY.

"At a few minutes after five o'clock the procession was formed and proceeded to the depôt, Judge Douglas being now the guest of the committee. The train soon started, and all along the road—at every station, at almost every farm-house and laborer's cabin—in every corn-field, and at every point where laborers were engaged—there was exhibited by cheers, by waving of handkerchiefs and other demonstrations, that cordial 'welcome home' to the great representative of popular rights.

"At the outer depôt of the Illinois Central Railroad the national flag had been raised by the operatives, and a swivel belched forth its roaring notes of welcome. The hardy hands of the mechanics resounded with applause, and cheers and huzzas continued until the train had passed on to the city.

"As the train passed along from Twelfth Street to the depôt, crowds of ladies were assembled on the door-steps of the residences on Michigan Avenue, waving banners and handkerchiefs; the Lake Park was crowded by persons hastily proceeding to the depôt. Long before the train could enter the station-house, thousands had crossed over the breakwater, got upon the track, and climbed into the cars, and when the latter reached the depôt they were literally crammed inside and covered on top by ardent and enthusiastic friends and supporters of the illustrious Illinoisian.

"Capt. Smith's artillery were, in the mean time, firing from Dearborn Park a salute of 150 guns (guns were also firing in the West and North Divisions), the booming of the cannon alone rising above the cheering plaudits of the assembled multitude.

"'The hotels and principal buildings of the city were adorned with flags. The Adams House, near the Central depôt, was most handsomely decorated. The national flag, a banner bearing the motto 'Douglas, the champion of Popular Sovereignty,' as well as numerous flags belonging to vessels in the harbor, were suspended across the street, presenting a grand display. The doors, windows, balconies, and roofs of the Adams House, as well as the private residences in the neighborhood, and the large stores and warehouses along Lake Street, were crowded with ladies and other persons, all cheering and welcoming the senator. At the depôt, a procession, consisting of the 'Montgomery Guards,' Capt. Gleeson, and the 'Emmett Guards,' Lieut. Stuart commanding, acting as a military escort, was then formed. Judge Douglas was in an open barouche drawn by six horses, and was followed by the Committee of Arrangements in other carriages. The procession proceeded up Lake to Wabash Avenue, down Wabash Avenue to Washington Street, and thence by Dearborn Street to the Tremont House.

"'Throughout the whole route of the procession the senator was greeted from house-top and window, from street, from awning-post and balcony, by every demonstration of grateful welcome.

THE SCENE AT THE TREMONT.

" As early as half past six o'clock people began to collect around the Tremont House. The omnibuses from Union Park, and from the southern and northern limits of the city, were crowded with suburban residents, and people came on foot from the remotest parts of the city, taking up eligible standing-places around the hotel. At about half past seven, the booming of cannon on the Lake shore having announced the arrival of the train, it was the signal for the assembling of thousands of others, who rapidly filled up every vacant spot in Lake Street, from State to Clark. Dearborn Street was also thronged from Water to Randolph. The area occupied by the people, packed together in one dense mass, was considerably over *fifty thousand square feet*. In addition to this, every window and roof within hearing distance was occupied, a large portion of the occupants being ladies. The assemblage of people who welcomed in vociferous and prolonged shouts of joy the return of Senator Douglas numbered at the least calculation *thirty thousand.*

"Chicago has never before witnessed such a sight. A field of human forms parted with difficulty as the procession passed through, and closed instantly behind it, with the surge and roar of the waters of the sea; an ocean of upturned faces, extending beyond the farthest limits to which the senator's powerful voice could reach, from which broke one spontaneous burst of applause as he appeared upon the balcony before them. Over all, the light of the illumination, and the glare and glitter of fireworks, spread an appearance which is indescribable.

"'The building just across the street from the Tremont, on Lake, occupied by Jno. Parmly, hat manufacturer, and others, was finely illuminated, and a handsome transparency was displayed, bearing the words, 'Welcome to STEPHEN A. DOUGLAS, the Defender of Popular Sovereignty.'

THE SPEECHES.

" Charles Walker, Esq., then appeared on the Lake Street balcony, and in a very neat address welcomed Senator Douglas to his constituents from a prolonged but glorious struggle, in which he had defended and maintained the right.

"Senator Douglas responded in a speech of over an hour, in which he reviewed the history of the past and the prospect of the future.''

Before giving the speech of Senator Douglas on this occasion, it should be stated that, on the evening of the 16th of June, when nominated as a candidate for the United States Senate, the Hon. ABRAHAM LINCOLN had addressed the Republican State Convention in a carefully prepared speech. As Mr. Lincoln's speech constituted one of the leading subjects of the great contest that followed, justice to that gentleman, and justice to the history of the memorable canvass, suggest that it should be here inserted.

SPEECH OF MR. LINCOLN.

On that evening Mr. Lincoln said:

Mr. President and Gentlemen of the Convention,—If we could first know where we are and whither we are tending, we could better judge what to do and how to do it. We are now far into the fifth year since a policy was initiated with the avowed object and confident promise of putting an end to slavery agitation. Under the operation of that policy, that agitation has not only not ceased, but has constantly augmented. In my opinion, it will not cease until a crisis shall have been reached and passed. "A house divided against itself can not stand." I believe this government can not endure permanently half slave and half free. I do not expect the Union to be dissolved—I do not expect the house to fall—but I do expect it will cease to be divided. It will become all one thing or all the other. Either the opponents of slavery will arrest the farther spread of it, and place it where the public mind shall rest in the belief that it is in the course of ultimate extinction, or its advocates will push it forward till it shall become alike lawful in all the states, old as well as new—North as well as South.

Have we no tendency to the latter condition?

Let any one who doubts carefully contemplate that now almost complete legal combination—piece of machinery so to speak—compounded of the Nebraska doctrine and the Dred Scott decision. Let him consider not only what work the machinery is adapted to do, and how well adapted, but also let him study the history of its construction, and trace if he can, or rather fail if he can, to trace the evidence of design and concert of action among its chief architects from the beginning.

The New-year of 1854 found slavery excluded from more than half the states by state Constitutions, and from most of the national territory by Congressional prohibition. Four days later commenced the struggle which ended in repealing that Congressional prohibition. This opened all the national territory to slavery, and was the first point gained.

But so far Congress only had acted; and an endorsement by the people, real or apparent, was indispensable, to save the point already gained, and give chance for more.

This necessity had not been overlooked, but had been provided for, as well as might be, in the notable argument of "squatter sovereignty," otherwise called "sacred right of self-government," which latter phrase, though expressive of the only rightful basis of any government, was so perverted in this attempted use of it as to amount to just this: that if any one man choose to enslave another, no third man shall be allowed to object. That argument was incorporated into the Nebraska Bill itself in the language which follows: "It being the true intent and meaning of this act not to legislate slavery into any Territory or state, nor to exclude it therefrom, but to leave the people thereof perfectly free to form and regulate their domestic institutions in their own way, subject only to the Constitution of the United States." Then opened the roar of loose declamation in favor of "squatter sovereignty," and "sacred right of self-government." "But," said opposition members, "let us amend the bill so as to expressly declare that the people of the Territory may exclude slavery." "Not we," said the friends of the measure; and down they voted the amendment.

While the Nebraska Bill was passing through Congress, a *law case* involving the question of a negro's freedom, by reason of his owner having voluntarily taken him first into a free state and then into a Territory covered by the Congressional prohibition, and held him as a slave for a long time in each, was passing through the U. S. Circuit Court for the District of Missouri, and both Nebraska Bill and lawsuit were brought to a decision in the same month of May, 1854. The negro's name was "Dred Scott," which name now designates the decision finally made in the case. Before the then next presidential election, the law case came to, and was argued in, the Supreme Court of the United States; but the decision of it was deferred until after the election. Still, before the election, Senator Trumbull, on the floor of the Senate, requests the leading advocate of the Nebraska Bill to state *his opinion* whether the people of a Territory can constitutionally exclude slavery from their limits; and the latter answers, "That is a question for the Supreme Court."

The election came. Mr. Buchanan was elected, and the endorsement, such as it was, secured. That was the second point gained. The endorsement, however, fell short of a clear popular majority by nearly four hundred thousand votes, and so, perhaps, was not overwhelmingly reliable and satisfactory. The outgoing President, in his last annual message, as impressively as possible echoed back upon the people the weight and authority of the endorsement. The Supreme Court met again; did not announce their decision, but ordered a re-argument. The presidential inauguration came, and still no decision of the court; but the incoming President, in his inaugural address, fervently exhorted the people to abide by the forthcoming decision, whatever it might be. Then, in a few days, came the decision. The reputed author of the Nebraska Bill finds an early occasion to make a speech at this capital endorsing the Dred Scott decision, and vehemently denouncing all opposition to it. The new President, too, seizes the early occasion of the Silliman Letter to indorse and strongly construe that decision, and to express his astonishment that any different view had ever been entertained!

At length a squabble springs up between the President and the author of the Nebraska Bill on the mere question of *fact* whether the Lecompton Constitution was or was not, in any just sense, made by the people of Kansas; and in that quarrel the latter declares that all he wants is a fair vote for the people, and that he cares not whether slavery be voted *down* or voted *up*. I do not understand his declaration that he cares not whether slavery be voted down or voted up to be intended by him other than as an apt definition of the policy he would impress upon the public mind—the principle for which he declares he has suffered so much, and is ready to suffer to the end. And well may he cling to that principle. If he has any parental feeling, well may he cling to it. That principle is the only shred left of his original Nebraska doctrine. Under the dred Scott decision, "squatter sovereignty" squatted out of existence, tumbled down like temporary scaffolding—like the mould at the foundry, served through one blast and fell back into loose sand—helped to carry an election, and then was kicked to the winds. His late joint struggle with the Republicans against the Lecompton Constitution involves nothing of the original Nebraska doctrine. The struggle was made on a point, the right of a people to make their own Constitution, upon which he and the Republicans have never differed.

The several points of the Dred Scott decision, in connection with Senator Douglas's "care not" policy, constitute the piece of machinery in its present state of advancement. The working points of that machinery are,

First. That no negro slave, imported as such from Africa, and no descendant of such slave, can ever be a citizen of any state, in the sense of that term as used in the Constitution of the United States. This point is made in order to deprive the negro, in every possible event, of the benefit of that provision of the United States Constitution which declares that "the citizens of each state shall be entitled to all privileges and immunities of citizens in the several states."

Secondly. That, "subject to the Constitution of the United States," neither Congress nor a Territorial Legislature can exclude slavery from any United States Territory. This point is made in order that individual men may fill up the Territories with slaves, without danger of losing them as property, and thus to enhance the chances of permanency to the institution through all the future.

Thirdly. That whether the holding a negro in actual slavery in a free state makes him free as against the holder, the United States Courts will not decide, but will leave to be decided by the courts of any slave state the negro may be forced into by the master. This point is made, not to be pressed immediately; but if acquiesced in for a while, and apparently endorsed by the people at an election, then to sustain the logical conclusion that what Dred Scott's master might do lawfully with Dred Scott in the free state of Illinois, every other master may lawfully do with any other one, or one thousand slaves, in Illinois, or in any other free state.

Auxiliary to all this, and working hand in hand with it, the Nebraska doctrine, or what is left of it, is to educate and mould public opinion, at least Northern public opinion, not to care whether slavery is voted down or voted up. This shows exactly where we now are, and partially, also, whither we are tending.

It will throw additional light on the latter to go back, and run the mind over the string of historical facts already stated. Several things will now appear less dark and mysterious than they did when they were transpiring. The people were to be left "perfectly free," "subject only to the Constitution." What the Constitution had to do with it outsiders could not then see. Plainly enough now, it was an exactly fitted niche for the Dred Scott decision to afterward come in, and declare the perfect freedom of the people to be just no freedom at all. Why was the amendment expressly declaring the right of the people voted down? Plainly enough now: the adoption of it would have spoiled the niche for the Dred Scott decision. Why was the court decision held up? Why even a senator's individual opinion withheld till after the presidential election? Plainly enough now: the speaking out then would have damaged the perfectly free argument upon which the election was to be carried. Why the outgoing President's felicitation on the endorsement? Why the delay of a re-argument? Why the incoming President's advance exhortation in favor of the decision? These things look like the cautious patting and petting of a spirited horse preparatory to mounting him, when it is dreaded that he may give the rider a fall. And why the hasty after-endorsement of the decision by the President and others?

We can not absolutely know that all these exact adaptations are the result of preconcert. But when we see a lot of framed timbers, different portions of which we know have been gotten out at different times and places and by different workmen—Stephen, Franklin, Roger, and James, for instance—and when we see these timbers joined together, and see they exactly make the frame of a house or a mill, all the tenons and mortices exactly fitting, and all the lengths and proportions of the different pieces exactly adapted to their respective places, and not a piece too many or too few—not omitting even scaffolding—or, if a single piece be lacking, we see the place in the frame exactly fitted and prepared yet to bring such piece in—in such a case, we find it impossible not to believe that Stephen, and Franklin, and Roger, and James all understood one another from the beginning, and all worked upon a common plan or draft drawn up before the first blow was struck.

It should not be overlooked that by the Nebraska Bill the people of a *state* as well as Territory were to be left "perfectly free," "subject only to the Constitution." Why mention a state? They were legislating for Territories, and not for or about states. Certainly the people of a state are and ought to be subject to the Constitution of the United States; but why is mention of this lugged into this merely Territorial law? Why are the people of a Territory and the people of a state therein lumped together, and their relation to the Constitution therein treated as being precisely the same? While the opinion of the court, by Chief Justice Taney, in the Dred Scott case, and the separate opinions of all the concurring judges, expressly declare that the Constitution of the United States neither permits Congress nor a Territorial Legislature to exclude slavery from any United States Territory, they all omit to declare whether or not the same Constitution permits a state, or the people of a state, to exclude it. *Possibly* this is a mere omission; but who can be quite sure, if M'Lean or Curtis had sought to get into the opinion a declaration of unlimited power in the people of a state to exclude slavery from their limits, just as Chase and Mace sought to get such declaration in behalf of the people of a Territory into the Nebraska Bill—I ask, who can be quite sure that it would not have been voted down in the one case as it had been in the other? The nearest approach to the point of declaring the power of a state over slavery is made by Judge Nelson. He approaches it more than once, using the precise idea, and almost the language too, of the Nebraska Act. On one occasion his exact language is, "except in cases where the power is restrained by the Constitution of the United States, the law of the state is supreme over the subject of slavery within its jurisdiction." In what cases the power of the states is so restrained by the United States Constitution is left an open question, precisely as the same question as to the restraint on the power of the Territories was left open in the Nebraska Act. Put this and that together, and we have another nice little niche, which we may, ere long, see filled with another Supreme Court decision, declaring that the Constitution of the United States does not permit a *state* to exclude slavery from its limits. And this may especially be expected if the doctrine of "care not whether slavery be voted down or voted up" shall gain upon the public mind sufficiently to give promise that such a decision can be maintained when made.

Such a decision is all that slavery now lacks of being alike lawful in all the states. Welcome or unwelcome, such decision is probably coming, and will soon be upon us, unless the power of the present political dynasty shall be met and overthrown. We shall lie down pleasantly dreaming that the people of Missouri are on the verge of making their state free, and we shall awake to the reality instead that the Supreme Court has made Illinois a slave state. To meet and overthrow the power of that dynasty is the work now before all those who would prevent that consummation. That is what we have to do. How can we best do it?

There are those who denounce us openly to their own friends, and yet whisper us softly that Senator Douglas is the aptest instrument there is with which to effect that object. They wish us to *infer* all from the fact that he now has a little quarrel with the present head of the dynasty, and that he has regularly voted with us on a single point, upon which he and we have never differed. They remind us that he is a very great man, and that the largest of us are very small ones. Let this be granted. But "a living dog is better than a dead lion." Judge Douglas, if not a dead lion for this work, is at least a caged and toothless one. How can he oppose the advances of slavery? He don't care any thing about it. His avowed mission is impressing the "public heart" to *care nothing about* it. A leading Douglas Democratic newspaper thinks Douglas's superior talent will be needed to resist the revival of the African slave-trade. Does Douglas believe an effort to revive that trade is approaching? He has not said so. Does he really think so? But if it is, how can he resist it? For years he has labored to prove it a sacred right of white men to take negro slaves into the new Territories. Can he possibly show that it is less a sacred right to buy them where they can be bought cheapest? And unquestionably they can be bought cheaper in Africa than in Virginia. He has done all in his power to reduce the whole question of slavery to one of a mere right of property; and, as such, how can he oppose the foreign slave-trade—how can he refuse that trade in that "property" shall be "perfectly free," unless he does it as a protection to the home production? And as the home producers will probably not ask the protection, he will be wholly without a ground of opposition.

Senator Douglas holds, we know, that a man may rightfully be wiser to-day than he was yesterday—that he may rightfully change when he finds himself wrong. But can we, for that reason, run ahead, and infer that he will make any particular change of which he himself has given no intimation? Can we safely base our action upon any such vague inference? Now, as ever, I wish not to misrepresent Judge Douglas's position, question his motives, or do aught that can be personally offensive to him. Whenever, if ever, he and we can come together on principle so that our cause may have assistance from his great ability, I hope to have interposed no adventitious obstacle. But clearly he is not now with us—he does not pretend to be—he does not promise ever to be.

Our cause, then, must be intrusted to, and conducted by its own undoubted friends—those whose hands are free, whose hearts are in the work—who *do* care for the result. Two years ago the Republicans of the nation mustered over thirteen hundred thousand strong. We did this under the single impulse of resistance to a common danger, with every external circumstance against us. Of strange, discordant, and even hostile elements, we gathered from the four winds, and formed and fought the battles through, under the constant hot fire of a disciplined, proud, and pampered enemy. Did we brave all then to falter now—now, when that same enemy is wavering, dissevered, and belligerent? The result is not doubtful. We shall not fail—if we stand firm, we *shall not fail*. Wise counsels may accelerate, or mistake delay it, but sooner or later the victory is sure to come.

In this speech was proclaimed the doctrine of an "irrepressible conflict." Mr. Lincoln, it is true, did not declare it in that phrase, but he declared it in terms not less strong when he declared,

"In my opinion, it (slavery agitation) will not cease until a crisis shall have been reached and passed. I believe this government can not endure permanently half slave and half free. * * * It will become all one thing or the other."

Mr. Seward, in his Rochester speech, expressed the same idea in more ornate terms, but not any more clearly or forcibly than it was expressed by Mr. Lincoln. And in a struggle between the originator and promulgator of that doctrine and the author of the Nebraska Bill, a Democratic federal administration took sides openly, through its federal officers and through its official organ at Washington, against the Democracy of Illinois.

In response to the cordial welcome given him by the multitude, Mr. Douglas said:

Mr. Chairman and Fellow-citizens:

I can find no language which can adequately express my profound gratitude for the magnificent welcome which you have extended to me on this occasion. This vast sea of human faces indicates how deep an interest is felt by our people in the great questions which agitate the public mind and which underlie the foundations of our free institutions. A reception like this, so great in numbers that no human voice can be heard to its countless thousands —so enthusiastic that no one individual can be the object of such enthusiasm, clearly shows that there is some great principle which sinks deep in the heart of the masses, and involves the rights and the liberties of a whole people, that has brought you together with a unanimity and a cordiality never before excelled, if, indeed, equaled on any occasion. (Cheers.) I have not the vanity to believe that it is any personal compliment to me.

(Voices, "It is!" "You have deserved it;" and great applause.)

It is an expression of your devotion to that great principle of self-government (cries of "Hear," "hear") to which my life for many years past has been, and in the whole future will be devoted. (Immense cheering.) If there is any one principle dearer and more sacred than all others in free governments, it is that which asserts the exclusive right of a free people to form and adopt their own fundamental law, and to manage and regulate their own internal affairs and domestic institutions. (Applause.)

When I found an effort being made during the recent session of Congress to force a Constitution upon the people of Kansas against their will, and to force that state into the Union with a Constitution which her people had rejected by more than 10,000, I felt bound, as a man of honor and a representative of Illinois—bound by every consideration of duty, of fidelity, and of patriotism, to resist to the utmost of my power the consummation of that fraud. (Cheers.) With others I did resist it, and resisted it successfully until the attempt was abandoned. (Great applause.) We forced them to refer that Constitution back to the people of Kansas, to be accepted or rejected as they shall decide at an election which is fixed for the first Monday of August next. It is true that the mode of reference and the form of the submission was not such as I could sanction with my vote, for the reason that it discriminated between free states and slave states; providing that if Kansas consented to come in under the Lecompton Constitution, it should be received with a population of 35,000; but that if she demanded another Constitution, more consistent with the sentiments of her people and their feelings, that it should not be received into the Union until she had 93,420 inhabitants. (Cries of "Hear," "hear," and cheers.) I did not consider that mode of submission fair, for the reason that any election is a mockery which is not free—that any election is a fraud upon the rights of the people which holds out inducements for affirmative votes, and threatens penalties for negative votes. (Hear, hear.) But, while I was not satisfied with the mode of submission—while I resisted it to the last, demanding a fair, a just, a free mode of submission, still, when the law passed placing it within the power of the people of Kansas at that election to reject the Lecompton Constitution, and then make another in harmony with their principles and their opinions (Bravo, and applause), I did not believe that either the penalties on the one hand, or the inducements on the other, would force that people to accept a Constitution to which they are irreconcilably opposed. (Cries of "Glorious," and renewed applause.) All I can say is, that if their votes can be controlled by such considerations, all the sympathy which has been expended upon them has been misplaced, and all the efforts that have been made in defense of their rights to self-government have been made in an unworthy cause. (Cheers.)

Hence, my friends, I regard the Lecompton battle as having been fought and the victory won, because the arrogant demand for the admission of Kansas under the Lecompton Constitution unconditionally, whether her people wanted it or not, has been abandoned, and the principle which recognizes the right of the people to decide for themselves has been substituted in its place. (Immense applause.)

Fellow-citizens.—While I devoted my best energies—all my energies, mental and physical—to the vindication of that great principle, and while the result has been such as will enable the people of Kansas to come into the Union with such a Constitution as they desire, yet the credit of this great moral victory is to be divided among a large number of men of various and different political creeds. (Prolonged applause.) I was rejoiced when I found in this great contest the Republican party coming up manfully and sustaining the principle that the people of each territory, when coming into the Union, have the right to decide for themselves (Cheers) whether slavery shall or shall not exist within their limits. (A voice, "Hope they will stick to it," and great cheering.) I have seen the time when that principle was controverted. I have seen the time when all parties did not recognize the right of a people to have slavery or freedom, to tolerate or prohibit slavery, as they deemed best, but claimed that power for the Congress of the United States, regardless of the wishes of the people to be affected by it; and when I found upon the Crittenden-Montgomery Bill the Republicans and the Americans of the North, and I may say, too, some glorious Americans and Old Line Whigs from the South (Cheers), like Crittenden and his patriotic associates, joined with a portion of the Democracy to carry out and vindicate the right of the people to decide whether slavery should or should not exist within the limits of Kansas, I was rejoiced within my secret soul, for I saw an indication that the American people, when they come to understand the principle, would give it their cordial support. (Cheers.)

The Crittenden-Montgomery Bill was as fair and as perfect an exposition of the doctrine of popular sovereignty as could be carried out by any bill that man ever devised. It proposed to refer the Lecompton Constitution back to the people of Kansas, and give them the right to accept or reject it as they pleased at a fair election, held in pursuance of law, and in the event of their rejecting it and forming another in its stead, to permit them to come into the Union on an equal footing with the original states. It was fair and just in all of its provisions. I gave it my cordial support, and was rejoiced when I found that it passed the House of Representatives, and at one time I entertained high hope that it would pass the Senate. (Applause.)

I regard the great principle of popular sovereignty as having been vindicated and made triumphant in this land as a permanent rule of public policy in the organization of territories and the admission of new states. (Cheers.) Illinois took her position upon this principle many years ago. You all recollect that in 1850, after the passage of the compromise measures of that year, when I returned to my home there was great dissatisfaction expressed at my course in supporting those measures. (Shame.) I appeared before the people of Chicago at a mass meeting, and vindicated each and every one of those measures; and by reference to my speech on that occasion, which was printed and circulated broadcast throughout the state at the time, you will find that I then and there said that those measures were all founded upon the great principle that every people ought to possess the right to form and regulate their own domestic institutions in their own way, and that that right being possessed by the people of the states, I saw no reason why the same principle should not be extended to all of the territories of the United States. A general election was held in this state a few months afterward for members of the Legislature, pending which all these questions were thoroughly canvassed and discussed, and the nominees of the different parties instructed in regard to the wishes of their constituents upon them. When that election was over, and the Legislature assembled, they proceeded to consider the merits of those compromise measures and the principles upon which they were predicated. And what was the result of their action? They passed resolutions, first repealing the Wilmot Proviso instructions, and in lieu thereof adopted another resolution, in which they declared the great principle which asserts the right of the people to make their own form of government and establish their own institutions. That resolution is as follows:

"*Resolved*, That our liberty and independence are based upon the right of the people to form for themselves such a government as they may choose; that this great principle, the birthright of freemen, the gift of Heaven, secured to us by the blood of our ancestors, ought to be extended to future generations, and no limitation ought to be applied to this power in the organization of any territory of the United States of either a territorial government or state Constitution, provided the government so established shall be Republican and in conformity with the Constitution of the United States."

That resolution, declaring the great principle of self-government as applicable to the territories and new states, passed the House of Representatives of this state by a vote of sixty-one in the affirmative to only four in the negative. Thus you find that an expression of public opinion, enlightened, educated, intelligent public opinion on this question by the representatives of Illinois, in 1851, approaches nearer to unanimity than has ever been obtained on any controverted question. That resolution was entered on the Journal of the Legislature of Illinois, and it has remained there from that day to this, a standing instruction to her senators and a request to her representatives in Congress to carry out that principle in all future cases. Illinois, therefore, stands pre-eminent as the state which stepped forward early and established a platform applicable to this slavery question, concurred in alike by Whigs and Democrats, in which it was declared to be the wish of our people that thereafter the people of the territories should be left perfectly free to form and regulate their domestic institutions in their own way, and that no limitation should be placed upon that right in any form. (Tremendous applause.) Hence, what was my duty in 1854, when it became necessary to bring forward a bill for the organization of the Territories of Kansas and Nebraska? Was it not my duty, in obedience to the Illinois platform, to your standing instructions to your senators, adopted with almost entire unanimity, to incorporate in that bill the great principle of self-government, declaring that it was "the true intent and meaning of the act not to legislate slavery into any state or territory, or to exclude it therefrom, but to leave the people thereof perfectly free to form and regulate their domestic institutions in their own way, subject only to the Constitution of the United States?" (Cries of "Yes, yes," and cheers.) I did incorporate that principle in the Kansas-Nebraska Bill, and perhaps I did as much as any living man in the enactment of that bill—(great applause)—thus establishing the doctrine in the public policy of the country. (Cries of "Good," and renewed applause.) I then defended that principle against assaults from one section of the Union.

During this last winter it became my duty to vindicate it against assaults from the other section of the Union. (Cheers.) I vindicated it boldly and fearlessly, as the people of Chicago can bear witness, when it was assailed by Free-soilers—(" Yes, yes," and cheers)—and during this winter I vindicated and defended it as boldly and as fearlessly when it was attempted to be violated by the almost united South. (Immense applause.) I pledged myself to you on every stump in Illinois in 1854, I pledged myself to the people of other states, North and South—wherever I spoke—and in the United States Senate and elsewhere, in every form in which I could reach the public mind or the public ear, I gave the pledge that I, so far as the power should be in my hands, would vindicate the principle of the right of the people to form their own institutions, to establish free states or slave states as they chose, and that that principle should never be violated either by fraud, by violence, by circumvention, or by any other means, if it was in my power to prevent it. (Applause.) I now submit to you, my fellow citizens, whether I have not redeemed that pledge in good faith! (Cries of "Yes, yes," and three tremendous cheers.) Yes, my friends, I have redeemed it in good faith, and it is a matter of heartfelt gratification to me to see these assembled thousands here to-night bearing their testimony to the fidelity with which I have advocated that principle and redeemed my pledges in connection with it. (Cheers.)

I will be entirely frank with you. My object was to secure the right of the people of each state and of each territory, North or South, to decide the question for themselves, to have slavery or not, just as they chose; and my opposition to the Lecompton Constitution was not predicated upon the ground that it was a Pro-slavery Constitution—(cheers)—nor would my action have been different had it been a Free-soil Constitution. My speech against the Lecompton fraud was made on the 9th of December, while the vote on the slavery clause in that Constitution was not taken until the 21st of the same month, nearly two weeks after. I made my speech against that Lecompton monstrosity solely on the ground that it was a violation of the fundamental principles of free government; on the ground that it was not the act and deed of the people of Kansas; that it did not embody their will; that they were averse to it; and hence I denied the right of Congress to force it upon them, either as a free state or a slave state. (Bravo.) I deny the right of Congress to force a slaveholding state upon an unwilling people. (Cheers.) I deny their right to force a free state upon an unwilling people. (Cheers.) I deny their right to force a good thing upon a people who are unwilling to receive it. (Cries of "Good, good," and cheers.) The great principle is the right of every community to judge and decide for itself whether a thing is right or wrong, whether it would be good or evil for them to adopt it; and the right of free action, the right of free thought, the right of free judgment upon the question is dearer to every true American than any other under a free government. My objection to the Lecompton contrivance was that it undertook to put a Constitution on the people of Kansas against their will, in opposition to their wishes, and thus violated the great principle upon which all our institutions rest. It is no answer to this argument to say that slavery is an evil, and hence should not be tolerated. You must allow the people to decide for themselves whether it is a good or an evil. You allow them to decide for themselves whether they desire a Maine liquor law or not; you allow them to decide for themselves what kind of common schools they will have; what system of banking they will adopt, or whether they will adopt any at all; you allow them to decide for themselves the relations between husband and wife, parent and child, and guardian and ward; in fact, you allow them to decide for themselves all other questions, and why not upon this question? (Cheers.) Whenever

S

you put a limitation upon the right of any people to decide what laws they want, you have destroyed the fundamental principle of self-government. (Cheers.)

In connection with this subject, perhaps, it will not be improper for me on this occasion to allude to the position of those who have chosen to arraign my conduct on this same subject. I have observed from the public prints that but a few days ago the Republican party of the State of Illinois assembled in convention at Springfield, and not only laid down their platform, but nominated a candidate for the United States Senate as my successor. (Hisses.) I take great pleasure in saying that I have known personally and intimately, for about a quarter of a century, the worthy gentleman who has been nominated for my place—(a voice, "He will never get it," and cheers)—and I will say that I regard him as a kind, amiable, and intelligent gentleman, a good citizen, and an honorable opponent; and whatever issue I may have with him will be of principle, and not involving personalities. (Cheers.) Mr. Lincoln made a speech before that Republican convention which unanimously nominated him for the Senate—a speech evidently well prepared and carefully written—in which he states the basis upon which he proposes to carry on the campaign during this summer. In it he lays down two distinct propositions, which I shall notice, and upon which I shall take a direct and bold issue with him. (Cries of "Good, good," and great applause.)

His first and main proposition I will give in his own language, Scripture quotation and all. (Laughter.) I give his exact language: "'A house divided against itself can not stand.' I believe this government can not endure, permanently, half *slave* and half *free*. I do not expect the Union to be *dissolved*; I do not expect the house to *fall*; but I do expect it to cease to be divided. It will become *all* one thing or *all* the other."

In other words, Mr. Lincoln asserts as a fundamental principle of this government that there must be uniformity in the local laws and domestic institutions of each and all the states of the Union, and he therefore invites all the non-slaveholding states to band together, organize as one body, and make war upon slavery in Kentucky, upon slavery in Virginia, upon slavery in the Carolinas, upon slavery in all of the slaveholding states in this Union, and to persevere in that war until it shall be exterminated. He then notifies the slaveholding states to stand together as a unit and make an aggressive war upon the free states of this Union with a view of establishing slavery in them all; of forcing it upon Illinois, of forcing it upon New York, upon New England, and upon every other free state, and that they shall keep up the warfare until it has been formally established in them all. In other words, Mr. Lincoln advocates boldly and clearly a war of sections, a war of the North against the South, of the free states against the slave states—a war of extermination—to be continued relentlessly until the one or the other shall be subdued, and all the states shall either become free or become slave.

Now, my friends, I must say to you frankly, that I take bold, unqualified issue with him upon that principle. I assert that it is neither desirable nor possible that there should be uniformity in the local institutions and domestic regulations of the different states of this Union. The framers of our government never contemplated uniformity in its internal concerns. The fathers of the Revolution, and the sages who made the Constitution, well understood that the laws and domestic institutions which would suit the granite hills of New Hampshire would be totally unfit for the rice plantations of South Carolina (Cheers); they well understood that the laws which would suit the agricultural districts of Pennsylvania and New York would be totally unfit for the large mining regions of the Pacific, or the lumber regions of Maine. (Bravo). They well understood that the great varieties of soil, of production, and of interests, in a republic as large as this, required different local and domestic regulations in each locality, adapted to the wants and interests of each separate state (cries of "Bravo," and "Good"), and for that reason it was provided in the federal Constitution that the thirteen original states should remain sovereign and supreme within their own limits in regard to all that was local, and internal, and domestic, while the federal government should have certain specified powers which were general and national, and could be exercised only by the federal authority. (Cheers).

The framers of the Constitution well understood that each locality, having separate and distinct interests, required separate and distinct laws, domestic institutions, and police regulations adapted to its own wants and its own condition; and they acted on the presumption, also, that these laws and institutions would be as diversified and as dissimilar as the states would be numerous, and that no two would be precisely alike, because the interests of no two would be precisely the same. Hence, I assert, that the great fundamental principle which underlies our complex system of state and federal governments contemplated diversity and dissimilarity in the local institutions and domestic affairs of each and every state then in the Union, or thereafter to be admitted into the confederacy. I therefore conceive that my friend, Mr. Lincoln, has totally misapprehended the great principles upon which our government rests. Uniformity in local and domestic affairs would be destructive of state rights, of state sovereignty, of personal liberty, and personal freedom. Uniformity is the parent of despotism the world over, not only in politics, but in religion. Wherever the doctrine of uniformity is proclaimed, that all the states must be free or all slave, that all labor must be white or all black, that all the citizens of the different states must have the same privileges or be governed by the same regulations, you have destroyed the greatest safeguard which our institutions have thrown around the rights of the citizen. ("Bravo," and great applause).

How could this uniformity be accomplished if it was desirable and possible? There is but one mode in which it could be obtained, and that must be by abolishing the state Legislatures, blotting out state sovereignty, merging the rights and sovereignty of the states in one consolidated empire, and vesting Congress with the plenary power to make all the police regulations, domestic and local laws, uniform throughout the limits of the republic. When you shall have done this you will have uniformity. Then the states will all be slave or all be free; then negroes will vote everywhere or no where; then you will have a Maine liquor law in every state or none; then you will have uniformity in all things local and domestic by the authority of the federal government. But, when you attain that uniformity, you will have converted these thirty-two sovereign, independent states into one consolidated empire, with the uniformity of despotism reigning triumphant throughout the length and breadth of the land. (Great applause).

From this view of the case, my friends, I am driven irresistibly to the conclusion that diversity, dissimilarity, variety in all our local and domestic institutions, is the great safeguard of our liberties; and that the framers of our institutions were wise, sagacious, and patriotic when they made this government a confederation of several states with a Legislature for each, and conferred upon each Legislature the power to make all local and domestic institutions to suit the people it represented, without interference from any other state or from the general Congress of the Union. If we expect to maintain our liberties, we must preserve the rights and sovereignty of the states; we must maintain and carry out that great principle of self-government incorporated in the compromise measures of 1850; endorsed by the Illinois Legislature of 1851; emphatically embodied and carried out in the

Kansas-Nebraska Bill, and vindicated this year by the refusal to bring Kansas into the Union with a Constitution distasteful to her people. (Cheers).

The other proposition discussed by Mr. Lincoln in his speech consists in a crusade against the Supreme Court of the United States on account of the Dred Scott decision. On this question, also, I desire to say to you, unequivocally, that I take direct and distinct issue with him. I have no warfare to make on the Supreme Court of the United States (Bravo), either on account of that or any other decision which they have pronounced from that bench. ("Good, good," and enthusiastic applause). The Constitution of the United States has provided that the powers of government (and the Constitution of each state has the same provision) shall be divided into three departments, executive, legislative, and judicial. The right and the province of expounding the Constitution, and constructing the law, is vested in the judiciary established by the Constitution. As a lawyer, I feel at liberty to appear before the court and controvert any principle of law while the question is pending before the tribunal; but when the decision is made, my private opinion, your opinion, all other opinions, must yield to the majesty of that authoritative adjudication. (Cries of "It is right," "Good, good," and cheers).

I wish you to bear in mind that this involves a great principle, upon which our rights, and our liberty, and our property all depend. What security have you for your property, for your reputation, and for your personal rights, if the courts are not upheld, and their decisions respected when once firmly rendered by the highest tribunal known to the Constitution? (Cheers.) I do not choose, therefore, to go into any argument with Mr. Lincoln in reviewing the various decisions which the Supreme Court has made, either upon the Dred Scott case, or any other. I have no idea of appealing from the decision of the Supreme Court upon a constitutional question to the decision of a tumultuous town meeting. (Cheers.) I am aware that once an eminent lawyer of this city, now no more, said that the State of Illinois had the most perfect judicial system in the world, subject to but one exception, which could be cured by a slight amendment, and that amendment was to so change the law as to allow an appeal from the decisions of the Supreme Court of Illinois, on all constitutional questions, to two justices of the peace. (Great laughter and applause.) My friend Mr. Lincoln, who sits behind me, reminds me that that proposition was made when I was a judge of the Supreme Court. Be that as it may, I do not think that fact adds any greater weight or authority to the suggestion. (Renewed laughter and applause.) It matters not with me who was on the bench, whether Mr. Lincoln or myself, whether a Lockwood or a Smith, a Taney or a Marshall; the decision of the highest tribunal known to the Constitution of the country must be final until it has been reversed by an equally high authority. (Cries of "Bravo," and applause.) Hence I am opposed to this doctrine of Mr. Lincoln, by which he proposes to take an appeal from the decision of the Supreme Court of the United States upon these high constitutional questions to a Republican caucus sitting in the country. (A voice—"Call it Free-soil," and cheers.) Yes, or to any other caucus or town meeting, whether it be Republican, American, or Democratic. (Cheers.) I respect the decisions of that august tribunal; I shall always bow in deference to them. I am a law-abiding man. I will sustain the Constitution of my country as our fathers have made it. I will yield obedience to the laws, whether I like them or not, as I find them on the statute-book. I will sustain the judicial tribunals and constituted authorities in all matters within the pale of their jurisdiction, as defined by the Constitution. (Applause.) But I am equally free to say that the reason assigned by Mr. Lincoln for resisting the decision of the Supreme Court in the Dred Scott case does not in itself meet my approbation. He objects to it because that decision declared that a negro descended from

African parents who were brought here and sold as slaves is not and can not be a citizen of the United States. He says it is wrong, because it deprives the negro of the benefits of that clause of the Constitution which says that citizens of one state shall enjoy all the privileges and immunities of citizens of the several states; in other words, he thinks it wrong because it deprives the negro of the privileges, immunities, and rights of citizenship, which pertain, according to that decision, only to the white man. I am free to say to you that in my opinion this government of ours is founded on the white basis. (Great applause.) It was made by the white man for the benefit of the white man, to be administered by white men in such manner as they should determine. (Cheers.) It is also true that a negro, an Indian, or any other man of an inferior race to a white man, should be permitted to enjoy, and humanity requires that he should have, all the rights, privileges, and immunities which he is capable of exercising consistent with the safety of society. I would give him every right and every privilege which his capacity would enable him to enjoy, consistent with the good of the society in which he lived. ("Bravo.") But you may ask me what are these rights and these privileges. My answer is that each state must decide for itself the nature and extent of these rights. ("Hear, hear," and applause.) Illinois has decided for herself. We have decided that the negro shall not be a slave, and we have at the same time decided that he shall not vote, or serve on juries, or enjoy political privileges. I am content with that system of policy which we have adopted for ourselves. (Cheers.) I deny the right of any other state to complain of our policy in that respect, or to interfere with it, or to attempt to change it. On the other hand, the State of Maine has decided that in that state a negro may vote on an equality with the white man. The sovereign power of Maine had the right to prescribe that rule for herself. Illinois has no right to complain of Maine for conferring the right of negro suffrage, nor has Maine any right to interfere with, or complain of Illinois because she has denied negro suffrage. ("That's so," and cheers.) The State of New York has decided by her Constitution that a negro may vote provided that he owns $250 worth of property, but not otherwise. The rich negro can vote, but the poor one can not. (Laughter.) Although that distinction does not commend itself to my judgment, yet I assert that the sovereign power of New York had a right to prescribe that form of the elective franchise. Kentucky, Virginia and other states, have provided that negroes, or a certain class of them in those states, shall be slaves, having neither civil or political rights. Without endorsing the wisdom of that decision, I assert that Virginia has the same power by virtue of her sovereignty to protect slavery within her limits as Illinois has to banish it forever from our own borders. ("Hear, hear," and applause.) I assert the right of each state to decide for itself on all these questions, and I do not subscribe to the doctrine of my friend, Mr. Lincoln, that uniformity is either desirable or possible. I do not acknowledge that the states must all be free or must all be slave. I do not acknowledge that the negro must have civil and political rights everywhere or nowhere. I do not acknowledge that the Chinese must have the same rights in California that we would confer upon him here. I do not acknowledge that the cooley imported into this country must necessarily be put upon an equality with the white race. I do not acknowledge any of these doctrines of uniformity in the local and domestic regulations in the different states. ("Bravo," and cheers.)

Thus you see, my fellow-citizens, that the issues between Mr. Lincoln and myself, as respective candidates for the United States Senate, as made up, are direct, unequivocal, and irreconcilable. He goes for uniformity in our domestic institutions, for a war of sections, until one or the other shall be subdued. I go for the great principle of the Kansas-Nebraska Bill, the right of the people to decide for themselves. (Senator Douglas was here interrupted by the wildest applause; cheer after cheer rent the air; the band struck up "Yankee Doodle;" rockets and pieces of fireworks blazed forth, and the enthusiasm was so intense and universal that it was some time before order could be restored and Mr. Douglas resume. The scene at this period was glorious beyond description.)

On the other point, Mr. Lincoln goes for a warfare upon the Supreme Court of the United States because of their judicial decision in the Dred Scott case. I yield obedience to the decisions of that court—to the final determination of the highest judicial tribunal known to our Constitution. He objects to the Dred Scott decision because it does not put the negro in the possession of the rights of citizenship on an equality with the white man. I am opposed to negro equality. (Immense applause.) I repeat that this nation is a white people—a people composed of European descendants—a people that have established this government for themselves and their posterity, and I am in favor of preserving not only the purity of the blood, but the purity of the government, from any mixture or amalgamation with inferior races. (Renewed applause.) I have seen the effects of this mixture of superior and inferior races—this amalgamation of white men and Indians and negroes; we have seen it in Mexico, in Central America, in South America, and in all the Spanish-American states, and its result has been degeneration, demoralization, and degradation below the capacity for self-government. ("True, true.")

I am opposed to taking any step that recognizes the negro man or the Indian as the equal of the white man. I am opposed to giving him a voice in the administration of the government. I would extend to the negro, and the Indian, and to all dependent races, every right, every privilege, and every immunity consistent with the safety and welfare of the white races (bravo); but equality they never should have, either political or social, or in any other respect whatever. (Cries of "Good," "good," and protracted cheers.)

My friends, you see that the issues are distinctly drawn. I stand by the same platform that I have so often proclaimed to you and to the people of Illinois heretofore. (Cries of "That's true," and applause.) I stand by the Democratic organization, yield obedience to its usages, and support its regular nominations. (Intense enthusiasm.) I indorse and approve the Cincinnati platform (renewed applause), and I adhere to and intend to carry out, as part of that platform, the great principle of self-government, which recognizes the right of the people in each state and territory to decide for themselves their domestic institutions. ("Good," "good," and cheers.) In other words, if the Lecompton issue shall arise again, you have only to turn back and see where you have found me during the last six months, and then rest assured that you will find me in the same position, battling for the same principle, and vindicating it from assault from whatever quarter it may come, so long as I have the power to do it. (Cheers.)

Fellow-citizens, you now have before you the outlines of the propositions which I intend to discuss before the people of Illinois during the pending campaign. I have spoken without preparation, and in a very desultory manner, and may have omitted some points which I desired to discuss, and may have been less implicit on others than I could have wished. I have made up my mind to appeal to the people against the combination which has been made against me. (Enthusiastic applause.) The Republican leaders have formed an alliance—an unholy, unnatural alliance—with a portion of the unscrupulous federal office-holders. I intend to fight that allied army wherever I meet them. (Cheers.) I know they deny the alliance while avowing the common purpose, but yet these men who are trying to divide the Democratic party for the purpose of electing a Republican senator in my place are just as much the agents, the tools, the supporters of Mr. Lincoln as if they were avowed Republicans, and expect their reward for their services when the Republicans come into power. (Cries of "That is true," and cheers.) I shall deal with these allied forces just as the Russians dealt with the allies at Sebastopol. The Russians, when they fired a broadside at the common enemy, did not stop to inquire, whether it hit a Frenchman, an Englishman, or a Turk, nor will I stop (Laughter and great applause); nor shall I stop to inquire whether my blows hit the Republican leaders or their allies, who are holding the federal offices, and yet acting in concert with the Republicans to defeat the Democratic party and its nominees. (Cheers, and cries of "Bravo!") I do not include all of the federal office-holders in this remark. Such of them as are Democrats, and show their Democracy by remaining inside of the Democratic organization and supporting its nominees, I recognize as Democrats; but those who, having been defeated inside of the organization, go outside, and attempt to divide and destroy the party in concert with the Republican leaders, have ceased to be Democrats, and belong to the allied army, whose avowed object is to elect the Republican ticket by dividing and destroying the Democratic party. (Cheers.)

My friends, I have exhausted myself (cries of "Don't stop yet), and I certainly have fatigued you ("No, no," and "Go on") in the long and desultory remarks which I have made. ("Go on longer," "We want to hear you," etc.) It is now two nights since I have been to bed, and I think I have a right to a little sleep. (Cheers, and a voice—"May you sleep soundly.") I will, however, have an opportunity of meeting you face to face, and addressing you on more than one occasion before the November election. (Cries of "We hope so," etc.) In conclusion, I must again say to you, justice to my own feelings demands it, that my gratitude for the welcome you have extended to me on this occasion knows no bounds, and can be described by no language which I can command. (Cries of "We did our duty," and cheers.) I see that I am literally at home when among my constituents. (Cries of "Welcome home," "You have done your duty," "Good," etc.) This welcome has amply repaid me for every effort that I have made in the public service during nearly twenty-five years that I have held office at your hands. (Cheers; a voice— "You will hold it longer.") It not only compensates me for the past, but it furnishes an inducement and incentive for future effort, which no man, no matter how patriotic, can feel who has not witnessed the magnificent reception you have extended to me to-night on my return.

At the conclusion of the remarks of Judge Douglas there was a spontaneous outburst of enthusiastic admiration. Cheers upon cheers followed, and the dense masses who had stood so long in solid ranks refused to separate, but continued for some time in vociferous applause.

Then followed another discharge of elegant fireworks. One piece, situated at the northwest corner of Dearborne and Lake Streets, was soon in a blaze, and as the fire ran from point to point on its surface, there was gradually revealed, in letters of dazzling and sparkling light, the glorious motto "POPULAR SOVEREIGNTY." This handsome and appropriate display renewed the enthusiasm of the multitude, and for more than an hour thousands of our people surrounded the hotel, cheering Douglas, Popular Sovereignty, and the Kansas-Nebraska Act.

CHAPTER XVII.

SAME SUBJECT CONTINUED.

MR. LINCOLN addressed a Republican meeting at the same place on the next evening, and the active campaign had now been formally opened. The Republican leaders were sanguine of success. They became extravagantly delighted with the Danites. On the 14th of July the leading Republican paper of Chicago addressed words of strong encouragement to that faction. It affected a fear of its strength, and had the effrontery to tell its readers that Douglas and his party were a mere handful and that the real party with whom the Republicans would have to contend would be the Danites.

It may not be out of place here to remark that as nearly as could be estimated by those not within the inner circles of Republican councils, there was about sixty thousand dollars of Republican money, besides considerable self respect recklessly sacrificed during that year in keeping the Danite party on its legs. It was an expensive item in the cost of the election, and we doubt very much if the organization and opposition of that faction did not give the Democratic party additional strength by enlisting the timid and negligent in the cause which was so fearfully threatened by the allies.

On the night of the 15th Judge Douglas was visited by a delegation of the German Democrats of Chicago—than whom a nobler band of patriots does not exist in the Union. It is true they form but a small portion of the German population of Chicago, but they are men of intelligence, education and experience. They understand the true principles of American freedom, and the Constitution has no more devoted supporters in the state. The speeches on the occasion were most happy.

On the morning of the 16th Judge Douglas left Chicago on his way to Springfield to meet the Democratic State Committee. The object and intention of his visit were well known. All along the road at every station he was greeted with all possible demonstrations of welcome. At Bloomington, where he arrived in the afternoon, he was met by a vast concourse of people ; he was greeted with a salute, which was re-echoed by a cannon carried down on the train by a large delegation from Joliet.

In the evening he made a speech of over two hours and a half. Of that speech an edition of eighty thousand was printed in pamphlet form and distributed all over Illinois, and copies were sent to all parts of the Union. It was also published in all the Democratic papers of the state, and thus distributed everywhere.

Particular reference is made to this speech because in it is contained an assertion of doctrine exactly similar in all practical operation and effect with that subsequently expressed at Freeport. At that time, however, July 16th, the allies thought there was no chance of Douglas' success, and it was not thought necessary to discover treason to Democratic faith in sentiments corresponding exactly with those uniformly expressed by him during the previous eight years of active discussion of the slavery question. The next day he proceeded on his way to Springfield. Present at his speech in Bloomington and on board the same train to Springfield was Mr. Lincoln. As the train proceeded it grew in length. At every station there was a mass of Democrats waiting to greet the champion of Democratic principles. Additional cars had to be added, and when the train reached Springfield it had twenty-five cars, each filled to overflowing with enthusiastic Democrats. Lincoln was perhaps the only Lincoln man on the train. During the day, which had been sultry, there fell heavy showers, yet the Democracy were not deterred in their determination to honor the man against whom there had been arraigned the force of such an extraordinary combination. Large trains filled to overflowing had come up from the lower part of the state. The vast multitude repaired to Edward's grove, and notwithstanding the ground was wet, and the trees dripping with the rain that had fallen, for three hours they remained listening to the voice of Stephen A. Douglas, who, in the name of Democratic truth, the Constitution and the vested rights of the people of the states and territories, bid Black Republicanism and its allies bold defiance. The writer of these pages witnessed that day of rejoicing, excitement and enthusiasm. It is imposible to describe it. It was the voluntary outpouring of popular enthusiasm towards a

man who had no patronage at his disposal, who was denounced as a political outcast, yet who with words of truth
and burning eloquence proclaimed the everlasting principles
of Democracy.   His speech on this occasion was published in
full, and an edition of fifty thousand copies in pamphlet form
was distributed in Illinois and other states.

At night Lincoln spoke in reply at the State House.

During the next few days Judge Douglas, acting with the
State Democratic Committee, fixed upon a list of appointments
for Democratic meetings, which list was published at once in
all the Democratic papers of the State.   This first list extended
only to the 21st of August, but was afterwards extended to
the last of October.   The complete list was as follows:

Clinton, on July 27th, then in succession at Monticello, Paris,
Hillsboro, Greenville, Edwardsville, Highland, Winchester,
Pittsfield, Beardstown, Havana, Lewiston, Peoria, Lacon,
Ottawa, Galena, Freeport, Junction, Joliet, Pontiac, Lincoln,
Jacksonville, Carlinville, Belleville, Waterloo, Chester, Jonesboro, Benton, Charleston, Danville, Urbana, Kankakee, Hene-
pin, Henry, Metamora, Pekin, Oquaka, Monmouth, Galesburg,
Macomb, Carthage, Quincy, Alton, Gillespie, Decatur, Springfield, Atlanta, Bloomington, Toulon, Genessee, Rock Island—
the last being on Friday, October 30—the election taking place
on Tuesday, the 3d of November.   These were his regular appointments, but in addition to these he spoke perhaps at
twenty other places, being points on his route, at which the
people would turn out, and insist upon his speaking to them.
His speeches at his regular appointments averaged about two
hours and a half each; except those at the joint discussions,
where the time was limited to one hour and a half.   A glance
at the map of the State will give an idea of the distance traveled, and the activity necessary to get from point to point
upon the list of designated places.   It was a task requiring a
wonderful display of fortitude and of physical endurance.   At
almost each of these places Senator Douglas was met at a distance from the town by committees, who in the name of the
Democracy welcomed him to the place.   To all these speeches
Judge Douglas made a response extending from ten to thirty
minutes.   He was then escorted to the place of meeting where
he delivered his regular speech.

On the 24th of July Mr. Douglas returned to Chicago, pre-

paratory to setting out to meet his appointments, the first of
which was fixed at Clinton on the 27th. Mr. Lincoln addressed
him a note proposing that they should canvass the State together. Lincoln or his friends had seen enough of the enthusiasm of the people along the line of Mr. Douglas' late journey
to satisfy every one that wherever Douglas was announced to
speak there would be no lack of auditors—men of all parties.
To allow Douglas to address these immense gatherings of
Democrats and Republicans, without any reply being made to
his remarks, was something that required attention if it could
not be prevented. Mr. Douglas responded, stating his regret
that Mr. Lincoln had not thought it proper to make the proposal at an earlier day, and before he (Mr. D.), had with the
Democratic State Committee arranged a series of exclusive
Democratic meetings, at which not only he, but the Democratic nominees for Congress and the Legislature were expected to speak. Mr. Lincoln had gone down to Springfield
with him, and from the 9th to the 24th had never said one
word upon the subject. He, however, agreed to meet Mr.
Lincoln once in each congressional district; and that, as they
had already both spoken at Chicago in the Second District
and Springfield in the Sixth District, they would have one
meeting in each of the other seven districts. He then left
Chicago and proceeded to Clinton; Mr. Lincoln was present
on that occasion; he next went to Monticello, where Lincoln
was again present. Lincoln subsequently accepted Douglas'
offer in a letter which, for its strange combination of phrases,
has become historical in Illinois as "Lincoln's conclusion."
Judge Douglas then named the following places for the joint
discussions :

Ottawa,	3d District,	August	21.
Freeport,	1st "	"	27.
Jonesboro,	9th "	Sept.	15.
Charleston,	7th "	"	18.
Galesburg,	4th "	Oct.	7.
Quincy,	5th "	"	13.
Alton,	8th "	"	15.

On the 7th of August Senator Trumbull spoke at Chicago,
and indulged in language of the lowest and most disreputable
personal abuse of Mr. Douglas. His special subject was the
alleged mutilation of the "Toombs Bill." That speech was so
boldly vituperative, and contained allegations so utterly reck-

less, that it failed in producing any impression save disgust for the author. His allegations were promptly exposed and triumphantly refuted.

Douglas' tour over the State was a succession of triumphs such as had rarely ever been witnessed in Illinois. Presidential aspirants in the Democratic party, who desired his defeat, hovered about Illinois, and were alarmed at the prospect. The arm of Federal power fell upon officials who dared say they would vote for Douglas. Brainard was appointed to the marine hospital in place of Dr. M'VICKAR, an accomplished physician and a Democrat of unimpeachable integrity.

An amusing incident occurred at this time, and it is questionable whether in the history of partizanship a parallel can be found for it. A venerable gentleman was holding a small, very small Federal office in Chicago. He was the father of twenty-one children; his age, his democracy and his patriarchal character could not save him from destruction. One of the respectable statesmen who, living far off from Illinois had taken such an interest in Illinois politics, and had become so anxious for Lincoln's success, reached Chicago, and in a few days it was ascertained that the fate of the venerable officeholder was sealed. On the morning when the papers for his removal and for the appointment of his successor were about to be sent off to Washington, the old man rushed into the hotel, entered unbidden the council chamber of the Danites, and addressing the exalted dispenser of Federal patronage, exclaimed, " He has come ! My wife have my twenty-second child this morning, and I have called him —— —— ——, and he look very much like you!"

The prefixes to the family name of the boy were the names of Mr. Buchanan's embassador to Illinois. Human nature could not resist that appeal ! He had already one boy named James Buchanan, and another Howell Cobb. Even Danite revenge yielded, and the old man was continued in office. The old man afterwards said that if Bright and Fitch would only give him ordinary time and notice he would be prepared for them when they should come to Illinois for the purpose of removing him. Since that time, however, his head has fallen, and the old gentleman is no longer an officer of the government.

MR. DOUGLAS VISITS HIS FIRST HOME IN ILLINOIS.

On August the 7th, 1858, Mr. Douglas reached Winchester. The people had taken the trouble to send all the way to Alton for a piece of artillery to add its reverberating tones to the welcome they had prepared for him. The attendance was very large. Winchester claimed Douglas as her own. The people of that little town regarded him as one whose history was to be forever identified with that of Winchester. He was greeted with the most unbounded expressions of delight. The Rev. Perry Bennett, of the Baptist church, in a chaste and eloquent speech welcomed him to his old home—his first home in Illinois. Mr. Douglas thus responded to the address:

"Ladies and gentlemen—fellow-citizens—To say that I am profoundly impressed with the keenest gratitude for the kind and cordial welcome you have given me in the eloquent and too partial remarks which have been addressed to me is but a feeble expression of the emotions of my heart. There is no spot on this vast globe which fills me with such emotions as when I come to this place, and recognize the faces of my old and good friends who now surround me and bid me welcome. Twenty-five years ago I entered this town on foot, with my coat upon my arm, without an acquaintance in a thousand miles, and without knowing where I could get money to pay a week's board. Here I made the first six dollars I ever earned in my life, and obtained the first regular occupation that I ever pursued. For the first time in my life I felt that the responsibilities of manhood were upon me, although I was under age, for I had none to advise with, and knew no one upon whom I had a right to call for assistance or friendship.

"Here I found the then settlers of the country my friends—my first start in life was taken here, not only as a private citizen, but my first election to public office by the people was conferred upon me by those whom I am now addressing and by their fathers. A quarter of a century has passed, and that penniless boy stands before you with his heart full and gushing with the sentiments which such associations and recollections necessarily inspire."

Mr. Douglas subsequently received a personal welcome from each of the vast multitude assembled at Winchester. Old times and old events were discussed familiarly; and men who had known him twenty-five years before crowded around him with an affectionate interest. He was a "Winchester boy," and Winchester people regarded him with fraternal love and admiration. Scott County, united with Morgan, sent up two members of the Legislature pledged to vote for the re-election of Stephen A. Douglas.

THE FREEPORT "TREASON."

During 1856, 1857, and 1858 the Democratic papers of Illinois and the Northwest, and Democratic speakers, including Mr. Douglas, in explaining and defending the Kansas-Nebraska Act, had been accustomed to quote arguments of southern statesmen to show that necessarily, in all communities, the local institutions must be sustained by the prevailing public sentiment, or it was useless to endeavor to maintain them. They had used this argument to prove that no matter what prohibitions Congress might enact against slavery in the territories, if the people desired to have slaves they would have them ; and local courts and laws would lean toward and protect the wishes and desires of the people. So, on the other hand, if slavery was not desired, it would be as effectually excluded by an adverse public sentiment as it could be by positive law. Upon this point they quoted as the views of a gentleman deservedly high in the estimation of the people of the South, and particularly of his own state, the following remarks of the Hon. James L. Orr, of South Carolina, made in 1856, in reference to the practical operation of the Nebraska Bill, and these views were constantly presented to the people from the stump and through the press :

OPINION OF MR. ORR IN 1856.

"I say, although I deny that squatter sovereignty exists in the territories of Kansas and Nebraska by virtue of this bill, it is a matter practically of little consequence whether it does or not; and I think I shall be able to satisfy the gentleman of that. The gentleman knows that, in every slaveholding community of this Union, we have local legislation and local police regulations appertaining to that institution, without which the institution would not only be valueless but a curse to the community. Without them the slaveholder could not enforce his rights when invaded by others. And if you had no local legislation for the purpose of giving protection, the institution would be of no value. I can appeal to every gentleman upon this floor, who represents a slaveholding constituency, to attest the truth of what I have stated upon that point.

"Now, the legislative authority of a territory is invested with a discretion to vote for or against laws. We think they ought to pass laws in every territory where the territory is open to settlement, and slaveholders go there, to protect slave property. But if they decline to pass such laws what is the remedy? None, sir. If the majority of the people are opposed to the institution, and if they do not desire it engrafted upon the territory, all they have to do is simply to decline to pass laws in the territorial Legislature for its protection, and then it is as well excluded as if the power was invested in the territorial Legislature, and exercised by them to prohibit it. Now I ask the gentleman what is the practical importance to result from the agitation and discussion of this question as to whether squatter sovereignty does or does not exist? Practically, it is a matter of little moment."

In June, 1857, Mr. Douglas, at the invitation of the members of the Grand Jury of the United States Court, and of other visitors at Springfield, delivered a speech at the State House upon the subject of Kansas and Utah affairs, and upon the Dred Scott decision. This speech was regarded at the time as the most thorough and complete vindication of the policy and principles of the Democratic party upon the topics embraced in it that he had ever made. The speech had a wide circulation, and was produced in most of the leading papers in the slaveholding states as the view of a high-minded, far-seeing, and national statesman. That speech has often been referred to by his enemies, even after the Lecompton difficulty had occurred, as a speech embracing the best and clearest views of constitutional law and of sound statesmanship. In that Springfield speech of June 12, 1857, a speech which has been held up as a model one, as containing nothing but sound Democratic doctrine, Mr. Douglas, in explaining what had been decided by the Supreme Court in the Dred Scott case, used the following clear and emphatic language. That the Supreme Court had decided—

"2d. That the act of the 6th of March, 1820, commonly called the Missouri Compromise Act, was unconstitutional and void before it was repealed by the Nebraska Act, and consequently did not and could not have the legal effect of extinguishing a master's right to a slave in that territory.

"While the right continues in full force under the guarantee of the Constitution, and can not be divested or alienated by an act of Congress, it necessarily remains a barren and worthless right unless sustained, protected, and enforced by appropriate police regulations and local legislation presenting adequate remedies for its violation. These regulations and remedies must necessarily depend entirely upon the will and wishes of the people of the Territory, as they can only be prescribed by the local Legislature.

"Hence the great principle of popular sovereignty and self-government is sustained and firmly established by the authority of this decision."

In his Bloomington speech, July 16th, 1858, he thus repeated the declaration of the same doctrine:

"I tell you, my friends, it is impossible, under our institutions, to force slavery on an unwilling people. If this principle of popular sovereignty inserted in the Nebraska Bill be fairly carried out, by letting the people decide the question for themselves by a fair vote, at a fair election, and with honest returns, slavery will never exist one day or one hour in any Territory against the unfriendly legislation of an unfriendly people. I care not how the Dred Scott decision may have settled the abstract question so far as the practical result is concerned; for, to use the language of an eminent southern senator on this very question:

"'I do not care a fig which way the decision shall be, for it is of no particular consequence; slavery can not exist a day or an hour in any territory or state unless it has affirmative laws sustaining and supporting it, furnishing police regulations and remedies, and an omission to furnish them would be as fatal as a constitutional prohibition. Without affirmative legislation in its favor, slavery could not exist any longer than a new-born infant could survive under the heat of the sun on a barren rock without protection. It would wilt and die for the want of support.'

"Hence, if the people of a territory want slavery, they will encourage it by passing affirmatory laws, and the necessary police regulations, patrol laws, and slave code; if they do not want it they will withhold that legislation, and by withholding it slavery is as dead as if it was prohibited by a constitutional prohibition—(cheers)—especially if, in addition, their legislation is unfriendly, as it would be if they were opposed to it. They could pass such local laws and police regulations as would drive slavery out in one day, or one hour, if they were opposed to it, and therefore, so far as the question of slavery in the territories is concerned, so far as the principle of popular sovereignty is concerned, in its practical operation, it matters not how the Dred Scott case may be decided with reference to the territories. My own opinion on that law point is well known. It is shown by my votes and speeches in Congress. But, be it as it may, the question was an abstract question, inviting no practical results, and whether slavery shall exist or shall not exist in any state or territory will depend upon whether the people are for it or against it, and whichever way they shall decide it in any territory or in any state will be entirely satisfactory to me. (Cheers.)"

In his speech at Springfield, July 18, 1858, he repeated substantially the same remarks upon this point—the impossibility of forcing or prohibiting slavery against the wishes of the people. Mr. Douglas and his friends also frequently quoted Mr. Buchanan's clear statement of the same doctrine, in his letter accepting the Cincinnati nomination, as follows:

"This legislation (Kansas-Nebraska Act) is founded upon principles as ancient as free government itself, and in accordance with them has simply declared that the people of a territory, like those of a state, shall decide for themselves whether slavery shall or shall not exist within their limits."

On August 21 the first joint discussion between Lincoln and Douglas took place; this occurred at Ottawa, in La Salle county, a strong Republican district, then and now represented in Congress by Mr. Lovejoy. The crowd in attendance was a large one, and about equally divided in political sentiment—the enthusiasm of the democracy having brought

out more than a due proportion of that party to hear and see
Douglas. His thrilling tones, his manly defiance towards the
enemies of the party, assured his friends, if any assurance was
wanting, that he was the same unconquered and unconquerable
Democrat that for twenty-five years he had been proved to
be. Douglas opened the discussion and spoke one hour;
Lincoln followed, his time being limited to an hour and a half,
yet he yielded thirteen minutes before the expiration of his
time. The speeches delivered on Saturday afternoon were
published in the *Chicago Times*, and *Press* and *Tribune*, on
Sunday afternoon. They had a wide circulation. The effect
of them was most damaging to Lincoln. It was, therefore,
deemed necessary to concoct some plan to break off the Democracy from Douglas, by placing the latter in the position of a
preacher of political heresy. The next joint meeting was to
be at Freeport, on Friday, the 27th, and during the interval
a meeting of the Danite and Republican leaders was held at
Chicago to prepare some trap for Douglas.

The speeches of Mr. Douglas, Mr. Orr, and the paragraphs
from Mr. Buchanan's inaugural, were taken by the Danite
and Republican leaders as the basis of a question to be propounded to Mr. Douglas at Freeport. If he answered negatively, the answer was to be used by the allies as a repudiation
of the principles of the Nebraska Bill, as in direct variance
with the established doctrine of the party as declared by
himself and by all others; and as more pro-slavery than even
the people of South Carolina asked for. If he answered in
the affirmative, then he was to be denounced as a preacher of
a political heresy, according to the Republican interpretation
of the Dred Scott decision. The questions were, therefore,
prepared, and when the parties met at Freeport, on the
27th, Mr. Lincoln, who had the opening, drew from his pocket
a paper containing four questions, all (so he said) that he had
had time to prepare for the occasion. Those questions were
as follows:

"1. If the people of Kansas shall, by means entirely unobjectionable in all
other respects, adopt a state Constitution, and ask admission into the Union
under it, before they have the requisite number of inhabitants, according to
the English bill, to wit: ninety-three thousand, will you vote to admit
them?

"2. Can the people of the United States territory, in any lawful way against the wishes of any citizen of the United States, exclude slavery from their limits prior to the formation of a state Constitution?

"3. If the Supreme Court of the United States shall decide that states can not exclude slavery from their limits, are you in favor of acquiescing in adopting and following such decision as a rule of political action?

"4. Are you in favor of acquiring additional territory in disregard of how such acquisition may affect the nation on the slavery question?

The second question was one involving the material point upon which the confederates proposed to make capital. The other questions really amounted to nothing, and were presented, with ostrich-like sagacity, under an impression that Douglas would not perceive the hidden purpose. In his speech he thus replied to the four questions:

"First he desires to know, If the people of Kansas shall form a Constitution by means entirely proper and unobjectionable, and ask admission into the Union as a state before they have the requisite population for a member of Congress, whether I will vote for that admission? Well, now, I regret exceedingly that he did not answer that interrogatory himself before he put it to me, in order that we might understand, and not be left to infer, on which side he is. Mr. Trumbull, during the last session of Congress, voted from the beginning to the end against the admission of Oregon, although a free state, because she had not the requisite population for a member of Congress. Mr. Trumbull would not consent, under any circumstances, to let a state, free or slave, come into the Union until it had the requisite population. As Mr. Trumbull is in the field fighting for Mr. Lincoln, I would like to have Mr. Lincoln answer his own question, and tell me whether he is fighting Trumbull on that issue or not. But I will answer his question. In reference to Kansas, it is my opinion that, as she has population enough to constitute a slave state, she has people enough for a free state. I will not make Kansas an exceptional case to the other states of the Union. I hold it to be a sound rule of universal application to require a territory to contain the requisite population for a member of Congress before it is admitted as a state into the Union. I made that proposition in the Senate in 1856, and I renewed it during the last session, in a bill providing that no territory of the United States should form a Constitution and apply for admission until it had the requisite population. On another occasion I proposed that neither Kansas, nor any other territory, should be admitted until it had the requisite population. Congress did not adopt any of my propositions containing this general rule, but did make an exception of Kansas. I will stand by that exception. Either Kansas must come in as a free state, with whatever population she may have, or the rule must be applied to all the other territories alike. I therefore answer at once, that it having been decided that Kansas has people enough for a slave state, I hold that she has enough for a free state. I hope Mr. Lincoln is satisfied with my answer; and now I would like to get his answer to his own interrogatory—whether or not he will vote to admit Kansas before she has the requisite population. I want to know whether he will vote to admit Oregon before that territory has the requisite population. Mr. Trumbull will not, and the same reason that commits Mr. Trumbull against the admission of Oregon commits him against Kansas, even if she should apply for admission as a free state. If there is any sincerity, any truth in the argument of Mr. Trumbull in the Senate against the admission of Oregon because she had not 93,420 people, although her population was larger than that of Kansas, he stands pledged against the admission of both Oregon and Kansas until they have 93,420 inhabitants. I would like Mr. Lincoln to answer this question. I would like him to take his own medicine. If he differs with Mr. Trumbull, let him answer his argument against the admission of Oregon, instead of poking questions at me.

"The next question propounded to me by Mr. Lincoln is, Can the people of a territory in any lawful way, against the wishes of any citizen of the United States, exclude slavery from their limits prior to the formation of a state Constitution? I answer emphatically, as Mr. Lincoln has heard me answer a hundred times from every stump in Illinois, that in my opinion the people of a territory can, by lawful means, exclude slavery from their limits prior to the formation of a state Constitution. Mr. Lincoln knew that I had answered that question over and over again. He heard me argue the Nebraska Bill on that principle all over the state in 1854, in 1855, and in 1856, and he has no excuse for pretending to be in doubt as to my position on that question. It matters not what way the Supreme Court may hereafter decide as to the abstract question whether slavery may or may not go into a territory under the Constitution, the people have the lawful means to introduce it or exclude it as they please, for the reason that slavery can not exist a day or an hour anywhere unless it is supported by local police regulations. Those police regulations can only be established by the local Legislature, and if the people are opposed to slavery they will elect representatives to that body who will, by unfriendly legislation, effectually prevent the introduction of it into their midst. If, on the contrary, they are for it, their legislation will favor its extension. Hence, no matter what the decision of the Supreme Court may be on that abstract question, still the right of the people to make a slave territory or a free territory is perfect and complete under the Nebraska Bill. I hope Mr. Lincoln deems my answer satisfactory on that point.

"In this connection I will notice the charge which he has introduced in relation to Mr. Chase's amendment. I thought that I had chased that amendment out of Mr. Lincoln's brain at Ottawa; but it seems that it still haunts his imagination, and he is not yet satisfied. I had supposed that he would be ashamed to press that question further. He is a lawyer, and has been a member of Congress, and has occupied his time and amused you by telling you about parliamentary proceedings. He ought to have known better than to try to palm off his miserable impositions upon this intelligent audience. The Nebraska Bill provided that the legislative power, and authority of the said territory, should extend to all rightful subjects of legislation consistent with the organic act and the Constitution of the United States. It did not make any exception as to slavery, but gave all the power that it was possible for Congress to give, without violating the Constitution, to the territorial Legislature, with no exception or limitation on the subject of slavery at all. The language of that bill which I have quoted gave the full power and the full authority over the subject of slavery, affirmatively and negatively, to introduce it or exclude it so far as the Constitution of the United States would permit. What more could Mr. Chase give by his amendment? Nothing. He offered his amendment for the identical purpose for which Mr. Lincoln is using it, to enable demagogues in the country to try and deceive the people. His amendment was to this effect. It provided that the Legislature should have the power to exclude slavery; and General Cass suggested, 'Why not give the power to introduce as well as exclude?' The answer was, they have the power already in the bill to do both. Chase was afraid his amendment would be adopted if he put the alternative proposition and so make it fair both ways, but would not yield. He offered it for the purpose of having it rejected. He offered it, as he has himself avowed over and over again, simply to make capital out of it for the stump. He expected that it would be capital for small politicians in the country, and that they would make an effort to deceive the people with it, and he was not mistaken, for Lincoln is carrying out the plan admirably. Lincoln knows that the Nebraska Bill, without Chase's amendment, gave all the power which the Constitution would permit. Could Congress confer any more? Could Congress go beyond the Constitution of the country? We gave all, a full grant, with no exception in regard to slavery one way or the other. We left that question as we left all others, to be decided by the people for themselves, just as they pleased. I will not occupy my time on this question. I have argued it before all over Illinois. I have argued it in this beautiful city of Freeport; I have argued it in the North, the South, the East, and the West, avowing the same sentiments and the same principles. I have not been afraid to avow my sentiments up here for fear I would be trotted down into Egypt.

"The third question which Mr. Lincoln presented is, If the Supreme Court of the United States shall decide that a state of this Union can not exclude slavery from its own limits, will I submit to it? I am amazed that Lincoln should ask such a question. ('A school-boy knows better.') Yes, a school-boy does know better. Mr. Lincoln's object is to cast an imputation upon the Supreme Court. He knows that there never was but one man in America, claiming any degree of intelligence or decency, who ever for a moment pretended such a thing. It is true that the Washington *Union*, in an article published on the 17th of last November, did put forth that doctrine, and I denounced the article on the floor of the Senate in a speech which Mr. Lincoln now pretends was against the President. The *Union* had claimed that slavery had a right to go into the free states, and that any provision in the Constitution or laws of the free states to the contrary were null and void. I denounced it in the Senate, as I said before, and I was the first man who did. Lincoln's friends, Trumbull, and Seward, and Hale, and Wilson, and the whole Black Republican side of the Senate were silent. They left it to me to denounce it. And what was the reply made to me on that occasion? Mr. Toombs, of Georgia, got up and undertook to lecture me on the ground that I ought not to have deemed the article worthy of notice, and ought not to have replied to it; that there was not one man, woman, or child South of the Potomac, in any slave state, who did not repudiate any such pretension. Mr. Lincoln knows that that reply was made on the spot, and yet now he asks this question. He might as well ask me, suppose Mr. Lincoln should steal a horse, would I sanction it; and it would be as genteel in me to ask him, in the event he stole a horse, what ought to be done with him. He casts an imputation upon the Supreme Court of the United States by supposing that they would violate the Constitution of the United States. I tell him that such a thing is not possible. It would be an act of moral treason that no man on the bench could ever descend to. Mr. Lincoln himself would never, in his partizan feelings, so far forget what was right as to be guilty of such an act.

"The fourth question of Mr. Lincoln is, Are you in favor of acquiring additional territory in disregard as to how such acquisition may affect the Union on the slavery question? This question is very ingeniously and cunningly put. The Black Republican creed lays it down expressly, that under no circumstances shall we acquire any more territory unless slavery is first prohibited in the country. I ask Mr. Lincoln whether he is in favor of that proposition. Are you (addressing Mr. Lincoln) opposed to the acquisition of any more territory, under any circumstances, unless slavery is prohibited in it? That he does not like to answer. When I ask him whether he stands up to that article in the platform of his party, he turns, Yankee-fashion, and without answering it, asks me whether I am in favor of acquiring territory without regard to how it may affect the Union on the slavery question. I answer that whenever it becomes necessary, in our growth and progress, to acquire more territory, that I am in favor of it, without reference to the question of slavery, and when we have acquired it, I will leave the people free to do as they please, either to make it slave or free territory, as they prefer.

This was the origin and history of the famous questions put to Mr. Douglas at Freeport, and of his reply. The answers were not exactly what the allies desired. They would have preferred that he should repudiate popular sovereignty, because they had southern authority and his own entire record to produce against him. The fidelity of Mr. Douglas to his own and oft-repeated doctrines—to the doctrines he had proclaimed in every county in the state during 1856, was looked upon by the allies as unpardonable. The scheme to entrap him had failed. His reply to Lincoln had a startling effect upon that gentleman. Douglas had refused to bid for the Danite vote by repudiating his own principles. Lincoln's half-hour rejoinder was a failure. He had expected a different answer, and had evidently intended in that half hour to expose Douglas' abandonment of popular sovereignty, and perhaps to quote upon him Mr. Orr's speech, Mr. Buchanan's letter, and a long list of other Democratic authorities.

Immediately the Republican papers of the state took up the matter: they were shocked that Democrats could support a man who did not believe the Kansas-Nebraska Act was a purely pro-slavery measure! *They read Douglas out of the Democratic party!*

The *Washington Union* took up the Republican cry, that Douglas had betrayed the Democratic party at Freeport, and the cry was continued from mouth to mouth, until, some time in the dog-days of 1859, it was heard for the last time in very feeble echoes, somewhere in the remote neighborhood of Grass Valley, California.

On the 23d of February, 1859, Mr. Douglas, in reply to a speech made by the Honorable A. G. Brown, of Mississippi, repeated the opinions expressed by him in his speeches in Illinois during 1856, 7, and 8, and in Congress from the time of the compromise measures of 1850. That speech has been widely circulated. Attached to the pamphlet edition is an appendix, making twenty-two pages of printed matter, in

which are grouped extracts from reports made by himself, and
from speeches made by the Hon. W. A. Richardson, of Illinois,
Hon. Louis Cass, Hon. Isaac Toucey, Hon. Howell Cobb, Hon.
John C. Breckinridge, Hon. J. L. Orr, Hon. A. H. Stephens,
Hon. J. P. Benjamin, Hon. J. M. Mason, Hon. J. A. Bayard,
Hon. G. E. Badger, Hon. John Pettit, Hon. A. P. Butler, Hon.
R. M. T. Hunter, Hon. Robert Toombs, Hon. J. A. Smith, Hon.
A. C. Dodge, Hon. T. F. Bowie, Hon. G. W. Jones, Hon. J. N.
Elliott, Hon. J. S. Caskie, Hon. A. G. Brown, Hon. W. C. Daw-
son, Hon. T. L. Clingman, Hon. Z. Kidwell, Hon. C. J. Faulk-
ner, Hon. J. H. Lumpkin, Hon. A. G. Talbott, Hon. Moses
Norris, Hon. J. B. Weller, Hon. W. H. English, Hon. M.
Macdonald, Hon. J. R. Thomson, Hon. R. Brodhead, Hon. W.
Bigler, Hon. L. O'B. Branch, and Hon. Harry Hibbard; also from
the Cincinnati platform, and the letter of Mr. Buchanan accepting the nomination—all showing the interpretation placed
upon the Kansas-Nebraska Act by these gentlemen at the
time of its passage and subsequently to its going into effect.
That speech and appendix present a compendium of authority
upon the proper construction to be placed upon the language
of the act.   Mr. Douglas demonstrates in that speech that the
"unsound doctrines" of his Freeport address were not new,
but were of very ancient date, and thoroughly understood by
the Senate and the country.

The next joint debate took place at Jonesboro, in Egypt,
on the 15th of September; the fourth at Charleston, in the
seventh district, on the 18th.   The fifth took place at Galesburg, in Knox county—strongly abolition—on October 7th;
the sixth at Quincy, on the 13th, and the last at Alton, on
the 15th.

Between these periods both candidates were busily engaged.
Lyman Trumbull was also at work.   His speeches were neither
argumentative nor poetical; they were not devoted to the advocacy of Lincoln or of Republicanism; they were fierce, malicious, vituperative, and scandalous denunciations of Judge
Douglas personally.   Trumbull neither served Lincoln nor
damaged Douglas.   He descended to the level of Lieb, Grund,
and Carpenter; and at this day of intelligence the people of
Illinois accept nothing on faith from men of that grade.

In the meantime the Republican papers kept constantly before the people the famous declaration of the *Washington Union:*

"Upon the issue of Douglas or Lincoln, Lincoln or Douglas, we confess to a serene indifference."

Chase, of Ohio, Colfax, of Indiana, Blair, of Missouri, H. F. Douglas (negro), and other Republican orators, were in Illinois urging their friends to "kill Douglas" now, or he would be President in 1860.

The Danites were also busy. They had candidates for Congress in all the districts. They talked of Judge Breese and Judge Skinner for the Senate. They had candidates for the Legislature in every district, except those which were overwhelmingly Democratic, and in these districts they united with the Republicans. In the close districts they were particularly active, and, to their own eternal shame, succeeded in electing four Republicans to the Legislature, where by a united vote Democrats could have been chosen. It is but just, however, to say, that the major portion of these men have since regretted their conduct, and are now warm friends and supporters of the Democratic organization.

The *Washington Union* throughout all this season continued its wholesale denunciation of Mr. Douglas. On the 3d of September it charged Douglas with degrading the office of senator by addressing the people of his own state in defense of his own official conduct, and in opposition to Republicanism. The Danites at an early day announced a "tremendous mass meeting," to come off at the state capital on September 7th; and handbills, printed in a variety of colors, announced that the "Hon. John C. Breckinridge, Vice-President of the United States, would address the meeting," and denounce the Democracy of Illinois. The mass meeting came off, but beyond a few hundred office-holders and expectants, no one attended, not even to hear Mr. Breckinridge upon that subject. The use of Mr. Breckinridge's name by these disorganizers was wholly unauthorized. In October following he timidly published a letter declaring his earnest hope that the Democracy of Illinois would sustain their regular nominees, including Mr. Douglas. This letter of Mr. Breckinridge, as well as an eloquent and stirring one from Governor Wise, were both written and published *long after* the Freeport speech, the doctrines of which have been represented since then as a justification for an unmanly and vindictive assault upon Mr. Douglas. All honor and credit to the illustrious Virginian who, rising above the petty instigations of rivalry, had the courage and independence to declare that he did not desire the election of Lincoln, and did desire the election of Douglas, the chosen leader of the Illinois Democracy. The Hon. James B. Clay, of Kentucky, also sent to his Democratic brethren of Illinois words of approval and of encouragement. The Hon. A. H. Stephens, of Georgia, was in Chicago during the summer, and an attempt was made by the Danites to use his name in approval of their proceedings. This, however, was unjust to that gentleman: he never, by word or deed, approved the election of the Republican candidates.

The labors of the campaign were excessive. The weather up to the tenth of October was oppressively warm. The most of Judge Douglas' appointments after that date were in northern Illinois. Then the weather changed; a cold blustering wind, often accompanied with rain, continued until the close. At Geneseo and Rock Island, where Mr. Douglas spoke on the Thursday and Friday preceding the election, it rained hard all day, yet he was listened to by thousands, many of whom had come hundreds of miles to hear him. On Saturday night, October 31, he reached Chicago pretty well fatigued, and voice almost exhausted from speaking so often in the open air, and exposed to the heavy rain. Sunday was a day of repose, and one he much needed. On Monday night he was again called out to address a mass meeting in Chicago, but a rain storm prevented his saying much.

Tuesday, at an early hour, the city was alive. Throughout the state an unusual excitement prevailed. In Chicago a rain continued at intervals all day. It is unnecessary to state here that the Republicans resorted to every possible means in the way of secret circulars to injure Mr. Douglas by representing him as being a Know-Nothing, and a Republican. All such attempts failed. The fate of Lincoln was sealed by the discussion at Ottawa, and nothing but a special interposition of Providence could have elected a Legislature favorable to his election to the Senate.

It only remains to add the result of the election:

Upon the state ticket the vote was—

Fondey, Democrat............121,609	
French " 122,413	
Average democratic vote..........	122,011
Dougherty, Danite..........	5,071
Total democratic vote..........	127,082
Miller, Republican............125,430	
Bateman " 124,556	
Average republican vote..........	124,993
Democratic majority in the state........	2,089

The Danite organs in the state, after the election, apologized and accounted for the smallness of their vote, by saying that the great bulk of their party, failing to see any other mode of "killing Douglas," had voted the Republican ticket direct.

The Legislature, including those holding over, stood thus:

	Senate.	House.	Totals.
Democrats	14	40	54
Republicans	11	35	46
Danites	00	00	00

Democratic majority on joint ballot 8.

This was the result of one of the most extraordinary political contests ever had in any state of the Union. It was a glorious personal as well as political triumph on the part of Mr. Douglas. It demonstrated the unpurchasable integrity of the Democracy of Illinois. It showed that they were without fear, and were above price. It showed also, and the fact was creditable to the intelligence of the American people, that no Federal authority can be successfully exercised to defeat the will and power of a free people.

The effort to defeat Mr. Douglas did not end with the decision of the people in November. It was at once noised about that among the Democratic senators holding over, were some who were under no obligation to vote for Mr. Douglas, and who were disposed to stand by the administration. The Legislature did not meet until January. The rumours concerning the fidelity of certain state senators were taken up and vouched for by Republican newspapers, and possibly found believers elsewhere. One federal officer in Illinois boasted that he held blank commissions to important federal offices, in which he was authorized to insert the names of such Democratic senators as would refuse to vote for Douglas. This boast was too degrading to the administration to find any Democrat in Illinois who would believe it. The effect, however, was soon felt. The senators holding over were sterling Democrats; they did not relish the free use of their names by the Danite chieftains, and they took occassion to express their sentiments very freely and decidedly upon the matter. It was stated that, during the interval between the election and the meeting of the Legislature, a politician of a neighboring state, who had been prominent as an outside friend and supporter of the Danites, found occasion to cross that part of Illinois represented in the state Senate by Captain Coffee, one of the best and honestest Democrats in the west. The distinguished stranger stopped at a town in the vicinity of Coffee's residence and inquired particularly after his health. Coffee happened to be away from home at the time, and when he returned the landlord told him of the visit made by the "eminent statesman" from another state, and of his particular inquiries after Captain Coffee's health. The answer was as emphatic as its purport was unmistakable: he said, "When——— calls here on his way back, you tell him for me, that I am a Democrat, and if he dare to ask me to vote against Douglas he may be sure that either he or I will be the worst whipped man that ever saw the state of Illinois." Captain Coffee's fidelity was never doubted by any Democrat, indeed his determination to vote for Douglas was soon publicly announced, and the distinguished gentleman has never returned that way since to hear any additional particulars touching Captain Coffee's health, which it is hoped may never be anything else than in a high state of preservation.

According to custom the Democratic members of the Legislature met in caucus the night before the organization. Douglas was nominated by acclamation, and three days thereafter was, in joint meeting, re-elected United States senator.

CHAPTER XVIII.

DOMESTIC AFFAIRS.

Mr. Douglas was first married on the 7th of April, 1847, in Rockingham county, North Carolina, to Miss Martha Denny Martin, only daughter of Col. Robert Martin, of that county. With his bride he returned to the State of Illinois, whose senator he had become but a month previously. Everywhere during his tour he was greeted with affection by his constituents, with all the attention that friendship could suggest, and all the respect which the gentleness and amiability of his accomplished bride could not fail to inspire. Her gentleness, and her strong native good judgment were of great service to him in many a season of perplexing and troublesome excitement. She made home an abiding place of peace and tranquility, where all the associations were of a refined and Christian character. In extending hospitality to the multitudes who thronged her husband's mansion, she was judicious and yet munificent. She won the respect of all his friends, and divided with him their unbounded admiration. After a happy life of nearly six years with a husband whose interest was the object of her wordly life, she died at his residence in Washington City, on the 19th of January, 1853, leaving three children, two boys, and one girl, the latter an infant, who survived its mother but a few months. The two boys are now bright, active, intelligent youths, and reside with their father.

In November, 1856, Mr. Douglas was married at Washington City to Miss Adele Cutts, the beautiful and accomplished daughter of Hon. James Madison Cutts, long a resident of that city.

DOUGLAS' PLANTATION AND SLAVES.

In speaking of the domestic affairs of Judge Douglas, it may not be out of place to introduce and dispose of a matter which on frequent occasions has served his political and personal enemies with a pretext for the most unscrupulous abuse. That matter is his "ownership of slaves."

In 1847, on the day after his marriage, Colonel Martin

placed in Mr. Douglas' hands a sealed package of papers. Upon an examination of these papers Mr. Douglas found among them a deed of certain plantations, including the servants upon them, in the State of Mississippi, which deed vested the title to both land and servants in him absolutely. He at once, without one moment's hesitation, sought Colonel Martin and returned him the deed, stating that while he was no abolitionist, and had no sympathy with them in their wild schemes and ultra views respecting slavery, yet he was a northern man by birth, education and residence, and was totally ignorant of that description of property, and as ignorant of the manner and rules by which it should be governed, and was therefore wholly incompetent to take charge of it and perform his duty towards it properly, particularly at a distance of fifteen hundred miles from where he resided, and where he should continue to reside at all times with the people to whom he owed so much. He said that he preferred Colonel Martin should retain the property, at least during his lifetime, and if in the meantime no disposition was made of it, he could then by will leave directions as to the manner in which he desired it disposed of.

Colonel Martin died on the 25th of May, 1848, leaving a will in which he provided for the disposal of his entire estate. In this will he recited the fact that he had a year previously offered the plantations in Mississippi, with the slaves upon them, to his son-in-law, Stephen A. Douglas, who had declined to receive them. He then declared substantially, that in the event of the death of his daughter, Martha D. Douglas, leaving surviving children, it was his wish and desire that the slaves upon those Mississippi plantations should remain and continue the property of those children; and he willed this in the firm belief that the negroes would be better off and better cared for as slaves in the family in which they had been born and raised than if set at liberty and sent to the free states; but he provided, that in the event of his said daughter dying, leaving no surviving children, the negroes should be sent to the coast of Africa and should be supported there one year, at the expense of his estate, and then be declared free.

This is the entire history of the manner in which Mr. Douglas became "the owner of plantations stocked with slaves;" and of the manner and the reasons by which the ownership of the slaves was continued by their grandfather to the children, after Mr. Douglas, for the reasons given, had declined the absolute gift of the entire property.

It has been thought proper and just toward Mr. Douglas that this matter should be stated clearly and distinctly. At the time that Col. Martin made him the valuable present, Mr. Douglas was not blessed with an over abundance of treasure. As a pecuniary gift this was of great value, and in his circumstances would, if converted into money, have enabled him, by judicious investments in Chicago and elsewhere in Illinois, to have laid the foundation for a princely fortune. The gift was clogged with no conditions. He was at liberty to convert plantations and slaves into cash at any moment. How many of those who have denounced him as a slaveholder, as being the " owner of human beings," and the " proprietor of human chattels," would have resisted the offer that he declined, is a question which the observer of the general hollowness of abolition pretensions will have no difficulty in answering.

A senator from Ohio, with a want of taste, a want of a becoming sense of the proprieties of life, shortly after the death of Mrs. Douglas, was shameless enough to introduce the matter into a debate in the Senate. The remarks made by Mr. Wade on that occasion elicited the following feeling, touching, manly reply from Mr. Douglas:

" Mr. President, the senator from Ohio [Mr. Wade] has invaded the circle of my private relations in search of materials for the impeachment of my official action. He has alluded to certain southern interests which he insinuates that I possess, and remarked, that where the treasure is there the heart is also. So long as the statement that I was one of the largest slaveholders in America was confined to the abolition newspapers and stump orators I treated it with silent contempt. I would gladly do so on this occasion, were it not for the fact that the reference is made in my presence by a senator for the purpose of imputing to me a mercenary motive for my official conduct. Under these circumstances, silence on my part in regard to the fact might be construed into a confession of guilt in reference to the impeachment of motive. I therefore say to the senator that his insinuation is false, and he knows it to be false, if he has ever searched the records or has any reliable information upon the subject. I am not the owner of a slave, and never have been, nor have I ever received and appropriated to my own use one dollar earned by slave labor. It is true that I once had tendered to me, under circumstances grateful to my feelings, a plantation with a large number of slaves upon it, which I declined to accept, not because I had any sympathy with abolitionists or the abolition movement, but for the reason that, being a northern man by birth, by education and residence, and intending always to remain such, it was impossible for me to know, understand, and provide for the wants, comforts and happiness of those people. I refused to accept them because I was unwilling to assume responsibilities which I was incapable of fulfilling. This fact is referred to in the will of my father-in-law as a reason for leaving the plantation and slaves to his only daughter, (who became the mother of my infant children), as her separate and exclusive estate, with the request that if she departed this life without surviving children the slaves should be emancipated and sent to Liberia at the expense of her estate; but in the event she should leave surviving children, the slaves should descend to them, under the belief, expressed in the will, that they would be happier and better off with the descendants of the family, with whom they had been born and raised, than in a distant land where they might find no friend to care for them. This brief statement, relating to private and domestic affairs, (which ought to be permitted to remain private and sacred), has been extorted and wrung from me with extreme reluctance, even in vindication of the purity of my motives in the performance of a high public trust. As the truth compelled me to negative the insinuation so offensively made by the senator from Ohio, God forbid that I should be understood by any one as being willing to cast from me any responsibility that now does, or ever has attached to any member of my family. So long as life shall last—and I shall cherish with religious veneration the memory and virtues of the sainted mother of my children—so long as my heart shall be filled with parental solicitude for the happiness of those motherless infants, I implore my enemies, who so ruthlessly invade the domestic sanctuary, to do me the favor to believe that I have no wish, no aspiration, to be considered purer or better than she who was, or they who are, slaveholders.

"Sir, whenever my assailants shall refuse to accept a like

amount of this species of property tendered to them, under similar circumstances, and shall perform a domestic trust with equal fidelity and disinterestedness, it will be time enough for them to impute mercenary motives to me in the performance of my official duties."

The "ownership of slaves" has for several years been one of the favorite themes upon which the lower and more disreputable class of the opposition have loved to dilate in denouncing Douglas to sympathetic audiences. Men of respectability, even among the abolitionists, have ceased to discourse of it. But in 1858, in the memorable contest to which a proper share of this book is devoted, the matter was revived and assumed a new and more intensified color by men who, in uniting with the abolitionists to accomplish a common end, felt compelled to resort to fabrications which no honorable Republican would stoop to invent.

It will be remembered that Illinois during that year was visited by several distinguished men, some of whom had such a profound regard for the rights of the South that they sought the election of Lincoln, with his negro equality doctrines, by the defeat of Douglas. In the list of statesmen who found, during 1858, a hitherto unknown salubriousness in the air of the northwest, was the Hon. JOHN SLIDELL of Louisiana, who being, as was well known, or at least, as it was supposed, a friend, confident, and adviser of the President in the days of the Danite rebellion, attracted by his venerable appearance, as well as by the classic purity of his language upon the subject of Douglas' reelection, the especial regard of the entire Danite faction, and of the more numerous and respectable party, the Republicans. It was understood—and when we say understood we mean that it was openly declared by the President's followers that Mr. Slidell was the main instrument by which certain changes in the federal offices in Illinois had been made. Dr. DANIEL BRAINARD, surgeon to the marine hospital, owed his appointment to the united and friendly exertions of FRANCIS J. GRUND, and Senator John Slidell. *Par nobile fratrum!* Immediately after Mr. Slidell's final leave of Chicago it was stated upon the streets and in public places that Senator Douglas (then absent in other parts of the state) was not only a slaveholder, but one that had no parallel in wickednesss, even in Uncle Tom's Cabin. We will not repeat the stories which were upon the lips of every one, because they eventually took shape, and appeared in a public and formal allegation. A few weeks before the election the leading Republican paper in Chicago charged that Mr. Douglas spent in riotous living an immense annual revenue, derived from his plantations in Mississippi; and not content with thus profiting by his property in human beings—his equals in all human attributes—he neglected them, placed them under cruel and tyrannical masters, who denied to the poor slaves food enough to keep them from suffering, and clothing enough to hide their nakedness. Upon this statement of facts, for which the authority of a distinguished southern senator was claimed, the paper produced a sensation article, which was extensively copied throughout all Illinois and the northwest. Mr. Douglas was absent from Chicago, and did not see the charge until after the election. Both Republican and administration orators made the most of the horrid condition of "Douglas' slaves;" and the gentleman to whom Mr. Douglas had intrusted the care and management of his children's estate was held up to the people as a monster of wickedness, and as a demon in cruelty.

The writer of these pages heard the same story repeated at a Republican convention in Chicago in September or October, 1858, by one of the persons nominated as a candidate for the Legislature. The candidate stated that there could be no doubt of the facts, for they were derived from a very distinguished southern man who had lately been in Chicago.

In the meantime the story had reached New Orleans, there attracting much attention. The authors of the story seemed to have overlooked the possibility that there would be ultimately an exposure of its want of truth. The New Orleans *Picayune* first noticed it, and pronounced it "an election canard." The Chicago *Press and Tribune* at once responded as follows:

"We have only to say that the story came to us from a personal friend of Mr. Slidell—a gentleman of character and influence in this city—and he assured us that he had the statement from Slidell himself, during his visit to Chicago, while the late canvass was going on. His name is at the service of any one authorized to demand it."

The Democratic paper at Chicago at once demanded the name of the "gentleman of character" who had made the statement. Upon the streets the name was publicly mentioned, but it had not been given up by the *Press and Tribune*. At last it was charged that Dr. DANIEL BRAINARD, a federal office-holder, was the man.

On the 18*th of December* Mr. Slidell published in the *Washington Union* a denial of having ever told Dr. Brainard or any one else such a story. He said:

I am constrained to believe either that Dr. Brainard did not make the statement attributed to him by the Chicago *Press and Tribune*, or that he has been guilty of a deliberate and malicious falsehood. I have no recollection of ever having spoken of Mr. Douglas' slaves; it is possible that I may have been asked if he had any property of that description. If so, I could only have answered that they were employed in cotton-planting on the Mississippi river, and were in possession of an old and valued friend, James A. McHatton, than whom a more honorable man or better master cannot be found in Louisiana."

On the 23d of December Dr. Brainard addressed a note to the editors of the *Press and Tribune*, denying having ever made the statements imputed to him. In the issue of that paper of December 24 the editors lifted the veil and exposed the whole fabrication. That paper said:

"We have on two occasions promised that, when called upon by one authorized to ask the name of the gentleman who related to us, on the authority of Mr. John Slidell, the story of the ill-treatment of Mr. Douglas' slaves, we would give it to the public. Mr. Slidell in his card above makes no demand of the kind; but as he denounces as a falsehood the story itself, we are impelled to make the following statement:

"In July last, about the time of Mr. Slidell's visit to Chicago, one of the editors of this paper was informed by Dr. Daniel Brainard, Professor of Surgery in the Rush Medical College, in a conversation invited by the doctor himself, in his own office, that Mr. Douglas' slaves in the South were 'the subjects of inhuman and disgraceful treatment—that they were hired out to a factor at fifteen dollars per annum each—that he, in turn, hired them out to others in lots, and that they were ill-fed, over-worked, and in every way so badly treated that they were spoken of in the neighborhood where they are held as a disgrace to all slaveholders and the system they support.' The authority given for these alleged facts, by Dr. Brainard, was the Hon. John Slidell, of Louisiana.

* * * * * *

"At that time, Dr. Brainard suggested that the case as stated was a proper one for newspaper comment; and he urged that Mr. Douglas should be denounced in the *Press and Tribune* for his inhumanity. Just before election, on the authority above stated, we did comment upon Mr. Douglas' share in this matter with considerable severity. Out of the article in which he was rebuked this controversy has grown.

"We had no doubt at the time this conversation took place, and have no doubt now, that Dr. Brainard was honest and truthful in his relation. We believe him to be a gentleman, at least the equal of John Slidell in ability and veracity. If we are mistaken in our recollection, that he had the particulars recited from Mr. Slidell himself, he will no doubt inform us and Mr. Slidell from whom he had them, and we shall then be one step nearer the author of a tale, which, according to Mr. Slidell's *latest* testimony, is false."

On December 28th Brainard published another letter, in which he admitted that he had had conversations with the editors of the Republican paper about the hardships, etc., of "Douglas' slaves," but denied having given Mr. Slidell as an authority. There the matter ended. The story failed to accomplish its original purpose, viz., to defeat Douglas' election. It resulted in obtaining Mr. Slidell's testimony that the slaves were in the possession of a gentleman "than whom a more honorable man or better master cannot be found in Louisiana." It also resulted in a question of veracity between two leaders of Douglas' active opponents—the Republican editor, and Dr. Brainard, a federal office-holder. Upon the subject there never has been and is now but one opinion in Chicago. Hundreds had heard the story as published by the Republican paper, and until Mr. Slidell's letter of denial no one had ever doubted that he had authorized it. This having been the most violent, will possibly be the last paroxysm of abolition regard for the moral and physical condition of "Douglas' plantation of human chattels." The total failure of the attempt to injure Mr. Douglas before his constituents by this malicious fabrication was but a sorry return for the self-abasement committed by those who participated in repeating the slander. Dr. Brainard still holds federal office in Chicago. He has never given up the name of his authority, and the point whether he did not furnish Mr. Slidell's name in the first instance is involved in a question of veracity between him and the Republican editor. The public have never doubted on which side was the truth.

Mr. Douglas is the owner of a very large landed estate in Illinois. His grounds at "Cottage Grove," near the southern limits of Chicago, are extensive and very valuable. In 1856 he deeded ten acres of this valuable land—worth possibly six thousand dollars an acre—to the Trustees of the Chicago University, an institution organized under the auspices and patronage of the Baptist denomination. Upon this land thus donated has already been erected a portion of the University buildings, and already a large class of students, under the direction of an accomplished faculty, are receiving instruction. The corner-stone of the University was laid with appropriate honors on the 4th of July, 1856, and the ceremonies were attended by an immense concourse of people.

In 1856 Mr. Douglas disposed of one hundred acres of land on the western limits of Chicago, for the round sum of $100,000. His contributions that year in aid of the election of Mr. Buchanan, particularly to aid the Democracy in carry-ing Pennsylvania, were liberal in the extreme. In Illinois he was present in person; he was aided by Richardson, Harris, McClernand, Morris, Marshall, Shaw, Smith, Logan and a host of Democrats; and though Illinois, unlike Pennsylvania, had no candidate on the national ticket, still when called upon by Douglas and his friends, gave to the son of Pennsylvania a free, unbought, and generous support—a support that no expendi-ture of money could have obtained—a support given volunta-rily by intelligent freemen to the candidates of their party, pledged to sustain the cherished principles of the Democratic platform.

CHAPTER XIX.

VARIOUS MATTERS.

In the spring of 1853 Mr. Douglas visited Europe, and spent several months in personal observation of the practical work-ings of the various systems of government. He stayed a con-siderable time in England, and though he had the pleasure and honor of being presented to several of the monarchs of Europe, it was done at no sacrifice of personal independence or yield-ing of American principle.

THE AMERICAN COSTUME.

He was presented to the Emperor of Russia, and was *not* presented to the Queen of England. The circumstances at-tending his success in the one case, and his failure in the other, furnish a practical lesson of the respect due to national eti-quette.

When he was in London there were several eminent gentle-men of the United States there at the same time; these as well as Mr. Douglas were about to be presented to her majesty at the next reception. When the time came, there came also the inexorable requirement that the Americans must put off that costume and dress which is universal at home, and put on another which is entirely discarded in their own country. Mr. Douglas protested, as did also his countrymen, but the requirements of royal etiquette could not be evaded. The alternative was to submit to a change of costume, or be denied a presentation to the queen. Mr. Douglas accepted the latter, and his companions put on the dress required by the court; they were presented and he was not.

Subsequently he visited St. Petersburg, and for two weeks examined personally all the public institutions of the capital, and sought a thorough knowledge of the manners, laws and government of that city and of the empire. He had not made known his official position. After this time he left his card at the residence of Count Nesselrode, and promptly received a cordial and pressing invitation to that minister's palace. The interview was a pleasant and agreeable one; the political affairs of the United States and of Europe were discussed unreservedly and with mutual gratification. At this, or a subsequent interview, Mr. Douglas announced his intended departure from the city, when Count Nesselrode inquired if he did not desire a presentation to the emperor. Mr. Douglas expressed the great pleasure such an honor would be to him, but suggested the difficulty of the "court dress." Count Nesselrode, after some consultation upon this point, frankly told Mr. Douglas that he was right; that a citizen of the United States entitled to be presented to a monarch in Europe, if received at all should be received in that dress in which he would be admitted to the presence of the President of the United States, and added that if Mr. Douglas desired to be presented to the emperor he could possibly arrange the interview within a few days.

Mr. Douglas thanked his distinguished friend for his kindness to him personally, and also for his manly and honorable tribute to the dignity of American citizenship.

The result was that in a few hours Mr. Douglas was visited by an officer of the imperial household, with a notice that he would be received by the emperor. Mr. Douglas had the good fortune to be placed in the hands of Baron Stoeckle, who is well known in the United States from his official position in the Russian embassy at Washington. The emperor was at that time celebrating, at some distance from St. Petersburg, a grand Russian national festival, and was reviewing the imperial army. Accompanied by Baron Stoeckle, Mr. Douglas proceeded in an imperial carriage and under an imperial escort to the neighborhood of the camp, where he left the carriage and proceeded on horseback towards the position on the field occupied by the emperor. At a proper distance he was met by officers of the imperial staff and conducted to the emperor.

He was the only American present at that magnificent display of the power and wealth of the empire; representatives from all quarters of the world were present to witness one of the grandest festivals of Russia, graced by the presence of the imperial household and of all the most distinguished individuals of the empire, and yet into this scene of royal magnificence Mr. Douglas was admitted and welcomed with a frank cordiality by the emperor, in the same black suit of cloth in which, just before his departure, he had visited Franklin Pierce.

The rule asserted by Mr. Douglas and confirmed and approved by Count Nesselrode—the veteran diplomatist and most eminent statesman of Europe—is the true one. Americans are the only people who are required to put on a masquerade dress to obtain admission to the presence of the Queen of England. The rule that persons of all nationalities may be admitted in that costume in which they would be received by their own sovereign is observed toward all persons except citizens of the United States. They are excepted. An officer in the service of a petty prince of a German kingdom, if presented, can obtain audience in the same suit that he would appear in before his prince, but an American will be excluded unless he puts off the dress in which he was admitted to the table of the President of the United States, and puts on the tinseled toggery prescribed by authority.

Against this unjust discrimination between his countrymen and citizens of other nations Mr. Douglas protested, and preferred a total exclusion from the presence of royalty to a submission to any such degrading rule.

Mr. Douglas visited Sebastopol and all the scenes shortly after made historical by the war then gathering in Europe. He visited all the principal points on the continent, storing his mind with practical information concerning the commerce, laws, and governments of the countries in which he sojourned, information which has since proved of great advantage to him.

His descriptions of what he saw in Europe, his conversations and interviews with the great and illustrious men whom he met during his trip, are of the most entertaining and instructive character. No one who has ever enjoyed an evening with him, when he discoursed of these things, has ever failed in expressing the delight and gratification afforded by Mr. Douglas' graphic delineations of men, and his charming pictures of scenes and events in Europe.

MR. DOUGLAS AND THE PRESIDENCY.

In 1848 the Democratic State Convention in Illinois unanimously recommended Mr. Douglas as a candidate for the presidency. He was then but thirty-five years of age, and had already attracted the attention of the nation by his abilities and great success as an orator. His services in Congress, during the four years he was a member of the House, and his one year's service in the Senate, had recommended him most strongly to a very large portion of the people of the country, as a man possessing more of the natural characteristics of Jacksonian power and Democracy than any other statesman.

Mr. Douglas, however, was a friend and supporter of General Cass. The doctrines declared in the celebrated Nicholson letter were doctrines of pure popular sovereignty. As in 1856, so in 1848, he preferred infinitely a platform embodying correct principles to any personal honors or distinctions. He and his friends were warm supporters of General Cass for the nomination.

The result of that convention is well known. The names of Buchanan, Woodbury, Calhoun, Dallas, Worth, and others were presented. The two-thirds rule was in force. On the first ballot Mr. Cass received 125 votes, Mr. Buchanan, 93, Mr. Woodbury, 58, and the other votes, making up the aggregate of 253, were scattered. Gen. Cass lacked 45 votes of having two-thirds, and two votes of a majority. On the second ballot he received 133, being a majority, but still less than two-thirds. The friends of other candidates then seeing that the distinguished statesman of Michigan was the choice of a majority, after the third ballot, yielded to what was the expressed wishes of a majority, and gave him on the 4th ballot the required two-thirds vote, and then nominated him by acclamation.

In 1852 the Democracy of Illinois again recommended Mr. Douglas to the Democracy of the nation for the Presidency; other states did the same. The Convention met at Baltimore, and having adopted the two-thirds rule proceeded to a ballot. The following ballotings will exhibit the state of the vote during the protracted contest.

	1st.	11th.	31st.	48th.
Cass,	116	101	64	73
Buchanan,	93	87	79	28
Douglas,	20	50	92	38
Marcy,	27	27	26	90
Butler,	2	1	16	1
Houston,	3	8	10	6
Pierce,	0	0	0	55

On the next ballot Gen. Pierce received 283 votes, and was then unanimously nominated. It will be seen that until the 49th ballot no candidate had received a majority of the Convention; had Mr. Buchanan, or Mr. Marcy, or Mr. Cass obtained a majority, the friends of the other candidates would undoubtedly have yielded their individual preferences, and given him the required two-thirds vote.

In 1856 the ever memorable Cincinnati Convention met in June. The two-thirds rule was again adopted. Mr. Douglas had been recommended by the conventions of several states, but as this was the first National Convention of the Democracy since the passage of the Kansas-Nebraska Act, he was more solicitous for the adoption of a platform that would approve the principles of that measure than he was for the nomination. His name, however, was submitted to the Convention by his friends. There were but four names before the Convention—Messrs. Buchanan, Pierce, Douglas, and Cass. The whole number of votes was 296, of which 149 would be a majority, and 198 two-thirds. There were seventeen ballotings. On the first ballot Mr. Buchanan had 135, Mr. Pierce 122, Mr. Douglas 33, Mr. Cass 6. On the thirteenth ballot, Mr. Buchanan received 150 votes, being a majority, and the first time that a majority vote had been obtained by any one. Mr. Douglas was at Washington, and the result of the several ballotings was announced in that city as soon as made. The

Convention adjourned that day without making a nomination, and when it assembled next day, the 16th ballot was taken with the following result : Buchanan 168, Douglas 122, Cass 6. Mr. Buchanan lacked thirty of the required two-thirds vote. The Convention was at a " dead lock."

The eventful scene that took place can hardly be described in words. A majority of the delegates had expressed their choice ; had recorded their wish for the nomination of Mr. Buchanan. It was true the two-thirds rule had been adopted, but that rule was never designed or intended to defeat the wishes of a majority when once clearly and unmistakably ascertained and declared. The vote of the states was announced and recorded. The choice of the majority was declared, and there were no questions asked whether that majority was made up of delegates from Democratic states, or from states hopelessly in the power of the opposition. It was regarded as the vote of the Democracy of the nation, a vote given by men in non-Democratic states as well as in Democratic states, with but one purpose and aim, and that was to nominate the man who in the estimation of the whole Democracy was the strongest candidate for the time. Mr. Buchanan's 168 votes on the sixteenth ballot were given for him as follows : from states that subsequently voted for him for President, 86 ; from states that voted for Frémont, 82. Mr. Douglas' 122 votes were given him—from states that voted for Buchanan, 84 ; from states that voted for Frémont, 38. General Cass received the vote of California. A majority of the delegates representing the Democratic states voted against Mr. Buchanan on the sixteenth ballot ; yet, he having a clear majority of the delegates from all the states, after the result of that ballot was announced, certain proceedings took place which are thus recorded in the official report of the action of the Convention :

"Mr. Preston, of Kentucky, said : Mr. President : As one of the friends of Mr. Douglas, I have become sufficiently satisfied, by the evidences presented here, that it is the wish of this Convention that James Buchanan should be the nominee for President of the United States. I believe that Judge Douglas himself, and the friends of Judge Douglas—and when I say this I speak with some degree of knowledge on the subject—I believe that the friends of Mr. Douglas will be among the first to come forward, and in a spirit of liberality put an end to the useless contest. I will now give way to the gentleman from Illinois, the friend of Mr. Douglas.

"During Mr. Preston's remarks there were loud expressions of dissatisfaction and cries of 'No, no !' 'Don't withdraw !' 'Don't withdraw.'

" Here W. A. Richardson, of Illinois, arose, and waving his hand, there was immediate and general silence. In a solemn and impressive manner that gentleman proceeded to address the Convention as follows:

" Mr. Richardson. Mr. President and gentlemen of the Convention: Before undertaking to advise any gentleman on this floor what he ought to do, I consider that I have a duty which I owe to my constituents, and which, since it is now imposed on me, I feel it is due to the Democratic party and friends of Stephen A. Douglas that I should discharge. Whatever may be the opinion of the gentlemen as to the contest, I am satisfied that I can not advance his interests or the interests of the common cause, or the principles of the Democratic party, by continuing him in this contest. I will, therefore, state that I have a dispatch from Judge Douglas, which I desire may be permitted to be read, and I shall then withdraw his name from before the Convention. I desire gentlemen, after that, to decide on what course they may deem it proper to pursue. (Tremendous applause—profound sensation.)

" The dispatch was sent to the chair to be read, and is as follows:

" 'LETTER OF S. A. DOUGLAS TO W. A. RICHARDSON, OF ILLINOIS.

" 'WASHINGTON, *June* 4, 1856.

" ' DEAR SIR: From the telegraphic reports in the newspapers, I fear that an embittered state of feeling is being engendered in the Convention, which may endanger the harmony and success of our party. I wish you and all my friends to bear in mind that I have a thousand fold more anxiety for the triumph of our principles than for my own personal elevation.

" ' If the withdrawal of my name will contribute to the harmony of our party or the success of our cause, I hope you will not hesitate to take the step. Especially it is my desire that the action of the Convention will embody and express the wishes, feelings and principles of the Democracy of the Republic; and hence, if Mr. Pierce or Mr. Buchanan, or any other statesman who is faithful to the great issue involved in the contest, *shall receive a majority of the Convention*, I earnestly hope that all my friends will unite in insuring him two-thirds, and then in making his nomination unanimous. Let no personal considerations disturb the harmony or endanger the triumph of our principles. S. A. DOUGLAS.

" ' To Hon. W. A. RICHARDSON, Burnett House, Cincinnati, Ohio.'

" The reading of this dispatch was interrupted by frequent and tremendous applause. It was some time before order could be restored. When the Convention had subsided into something like order, the president announced that they would proceed with the seventeenth ballot."

On the next, or seventeenth ballot, Mr. Buchanan was nominated unanimously. The friends of Mr. Douglas at once conceding the justice of the suggestions in his letter, that Mr. Buchanan having received the votes of a majority of the Convention ought to be given the required two-thirds.

On the 4th of January, 1860, the Democratic State Convention of Illinois, in consequence of the call of the National Convention at an earlier day than usual, met some months in advance of the ordinary period, to appoint delegates to Charleston. The Convention was large, harmonious, and included within its members the veterans who had done service in the party for twenty or thirty years. The following resolutions, reported by a committee of which the Hon. O. B. Ficklin was chairman, were adopted unanimously.

Whereas, The Democratic party assembled in national convention in June, 1856, by the unanimous vote of all the delegates from every state in the Union, adopted a platform of principles, as the only authoritative exposition of Democratic doctrines, which remains unaltered and unalterable until the meeting of the Charleston convention.

And whereas, We have good reasons for the belief, that if we depart from the doctrines of that platform by attempting to force upon the party new issues and tests, the Democracy of the several states may never be able to agree upon another platform of principles with the same unanimity.

And whereas, The Democratic party is the only political organization which can maintain in their purity the principles of self-government, the reserved rights of the states, and the perpetuity of the Union under the Constitution.

And whereas, The unity, integrity, and supremacy of the Democratic party depend upon its faithful adherence to those fundamental principles upon which we have achieved so many glorious triumphs, and to which we are solemnly and irrevocably pledged. Therefore,

Resolved, That the Democracy of Illinois, in state convention assembled, do reassert and affirm the Cincinnati platform, in the words, spirit, and meaning with which the same was adopted, understood, and ratified by the people in 1856, and do reject and utterly repudiate all such new issues and tests as the revival of the African slave trade, or a congressional slave code for the territories, or the doctrine that slavery is a federal institution deriving its validity in the several states and territories in which it exists from the Constitution of the United States, instead of being a mere municipal institution, existing in such states and territories "under the laws thereof."

Resolved, That there can be no exception to the rule that every right guaranteed by the Constitution must be protected by law, in all cases where legislation is necessary for its protection and enjoyment, and, in obedience to this principle, it was the imperative duty of Congress to enact an efficient law for the surrender of fugitive slaves.

Resolved, That no considerations of political expediency or partizan policy can release any member of Congress or American citizen from his sworn obligations of fidelity to the Constitution, or excuse him for not advocating and supporting all legislation which may be necessary for the protection and enjoyment of every right guaranteed by that instrument.

Resolved, That the Democratic party of the Union is pledged in faith and honor, by the Cincinnati platform and its indorsement of the Kansas-Nebraska act, to the following propositions:

1st. That all questions pertaining to African slavery in the territories shall be for ever banished from the halls of Congress.

2d. That the people of the territories respectively shall be left perfectly free to make just such laws and regulations in respect to slavery and all other matters of local concern as they may determine for themselves, subject to no other limitations or restrictions than those imposed by the Constitution of the United States.

3d. That all questions affecting the validity or constitutionality of any territorial enactments, shall be referred for final decision to the Supreme Court of the United States as the only tribunal provided by the Constitution which is competent to determine them.

Resolved, That in the opinion of the Democracy of Illinois, Mr. Buchanan truly interpreted the Cincinnati platform in his letter accepting the presidential nomination, when he said, " the people of a territory, like those of a state, shall decide for themselves whether slavery shall or shall not exist within their limits."

Resolved, That we recognize the paramount judicial authority of the Supreme Court of the United States, as provided in the Constitution, and hold it to be the imperative duty of all good citizens to respect and obey the decision of that tribunal, and to aid, by all lawful means, in carrying them into faithful execution.

Resolved, That the Democracy of Illinois repel, with just indignation, the injurious and unfounded imputation upon the integrity and impartiality of the Supreme Court, which is contained in the assumption on the part of the so-called Republicans that, in the Dred Scott case, that august tribunal decided against the right of the people of the territory to decide the slavery question for themselves, without giving them an opportunity of being heard by counsel in defense of their rights of self-government, and when there was no territorial law, enactment or fact before the court upon which that question could possibly arise.

Resolved, That whenever Congress or the Legislature of any state or territory shall make any enactment, or do any act which attempts to divest, impair, or prejudice any right which the owner of slaves, or any other species of property, may have or claim in any territory or elsewhere, by virtue of the Constitution or otherwise, and the party aggrieved shall bring his case before the Supreme Court of the United States, the Democracy of Illinois, as in duty bound by their obligations of fidelity to the Constitution, will cheerfully and faithfully respect and abide by the decision, and use all lawful means to aid in giving it full effect according to its true intent and meaning.

Resolved, That the Democracy of Illinois view with inexpressible horror and indignation the murderous and treasonable conspiracy of John Brown and his confederates to incite a civil insurrection in the slaveholding states; and heartily rejoice that the attempt was promptly suppressed, and the majesty of the law vindicated, by inflicting upon the conspirators, after a fair and impartial trial, that just punishment which the enormity of their crimes so richly merited.

Resolved, That the Harper's Ferry outrage was the natural consequence and logical result of the doctrines and teachings of the Republican party, as explained and enforced in their platforms, partizan presses, books and pamphlets, and in the speeches of their leaders, in and out of Congress; and for this reason an honest and law-abiding people should not be satisfied with the disavowal or disapproval by the Republican leaders of John Brown's *acts,* unless they also repudiate the doctrines and teachings which produced those monstrous crimes, and denounce all persons who profess to sympathize with murderers and traitors, lamenting their fate and venerating their memory as martyrs who lost their lives in a just and holy cause.

Resolved, That the delegates representing Illinois in the Charleston convention be instructed to vote for and use all honorable means to secure the readoption of the Cincinnati platform, without any additions or subtractions.

Resolved, That no honorable man can accept a seat as a delegate in the national Democratic convention, or should be recognized as a member of the Democratic party, who will not abide the decisions of such convention and support its nominees.

Resolved, That we affirm and repeat the principles set forth in the resolutions of the last state convention of the Illinois Democracy, held in this city on the 21st day of April, 1858, and will not hesitate to apply those principles wherever a proper case may arise.

Resolved, That the Democracy of the State of Illinois is unanimously in favor of Stephen A. Douglas for the next presidency, and the delegates from this state are instructed to vote for him, and make every honorable effort to procure his nomination.

The Democratic State Conventions of Ohio, Indiana, Wisconsin, Minnesota, Michigan, and Iowa, have since adopted resolutions substantially of the same character, and in other states, where delegates are appointed by districts, resolutions expressing the same doctrine and instructions in favor of Douglas' nomination at Charleston have also been adopted. In Pennsylvania, Tennessee, New Jersey and New York, and in other states where no expression has been made in favor of any particular person for the presidency, the state conventions have asserted principles and proclaimed doctrines so much in accordance with those of Mr. Douglas, that he and his friends would be somewhat embarrassed if forced to chose between them, in selecting the particular one they would prefer. The resolutions so enthusiastically adopted by the Tennessee Democracy in their state Convention are resolutions that can be adopted and as heartily and emphatically approved and sustained by the Democracy of the northwest, as they can be by those gallant Democrats who learned Democracy from the precept and example of Jackson and Polk.

THE DEMOCRATIC ORGANIZATION IN ILLINOIS.

As has been stated elsewhere in this volume, there was no organization of the Democracy of Illinois until 1837. On the 22d of July of that year, the Legislature being then in session, a meeting of the Democratic members and other Democrats was held at the State House in Vandalia to adopt such measures as would produce "concert of action" in the party, and to enable it to combine all its members against the strong and united opposition. A call for a state Convention, to meet at Vandalia in December following, was agreed upon, and a committee of thirty were selected to prepare and publish an address to the people of the state. On that committee were James Semple, afterwards United States senator, W. A. Richardson, James Shields, now of Minnesota, John A. McClernand, now of the House of Representatives, Robert Smith, ex-member of Congress, and other leading Democrats. A Central Committee, consisting of five members from each congressional district, was also appointed, viz: 1st. W. A. Richardson, J. W. Stephenson, E. D. Taylor, Newton Cloud, J. D. Early; 2d. W. L. D. Ewing, William Walters, II. Smith, Joseph Kitchell, Dr. Turney; 3d. H. M. Rollings, H. L. Webb, R. G. Murphy, A. M. Jenkins, and S. M. Hubbard. This was the first State Committee appointed by the Democracy of Illinois.

The Convention met in December, 1837, and nominated J. W. Stephenson for governor, and J. S. Hacker for lieutenant-governor. The candidates having both withdrawn in April, the Convention was called to reassemble, and did reassemble, on the 5th of June, 1838. The Convention nominated Thomas Carlin for governor and S. H. Anderson for lieutenant-governor; and appointed as the State Committee V. Hickox, John Taylor, Robert Allen, John Calhoun, C. R. Hurst, J. S. Roberts, and David Prickett. This committee, in 1839, called a state Convention, to meet in the December following; and on the 9th of December the second Democratic State Convention in Illinois met at Springfield, to which place the seat of government had been removed. This body appointed as the State Committee, until the next state Convention, E. D. Taylor, V. Hickox, James Shields, J. R. Diller, M. Carpenter, William Walters, and G. R. Webber; and in September, 1841, they issued a call for a state Convention to meet in December following.

On the 13th of December, 1841, the Third Democratic State Convention met at Springfield. Having nominated candidates, it renewed the state authority by appointing the following State Committee: D. B. Campbell, James Shepherd, and G. R. Weber, of Sangamon; James H. Ralston, of Adams; Thompson Campbell, of Jo Daviess; N. W. Nunnally, of Edgar; and John A. McClernand, of Gallatin. A. W. Snyder was nominated for governor, and John Moore for lieutenant-governor. Snyder died during the canvass, and the Hon. Thomas Ford, a judge of the Supreme Court, was selected as the candidate in his stead. The State Committee appointed by the Convention of 1841 called, in 1842, a state Convention (the 4th), to meet in February, 1844, to appoint delegates to the Baltimore Convention. It made no change in the State Committee.

The Fifth Democratic State Convention met (pursuant to the call of the committee) on February 10, 1846. It nominated

A. C. French for governor, and Joseph B. Wells for lieutenant-governor. It appointed as the State Committee: J. R. Diller, William Walters, B. C. Webster, E. D. Jones, Peter Sweat, M. McConnell, and John Moore. In 1847, a Convention having met and prepared a new Constitution for the state, which went into operation in April, 1848, the office of governor was to become vacant on the 1st of January, 1849.

The Sixth Democratic State Convention met (pursuant to the call of the State Committee) on the 24th of April, 1848, and nominated A. C. French for reëlection as governor, and William McMurtry for lieutenant-governor—besides a number of candidates for other state offices. It also appointed the delegates to the Baltimore Convention. The following gentlemen were appointed the State Committee: V. Hickox, of Sangamon; E. F. Sweeney, of Warren; Thomas Dyer, of Cook; James Bigler, of Brown; J. P. Cooper, of Clark; F. D. Preston, of Gallatin; Robert Dunlap, of Madison; J. R. Diller, of Sangamon; James Dunlap, of Morgan; H. E. Roberts, of Sangamon.

The Seventh State Convention met (pursuant to the call of the State Committee) April 19, 1852. It nominated J. A. Matteson for governor, and the full list of candidates for other offices. It appointed the delegates to the Baltimore Convention, and selected as the State Committee the following gentlemen—four from the State at large and one from each Congressional District, viz.: At large, John A. McClernand, of Gallatin; J. McRoberts, of Will; C. Sweeney, of Jo Daviess, and T. L. Harris, of Menard; 1st district, W. H. Snyder, of St. Clair; 2d district, F. D. Preston, of Jefferson; 3d district, B. W. Henry, of Shelby; 4th district, E. Wilcox, of Kane; 5th district, M. W. Delahay, of Green; 6th district, James Sibley, of Hancock; 7th district, C. H. Lanphier, of Sangamon.

On the 1st of May, 1856, the Eighth Democratic State Convention met (pursuant to the call of the committee) at Springfield. The Convention nominated W. A. Richardson for governor, and nominated an entire state ticket; appointed delegates to the Cincinnati Convention, and selected the following State Committee: For the state at large, Alexander Starne, and Charles H. Lanphier; 1st district, F. W. S. Brawley; 2d district, John Dement; 3d district, William Reddick;

4th district, Robert Holloway; 5th district, W. H. Carlin; 6th district, Virgil Hickox; 7th district, W. D. Latshaw; 8th district, A. H. Trapp; 9th district, S. S. Taylor.

The Ninth Democratic State Convention met (pursuant to the call of the above named committee) at Springfield, on the 21st of April, 1858, and nominated W. B. Fondey for State Treasurer and A. C. French for Superintendent of Public Instruction. It appointed as the State Committee the following persons: *At large*, John Moore, C. H. Lanphier. 1st district, C. J. Horsman; 2d district, J. W. Sheahan; 3d district, N. Elwood; 4th district, John McDonald; 5th district, Alexander Starne; 6th district, V. Hickox; 7th district, S. A. Buckmaster; 8th district, O. B. Ficklin; 9th district, John White.

The Tenth Democratic State Convention met (pursuant to the call of the above committee) at Springfield, January 4, 1860, and appointed delegates to Charleston. The Convention did not nominate candidates for state officers, and by resolution continued the existing State Committee in office, until the meeting of the Convention to be held to nominate candidates for state offices, and an electoral ticket.

That committee have called the Eleventh Democratic State Convention to meet at Springfield, on the 13th of June, to nominate candidates for Governor, Lieutenant-governor, Secretary of State, Auditor of Public Accounts, State Treasurer, and Superintendant of Public Instruction, also eleven candidates for Presidential electors—electors pledged to vote for the nominees of the Charleston Convention.

For twenty-two years the authority of the Democratic State Committee has been transmitted in unbroken succession from each State Convention to the following one.

CHAPTER XX.

UTAH AND THE MORMONS.—MINNESOTA.—OREGON.—SLAVE TRADE.

An attempt has been frequently made by the enemies of popular right to show the failure of popular sovereignty by pointing to the enormities and outrages perpetrated by the Mormons in Utah. There is no question that the practices in Utah are dangerous to the peace of the Union, and dangerous to the moral and political character of the republic. That the political and social condition of the Mormon settlements in Utah are destined to be, especially if weak and timorous counsels prevail, a source of great vexation and trouble to the American people. Polygamy exists in Utah, but polygamy is not the result of popular sovereignty. Polygamy existed in Utah before the passage of the territorial act of 1850, and polygamy will exist among the Mormons so long and wherever they have the political power. The Mormons are in a majority in Kansas, they constitute so nearly the entire population that Utah may be regarded as a Mormon community. They have peculiar doctrines, which form part of what they call their "religious faith." They have an ecclesiastical organization, with its courts, tribunals, officers, decrees, mandates and punishments, to all of which the people, as members of a religious society, yield implicit obedience. In the list of powers claimed and exercised by this ecclesiastical authority is that of summary divorce, and of sealing in marriage. It is by the authority of this theocratical government, which rules above and independently of the civil government of the Territory, that polygamy and its attendant vices are encouraged, fostered and promoted.

If Utah were a state, we suppose there is no one who would admit that Congress or the federal government had the constitutional power or authority to legislate for the prohibition or punishment of polygamy, or any other crime of that nature within the limits of the state. It would be one of those instances where the federal government would be restrained, by a total absence of all power, to interpose its authority.

The question whether Congress has the power, or having it ought to exercise the power of passing laws for the prohibition, or for the protection of particular institutions in the territories is one upon which there is, has been, and possibly will always be a variety of opinions. The Mormons, however, are not dangerous to the peace of the Union only because of their polygamy. That is a social evil, which, however infamous and dangerous it may be, is nevertheless one which is confined within their own territorial limits, and to their own people, There is a large class of people who seem to be horrified at the existence of slavery in some of the states, and who do not hesitate to attribute to that institution a character as revolting in many respects as is attributed to polygamy. Indeed the Republican party have in their platform linked slavery and polygamy as "twin relics of barbarism," which ought to be rooted out by all constitutional means. They disclaim all purpose of interfering with slavery in the states, and we suppose would be equally forbearing to polygamy in the same localities. But against both in the territories they propose to wage a constant war—an "irrepressible conflict."

These men represent that in the slaveholding states, marriage is an institution unknown amongst slaves, and that owners have, and exercise the power of giving slave women to men as wives, and then of separating them, and forming new arrangements by which the husband of one woman is transferred to other women, and the wives of certain men transferred to other men. The anti-slavery orators affect to see but little difference between the moral statutes established amongst slaves, and that existing under the polygamous institutions of the Mormons. Hence, they style them, "those twin relics of barbarism, polygamy and slavery," against whose existence in the territories there must ever exist an "irrepressible conflict." The Supreme Court has decided that any act of Congress prohibiting slavery in the territories must be void, but no decision in terms that such a power exercised against polygamy has been made. Where the power to prohibit slavery is denied, and where the power to prohibit polygamy is granted to Congress by the Constitution, is a question for constitutional lawyers to determine. The Democratic party unanimously agree that Congress possesses no such power to prohibit slavery; and Congress having no power over one of the "twin relics," it is yet to be determined whether the party agree that Congress has the power to prohibit the other "twin relic." If Congress has no power to prohibit slavery, yet has the power to prohibit polygamy or other intercourse between the sexes unless sanctioned by marriage, then Congress may, we presume, legislate upon the marriage relations to be preserved amongst all the slaves who may be taken to the territories, and if Congress may legislate respecting the marriage relations between slaves in the territories, Congress will shortly find that, from the same source whence it derives that authority, it can also obtain the authority to legislate upon the relation between slaves and the white people, and between slaves and their owners. The ultimate end to which the doctrine of intervention by Congress with the internal affairs of the people of the territory must lead is evident. It can not be exercised in one case without necessarily carrying with it an expression of authority to exercise it in all cases. The only safe rule is to abstain from the exercise of all doubtful powers and to leave the people of the territories, as long as they remain faithful to their political obligations, alone to work out their own destiny.

But, it may be asked, is there no remedy for the evils in Utah? Must these Mormons go on in their works of evil wholly unchecked and unrestrained by any authority. To these questions it is only necessary to say that polygamy is not the only crime which the Mormons commit against the peace, law, and good order of the republic. They set up their ecclesiastical government in open and direct hostility to the government of the United States; they set up the decrees of their apostles as the "higher law," which it is their duty as well as their pleasure to obey, even when the laws and their obligations as citizens of the United States require a different rule of government. In short, the Mormons, though living upon the soil of the United States, are not of the United States; though living nominally under the government of the United States, that government is not their government, but their government is another established by themselves, of a social and religious character, to which they submit in preference and to the exclusion of all other governments. They are a people and a government wholly independent in all things of the people and government of the United States, and recognize no authority on the part of the government, laws or Constitution of the United States to require of them the performance of any duty, or abstinence from any acts made unlawful by United States law. They are in organization, sentiment and feeling, as much and as essentially aliens to the United States as if they resided upon the plains of Asia. A territorial government was established in 1850 for the people of Utah, but it was designed and prepared for a people knowing no allegiance on earth save to the American Union. It was not intended for a people who repudiate the Constitution and the Union, declare themselves free and independent of United States authority, and claim for their apostles a power civil and religious far above that of the Constitution and government of the United States.

The searcher after an appropriate remedy for the evils in Utah will not find a practicable or a sufficient one in the exercise of the doubtful power of prohibiting polygamy. Let him go further and he will find the primal cause for all the abominations of Utah, and that cause is the entire disloyalty of the people; their utter repudiation of the American Constitution and laws, and their total want of political fidelity. The territorial government was designed for a portion of the American people; the people of Utah are not Americans in any sense of the word, they are a distinct race and a separate people, having no relations with any other race or people. They are a Mormon people, who bid defiance to, and hold in scorn and contempt, all other people; their government is a Mormon government, having no relations of any kind, much less allegiance to any other government on earth. The existing territorial government is used by these men only to draw money from the Federal treasury—" quartering upon the Gentiles"—and to cover up and hide as far as possible their enormities. The Act of Congress making polygamy a crime will be treated as a farce. The jurors and sheriffs and witnesses must be Mormons. The party accused of polygamy must be indicted by a grand jury each member of which has from five to twenty wives; he must next be tried by a jury each member of which has a dozen wives. That will be the practical execution of the act to prohibit one of the twin relics of barbarism. The barbarians will be the judges of each other's barbarity.

The only practical remedy for these evils is to treat these

alien barbarians as the government would treat any other nation of aliens who, settling upon American soil, would raise the
standard of independence, declare themselves a nation of themselves, and free of all allegiance to the government or people
of the United States. Since the Mormons will not become
American citizens, will not subject themselves to American
laws and American authority, let the territorial government
be abolished; let the Mormons become as all other aliens
would become, mere residents of the territory which is under
the exclusive control and jurisdiction of the United States,
and subject beyond all question to the laws of Congress.

As long ago as June, 1857, Mr. Douglas foresaw the evils
to result from the persistent refusal of the Mormons to Americanize themselves, and he then proposed a remedy which time
has proved to be the only effective one. In his famous speech
at Springfield, on the 12th of June, 1857, after having spoken
of Kansas affairs and the Dred Scott decision, he thus referred
to matters in Utah :

Mr. President, I will now respond to the call which has been made upon
me for my opinion of the condition of things in Utah, and the appropriate
remedy for existing evils.

The Territory of Utah was organized under one of the acts known as the
Compromise measures of 1850, on the supposition that the inhabitants were
American citizens, owing and acknowledging allegiance to the United States,
and consequently entitled to the benefits of self-government while a territory, and to admission into the Union, on an equal footing with the original
states, so soon as they should number the requisite population. It was conceded on all hands, and by all parties, that the peculiarities of their religious
faith and ceremonies interposed no valid and constitutional objection to their
reception into the Union, in conformity with the federal Constitution, so long
as they were in all other respects entitled to admission. Hence the great
political parties of the country indorsed and approved the Compromise measures of 1850, including the act for the organization of the Territory of Utah,
with the hope and in the confidence that the inhabitants would conform to
the Constitution and laws, and prove themselves worthy, respectable and
law-abiding citizens. If we are permitted to place credence in the rumors
and reports from that country (and it must be admitted that they have increased and strengthened, and assumed consistency and plausibility by each
succeeding mail), seven years' experience has disclosed a state of facts entirely different from that which was supposed to exist when Utah was organized. These rumors and reports would seem to justify the belief that the
following facts are susceptible of proof:

1st. That nine tenths of the inhabitants are aliens by birth, who have refused to become naturalized, or to take the oath of allegiance, or to do any
other act recognizing the government of the United States as the paramount
authority in that territory.

2d. That all the inhabitants, whether native or alien born, known as Mormons (and they constitute the whole people of the territory), are bound by

horrid oaths and terrible penalties to recognize and maintain the authority of Brigham Young, and the government of which he is the head, as paramount to that of the United States, in civil as well as religious affairs; and that they will, in due time, and under the direction of their leaders, use all means in their power to subvert the government of the United States, and resist its authority.

3d. That the Mormon government, with Brigham Young at its head, is now forming alliances with the Indian tribes of Utah and the adjoining territories—stimulating the Indians to acts of hostility—and organizing bands of his own followers, under the name of "Danites or Destroying Angels," to prosecute a system of robbery and murder upon American citizens, who support the authority of the United States, and denounce the infamous and disgusting practices and institutions of the Mormon government.

If, upon a full investigation, these representations shall prove true, they will establish the fact that the inhabitants of Utah, as a community, are outlaws and alien enemies, unfit to exercise the right of self-government under the organic act, and unworthy to be admitted into the Union as a state, when their only object in seeking admission is to interpose the sovereignty of the state as an invincible shield to protect them in their treason and crime, debauchery and infamy. (Applause.)

Under this view of the subject, I think it is the duty of the President, as I have no doubt it is his fixed purpose, to remove Brigham Young and all his followers from office, and to fill their places with bold, able, and true men, and to cause a thorough and searching investigation into all the crimes and enormities which are alleged to be perpetrated daily in that territory, under the direction of Brigham Young and his confederates; and to use all the military force necessary to protect the officers in the discharge of their duties, and to enforce the laws of the land. (Applause.)

When the authentic evidence shall arrive, if it shall establish the facts which are believed to exist, it will become the duty of Congress to apply the knife and cut out this loathsome, disgusting ulcer. (Applause.) No temporizing policy—no half-way measure will then answer. It has been supposed by those who have not thought deeply upon the subject, that an act of Congress prohibiting murder, robbery, polygamy, and other crimes, with appropriate penalties for those offenses, would afford adequate remedies for all the enormities complained of. Suppose such a law to be on the statute-book, and I believe they have a criminal code, providing the usual punishments for the entire catalogue of crimes, according to the usages of all civilized and Christian countries, with the exception of polygamy, which is practiced under the sanction of the Mormon church, but is neither prohibited nor authorized by the laws of the territory.

Suppose, I repeat, that Congress should pass a law prescribing a criminal code and punishing polygamy among other offences, what effect would it have—what good would it do? Would you call on twenty-three grand jurymen with twenty-three wives each, to find a bill of indictment against a poor miserable wretch for having two wives? (Cheers and laughter.) Would you rely upon twelve petit jurors with twelve wives each to convict the same loathsome wretch for having two wives? (Continued applause.) Would you expect a grand jury composed of twenty-three "Danites" to find a bill of indictment against a brother "Danite" for having, under their direction, murdered a Gentile, as they call all American citizens? Much less would you expect a jury of twelve "destroying angels" to find another "destroying angel" guilty of the crime of murder, and cause him to be hanged for no other offense than that of taking the life of a Gentile! No. If there is any truth in the reports we receive from Utah, Congress may pass what laws it chooses, but you can never rely upon the local tribunals and juries to punish crimes committed by Mormons in that territory. Some other and more effectual remedy must be devised and applied. In my opinion the first step should be the absolute and unconditional repeal of the organic act—blotting the territorial government out of existence—upon the ground that they are alien enemies and outlaws, denying their allegiance and defying the authority of the United States. (Immense applause.)

The territorial government once abolished, the country would revert to its primitive condition, prior to the act of 1850, "under the sole and exclusive jurisdiction of the United States," and should be placed under the operation of the act of Congress of the 30th of April, 1790, and the various acts supplemental thereto and amendatory thereof, "providing for the punishment of crimes against the United States within any fort, arsenal, dock-yard, magazine, or ANY OTHER PLACE OR DISTRICT OF COUNTRY, UNDER THE SOLE AND EXCLUSIVE *jurisdiction of the United States.* All offenses against the provisions of these acts are required by law to be tried and punished by the United States courts in the states or territories where the offenders shall be " FIRST APPREHENDED OR BROUGHT FOR TRIAL." Thus it will be seen that, under the plan proposed, Brigham Young and his confederates could be " apprehended and brought for trial" to Iowa or Missouri, California or Oregon, or to any other adjacent state or territory, where a fair trial could be had, and justice administered impartially—where the witnesses could be protected and the judgment of the court could be carried into execution, without violence or intimidation. I do not propose to introduce any new principles into our jurisprudence, nor to change the modes of proceeding or the rules of practice in our courts. I only propose to place the district of country embraced within the territory of Utah under the operation of the same laws and rules of proceeding that Kansas, Nebraska, Minnesota, and our other territories were placed, *before they became organized territories.* The whole country embraced within those territories was under the operation of that same system of laws, and all the offenses committed within the same were punished in the manner now proposed, so long as the country remained " under the sole and exclusive jurisdiction of the United States;" but the moment the country was organized into territorial governments, with legislative, executive and judicial departments, it ceased to be under the sole and exclusive jurisdiction of the United States, within the meaning of the act of Congress, for the reason that it had passed under another and different jurisdiction. Hence, if we abolish the territorial government of Utah, preserving all existing rights, and place the country under the sole and exclusive jurisdiction of the United States, offenders can be apprehended, and brought into the adjacent states or territories, for trial and punishment, in the same manner and under the same rules and regulations, which obtained, and have been uniformly practiced, under like circumstances since 1790.

If the plan proposed shall be found an effective and adequate remedy for the evils complained of in Utah, no one, no matter what his political creed or partizan associations, need be apprehensive that it will violate any cherished theory or constitutional right in regard to the government of the territories. It is a great mistake to suppose that all the territory or land belonging to the United States must necessarily be governed by the same laws and under the same clause of the Constitution, without reference to the purpose to which it is dedicated or the use which it is proposed to make of it. While all that portion of country which is or shall be set apart to become new States, must necessarily be governed under and consistent with that clause of the Constitution which authorizes Congress to admit new states, it does not follow that other territory, not intended to be organized and admitted into the Union as states, must be governed under the same clause of the Constitution, with all the rights of self-government and state equality. For instance, if we should purchase Vancouver's Island from Great Britain, for the purpose of removing all the Indians from our Pacific territories, and locating them on that island, as their permanent home, with guarantees that it should never be settled or occupied by white men, will it be contended that the purchase should be made and the island governed under the power to admit new states, when it was not acquired for that purpose, or intended to be applied to that object? Being acquired for Indian purposes, is it not more reasonable to assume that the power to acquire was derived from the Indian clause, and the island must necessarily be governed under and consistent with that clause of the Constitution which relates to Indian affairs. Again, suppose we deem it expedient to buy a small island in the Mediterranean or Caribbean sea, for a naval station, can it be said, with any force or plausibility, that the purchase should be made or the island governed under the power to admit new states? On the contrary, is it not obvious that the right to acquire and govern in that case is derived from the power "to provide and maintain a navy," and must be exercised consistent with that power? So, if we purchase land for forts, arsenals, or other military purposes, or set apart and dedicate any territory which we now own for a military reservation, it immediately passes under the military power, and must be governed in harmony with it. So, if land be purchased for a mint, it must be governed under the power to coin money; or if purchased for a post-office, it must be governed under the power to establish post-offices and post-roads; or for a custom-house, under the power to regulate commerce; or for a court-house, under the judiciary power. In short, the clause of the Constitution under which any land or territory belonging to the United States must be governed, is indicated by the object for which it was acquired and the object to which it is dedicated. So long, therefore, as the organic act of Utah shall remain in force, setting apart that country for a new state, and pledging the faith of the United States to receive it into the Union as soon as it should have the requisite population, we are bound to extend to it all the rights of self-government, agreeably to the clause of the Constitution providing for the admission of new states. Hence the necessity of repealing the organic act, withdrawing the pledge of admission, and placing it under the sole and exclusive jurisdiction of the United States, in order that persons and property may be protected, and justice administered, and crimes punished under the laws prescribed by Congress in such cases.

While the power of Congress to repeal the organic act and abolish the territorial government cannot be denied, the question may arise whether we possess the moral right of exercising the power, after the charter has been once granted, and the local government organized under its provisions. This is a grave question—one which should not be decided hastily, nor under the influence of passion or prejudice. In my opinion, I am free to say there is no moral right to repeal the organic act of a territory, and abolish the government organized under it, unless the inhabitants of that territory, as a community, have done such acts as amount to a forfeiture of all rights under it—such as becoming alien enemies, outlaws, disavowing their allegiance, or resisting the authority of the United States. These and kindred acts, which we have every reason to believe are daily perpetrated in that territory, would not only give us the moral right, but make it our imperative duty to abolish the territorial government, and place the inhabitants under the sole and exclusive jurisdiction of the United States, to the end that justice may be done, and the dignity and authority of the government vindicated.

I have thus presented plainly and frankly my views of the Utah question— the evils and the remedy—upon the facts as they have reached us, and are supposed to be substantially correct. If official reports and authentic information shall change or modify these facts, I shall be ready to conform my action to the real facts as they shall be found to exist. I have no such pride of opinion as will induce me to persevere in an error one moment after my judgment is convinced. If, therefore, a better plan can be devised—one more consistent with justice and sound policy, or more effective as a remedy for acknowledged evils, I will take great pleasure in adopting it, in lieu of the one I have presented to you to-night.

In conclusion, permit me to present my grateful acknowledgements for your patient attention, and the kind and respectful manner in which you have received my remarks.

Had the remedy thus indicated by Mr. Douglas in 1857 been adopted in place of the " war measures," to-day the Mormons would have been divested of that political government which serves them merely to carry out more fully their treasonable and disgusting enormities. To that remedy the government must come at last, and with a new government in the gold regions, the Mormons will eventually be forced either to leave the country or reform their code of civil and political morals to a standard more becoming the age, and more suitable to the enlightenment of the people of the United States.

MINNESOTA AND OREGON.

Pending the Lecompton controversy in Congress, the President on the 11th day of January, 1858, communicated to Congress copies of the Constitution of the State of Minnesota, and an application for admission into the Union. It was referred in the Senate to the Committee on Territories. On the 26th of the same month Mr. Douglas reported a bill for the admission of the State. He was indefatigable in his efforts to have the bill taken up, but it was not until after the Kansas bill had passed that he could succeed. Eventually the bill was taken up, and passed with but very little objection. The vote in the Senate being, yeas, 49; nays, 3; and in the House, yeas, 157; nays, 38.

On the 5th of April Mr. Douglas, from the Committee, on Territories, reported a bill for the admission of Oregon into the Union as a State. On the 18th of May, the bill having been debated in the meantime, and the principal objection urged was that of Mr. Trumbull, that the Constitution of the State prohibited the immigration of negroes, the question was taken on Trumbull's motion to postpone the bill till next session. This motion was rejected, the yeas being, Bell, Chandler, Clay, Crittenden, Durkee, Fessenden, Fitzpatrick, Hale, Hamlin,

Hammond, Hunter, Iverson, Kennedy, Mason, Trumbull and Wade. Democrats 6, Republicans 7, Americans 3. The bill then passed, yeas 35; nays 17; the nays being the same who voted to postpone, excepting Mr. Chandler, and with the addition of Mr. Davis, of Mississippi, and Mr. Henderson, of Texas. The House did not act on the bill until the next session, when the bill was passed, and Oregon was admitted.

At this point it may not be out of place to recapitulate the action of Mr. Douglas upon the subject of territorial bills, and the admission of new states. When a member of the house he was a warm supporter of the bills to establish a territorial government in Oregon. He found that measure unacted upon when he entered the Senate. He voted for it there when it passed. He, as a member of the house, supported the resolutions for the annexation of Texas, and the bill for her admission into the Union. In the house he supported and voted for the bills admitting Iowa and Florida as states of the Union. On the latter bill he made one of his most forcible speeches on a proposal that Florida be required as a condition of her admission to abolish a provision in her Constitution limiting the authority for emancipating slaves. He denied the right or power of Congress to legislate upon the provisions of any constitution adopted by a state. He reported the several bills respecting the admission of Wisconsin, and voted for the admission of that state. He wrote the bills establishing the territorial governments of Utah, New Mexico, Washington, Kansas, Minnesota and Nebraska. He prepared the acts for the admission of California, Minnesota, and Oregon, into the Union as states.

THE AFRICAN SLAVE TRADE.

Mr. Douglas has always been decided in his opposition to the revival of the African slave trade. He has been always as decided in his efforts to enforce the existing, and willing to provide additional laws if necessary against that traffic. When this matter was discussed some time ago, Mr. Douglas, in answer to a letter from a gentleman in Virginia, thus expressed his views:

WASHINGTON, *August* 2, 1859.

Col. John L. Peyton, Staunton, Va.:

MY DEAR SIR: You do me no more than justice in your kind letter, for which accept my thanks, in assuming that I do not concur with the admin-

U 2

istration in their views respecting the rights of naturalized citizens, as defined in the "Le Clerc letter," which, it is proper to observe, has since been materially modified.

Under our Constitution there can be no just distinction between the rights of native born and naturalized citizens to claim the protection of our government at home and abroad. Unless the naturalization releases the person naturalized from all obligations which he owed to his native country, by virtue of his allegiance, it leaves him in the sad predicament of owing allegiance to two countries, without receiving protection from either—a dilemma in which no American citizen should be placed.

Neither have you misapprehended my opinions in respect to the African slave trade. That question seriously disturbed the harmony of the Convention which framed the federal Constitution. Upon it the delegates divided into two parties, under circumstances which, for a time, rendered harmonious action hopeless. The one demanded the instant and unconditional prohibition of the African slave trade, on moral and religious grounds, while the other insisted that it was a legitimate commerce, involving no other consideration than a sound public policy, which each state ought to be permitted to determine for itself, so long as it was sanctioned by its own laws. Each party stood resolutely and firmly by its own position, until both became convinced that this vexed question would break up the Convention, destroy the federal Union, blot out the glories of the Revolution, and throw away all its blessings, unless some fair and just compromise could be formed on the common ground of such mutual concessions as were indispensable to the preservation of their liberties, Union, and independence.

Such a compromise was effected and incorporated into the Constitution, by which it was understood that the African slave trade might continue a legitimate commerce in those states whose laws sanctioned it until the year 1808, from and after which time Congress might and would prohibit it for ever, throughout the dominion and limits of the United States, and pass all laws which might become necessary to make such prohibition effectual. The harmony of the Convention was restored, and the Union saved by this compromise, without which the Constitution could never have been made.

I stand firmly by this compromise and by all the other compromises of the Constitution, and shall use my best efforts to carry each and all of them into faithful execution, in the sense and with the understanding in which they were originally adopted. In accordance with this compromise, I am irreconcilably opposed to the revival of the African slave trade, in any form and under any circumstances.

am, with great respect, yours truly,
S. A. DOUGLAS.

————————

CHAPTER XXI.

THE CINCINNATI PLATFORM.

At no period of his life did Mr. Douglas experience more anxiety than just previous to the assembling of the Cincinnati Convention. This anxiety was not produced by any anticipations as to the action of that body respecting his nomination for the presidency. He had, in obedience to an established and recognized principle of the party, introduced and carried through Congress the Kansas-Nebraska Act, including the repeal of the Missouri Compromise. That act had failed to command the votes of a large body of the Democratic representatives in Congress. It had been met by a fierce and unrelenting combination in the northern states, against which the Democracy, except in a few isolated cases, had been unable to stand. The elections of 1854-5 had been most disastrous, and the thousands who regard present defeat as more fatal than the ultimate and successful establishment of a right principle heaped upon him their denunciations. His anxiety was lest the timid and temporizing would endeavor in that Convention to avoid or oppose a clear and unequivocal endorsement of the great principle of self-government and non-interference by Congress with the subject of slavery in the territories. When that Convention met, and when the representatives of the Democracy of all the states, without a dissenting voice, indorsed that great act of legislation, and proclaimed that thenceforth Congress washed its hands of all interference with the domestic affairs of the people of the territories—those inchoate states, as President Pierce styled them—all anxiety was removed, and once more he had the assurance of the Democracy that his adherence to the cause of right and truth had received, as well it had merited, the approbation of the Democracy of the nation.

There never was a platform of the Democracy that commended itself more generally to the approval of the people than that adopted at Cincinnati. It commanded the approbation of at least one half of the Republican party at the North. The latter, however, could not be induced to believe that the Democracy would carry out that platform in good faith. The action of the Lecompton Convention, the propositions for a revival of the slave trade, and for a slave code for the territories, have not had the effect to remove the doubts previously entertained by those who questioned the honesty of the intentions of those who adopted the Cincinnati platform. The only way in which these doubts can ever be removed, and the people of the northwest again united under a common organization for the protection and security of the Constitution and the Union, is by placing the administration of that platform in the hands of a man who is known to entertain for it a devotion and an affection unequalled by that of any other person. A good platform with candidates whose political fidelity is not established in the minds of the people is one thing, and a very different thing from the same platform with candidates who are known to the people as men who, at all hazards, and under all circumstances, will stand by principle, and never, even to court popular favor, abandon the established doctrines of free constitutional government.

Since June, 1856, Mr. Douglas has been unremitting in his defense of that platform. He stands upon it now, and clings to it as the best exposition of political faith ever produced in the United States since the adoption of the Constitution; and, when fairly executed, the safest and only reliable chart for avoiding those calamities that must ever attend any Federal legislation repecting African slavery. It is the best and most comprehensive declaration of the rights of the States that has ever been put in form, and there can be no violation of that platform that does not equally violate the vested and constitutional rights of the states of the Confederacy.

To the support and maintenance of that platform he has devoted much of his time, and expended his health and personal labor. In 1856, after its adoption, the Democratic National Committee at Washington regarded his report made upon Kansas affairs, on March 12th preceding, such an admirable epitome of the principles of the Democracy, subsequently asserted in the Cincinnati platform, that they had no less than *three hundred thousand* copies of it printed and circulated. The doctrines of that report were then deemed the best kind of Democracy, although they declared that no law or state government should be forced upon the people that did not receive a sanction from these people.

In the defense of the Cincinnati platform all questions were narrowed down to the one—the great fundamental principle of the right of the people of every distinct political community, which may be loyal to the Constitution, to regulate their own domestic affairs and local institutions, free of all interference by other states, or by the Federal government, and subject to no other restraint than may exist in the Constitution of the United States. In the defense of this principle Mr. Douglas, during the recess of 1859, prepared an elaborate essay, which was published in the September number of *Harper's New Monthly Magazine*. It had not only the extensive circulation of that popular publication, but soon found its way through an extra or supplemental edition, in pamphlet form, to all parts of the country. It was also published extensively in the public journals. We are authorized by Messrs. Harper & Brothers to republish that argument in this volume. It was as follows:

THE DIVIDING LINE BETWEEN FEDERAL AND LOCAL AUTHORITY.

[Reprinted from Harper's Magazine, September, 1859.]

Under our complex system of government it is the first duty of American statesmen to mark distinctly the dividing line between federal and local authority. To do this with accuracy involves an inquiry, not only into the powers and duties of the federal government under the Constitution, but also into the rights, privileges, and immunities of the people of the territories, as well as of the states composing the Union. The relative powers and functions of the federal and state governments have become well understood and clearly defined by their practical operation and harmonious action for a long series of years; while the disputed question—involving the right of the people of the territories to govern themselves in respect to their local affairs and internal polity—remains a fruitful source of partisan strife and sectional controversy. The political organization which was formed in 1854, and has assumed the name of the Republican party, is based on the theory that African slavery, as it exists in this country, is an evil of such magnitude—social, moral, and political—as to justify and require the exertion of the entire power and influence of the federal government to the full extent that the Constitution, according to their interpretation, will permit for its ultimate extinction. In the platform of principles adopted at Philadelphia by the Republican National Convention in 1856, it is affirmed:

"That the Constitution confers upon Congress sovereign power over the territories of the United States for their government, and that in the exercise of this power it is both the right and the duty of Congress to prohibit in the territories those twin relics of barbarism, polygamy and slavery."

According to the theory of the Republican party there is an irrepressible conflict between freedom and slavery, free labor and slave labor, free states and slave states, which is irreconcilable, and must continue to rage with increasing fury until the one shall become universal by the annihilation of the other. In the language of the most eminent and authoritative expounder of their political faith,

"It is an irrepressible conflict between opposing and enduring forces; and it means that the United States must and will, sooner or later, become either entirely a slaveholding nation or entirely a free-labor nation. Either the cotton and rice fields of South Carolina, and the sugar plantations of Louisiana will ultimately be tilled by free labor, and Charleston and New Orleans become marts for legitimate merchandise alone, or else the rye fields and wheat fields of Massachusetts and New York must again be surrendered by their farmers to slave culture and to the production of slaves, and Boston and New York become once more markets for trade in the bodies and souls of men."

In the Illinois canvass of 1858 the same proposition was advocated and defended by the distinguished Republican standard-bearer in these words:

"In my opinion it [the slavery agitation] will not cease until a crisis shall have been reached and passed. 'A house divided against itself can not stand.' I believe this government can not endure permanently half slave and half free. I do not expect the house to fall, but I do expect it will cease to be divided. It will become all one thing or all the other. Either the opponents of slavery will arrest the further spread of it, and place it where the public mind shall rest in the belief that it is in the course of ultimate extinction, or its advocates will push forward till it shall become alike lawful in all the States—old as well as new, North as well as South."

Thus it will be seen, that under the auspices of a political party, which claims sovereignty in Congress over the subject of slavery, there can be no peace on the slavery question—no truce in the sectional strife—no fraternity between the North and South, so long as this Union remains as our fathers made it—divided into free and slave states, with the right on the part of each to retain slavery so long as it chooses, and to abolish it whenever it pleases.

On the other hand, it would be uncandid to deny that, while the Democratic party is a unit in its irreconcilable opposition to the doctrines and principles of the Republican party, there are radical differences of opinion in respect to the powers and duties of Congress, and the rights and immunities of the people of the territories under the Federal Constitution, which seriously disturb its harmony and threaten its integrity. These differences of opinion arise from the different interpretations placed upon the Constitution by persons who belong to one of the following classes:

First.—Those who believe that the Constitution of the United States neither establishes or prohibits slavery in the states or territories beyond the power of the people legally to control it, but "but leaves the people thereof perfectly free to form and regulate their domestic institutions in their own way, subject only to the Constitution of the United States."

Second.—Those who believe that the Constitution establishes slavery in the territories, and withholds from Congress and the territorial Legislature the power to control it; and who insist that, in the event the territorial Legislature fails to enact the requisite laws for its protection, it becomes the imperative duty of Congress to interpose its authority and furnish such protection.

Third.—Those who, while professing to believe that the Constitution establishes slavery in the territories beyond the power of Congress or the territorial Legislature to control it, at the same time protest against the duty of Congress to interfere for its protection; but insist that it is the duty of the Judiciary to protect and maintain slavery in the territories without any law upon the subject.

By a careful examination of the second and third propositions, it will be seen that the advocates of each agree on the theoretical question, that the Constitution establishes slavery in the territories, and compels them to have it whether they want it or not; and differ on the practical point, whether a right secured by the Constitution shall be protected by an act of Congress when all other remedies fail. The reason assigned for not protecting by law a right secured by the Constitution is, that it is the duty of the courts to protect slavery in the territories without any legislation upon the subject. How the courts are to afford protection to slaves or any other property, where there is no law providing remedies and imposing penalties and conferring jurisdiction upon the courts to hear and determine the cases as they arise, remains to be explained.

The acts of Congress, establishing the several territories of the United States, provide that: "The jurisdiction of the several courts herein provided for, both appellate and original, and that of the Probate Courts and Justices of the Peace, shall be as limited by law"—meaning such laws as the territorial Legislatures shall from time to time enact. It will be seen that the judicial tribunals of the territories have just such jurisdiction, and only such, in respect to the rights of persons and property pertaining to the citizens of the territory as the territorial Legislature shall see fit to confer; and consequently, that the courts can afford protection to persons and property no further than the Legislature shall, by law, confer the jurisdiction, and prescribe the remedies, penalties, and modes of proceeding.

It is difficult to conceive how any person who believes that the Constitution confers the right of protection in the enjoyment of slave property in the territories, regardless of the wishes of the people and of the action of the territorial Legislature, can satisfy his conscience and his oath of fidelity to the Constitution in withholding such Congressional legislation as may be essential to the enjoyment of such right under the Constitution. Under this view of the subject it is impossible to resist the conclusion that, if the Constitution does establish slavery in the territories, beyond the power of the people to control it by law, it is the imperative duty of Congress to supply all the legislation necessary for its protection; and if this proposition is not true, it necessarily results that the Constitution neither establishes nor prohibits slavery any where, but leaves the people of each state and territory entirely free to form and regulate their domestic affairs to suit themselves, without the intervention of Congress or of any other power whatsoever.

But it is urged with great plausibility by those who have entire faith in the soundness of the proposition, that "a territory is the mere creature of Congress; that the creature can not be clothed with any powers not possessed by the creator; and that Congress, not possessing the power to legislate in respect to African slavery in the territories, can not delegate to a territorial Legislature any power which it does not itself possess."

This proposition is as plausible as it is fallacious. But the reverse of it is true as a general rule. Congress can not delegate to a territorial Legislature, or to any other body of men whatsoever, any power which the Constitution has vested in Congress. In other words: *Every power conferred on Congress by the Constitution must be exercised by Congress in the mode prescribed in the Constitution.*

Let us test the correctness of this proposition by reference to the powers of Congress as defined in the Constitution:

"The Congress shall have power—

"To lay and collect taxes, duties, imposts, and excises," etc.;

"To borrow money on the credit of the United States;"

"To regulate commerce with foreign nations," etc.;

"To establish a uniform rule of naturalization," etc.;

"To coin money, and regulate the value thereof;"

"To establish post-offices and post-roads;"

"To constitute tribunals inferior to the Supreme Court;"

"To declare war," etc.;

"To provide and maintain a navy."

The list might be extended so as to embrace all the powers conferred on Congress by the Constitution; but enough has been cited to test the principle. Will it be contended that Congress can delegate any one of these powers to a territorial Legislature or to any tribunal whatever? Can Congress delegate to Kansas the power to "regulate commerce," or to Nebraska the power "to establish uniform rules of naturalization," or to Illinois the power "to coin money and regulate the value thereof," or to Virginia the power "to establish post-offices and post-roads?"

The mere statement of the question carries with it the emphatic answer, that Congress can not delegate any power which it does possess; but that every power conferred on Congress by the Constitution must be exercised by Congress in the manner prescribed in that instrument.

On the other hand, there are cases in which Congress may establish tribunals and local governments, and invest them with powers which Congress does not possess and can not exercise under the Constitution. For instance, Congress may establish courts inferior to the Supreme Court, and confer upon them the power to hear and determine causes, and render judgments affecting the life, liberty, and property of the citizen, without itself having the power to hear and determine such causes, render judgments, or revise or annul the same. In like manner Congress may institute governments for the territories, composed of an executive, judicial, and legislative department; and may confer upon the governor all the executive powers and functions of the territory, without having the right to exercise any one of those powers or functions itself.

Congress may confer upon the judicial department all the judicial powers and functions of the territory, without having the right to hear and determine a cause, or render a judgment, or to revise or annul any decision made by the courts so established by Congress. Congress may also confer upon the legislative department of the territory certain legislative powers which it can not itself exercise, and only such as Congress can not exercise under the Constitution. The powers which Congress may thus *confer* but can not *exercise*, are such as relate to the domestic affairs and internal polity of the territory, and do not affect the general welfare of the Republic.

This dividing line between Federal and local authority was familiar to the framers of the Constitution. It is clearly defined and distinctly marked on every page of history which records the great events of that immortal struggle between the American colonies and the British government, which resulted in the establishment of our national independence. In the beginning of that struggle the colonies neither contemplated nor desired independence. In all their addresses to the Crown, and to the Parliament, and to the people of Great Britain, as well as to the people of America, they averred that as loyal British subjects they deplored the causes which impelled their separation from the parent country. They were strongly and affectionately attached to the Constitution, civil and political institutions and jurisprudence of Great Britain, which they proudly claimed as the birth-right of all Englishmen, and desired to transmit them unimpaired as a precious legacy to their posterity. For a long series of years they remonstrated against the violation of their inalienable rights of self-government under the British Constitution, and humbly petitioned for the redress of their grievances.

They acknowledged and affirmed their allegiance to the Crown, their affection for the people, and their devotion to the Constitution of Great Britain; and their only complaint was that they were not permitted to enjoy the rights and privileges of self-government, in the management of their internal affairs and domestic concerns, in accordance with the guaranties of that Constitution and of the colonial charters granted by the Crown in pursuance of it. They conceded the right of the Imperial government to make all laws and perform all acts concerning the colonies, which were in their nature *Imperial* and not *colonial*—which affected the general welfare of the Empire, and did not interfere with the "internal polity" of the colonies. They recognized the right of the Imperial government to declare war and make peace; to coin money and determine its value; to make treaties and conduct intercourse with foreign nations; to regulate commerce between the several colonies, and between each colony and the parent country, and with foreign countries; and in general they recognized the right of the Imperial government of Great Britain to exercise all the powers and authority which, under our Federal Constitution, are delegated by the people of the several States to the government of the United States.

Recognizing and conceding to the Imperial government all these powers—*including the right to institute governments for the colonies,* by granting charters under which the inhabitants residing within the limits of any specified territory might be organized into a political community, with a government consisting of its appropriate departments, executive, legislative, and judicial; conceding all these powers, the colonies emphatically denied that the imperial government had any rightful authority to impose taxes upon them without their consent, or to interfere with their internal polity; claiming that it was the birth-right of all Englishmen—inalienable when formed into a political community—to exercise and enjoy all the rights, privileges, and immunities of self-government in respect to all matters and things which were local and not general—internal and not external—colonial and not imperial—as fully as if they were inhabitants of England, with a fair representation in Parliament.

Thus it appears that our fathers of the Revolution were contending, not for independence in the first instance, but for the inestimable right of local self-government under the British Constitution; the right of every distinct political community—dependent colonies, territories, and provinces, as well as sovereign states—to make their own local laws, form their own domestic institutions, and manage their own internal affairs in their own way, subject only to the Constitution of Great Britain as the paramount law of the empire.

The government of Great Britain had violated this inalienable right of local self-government by a long series of acts on a great variety of subjects. The first serious point of controversy arose on the slavery question as early as 1699, which continued a fruitful source of irritation until the Revolution, and formed one of the causes for the separation of the colonies from the British Crown.

For more than forty years the Provincial Legislature of Virginia had passed laws for the protection and encouragement of African slavery within her limits. This policy was steadily pursued until the white inhabitants of Virginia became alarmed for their own safety, in view of the numerous and formidable tribes of Indian savages which surrounded and threatened the feeble white settlements, while ship loads of African savages were being daily landed in their midst. In order to check and restrain a policy which seemed to threaten the very existence of the colony, the Provincial Legislature enacted a law imposing a tax upon every slave who should be brought into Virginia. The British merchants, who were engaged in the African slave trade, regarding this legislation as injurious to their interests and in violation of their rights, petitioned the King of England and his Majesty's ministers to annul the obnoxious law and protect them in their right to carry their slaves into Virginia and all other British colonies which were the common property of the empire—acquired by the common blood and common treasure—and from which a few adventurers, who had settled on the imperial domain by his Majesty's sufferance, had no right to exclude them or discriminate against their property by a mere provincial enactment. Upon a full consideration of the subject the King graciously granted the prayer of the petitioners; and accordingly issued peremptory orders to the royal governor of Virginia, and to the governors of all the other British colonies in America, forbidding them to sign or approve any colonial or provincial enactment injurious to the African slave trade, unless such enactment should contain a clause suspending its operation until his Majesty's pleasure should be made known in the premises.

Judge Tucker, in his Appendix to Blackstone, refers to thirty-one acts of the Provincial Legislature of Virginia, passed at various periods from 1662 to 1772, upon the subject of African slavery, showing conclusively that Virginia always considered this as one of the questions affecting her "internal polity," over which she, in common with the other colonies, claimed "the right of exclusive legislation in their Provincial Legislatures" within their respective limits. Some of these acts, particularly those which were enacted prior to the year 1699, were evidently intended to foster and encourage, as well as to regulate and control African slavery, as one of the domestic institutions of the colony. The act of 1699, and most of the enactments subsequent to that date, were as obviously designed to restrain and check the growth of the institution, with the view of confining it within the limit of the actual necessities of the community, or its ultimate extinction, as might be deemed most conducive to the public interests, by a system of unfriendly legislation, such as imposing a tax on all slaves introduced into the colony, which was increased and renewed from time to time, as occasion required, until the period of the Revolution. Many of these acts never took effect, in consequence of the King withholding his assent, even after the governor had approved the enactment, in cases where it contained a clause suspending its operation until his Majesty's pleasure should be made known in the premises.

In 1772 the Provincial Legislature of Virginia, after imposing another tax of five per cent. on all slaves imported into the colony, petitioned the King to remove all those restraints which inhibited his Majesty's governors assenting to such laws as might check so very pernicious a commerce as slavery. Of this petition Judge Tucker says:

"The following extract from a petition to the Throne, presented from the House of Burgesses of Virginia, April 1st, 1772, will show the sense of the people of Virginia on the subject of slavery at that period:

"'The importation of slaves into the colony from the coast of Africa hath long been considered as a trade of great inhumanity; and under its present encouragement we have too much reason to fear will endanger the very existence of your Majesty's American dominions.'"

Mark the ominous words! Virginia tells the King of England in 1772, four years prior to the Declaration of Independence, that his Majesty's American dominions are in danger: not because of the stamp duties—not because of the tax on tea—not because of his attempts to collect revenue in America! These have since been deemed sufficient to justify rebellion and revolution. But none of these are referred to by Virginia in her address to the Throne—there being another wrong which, in magnitude and enormity, so far exceeded these and all other causes of complaint, that the very existence of his Majesty's American dominions depended upon it! That wrong consisted in forcing African slavery upon a dependent colony without her consent, and in opposition to the wishes of her own people!

The people of Virginia at that day did not appreciate the force of the argument used by the British merchants, who were engaged in the African slave-trade, and which was afterward indorsed, at least by implication, by the King and his ministers; that the colonies were the common property of the empire—acquired by the common blood and treasure—and therefore all British subjects had the right to carry their slaves into the colonies and hold them in defiance of the local law and in contempt of the wishes and safety of the colonies.

The people of Virginia, not being convinced by this process of reasoning, still adhered to the doctrine which they held in common with their sister colonies, that it was the birth-right of all freemen—inalienable when formed into political communities—to exercise exclusive legislation in respect to all matters pertaining to their internal polity—slavery not excepted; and rather than surrender this great right they were prepared to withdraw their allegiance from the Crown.

Again referring to this petition to the King, the same learned Judge adds:

"This petition produced no effect, as appears from the first clause of our (Virginia) Constitution, where, among other acts of misrule, the inhuman use of the royal negative in refusing us (the people of Virginia) permission to exclude slavery from us by law, is enumerated among the reasons for separating from Great Britain."

This clause in the Constitution of Virginia, referring to the inhuman use of the royal negative, in refusing the colony of Virginia permission to exclude slavery from her limits by law, as one of the reasons for separating from Great Britain, was adopted on the 12th day of June, 1776, three weeks and one day previous to the Declaration of Independence by the Continental Congress; and after remaining in force as a part of the Constitution for a period of fifty-four years, was re-adopted, without alteration, by the Convention which framed the new Constitution in 1830, and then ratified by the people as a part of the new Constitution; and was again re-adopted by the Convention which amended the Constitution in 1850, and again ratified by the people as a part of the amended Constitution, and at this day remains a portion of the fundamental law of Virginia—proclaiming to the world and to posterity that one of the reasons for separating from Great Britain was "the inhuman use of the royal negative in refusing us (the colony of Virginia) permission to exclude slavery from us by law !"

The legislation of Virginia on this subject may be taken as a fair sample of the legislative enactments of each of the thirteen colonies, showing conclusively that slavery was regarded by them all as a domestic question to be regarded and determined by each colony to suit itself, without the intervention of the British Parliament or "the inhuman use of the royal negative." Each colony passed a series of enactments, beginning at an early period of its history and running down to the commencement of the Revolution, either protecting, regulating, or restraining African slavery within its respective limits and in accordance with their wishes and supposed interests. North and South Carolina, following the example of Virginia, at first encouraged the introduction of slaves, until the number increased beyond their wants and necessities, when they attempted to check and restrain the further growth of the institution, by imposing a high rate of taxation upon all slaves which should be brought into those colonies; and finally, in 1764, South Carolina passed a law imposing a penalty of one hundred pounds (or five hundred dollars) for every negro slave subsequently introduced into that colony.

The colony of Georgia was originally founded on strict anti-slavery principles, and rigidly maintained this policy for a series of years, until the inhabitants became convinced by experience that, with their climate and productions, slave labor, if not essential to their existence, would prove beneficial and useful to their material interests. Maryland and Delaware protected and regulated African slavery as one of their domestic institutions. Pennsylvania, under the advice of William Penn, substituted fourteen years' service and perpetual adscript to the soil for hereditary slavery, and attempted to legislate, not for the total abolition of slavery, but for the sanctity of marriage among slaves, and for their personal security. New Jersey, New York, and Connecticut recognized African slavery as a domestic institution lawfully existing within their respective limits, and passed the requisite laws for its control and regulation.

Rhode Island provided by law that no slave should serve more than ten years, at the end of which time he was to be set free; and if the master should refuse to let him go free, or sold him elsewhere for a longer period of service, he was subject to a penalty of forty pounds, which was supposed at that period to be nearly double the value of the slave.

Massachusetts imposed heavy taxes upon all slaves brought into the colony, and provided in some instances for sending the slaves back to their native land; and finally prohibited the introduction of any more slaves into the colony under any circumstances.

When New Hampshire passed laws which were designed to prevent the introduction of any more slaves, the British cabinet issued the following order to Governor Wentworth: "You are not to give your assent to, or pass any law imposing duties upon negroes imported into New Hampshire."

While the legislation of the several colonies exhibits dissimilarity of views, founded on a diversity of interests, on the merits and policy of slavery, it shows conclusively that they all regarded it as a domestic question affecting their internal polity in respect to which they were entitled to a full and exclusive power of legislation in the several provincial Legislatures. For a few years immediately preceding the American Revolution the African slave-trade was encouraged and stimulated by the British government and carried on with more vigor by the English merchants than at at any other period in the history of the colonies; and this fact, taken in connection with the extraordinary claim asserted in the memorable preamble to the act repealing the stamp duties, that "Parliament possessed the right to bind the colonies in all cases whatever," not only in respect to all matters affecting the general welfare of the empire, but also in regard to the domestic relations and internal policy of the colony—produced a powerful impression upon the minds of the colonists, and imparted peculiar prominence to the principle involved in the controversy.

Hence the enactments by the several colonial Legislatures calculated and designed to restrain and prevent the increase of slaves; and, on the other hand, the orders issued by the Crown instructing the colonial governors not to sign or permit any legislative enactment prejudicial or injurious to the African slave trade, unless such enactment should contain a clause suspending its operation until the royal pleasure should be made known in the premises; or, in other words, until the king should have an opportunity of annulling the acts of the colonial Legislatures by the "inhuman use of the royal negative."

Thus the policy of the colonies on the slavery question had assumed a direct antagonism to that of the British government; and this antagonism not only added to the importance of the principle of local self-government in the colonies, but produced a general concurrence of opinion and action in respect to the question of slavery in the proceedings of the Continental Congress, which assembled at Philadelphia for the first time on the 5th of September, 1774.

On the 14th of October the Congress adopted a bill of rights for the colonies, in the form of a series of resolutions, in which, after conceding to the British government the power to regulate commerce and do such other things as affected the general welfare of the empire without interfering with the internal polity of the colonies, they declared "That they are entitled to a free and exclusive power in their several provincial Legislatures, where their right of representation can alone be preserved, in all cases of taxation and internal polity." Having thus defined the principle for which they were contending, the Congress proceeded to adopt the following "Peaceful Measures," which they still hoped would be sufficient to induce compliance with their just and reasonable demands. These "Peaceful Measures" consisted of addresses to the king, to the Parliament, and to the people of Great Britain, together with an Association of Non-Intercourse to be observed and maintained so long as their grievances should remain unredressed.

The second article of this Association, which was adopted without opposition and signed by the delegates from all the colonies, was in these words:

"That we will neither import nor purchase any slave imported after the first day of December next; after which time we will wholly discontinue the slave trade, and will neither be concerned in it ourselves, nor will we hire our vessels, nor sell our commodities or manufactures to those who are engaged in it."

This bill of rights, together with these articles of association, were subsequently submitted to and adopted by each of the thirteen colonies in their respective provincial Legislatures.

Thus was distinctly formed between the colonies and the parent country that issue upon which the Declaration of Independence was founded and the battles of the Revolution were fought. It involved the specific claim on the part of the colonies—denied by the King and Parliament—to the exclusive right of legislation touching all local and internal concerns, *slavery included*. This being the principle involved in the contest, a majority of the colonies refused to permit their delegates to sign the Declaration of Independence except upon the distinct condition and express reservation to each colony of the exclusive right to manage and control its local concerns and police regulations without the intervention of any general Congress which might be established for the United Colonies.

Let us cite one of these reservations as a specimen of all, showing conclusively that they were fighting for the inalienable right of local self-government, with the clear understanding that when they had succeeded in throwing off the despotism of the British Parliament, no congressional despotism was to be substituted for it:

" We, the delegates of Maryland, in convention assembled, do declare that the King of Great Britain has violated his compact with this people, and that they owe no allegiance to him. We have, therefore, thought it just and necessary to empower our deputies in Congress to join with a majority of the United Colonies in declaring them free and independent States, in framing such further confederation between them, in making foreign alliances, and in adopting such other measures as shall be judged necessary for the preservation of their liberties:

" *Provided*, the sole and exclusive right of regulating the internal polity and government of this colony be reserved to the people thereof.

" We have also thought proper to call a new Convention for the purpose of establishing a government in this colony.

" No ambitious views, no desire of independence, induced the people of Maryland to form an union with the other colonies. To procure an exemption from parliamentary taxation, and to continue to the Legislatures of these colonies the sole and exclusive right of regulating their internal polity, was our original and only motive. To maintain inviolate our liberties, and to transmit them unimpaired to posterity, was our duty and our first wish; our next, to continue connected with and dependent on Great Britain. For the truth of these assertions we appeal to that Almighty Being who is emphatically styled the Searcher of hearts, and from whose omniscience none is concealed. Relying on his Divine protection and assistance, and trusting to the justice of our cause, we exhort and conjure every virtuous citizen to join cordially in defense of our common rights, and in maintenance of the freedom of this and her sister colonies."

The first plan of Federal government adopted for the United States was formed during the Revolution, and is usually known as "The Articles of Confederation." By these articles it was provided that "Each state retains its sovereignty, freedom and independence, and every power, jurisdiction and right which is not by this Confederation expressly delegated to the United States in Congress assembled."

At the time the Articles of Confederation were adopted—July 9, 1778—the United States held no lands or territory in common. The entire country—including all the waste and unappropriated lands—embraced within or pertaining to the confederacy, belonged to and was the property of the several states within whose limits the same was situated.

On the 6th day of September, 1780, Congress " recommended to the several states of the Union having claims to waste and unappropriated lands in the western country, a liberal cession to the United States of a portion of their respective claims for the common benefit of the Union."

On the 20th day of October, 1783, the Legislature of Virginia passed an act authorizing the delegates in Congress from that state to convey to the United States "the territory or tract of country within the limits of the Virginia charter, lying and bearing to the northwest of the river Ohio"—which grant was to be made upon the "condition that the territory so ceded shall be laid out and formed into States;" and that "the states so formed shall be distinct Republican states, and admitted members of the Federal Union, having the same rights of sovereignty, freedom, and independence as the other states."

On the 1st day of March, 1784, Thomas Jefferson and his colleagues in Congress executed the deed of cession in pursuance of the act of the Virginia Legislature, which was accepted and ordered to "be recorded and enrolled among the acts of the United States in Congress assembled." This was the first territory ever acquired, held, or owned by the United States. On the same day of the deed of cession Mr. Jefferson, as chairman of a committee which had been appointed, consisting of Mr. Jefferson, of Virginia, Mr. Chase, of Maryland, and Mr. Howell, of Rhode Island, submitted to Congress "a plan for the temporary government of the territory ceded or to be ceded by the individual states of the United States."

It is important that this Jeffersonian plan of government for the territories should be carefully considered for many obvious reasons. It was the first plan of government for the territories ever adopted in the United States. It was drawn by the author of the Declaration of Independence, and revised and adopted by those who shaped the issues which produced the Revolution, and formed the foundations upon which our whole American system of government rests. It was not intended to be either local or temporary in its character, but was designed to apply to all "territory ceded or to be ceded," and to be universal in its application and eternal in its duration, wherever and whenever we might have territory requiring a government. It ignored the right of Congress to legislate for the people of the territories without their consent, and recognized the inalienable right of the people of the territories, when organized into political communities, to govern themselves in respect to their local concerns and internal policy. It was adopted by the Congress of the Confederation on the 23d day of April, 1784, and stood upon the statute book as a general and permanent plan for the government of all territory which we then owned or should subsequently acquire, with a provision declaring it to be a "Charter of Compact," and that its provisions should "stand as fundamental conditions between the thirteen original states and those newly described, unalterable but by the joint consent of the United States in Congress assembled, and of the particular state within which such alteration is proposed to be made." Thus this Jeffersonian plan for the government of the territories—this "Charter of Compact"—"these fundamental conditions," which were declared to be "unalterable" without the consent of the people of "the particular states (territories) within which such alteration is proposed to be made," stood on the statute book when the Convention assembled at Philadelphia in 1787 and proceeded to form the Constitution of the United States.

Now let us examine the main provisions of the Jeffersonian plan:

First.—"That the territory ceded or to be ceded by the individual states to the United States, whenever the same shall have been purchased of the Indian inhabitants and offered for sale by the United States, shall be formed into *additional states*," etc. etc.

The plan proceeds to designate the boundaries and territorial extent of the proposed "additional states," and then provides:

Second.—"That the settlers within the territory so to be purchased and offered for sale shall, either on their own petition or on the order of Congress, receive authority from them, with appointments of time and place, for their free males of full age to meet together for the purpose of establishing a temporary government to adopt the Constitution and laws of any one of these states (the original states), so that such laws nevertheless shall be subject to alteration by their ordinary Legislature; and to erect, subject to like alteration, counties or townships for the election of members for their Legislature."

Having thus provided a mode by which the first inhabitants or settlers of the territory may assemble together and choose for themselves the Constitution and laws of some one of the original thirteen states, and declare the same in force for the government of their territory temporarily, with the right on the part of the people to change the same, through their local Legislature, as they may see proper, the plan then proceeds to point out the mode in which they may establish for themselves "a permanent Constitution and government," whenever they shall have twenty thousand inhabitants, as follows:

Third.—"That such temporary government only shall continue in force in any *State* until it shall have acquired twenty thousand free inhabitants, when, giving due proof thereof to Congress, they shall receive from them authority, with appointments of time and place, to call a Convention of Representatives to establish a permanent Constitution and government for themselves."

Having thus provided for the first settlers "a temporary government" in these "additional states," and for "a permanent Constitution and government" when they shall have acquired twenty thousand inhabitants, the plan contemplates that they shall continue to govern themselves *as states*, having, as provided in the Virginia deed of cession, "the same rights of sovereignty, freedom, and independence," in respect to their domestic affairs and internal polity, "as the other States," until they shall have a population equal to the least numerous of the original thirteen States; and in the mean time shall keep a sitting member in Congress, with a right of debating but not of voting, when they shall be admitted into the Union on an equal footing with the other states, as follows:

Fourth.—"That whenever any of the said states shall have of free inhabitants as many as shall then be in any one of the least numerous of the thirteen original states, such *state* shall be admitted by its delegates into the Congress of the United States on an equal footing with the said original states." . . . .

And—

"Until such admission by their delegates into Congress any of the said *states*, after the establishment of their temporary government, shall have authority to keep a sitting member in Congress, with the right of debating, but not of voting."

Attached to the provision which appears in this paper under the "third" head is a proviso, containing five propositions, which when agreed to and accepted by the people of said additional states, were to "be formed into a charter of compact," and to remain forever "unalterable," except by the consent of such states as well as of the United States—to wit:

"*Provided* that both the temporary and permanent governments be established on these principles as their basis:

1*st.*—"That they shall forever remain a part of the United States of America."

2*d.*—"That in their persons, property, and territory they shall be subject to the government of the United States in Congress assembled, and to the Articles of Confederation in all those cases in which the original states shall be so subject."

3*d.*—"That they shall be subject to pay a part of the federal debts contracted, or to be contracted—to be apportioned on them by Congress according to the same common rule and measure by which apportionments thereof shall be made on the other states."

4th.—"That their respective governments shall be in republican form, and shall admit no person to be a citizen who holds any hereditary title."

The fifth article, which relates to the prohibition of slavery after the year 1800, having been rejected by Congress, never became a part of the Jeffersonian plan of government for the territories, as adopted April 23, 1784.

The concluding paragraph of this plan of government, which emphatically ignores the right of Congress to bind the people of the territories without their consent, and recognizes the people therein as the true source of all legitimate power in respect to their internal polity, is in these words:

"That all the preceding articles shall be formed into a *charter of compact*, shall be duly executed by the President of the United States, in Congress assembled, under his hand and the seal of the United States, shall be promulgated, and shall stand as fundamental conditions between the thirteen original states and those newly described, unalterable but by the joint consent of the United States in Congress assembled, and of the particular state within which such alteration is proposed to be made."

This Jeffersonian plan of government embodies and carries out the ideas and principles of the fathers of the Revolution—that the people of every separate political community (dependent colonies, provinces, and territories, as well as sovereign states) have an inalienable right to govern themselves in respect to their internal polity, and repudiates the dogma of the British ministry and the Tories of that day, that all colonies, provinces, and territories were the property of the empire, acquired with the common blood and common treasure; and that the inhabitants thereof have no rights, privileges, or immunities except such as the Imperial government should graciously condescend to bestow upon them. This plan recognizes by law and irrevocable "compact" the existence of two distinct classes of states under our American system of government—the one being members of the Union, and consisting of the original thirteen and such other states, having the requisite population, as Congress should admit into the Federal Union, with an equal vote in the management of Federal affairs, as well as the exclusive power in regard to their internal polity respectively—the others, not having the requisite population for admission into the Union, could have no vote or agency in the control of the Federal relations, but possessed the same exclusive power over their domestic affairs and internal policy respectively as the original states, with the right, while they have less than twenty thousand inhabitants, to choose for their government the Constitution and laws of any one of the original states; and when they should have more than twenty thousand, but less than the number required to entitle them to admission into the Union, they were authorized to form for themselves "a permanent Constitution and government;" and in either case they were entitled to keep a delegate in Congress with the right of debating, but not of voting. This "Charter of Compact," with its "fundamental conditions," which were declared to be "unalterable" without "the joint consent" of the people interested in them, as well as of the United States, thus stood on the statute book unrepealed and irrepealable—furnishing a complete system of government for all "the territories ceded or to be ceded" to the United States, without any other legislation upon the subject, when, on the 14th day of May, 1787, the Federal Convention assembled in Philadelphia and proceeded to form the Constitution under which we now live. Thus it will be seen that the dividing line between Federal and local authority, in respect to the rights of those political communities which, for the sake of convenience and in contradistinction to the states represented in Congress, we now call territories, but which were then known as "*states*," or "*new states,*" was so distinctly marked at that day that no intelligent man could fail to perceive it.

It is true that the government of the Confederation had proved totally inadequate to the fulfillment of the ends for which it was devised; not because of the relations between the territories, or new states and the United States, but in consequence of having no power to enforce its decrees on the Federal questions which were clearly within the scope of its expressly delegated powers. The radical defects in the Articles of Confederation were found to consist in the fact that it was a mere league between sovereign states, and not a Federal government with its appropriate departments—executive, legislative, and judicial—each clothed with authority to perform and carry into effect its own peculiar functions. The Confederation having no power to enforce compliance with its resolves, "the consequence was, that though in theory the resolutions of Congress were equivalent to laws, yet in practice they were found to be mere recommendations, which the states, like other sovereignties, observed or disregarded according to their own good-will and gracious pleasure." Congress could not impose duties, collect taxes, raise armies, or do any other act essential to the existence of government, without the voluntary consent and coöperation of each of the states. Congress could resolve, but could not carry its resolutions into effect—could recommend to the states to provide a revenue for the necessities of the Federal government, but could not use the means necessary to the collection of the revenue when the states failed to comply—could recommend to the states to provide an army for the general defense, and apportion among the states their respective quotas, but could not enlist the men and order them into the Federal service. For these reasons, a Federal government, with its appropriate departments, acting directly upon the individual citizens, with authority to enforce its decrees to the extent of its delegated powers, and not dependent upon the voluntary action of the several states in their corporate capacity, became indispensable as a substitute for the government of the Confederation.

In the formation of the Constitution of the United States the federal Convention took the British Constitution, as interpreted and expounded by the colonies during their controversy with Great Britain, for their model—making such modifications in its structure and principles as the change in our condition had rendered necessary. They intrusted the executive functions to a President in the place of a King; the legislative functions to a Congress composed of a Senate and House of Representatives, in lieu of the Parliament consisting of the House of Lords and Commons; and the judicial functions to a Supreme Court and such inferior courts as Congress should from time to time ordain and establish.

Having thus divided the powers of government into the three appropriate departments, with which they had always been familiar, they proceeded to confer upon the federal government substantially the same powers which they as colonies had been willing to concede to the British government, and to reserve to the states and to the people the same rights and privileges which they as colonies had denied to the British government during the entire struggle which terminated in our independence, and which they had claimed for themselves and their posterity as the birth-right of all freemen, inalienable when organized into political communities, and to be enjoyed and exercised by colonies, territories, and provinces as fully and completely as by sovereign states. Thus it will be seen that there is no organic feature or fundamental principle embodied in the Constitution of the United States which had not been familiar to the people of the colonies from the period of their earliest settlement, and which had not been repeatedly asserted by them when denied by Great Britain during the whole period of their colonial history.

Let us pause at this point for a moment, and inquire whether it be just to those illustrious patriots and sages who formed the Constitution of the United States to assume that they intended to confer upon Congress that unlimited and arbitrary power over the people of the American territories, which they had resisted with their blood when claimed by the British Parliament over British colonies in America? Did they confer upon Congress the right to bind the people of the American territories in all cases whatsoever, after having fought the battles of the Revolution against a "Preamble" declaring the right of Parliament "to bind the colonies in all cases whatsoever?"

If, as they contended before the Revolution, it was the birth-right of all Englishmen, inalienable when formed into political communities, to exercise exclusive power of legislation in their local Legislatures in respect to all things affecting their internal polity—slavery not excepted—did not the same right, after the Revolution, and by virtue of it, become the birth-right of all Americans, in like manner inalienable when organized into political communities—no matter by what name, whether colonies, territories, provinces, or new states?

Names often deceive persons in respect to the nature and substance of things. A single instance of this kind is to be found in that clause of the Constitution which says:

"Congress shall have power to dispose of, and make all needful rules and regulations respecting the territory or other property belonging to the United States."

This being the only clause of the Constitution in which the word "territory" appears, that fact alone has doubtless led many persons to suppose that the right of Congress to establish temporary governments for the territories, in the sense in which the word is now used, must be derived from it, overlooking the important and controlling facts that at the time the Constitution was formed the word "territory" had never been used or understood to designate a political community or government of any kind in any law, compact, deed of cession, or public document; but had invariably been used either in its geographical sense to describe the superficial area of a State or district of country, as in the Virginia deed of cession of the "territory or *tract of country*" northwest of the river Ohio; or as meaning land in its character as property, in which latter sense it appears in the clause of the Constitution referred to, when providing for the disposition of the "territory or other property belonging to the United States." These facts, taking in connection with the kindred one that during the whole period of the confederation and the formation of the Constitution the temporary governments which we now call "territories," were invariably referred to in the deeds of cession, laws, compacts, plans of government, resolutions of Congress, public records, and authentic documents as "states," or "new states," conclusively show that the words "territory and other property" in the Constitution were used to designate the unappropriated lands and other property which the United States owned, and not the people who might become residents on those lands, and be organized into political communities after the United States had parted with their title.

It is from this clause of the Constitution alone that Congress derives the power to provide for the surveys and sale of the public lands and all other property belonging to the United States, not only in the territories, but also in the several states of the Union. But for this provision Congress would have no power to authorize the sale of the public lands, military sites, old ships, cannon, muskets, or other property, real or personal, which belong to the United States and are no longer needed for any public purpose. It refers exclusively to property in contradistinction to persons and communities. It confers the same power "to make all needful rules and regulations" in the states as in the territories, and extends wherever there may be any land or other property belonging to the United States to be regulated or disposed of; but does not authorize Congress to control or interfere with the domestic institutions and internal polity of the people (either in the states or the territories) who may reside upon lands which the United States once owned. Such a power, had it been vested in Congress, would annihilate the sovereignty and freedom of the states as well as the great principle of self-government in the territories, wherever the United States happen to own a portion of the public land within their respective limits, as, at present, in the States of Alabama, Florida, Mississippi, Louisiana, Arkansas, Missouri, Illinois, Indiana, Ohio, Michigan, Wisconsin, Iowa, Minnesota, California, and Oregon, and in the Territories of Washington, Nebraska, Kansas, Utah, and New Mexico. The idea is repugnant to the spirit and genius of our complex system of government; because it effectually blots out the dividing line between federal and local authority, which forms an essential barrier for the defense of the independence of the states and the liberties of the people against federal invasion. With one anomalous exception, all the powers conferred on Congress are *federal*, and not *municipal*, in their character—affecting the general welfare of the whole country without interfering with the internal polity of the people—and can be carried into effect by laws which apply alike to states and territories. The exception, being in derogation of one of the fundamental principles of our political system (because it authorizes the federal government to control the municipal affairs and internal polity of the people in certain specified, limited localities), was not left to vague inference or loose construction, nor expressed in dubious or equivocal language; but is found plainly written in that section of the Constitution which says:

"Congress shall have power to exercise exclusive legislation in all cases whatsoever, over such district (not exceeding ten miles square) as may, by cession of particular states, and the acceptance of Congress, become the seat of the government of the United States, and to exercise like authority over all places purchased by the consent of the Legislature of the state in which the same shall be for the erection of forts, magazines, arsenals, dockyards, and other needful buildings."

No such power "to exercise exclusive legislation in all cases whatsoever," nor indeed any legislation in any case whatsoever, is conferred on Congress in respect to the municipal affairs and internal polity, either of the states or of the territories. On the contrary, after the Constitution had been finally adopted, with its federal power delegated, enumerated, and defined, in order to guard in all future time against any possible infringement of the reserved rights of the states, or of the people, an amendment was incorporated into the Constitution which marks the dividing line between federal and local authority so directly and indelibly that no lapse of time, no partisan prejudice, no sectional aggrandizement, no frenzied fanaticism can efface it. The amendment is in these words:

"The powers not delegated to the United States by the Constitution, nor prohibited by it to the states, are reserved to the states respectively, or to the people."

This view of the subject is confirmed, if indeed any corroborative evidence is required, by reference to the proceedings and debates of the Federal Convention, as reported by Mr. Madison. On the 18th of August, after a series of resolutions had been adopted as the basis of the proposed Constitution and referred to the Committee of Detail for the purpose of being put in proper form, the record says:

"Mr. Madison submitted, in order to be referred to the Committee of Detail, the following powers, as proper to be added to those of the general Legislature (Congress):

"To dispose of the unappropriated lands of the United States.

"To institute temporary governments for the new states arising therein.

"To regulate affairs with the Indians, as well within as without the limits of the United States.

"To exercise exclusively legislative authority at the seat of the general government, and over a district around the same not exceeding——square miles, the consent of the Legislature of the state or states comprising the same being first obtained."

Here we find the original and rough draft of these several powers as they now exist, in their revised form, in the Constitution. The provision empowering Congress "to dispose of the unappropriated lands of the United States" was modified and enlarged so as to include "other property belonging to the United States," and to authorize Congress to "make all needful rules and regulations" for the preservation, management, and sale of the same.

The provision empowering Congress "to institute temporary governments for the new states arising in the unappropriated lands of the United States," taken in connection with the one empowering Congress "to exercise exclusively legislative authority at the seat of the general government, and over a district of country around the same," clearly shows the difference in the extent and nature of the powers intended to be conferred in the new states or territories on the one hand, and in the District of Columbia on the other. In the one case it was proposed to authorize Congress "to institute temporary governments for the new states," or territories, as they are now called, just as our Revolutionary fathers recognized the right of the British crown to institute local governments for the colonies, by issuing charters, under which the people of the colonies were "entitled (according to the Bill of Rights adopted by the Continental Congress) to a free and exclusive power of legislation, in their several Provincial Legislatures, where their right of representation can alone be preserved, in all cases of taxation and internal polity;" while, in the other case, it was proposed to authorize Congress to exercise, exclusively, legislative authority over the municipal and internal polity of the people residing within the district which should be ceded for that purpose as the seat of the general government.

Each of these provisions was modified and perfected by the Committees of Detail and Revision, as will appear by comparing them with the corresponding clauses as finally incorporated into the Constitution. The provision to authorize Congress to institute temporary governments for the new states or territories, and to provide for their admission into the Union, appears in the Constitution in this form:

"New states may be admitted by the Congress into this Union."

The power to admit "new states," and "to make all laws which shall be necessary and proper" to that end, may fairly be construed to include the right to institute temporary governments for such new states or territories, the same as Great Britain could rightfully institute similar governments for the colonies; but certainly not to authorize Congress to legislate in respect to their municipal affairs and internal concerns, without violating that great fundamental principle in defense of which the battles of the Revolution were fought.

If judicial authority were deemed necessary to give force to principles so eminently just in themselves, and which form the basis of our entire political system, such authority may be found in the opinion of the Supreme Court of the United States, in the Dred Scott case. In that case the Court say:

"This brings us to examine by what provision of the Constitution the present Federal government, under its delegated and restricted powers, is authorized to acquire territory outside of the original limits of the United States, and what powers it may exercise therein over the person or property of a citizen of the United States, while it remains a territory, and until it shall be admitted as one of the States of the Union.

"There is certainly no power given by the Constitution to the Federal government to establish or maintain colonies, bordering on the United States or at a distance, to be ruled and governed at its own pleasure; nor to enlarge its territorial limits in any way except by the admission of new states . . .

"The power to expand the territory of the United States by the admission of new states is plainly given; and in the construction of this power by all the departments of the government, it has been held to authorize the acquisition of territory, not fit for admission at the time, but to be admitted as soon as its population and situation would entitle it to admission. It is acquired to become a state, and not to be held as a colony and governed by Congress with absolute authority; and as the propriety of admitting a new state is committed to the sound discretion of Congress, the power to acquire territory for that purpose, to be held by the United States until it is in a suitable condition to become a state upon an equal footing with the other states, must rest upon the same discretion."

Having determined the question that the power to acquire territory for the purpose of enlarging our territorial limits and increasing the number of states is included within the power to admit new states and conferred by the same clause of the Constitution, the Court proceeded to say that "the power to acquire necessarily carries with it the power to preserve and apply to the purposes for which it was acquired." And again, referring to a former decision of the same Court in respect to the power of Congress to institute governments for the territories, the Court say:

"The power stands firmly on the latter alternative put by the Court—that is, as the inevitable consequence of the right to acquire territory."

The power to acquire territory, as well as the right, in the language of Mr. Madison, " to institute temporary governments for the new states arising therein" (or territorial governments, as they are now called), having been traced to that provision of the Constitution which provides for the admission of "new states," the Court proceed to consider the nature and extent of the power of Congress over the people of the territories:

"All we mean to say on this point is, that, as there is no express regulation in the Constitution defining the power which the general government may exercise over the person or property of a citizen in a territory thus acquired, the Court must necessarily look to the provisions and principles of the Constitution, and its distribution of powers, for the rules and principles by which its decision must be governed.

"Taking this rule to guide us, it may be safely assumed that citizens of the United States, who emigrate to a territory belonging to the people of the United States, can not be ruled as mere colonists, dependent upon the will of the general government, and to be governed by any laws it may think proper to impose. . . . The territory being a part of the United States, the government and the citizen both enter it under the authority of the Constitution, with their respective rights defined and marked out; and the federal government can exercise no power over his person or property beyond what that instrument confers, nor lawfully deny any right which it has reserved."

Hence, inasmuch as the Constitution has conferred on the Federal government no right to interfere with the property, domestic relations, police regulations, or internal polity of the people of the territories, it necessarily follows, under the authority of the Court, that Congress can rightfully exercise no such power over the people of the territories. For this reason alone, the Supreme Court were authorized and compelled to pronounce the eighth section of the act approved March 6, 1820 (commonly called the Missouri Compromise), inoperative and void—there being no power delegated to Congress in the Constitution authorizing Congress to prohibit slavery in the territories.

In the course of the discussion of this question the Court gave an elaborate exposition of the structure, principles, and powers of the Federal government; showing that it possesses no powers except those which are delegated, enumerated, and defined in the Constitution; and that all other powers are either *prohibited* altogether or are *reserved* to the states, or to the people. In order to show that the prohibited as well as the delegated powers are enumerated and defined in the Constitution, the Court enumerated certain powers which can not be exercised either by Congress or by the territorial Legislatures, or by any other authority whatever, for the simple reason that they are forbidden by the Constitution.

Some persons, who have not examined critically the opinion of the Court in this respect, have been induced to believe that the *slavery question* was included in this class of prohibited powers, and that the Court had decided in the Dread Scott case that the territorial Legislature could not legislate in respect to slave property the same as all other property in the territories. A few extracts from the opinin of the Court will correct this error, and show clearly the class of powers to which the Court referred, as being forbidden alike to the Federal government, to the states, and to the territories. The Court say :

"A reference to a few of the provisions of the Constitution will illustrate this proposition. For example, no one, we presume, will contend that Congress can make any law in a territory respecting the establishment of religion, or the free exercise thereof, or abridging the freedom of speech or of the press, or the right of the people of the territory peaceably to assemble, and to petition the government for the redress of grievances.

"Nor can Congress deny to the people the right to keep and bear arms, nor the right to trial by jury, nor compel any one to be a witness against himself in a criminal proceeding. . . . So, too, it will hardly be contended that Congress could by law quarter a soldier in a house in a territory without the consent of the owner in a time of peace; nor in time of war but in a manner prescribed by law. Nor could they by law forfeit the property of a citizen in a territory who was convicted of treason, for a longer period than the life of the person convicted, nor take private property for public use without just compensation.

"The powers over persons and property, of which we speak, are not only not granted to Congress, but are in express terms denied, and they are forbidden to exercise them. And this prohibition is not confined to the states, but the words are general, and extend to the whole territory over which the Constitution gives it power to legislate, including those portions of it remaining under territorial governments, as well as that covered by states.

"It is a total absence of power, everywhere within the dominion of the United States, and places the citizens of a territory, so far as these rights are concerned, on the same footing with citizens of the states, and guards them as firmly and plainly against any inroads which the general government might attempt, under the plea of implied or incidental powers. And if Congress itself can not do this—if it is beyond the powers conferred on the Federal government—it will be admitted, we presume, that it could not authorize a territorial government, established by its authority, to violate the provisions of the Constitution."

Nothing can be more certain than that the Court where here speaking only of *forbidden powers*, which were denied alike to Congress, to the state legislatures, and to the territorial legislatures, and that the prohibition extends "every where within the dominion of the United States," applicable equally to states and territories, as well as to the United States.

If this sweeping prohibition—this just but inexorable restriction upon the powers of government—federal, state, and territorial—shall ever be held to include the slavery question, thus negativing the right of the people of the states and territories, as well as the federal government, to control it by law (and it will be observed that in the opinion of the Court "the citizens of a territory, so far as these rights are concerned, are on the same footing with the citizens of the states"), then, indeed, will the doctrine become firmly established that the principles of law applicable to African slavery are *uniform throughout the dominion of the United States*, and that there "is an irrepressible conflict between opposing and enduring forces, which means that the United States must and will, sooner or later, become either entirely a slaveholding nation or entirely a free-labor nation."

Notwithstanding the disastrous consequences which would inevitably result from the authorative recognition and practical operation of such a doctrine, there are those who maintain that the Court referred to and included the slavery question within that class of forbidden powers which (although the same in the territories as in the states) could not be exercised by the people of the territories.

If this proposition were true, which fortunately for the peace and welfare of the whole country it is not, the conclusion would inevitably result, which they logically deduce from the premises—that the Constitution by the recognition of slavery establishes it in the territories beyond the power of the people to control it by law, and guarantees to every citizen the right to go there and be protected in the enjoyment of his slave property; and when all other remedies fail for the protection of such rights of property, it becomes the imperative duty of Congress (to the performance of which every member is bound by his conscience and his oath, and from which no consideration of political policy or expediency can release him) to provide by law such adequate and complete protection as is essential to the full enjoyment of an important right secured by the Constitution. If the proposition be true, that the Constitution establishes slavery in the territories beyond the power of the people legally to control it, another result, no less startling, and from which there is no escape, must inevitably follow. The Constitution is uniform "every where within the dominions of the United States"—is the same in Pennsylvania as in Kansas—and if it be true, as stated by the President in a special message to Congress, "that slavery exists in Kansas by virtue of the Constitution of the United States," and that "Kansas is therefore at this moment as much a slave state as Georgia or South Carolina," why does it not exist in Pennsylvania by virtue of the same Constitution?

If it be said that Pennsylvania is a Sovereign State, and therefore has a right to regulate the slavery question within her own limits to suit herself, it must be borne in mind that the sovereignty of Pennsylvania, like that of every other state, is limited by the Constitution, which provides that:

"This Constitution, and all laws of the United States which shall be made in pursuance thereof, and all treaties made, or which shall be made, under the authority of the United States, shall be the *supreme law of the land*, and the judges in every state shall be bound thereby, *any thing in the Constitution or laws of any state to the contrary notwithstanding*."

Hence, the State of Pennsylvania, with her Constitution and laws, and domestic institutions, and internal policy, is subordinate to the Constitution of the United States, in the same manner, and to the same extent, as the Territory of Kansas. The Kansas-Nebraska Act says that the Territory of Kansas shall exercise legislative power over, "all rightful subjects of legislation

consistent with the Constitution," and that the people of said territory shall
be left "perfectly free to form and regulate their domestic institutions in their
own way, subject only to the Constitution of the United States." The provisions of this act are believed to be in entire harmony with the Constitution,
and under them the people of Kansas possess every right, privilege, and immunity, in respect to their internal polity and domestic relations which the
people of Pennsylvania can exercise under their Constitution and laws. Each
is invested with full, complete, and exclusive powers in this respect, "subject
only to the Constitution of the United States."

The question recurs then, if the Constitution does establish slavery in Kansas or any other territory beyond the power of the people to control it by law,
how can the conclusion be resisted that slavery is established in like manner
and by the same authority in all the states of the Union? And if it be the
imperative duty of Congress to provide by law for the protection of slave
property in the territories upon the ground that "slavery exists in Kansas"
(and consequently in every other territory), "by virtue of the Constitution of
the United States," why is it not also the duty of Congress, for the same
reason, to provide similar protection to slave property in all the states of the
Union, when the Legislatures fail to furnish such protection?

Without confessing or attempting to avoid the inevitable consequences of
their own doctrine, its advocates endeavor to fortify their position by citing
the Dred Scott decision to prove that the Constitution recognizes property in
slaves—that there is no legal distinction between this and every other description of property—that slave property and every other kind of property
stand on an equal footing—that Congress has no more power over the one
than over the other—and, consequently, can not discriminate between them.
Upon this point the Court say:

"Now as we have already said in an earlier part of this opinion, upon a different point, the right of property in a slave is distinctly and expressly affirmed
in the Constitution. . . . And if the Constitution recognizes the right
of property of the master in a slave, and makes no distinction between that
description of property and other property owned by a citizen, no tribunal
acting under the authority of the United States, whether it be legislative,
executive, or judicial, has a right to draw such a distinction, or deny to it the
benefit of the provisions and guarantees which have been provided for the
protection of private property against the encroachments of the government.
. . . And the government in express terms is pledged to protect it in
all future time, *if the slave escapes from his owner.* This is done in plain
words—too plain to be misunderstood. And no word can be found in the
Constitution which gives Congress a *greater* power over slave property, or
which entitles property of that kind to *less* protection than property of any
other description. The only power conferred is the power coupled with the
duty of guarding and protecting the owner in his rights."

The rights of the owner which it is thus made the duty of the Federal government to guard and protect are those expressly provided for in the Constitution, and defined in clear and explicit language by the Court—that "the
government, in express terms, is pledged to protect it (slave property) in all
future time, *if the slave escapes from his owner.*" This is the only contingency,
according to the plain reading of the Constitution as authoritatively interpreted by the Supreme Court, in which the Federal government is authorized,
required, or permitted to interfere with slavery in the states or territories;
and in that case only for the purpose "of guarding and protecting the owner
in his rights" to reclaim his slave property. In all other respects slaves
stand on the same footing with all other property—"the Constitution makes
no distinction between that description of property and other property owned
by a citizen;" and "no word can be found in the Constitution which gives

Congress a greater power over slave property, or which entitles property of that kind to less protection than property of any other description." This is the basis upon which all rights pertaining to slave property, either in the states or the territories, stand under the Constitution as expounded by the Supreme Court in the Dred Scott case.

Inasmuch as the Constitution has delegated no power to the Federal government in respect to any other kind of property belonging to the citizen—neither introducing, establishing, prohibiting, nor excluding it any where within the dominion of the United States, but leaves the owner thereof perfectly free to remove into any state or territory and carry his property with him, and hold the same subject to the local law, and relying upon the local authorities for protection, it follows, according to the decision of the Court, that slave property stands on the same footing, is entitled to the same rights and immunities, and in like manner is dependent upon the local authorities and laws for protection.

The Court refer to that clause of the Constitution which provides for the rendition of fugitive slaves as their authority for saying that the "right of property in slaves is distinctly and expressly affirmed in the Constitution." By reference to that provision it will be seen that, while the word "slaves" is not used, still the Constitution not only recognizes the right of property in slaves, as stated by the Court, but explicitly states what class of persons shall be deemed slaves, and under what laws or authority they may be held to servitude, and under what circumstances fugitive slaves shall be restored to their owners, all in the same section, as follows:

"No person held to service or labor in one state, *under the laws thereof,* escaping into another, shall, in consequence of any law or regulation therein, be discharged from such service or labor, but shall be delivered up on claim of the party to whom such service or labor may be due."

Thus it will be seen that a slave, within the meaning of the Constitution, is a "person held to service or labor in one state, *under the laws thereof*"—not under the Constitution of the United States, nor by the laws thereof, nor by virtue of any Federal authority whatsoever, but under the laws of the particular state where such service or labor may be due.

It was necessary to give this exact definition of slavery in the Constitution in order to satisfy the people of the South as well as of the North. The slaveholding states would never consent for a moment that their domestic relations—and especially their right of property in their slaves—should be dependent upon Federal authority, or that Congress should have any power over the subject—either to extend, confine, or restrain it; much less to protect or regulate it—lest, under the pretense of protection and regulation, the Federal government, under the influence of the strong and increasing anti-slavery sentiment which prevailed at that period, might destroy the institution, and divest those rights of property in slaves which were sacred under the laws and Constitutions of their respective states so long as the Federal government had no power to interfere with the subject.

In like manner the non-slaveholding states, while they were entirely willing to provide for the surrender of all fugitive slaves—as is conclusively shown by the unanimous vote of all the states in the Convention for the provision now under consideration—and to leave each state perfectly free to hold slaves under its own laws, and by virtue of its own separate and exclusive authority, so long as it pleased, and to abolish it when it chose, were unwilling to become responsible for its existence by incorporating it into the Constitution as a national institution, to be protected and regulated, extended and controlled by Federal authority, regardless of the wishes of the people, and in defiance of the local laws of the several states and territories. For these opposite reasons the southern and northern states united in giving a unanimous vote in the Convention for that provision of the Constitution which recognizes slavery as a local institution in the several states where it exists, "under the laws thereof," and provides for the surrender of fugitive slaves.

It will be observed that the term "state" is used in this provision, as well as in various other parts of the Constitution, in the same sense in which it was used by Mr. Jefferson in his plan for establishing governments for the new states in the territory ceded and to be ceded to the United states, and by Mr. Madison in his proposition to confer on Congress power " to institute temporary governments for the *new states* arising in the unappropriated lands of the United States," to designate the political communities, territories as well as states, within the dominion of the United States. The word "states" is used in the same sense in the ordinance of the 13th July, 1787, for the government of the territory northwest of the River Ohio, which was passed by the remnant of the Congress of the Confederation, sitting in New York while its most eminent members were at Philadelphia, as delegates to the Federal Convention, aiding in the formation of the Constitution of the United States.

In this sense the word "states" is used in the clause providing for the rendition of fugitive slaves, applicable to all political communities under the authority of the United States, including the territories as well as the several states of the Union. Under any other construction the right of the owner to recover his slave would be restricted to the *states* of the Union, leaving the territories a secure place of refuge for all fugitives. The same remark is applicable to the clause of the Constitution which provides that "a person charged in any *state* with treason, felony, or other crime, who shall flee from justice, and be found in *another state*, shall, on the demand of the executive authority of the *state* from which he fled, be delivered up to be removed to the state having jurisdiction of the crime." Unless the term state, as used in these provisions of the Constitution, shall be construed to include every distinct political community under the jurisdiction of the United States, and to apply to territories as well as to the states of the Union, the territories must become a sanctuary for all the fugitives from service and justice, for all the felons and criminals who shall escape from the several *states* and seek refuge and immunity in the *territories.*

If any other illustration were necessary to show that the political communities which we now call territories (but which, during the whole period of the Confederation and the formation of the Constitution, were always referred to as "states" or "new states"), are recognized as "states" in *some* of the provisions of the Constitution, they may be found in those clauses which declare that " no *state*" shall enter into any "treaty, alliance, or confederation ; grant letters of marque and reprisal; coin money ; emit bills of credit; make any thing but gold and silver and coin a tender in payment of debts ; pass any bill of attainder, *ex post facto* law, or law impairing the obligation of contracts, or grant any title of nobility."

It must be borne in mind that in each of these cases where the power is not expressly delegated to Congress the prohibition is not imposed upon the Federal government, but upon the *states.* There was no necessity for any such prohibition upon Congress or the Federal government, for the reason that the omission to delegate any such powers in the Constitution was of itself a prohibition, and so declared in express terms by the tenth amendment, which declares that " the powers not delegated to the United States by the Constitution, nor prohibited by it to the states, are reserved to the states respectively, or to the people."

Hence it would certainly be competent for the states and territories to exercise these powers but for the prohibition contained in those provisions of the Constitution; and inasmuch as the prohibition only extends to the "states," the people of the "territories" are still at liberty to exercise them, unless the territories are included within the term *states*, within the meaning of these provisions of the Constitution of the United States.

It only remains to be shown that the Compromise measures of 1850 and the Kansas-Nebraska Act of 1854 are in perfect harmony with, and a faithful embodiment of the principles herein enforced. A brief history of these measures will disclose the principles upon which they are founded.

On the 29th of January, 1850, Mr. Clay introduced into the Senate a series of resolutions upon the slavery question which were intended to form the basis of the subsequent legislation upon that subject. Pending the discussion of these resolutions the chairman of the Committee on Territories prepared and reported to the Senate, on the 25th of March, two bills—one for the admission of California into the Union of states, and the other for the organization of the territories of Utah and New Mexico, and for the adjustment of the disputed boundary of the State of Texas, which were read twice and printed for the use of the Senate. On the 19th of April a select committee of thirteen was appointed, on motion of Mr. Foote, of Mississippi, of which Mr. Clay was made chairman, and to which were referred all pending propositions relating to the slavery question. On the 8th of May, Mr. Clay, from the select committee of thirteen, submitted to the Senate an elaborate report covering all the points in controversy, accompanied by a bill, which is usually known as the "Omnibus Bill." By reference to the provisions of of this bill, as it appears on the files of the Senate, it will be seen that it is composed of the two printed bills which had been reported by the Committee on Territories on the 25th of March previous; and that the only material change in its provisions, involving an important and essential principle, is to be found in the tenth section, which prescribes and defines the powers of the territorial Legislature. In the bill, as reported by the Committee on Territories, the legislative power of the territories extended to "rightful subjects of legislation consistent with the Constitution of the United States," *without excepting African slavery* ; while the bill, as reported by the committee of thirteen, conferred the same power on the territorial Legislature, *with the exception of African slavery.* This portion of the section in its original form read thus:

"*And be it further enacted* that the legislative power of the territory shall extend to all rightful subjects of legislation consistent with the Constitution of the United States and the provisions of this act; but no law shall be passed interfering with the primary disposition of the soil."

To which the committee of thirteen added these words: "*Nor in respect to African slavery.*" When the bill came up for action on the 15th of May, Mr. Davis, of Mississippi, said:

"I offer the following amendment. To strike out, in the sixth line of the tenth section, the words '*in respect to African slavery,*' and insert the words '*with those rights of property growing out of the institution of African slavery as its exists in any of the states of the Union.*' The object of the amendment is to prevent the territorial Legislature from legislating against the rights of property growing out of the institution of slavery. . . . . . It will leave to the territorial Legislatures those rights and powers which are essentially necessary, not only to the preservation of property, but to the peace of the territory. It will leave the right to make such police regulations as are necessary to prevent disorder, and which will be absolutely necessary with such property as that to secure its beneficial use to its owner. With this brief explanation I submit the amendment."

Mr. Clay, in reply to Mr. Davis, said:

"I am not perfectly sure that I comprehend the full meaning of the amendment offered by the senator from Mississippi. If I do, I think he accomplishes nothing by striking out the clause now in the bill and inserting that which he proposes to insert. The clause now in the bill is, that the territorial legislation shall not extend to any thing respecting African slavery within the territories. The effect of retaining the clause as reported by the committee will be this: That if in any of the territories slavery now exists, it shall not be abolished by the territorial Legislature; and if in any of the territories slavery does not now exist, it can not be introduced by the territorial Legislature. The clause itself was introduced into the bill by the committee for the purpose of tying up the hands of the territorial Legislature in respect to legislating at all, one way or the other, upon the subject of African slavery. It was intended to leave the legislation and the law of the respective territories in the condition in which the act will find them. I stated on a former occasion that I did not, in committee, vote for the amendment to insert the clause, though it was proposed to be introduced by a majority of the committee. I attached very little consequence to it at the time, and I attach very little to it at present. It is perhaps of no particular importance whatever. Now, sir, if I understand the measure proposed by the senator from Mississippi, it aims at the same thing. I do not understand him as proposing that if any one shall carry slaves into the territory—although by the laws of the territory he can not take them there—the legislative hands of the territorial government should be so tied as to prevent it saying he shall not enjoy the fruits of their labor. If the senator from Mississippi means to say that—"

Mr. Davis:

"I do mean to say it."

Mr. Clay:

"If the object of the senator is to provide that slaves may be introduced into the territory contrary to the *lex loci*, and, being introduced, nothing shall be done by the Legislature to impair the rights of owners to hold the slaves thus brought contrary to the local laws, *I certainly can not vote for it*. In doing so I shall repeat again the expression of opinion which I announced at an early period of the session."

Here we find the line distinctly drawn between those who contended for the right to carry slaves into the territories and hold them in defiance of the local law, and those who contended that such right was subject to the local law of the territory. During the progress of the discussion on the same day Mr. Davis, of Mississippi, said:

"We are giving, or proposing to give, a government to a territory, which act rests upon the basis of our right to make such provision. We suppose we have a right to confer power. If so, we may mark out the limit to which they may legislate, and are bound not to confer power beyond that which exists in Congress. If we give them power to legislate beyond that we commit a fraud or usurpation, as it may be done openly, covertly, or indirectly."

To which Mr. Clay replied:

"Now, sir, I only repeat what I have had occasion to say before, that while I am willing to stand aside and make no legislative enactment one way or the other—to lay off the territories without the Wilmot proviso, on the one hand, with which I understand we are threatened, or without an attempt to introduce a clause for the introduction of slavery into the territories. While I am for rejecting both the one and the other, I am content that the law as it exists shall prevail; and if there be any diversity of opinion as to what it means, I am willing that it shall be settled by the highest judicial authority of the country. While I am content thus to abide the result, I must say that I can not vote for any express provision recognizing the right to carry slaves there."

To which Mr. Davis rejoined, that—

"It is said our Revolution grew out of a preamble; and I hope we have something of the same character of the hardy men of the Revolution who first commenced the war with the mother country—something of the spirit of that bold Yankee who said he had a right to go to Concord, and that go he would; and who, in the maintenance of that right, met his death at the hands of a British sentinel. Now, sir, if our right to carry slaves into these territories be a constitutional right, it is our first duty to maintain it."

Pending the discussion which ensued, Mr. Davis, at the suggestion of a friends, modified his amendment from time to time, until it assumed the following shape:

"Nor to introduce nor exclude African slavery. Provided that nothing herein contained shall be construed so as to prevent the territorial Legislature from passing such laws as may be necessary for the protection of the rights of property of every kind which may have been, or may be hereafter, conformably to the Constitution of the United States, held in or introduced into said territory."

To which, on the same day, Mr. Chase, of Ohio, offered the following amendment:

"Provided further, That nothing herein contained shall be construed as authorizing or permitting the introduction of slavery or the holding of persons as property within said territory."

Upon these amendments—the one affirming the pro-slavery and the other the anti-slavery position, in opposition to the right of the people of the territories to decide the slavery question for themselves—Mr. Douglas said:

"The position that I have ever taken has been, that this, and all other questions relating to the domestic affairs and domestic policy of the territories, ought to be left to the decision of the people themselves; and that we ought to be content with whatever way they may decide the question, because they have a much deeper interest in these matters than we have, and know much better what institutions suit them than we, who have never been there, can decide for them. I would therefore have much preferred that that portion of the bill should have remained as it was reported from the Committee on Territories, with no provision on the subject of slavery, the one way or the other. And I do hope yet that that clause will be stricken out. I am satisfied, sir, that it gives no strength to the bill. I am satisfied, even if it did give strength to it, that it ought not to be there, *because it is a violation of principle*—a violation of that principle upon which we have all rested our defense of the course we have taken on this question. I do not see how those of us who have taken the position we have taken—that of *non-intervention*—and have argued in favor of the right of the people to legislate for themselves on this question, can support such a provision without abandoning all the arguments which we used in the presidential campaign in the year 1848, and the principles set forth by the honorable senator from Michigan (Mr. Cass), in that letter which is known as the 'Nicholson Letter.' We are required to abandon that platform; we are required to abandon those principles, and to stultify ourselves, and to adopt the opposite doctrine—and for what? In order to say that *the people of the territories shall not have such institutions as they shall deem adopted to their condition and their wants*. I do not see, sir, how such a provision can be acceptable either to the people of the North or the South."

Upon the question, how many inhabitants a territory should contain before it should be formed into a political community, with the rights of self-government, Mr. Douglas said:

"The senator from Mississippi puts the question to me as to what number of people there must be in a territory before this right to govern themselves accrues. Without determining the precise number, I will assume that the right ought to accrue to the people at the moment they have enough to constitute a government; and, sir, the bill assumes that there are people enough there to require a government, and enough to authorize the people to govern themselves. . . . . . Your bill concedes that a representative government is necessary—a government founded upon the principles of popular sovereignty and the right of a people to enact their own laws; and for this reason you give them a Legislature composed of two branches, like the Legislatures of the different states and territories of the Union. You confer upon them the right to legislate on 'all rightful subjects of legislation,' except negroes. Why except negroes? Why except African slavery? If the inhabitants are competent to govern themselves upon all other subjects, and in reference to all other descriptions of property—if they are competent to make laws and determine the relations between husband and wife, and parent and child, and municipal laws affecting the rights and property of citizens generally, they are competent also to make laws to govern themselves in relation to slavery and negroes."

With reference to the protection of property in slaves, Mr. Douglas said:

"I have a word to say to the honorable senator from Mississippi (Mr. Davis). He insists that I am not in favor of protecting property, and that his amendment is offered for the purpose of protecting property under the Constitution. Now, sir, I ask you what authority he has for assuming that? Do I not desire to protect property because I wish to allow the people to pass such laws as they deem proper respecting their rights to property without any exception? He might just as well say that I am opposed to protecting property in merchandise, in steamboats, in cattle, in real estate, as to say that I am opposed to protecting property of any other description; for I desire to put them all on an equality, and allow the people to make their own laws in respect to the whole of them."

Mr. Cass said (referring to the amendments offered by Mr. Davis and Mr. Chase):

"Now with respect to the amendments. I shall vote against them both; and then I shall vote in favor of striking out the restriction in the bill upon the power of the territorial governments. I shall do so upon this ground. I was opposed, as the honorable senator from Kentucky has declared he was, to the insertion of this prohibition by the committee. I consider it inexpedient and unconstitutional. I have already stated my belief that the rightful power of internal legislation in the territories belongs to the people."

After further discussion the vote was taken by yeas and nays on the amendment of Mr. Chase, and decided in the negative: yeas, 25; nays, 30. The question recurring on the amendment of Mr. Davis, of Mississippi, it was also rejected: yeas, 25; nays, 30. Whereupon Mr. Seward offered the following amendment:

"Neither slavery nor involuntary servitude, otherwise than by conviction for crime, shall ever be allowed in either of said Territories of Utah and New Mexico."

Which was rejected: yeas, 23; nays, 33.

After various other amendments had been offered and voted upon—all relating to the power of the territorial Legislature over slavery—Mr. Douglas moved to strike out all relating to African slavery, so that the territorial Legislature should have the same power over that question as over all other rightful subjects of legislation consistent with the Constitution—which amendment was rejected. After the rejection of this amendment, the discussion was renewed with great ability and depth of feeling in respect to the powers which the territorial Legislature should exercise upon the subject of slavery. Various propositions were made, and amendments offered and rejected—all relating to this one controverted point—when Mr. Norris, of New Hampshire, renewed the motion of Mr. Douglas, to strike out the restriction on the territorial Legislature in respect to African slavery. On the 31st of July this amendment was adopted by a vote of 32 to 19—restoring this section of the bill to the form in which it was reported from the Committee on Territories on the 25th of March, and conferring on the territorial Legislature power over "all rightful subjects of legislation consistent with the Constitution of the United States," *without excepting African slavery.*

Thus terminated this great struggle in the affirmance of the principle, as the basis of the compromise measures of 1850, so far as they related to the organization of the territories, *that the people of the territories should decide the slavery question for themselves through the action of their territorial Legislatures.*

This controverted question having been definitely settled, the Senate proceeded on the same day to consider the other portions of the bill, and after striking out all except those provisions which provided for the organization of the Territory of Utah, ordered the bill to be engrossed for a third reading, and on the next day—August 1, 1850—the bill was read a third time, and passed.

On the 14th of August the bill for the organization of the Territory of New Mexico was taken up, and amended so as to conform fully to the provisions of the Utah Act in respect to the power of the territorial Legislature over "all rightful subjects of legislation consistent with the Constitution," without excepting African slavery, and was ordered to be engrossed for a third reading without a division; and on the next day the bill was passed—yeas, 27; nays, 10.

These two bills were sent to the House of Representatives, and passed that body without any alteration in respect to the power of the territorial Legislatures over the subject of slavery, and were approved by President Filmore September 9, 1850.

In 1852, when the two great political parties—Whig and Democratic—into which the country was then divided, assembled in National Convention at Baltimore for the purpose of nominating candidates for the Presidency and Vice-Presidency, each convention adopted and affirmed the principles embodied in the compromise measures of 1850 as rules of action by which they would be governed in all future cases in the organization of territorial governments and the admission of new states.

On the 4th of January, 1854, the Committee on Territories of the Senate, to which had been referred a bill for the organization of the Territory of Nebraska, reported the bill back, with an amendment, in the form of a substitute for the entire bill, which, with some modifications, is now known on the statute book as the "Kansas-Nebraska Act," accompanied by a report explaining the principles upon which it was proposed to organize those territories, as follows:

"The principal amendments which your committee deem it their duty to commend to the favorable action of the Senate, in a special report, are those in which the principles established by the compromise measures of 1850, so far as they are applicable to territorial organizations, are proposed to be affirmed and carried into practical operation within the limits of the new territory. The wisdom of those measures is attested, not less by their salutary and beneficial effects in allaying sectional agitation and restoring peace and harmony to an irritated and distracted people, than by the cordial and almost universal approbation with which they have been received and sanctioned by the whole country.

"In the judgment of your committee, those measures were intended to have a far more comprehensive and enduring effect than the mere adjustment of the difficulties arising out of the recent acquisition of Mexican territory. They were designed to establish certain great principles, which would not only furnish adequate remedies for existing evils, but, in all time to come, avoid the perils of a similar agitation, by withdrawing the question of slavery from the halls of Congress and the political arena, and committing it to the arbitrament of those who were immediately interested in and alone responsible for its consequences. With a view of conforming their action to the settled policy of the government, sanctioned by the approving voice of the American people, your committee have deemed it their duty to incorporate and perpetuate, in their territorial bill, the principles and spirit of those measures."

After presenting and reviewing certain provisions of the bill, the committee conclude as follows:

"From these provisions it is apparent that the compromise measures of 1850 affirm and rest upon the following propositions:

"'First.—That all questions pertaining to slavery in the territories, and in the new states to be formed therefrom, are to be left to the decision of the people residing therein, by their appropriate representatives to be chosen by them for that purpose.

"'Second.—That all cases involving title to slaves and questions of personal freedom, are referred to the adjudication of the local tribunals, with the right of appeal to the Supreme Court of the United States.

"'Third.—That the provision of the Constitution of the United States in respect to fugitives from service, is to be carried into faithful execution in all the organized territories, the same as in the states. The substitute for the bill which your committee have prepared, and which is commended to the favorable action of the Senate, proposes to carry these propositions and principles into practical operation, in the precise language of the Compromise Measures of 1850.'"

By reference to that section of the "Kansas-Nebraska Act" as it now stands on the statute book, which described and defined the power of the territorial Legislature, it will be seen that it is "in the precise language of the Compromise Measures of 1850," extending the legislative power of the territory "to all rightful subjects of legislation consistent with the Constitution," without excepting African slavery.

It having been suggested, with some plausibility, during the discussion of the bill, that the act of Congress of March 6, 1820, prohibiting slavery north of the parallel of 36° 30' would deprive the people of the territory of the power of regulating the slavery question to suit themselves while they should remain in a territorial condition, and before they should have the requisite population to entitle them to admission into the Union as a state, an amendment was prepared by the chairman of the Committee, and incorporated into the bill to remove this obstacle to the free exercise of the principle of popular sovereignty in the territory, while it remained in a territorial condition, by repealing the said act of Congress, and declaring the true intent and meaning of all the friends of the bill in these words:

"That the Constitution and all laws of the United States which are not locally inapplicable, shall have the same force and effect within the territory as elsewhere within the United States, except the eighth section of the act preparatory to the admission of Missouri into the Union, approved March 6, 1820, which being inconsistent with the principle of non-intervention by Congress with slavery in the states and territories, as recognized by the legislation of 1850, commonly called the 'Compromise Measures,' is hereby declared inoperative and void—*it being the true intent and meaning of this act not to legislate slavery into any territory or state, nor to exclude it therefrom, but to leave the people thereof perfectly free to form and regulate their domestic institutions in their own way, subject only to the Constitution of the United States.*"

To which was added, on motion of Mr. Badger, the following:

"*Provided,* That nothing herein contained shall be construed to revive or put in force any law or regulation which may have existed prior to the act of the sixth of March, 1820, either protecting, establishing, or abolishing slavery."

In this form, and with this distinct understanding of its "true intent and meaning," the bill passed the two houses of Congress, and became the law of the land by the approval of the President, May 30, 1854.

In 1856, the Democratic party, assembled in National Convention at Cincinnati, declared by a unanimous vote of the delegates from every State in the Union, that

"The American Democracy recognize and adopt the principles contained in the organic laws establishing the territories of Kansas and Nebraska as embodying the only sound and safe solution of the 'slavery question,' upon which the great national idea of the people of this whole country can repose in its determined conservatism of the Union—non-interference by Congress with slavery in state and territory, or in the District of Columbia.

"That this was the basis of the Compromises of 1850, confirmed by both the Democratic and Whig parties in National Conventions—ratified by the people in the election of 1852—and rightly applied to the organization of the territories in 1854; That by the uniform application of this Democratic principle to the organization of territories and to the admission of new states, with or without domestic slavery as they may elect, the equal rights of all will be preserved intact—the original compacts of the Constitution maintained inviolate—and the perpetuity and expansion of this Union insured to its utmost capacity of embracing in peace and harmony any future American State that may be constituted or annexed with a Republican form of government."

In accepting the nomination of this Convention, Mr. Buchanan, in a letter dated June 16, 1856, said:

"The agitation on the question of domestic slavery has too long distracted and divided the people of this Union, and alienated their affections from each other. This agitation has assumed many forms since its commencement, but it now seems to be directed chiefly to the territories; and judging from its present character, I think we may safely anticipate that it is rapidly approaching a 'finality.' The recent legislation of Congress respecting domestic slavery, derived, as it has been, from the original and pure fountain of legitimate political power, the will of the majority, promises, ere long, to allay the dangerous excitement. This legislation is founded upon principles as ancient as free government itself, and in accordance with them has simply declared that the people of a territory, like those of a state, *shall decide for themselves whether slavery shall or shall not exist within their limits.*"

This exposition of the history of these measures shows conclusively that the authors of the Compromise Measures of 1850, and of the Kansas-Nebraska Act of 1854, as well as the members of the Continental Congress of 1774 and the founders of our system of government subsequent to the Revolution, regarded the people of the territories and colonies as political communities which were entitled to a free and exclusive power of legislation in their provincial legislatures, where their representation could alone be preserved, in all cases of taxation and internal polity. This right pertains to the people collectively as a law-abiding and peaceful community, and not to the isolated individuals who may wander upon the public domain in violation of law. It can only be exercised where there are inhabitants sufficient to constitute a government, and capable of performing its various functions and duties—a fact to be ascertained and determined by Congress. Whether the number shall be fixed at ten, fifteen, or twenty thousand inhabitants does not affect the principle.

The principle, under our political system, is *that every distinct political com-*

munity, loyal to the Constitution and the Union, is entitled to all the rights, privileges, and immunities of self-government in respect to their local concerns and internal polity, subject only to the Constitution of the United States.

THE CONTROVERSY WITH BLACK.

The appearance of this article in Harper's Magazine was rather a surprise to the enemies of popular right. The ability of its argument and the great force of its reasoning, carrying conviction to all candid minds, caused no little alarm. It was deemed necessary, on the part of those who professed doctrines which General Cass so emphatically declared were " far better suited to the meridian of Constantinople than to that of Washington," that there should be a reply. And with that blindness and blundering which seems to have marked every step and every movement of the Administration in the warfare upon popular sovereignty and its champion, instead of committing the office of replying to a competent or even well informed person, the task was intrusted to Attorney General Black. The country sustained a loss in this selection. Had the task of replying to Judge Douglas been assumed by a lawyer or statesman fitted by natural gifts or legal acquirements and political experience to discuss *principles* of government and their bearings and application towards the great point at issue, the literature—the political and legal literature of the country, would have been enriched by the productions on both sides, and the public would have been aided by the profound reasoning of the disputants in arriving at a correct conclusion. But Attorney General Black discussed the question not as a lawyer, not as a statesman, but after the style of a county court pettifogger arguing a case of slander. Had the discussion of this topic been conducted by Senator Davis, of Mississippi, instead of by Attorney General Black, the country would have had the views of a man thoroughly acquainted with the subject, well informed as a statesman, and one representing a people deeply interested in the matter ; and whose views would have been presented in a manner and in language becoming a dignified gentleman, a scholar, and a constitutional lawyer. Had it been conducted by Mr. Toucey, who once filled the office of attorney general with great distinction, the country would have had an argument not only embellished with dignity and learning, but possibly as clear and as convincing even as his beautiful and thrilling defence of the opposite doctrine delivered in the Senate in 1854 and in 1856.

It is related of an editor in one of the western cities who for a long time believed himself possessed of great powers of oratory, and who upon all occasions and at all times felt called upon to "respond for the press," that on one occasion, while standing in a crowd at a depot, when a lady complained to her attendant of the almost suffocating pressure they were experiencing, the editor, who had overheard only the first syllable of the word " pressure," immediately mounted a pile of trunks, and in behalf of the " press" gave utterance to his opinions. Judge Black seems to labor under a like impression, not only as to his capacity to discuss legal questions, but also as to the necessity for him, whenever a legal question is discussed, to enter into the debate, no matter where and by whom originated. With a recklessness that amounted almost to absurdity he rushed into print in reply to the Harper article of Judge Douglas. This reply appeared anonymously in the Washington *Union*, and was soon laughed at by the lawyers of the country. Subsequently the name of the author was given, and the reply, printed in pamphlet form, and franked by the attorney general, was distributed broad-cast over the country. Judge Douglas was then in Chicago. He had agreed, in reply to an invitation of the Democrats of Ohio, to deliver three speeches in that State. One of these was at Wooster. On his way to that place a copy of Black's reply was placed in his hands, and in his speech he discussed somewhat severely some of the personal passages of the document ; and made a remark that the author of that reply had, in 1858, written letters to Illinois urging reasons for the defeat of Douglas and, consequently, the election of Lincoln.

It is only just, as a matter of history, that it should be stated that shortly after the publication of this speech letters from a cabinet officer were received by persons in Illinois, requesting the return of the originals of certain political letters written by the same cabinet officer during the great contest between the Democracy and the allied Danites and Republicans.

The limits of this volume preclude the possibility of giving herein Judge Douglas' reply to Judge Black's pamphlet. It was a complete and thorough review and exposure of the mistakes and blunders of the attorney general. Judge Black, late in October, rejoined in a pamphlet, and Mr. Douglas was preparing an elaborate reply to that when he was stricken down with a painful and protracted disease. For weeks he hoped to be able to resume the work, but on November 16th, seeing no hope of being able to complete it within a reasonable period, he sent what had been written to the printer.

THE GWIN CONTROVERSY.

Sometime during the summer of 1859, Senator Gwin made a speech at Grass Valley, California, in which he told the Democrats there, that Judge Douglas had been removed from the chairmanship of the Committee on Territories because of the doctrines of his Freeport speech.

Copies of Mr. Gwin's speech, as published in the San Francisco *National*, were sent to Mr. Douglas. He at once replied to that speech in a letter to the editor of that paper. Mr Douglas again asserted that the views entertained by him and expressed in his Freeport speech were the same expressed by him during the entire period commencing with the compromise measures of 1850. He cited numerous authorities to show that *he* always was of that opinion, and also that the Nebraska bill was understood by others in the same light. After quoting from speeches of Secretaries Cass and Toucey he made the following quotation from a speech delivered by Hon. Mr. Cobb—Howell Cobb, now Secretary of the Treasury, at West Chester, Pennsylvania, on the 19th of September, 1856:

Fellow-citizens: There never has been, in all the history of this slavery matter, a more *purely theoretical issue* than the one involved in the question propounded to me by my friend, and I will show it to you. *I will state to you the positions of the advocates of this doctrine of non-intervention, on which there are different opinions held; but I will show you that it is the purest abstraction, in a practical point of view, that ever was proposed for political discussion.* There are those who hold that the Constitution carries all the institutions of this country into all the territories of the Union; that slavery, being one of the institutions recognized by the Constitution, goes with the Constitution into the territories of the United States; and that when the territorial government is organized the people have no right to prohibit slavery there, until they come to form a state Constitution. That is what my friend calls "southern doctrine." There is another class who hold that the people of the territories, in their territorial state, and whilst acting as a territorial Legislature, have a right to decide upon the question whether slavery shall exist there during their territorial state; and that has been dubbed "squatter sovereignty." Now, you perceive that there is but one point of difference between the advocates of the two doctrines. Each holds that the people have the right to decide the question in the territory; one holds that it can be done through the territorial Legislature, and whilst it has a territorial existence, the other holds that it can be done only when they come to form a state Constitution. BUT THOSE WHO HOLD THAT THE TERRITORIAL LEGISLATURE CANNOT PASS A LAW PROHIBITING SLAVERY, ADMIT THAT UNLESS THE TERRITORIAL LEGISLATURE PASS LAWS FOR ITS PROTECTION, SLAVERY WILL NOT GO THERE. THEREFORE, PRACTICALLY A MAJORITY OF THE PEOPLE REPRESENTED IN THE TERRITORIAL LEGISLATURE DECIDES THE QUESTION. WHETHER THEY DECIDE IT BY PROHIBITING IT, AC- CORDING TO THE ONE DOCTRINE, OR BY REFUSING TO PASS LAWS TO PROTECT IT, AS CONTENDED FOR BY THE OTHER PARTY, IS IMMATERIAL. THE MAJORITY OF THE PEOPLE BY THE ACTION OF THE TERRITORIAL LEGISLATURE WILL DECIDE THE QUESTION; AND ALL MUST ABIDE THE DECISION WHEN MADE. (Great applause.)

Commenting upon these quotations, Judge Douglas said :

Here we find the doctrines of the Freeport speech, including "non-action" and "unfriendly legislation" as a lawful and proper mode for the exclusion of slavery from a territory clearly defined by Mr. Cobb, and the election of Mr. Buchanan advocated on those identical doctrines. Mr. Cobb made similar speeches during the presidential canvass in other sections of Pennsylvania, in Maine, Indiana, and most of the northern states, and was appointed Secretary of the Treasury by Mr. Buchanan as a mark of gratitude for the efficient ser- vices which had been thus rendered. Will any senator who voted to remove me from the chairmanship of the Territorial Committee for expressing opinions for which Mr. Cobb, Mr. Toucey and General Cass were rewarded, pretend that he did not know that they or either of them had ever uttered such opin- ions when their nominations were before the Senate? I am sure that no sen- ator will make so humiliating a confession. Why, then, were those distin- guished gentlemen appointed by the President and confirmed by the Senate as cabinet ministers if they were not good Democrats—sound on the slavery question, and faithful exponents of the principles and creed of the party? Is it not a significant fact that the President and the most distinguished and honored of his cabinet should have been solemnly and irrevocably pledged to this monstrous heresy of "popular sovereignty," for asserting which the Sen- ate, by Mr. Gwin's frank avowal, condemned me to the extent of their power?

THE PLATFORM UNCHANGED.

In reply to an unworthy taunt by Judge Black in one of his letters, Mr. Douglas thus expressed his veneration for the Cin- cinnati platform.

While I could have no hesitation in voting for the nominee of my own party, with whom I might differ on certain points, in preference to the candi- date of the Black Republican party, whose whole creed is subversive of the Constitution and destructive of the Union, I am under no obligation to be- come a candidate upon a platform that I would not be willing to carry out in good faith, nor to accept the presidency on the implied pledge to carry into effect certain principles, and then administer the government in direct conflict with them. In other words, I prefer the position of senator, or even that of a private citizen, where I would be at liberty to defend and maintain the well- defined principles of the Democratic party, to accepting a presidential nomi- nation upon a platform incompatible with the principle of self-government in the territories, or the reserved rights of the states, or the perpetuity of the Union under the Constitution. In harmony with these views, I said in those very speeches in Ohio, to which Judge Black refers in his appendix, that I was in favor of conducting the great struggle of 1860 upon "the Cincinnati platform WITHOUT THE ADDITION OF A WORD OR THE SUBTRACTION OF A LETTER." Yet, in the face of all these facts, the attorney general does not hesitate to represent me as attempting to establish a new school of politics, to force new issues upon the party, and prescribe new tests of Democratic faith.

In conclusion, I have only to suggest to Judge Black and his confederates in this crusade, whether it would not be wiser for them, and more consistent with fidelity to the party which placed them in power, to exert their energies and direct all their efforts to the redemption of Pennsylvania from the thraldom of Black Republicanism than to continue their alliance with the Black Republicans in Illinois, with the vain hope of dividing and defeating the Democratic party in the only western or northern state which has never failed to cast her electoral vote for the regular nominee of the Democratic party at any Presidential election.

CHAPTER XXII.

THE INVASION OF STATES.

WHEN Congress assembled in December, 1859, the bloody history of the Harper's Ferry invasion was fresh in the minds of the people. That history was soon commented upon in the Senate, it formed a leading topic in the House of Representatives during the protracted struggle over the election of Speaker. As soon as both houses had organized, Mr. Douglas submitted a resolution having in view some practical legislation to prevent a recurrence of such an event. On that resolution a debate ensued, in which Mr. Douglas took a conspicuous part. We give his remarks entire, omitting all comment, as they are their own best commentaries.

On the 23d of January—the hour having arrived for the consideration of the special order—the Senate proceeded to consider the following resolution, submitted by Mr. Douglas on the 16th instant:

Resolved, That the Committee on the Judiciary be instructed to report a bill for the protection of each state and territory of the Union against invasion by the authorities or inhabitants of any other state or territory ; and for the suppression and punishment of conspiracies or combinations in any state or territory with intent to invade, assail, or molest the government, inhabitants, property, or institutions of any state or territory of the Union.

Mr. DOUGLAS. Mr. President, on the 25th of November last, the Governor of Virginia addressed an official communication to the President of the United States, in which he said:

"I have information from various quarters, upon which I rely, that a conspiracy of formidable extent, in means and numbers, is formed in Ohio, Pennsylvania, New York, and other states, to rescue John Brown and his associates, prisoners at Charleston, Virginia. The information is specific enough to be reliable.   *   *   *   *   *   *

"Places in Maryland, Ohio, and Pennsylvania, have been occupied as depots and rendezvous by these desperadoes, and unobstructed by guards or otherwise, to invade this state, and we are kept in continual apprehension of outrage from fire and rapine. I apprise you of these facts in order that you may take steps to preserve peace between the states."

To this communication, the President of the United States, on the 28th of November, returned a reply, from which I read the following sentence:

"I am at a loss to discover any provision in the Constitution or laws of the United States which would authorize me to 'take steps' for this purpose." [That is, to preserve the peace between the States.]

This announcement produced a profound impression upon the public mind and especially in the slaveholding states. It was generally received and regarded as an authorative announcement that the Constitution of the United States confers no power upon the federal government to protect each of the states of this Union against invasion from the other states. I shall not stop to inquire whether the President meant to declare that the existing laws confer no authority upon him, or that the Constitution empowers Congress to enact no laws which would authorize the Federal interposition to protect the states from invasion; my object is to raise the inquiry, and to ask the judgment of the Senate and of the House of Representatives on the question, whether it is not within the power of Congress, and the duty of Congress, under the Constitution, to enact all laws which may be necessary and proper for the protection of each and every state against invasion, either from foreign powers or from any portion of the United States.

The denial of the existence of such a power in the Federal government has induced an inquiry among conservative men—men loyal to the Constitution and devoted to the Union—as to what means they have of protection, if the Federal government is not authorized to protect them against external violence. It must be conceded that no community is safe, no state can enjoy peace, or prosperity, or domestic tranquility, without security against external violence. Every state and nation of the world, outside of this Republic, is supposed to maintain armies and navies for this precise purpose. It is the only legitimate purpose for which armies and navies are maintained in time of peace. They may be kept up for ambitious purposes, for the purposes of aggression and foreign war; but the legitimate purpose of a military force in time of peace is to insure domestic tranquility against violence or aggression from without. The states of this Union would possess that power, were it not for the restraints imposed upon them by the Federal Constitution. When that Constitution was made, the states surrendered to the Federal government the power to raise and support armies, and the power to provide and maintain navies, and not only thus surrendered the means of protection from invasion, but consented to a prohibition upon themselves which declares that no state shall keep troops or vessels of war in time of peace.

The question now recurs, whether the states of this Union are in that helpless condition, with their hands tied by the Constitution, stripped of all means of repelling assaults and maintaining their existence, without a guarantee from the federal government, to protect them against violence. If the people of this country shall settle down into the conviction that there is no power in the Federal government under the Constitution to protect each and every state from violence, from aggression, from invasion, they will demand that the cord be severed, and that the weapons be restored to their hands with which they may defend themselves. This inquiry involves the question of the perpetuity of the Union. The means of defence, the means of repelling assaults, the means of providing against invasion, must exist as a condition of the safety of the states and the existence of the Union.

Now, sir, I hope to be able to demonstrate that there is no wrong in this Union for which the Constitution of the United States has not provided a remedy. I believe, and I hope I shall be able to maintain, that a remedy is furnished for every wrong which can be perpetrated within the Union, if the Federal government performs its whole duty. I think it is clear, on a careful examination of the Constitution, that the power is conferred upon Congress, first, to provide for repelling invasion from foreign countries; and, secondly, to protect each state of this Union against invasion from any other state, territory, or place, within the jurisdiction of the United States. I will first turn your attention, sir, to the power conferred upon Congress to protect the United States—including states, territories, and the District of Columbia; including every inch of ground within our limits and jurisdiction—against foreign invasion. In the eighth section of the first article of the Constitution, you find that Congress has power—

"To raise and support armies; to provide and maintain a navy; to make rules for the government and regulation of the land and naval forces; to provide for calling forth the militia to execute the laws of the Union, suppress insurrections, and repel invasions."

These various clauses confer upon Congress power to use the whole military force of the country for the purpose specified in the Constitution. They shall provide for the execution of the laws of the Union; and, secondly, suppress insurrections. The insurrections there referred to are insurrections against the authority of the United States—insurrections against a state authority being provided for in a subsequent action, in which the United States can not interfere, except upon the application of the state authorities. The invasion which is to be repelled by this clause of the Constitution is an invasion of the United States. The language is, Congress shall have power to "repel invasions." That gives the authority to repel the invasion, no matter whether the enemy shall land within the limits of Virginia, within the District of Columbia, within the Territory of New Mexico, or anywhere else within the jurisdiction of the United States. The power to protect every portion of the country against invasion from foreign nations having thus been specifically conferred, the framers of the Constitution then proceeded to make guarantees for the protection of *each of the states* by Federal authority. I will read the fourth section of the fourth article of the Constitution:

"The United States shall guaranty to every state in this Union a Republican form of government, and shall protect each of them against invasion; and, on application of the Legislature, or of the Executive, (when the Legislature can not be convened), against domestic violence."

This clause contains three distinct guarantees: first, the United States shall guaranty to every state in this Union a Republican form of government; second, the United States shall protect each of them against invasion; third, the United States shall, on application of the Legislature, or of the Executive, when the Legislature can not be convened, protect them against domestic violence. Now, sir, I submit to you whether it is not clear, from the very language of the Constitution, that this clause was inserted for the purpose of making it the duty of the Federal government to protect each of the states against invasion from any other state, territory, or place within the jurisdiction of the United States? For what other purpose was the clause inserted? The power and duty of protection as against foreign nations had already been provided for. This clause occurs among the guarantees from the United States to each state, for the benefit of each state, for the protection of each state, and necessarily from other states, inasmuch as the guarantee had been given previously as against foreign nations.

If any further authority is necessary to show that such is the true construction of the Constitution, it may be found in the forty-third number of the *Federalist*, written by James Madison. Mr. Madison quotes the clause of the Constitution which I have read, giving these three guarantees; and, after discussing the one guarantying to each state a Republican form of government, proceeds to consider the second, which makes it the duty of the United States to protect each of the states against invasion. Here is what Mr. Madison says upon that subject:

"A protection against invasion is due *from every society to the parts composing it.* The latitude of the expression here used seems to secure each state, not only against foreign hostility, but against ambitious or vindictive enterprises of its more powerful neighbors. The history both of ancient and modern confederacies proves that the weaker members of the Union ought not to be insensible to the policy of this article."

The number of the *Federalist*, like all the others of that celebrated work, was written after the Constitution was made, and before it was ratified by the states, and with a view to securing its ratification; hence the people of the several states, when they ratified this instrument, knew that this clause was intended to bear the construction which I now place upon it. It was intended to make it the duty of every society to protect each of its parts; the duty of the Federal government to protect each of the states; and, he says, the smaller states ought not to be insensible to the policy of this article of the Constitution.

Then, sir, if it be made the imperative duty of the Federal government, by the express provision of the Constitution, to protect each of the states against invasion or violence from the other states, or from combinations of desperadoes within their limits, it necessarily follows that it is the duty of Congress to pass all laws necessary and proper to render that guarantee effectual. While Congress, in the early history of the government, did provide legislation, which is supposed to be ample to protect the United States against invasion from foreign countries and the Indian tribes they have failed, up to this time, to make any law for the protection of each of the states against invasion from within the limits of the Union. I am unable to account for this omission; but I presume the reason is to be found in the fact that no Congress ever dreamed that such legislation would ever become necessary for the protection of one state of this Union against invasion and violence from her sister states. Who, until the Harper's Ferry outrage, ever conceived that American citizens could be so forgetful of their duties to themselves, to the country, to the Constitution, as to plan an invasion of another state, with the view of inciting servile insurrection, murder, treason, and every other crime that disgraces humanity? While, therefore, no blame can justly be attached to our predecessors in failing to provide the legislation necessary to render this guarantee of the Constitution effectual; still, since the experience of last year, we cannot stand justified in omitting longer to perform this imperative duty.

The question then remaining is, what legislation is necessary and proper to render this guarantee of the Constitution effectual? I presume there will be very little difference of opinion that it will be necessary to place the whole military power of the government at the disposal of the President, under proper guards and restrictions against abuse, to repel and suppress invasion when the hostile force shall be actually in the field. But, sir, this is not sufficient. Such a legislation would not be a full compliance with this guarantee of the Constitution. The framers of that instrument meant more when they gave the guarantee. Mark the difference in language between the provision for protecting the United States against invasion and that for protecting the states. When it provided for protecting the United States it said Congress shall have power to "*repel* invasion." When it came to make this guarantee to the states it changed the language, and said the United States shall "*protect*" each of the states against invasion. In the one instance the duty of the government is to repel, in the other the guarantee is that they will protect. In other words, the United States are not permitted to wait until the enemy shall be upon your borders; until the invading army shall have been organized and drilled, and placed in march with a view to the invasion; but they must

Y

pass all laws necessary and proper to insure protection and domestic tranquility to each state and territory of this Union against invasion or hostility from other states and territories.

Then, sir, I hold that it is not only necessary to use the military power when the actual case of invasion shall occur, but to authorize the judicial department of the government to suppress all conspiracies and combinations in the several states with intent to invade a state or molest or disturb its government, its peace, its citizens, its property, or its institutions. You must punish the conspiracy, the combination with intent to do the act, and then you will suppress it in advance. There is no principle more familiar to the legal profession than that wherever it is proper to declare an act to be a crime, it is proper to punish a conspiracy or combination with intent to perpetrate the act. Look upon your statute books, and I presume you will find an enactment to punish the counterfeiting of the coin of the United States; and then another section to punish a man for having counterfeit coin in his possession *with intent* to pass it; and another section to punish him for having the molds, or dies, or instruments for counterfeiting, *with intent* to use them. This is a familiar principle in legislative and judicial proceedings. If the act of invasion is criminal, the conspiracy to invade should also be made criminal. If it be unlawful and illegal to invade a state, and run off fugitive slaves, why not make it unlawful to form conspiracies and combinations in the several states with intent to do the act? We have been told that a notorious man who has recently suffered death for his crimes upon the gallows, boasted in Cleveland, Ohio, in a public lecture, a year ago, that he had then a body of men employed in running away horses from the slaveholders of Missouri, and pointed to a livery stable in Cleveland which was full of the stolen horses at that time.

I think it is within our competency, and consequently our duty, to pass a law making every conspiracy or combination in any state or territory of this Union to invade another with intent to steal or run away property of any kind, whether it be negroes, horses, or property of any other description, into another state, a crime, and punish the conspirators by indictment in the United States courts, and confinement in the prisons or penitentiaries of the state or territory where the conspiracy may be formed and quelled. Sir, I would carry these provisions of law as far as our constitutional power will reach. I would make it a crime to form conspiracies with a view of invading states or territories to control elections, whether they be under the garb of Emigrant Aid Societies of New England, or Blue Lodges of Missouri. (Applause in the galleries.) In other words, this provision of the Constitution means more than the mere repelling of an invasion when the invading army shall reach the border of a state. The language is, it shall protect the state against invasion; the meaning of which is, to use the language of the preamble to the Constitution, to insure to each state domestic tranquility against external violence. There can be no peace, there can be no prosperity, there can be no safety in any community, unless it is secured against violence from abroad. Why sir, it has been a question seriously mooted in Europe, whether it was not the duty of England, a power foreign to France, to pass laws to punish conspiracies in England against the lives of the princes of France. I shall not argue the question of comity between foreign states. I predicate my argument upon the Constitution by which we are governed, and which we have sworn to obey, and demand that the Constitution be executed in good faith so as to punish and suppress every combination, every conspiracy, either to invade a state, or to molest its inhabitants, or to disturb its property, or to subvert its institutions and its government. I believe this can be effectually done by authorizing the United States courts in the several states to take jurisdiction of the offence, and punish the violation of the law with appropriate punishments.

It cannot be said that the time has not yet arrived for such legislation. It cannot be said with truth that the Harper's Ferry case will not be repeated, or is not in danger of repetition. It is only necessary to inquire into the causes which produced the Harper's Ferry outrage, and ascertain whether those causes are yet in active operation, and then you can determine whether there is any ground for apprehension that that invasion will be repeated. Sir, what were the causes which produced the Harper's Ferry outrage? Without stopping to adduce evidence in detail, I have no hesitation in expressing my firm and deliberate conviction that the Harper's Ferry crime was the natural, logical, inevitable result of the doctrines and teachings of the Republican party, as explained and enforced in their platform, their partisan presses, their pamphlets and books, and especially in the speeches of their leaders in and out of Congress. (Applause in the galleries.)

Mr. Mason. I trust the order of the Senate will be preserved. I am sure it is only necessary to suggest to the presiding officer the indispensable necessity of preserving the order of the Senate; and I give notice that, if it is disturbed again, I shall insist upon the galleries being cleared entirely.

Mr. Douglas. Mr. President——

The Vice-President. The Senator will pause for a single moment. It is impossible for the chair to preserve order without the concurrence of the vast assembly in the galleries. He trusts that there will be no occasion to make a reference to this subject again.

Mr. Toombs. I hope that the presiding officer will place officers in the galleries, and put a stop to this thing. It is a very bad sign of the times. It is unbecoming this body, or the deliberations of any free people.

The Vice-President. The presiding officer has not the force at his command to place officers in the gallery.

Mr. Douglas. If the Senate will pardon me for a digression an instant, I was about to suggest to the presiding officer that I thought it would be necessary to place officers in different parts of the gallery, with instructions that if they saw any person giving any signs of approbation or disapprobation calculated to disturb our proceedings, they should instantly put the guilty person out of the gallery.

The Vice-President. That has been done.

Mr. Douglas. I was remarking that I considered this outrage at Harper's Ferry as the logical, natural consequence of the teachings and doctrines of the Republican party. I am not making this statement for the purpose of crimination or partisan effect. I desire to call the attention of members of that party to a reconsideration of the doctrines that they are in the habit of enforcing, with a view to a fair judgment whether they do not lead directly to those consequences, on the part of those deluded persons who think that all they say is meant, in real earnest, and ought to be carried out. The great principle that underlies the Republican party is violent, irreconcilable, eternal warfare upon the institution of American slavery, with the view of its ultimate extinction throughout the land; sectional war is to be waged until the cotton field of the south shall be cultivated by free labor, or the rye fields of New York and Massachusetts shall be cultivated by slave labor. In furtherance of this article of their creed, you find their political organization not only sectional in its location, but one whose vitality consists in appeals to northern passion, northern prejudice, northern ambition against southern states, southern institutions, and southern people. I have had some experience in fighting this element within the last few years, and I find that the source of their power consists in exciting the prejudices and the passions of the northern section against those of the southern section. They not only attempt to excite the North against the South, but they invite the South to assail and abuse and traduce the North. Southern abuse, by violent men, of northern statesmen and northern people, is essential to the triumph of the Republican cause. Hence the course of argument which we have to meet is not only repelling the appeals to northern passion and prejudice, but we have to encounter their appeals to southern men to assail us, in order that they may justify their assaults upon the plea of self-defence.

Sir, when I returned home in 1858, for the purpose of canvassing Illinois, with a view to a re-election, I had to meet this issue of the "irrepressible conflict." It is true that the Senator from New York had not then made his Rochester speech, and did not for four months afterwards. It is true that he had not given the doctrine that precise name and form; but the principle was in existence, and had been proclaimed by the ablest and the most clear-headed men of the party. I will call your attention, sir, to a single passage from a speech, to show the language in which this doctrine was stated in Illinois before it received the name of the "irrepressible conflict." The Republican party assembled in state convention in June 1858, in Illinois, and unanimously adopted Abraham Lincoln as their candidate for United States senator. Mr. Lincoln appeared before the convention, accepted the nomination, and made a speech—which had been previously written and agreed to in caucus by most of the leaders of the party. I will read a single extract from that speech:

"In my opinion, it [the slavery agitation] will not cease until a crisis shall have been reached and passed. 'A house divided against itself can not stand.' I believe this government can not endure permanently, half slave and half free. I do not expect the house to fall, but I do expect it will cease to be divided. It will become all one thing or all the other. Either the opponents of slavery will arrest the further spread of it, and place it where the public mind shall rest in the belief that it is in the course of ultimate extinction; or its advocates will push forward till it shall become alike lawful in all the states—old as well as new, North as well as South."

Sir, the moment I landed upon the soil of Illinois, at a vast gathering of many thousands of my constituents to welcome me home, I read that passage, and took direct issue with the doctrine contained in it as being revolutionary and treasonable, and inconsistent with the perpetuity of this republic. That is not merely the individual opinion of Mr. Lincoln; nor is it the individual opinion merely of the senator from New York, who four months afterward asserted the same doctrine in different language; but, so far as I know, it is the general opinion of the members of the Abolition or Republican party. They tell the people of the North that unless they rally as one man, under a sectional banner, and make war upon the South with a view to the ultimate extinction of slavery, slavery will overrun the whole North and fasten itself upon all the free states. They then tell the South, unless you rally as one man, binding the whole southern people into a sectional party, and establish slavery all over the free states, the inevitable consequence will be that we shall abolish it in the slaveholding states. The same doctrine is held by the senator from New York in his Rochester speech. He tells us that the states must all become free, or all become slave; that the South, in other words, must conquer and subdue the North, or the North must triumph over the South, and drive slavery from within its limits.

Mr. President, in order to show that I have not misinterpreted the position of the senator from New York, in notifying the South that, if they wish to maintain slavery within their limits, they must also fasten it upon the northern states, I will read an extract from his Rochester speech:

"It is an irrepressible conflict between opposing and enduring forces; and it means that the United States must and will, sooner or later, become either entirely a slaveholding nation, or entirely a free-labor nation. Either the cotton and rice fields of South Carolina, and the sugar plantations of

Louisiana, will ultimately be tilled by free labor, and Charleston and New Orleans become marts for legitimate merchandise alone, or else the rye fields and wheat fields of Massachusetts and New York must again be surrendered by their farmers to slave culture and to the production of slaves, and Boston and New York become once more markets for trade in the bodies and souls of men."

Thus, sir, you perceive that the theory of the Republican party is, that there is a conflict between two different systems of institutions in the respective classes of states—not a conflict in the same states, but an irrepressible conflict between the free states and the slave states; and they argue that these two systems of state can not permanently exist in the same Union; that the sectional warfare must continue to rage and increase with increasing fury until the free states shall surrender, or the slave states shall be subdued. Hence, while they appeal to the passions of our own section, their object is to alarm the people of the other section, and drive them to madness, with the hope that they will invade our rights as an excuse for some of our people to carry on aggressions upon their rights. I appeal to the candor of senators, whether this is not a fair exposition of the tendency of the doctrines proclaimed by the Republican party. The creed of that party is founded upon the theory that, because slavery is not desirable in our states, it is not desirable anywhere; because free labor is a good thing with us, it must be the best thing everywhere. In other words, the creed of their party rests upon the theory that there must be *uniformity* in the domestic institutions and internal polity of the several states of this Union. There, in my opinion, is the fundamental error upon which their whole system rests. In the Illinois canvass, I asserted, and now repeat, that uniformity in the domestic institutions of the different states is neither possible nor desirable. That is the very issue upon which I conducted the canvass at home, and it is the question which I desire to put to the Senate. I repeat, that uniformity in domestic institutions of the different states is neither possible nor desirable.

Was such the doctrine of the framers of the Constitution? I wish the country to bear in mind that when the Constitution was adopted the Union consisted of thirteen states, twelve of which were slaveholding states, and one a free state. Suppose this doctrine of uniformity on the slavery question had prevailed in the Federal Convention, do the gentlemen on that side of the house think that freedom would have triumphed over slavery? Do they imagine that the one free state would have outvoted the twelve slaveholding states, and thus have abolished slavery throughout the land by a constitutional provision? On the contrary, if the test had then been made, if this doctrine of uniformity on the slavery question had then been proclaimed and believed in, with the twelve slaveholding states against one free state, would it not have resulted in a constitutional provision fastening slavery irrevocably upon every inch of American soil, North as well as South? Was it quite fair in those days for the friends of free institutions to claim that the Federal government must not touch the question, but must leave the people of each state to do as they pleased, until under the operation of that principle they secured the majority, and then wield that majority to abolish slavery in the other states of the Union?

Sir, if uniformity in respect to domestic institutions had been deemed desirable when the Constitution was adopted, there was another mode by which it could have been obtained. The natural mode of obtaining uniformity was to have blotted out the state governments, to have abolished the state Legislatures, to have conferred upon Congress legislative power over the municipal and domestic concerns of the people of all the states, as well as upon Federal questions affecting the whole Union; and if this doctrine of uniformity had been entertained and favored by the framers of the Constitution, such would have been the result. But, sir, the framers of that instrument knew at that day, as well as we now know, that in a country as broad as this, with so great a variety of climate, of soil, and of production, there must necessarily be a corresponding diversity of institutions and domestic regulations, adapted to the wants and necessities of each locality. The framers of the Constitution knew that the laws and institutions which were well adapted to the mountains and valleys of New England, were ill-suited to the rice plantations and the cotton-fields of the Carolinas. They knew that our liberties depended upon reserving the right to the people of each state to make their own laws and establish their own institutions, and control them at pleasure, without interference from the Federal government, or from any other state or territory, or any foreign country. The Constitution, therefore, was based, and the Union was founded, on the principle of dissimilarity in the domestic institutions and internal polity of the several states. The Union was founded on the theory that each state had peculiar interests, requiring peculiar legislation, and peculiar institutions, different and distinct from every other state. The Union rests on the theory that no two states would be precisely alike in their domestic policy and institutions.

Hence, I assert that this doctrine of uniformity in the domestic institutions of the different states is repugnant to the Constitution, subversive of the principles upon which the Union was based, revolutionary in its character, and leading directly to despotism if it is ever established. Uniformity in local and domestic affairs in a country of great extent is despotism always. Show me centralism prescribing uniformity from the capital to all of its provinces in their local and domestic concerns, and I will show you a despotism as odious and as insufferable as that of Austria or of Naples. Dissimilarity is the principle upon which the Union rests. It is founded upon the idea that each state must necessarily require different regulations; that no two states have precisely the same interests, and hence do not need precisely the same laws; and you cannot account for this confederation of states upon any other principle.

Then, sir, what becomes of this doctrine that slavery must be established in all the states or prohibited in all the states? If we only conform to the principles upon which the Federal Union was formed, there can be no conflict. It is only necessary to recognize the right of the people of every state to have just such institutions as they please, without consulting your wishes, your views, or your prejudices, and there can be no conflict.

And, sir, inasmuch as the Constitution of the United States confers upon Congress the power coupled with the duty of protecting each state against external aggression, and inasmuch as that includes the power of suppressing and punishing conspiracies in one state against the institutions, property, people, or government of every other state, I desire to carry out that power vigorously. Sir, give us such a law as the Constitution contemplates and authorizes, and I will show the senator from New York that there is a constitutional mode of repressing the "irrepressible conflict." I will open the prison door to allow conspirators against the peace of the Republic and the domestic tranquility of our states to select their cells wherein to drag out a miserable life, as a punishment for their crimes against the peace of society.

Can any man say to us that although this outrage has been perpetrated at Harper's Ferry, there is no danger of its recurrence? Sir, is not the Republican party still embodied, organized, confident of success, and defiant in its pretensions? Does it not now hold and proclaim the same creed that it did before this invasion? It is true that most of its representatatives here disavow the *acts* of John Brown at Harper's Ferry. I am glad that they do so; I am rejoiced that they have gone thus far; but I must be permitted to say to them that it is not sufficient that they disavow the act, unless they also repudiate and denounce the doctrines and teachings which produced the act. Those doctrines remain the same; those teachings are being poured into the minds of men throughout the country by means of speeches and pamphlets and books and through partisan presses. The causes that produced the Harper's Ferry invasion are now in active operation. It is true that the people of all the border states are required by the Constitution to have their hands tied, without the power of self-defence, and remain patient under a threatened invasion in the day or in the night? Can you expect people to be patient, when they dare not lie down to sleep at night without first stationing sentinels around their houses to see if a band of marauders and murderers are not approaching with torch and pistol? Sir, it requires more patience than freemen ever should cultivate, to submit to constant annoyance, irritation and apprehension. If we expect to preserve this Union, we must remedy, within the Union and in obedience to the Constitution, every evil for which disunion would furnish a remedy. If the Federal government fails to act, either from choice or from an apprehension of the want of power, it can not be expected that the states will be content to remain unprotected.

Then, sir, I see no hope of peace, of fraternity, of good feeling, between the different portions of the United States, except by bringing to bear the power of the federal government to the extent authorized by the Constitution —to protect the people of all the states against any external violence or aggression. I repeat, that if the theory of the Constitution shall be carried out by conceding the right of the people of every state to have just such institutions as they choose, there cannot be a conflict, much less an "irrepressible conflict," between the free and the slaveholding states.

Mr. President, the mode of preserving peace is plain. This system of sectional warfare must cease. The Constitution has given the power, and all we ask of Congress is to give the means, and we, by indictments and convictions in the Federal courts of our several states, will make such examples of the leaders of these conspiracies as will strike terror into the hearts of the others, and there will be an end of this crusade. Sir, you must check it by crushing out the conspiracy, the combination, and then there can be safety. Then we shall be able to restore that spirit of fraternity which inspired our revolutionary fathers upon every battle-field; which presided over the deliberations of the convention that framed the Constitution, and filled the hearts of the people who ratified it. Then we shall be able to demonstrate to you that there is no evil unredressed in the Union for which disunion would furnish a remedy. Then, sir, let us execute the Constitution in the spirit in which it was made. Let Congress pass all the laws necessary and proper to give full and complete effect to every guarantee of the Constitution. Let them authorize the punishment of conspiracies and combinations in any state or territory against the property, institutions, people or government of any other state or territory, and there will be no excuse, no desire, for disunion. Then, sir, let us leave the people of every state perfectly free to form and regulate their domestic institutions in their own way. Let each of them retain slavery just as long as it pleases, and abolish it when it chooses. Let us act upon that good old golden principle which teaches all men to mind their own business and let their neighbors alone. Let this be done and this Union can endure forever as our fathers made it, composed of free and slave states, just as the people of each state may determine for themselves.

REPLY TO FESSENDEN.

Mr. Fessenden having replied at some length to Mr. Douglas, he made the following rejoinder:

Mr. Douglas. Mr. President, I shall not follow the senator from Maine through his entire speech, but simply notice such points as demand of me some reply. He does not know why I introduced my resolution; he cannot conceive any good motive for it; he thinks there must be some other motive besides the one that has been avowed. There are some men, I know, who cannot conceive that a man can be governed by a patriotic or proper motive; but it is not among that class of men that I look for those who are governed by motives of propriety. I have no impeachment to make of his motives. I brought in this resolution because I thought the time had arrived when we should have a measure of practical legislation. I had seen expressions of opinion against the power from authorities so high that I felt it my duty to bring it to the attention of the Senate. I had heard that the senator from Virginia had intimated some doubt on the question of power, as well as of policy. Other senators discussed the question here for weeks when I was confined to my sick bed. Was there any thing unreasonable in my coming before the Senate at this time, expressing my own opinion and confining myself to the practical legislation indicated in the resolution? Nor, sir, have I in my remarks gone outside of the legitimate argument pertaining to the necessity for this legislation. I first showed that there had been a great outrage; I showed what I believed to be the causes that had produced the outrage, and that the causes which produced it were still in operation; and argued that, so long as the party to which the gentlemen belong remains embodied in full force, those causes will still threaten the country. That was all.

The senator from Maine thinks he will vote for the bill that will be proposed to carry out the objects referred to in my resolution. Sir, whenever that senator and his associates on the other side of the chamber will record their votes for a bill of the character described in my resolution and speech, I shall congratulate the country upon the progress they are making towards sound principles. Whenever he and his associates will make it a felony for two or more men to conspire to run off fugitive slaves, and punish the conspirators by confinement in the penitentiary, I shall consider that wonderful changes have taken place in this country. I tell the senator that it is the general tone of sentiment in all those sections of the country where the Republican party predominate, so far as I know, not only not to deem it a crime to rescue a fugitive slave, but to raise mobs to aid in the rescue. He talks about slandering the Republican party when we intimate that they are making a warfare upon the rights guarantied by the Constitution. Sir, where, in the towns and cities with Republican majorities, can you execute the fugitive slave law? Is it in the town where the senator from New York resides? Do you not remember the Jerry rescuers? Is it at Oberlin, where the mob was raised that made the rescue last year and produced the riot?

Mr. Fessenden. I stated, and I believe it was all I said on that matter, that I was disposed to agree with the senator in his views as to the question of power; and that, with my views, I should go very far—far enough to accomplish the purpose—to prevent the forming of conspiracies in one state to attack another. I did not understand the senator to say any thing about conspiracies to run away with slaves; nor did I understand him to say any thing about the fugitive slave law. How I should act in reference to that matter I do not know; I will meet it when it comes; but I ask the senator whether that was a part of his first speech, or whether it is a part of his reply?

Mr. Douglas. The senator will find it several times repeated in my first speech, and the question asked: Why not make it a crime to form conspiracies and combinations to run off fugitive slaves, as well as to run off horses, or any other property? I am talking about conspiracies which are so common in all our northern states, to invade and enter, through their agents, the slave states, and seduce away slaves and run them off by the underground railroad, in order to send them to Canada. It is these conspiracies to perpetrate crime with impunity that keep up the irritation. John Brown could boast, in a public house in Cleveland, that he and his band had been engaged all the winter in stealing horses and running them off from the slaveholders in Missouri, and that the livery stables were then filled with stolen horses, and yet the conspiracy to do it could not be punished.

Sir, I desire a law that will make it a crime, punishable by imprisonment in the penitentiary, after conviction in the United States court, to make a conspiracy in one state, against the people, property, government, or institutions, of another. Then we shall get at the root of the evil. I have no doubt that gentlemen on the other side will vote for a law which pretends to comply with the guarantees of the Constitution, without carrying any force or efficiency in its provisions. I have heard men abuse the fugitive slave law, and express their willingness to vote for amendments: but when you come to the amendments which they desired to adopt, you found they were such as would never return a fugitive to his master. They would go for any fugitive slave law that had a hole in it big enough to let the negro drop through and escape; but none that would comply with the obligations of the Constitution. So we shall find that side of the chamber voting for a law that will, in terms, disapprove of unlawful expeditions against neighboring states, without being efficient in affording protection.

But the senator says it is a part of the policy of the northern Democracy to represent the Republicans as being hostile to southern institutions. Sir, it is a part of the policy of the northern Democracy, as well as their duty, to speak the truth on that subject. I did not suppose that any man would have the audacity to arraign a brother senator here for representing the Republican party as dealing in denunciation and insult of the institutions of the South. Look to your Philadelphia platform, where you assert the sovereign power of Congress over the territories for their government, and demand that it shall be exerted against those twin relicts of barbarism—polygamy and slavery.

Mr. Fessenden. Let me suggest to the senator that he is entirely changing the issue between him and me. I did not desire to say, and I did not say, that the Republicans of the North were not unfriendly to the institution of slavery. I admitted myself that I was; I trust they all are. It is not in that respect that I accuse the Democracy of the North of misrepresenting the position of the Republican party. It was in representing that they desired to interfere with the institution in the southern states. That is the ground—that they were opposed to southern rights. That they do not think well of slavery, as it exists in this country, I do not undertake to deny. I do not know that southern gentlemen expect us to be friendly to it. I apprehend that they would not think very well of us if we pretended to be friendly to it. If we were friendly to the institution, we should try to adopt, we certainly should not oppose it; but what I charged upon the northern Democracy was, that they misrepresented our position. That we were opposed to the extension of slavery over free territory, that we called it a relic of barbarism, I admit; but I do deny that the Republican party, or the Republicans generally, have ever exhibited a desire or made a movement towards interfering with the right of southern men the states, or any constitutional rights that they have any where. That is the charge I made.

Mr. Douglas. Mr. President, for what purpose does the Republican party appeal to northern passions and northern prejudices against southern institutions and the southern people, unless it is to operate upon those institutions? They represent southern institutions as no better than polygamy; the slaveholder as no better than the polygamist; and complain that we should intimate that they did not like to associate with the slaveholder any better than with the polygamist. I can see a monstrous lowering of the flag in the senator's speech and explanation. I would respect the concession, if the fact was acknowledged. This thing of shrinking from position that every northern man knows to be true, and arraigning men for slander for telling the truth to them——

Mr. Fessenden. I know it not to be true.

Mr. Douglas. You may know it down in Maine, but you do not know it in Illinois. I have always noted that those men who were so far off from the slave states that they did not know any thing about them, are most anxious for the fate of the poor slave. Those men who are so far off that they do not know what a negro is, are distressed to death about the condition of the poor negro. (Laughter.) But, sir, go into the border states, where we associate across the line, where the civilities of society are constantly interchanged; where we trade with each other, and have social and commercial intercourse, and there you will find them standing by each other like a band of brothers. Take southern Illinois, southern Indiana, southern Ohio, and that part of Pennsylvania bordering on Maryland, and there you will find social intercourse, commercial intercourse, good feeling; because those people know the condition of the slave on the opposite side of the line; but just in proportion as you recede from the slave states, just in proportion as the people are ignorant of the facts, just in that proportion party leaders can impose on their sympathies and honest prejudices.

Sir, I know it is the habit of the Republican party, as a party, wherever I have met them, to make the warfare in such a way as to try to rally the whole north on sectional grounds against the south. I know that is to be the issue, and it is proven by the speech of the senator from New York, which I quoted before, and that of Mr. Lincoln, so far as they are authority. I happen to have those speeches before me. The senator from Maine has said that neither of these speeches justified the conclusion that they asserted that the free states and the slave states cannot coëxist permanently in the same Republic. Let us see whether they do or not. Mr. Lincoln says:

"A house divided against itself cannot stand. I believe this government cannot endure permanently, half slave and half free."

Then he goes on to say they must all be one thing or all the other, or else the Union cannot endure. What is the meaning of that language, unless it is that the Union cannot permanently exist, half slave and half free—that it must all become one thing or all become the other? That is the declaration.

The declaration is that the North must combine as a sectional party, and carry on the agitation so fiercely, up to the very borders of the slaveholding states, that the master dare not sleep at night for fear that the robbers, the John Browns, will come and set his house on fire, and murder the women and children, before morning. It is to surround the slaveholding states by a cordon of free states, to use the language of the senator; to hem them in, in order that you may smother them out. The senator avowed, in his speech to-day, their object to be to hem in the slave states, in order that slavery may die out. How die out? Confine it to its present limits; let the ratio of increase go on by the laws of nature; and just in proportion as the lands in the slaveholding states wear out, the negroes increase, and you will soon reach that point where the soil will not produce enough to feed the slaves; then hem them in, and let them starve out—let them die out by starvation. That is the policy—hem them in, and starve them out. Do as the French did in Algeria, when the Arabs took to the caverns—smoke them out, by making fires at the mouths of the caverns, and keep them burning until they die. The policy is, to keep up this agitation along the line; make slave property insecure in the border states; keep the master constantly in apprehension of assault, till he will consent to abandon his native country, leaving his slaves behind him, or to remove them further south. If you can force Kentucky thus to abolish slavery, you make Tennessee the border state, and begin the same operation upon her.

But, sir, let us see whether the senator from New York did not proclaim the doctrine that free states and slave states cannot permanently exist in the same Republic. He said :

"It is an irrepressible conflict between opposing and enduring forces; and it means that the United States must and will, sooner or later, become either entirely a slaveholding nation or entirely a free labor nation."

The opposing conflict is between the States; the Union can not remain as it now is, part free and part slave. The conflict between free states and slave states must go on until there is not a slave state left, or until they are all slave states. That is the declaration of the senator from New York. The senator from Maine tried to make the senate believe that I had misrepresented the senator from New York and Mr. Lincoln, of Illinois, in stating that they referred to a conflict between states. He said that all they meant was that it was a conflict between free labor and slave labor in the same state. Now, sir, let me submit to that man's candor whether he will insist on that position. They both say the contest will go on until the states become all free or all slave. Then, when is the contest going to end? When they become all slave? Will there not be the same conflict between free labor and slave labor, after every state has become a slave state, that there is now? If that was the meaning, would the conflict between slave labor and free labor cease even when every state had become slaveholding? Have not all the slaveholding states a large number of free laborers within their limits; and if there is an irrepressible conflict between free labor and slave labor, will you remove that conflict by making the states all slave? Yet, the senator from New York says they must become all slave or all free before the conflict ceases. Sir, that shows that the senator from New York meant what I represented him as meaning. It shows that a man who knows the meaning of words, and has the heart to express them as they read, can not fail to know that that was the meaning of those senators. The boldness with which a charge of misrepresentation may be made in this body will not give character to it when it is contradicted by the facts. I dislike to have to repel these charges of unfairness and misrepresentation; yet the senator began with a series of inuendoes, with a series of complaints of misrepresentation, showing that he was afraid to meet the real issues of his party, and would make up for that by personal assaults and inuendos against the opposite party.

He goes back to a speech of mine in opposition to the Lecompton Constitution, in which I said that if you would send that Constitution back and let the people of Kansas vote for or against it, if they voted for a free state or a slave state I would go for it without caring whether they voted slavery up or down. He thinks it is a great charge against me that I do not care whether the people vote it up or vote it down.

Mr. Fessenden. The senator is mistaken as to the speech to which I referred. It was one of his speeches made on his southern tour that I referred to.

Mr. Douglas. The idea is taken from a speech in the Senate—the first speech I made against the Lecompton Constitution. It was quoted all over Illinois by Mr. Lincoln in the canvass, and I repeated the sentiment each time it was quoted against me, and repeated it in the South as well as the North. I say this : if the people of Kansas want a slave state, it is their business and not mine ; if they want a free state, they have a right to have it ; and hence, I do not care, so far as regards my action, whether they make it a free state or not ; it is none of my business. But the senator says he does care, he has a preference between freedom and slavery. How long would this preference last if he was a sugar planter in Louisiana, residing on his estate, instead of living in Maine? Sir, I hold the doctrine that a wise statesman will adapt his laws to the wants, conditions, and interests of the people to be governed by them. Slavery may be very essential in one climate and totally useless in another. If I were a citizen of Louisiana I would vote for retaining and maintaining slavery, because I believe the good of that people would require it. As a citizen of Illinois I am utterly opposed to it, because our interests would not be promoted by it. I should like to see the Abolitionist who would go and live in a southern country that would not get over his scruples very soon and have a plantation as quickly as he could get the money to buy it.

I have said and repeat that this question of slavery is one of climate, of political economy, of self-interest, not a question of legislation. Wherever the climate, the soil, the health of the country are such that it can not be cultivated by white labor, you will have African labor, and compulsory labor at that. Wherever white labor can be employed cheapest and most profitably, there African labor will retire and white labor will take its place.

You cannot force slavery by all the acts of Congress you may make on one inch of territory against the will of the people, and you cannot by any law you can make keep it out from one inch of American territory where the people want it. You tried it in Illinois. By the ordinance of 1787 slavery was prohibited, and yet our people, believing that slavery would be profitable to them, established hereditary servitude in the territory by territorial legislation, in defiance of your Federal ordinance. We maintained slavery there just so long as Congress said we should not have it, and we abolished it at just the moment you recognized us as a state, with the right to do as we pleased. When we established it, it was on the supposition that it was our interest to do so. When we abolished it, we did so because experience proved that it was not our interest to have it. I hold that slavery is a question of political economy, to be determined by climate, by soil, by production, by self-interest, and hence the people to be affected by it are the most impartial jury to try the fact whether their interest requires them to have it or not.

But the senator thinks it is a great crime for me to say that I do not care whether they have it or not. I care just this far: I want every people to have that kind of government, that system of laws, that class of institutions, which will best promote their welfare, and I want them to decide for themselves; and so that they decide it to suit themselves, I am satisfied, without stopping to inquire or caring which way they decide it. That is what I meant by that declaration, and I am ready to stand by it.

The senator has made the discovery—I suppose it is very new, for he would not repeat anything that was old, after calling me to account for expressing an idea that had been heard of before—that I re-opened the agitation by bringing in the Nebraska Bill in 1854; and he tries to put the responsibility of the crimes perpetrated by his political friends, and in violation of the law, upon the provisions of the law itself. We passed a bill to allow the people of Kansas to form and regulate their own institutions to suit themselves. No sooner had we placed that law on the statute book, than his political friends formed conspiracies and combinations in the different New England states to import a set of desperadoes into Kansas to control the elections and the institutions of that country in fraud of the laws of Congress.

Sir, I desire to make the legislation broad enough to reach conspiracies and combinations of that kind; and I would also include combinations and conspiracies on the other side. My object is to establish firmly the doctrine that each state is to do its own voting, establish its own institutions, make its own laws, without interference, directly or indirectly, from any outside power. The gentleman says that is squatter sovereignty. Call it squatter sovereignty, call it popular sovereignty, call it what you please, it is the great principle of self-government on which this Union was formed, and by the preservation of which alone it can be maintained. It is the right of the people of every state to govern themselves and make their own laws, and be protected from outside violence or interference, directly or indirectly. Sir, I confess the object of the legislation I contemplate is to put down this outside interference; it is to repress this "irrepressible conflict;" it is to bring the government back to the true principles of the Constitution, and let each people in this Union rest secure in the enjoyment of domestic tranquility without apprehension from neighboring states. I will not occupy further time.

On the 29th of February, Mr. Seward having addressed the Senate, Mr. Douglas said :

MR. PRESIDENT: I trust I shall be pardoned for a few remarks upon so much of the senator's speech as consists in an assault on the Democratic party, and especially with regard to the Kansas-Nebraska Bill, of which I was the responsible author. It has become fashionable now-a-days for each gentleman making a speech against the Democratic party to refer to the Kansas-Nebraska Act as the cause of all the disturbances that have since ensued. They talk about the repeal of a sacred compact that had been undisturbed for more than a quarter of a century, as if those who complained of violated faith had been faithful to the provisions of the Missouri Compromise. Sir, wherein consisted the necessity for the repeal or abrogation of that act, except it was that the majority in the northern states refused to carry out the Missouri Compromise in good faith? I stood willing to extend it to the Pacific ocean, and abide by it forever, and the entire South, without one exception in this body, was willing thus to abide by it; but the free-soil element of the northern states was so strong as to defeat that measure, and thus open the slavery question anew. The men who now complain of the abrogation of that act were the very men who denounced it, and denounced all of us who were willing to abide by it so long as it stood upon the statute book. Sir, it was the defeat in the House of Representatives of the enactment of the bill to extend the Missouri Compromise to the Pacific ocean, after it had passed the Senate on my own motion, that opened the controversy of 1850, which was terminated by the adoption of the measures of that year.

We carried those Compromise measures over the head of the senator from New York and his present associates. We, in those measures, established a great principle, rebuking his doctrine of intervention by the Congress of the United States to prohibit slavery in the territories. Both parties, in 1852, pledged themselves to abide by that principle, and thus stood pledged not to prohibit slavery in the territories by act of Congress. The Whig party affirmed that pledge, and so did the Democracy. In 1854 we only carried out, in the Kansas-Nebraska Act, the same principle that had been affirmed in the Compromise measures of 1850. I repeat that their resistance to carrying out in good faith the settlement of 1820, their defeat of the bill for extending it to the Pacific ocean, was the sole cause of the agitation of 1850, and gave rise to the necessity of establishing the principle of non-intervention by Congress with slavery in the territories.

Hence I am not willing to sit here and allow the senator from New York, with all the weight of authority he has with the powerful party of which he is the head, to arraign me and the party to which I belong with the responsibility for that agitation which rests solely upon him and his associates. Sir, the Democratic party was willing to carry out the Compromise in good faith. Having been defeated in that for the want of numbers, and having established the principle of non-intervention in the Compromise measures of 1850, in lieu of it, the Democratic party from that day to this has been faithful to the new principle of adjustment. Whatever agitation has grown out of the question since, has been occasioned by the resistance of the party of which that senator is the head, to this great principle which has been ratified by the American people at two presidential elections. If he was willing to acquiesce in the solemn and repeated judgment of that American people to which he appeals, there would be no agitation in this country now.

But, sir, the whole argument of that senator goes far beyond the question of slavery, even in the territories. His entire argument rests on the assumption that the negro and the white man were equal by Divine law, and hence that all laws and constitutions and governments in violation of the principle of negro equality are in violation of the law of God. That is the basis upon which his speech rests. He quotes the Declaration of Independence to show that the fathers of the Revolution understood that the negro was placed on an equality with the white man, by quoting the clause, "We hold these truths to be self-evident, that all men are created equal, and are endowed by their Creator with certain inalienable rights, among which are life, liberty, and the pursuit of happiness." Sir, the doctrine of that senator and of his party is—and I have had to meet it for eight years—that the Declaration of Independence intended to recognize the negro and the white man as equal under the Divine law, and hence that all the provisions of the Constitution of the United States which recognizes slavery are in violation of the Divine law. In other words, it is an argument against the Constitution of the United States upon the ground that it is contrary to the law of God. The senator from New York has long held that doctrine. The senator from New York has often proclaimed to the world that the Constitution of the United States was in violation of the Divine law, and that senator will not contradict the statement. I have an extract from one of his speeches now before me, in which that proposition is distinctly put forth. In a speech made in the State of Ohio, in 1848, he said:

"Slavery is the sin of not some of the states only, but of them all; of not one nationality, but of all nations. It perverted and corrupted the moral sense of mankind deeply and universally, and this perversion became a universal habit. Habits of thought become fixed principles. No American state has yet delivered itself entirely from these habits. We, in New York, are guilty of slavery still by withholding the rights of suffrage from the race we have emancipated. You, in Ohio, are guilty in the same way by a system of black laws still more aristocratic and odious. It is written in the Constitution of the United States that five slaves shall count equal to three freemen as a basis of representation; and it is written also, IN VIOLATION OF DIVINE LAW, that we shall surrender the fugitive slave who takes refuge at our fireside from his relentless pursuers."

There you find his doctrine clearly laid down, that the Constitution of the United States is "*in violation of the Divine law,*" and therefore is not to be obeyed. You are told that the clause relating to fugitives slaves, being in violation of the Divine law, is not binding on mankind. This has been the doctrine of the senator from New York for years. I have not heard it in the Senate to-day for the first time. I have met in my own State, for the last ten years, this same doctrine, that the Declaration of Independence recognized the negro and the white man as equal; that the negro and white man are equals by Divine law, and that every provision of our Constitution and laws which establishes inequality between the negro and the white man is void, because contrary to the law of God.

The senator from New York says, in the very speech from which I have quoted, that New York is yet a slave state. Why? Not that she has a slave within her limits, but because the Constitution of New York does not allow a negro to vote on an equality with a white man. For that reason, he says, New York is still a slave state; for that reason every other state that discriminates between the negro and the white man is a slave state, leaving but a very few states in the Union that are free from his objection. Yet, notwithstanding the senator is committed to these doctrines, notwithstanding the leading men of his party are committed to them, he argues that they have been accused of being in favor of negro equality, and says the tendency of their doctrine is the equality of the white man. He introduces the objection, and fails to answer it. He states the proposition, and dodges it, to leave the inference that he does not indorse it. Sir, I desire to see these gentlemen carry out their principles to the logical conclusion. If they will persist in the declaration that the negro is made the equal of the white man, and that any inequality is in violation of the Divine law, then let them carry it out in their legislation by conferring on the negroes all the rights of citizenship the same as on white men. For one, I never held to any such doctrine. I hold that the Declaration of Independence was only referring to the white man—to the governing race of this country, who were in conflict with Great Britain, and had no reference to the negro race at all when it declared that all men were created equal.

Sir, if the signers of that declaration had understood the instrument then as the senator from New York now construes it, were they not bound on that day, at that very hour, to emancipate all their slaves? If Mr. Jefferson had meant that his negro slaves were created by the Almighty his equals, was he not bound to emancipate the slaves on the very day that he signed his name to the Declaration of Independence? Yet no one of the signers of that declaration emancipated his slaves. No one of the states on whose behalf the declaration was signed emancipated its slaves until after the Revolution was over. Every one of the original colonies, every one of the thirteen original states, sanctioned and legalized slavery until after the Revolution was closed. These facts show conclusively that the Declaration of Independence was never intended to bear the construction placed upon it by the senator from New York, and by that enormous tribe of lecturers that go through the country delivering lectures in country school houses and basements of churches to Abolitionists, in order to teach the children that the Almighty had put his seal of condemnation upon any inequality between the white man and the negro.

Mr. President, I am free to say here—what I have said over and over again at home—that, in my opinion, this government was made by white men for the benefit of white men and their posterity forever, and should be administered by white men, and by none other whatsoever.

Mr. Doolittle. I will ask the honorable senator, then, why not give the territories to white men?

Mr. Douglas. Mr. President, I am in favor of throwing the territories open to all the white men, and all the negroes, too, that choose to go, and then allow the white man to govern the territory. I would not let one of the negroes, free or slave, either vote or hold office anywhere, where I had the right, under the Constitution, to prevent it. I am in favor of each state and each territory of this Union taking care of its own negroes, free or slave. If they want slavery, let them have it; if they desire to prohibit slavery, let them do it; it is their business, not mine. We in Illinois tried slavery while we were a territory, and found it was not profitable; and hence we turned philanthropists and abolished it, just as our British friends across the ocean did. They established slavery in all their colonies, and when they found they could not make any more money out of it, abolished it. I hold that the question of slavery is one of political economy, governed by the laws of climate, soil, productions, and self-interest, and not by mere statutory provision. I repudiate the doctrine, that because free institutions may be best in one climate, they are, necessarily, the best every where; or that because slavery may be indispensable in one locality, therefore it is desirable every where. I hold that a wise statesman will always adapt his legislation to the wants, interests, condition and necessities of the people to be governed by it. One people will bear different institutions from another. One climate demands different institutions from another. I repeat, then, what I have often had occasion to say, that I do not think uniformity is either possible or desirable. I wish to see no two states precisely alike in their domestic institutions in this Union. Our system rests on the supposition that each state has something in her condition or climate, or her circumstances, requiring laws and institutions different from every other state of the Union. Hence I answer the question of the senator from Wisconsin, that I am willing that a territory settled by white men shall have negroes, free or slave, just as the white men shall determine, but not as the negro shall prescribe.

The senator from New York has coined a new definition of the states of the Union—labor states and capital states. The capital states, I believe, are the slaveholding states; the labor states are the non-slaveholding states. It has taken that senator a good many years to coin that phrase and bring it into use. I have heard him discuss these favorite theories of his for the last ten years, I think, and I never heard of capital states and labor states before. It strikes me that something has recently occurred up in New England that makes it politic to get up a question between capital and labor, and take the side of the numbers against the few. We have seen some accounts in the newspapers of combinations and strikes among the journeymen shoemakers in the towns there—labor against capital. The senator has a new word ready coined to suit their case, and make the laborers believe that he is on the side of the most numerous class of voters.

What produced that strike among the journeymen shoemakers? Why are the mechanics of New England, the laborers and the employees, now reduced to the starvation point? Simply because, by your treason, by your sectional agitation, you have created a strife between the North and the South, have driven away your southern customers, and thus deprive the laborers of the means of support. This is the fruit of your Republican dogmas. It is another step, following John Brown, of the "irrepressible conflict." Therefore, we now get this new coinage of "labor states"—he is on the side of the shoe- makers, (laughter), and "capital states"—he is against those that furnish the hides. (Laughter.) I think those shoemakers will understand this business. They know why it is that they do not get so many orders as they did a few months ago. It is not confined to the shoemakers; it reaches every mechanic's shop and every factory. All the large laboring establishments of the North feel the pressure produced by the doctrine of the "irrepressible conflict." This new coinage of words will not save them from the just responsibility that follows the doctrines they have been inculcating. If they had abandoned the doctrine of the "irrepressible conflict," and proclaimed the true doctrine of the Constitution, that each state is entirely free to do just as it pleases, have slavery as long as it chooses, and abolish it when it wishes, there would be no conflict; the northern and southern states would be brethren; there would be fraternity between us, and your shoemakers would not strike for higher prices.

Mr. Clark. Will the senator pardon me for interrupting him a moment?

will not give way for a speech; I will for a suggestion.
sire simply to make one single suggestion in regard to what
llinois said in reference to the condition of the laboring
ies. I come from a city where there are three thousand
·o never was a time when they were more contented and
ictories than now, and when their business was better than

was speaking of the scarcity of labor growing up in our
ring towns, as a legitimate and natural consequence of the
:mand for the manufactured article; and then the question
reduced this demand, except the "irrepressible conflict"
ɔ southern trade away from northern cities into southern
cities? Sir, the feeling among the masses of the south
he dress of the senator from Virginia. (Mr. Mason); they
·ear the homespun of their own productions rather than
ı. That is the feeling which has produced this state of
ifacturing towns.
New York has also referred to the recent action of the
xico, in establishing a code for the protection of prop-
he congratulates the country upon the final success of
·eo institutions in Kansas. He could not fail, however,
ireserve what he thought was a striking antithesis, that
· in Kansas meant state sovereignty in Missouri. No,
gnty in Kansas was stricken down by unholy combination
ship men to Kansas—rowdies and vagabonds—with the
nd Sharpe's rifle in the other, to shoot down the friends
Popular sovereignty in Kansas was stricken down by the
northern states to carry elections under pretence of emi-
In retaliation, Missouri formed aid societies too; and she,
iple, sent men into Kansas and then occurred the conflict.
: blame upon Missouri merely because she followed your
pted to resist its consequences. I condemn both; but I
l-fold more those who set the example and struck the first
10 thought they would act upon the principle of fighting
vn weapons, and resorted to the same means that you had

:tanding the efforts of the emigrant aid societies, the peo-
had their own way, and the people of New Mexico have
Kansas had adopted a free state; New Mexico has es-
rritory. I am content with both. If the people of New
y, let them have it, and I never will vote to repeal their
isas does not want slavery, I will not help anybody to
t each do as it pleases. When Kansas comes to the con-
will suit her, and promote her interest better than the
pass her own slave code; I will not pass it for her.
xico gets tired of her code, she must repeal it for herself;
for her. Non-intervention by Congress with slavery in
platform on which I stand.
ɔw why will not the senator from New York carry out
ir logical conclusion? Why is there not a man in that
body or in the House of Representatives, bold enough to
which that party has made to the country? I believe
iiladelphia platform, that Congress had sovereign power
for their government, and that it was the duty of Con-
the territories those twin relics of barbarism, slavery and
ɔ you not carry out your pledges? Why do you not in-

troduce your bill? The senator from New York says they have no new measures to originate; no new movement to make; no new bill to bring forward. Then what confidence shall the American people repose in your faith and sincerity, when, having the power in one house, you do not bring forward a bill to carry out your principles? The fact is, these principles are avowed to get votes in the North, but not to be carried into effect by acts of Congress. You are afraid of hurting your party if you bring in your bill to repeal the slave code of New Mexico; afraid of driving off the conservative men; you think it is wise to wait until after the election. I should be glad to have confidence enough in the sincerity of the other side of the chamber to suppose they had courage to bring forward a law to carry out their principles to their logical conclusions. I find nothing of that. They wish to agitate, to excite the people of the North against the South to get votes for the Presidential election; but they shrink from carrying out their measures, lest they might throw off some conservative voters who do not like the Democratic party.

But, sir, if the senator from New York, in the event that he is made President, intends to carry out his principles to their logical conclusion, let us see where they will lead him. In the same speech that I read from a few minutes ago, I find the following. Addressing the people of Ohio, he said:

"You blush not at these things, because they have become as familiar as household words; and your pretended free-soil allies claim peculiar merit for maintaining these miscalled guarantees of slavery, which they find in the national compact. Does not all this prove that the Whig party have kept up with the spirit of the age; that it is as true and faithful to human freedom as the inert conscience of the American people will permit it to be? What then, you say, can nothing be done for freedom, because the public conscience remains inert? Yes, much can be done, everything can be done. *Slavery can be limited to its present bounds.*"

That is the first thing that can be done—slavery can be limited to its present bounds. What else?

"IT CAN BE AMELIORATED. IT CAN AND MUST BE ABOLISHED, AND YOU AND I CAN AND MUST DO IT."

There you find our two propositions; first, slavery was to be limited to the states in which it was then situated. It did not then exist in any territory. Slavery was confined to the states. The first proposition was that slavery must be restricted and confined to those states. The second was that he, as a New Yorker, and they, the people of Ohio, must and would abolish it; that is to say abolish it in the states. They could abolish it no where else. Every appeal they make to northern prejudice and passion is against the institution of slavery everywhere, and they would not be able to retain their Abolition allies, the rank and file, unless they held out the hope that it was the mission of the Republican party, if successful, to abolish slavery in the states as well as in the territories of the Union.

And again, in the same speech, the senator from New York advised the people to disregard constitutional obligations in these words:

"But we must begin deeper and lower than the composition and combination of factions or parties, wherein the strength and security of slavery lie. You answer that it lies in the Constitution of the United States and the Constitutions and laws of slaveholding states. Not at all. It is in the erroneous sentiment of the American people. Constitutions and laws can no more rise above the virtue of the people than the limpid stream can climb above its native spring. Inculcate the love of freedom and the *equal rights of man under the paternal roof; see to it that they are taught in the schools and in the churches; reform your own code; extend a cordial welcome to the fugitive who lays his weary limbs at your door, and defend him as you would your paternal gods, correct your own error that slavery is a constitutional guarantee which may not be released, and ought not to be relinquished."*

I know they tell us that all this is to be done according to the Constitution; they would not violate the Constitution except so far as the Constitution violates the law of God—that is all—and they are to be the judges of how far the Constitution does violate the law of God. They say that every clause of the Constitution that recognizes property in slaves is in violation of the Divine law, and hence should not be made; and with that interpretation of the Constitution they turn to the South and say, "We will give you all your rights under the Constitution as we explain it!"

Then the senator devoted about a third of his speech to a very beautiful homily on the glories of our Union. All that he has said, all that any other man has ever said, all that the most eloquent tongue can ever utter, in behalf of the blessings and the advantages of this glorious Union, I fully indorse. But still, sir, I am prepared to say that the Union is glorious only when the Constitution is preserved inviolate. He eulogized the Union. I, too, am for the Union; I indorse the eulogies; but still, what is the Union worth, unless the Constitution is preserved and maintained inviolate in all its provisions?

Sir, I have no faith in the Union loving sentiments of those will not carry out the Constitution in good faith, as our fathers made it. Professions of fidelity to the Union will be taken for naught, unless they are accompanied by obedience to the Constitution upon which the Union rests. I have a right to insist that the Constitution shall be maintained inviolate in all its parts, not only that which suits the temper of the North, but every clause of that Constitution, whether you like it or dislike it. Your oath to support the Constitution binds you to every line, word, and syllable of the instrument. You have no right to say that any given clause is in violation of the Divine law, and that, therefore, you will not observe it. The man who disobeys any one clause on the pretext that it violates the Divine law, or on any other pretext, violates his oath of office.

But, sir, what a commentary is this pretext that the Constitution is a violation of the Divine law upon those revolutionary fathers whose eulogies we have heard here to-day! Did the framers of that instrument make a Constitution in violation of the law of God? If so, how do your consciences allow you to take the oath of office? If the senator from New York still holds to his declaration that the clause in the Constitution relative to fugitive slaves is a violation of the Divine law, how dare he, as an honest man, take an oath to support the instrument? Did he understand that he was defying the authority of Heaven when he took the oath to support that in-instrument?

Thus, we see, the radical difference between the Republican party and the Democratic party, is this: we stand by the Constitution as our fathers made it, and by the decisions of the constituted authorities as they are pronounced in obedience to the Constitution. They repudiate the instrument, substitute their own will for that of the constituted authorities, annul such provisions as their fanaticism, or prejudice, or policy, may declare to be in violation of God's law, and then say, "We will protect all your rights under the Constitution as expounded by ourselves; but not as expounded by the tribunal created for that purpose."

Mr. President, I shall not occupy further time in the discussion of this question to-night. I did not intend to utter a word; and I should not have uttered a word upon the subject, if the senator from New York had not made a broad arraignment of the Democratic party, and especially of that portion of the action of the party for which I was most immediately responsible. Everybody knows that I brought forward and helped to carry through the

Kansas-Nebraska Act, and that I was active in support of the Compromise measures of 1850. I have heard bad faith attached to the Democratic party for that act too long to be willing to remain silent and seem to sanction it by tacit acquiescence.

CHAPTER XXIII.

PUBLIC DEMONSTRATIONS—COMMITTEE SERVICE—PUBLIC LANDS.

IMMEDIATELY after the election in 1858, Judge Douglas, for the purpose of recruiting his health, le Chicago with his family for Washington by the way of the Mississippi river. When in St. Louis he was the recipient of many public honors and courtesies. On his way South, he was met some fifty miles north of Memphis by a delegation of the citizens of that prosperous city, who earnestly invited him to remain over there and partake of the hospitalities which it would be their pride as well as pleasure to extend to him and his family. Gratified beyond measure by this most unexpected greeting at the hands of the people of a southern city, he accepted the cordial invitation, and on the day after his arrival, addressed a very large assemblage of citizens, to whom he repeated the policy and principles he had advocated in the campaign that had just closed in Illinois. He declared that he could speak no sentiments in Tennessee that he could not speak as freely in Illinois, and that any opinions that could not be uttered in the one state as acceptably as in the other were necessarily unsound and anti-Democratic.

He on the next day proceeded down the river to New Orleans, where a grand reception awaited him. He reached there at night, and as the steamer neared the city he was greeted with a salute and an illumination. He was escorted to the hotel by the military and a vast concourse of people. At the hotel he was welcomed by the mayor as the guest of the city, and also welcomed by the Hon. Pierre Soulé on the part of the citizens. To these addresses, in which he was congratulated upon his recent victory in Illinois, he responded in a suitable manner.

On the 6th of December he addressed a mass meeting in Odd Fellows Hall, in a speech of which we have already given some extracts, and in which he repeated the famous doctrines so often defended by him in the Illinois campaign.

After leaving New Orleans he staid some days at Havana,

and then proceeded to New York by steamer. In the mean-time the authorities of New York in anticipation of his arrival had unanimously voted that, "it is eminently due to this es-teemed patriot and distinguished senator that the city of New York, through its constituted authorities, should extend to him a cordial welcome on his arrival, in order to express their ad-miration of the man, and of the principles which he has so long and so ably defended," and therefore appointed a committe to extend to Mr. Douglas the hospitalities of the city. When he reached New York he was met by committees of the city coun-cils and escorted to the Everett House.

As soon as his presence in New York was ascertained, a meeting of citizens was held at Philadelphia to adopt measures for his reception there. The city council voted the use of In-dependence Hall for that purpose. On his arrival there on the 4th of January, 1859, he was escorted to the venerated hall, and was there formally welcomed by Mayor Henry on behalf of the authorities, and by W. E. Lehman, Esq., on behalf of the people. The speeches on this occasion have been pre-served, and in a more comprehensive biography of Mr. Douglas will form a most interesting chapter.

When leaving Philadelphia he was accompanied by a large delegation of his friends, who continued with him until he had crossed the Susquehanna, when he was met by a committee of citizens of Baltimore, who, in behalf of the people of that city, welcomed him to the soil of Maryland.

In the evening of January the 5th, he was greeted with a serenade at the Gilmore House, and having been introduced to the assemblage of persons in Monument Square, addresssd them—returning his acknowledgments for the honors received by him, and again repeating the truths and arguments he had been accustomed to express to the people of Illinois.

On his arrival at Washington he was welcomed by thou-sands of the people of that city—people who held no office and expected none, and therefore had no dread of official frowns. On reaching his own house he made a suitable acknowledg-ment for the kindness of his old friends and neighbors. His whole journey from Chicago to Washington was a succession of popular manifestations of admiration for the man who had had the boldness to maintain the right, and had the ability to overcome and vanquish all the opposition arrayed against him.

SERVICES ON COMMITTEES IN CONGRESS.

While Mr. Douglas was at Havana, Congress had assembled, and a caucus of the Democratic senators had arranged the Senate committees. In this arrangement Mr. GREEN, of Missouri, was named as chairman of the Committee on Territories in place of Mr. Douglas. This, it will be remembered, was done while Mr. Douglas was absent. No reason was given for it until late in the year, when Mr. Gwin stated the reason in his speech at Grass Valley, California.

When Mr. Douglas first took his seat in the House of Representatives he was assigned a place on the Committee on Elections, from which committee at that session he made the celebrated report upon the constitutional powers of Congress to regulate the manner and time of holding elections in the states. The Whig Congress of 1841 and 1842 had passed a law requiring the states to elect members of Congress by districts. New Hampshire, Georgia and some other states had disregarded this law and had elected their representatives by general ticket. The question whether the members thus elected against the provisions of the act of the previous Congress was one that was considered of great importance. Mr. Douglas made an elaborate report upon the subject, being a complete vindication of the rights of the states, and his report was adopted as the judgment of the house by a most decided majority. At the next session he was placed on the Judiciary Committee, from which he reported the bill extending the admiralty and maritime jurisdiction of the United States district and circuit courts to all cases arising on the lakes—thus giving to the internal commerce and navigation the same judicial protection that was enjoyed on the coast.

At the opening of the next Congress, Mr. Douglas was made chairman of the Committee on Territories in the House of Representatives, and held that position until he closed his services in that body. When he took his seat in the Senate he was made chairman of the Committee on Territories, and had been regularly elected to the position every year from December 1847, to December 1857, inclusive. In December 1858, for the reasons given by Mr. Gwin, he was displaced. It has been stated that he was tendered the chairmanship of another committee but he declined it—if politically unfitted for the one he was equally so for the other.

During his service in the Senate he was for many years a member of the Committee on Foreign Relations, and also a Regent of the Smithsonian Institution.

THE PUBLIC LANDS.

Mr. Douglas, as has been shown, successfully supported the act making the great donation of public land to Illinois for rail road purposes, and has supported acts making like grants to other states.

He has always supported a liberal policy in the administration of the public lands—a policy looking always to their occupancy and cultivation by actual settlers. He has reported and defended those provisions in the Oregon, Washington and other territoritorial acts granting lands to actual settlers on condition of occupancy, &c.

In 1850 he introduced into the Senate a proposition having for its effect a liberal donation to the head of every family, male or female—of the public land on the condition of settlement and cultivation. The principle involved in his proposition was something similar to that embraced in the "Homestead bill" so long pending in Congress, and of which Mr. Douglas is an earnest supporter.

He has always as a legislator, as a judge, and as a statesman been a firm friend and maintainer of the rights and interests of the agriculturists of the country. Hence it is that he has always opposed the extension and renewal by Congress for extraordinary periods the patents of inventors for agricultural implements, an opposition which has provoked a hostility that is as unjust as it is selfish.

On the 18th of September, 1851, he delivered by invitation an address at Rochester, New York, before the New York Agricultural Society, an address abounding in lofty sentiment and practical teaching. A copy of that address is published in the annual reports of the proceedings of the society.

CONCLUSION.

In the foregoing pages have been crowded brief statements of some of the leading incidents of the marked career of Mr. Douglas. His history is a voluminous one, and to do full justice to it would require four times the space that has been taken in this work. At some future time, some of the events herein only slightly touched upon may be elaborated to an extent that their importance will justify and that truth will require. The record, even prepared as it is imperfectly, will not fail to point out Mr. Douglas as a most remarkable man.

At this day he occupies the most extraordinary position of being the only man in his own party whose nomination for the Presidency is deemed equivalent to an election. Friends of other statesmen claim that other men, if nominated, may be elected—a claim that admits of strong and well supported controversy; but friend and foe—all Democrats, unite in the opinion that Douglas' nomination will place success beyond all doubt.

THE END.

www.ingramcontent.com/pod-product-compliance
Lightning Source LLC
Chambersburg PA
CBHW021940110726
47901CB00003B/919